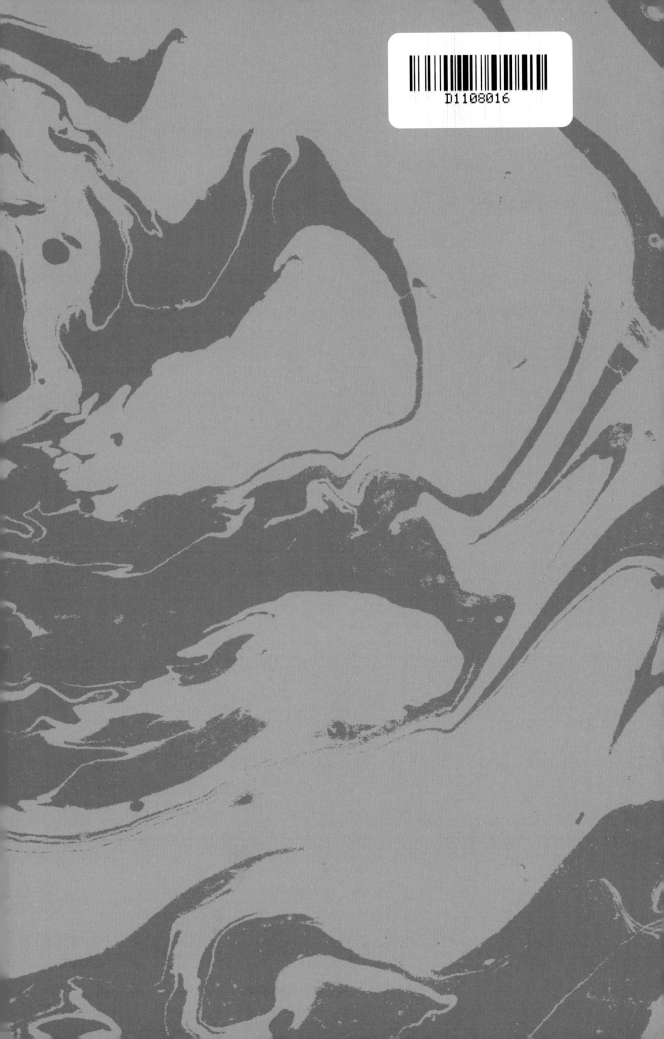

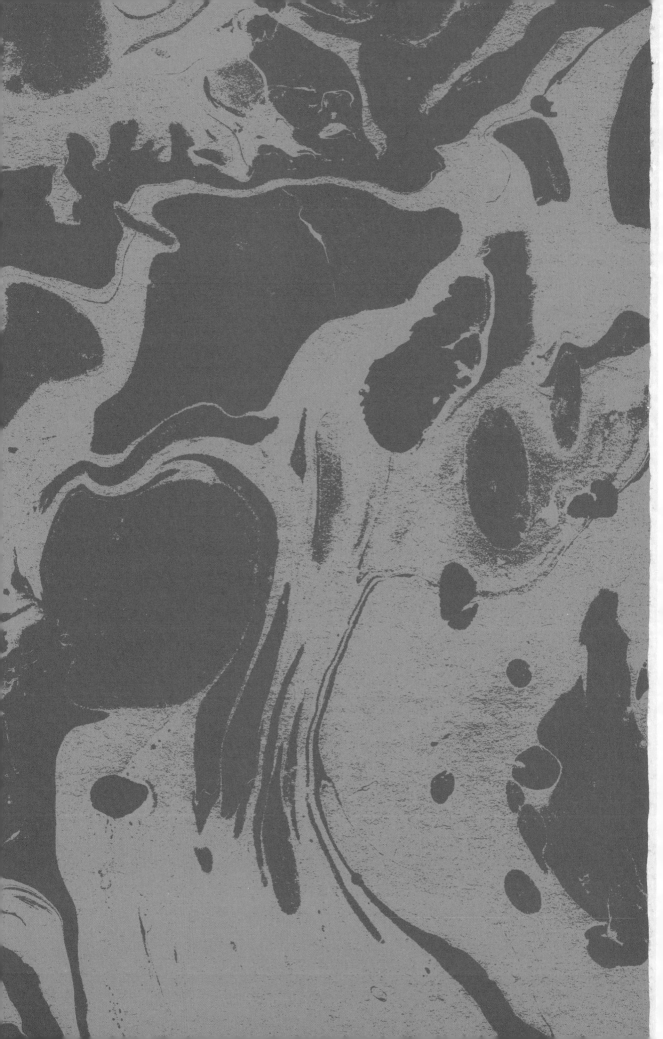

OBLIVION SONG

CREATED BY
ROBERT KIRKMAN
AND
LORENZO DE FELICI

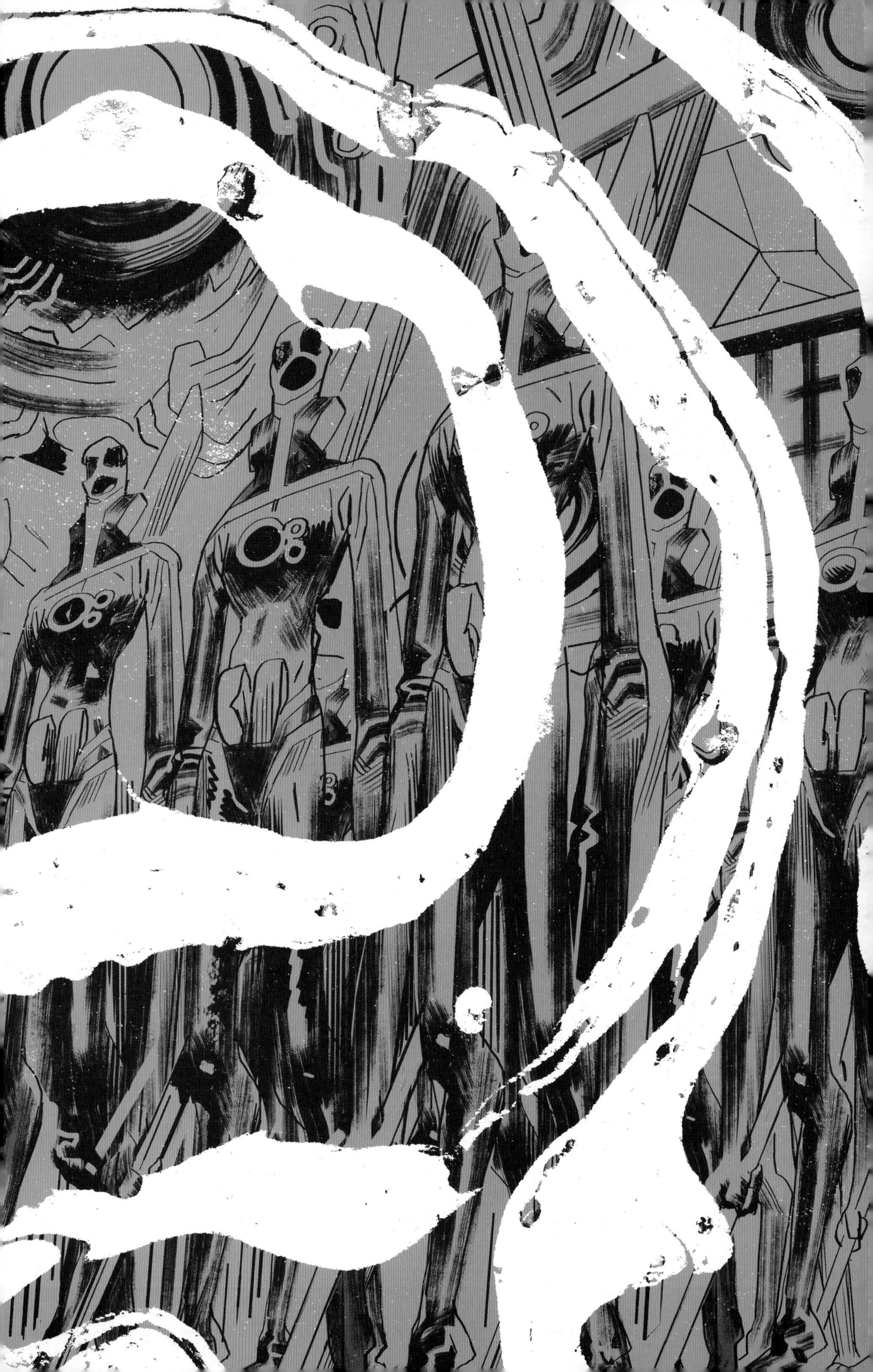

ROBERT KIRKMAN
WRITER/CREATOR

LORENZO DE FELICI
ARTIST/CREATOR

ANNALISA LEONI
COLORIST/BONUS STORY ARTIST

RUS WOOTON
LETTERER

SEAN MACKIEWICZ
EDITOR

ANDRES JUAREZ
LOGO & COLLECTION DESIGN

FOR SKYBOUND ENTERTAINMENT

ROBERT KIRKMAN *Chairman* ▪ DAVID ALPERT *CEO* ▪ SEAN MACKIEWICZ *SVP, Publisher*
SHAWN KIRKHAM *SVP, Business Development* ▪ BRIAN HUNTINGTON *VP of Online Content*
ANDRES JUAREZ *Art Director* ▪ ARUNE SINGH *Director of Brand, Editorial* ▪ ALEX ANTONE *Senior Editor*
AMANDA LaFRANCO *Editor* ▪ JILLIAN CRAB *Graphic Designer* ▪ MORGAN PERRY *Brand Manager, Editorial*
DAN PETERSEN *Sr. Director of Operations & Events*
Foreign Rights & Licensing Inquiries: contact@skybound.com
SKYBOUND.COM

IMAGE COMICS, INC.

TODD McFARLANE *President* ▪ JIM VALENTINO *Vice President* ▪ MARC SILVESTRI *Chief Executive
Officer* ▪ ERIK LARSEN *Chief Financial Officer* ▪ ROBERT KIRKMAN *Chief Operating Officer*
ERIC STEPHENSON *Publisher / Chief Creative Officer* ▪ NICOLE LAPALME *Controller* ▪ LEANNA
CAUNTER *Accounting Analyst* ▪ SUE KORPELA *Accounting & HR Manager* ▪ DIRK WOOD *Director of
International Sales & Licensing* ▪ ALEX COX *Director of Direct Market Sales* ▪ CHLOE RAMOS *Book
Market & Library Sales Manager* ▪ EMILIO BAUTISTA *Digital Sales Coordinator* ▪ JON SCHLAFFMAN *Specialty
Sales Coordinator* ▪ KAT SALAZAR *Director of PR & Marketing* ▪ DREW FITZGERALD *Marketing Content Associate*
▪ HEATHER DOORNINK *Production Director* ▪ DREW GILL *Art Director* ▪ HILARY DILORETO *Print Manager*
TRICIA RAMOS *Traffic Manager* ▪ MELISSA GIFFORD *Content Manager* ▪ ERIKA SCHNATZ *Senior Production
Artist* ▪ RYAN BREWER *Production Artist* ▪ DEANNA PHELPS *Production Artist* ▪ IMAGECOMICS.COM

OBLIVION SONG BOOK THREE.
First Printing. ISBN: 978-1-5343-2231-8

CHAPTER

FIVE

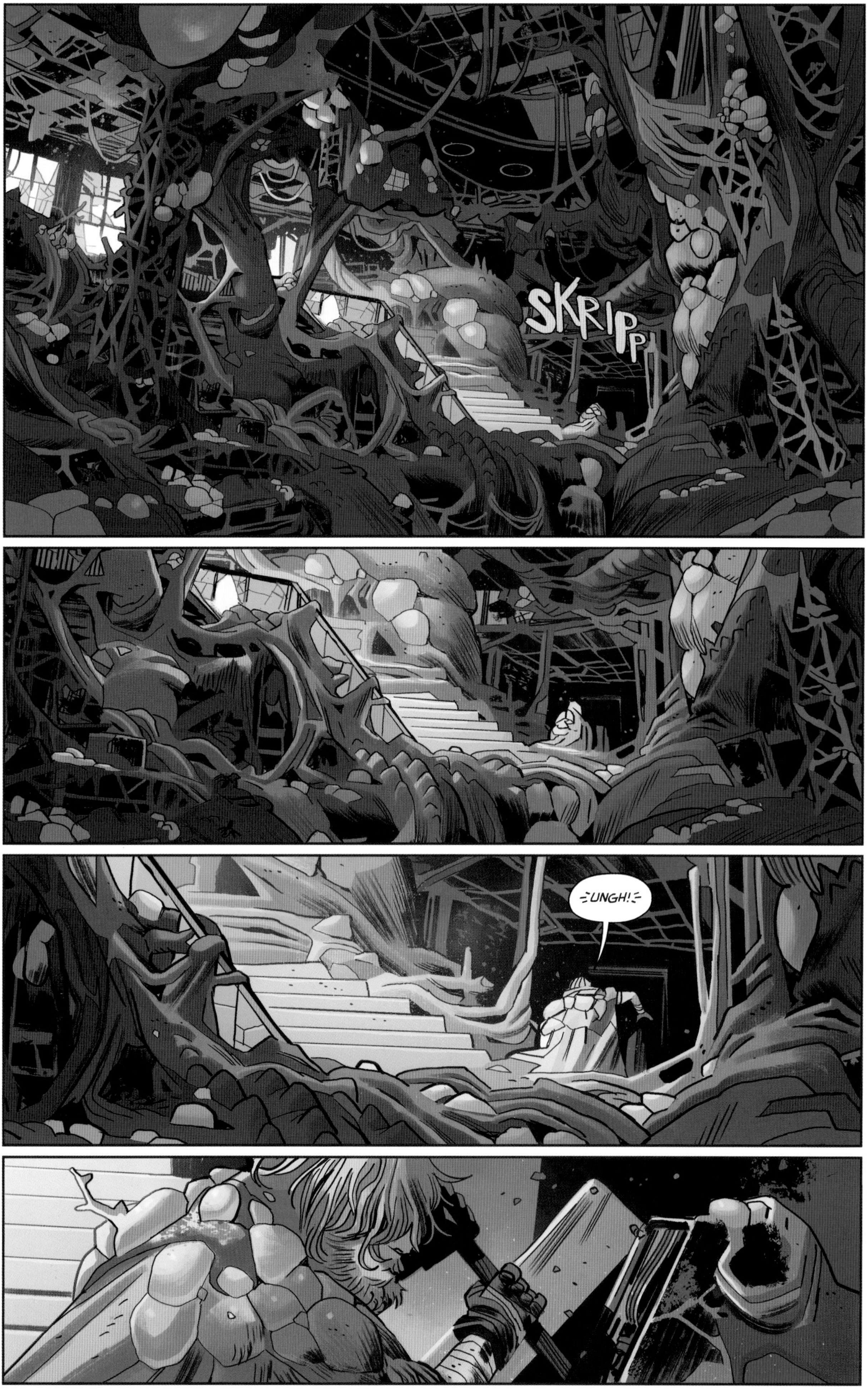
SKRIPP
UNGH!

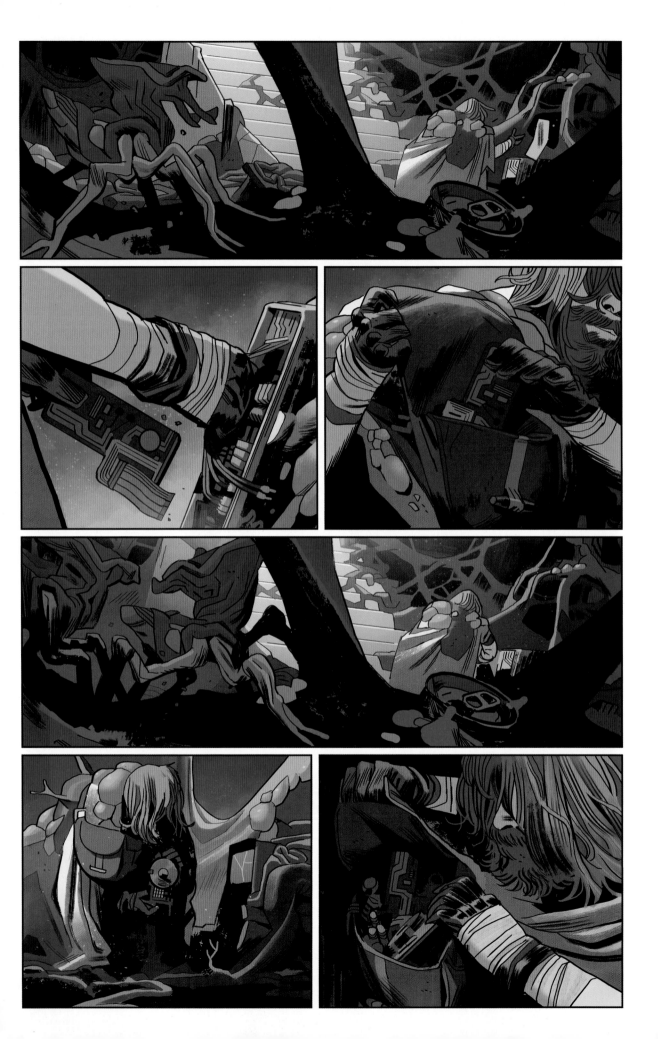

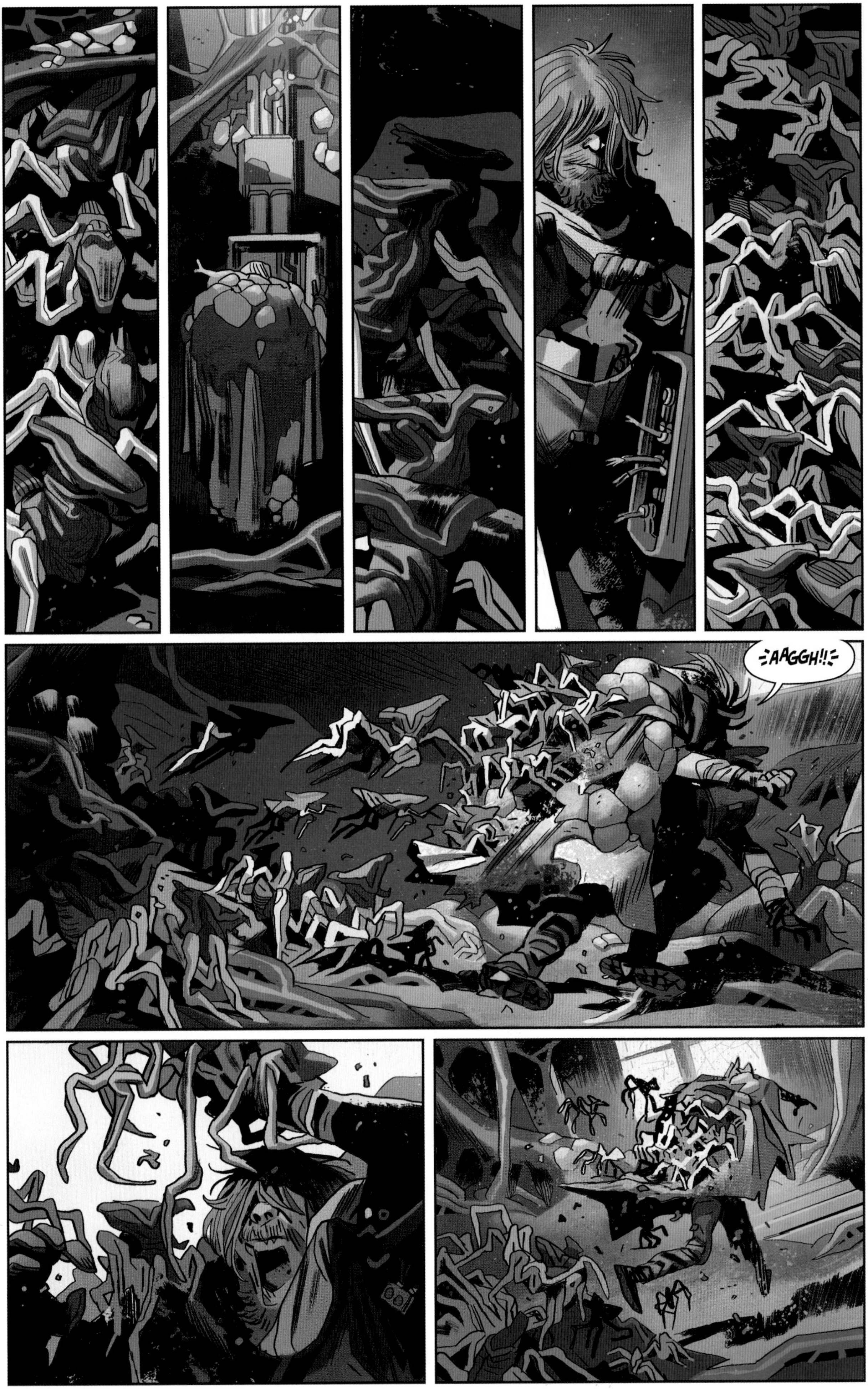
AAGGH!!

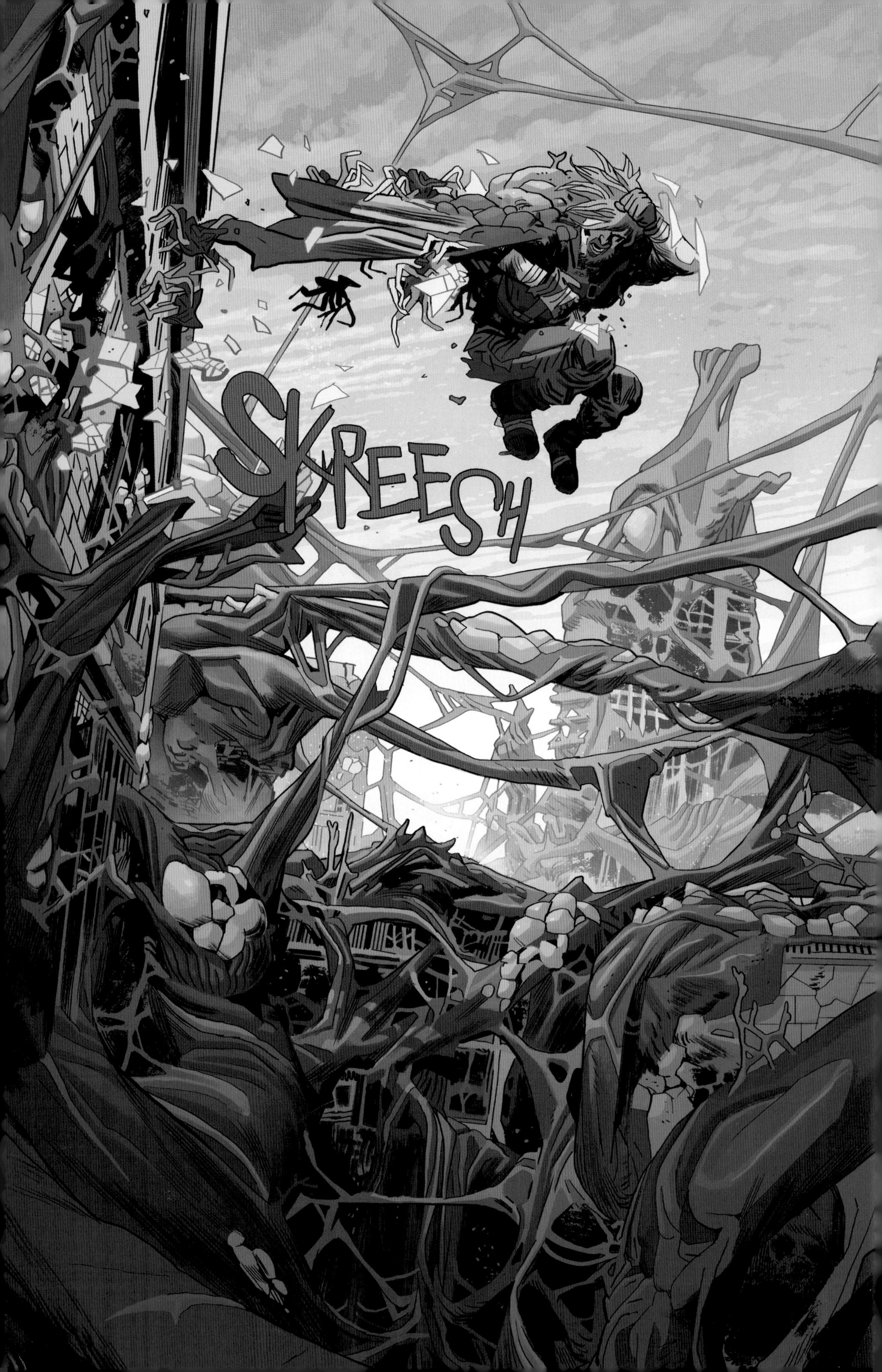
SKREESH

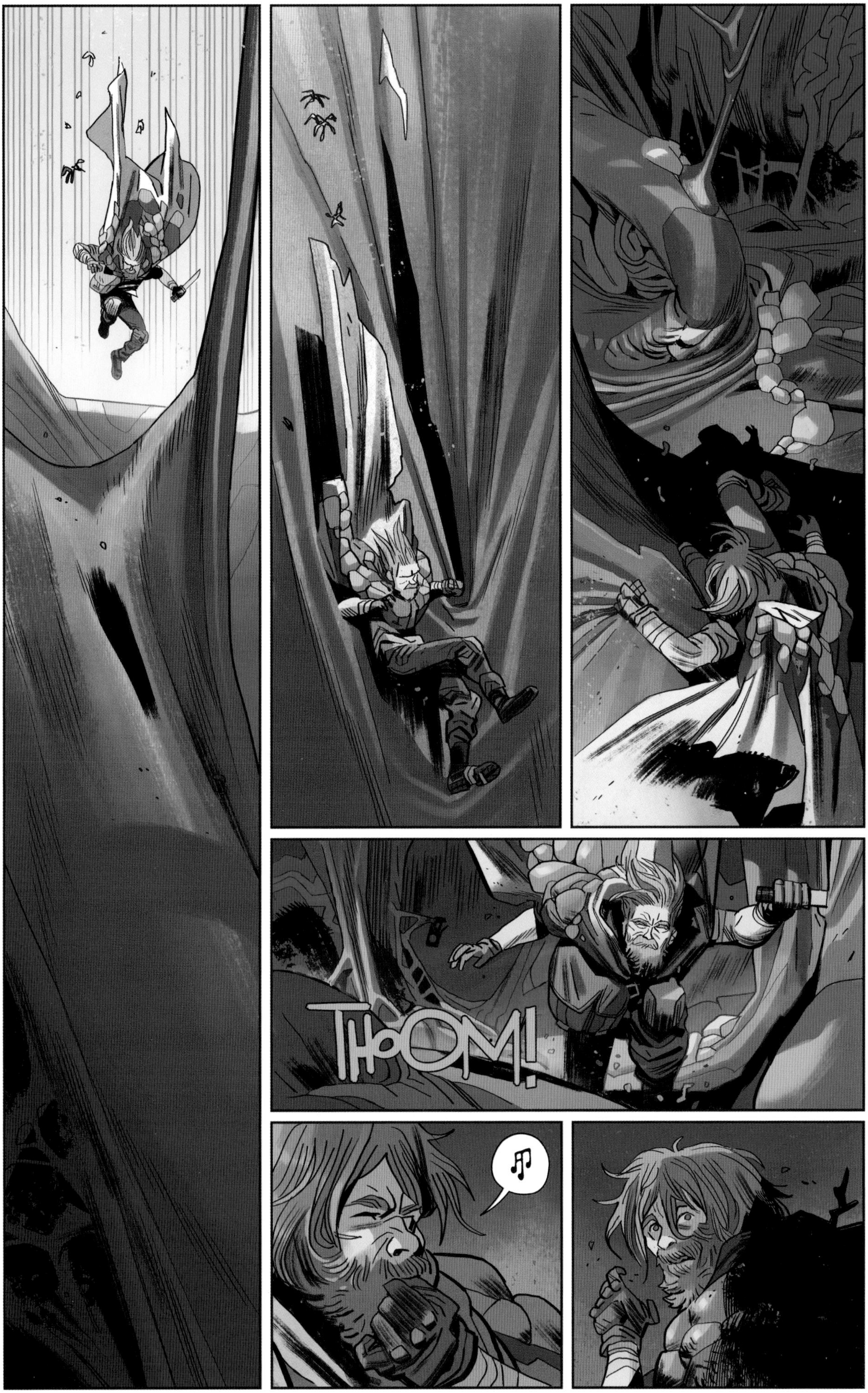
THOOM!
♫

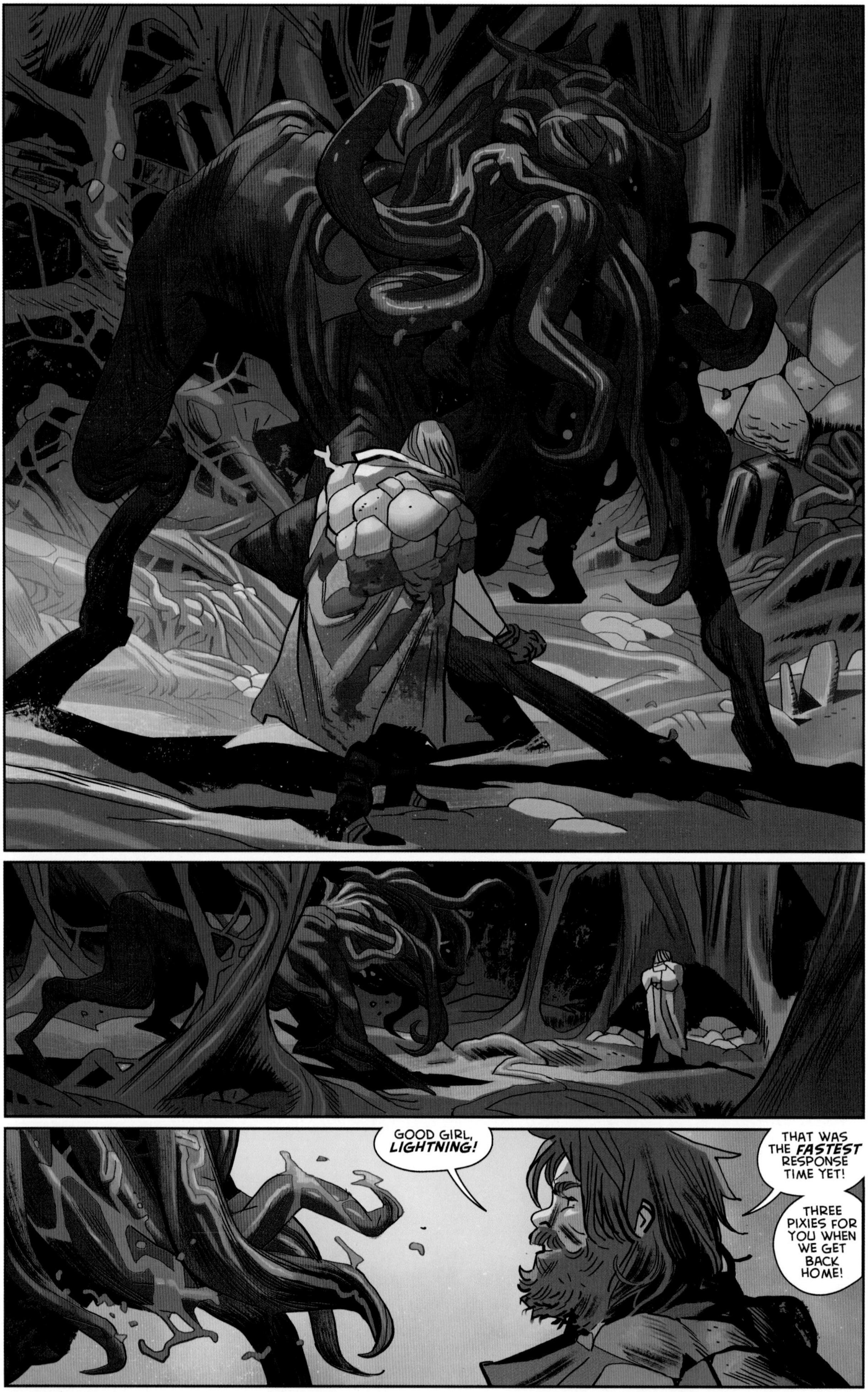
GOOD GIRL, LIGHTNING!
THAT WAS THE FASTEST RESPONSE TIME YET!
THREE PIXIES FOR YOU WHEN WE GET BACK HOME!

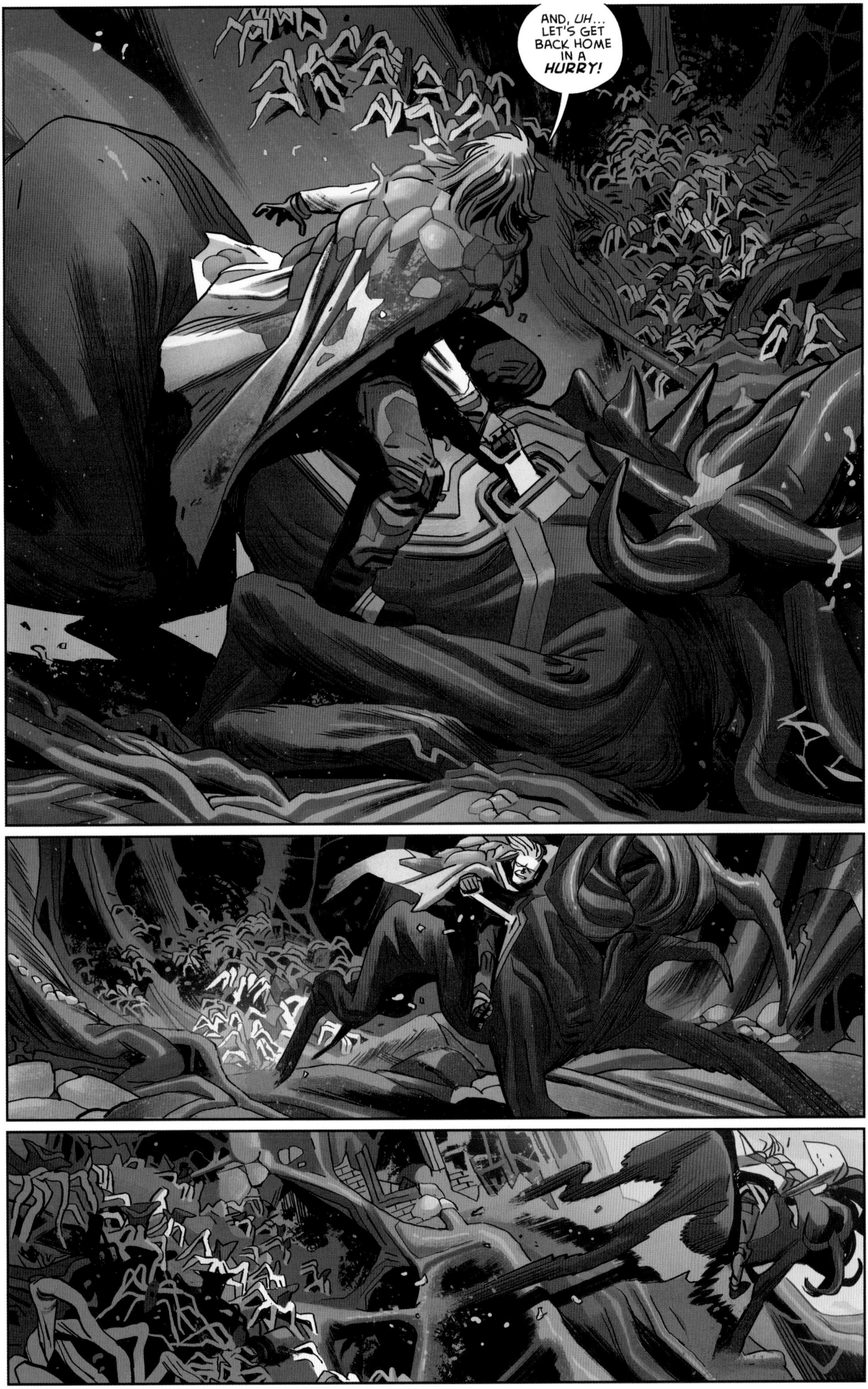
AND, *UH*... LET'S GET BACK HOME IN A ***HURRY!***

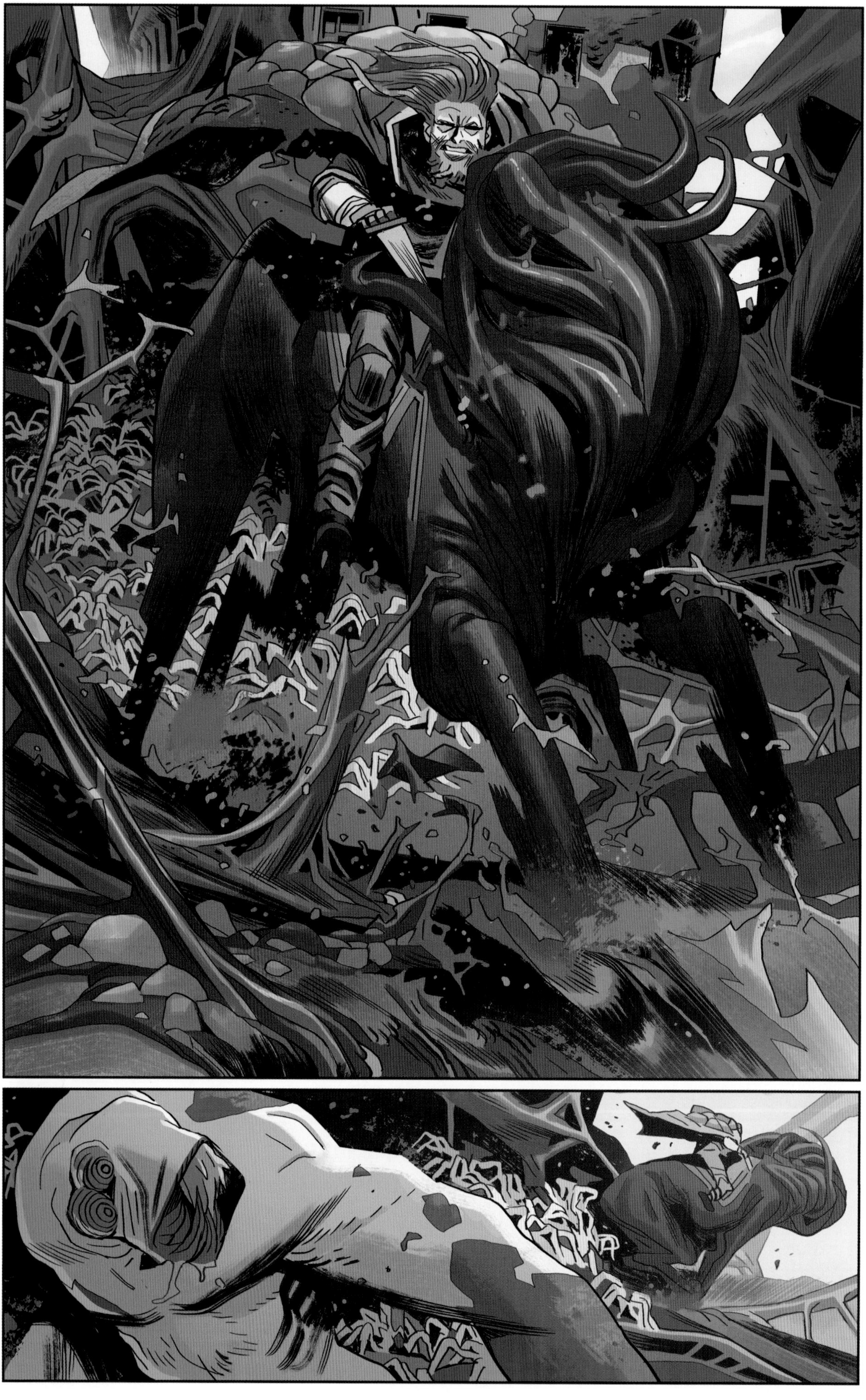

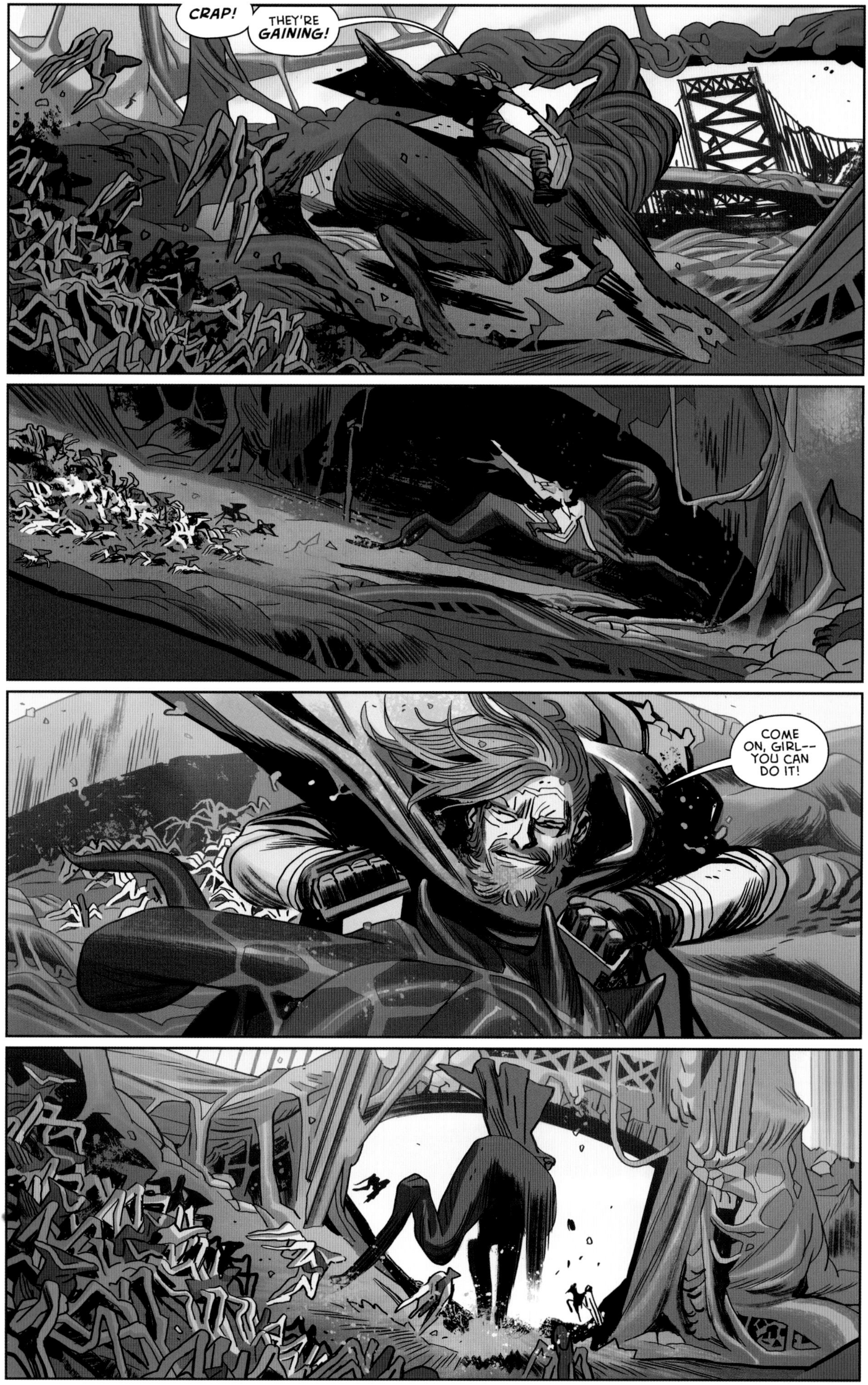
CRAP!
THEY'RE GAINING!
COME ON, GIRL-- YOU CAN DO IT!

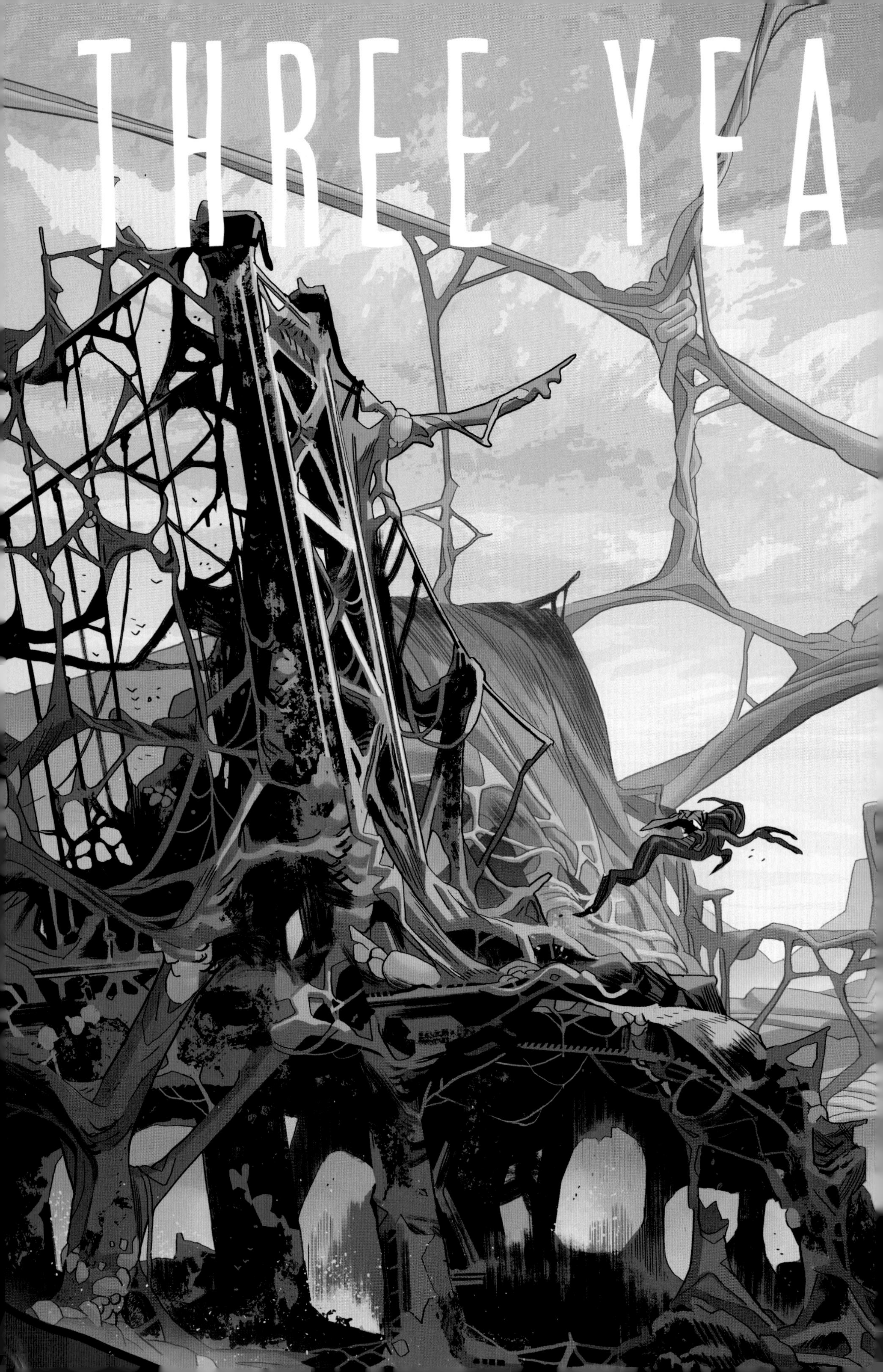
THREE YEA

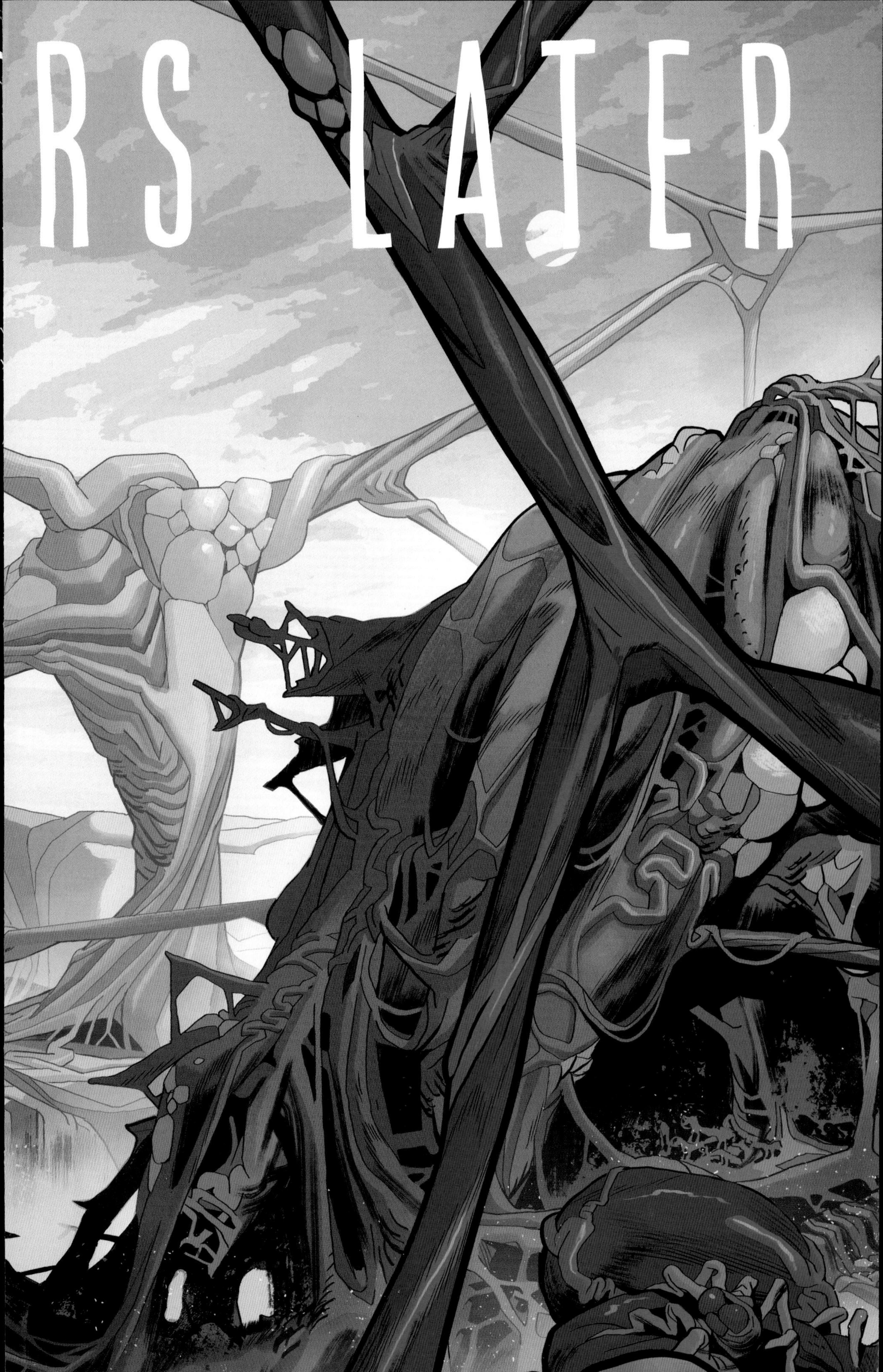
RS LATER

THUDD

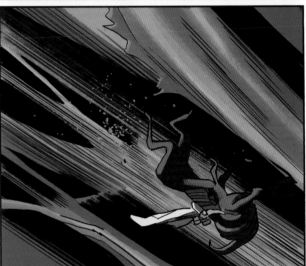

I THINK WE LOST THEM...

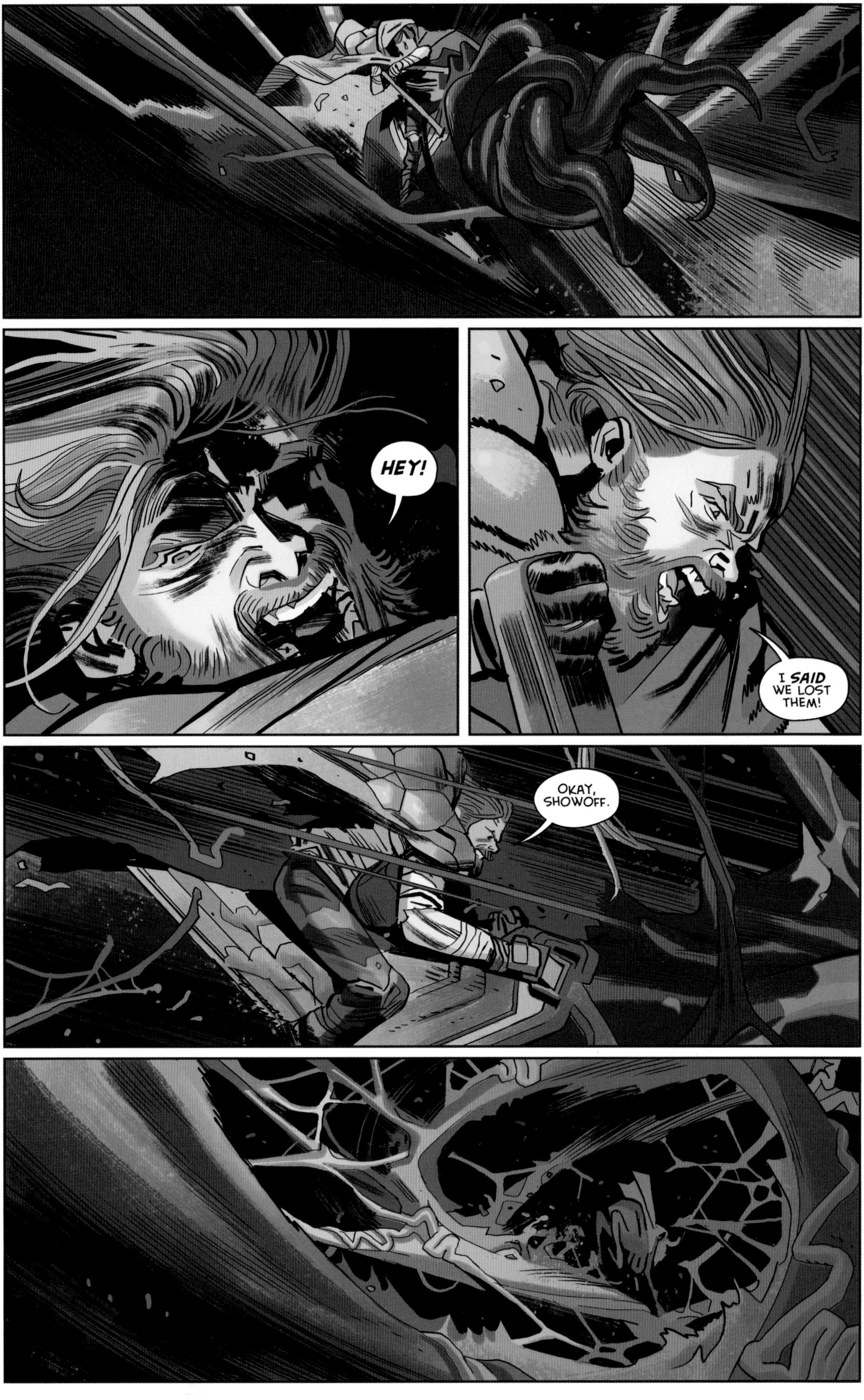
HEY!
I SAID WE LOST THEM!
OKAY, SHOWOFF.

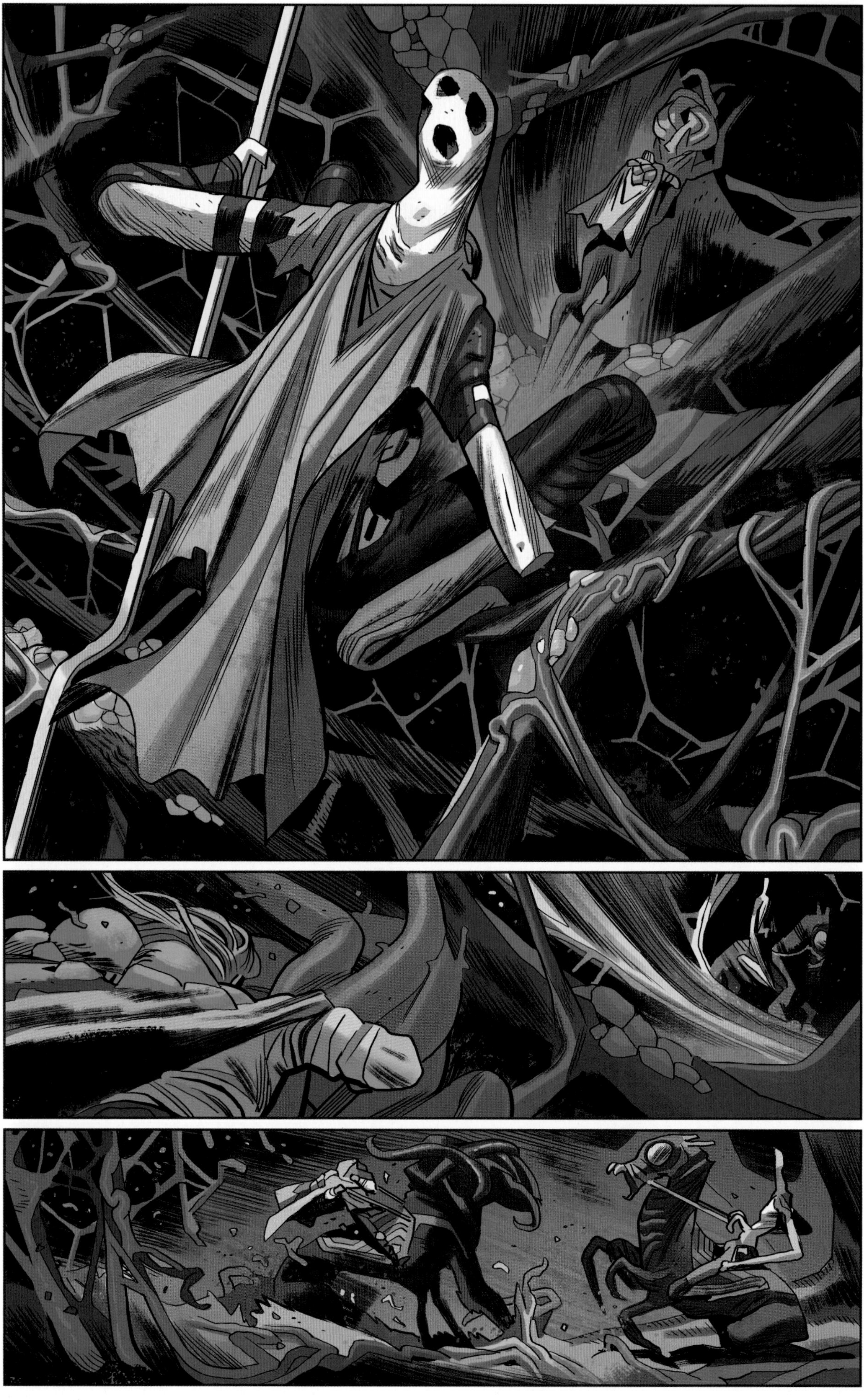

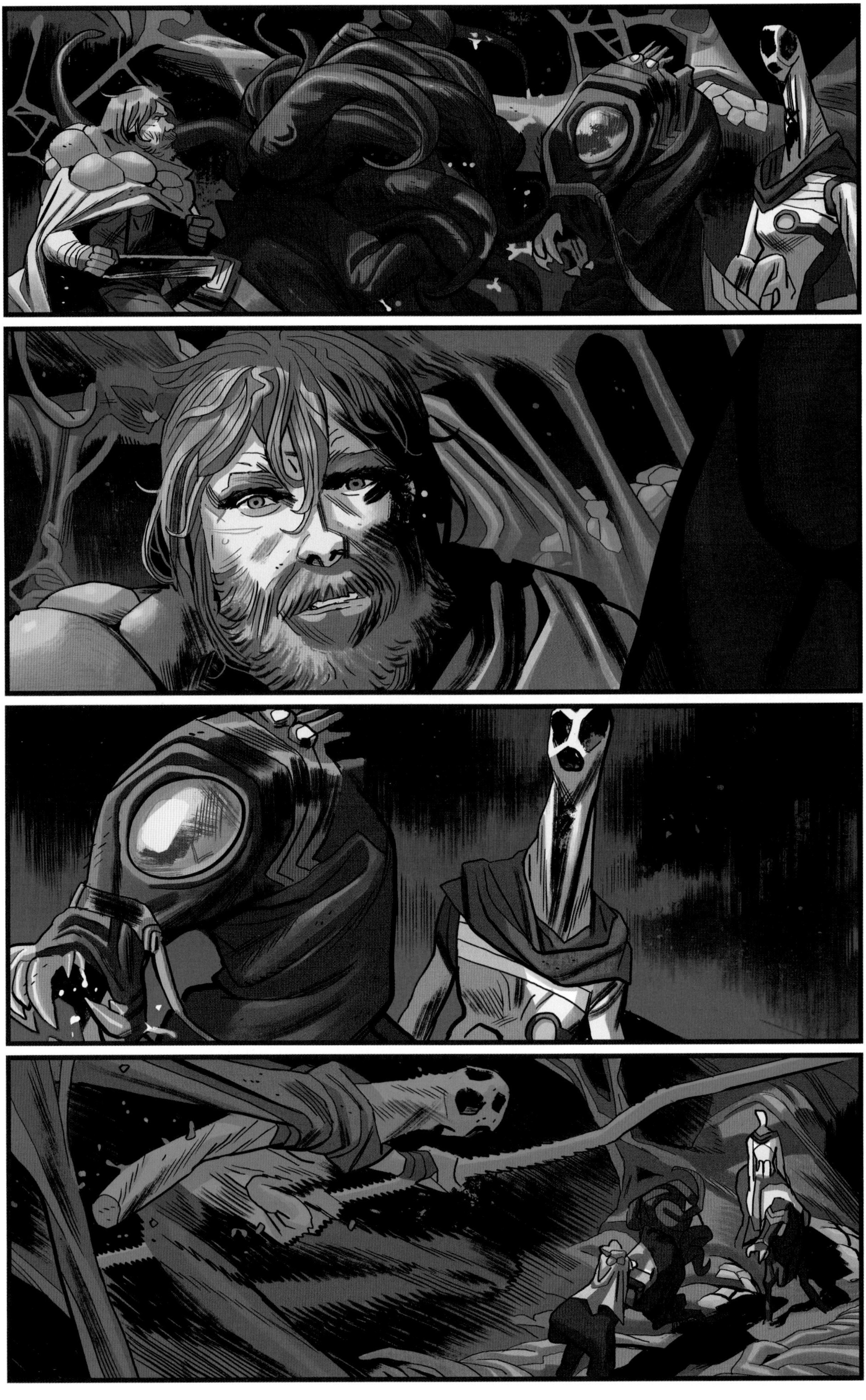

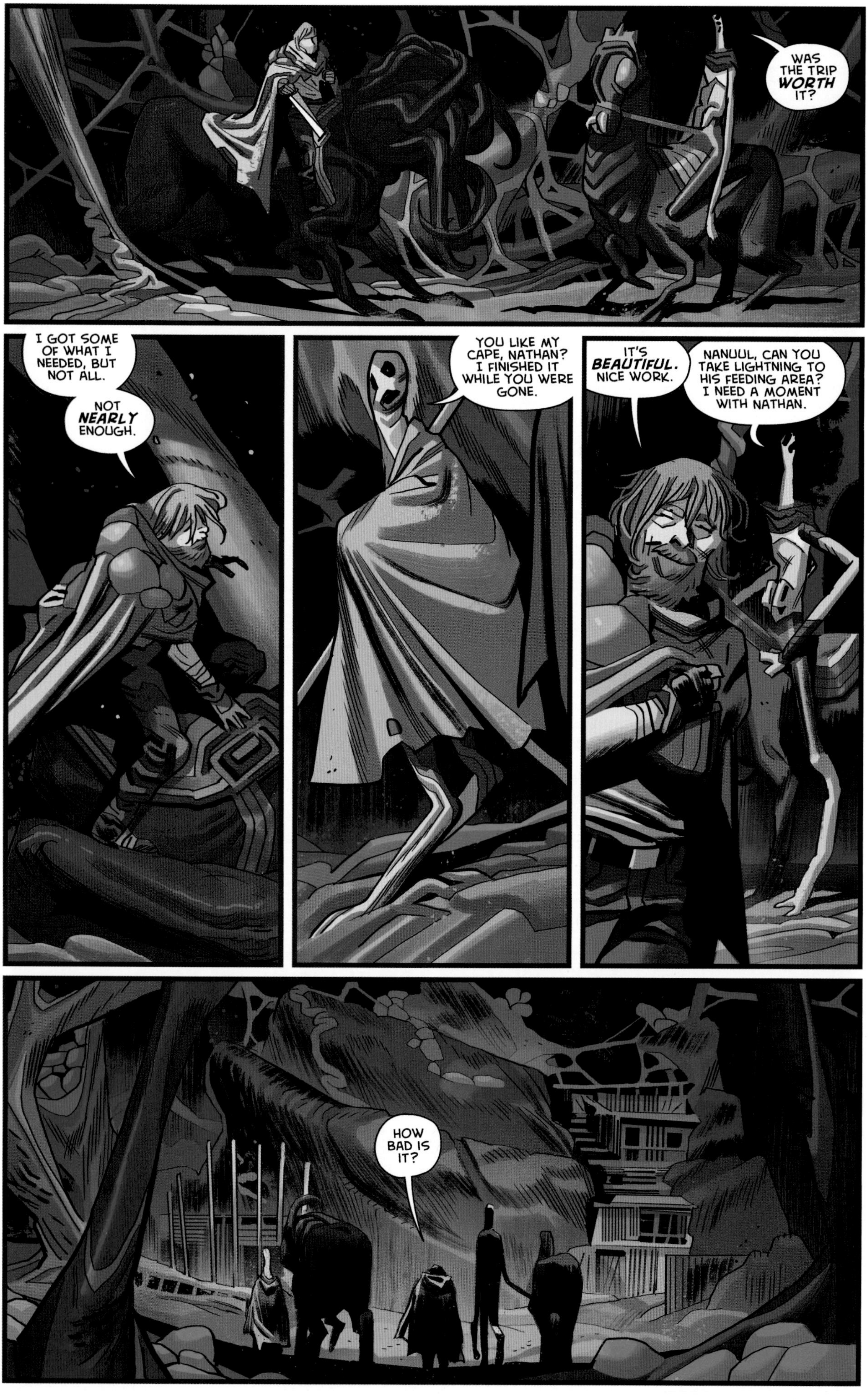
WAS THE TRIP *WORTH* IT?
I GOT SOME OF WHAT I NEEDED, BUT NOT ALL.
NOT *NEARLY* ENOUGH.
YOU LIKE MY CAPE, NATHAN? I FINISHED IT WHILE YOU WERE GONE.
IT'S *BEAUTIFUL.* NICE WORK.
NANUUL, CAN YOU TAKE LIGHTNING TO HIS FEEDING AREA? I NEED A MOMENT WITH NATHAN.
HOW BAD IS IT?

HOW CLOSE DO YOU THINK YOU CAN GET TO A *PROTOTYPE* WITH WHAT YOU HAVE?

I'M SORRY, GAKAAL. I'M NOT SURE I CAN, AT ALL.

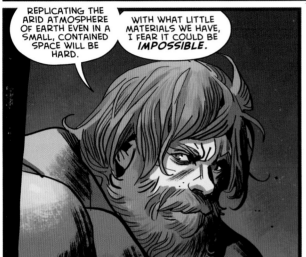

REPLICATING THE ARID ATMOSPHERE OF EARTH EVEN IN A SMALL, CONTAINED SPACE WILL BE HARD.

WITH WHAT LITTLE MATERIALS WE HAVE, I FEAR IT COULD BE *IMPOSSIBLE.*

...

WHAT IS IT?

SIGNAL CAME THROUGH TODAY. THE SCIENCE COMMISSION CLAIMS THEY'RE *CLOSE* TO MAKING YOUR DEVICE WORK.

...

EVEN IF WE SOMEHOW SHOWED PROGRESS NOW, THEY'D PROBABLY JUST BACK *BOTH* PLANS.

I FEAR IT'S *TOO LATE.* THEY'RE GOING TO HAVE ACCESS TO YOUR WORLD NO MATTER WHAT.

IT'S ONLY A MATTER OF TIME.

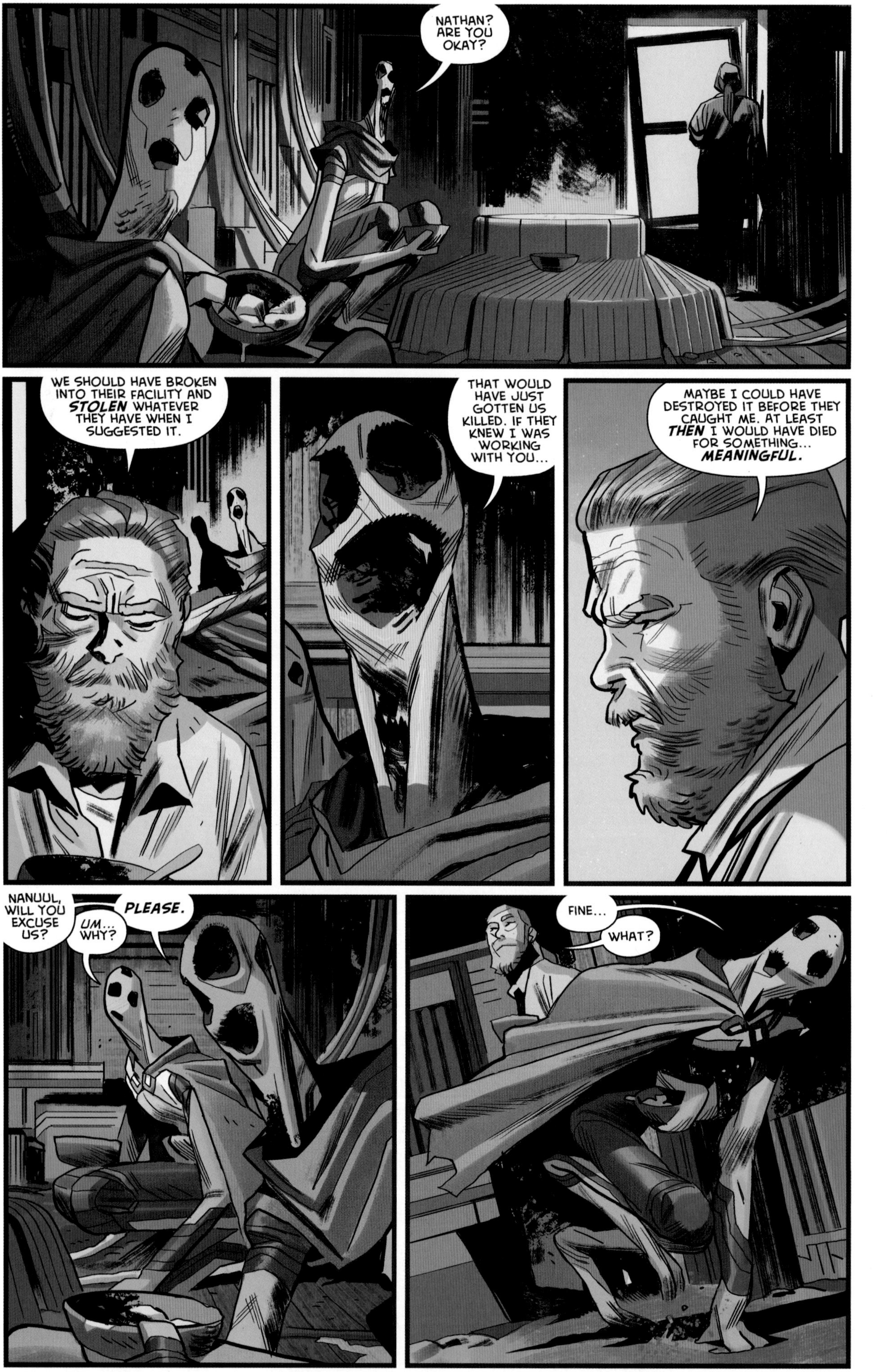
NATHAN? ARE YOU OKAY?
WE SHOULD HAVE BROKEN INTO THEIR FACILITY AND STOLEN WHATEVER THEY HAVE WHEN I SUGGESTED IT.
THAT WOULD HAVE JUST GOTTEN US KILLED. IF THEY KNEW I WAS WORKING WITH YOU...
MAYBE I COULD HAVE DESTROYED IT BEFORE THEY CAUGHT ME. AT LEAST THEN I WOULD HAVE DIED FOR SOMETHING... MEANINGFUL.
NANUUL, WILL YOU EXCUSE US?
UM... WHY?
PLEASE.
FINE...
WHAT?

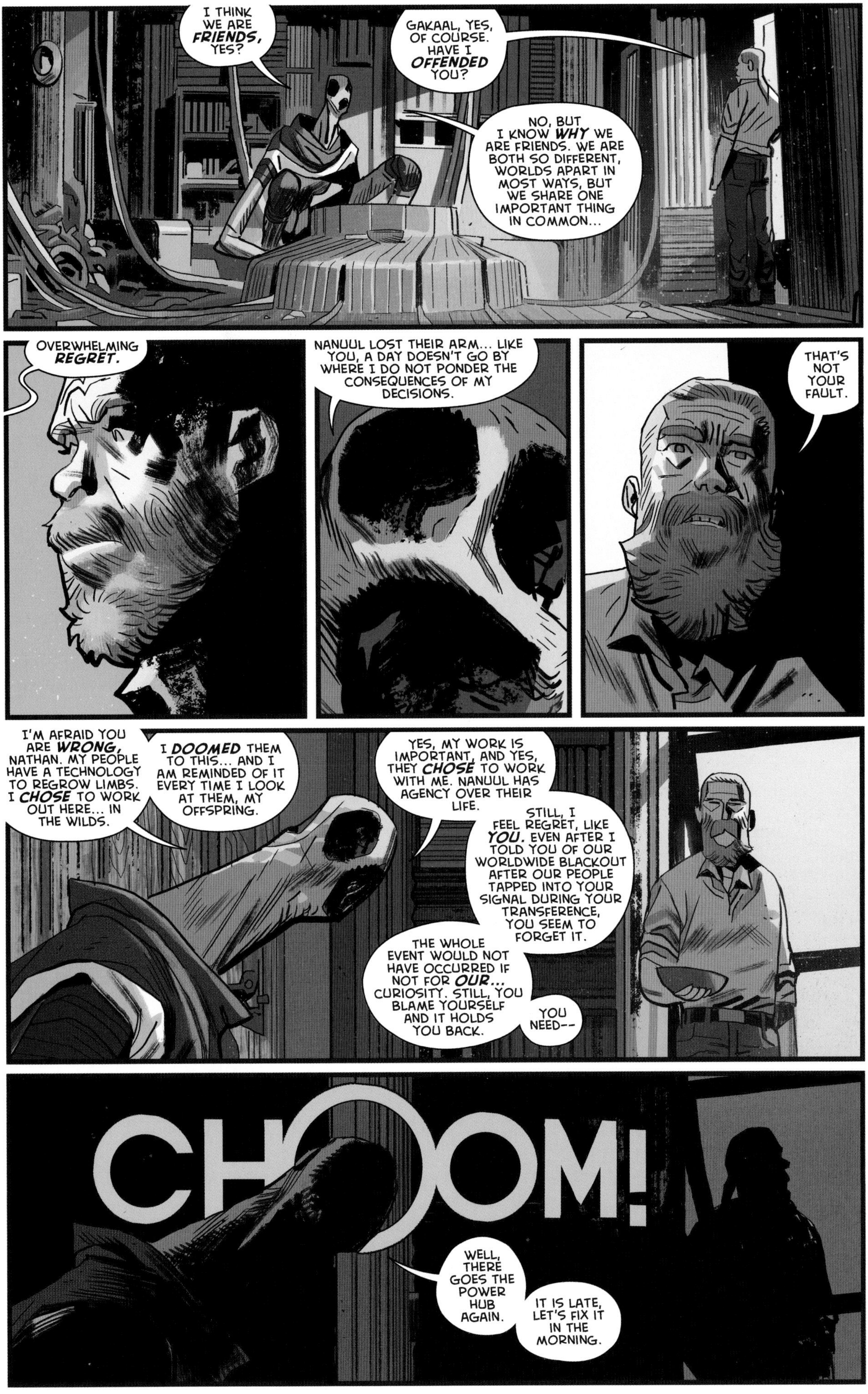
I THINK WE ARE FRIENDS, YES?
GAKAAL, YES, OF COURSE. HAVE I OFFENDED YOU?
NO, BUT I KNOW WHY WE ARE FRIENDS. WE ARE BOTH SO DIFFERENT, WORLDS APART IN MOST WAYS, BUT WE SHARE ONE IMPORTANT THING IN COMMON...
OVERWHELMING REGRET.
NANUUL LOST THEIR ARM... LIKE YOU, A DAY DOESN'T GO BY WHERE I DO NOT PONDER THE CONSEQUENCES OF MY DECISIONS.
THAT'S NOT YOUR FAULT.
I'M AFRAID YOU ARE WRONG, NATHAN. MY PEOPLE HAVE A TECHNOLOGY TO REGROW LIMBS. I CHOSE TO WORK OUT HERE... IN THE WILDS.
I DOOMED THEM TO THIS... AND I AM REMINDED OF IT EVERY TIME I LOOK AT THEM, MY OFFSPRING.
YES, MY WORK IS IMPORTANT, AND YES, THEY CHOSE TO WORK WITH ME. NANUUL HAS AGENCY OVER THEIR LIFE.
STILL, I FEEL REGRET, LIKE YOU. EVEN AFTER I TOLD YOU OF OUR WORLDWIDE BLACKOUT AFTER OUR PEOPLE TAPPED INTO YOUR SIGNAL DURING YOUR TRANSFERENCE, YOU SEEM TO FORGET IT.
THE WHOLE EVENT WOULD NOT HAVE OCCURRED IF NOT FOR OUR... CURIOSITY. STILL, YOU BLAME YOURSELF AND IT HOLDS YOU BACK.
YOU NEED--
CHOOM!
WELL, THERE GOES THE POWER HUB AGAIN.
IT IS LATE, LET'S FIX IT IN THE MORNING.

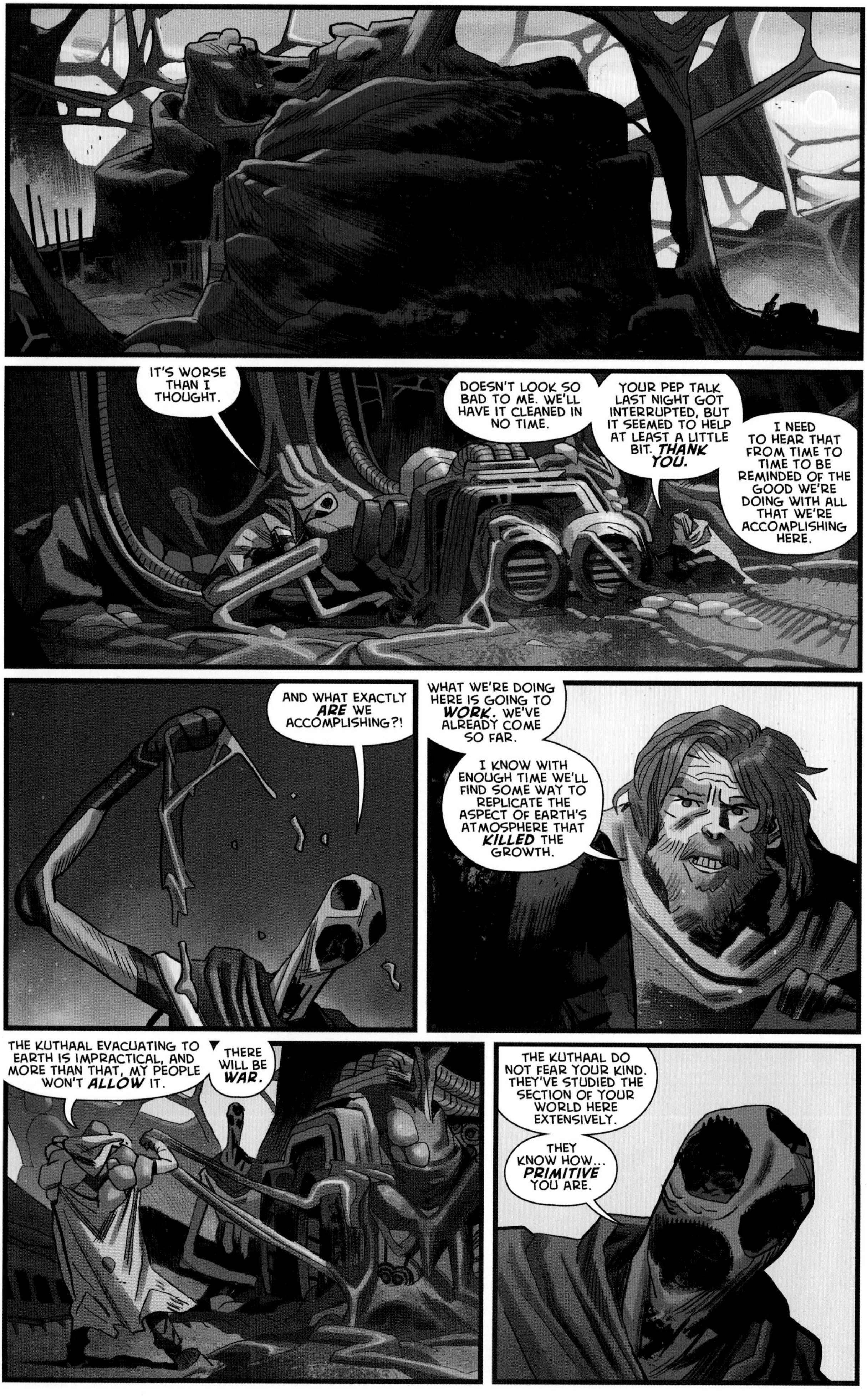
IT'S WORSE THAN I THOUGHT.
DOESN'T LOOK SO BAD TO ME. WE'LL HAVE IT CLEANED IN NO TIME.
YOUR PEP TALK LAST NIGHT GOT INTERRUPTED, BUT IT SEEMED TO HELP AT LEAST A LITTLE BIT. THANK YOU.
I NEED TO HEAR THAT FROM TIME TO TIME TO BE REMINDED OF THE GOOD WE'RE DOING WITH ALL THAT WE'RE ACCOMPLISHING HERE.
AND WHAT EXACTLY ARE WE ACCOMPLISHING?!
WHAT WE'RE DOING HERE IS GOING TO WORK. WE'VE ALREADY COME SO FAR.
I KNOW WITH ENOUGH TIME WE'LL FIND SOME WAY TO REPLICATE THE ASPECT OF EARTH'S ATMOSPHERE THAT KILLED THE GROWTH.
THE KUTHAAL EVACUATING TO EARTH IS IMPRACTICAL, AND MORE THAN THAT, MY PEOPLE WON'T ALLOW IT.
THERE WILL BE WAR.
THE KUTHAAL DO NOT FEAR YOUR KIND. THEY'VE STUDIED THE SECTION OF YOUR WORLD HERE EXTENSIVELY.
THEY KNOW HOW... PRIMITIVE YOU ARE.

...

DON'T WORRY, FRIEND, I'M SURE IT WON'T COME TO THAT.

NO MATTER HOW CONFIDENT MY PEOPLE ARE, I DO NOT THINK THEY'LL BE ABLE TO REPLICATE YOUR DEVICE IN TIME.

OUR WORLD WILL *DIE.*

THERE'S NOTHING WE CAN DO TO STOP THE GROWTH. IT'S TOO STRONG AND WE DON'T HAVE THE RESOURCES TO FIGHT IT.

DON'T SAY THAT. WE'VE BEEN WORKING TOO HARD FOR TOO LONG FOR YOU TO GIVE UP NOW.

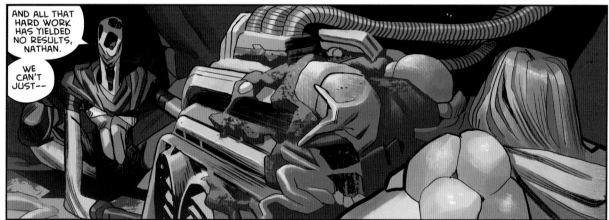

AND ALL THAT HARD WORK HAS YIELDED NO RESULTS, NATHAN.

WE CAN'T JUST--

KRAGOOM WROOM!

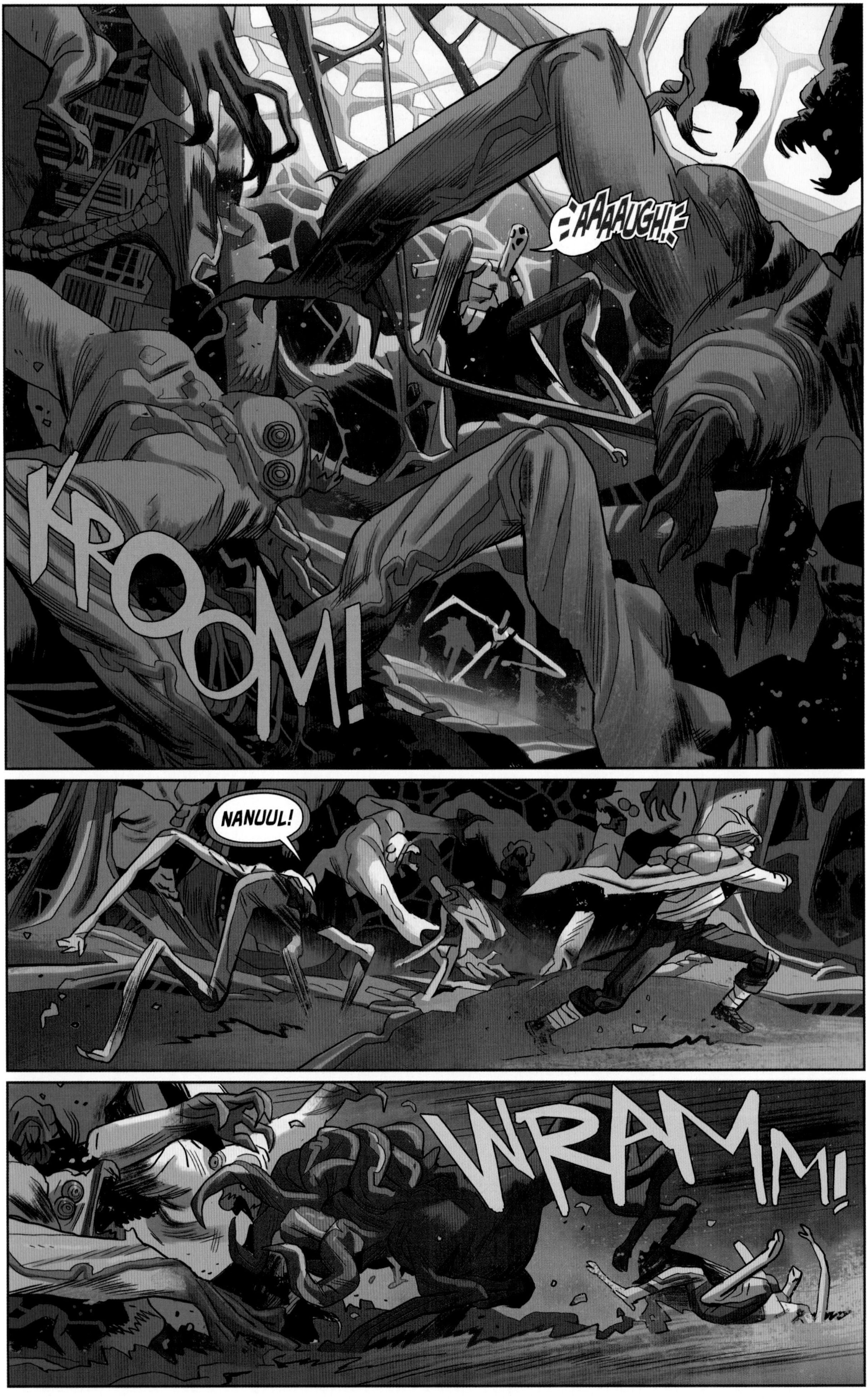
AAAAUGH!
KROOOM!
NANUUL!
WRAMM!

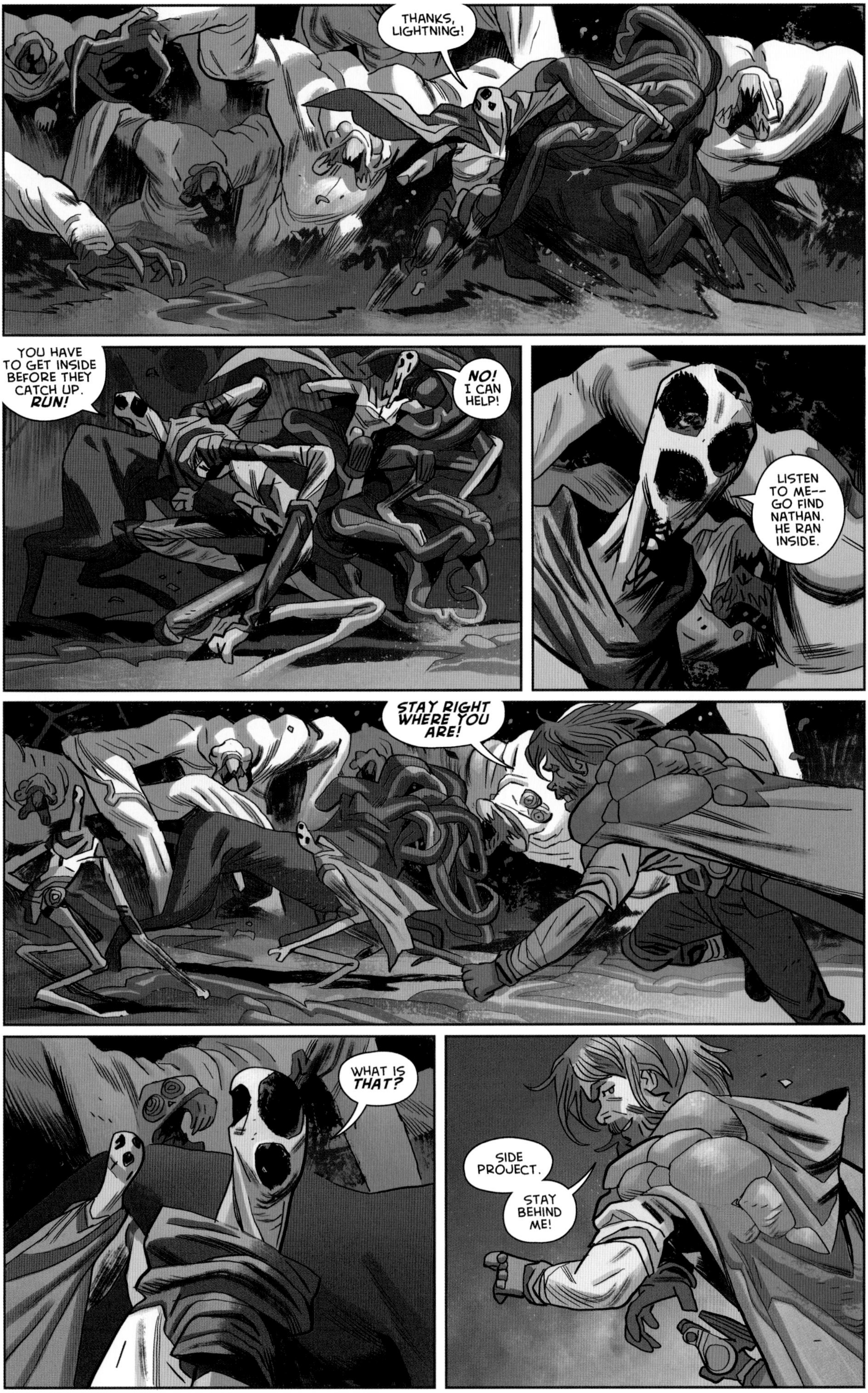
THANKS, LIGHTNING!
YOU HAVE TO GET INSIDE BEFORE THEY CATCH UP. RUN!
NO! I CAN HELP!
LISTEN TO ME-- GO FIND NATHAN. HE RAN INSIDE.
STAY RIGHT WHERE YOU ARE!
WHAT IS THAT?
SIDE PROJECT.
STAY BEHIND ME!

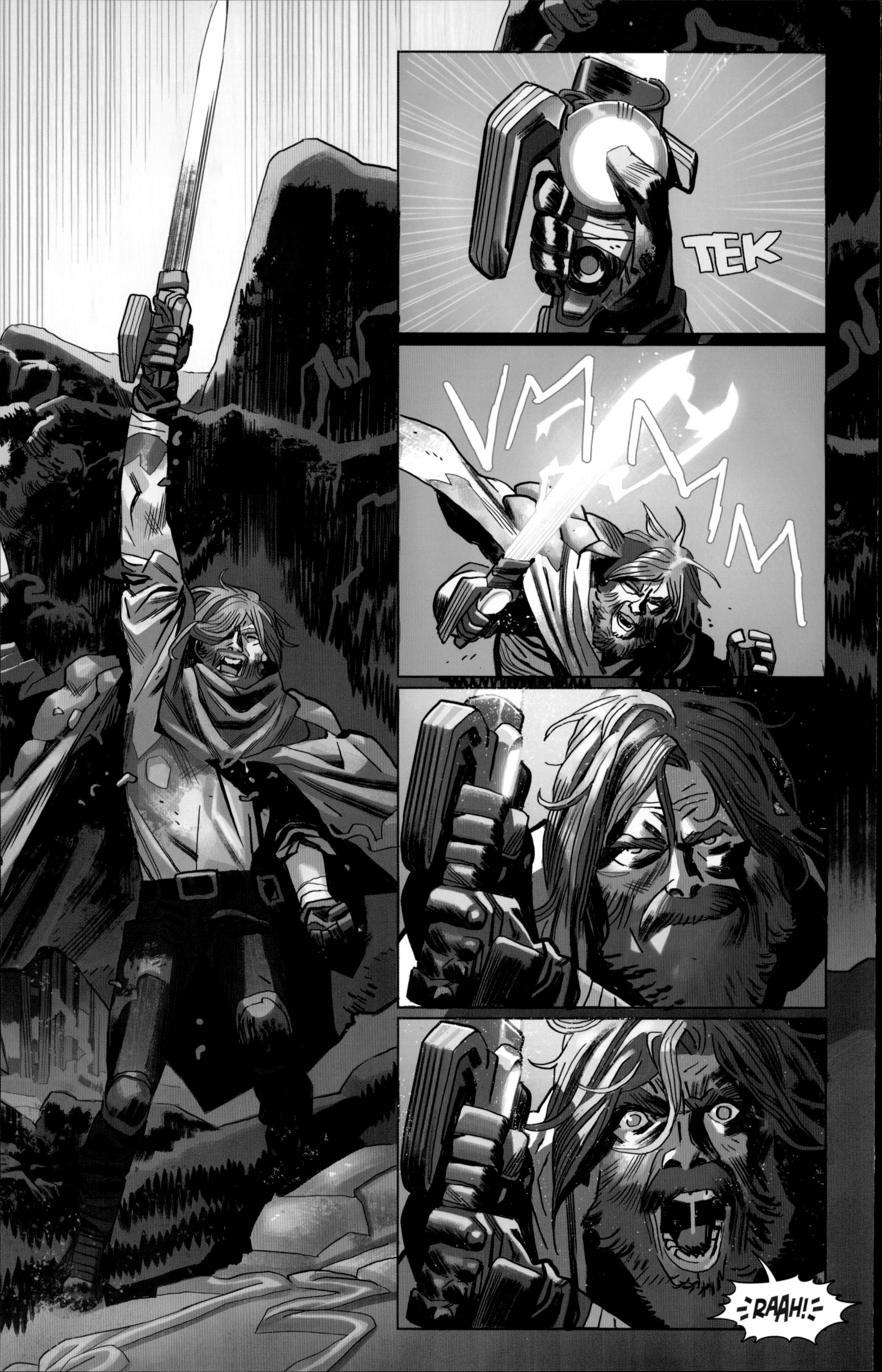
TEK
VMMMM
RAAH!

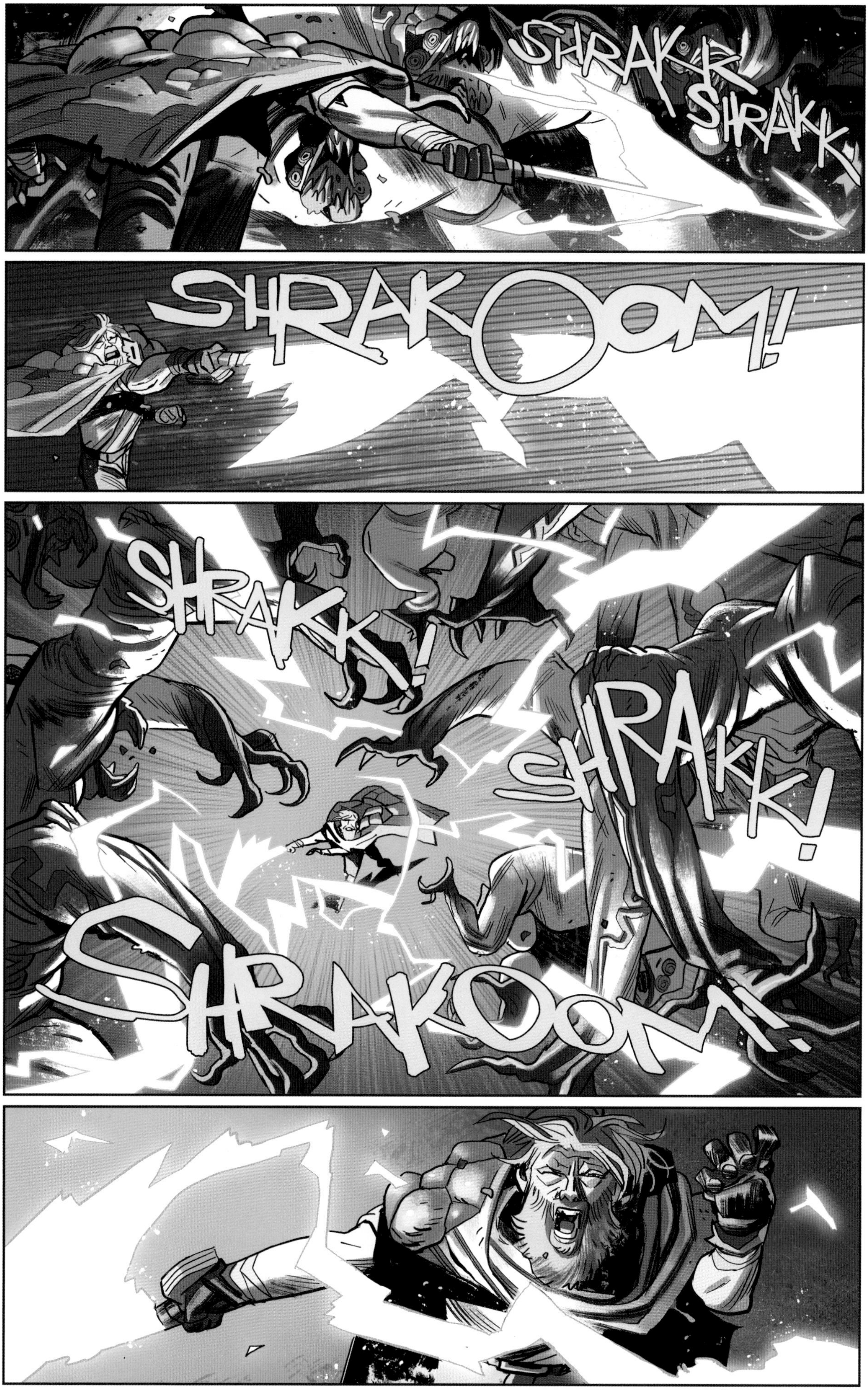
SHRAKKK
SHRAKKK
SHRAKOOM!
SHRAKK!
SHRAKK!
SHRAKOOM!

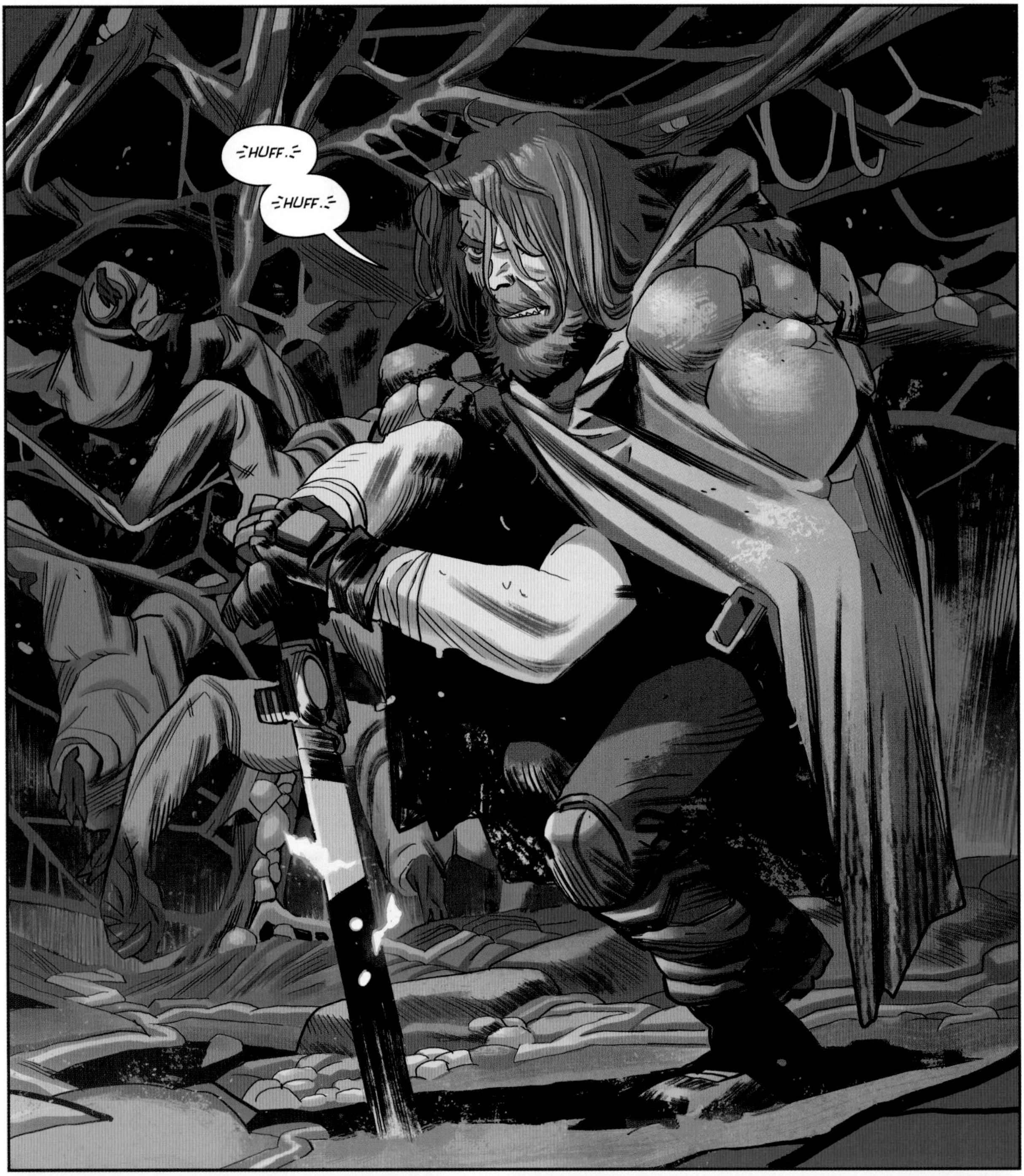
HUFF.
HUFF.
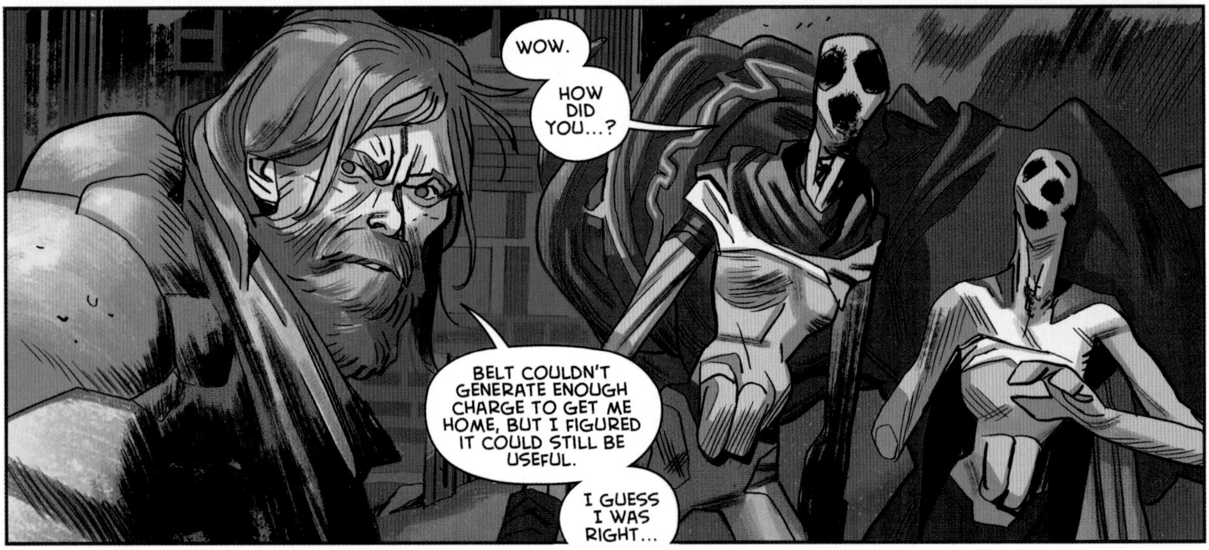
WOW.
HOW DID YOU...?
BELT COULDN'T GENERATE ENOUGH CHARGE TO GET ME HOME, BUT I FIGURED IT COULD STILL BE USEFUL.
I GUESS I WAS RIGHT...

OKAY. THERE.

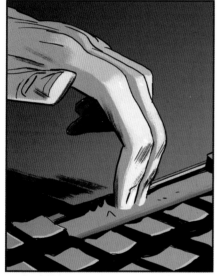

WHIRRRRRRR

C'MON.

C'MON...

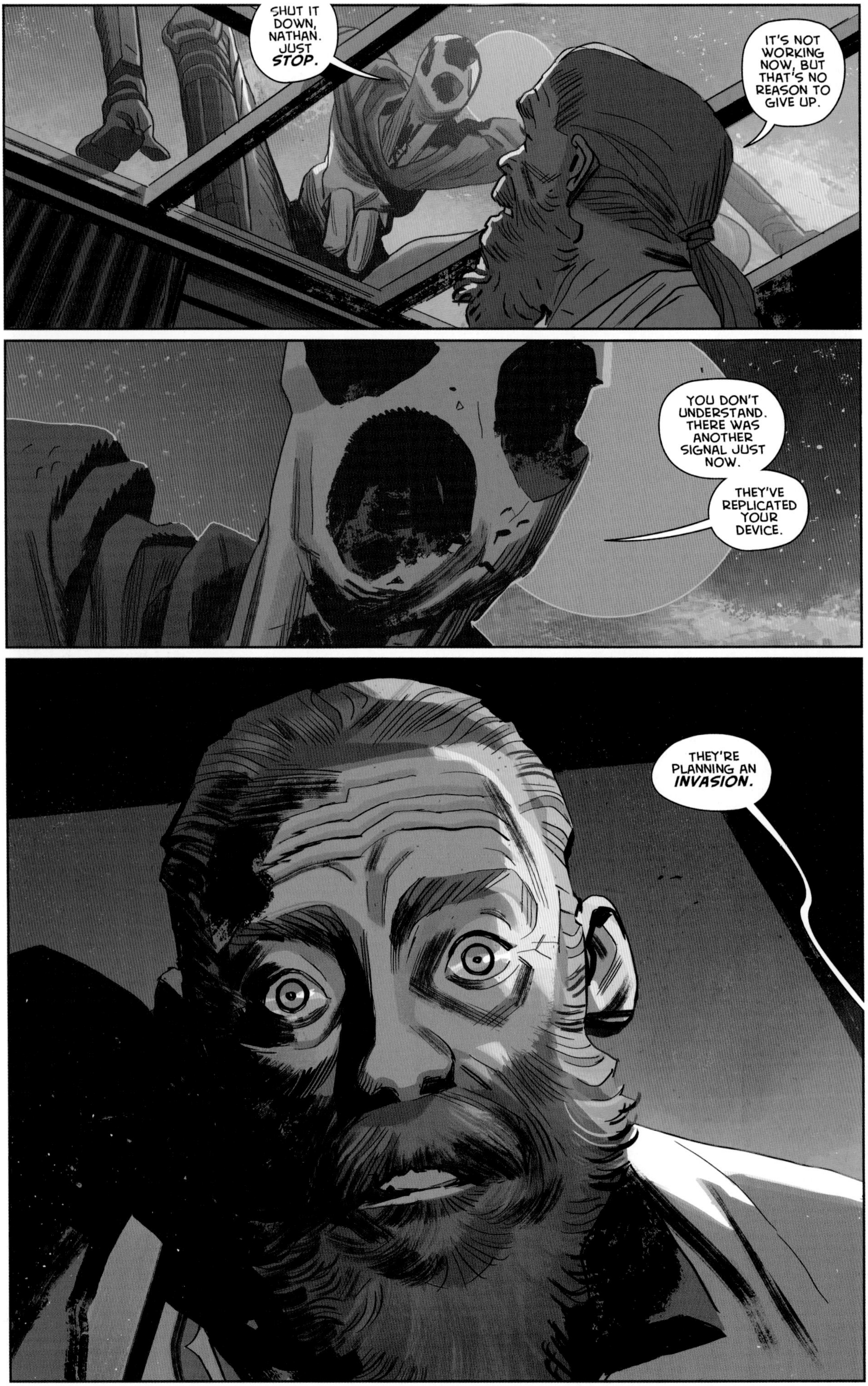
SHUT IT DOWN, NATHAN. JUST **STOP**.
IT'S NOT WORKING NOW, BUT THAT'S NO REASON TO GIVE UP.
YOU DON'T UNDERSTAND. THERE WAS ANOTHER SIGNAL JUST NOW.
THEY'VE REPLICATED YOUR DEVICE.
THEY'RE PLANNING AN **INVASION**.

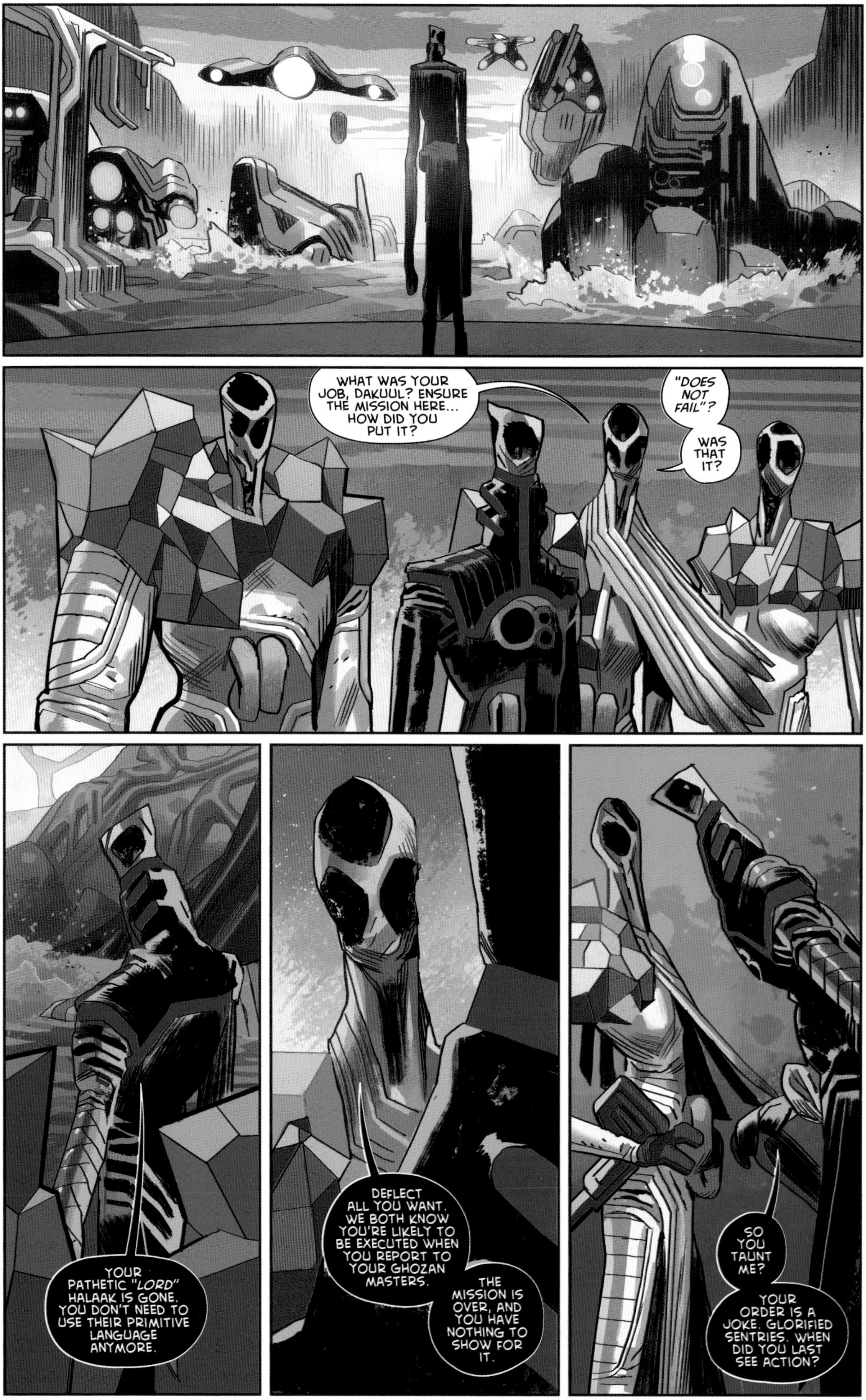
WHAT WAS YOUR JOB, DAKUUL? ENSURE THE MISSION HERE... HOW DID YOU PUT IT?
"DOES NOT FAIL"?
WAS THAT IT?
YOUR PATHETIC "LORD" HALAAK IS GONE. YOU DON'T NEED TO USE THEIR PRIMITIVE LANGUAGE ANYMORE.
DEFLECT ALL YOU WANT. WE BOTH KNOW YOU'RE LIKELY TO BE EXECUTED WHEN YOU REPORT TO YOUR GHOZAN MASTERS.
THE MISSION IS OVER, AND YOU HAVE NOTHING TO SHOW FOR IT.
SO YOU TAUNT ME?
YOUR ORDER IS A JOKE. GLORIFIED SENTRIES. WHEN DID YOU LAST SEE ACTION?

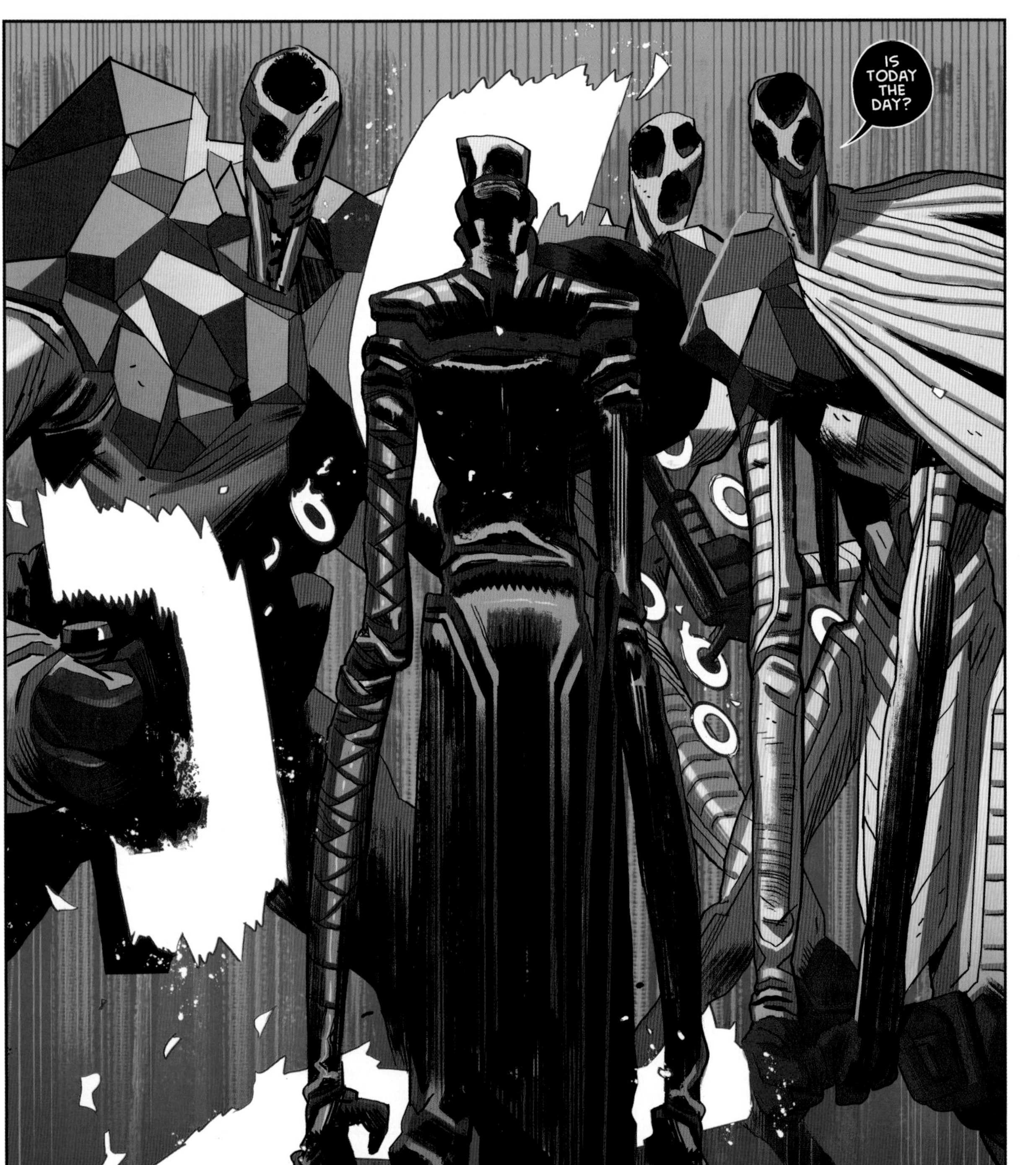
IS TODAY THE DAY?

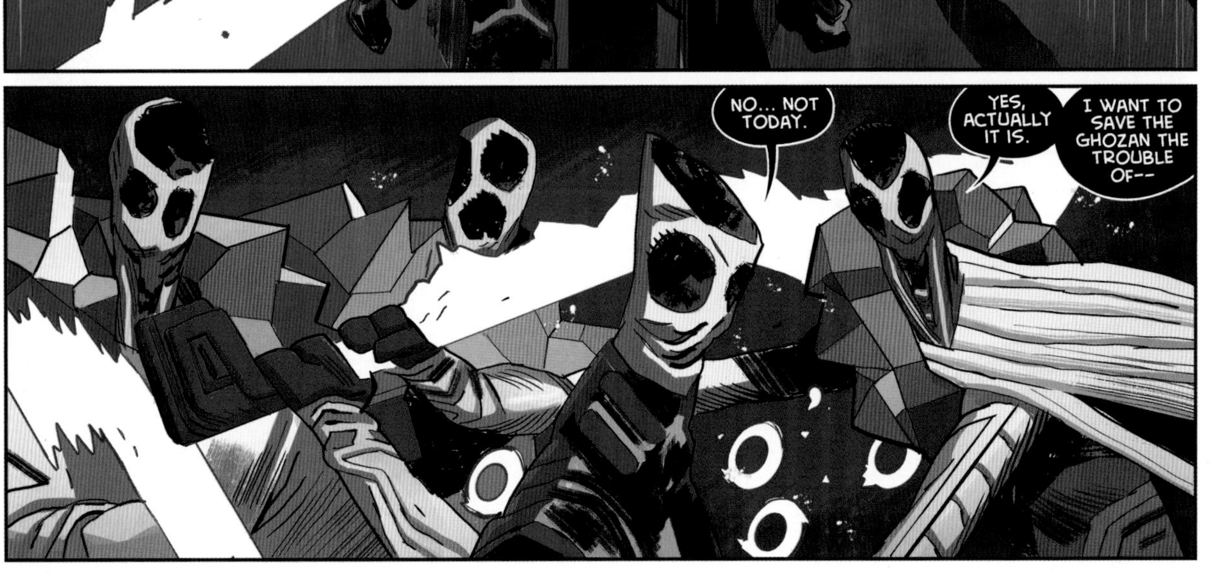
NO... NOT TODAY.
YES, ACTUALLY IT IS.
I WANT TO SAVE THE GHOZAN THE TROUBLE OF--

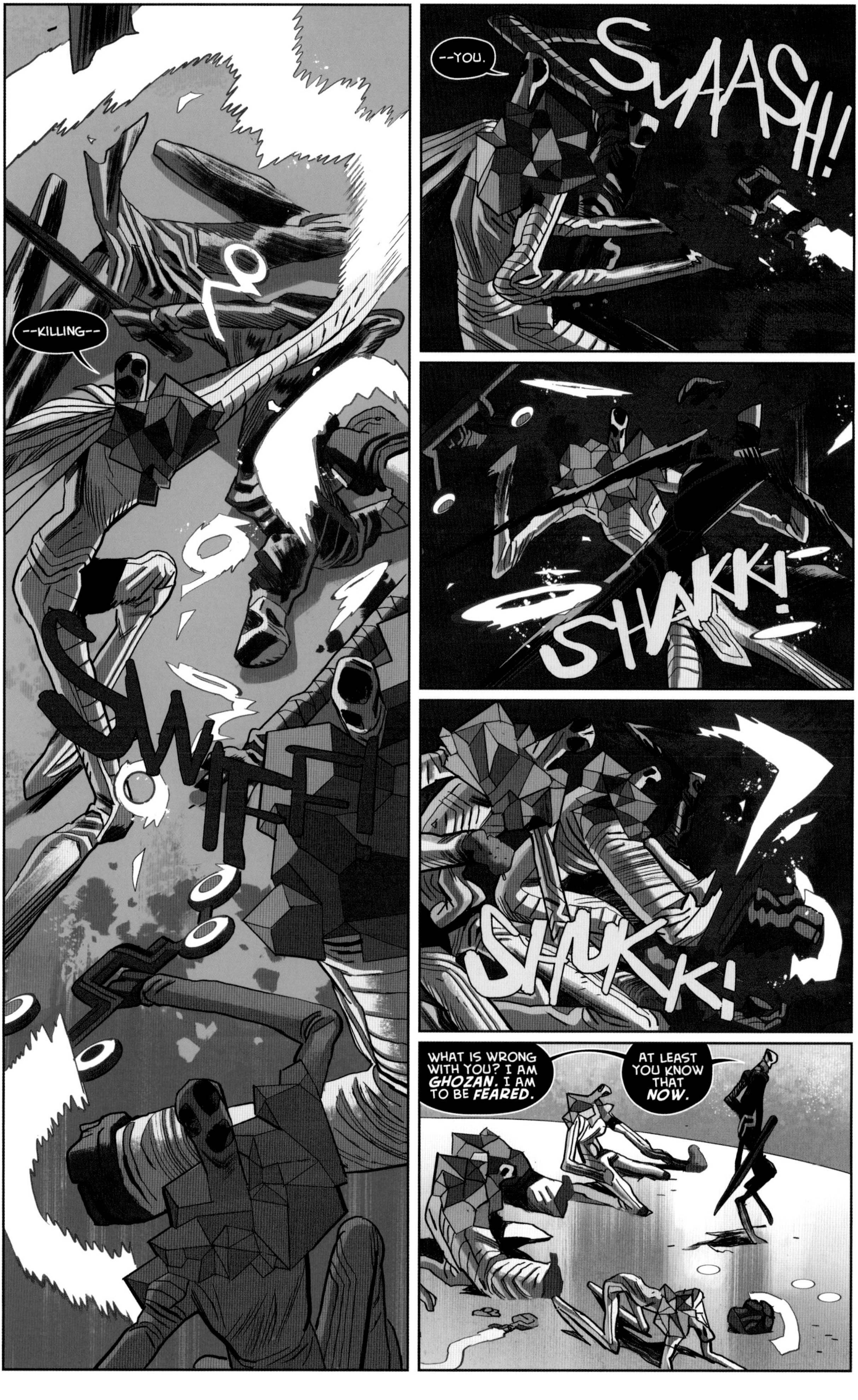
--KILLING--
SWIFF!
--YOU.
SWAASH!
SHAKK!
SHUKK!
WHAT IS WRONG WITH YOU? I AM GHOZAN. I AM TO BE FEARED.
AT LEAST YOU KNOW THAT NOW.

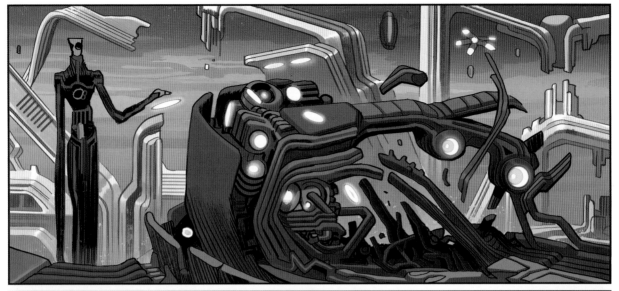

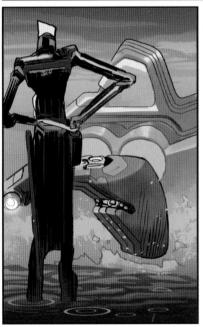

"NOTHING TO SHOW FOR IT..."

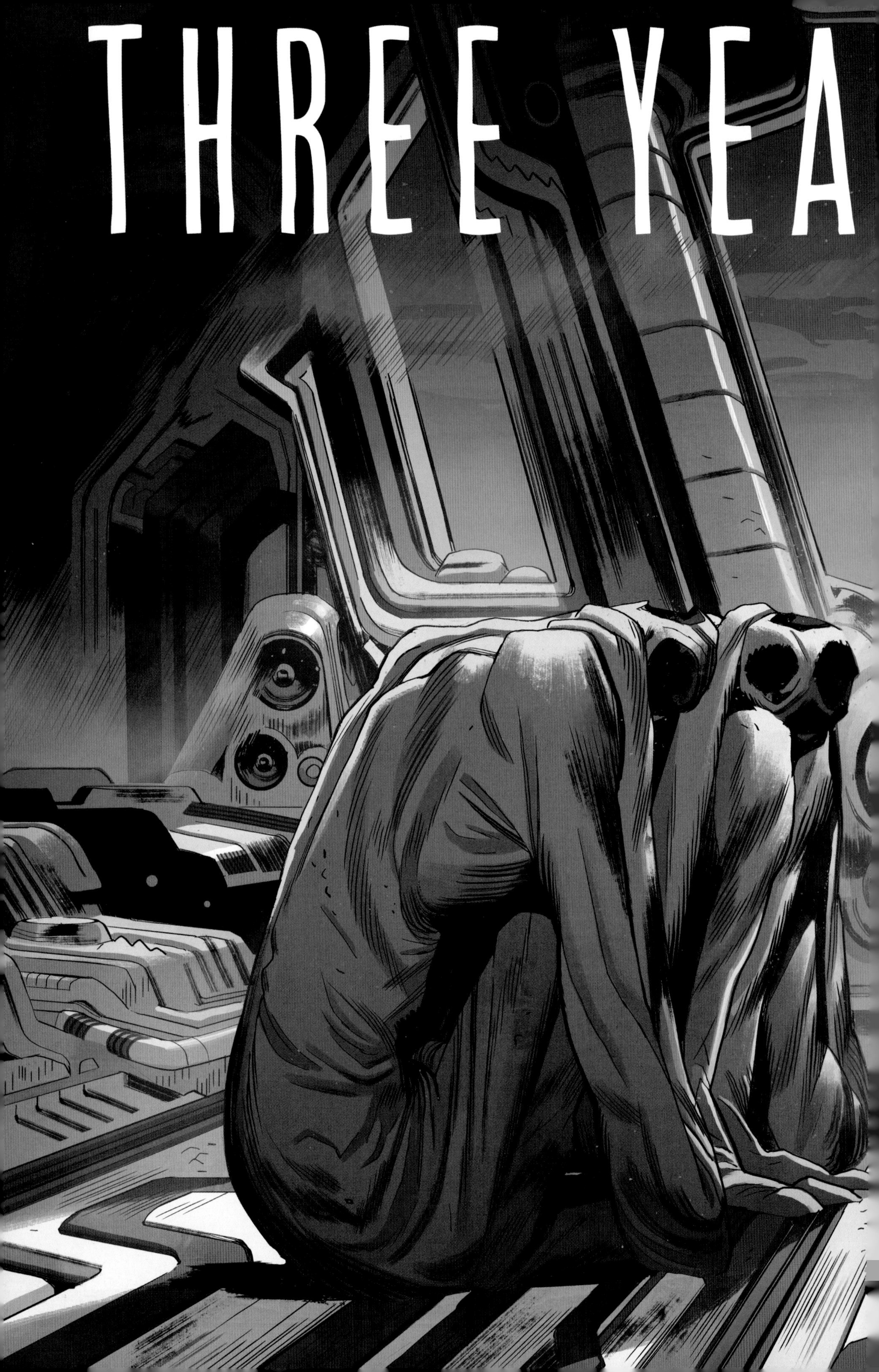
THREE YEA

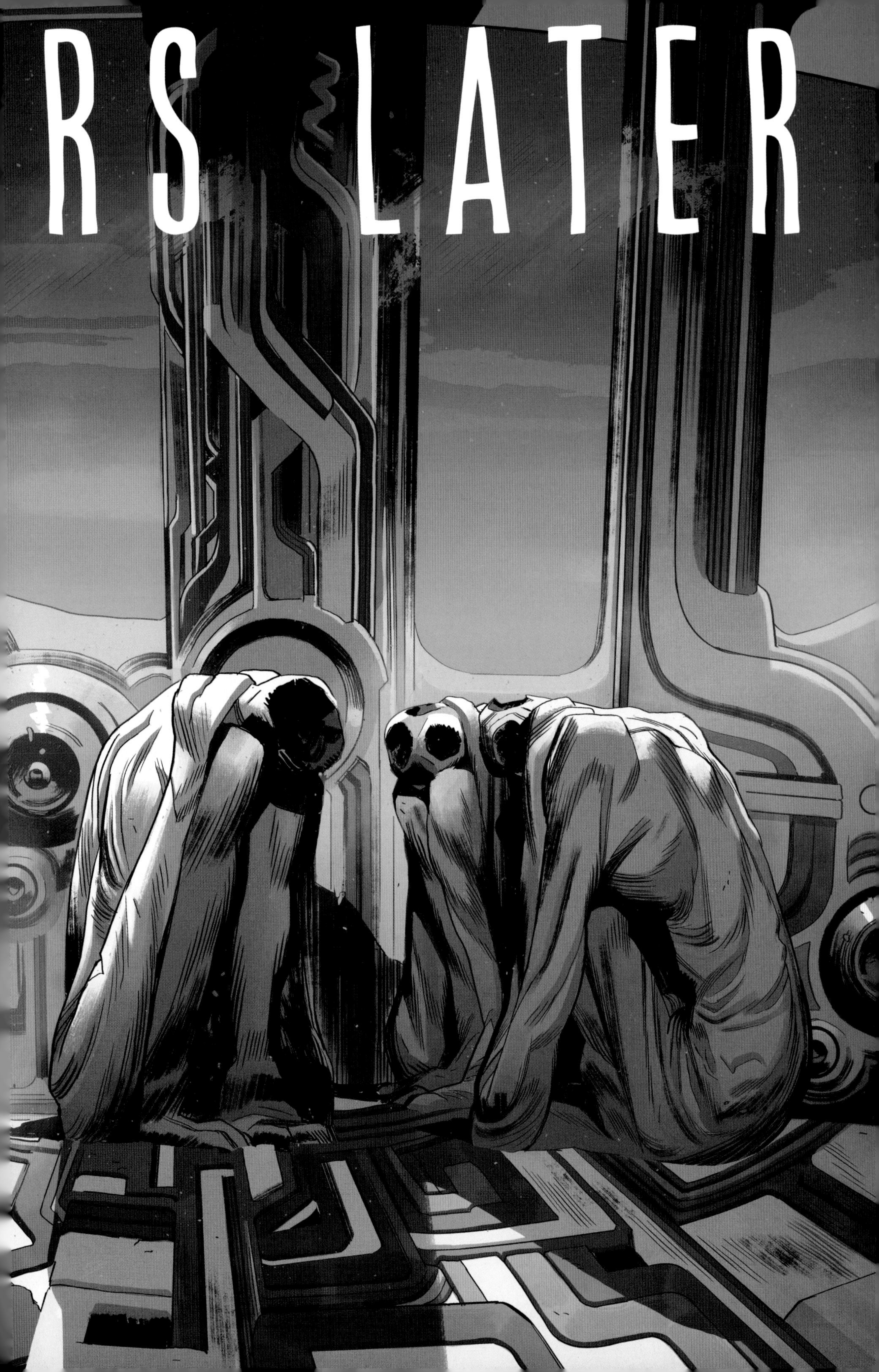
RS LATER

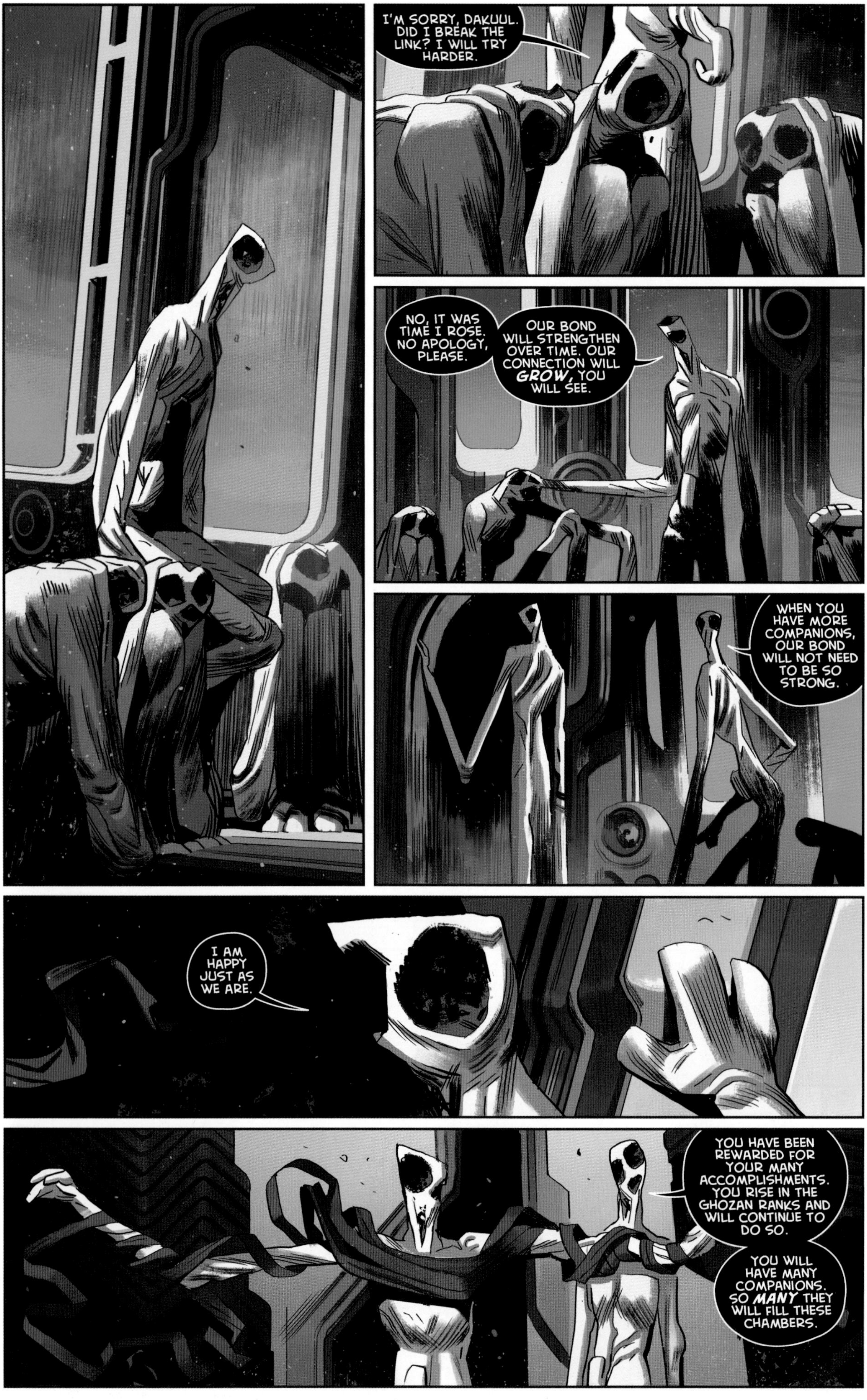
I'M SORRY, DAKUUL. DID I BREAK THE LINK? I WILL TRY HARDER.
NO, IT WAS TIME I ROSE. NO APOLOGY, PLEASE.
OUR BOND WILL STRENGTHEN OVER TIME. OUR CONNECTION WILL GROW, YOU WILL SEE.
WHEN YOU HAVE MORE COMPANIONS, OUR BOND WILL NOT NEED TO BE SO STRONG.
I AM HAPPY JUST AS WE ARE.
YOU HAVE BEEN REWARDED FOR YOUR MANY ACCOMPLISHMENTS. YOU RISE IN THE GHOZAN RANKS AND WILL CONTINUE TO DO SO.
YOU WILL HAVE MANY COMPANIONS. SO MANY THEY WILL FILL THESE CHAMBERS.

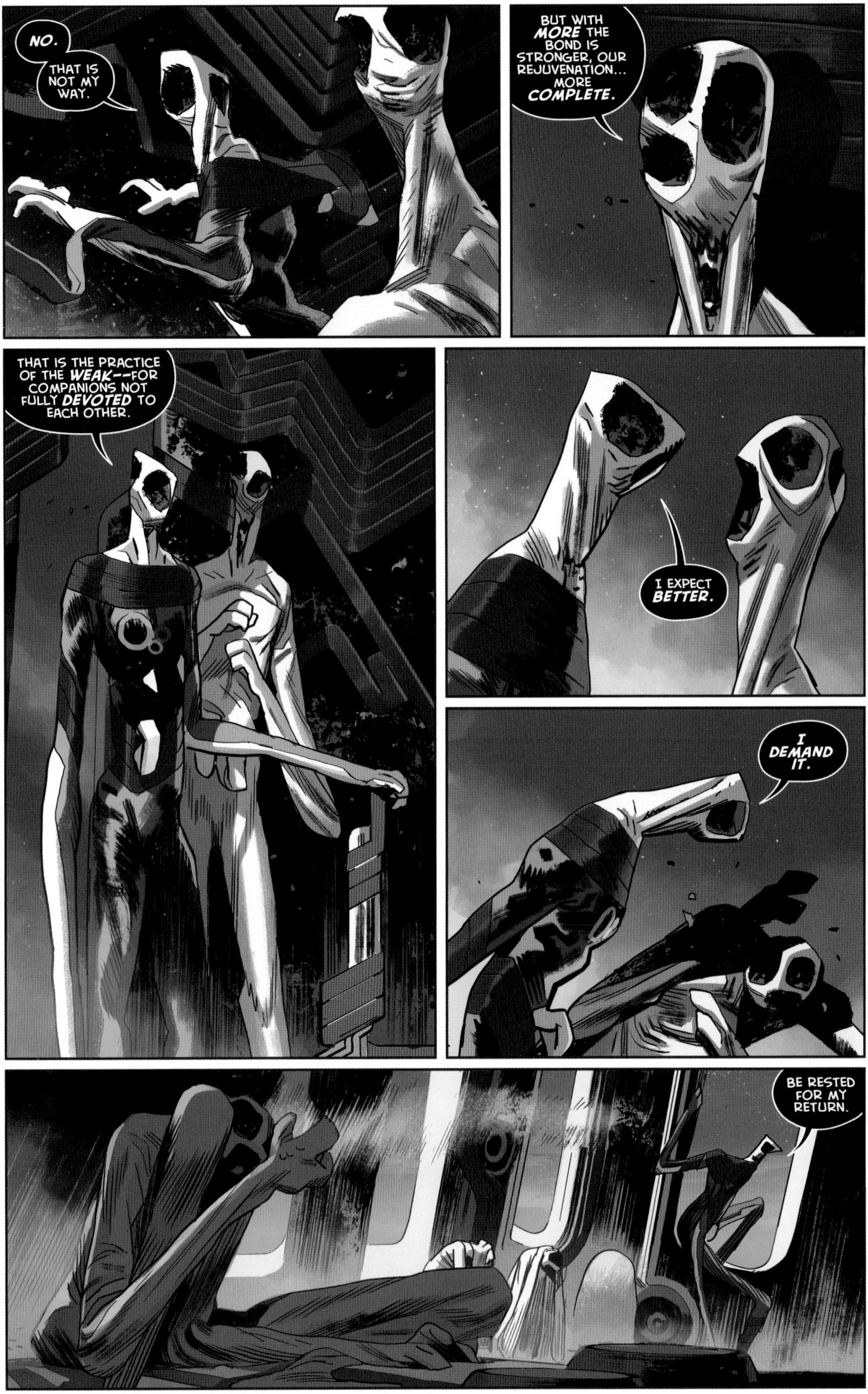
NO.
THAT IS NOT MY WAY.
BUT WITH MORE THE BOND IS STRONGER, OUR REJUVENATION... MORE COMPLETE.
THAT IS THE PRACTICE OF THE WEAK--FOR COMPANIONS NOT FULLY DEVOTED TO EACH OTHER.
I EXPECT BETTER.
I DEMAND IT.
BE RESTED FOR MY RETURN.

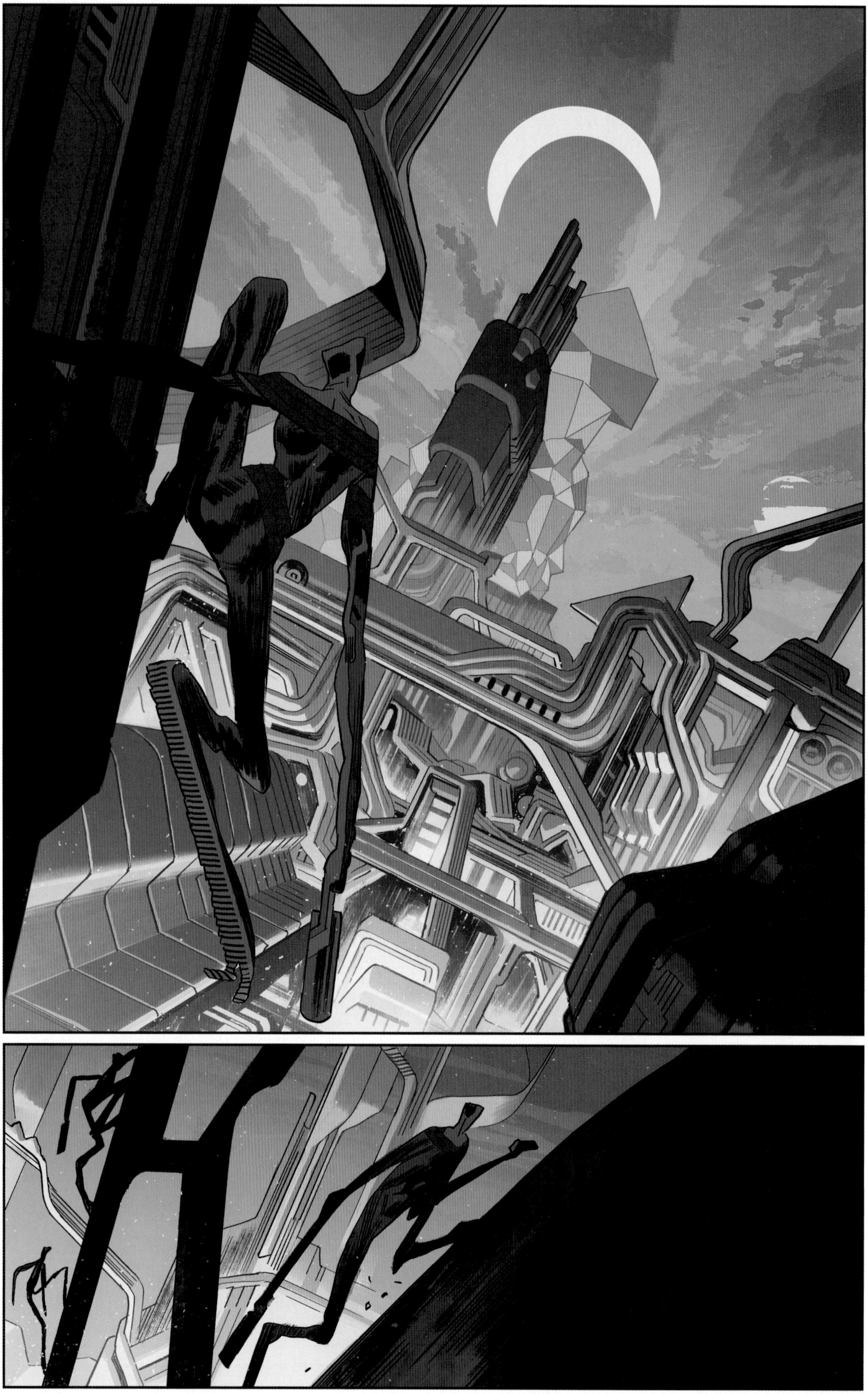

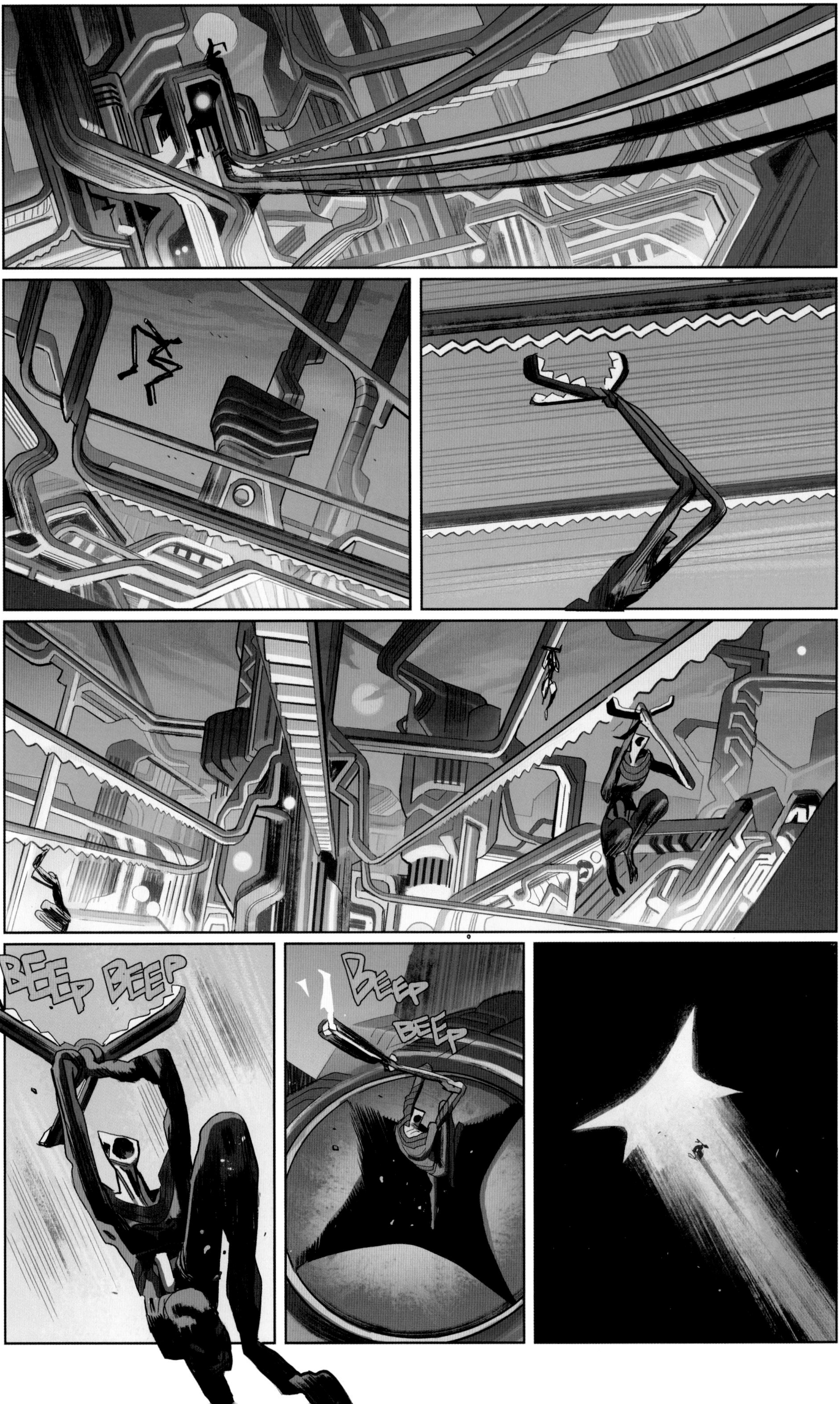
BEEP BEEP
BEEP
BEEP

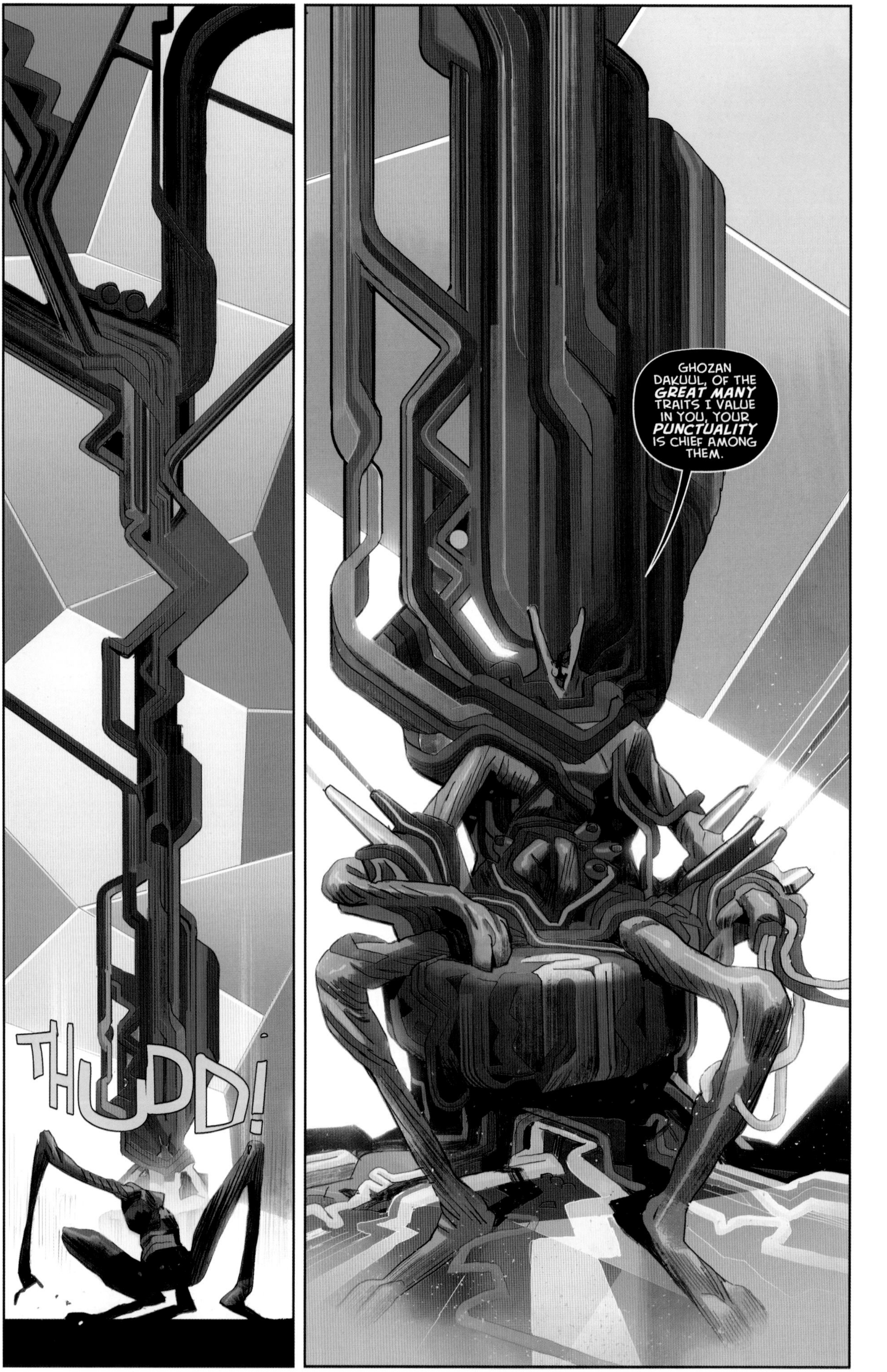
THUDD!
GHOZAN DAKUUL, OF THE **GREAT MANY** TRAITS I VALUE IN YOU, YOUR **PUNCTUALITY** IS CHIEF AMONG THEM.

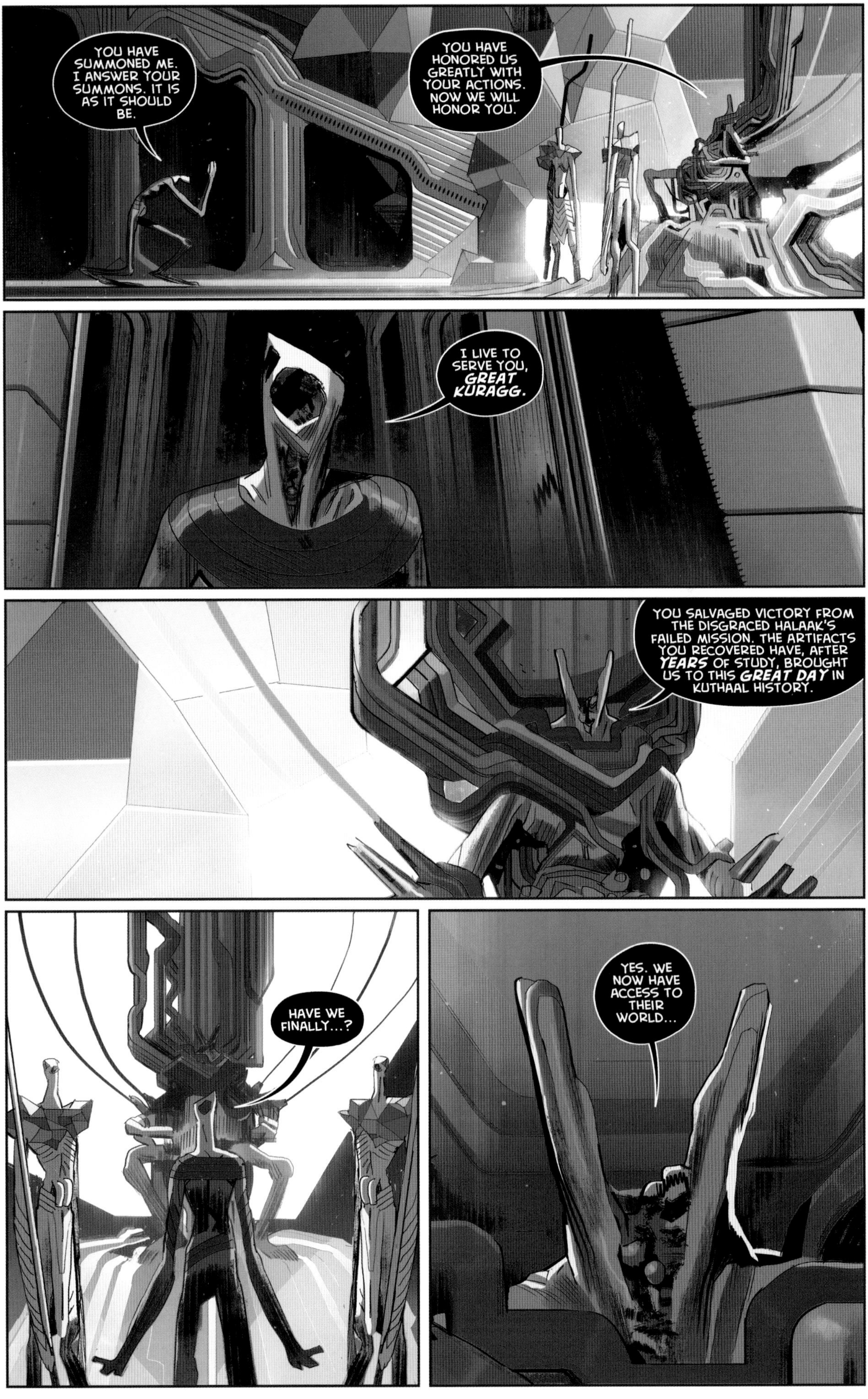
YOU HAVE SUMMONED ME. I ANSWER YOUR SUMMONS. IT IS AS IT SHOULD BE.
YOU HAVE HONORED US GREATLY WITH YOUR ACTIONS. NOW WE WILL HONOR YOU.
I LIVE TO SERVE YOU, GREAT KURAGG.
YOU SALVAGED VICTORY FROM THE DISGRACED HALAAK'S FAILED MISSION. THE ARTIFACTS YOU RECOVERED HAVE, AFTER YEARS OF STUDY, BROUGHT US TO THIS GREAT DAY IN KUTHAAL HISTORY.
HAVE WE FINALLY...?
YES. WE NOW HAVE ACCESS TO THEIR WORLD...

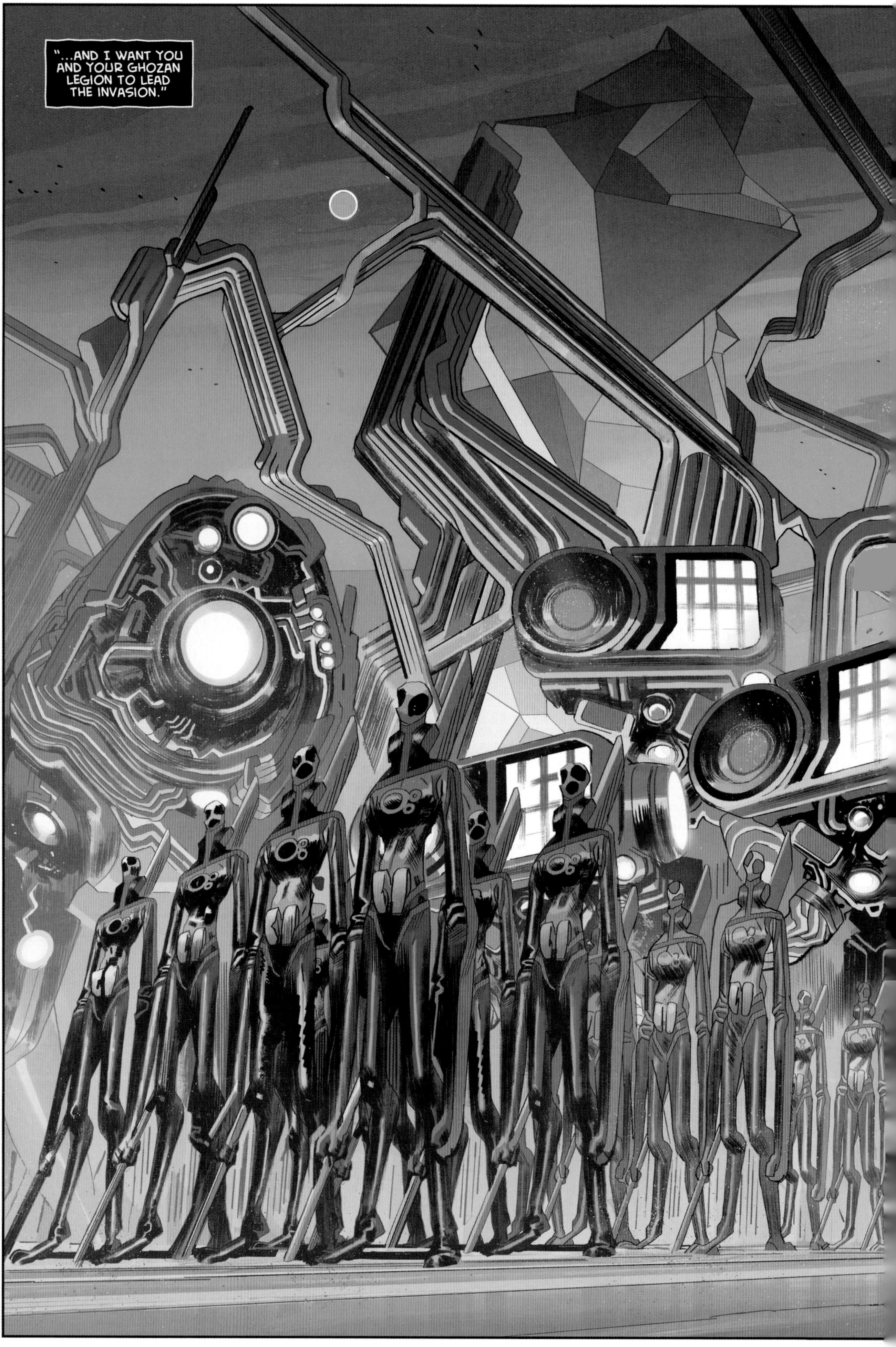
"...AND I WANT YOU AND YOUR GHOZAN LEGION TO LEAD THE INVASION."

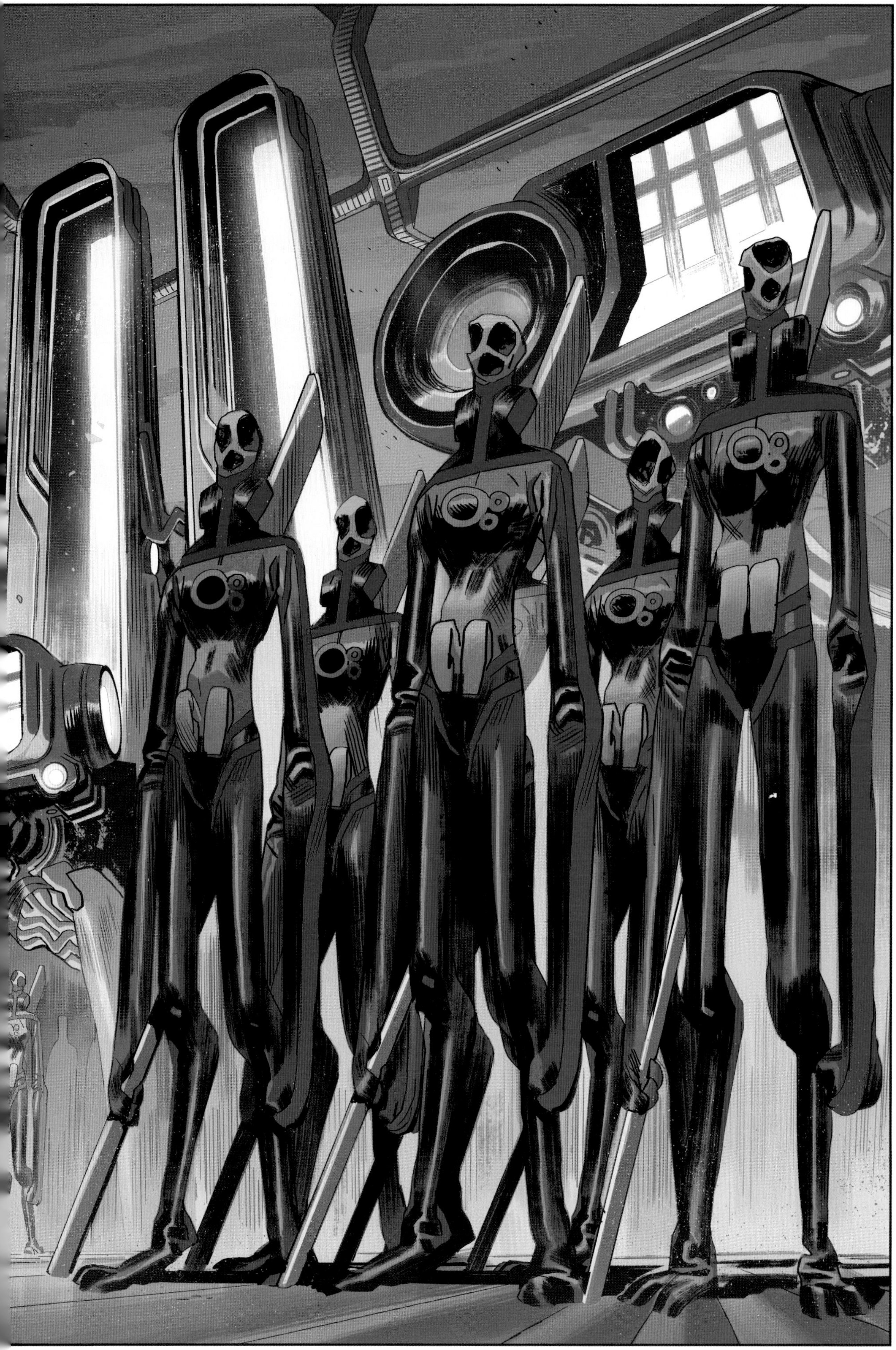

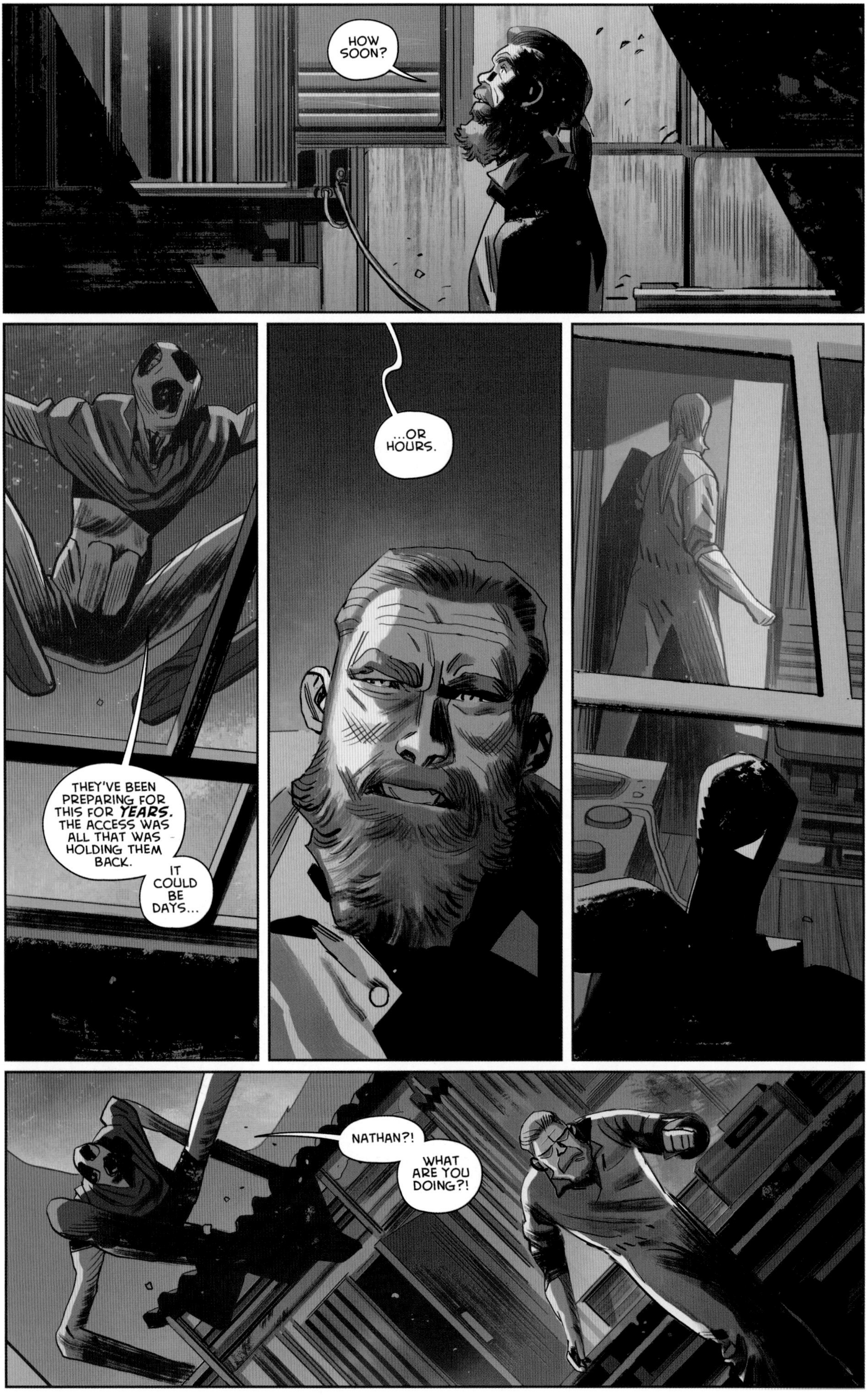
HOW SOON?
THEY'VE BEEN PREPARING FOR THIS FOR YEARS. THE ACCESS WAS ALL THAT WAS HOLDING THEM BACK.
IT COULD BE DAYS...
...OR HOURS.
NATHAN?!
WHAT ARE YOU DOING?!

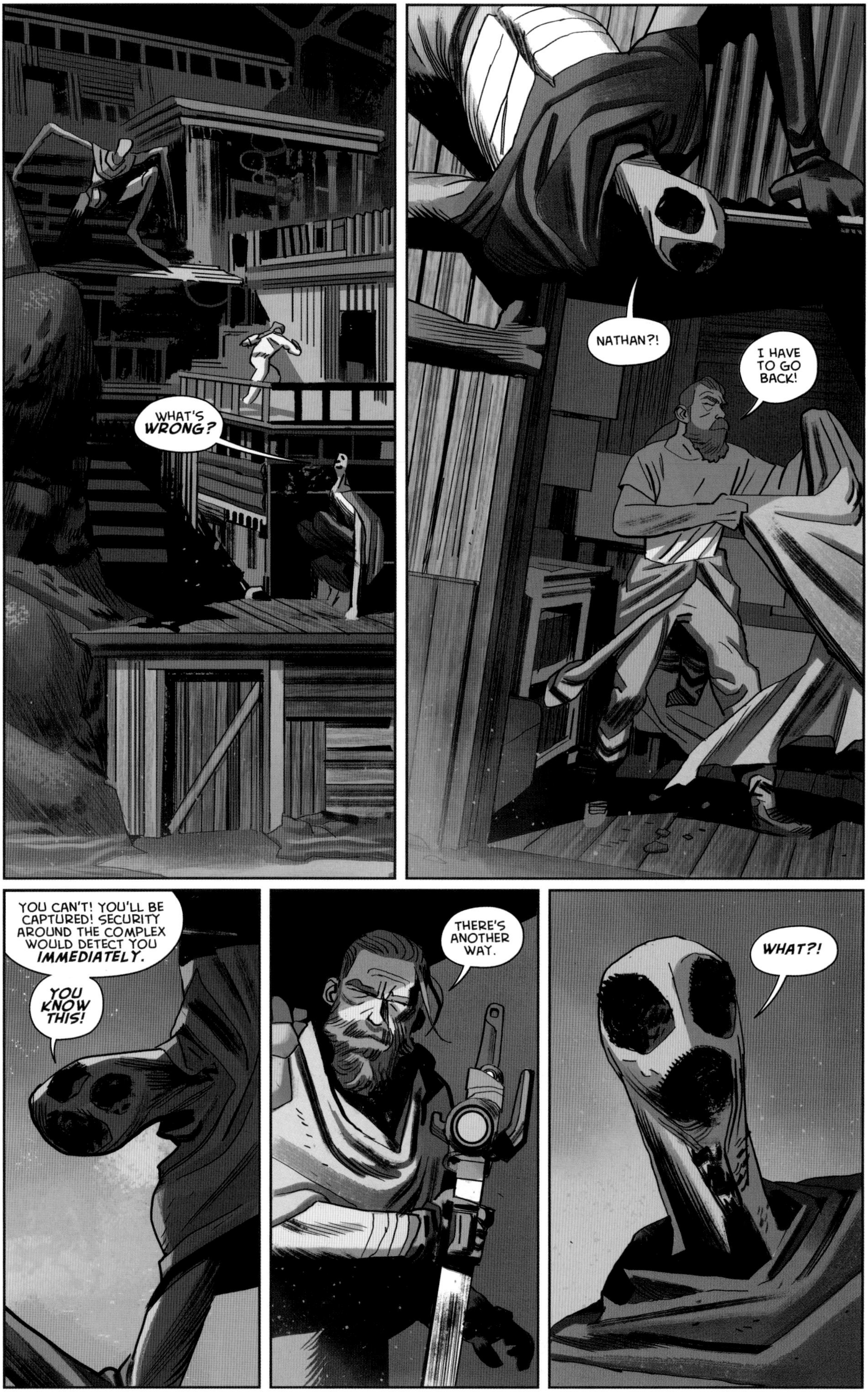
WHAT'S WRONG?
NATHAN?!
I HAVE TO GO BACK!
YOU CAN'T! YOU'LL BE CAPTURED! SECURITY AROUND THE COMPLEX WOULD DETECT YOU IMMEDIATELY.
YOU KNOW THIS!
THERE'S ANOTHER WAY.
WHAT?!

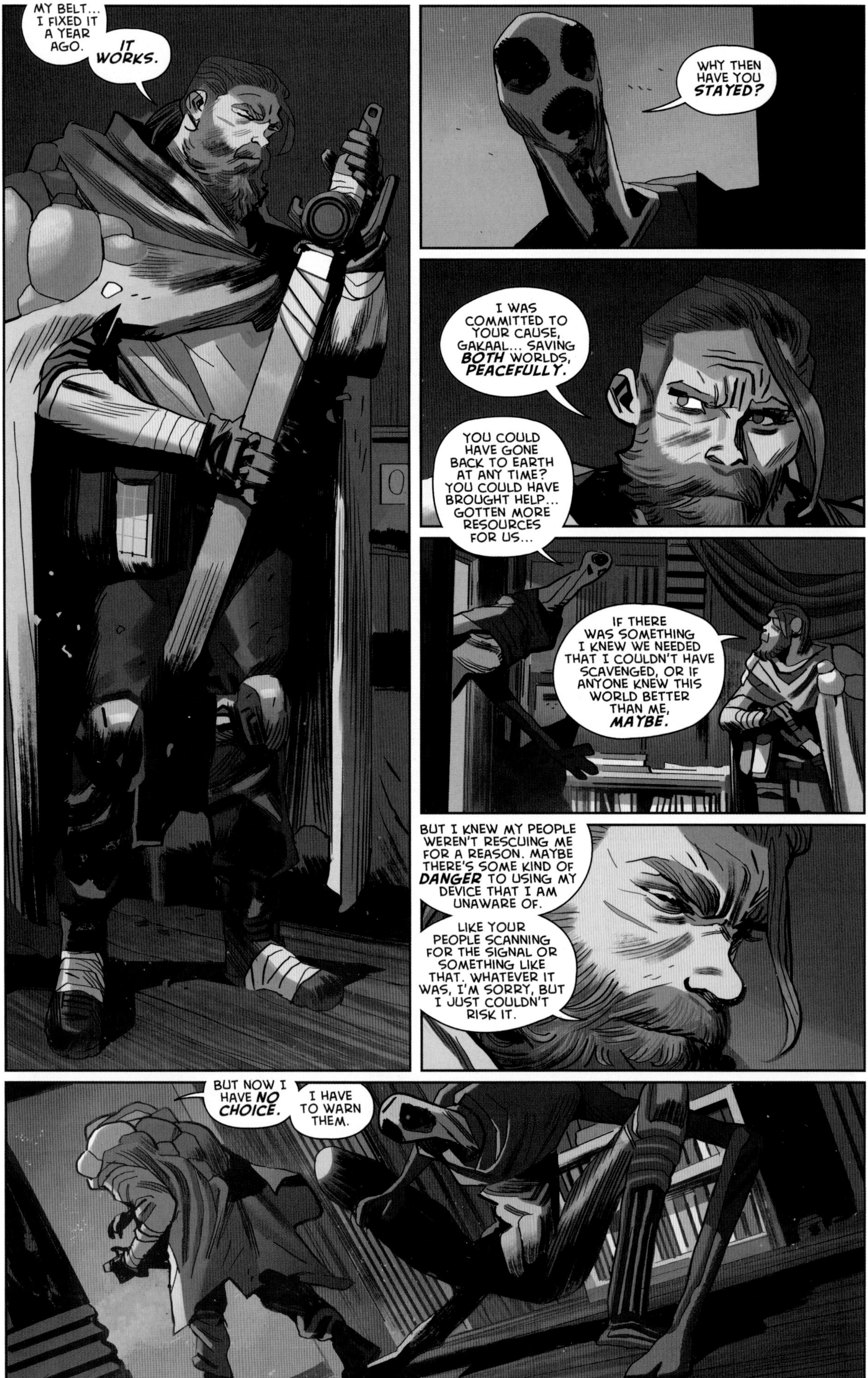
MY BELT... I FIXED IT A YEAR AGO.
IT WORKS.
WHY THEN HAVE YOU STAYED?
I WAS COMMITTED TO YOUR CAUSE, GAKAAL... SAVING BOTH WORLDS, PEACEFULLY.
YOU COULD HAVE GONE BACK TO EARTH AT ANY TIME? YOU COULD HAVE BROUGHT HELP... GOTTEN MORE RESOURCES FOR US...
IF THERE WAS SOMETHING I KNEW WE NEEDED THAT I COULDN'T HAVE SCAVENGED, OR IF ANYONE KNEW THIS WORLD BETTER THAN ME, MAYBE.
BUT I KNEW MY PEOPLE WEREN'T RESCUING ME FOR A REASON. MAYBE THERE'S SOME KIND OF DANGER TO USING MY DEVICE THAT I AM UNAWARE OF.
LIKE YOUR PEOPLE SCANNING FOR THE SIGNAL OR SOMETHING LIKE THAT. WHATEVER IT WAS, I'M SORRY, BUT I JUST COULDN'T RISK IT.
BUT NOW I HAVE NO CHOICE.
I HAVE TO WARN THEM.

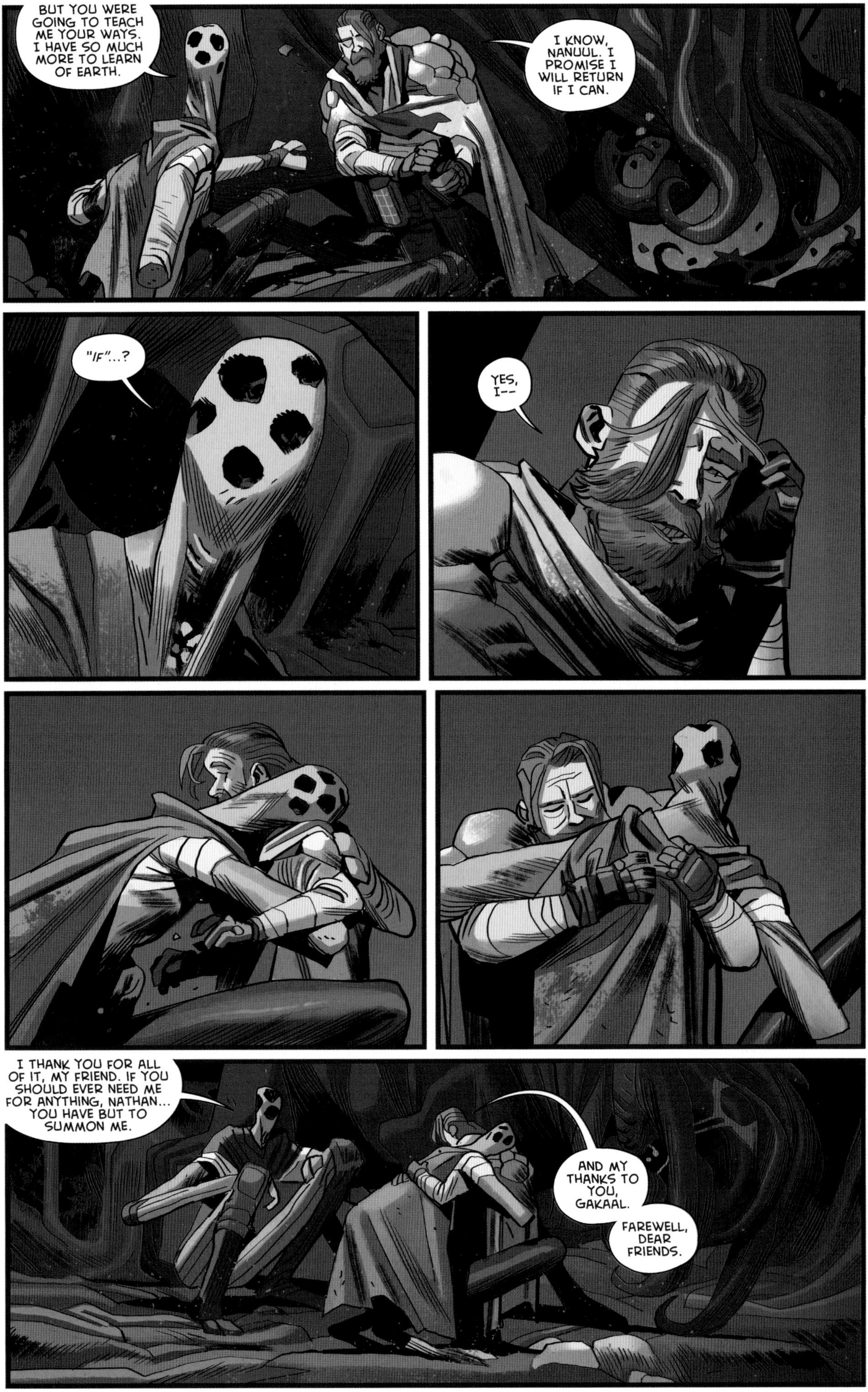
BUT YOU WERE GOING TO TEACH ME YOUR WAYS. I HAVE SO MUCH MORE TO LEARN OF EARTH.
I KNOW, NANUUL. I PROMISE I WILL RETURN IF I CAN.
"IF"...?
YES, I--
I THANK YOU FOR ALL OF IT, MY FRIEND. IF YOU SHOULD EVER NEED ME FOR ANYTHING, NATHAN... YOU HAVE BUT TO SUMMON ME.
AND MY THANKS TO YOU, GAKAAL.
FAREWELL, DEAR FRIENDS.

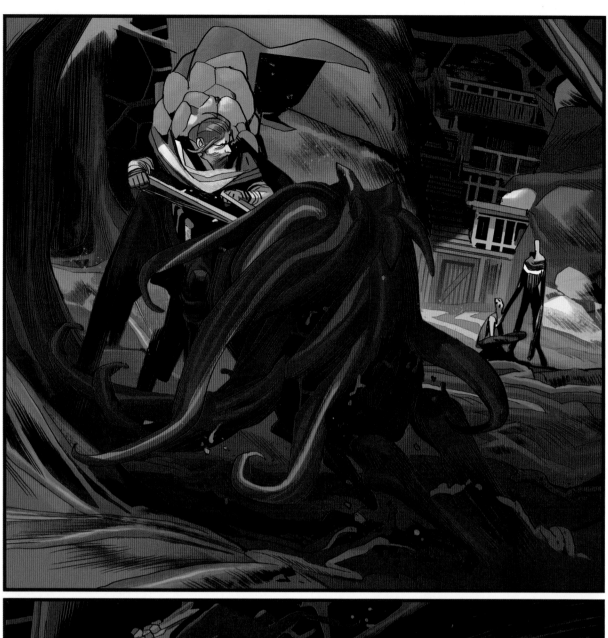

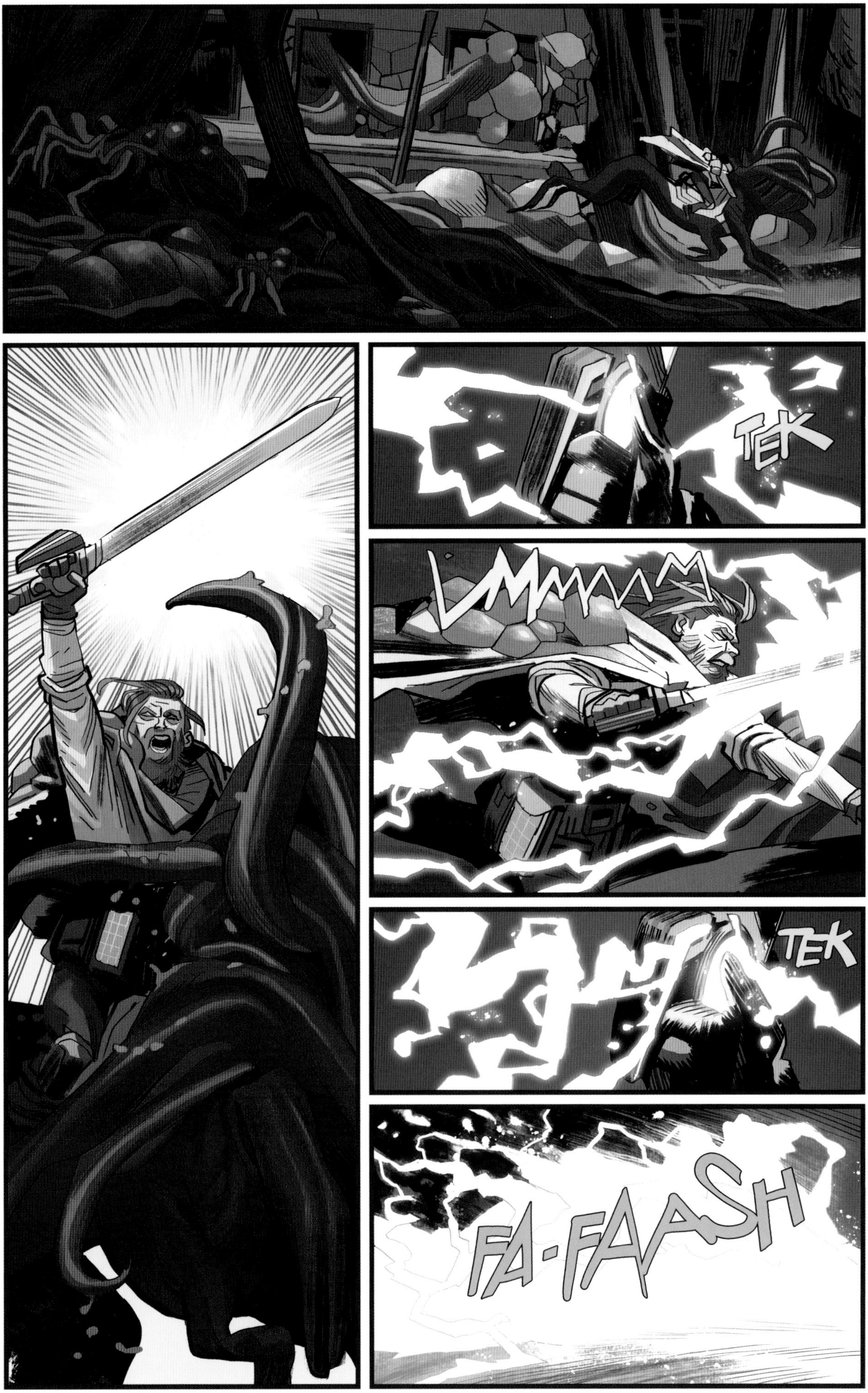
TEK
VMMMMM
TEK
FA-FAASH

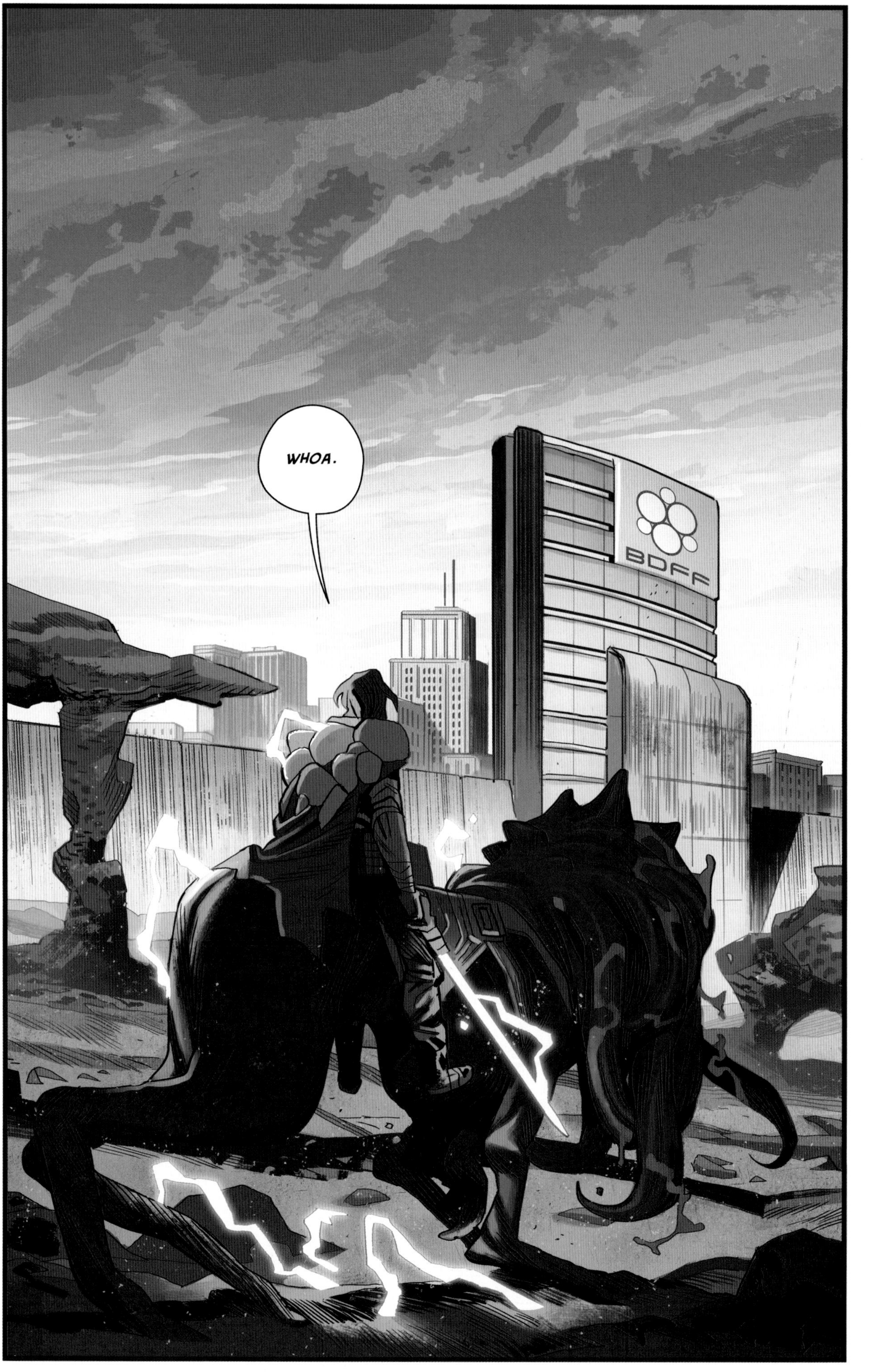
WHOA.
BDFF

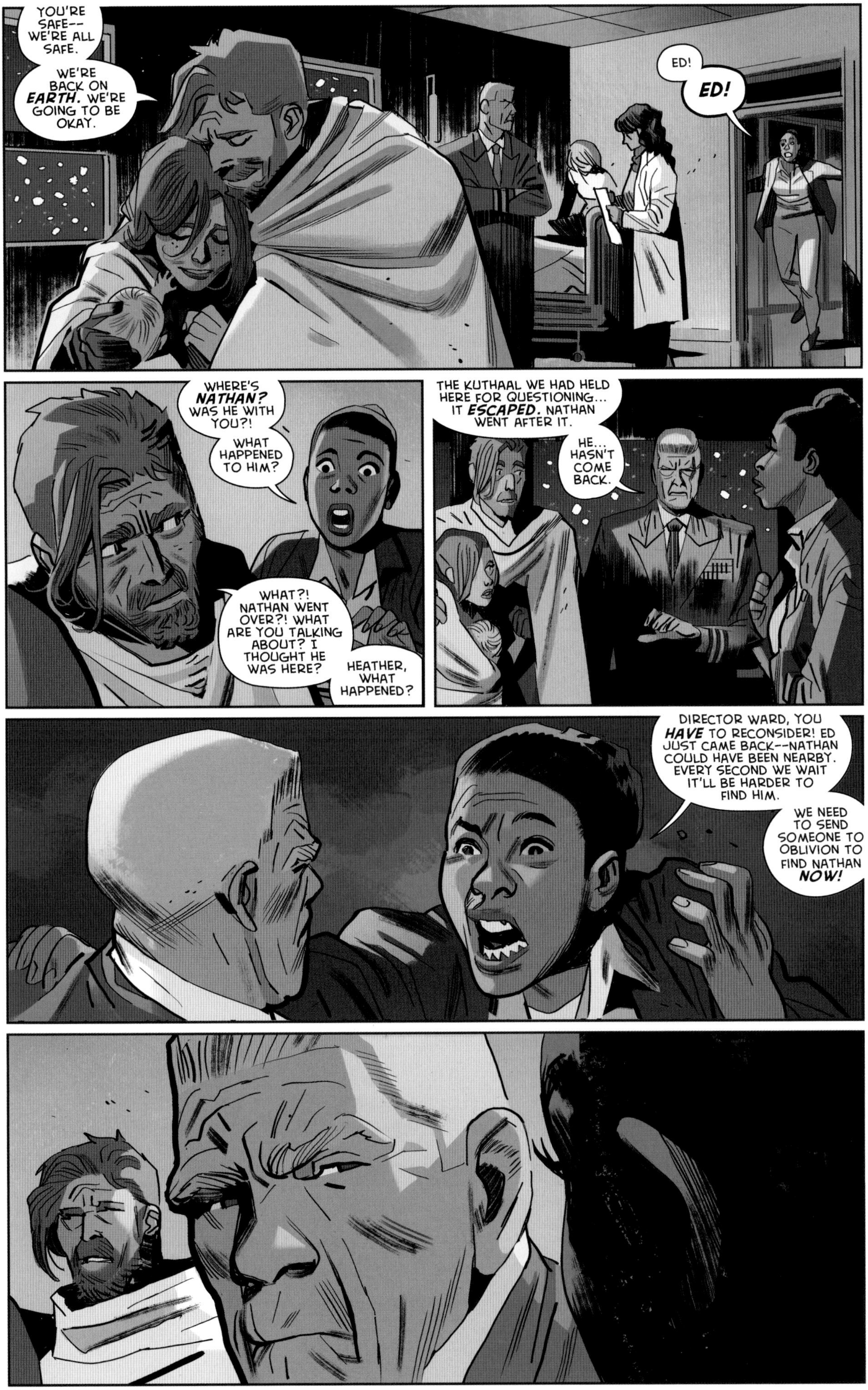
YOU'RE SAFE-- WE'RE ALL SAFE.
WE'RE BACK ON EARTH. WE'RE GOING TO BE OKAY.
ED!
ED!
WHERE'S NATHAN? WAS HE WITH YOU?!
WHAT HAPPENED TO HIM?
WHAT?! NATHAN WENT OVER?! WHAT ARE YOU TALKING ABOUT? I THOUGHT HE WAS HERE?
HEATHER, WHAT HAPPENED?
THE KUTHAAL WE HAD HELD HERE FOR QUESTIONING... IT ESCAPED. NATHAN WENT AFTER IT.
HE... HASN'T COME BACK.
DIRECTOR WARD, YOU HAVE TO RECONSIDER! ED JUST CAME BACK--NATHAN COULD HAVE BEEN NEARBY. EVERY SECOND WE WAIT IT'LL BE HARDER TO FIND HIM.
WE NEED TO SEND SOMEONE TO OBLIVION TO FIND NATHAN NOW!

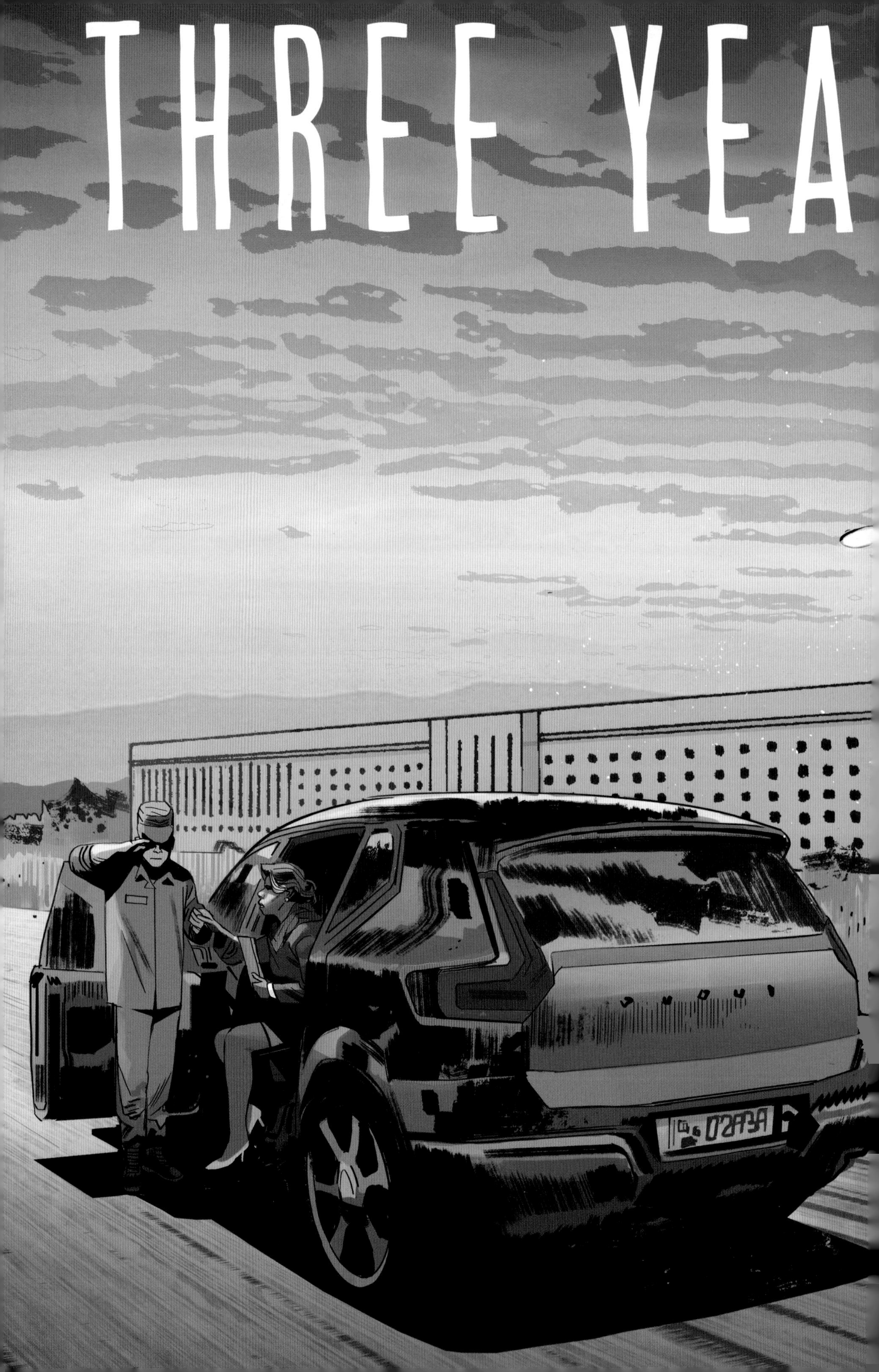
THREE YEA

RS LATER

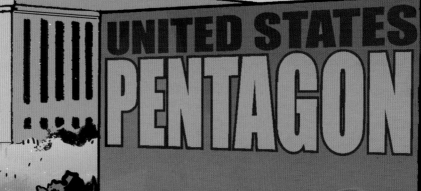 UNITED STATES PENTAGON

Parking in Rear

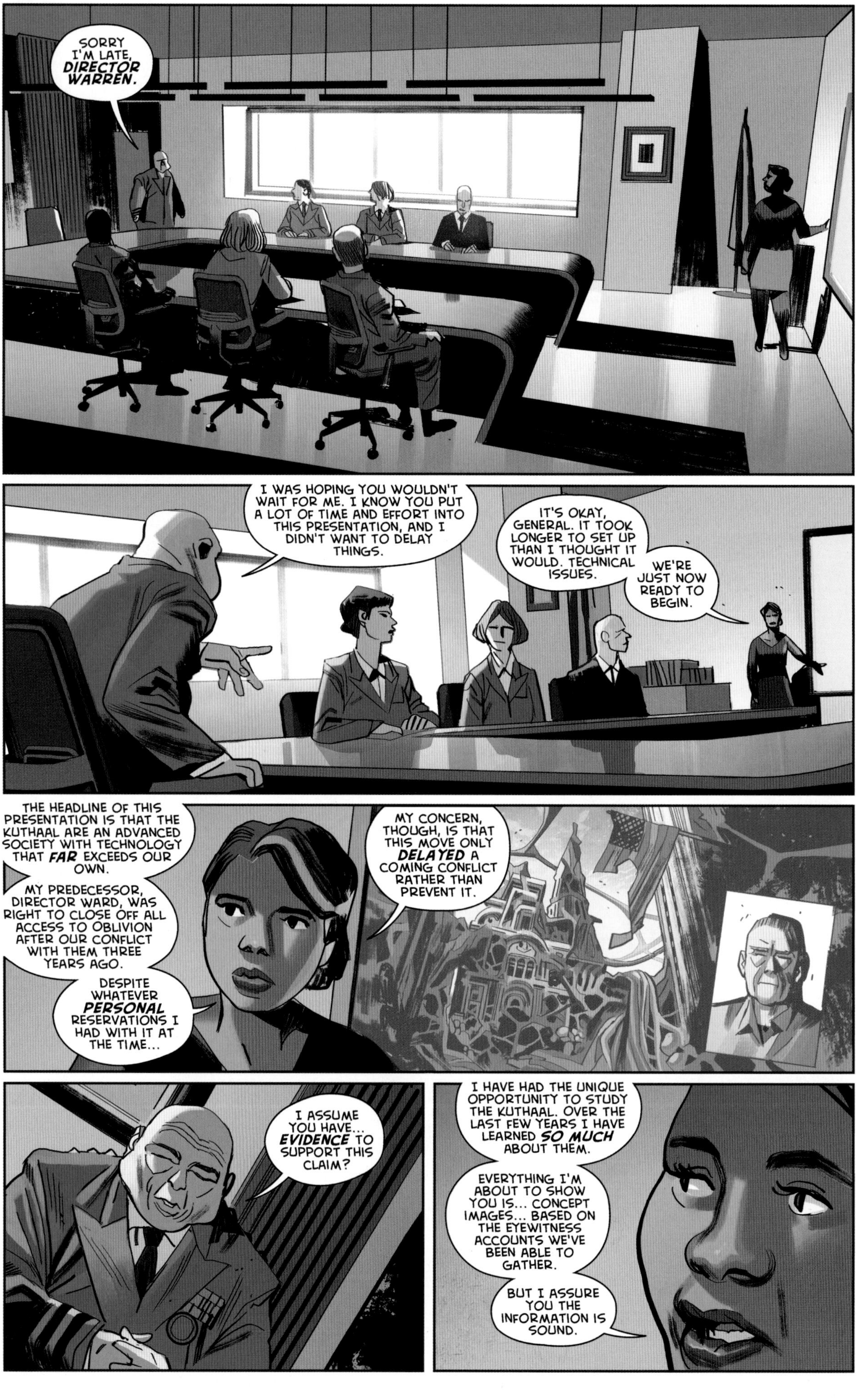
SORRY I'M LATE, DIRECTOR WARREN.
I WAS HOPING YOU WOULDN'T WAIT FOR ME. I KNOW YOU PUT A LOT OF TIME AND EFFORT INTO THIS PRESENTATION, AND I DIDN'T WANT TO DELAY THINGS.
IT'S OKAY, GENERAL. IT TOOK LONGER TO SET UP THAN I THOUGHT IT WOULD. TECHNICAL ISSUES.
WE'RE JUST NOW READY TO BEGIN.
THE HEADLINE OF THIS PRESENTATION IS THAT THE KUTHAAL ARE AN ADVANCED SOCIETY WITH TECHNOLOGY THAT FAR EXCEEDS OUR OWN.
MY PREDECESSOR, DIRECTOR WARD, WAS RIGHT TO CLOSE OFF ALL ACCESS TO OBLIVION AFTER OUR CONFLICT WITH THEM THREE YEARS AGO.
DESPITE WHATEVER PERSONAL RESERVATIONS I HAD WITH IT AT THE TIME...
MY CONCERN, THOUGH, IS THAT THIS MOVE ONLY DELAYED A COMING CONFLICT RATHER THAN PREVENT IT.
I ASSUME YOU HAVE... EVIDENCE TO SUPPORT THIS CLAIM?
I HAVE HAD THE UNIQUE OPPORTUNITY TO STUDY THE KUTHAAL. OVER THE LAST FEW YEARS I HAVE LEARNED SO MUCH ABOUT THEM.
EVERYTHING I'M ABOUT TO SHOW YOU IS... CONCEPT IMAGES... BASED ON THE EYEWITNESS ACCOUNTS WE'VE BEEN ABLE TO GATHER.
BUT I ASSURE YOU THE INFORMATION IS SOUND.

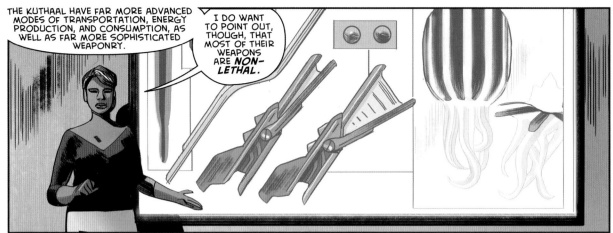

THE KUTHAAL HAVE FAR MORE ADVANCED MODES OF TRANSPORTATION, ENERGY PRODUCTION, AND CONSUMPTION, AS WELL AS FAR MORE SOPHISTICATED WEAPONRY.

I DO WANT TO POINT OUT, THOUGH, THAT MOST OF THEIR WEAPONS ARE *NON-LETHAL.*

WELL, THAT'S GOOD NEWS.

NEUTRAL AT BEST, I'M SORRY TO SAY.

AND WHY DO YOU SAY THAT?

IT DOESN'T MATTER IF THEIR WEAPONS DON'T KILL US IF THEY ARE EFFECTIVE ENOUGH TO INCAPACITATE US *IMMEDIATELY* IN WAYS WE HAVE NO DEFENSE FOR.

I CAN GLEAN *NO ADVANTAGE* FROM THE INFORMATION I'VE GATHERED.

A HEAD-TO-HEAD CONFLICT WOULD *NOT* GO OUR WAY.

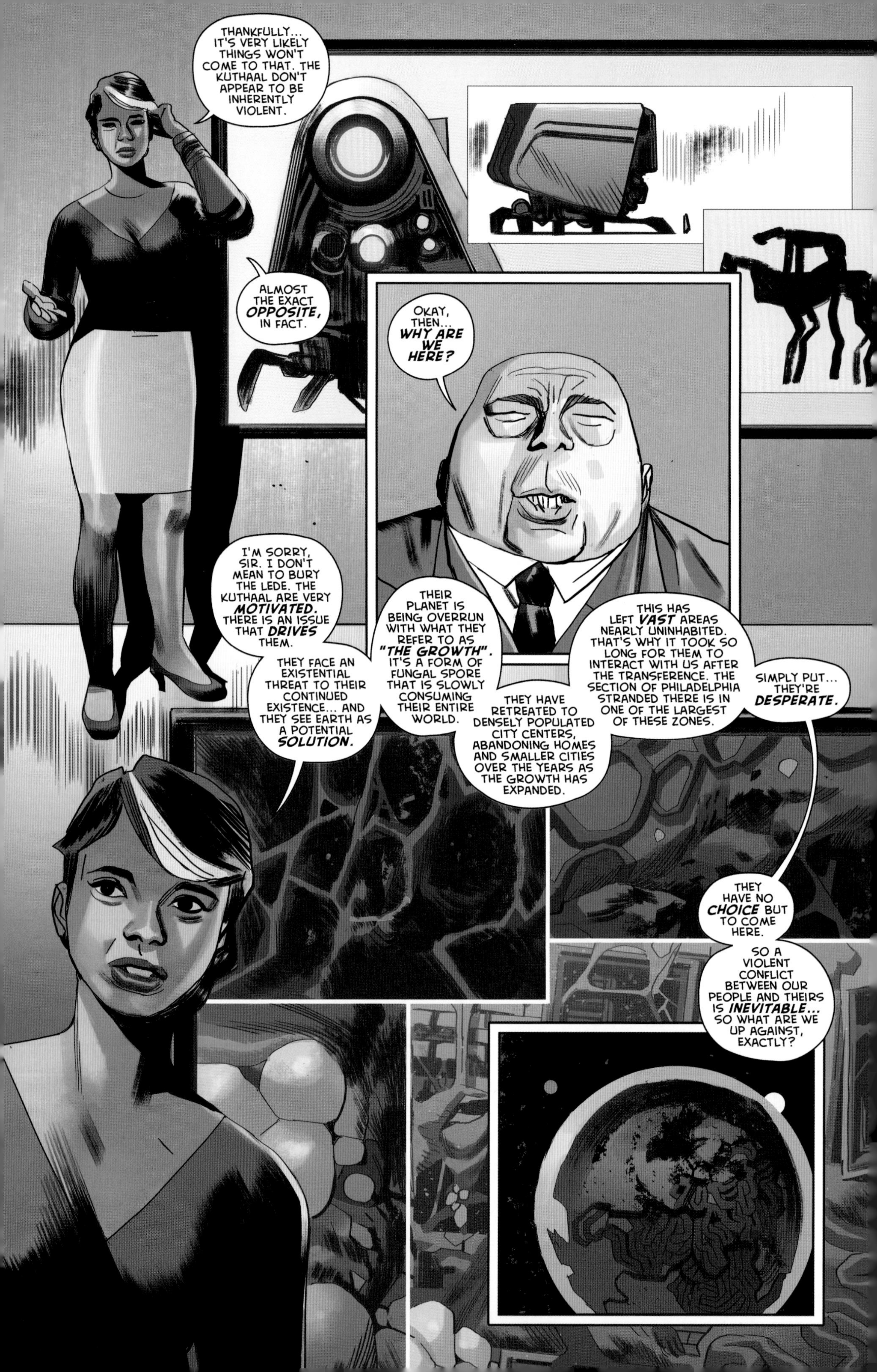
THANKFULLY... IT'S VERY LIKELY THINGS WON'T COME TO THAT. THE KUTHAAL DON'T APPEAR TO BE INHERENTLY VIOLENT.
ALMOST THE EXACT OPPOSITE, IN FACT.
OKAY, THEN... WHY ARE WE HERE?
I'M SORRY, SIR. I DON'T MEAN TO BURY THE LEDE. THE KUTHAAL ARE VERY MOTIVATED. THERE IS AN ISSUE THAT DRIVES THEM.
THEY FACE AN EXISTENTIAL THREAT TO THEIR CONTINUED EXISTENCE... AND THEY SEE EARTH AS A POTENTIAL SOLUTION.
THEIR PLANET IS BEING OVERRUN WITH WHAT THEY REFER TO AS "THE GROWTH". IT'S A FORM OF FUNGAL SPORE THAT IS SLOWLY CONSUMING THEIR ENTIRE WORLD.
THEY HAVE RETREATED TO DENSELY POPULATED CITY CENTERS, ABANDONING HOMES AND SMALLER CITIES OVER THE YEARS AS THE GROWTH HAS EXPANDED.
THIS HAS LEFT VAST AREAS NEARLY UNINHABITED. THAT'S WHY IT TOOK SO LONG FOR THEM TO INTERACT WITH US AFTER THE TRANSFERENCE. THE SECTION OF PHILADELPHIA STRANDED THERE IS IN ONE OF THE LARGEST OF THESE ZONES.
SIMPLY PUT... THEY'RE DESPERATE.
THEY HAVE NO CHOICE BUT TO COME HERE.
SO A VIOLENT CONFLICT BETWEEN OUR PEOPLE AND THEIRS IS INEVITABLE... SO WHAT ARE WE UP AGAINST, EXACTLY?

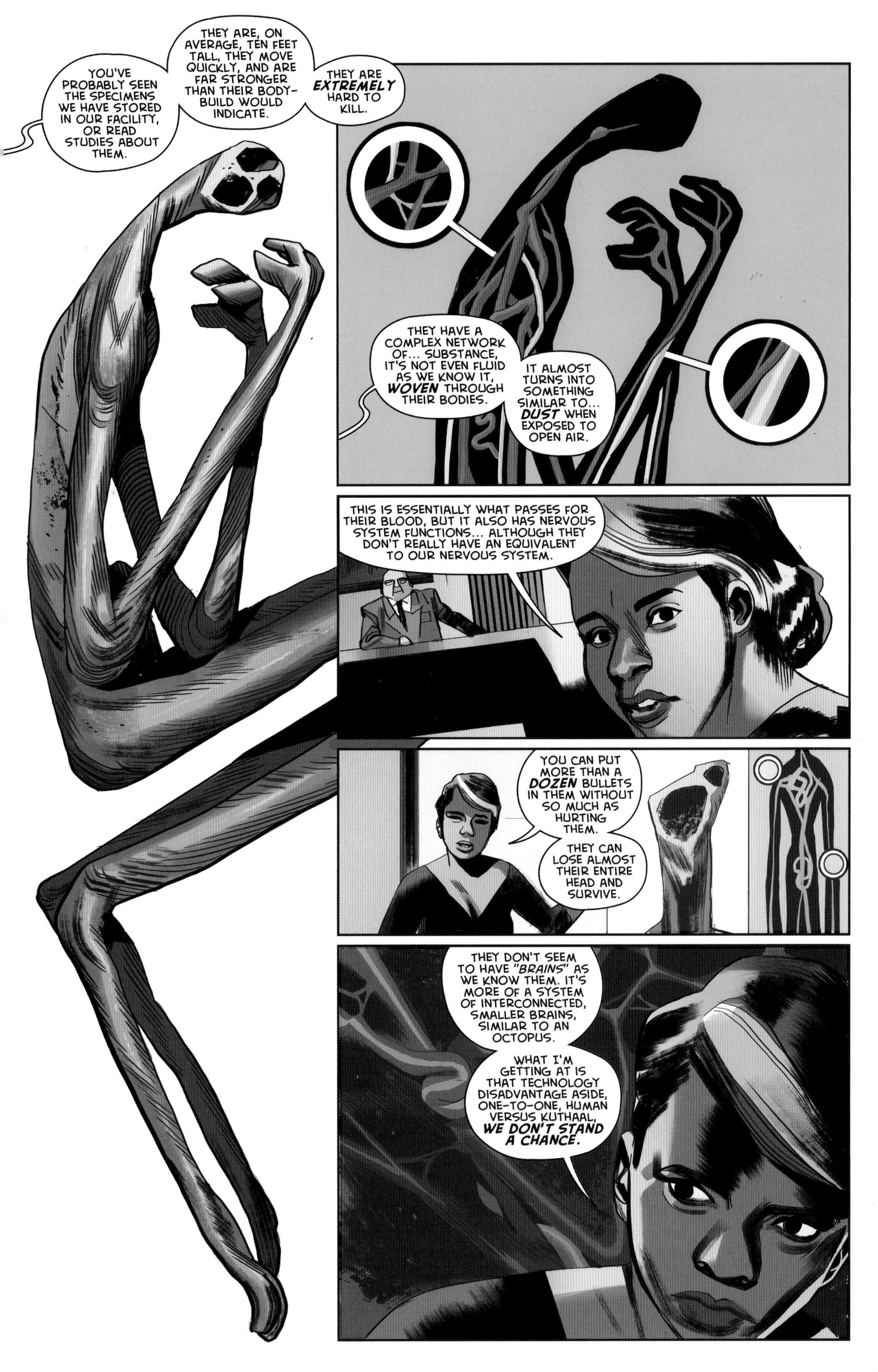

YOU'VE PROBABLY SEEN THE SPECIMENS WE HAVE STORED IN OUR FACILITY, OR READ STUDIES ABOUT THEM.
THEY ARE, ON AVERAGE, TEN FEET TALL, THEY MOVE QUICKLY, AND ARE FAR STRONGER THAN THEIR BODY-BUILD WOULD INDICATE.
THEY ARE ***EXTREMELY*** HARD TO KILL.
THEY HAVE A COMPLEX NETWORK OF... SUBSTANCE, IT'S NOT EVEN FLUID AS WE KNOW IT, ***WOVEN*** THROUGH THEIR BODIES.
IT ALMOST TURNS INTO SOMETHING SIMILAR TO... ***DUST*** WHEN EXPOSED TO OPEN AIR.
THIS IS ESSENTIALLY WHAT PASSES FOR THEIR BLOOD, BUT IT ALSO HAS NERVOUS SYSTEM FUNCTIONS... ALTHOUGH THEY DON'T REALLY HAVE AN EQUIVALENT TO OUR NERVOUS SYSTEM.
YOU CAN PUT MORE THAN A ***DOZEN*** BULLETS IN THEM WITHOUT SO MUCH AS HURTING THEM.
THEY CAN LOSE ALMOST THEIR ENTIRE HEAD AND SURVIVE.
THEY DON'T SEEM TO HAVE *"BRAINS"* AS WE KNOW THEM. IT'S MORE OF A SYSTEM OF INTERCONNECTED, SMALLER BRAINS, SIMILAR TO AN OCTOPUS.
WHAT I'M GETTING AT IS THAT TECHNOLOGY DISADVANTAGE ASIDE, ONE-TO-ONE, HUMAN VERSUS KUTHAAL, ***WE DON'T STAND A CHANCE.***

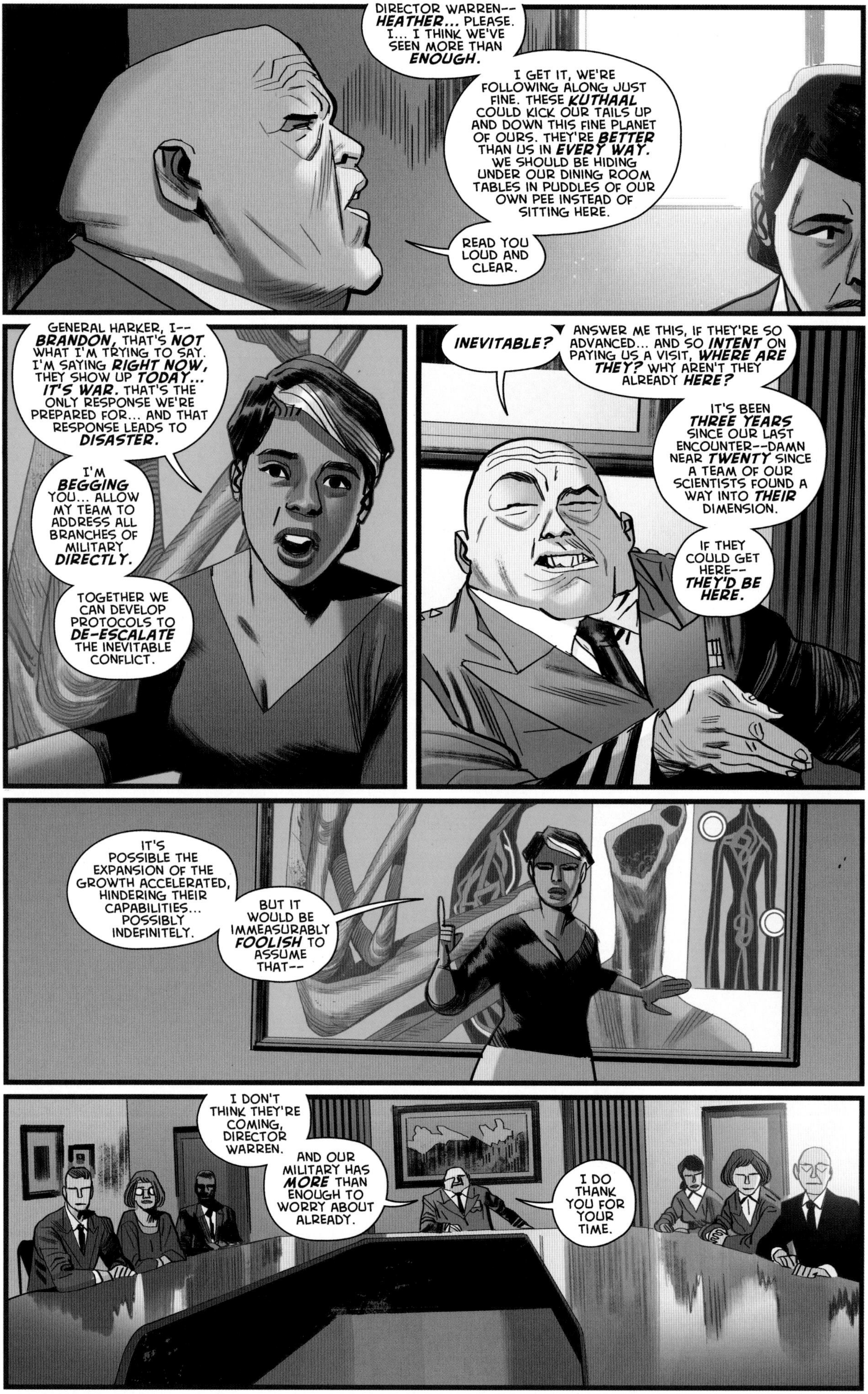
DIRECTOR WARREN-- HEATHER... PLEASE. I... I THINK WE'VE SEEN MORE THAN ENOUGH.
I GET IT, WE'RE FOLLOWING ALONG JUST FINE. THESE KUTHAAL COULD KICK OUR TAILS UP AND DOWN THIS FINE PLANET OF OURS. THEY'RE BETTER THAN US IN EVERY WAY. WE SHOULD BE HIDING UNDER OUR DINING ROOM TABLES IN PUDDLES OF OUR OWN PEE INSTEAD OF SITTING HERE.
READ YOU LOUD AND CLEAR.
GENERAL HARKER, I-- BRANDON, THAT'S NOT WHAT I'M TRYING TO SAY. I'M SAYING RIGHT NOW, THEY SHOW UP TODAY... IT'S WAR. THAT'S THE ONLY RESPONSE WE'RE PREPARED FOR... AND THAT RESPONSE LEADS TO DISASTER.
I'M BEGGING YOU... ALLOW MY TEAM TO ADDRESS ALL BRANCHES OF MILITARY DIRECTLY.
TOGETHER WE CAN DEVELOP PROTOCOLS TO DE-ESCALATE THE INEVITABLE CONFLICT.
INEVITABLE?
ANSWER ME THIS, IF THEY'RE SO ADVANCED... AND SO INTENT ON PAYING US A VISIT, WHERE ARE THEY? WHY AREN'T THEY ALREADY HERE?
IT'S BEEN THREE YEARS SINCE OUR LAST ENCOUNTER--DAMN NEAR TWENTY SINCE A TEAM OF OUR SCIENTISTS FOUND A WAY INTO THEIR DIMENSION.
IF THEY COULD GET HERE-- THEY'D BE HERE.
IT'S POSSIBLE THE EXPANSION OF THE GROWTH ACCELERATED, HINDERING THEIR CAPABILITIES... POSSIBLY INDEFINITELY.
BUT IT WOULD BE IMMEASURABLY FOOLISH TO ASSUME THAT--
I DON'T THINK THEY'RE COMING, DIRECTOR WARREN.
AND OUR MILITARY HAS MORE THAN ENOUGH TO WORRY ABOUT ALREADY.
I DO THANK YOU FOR YOUR TIME.

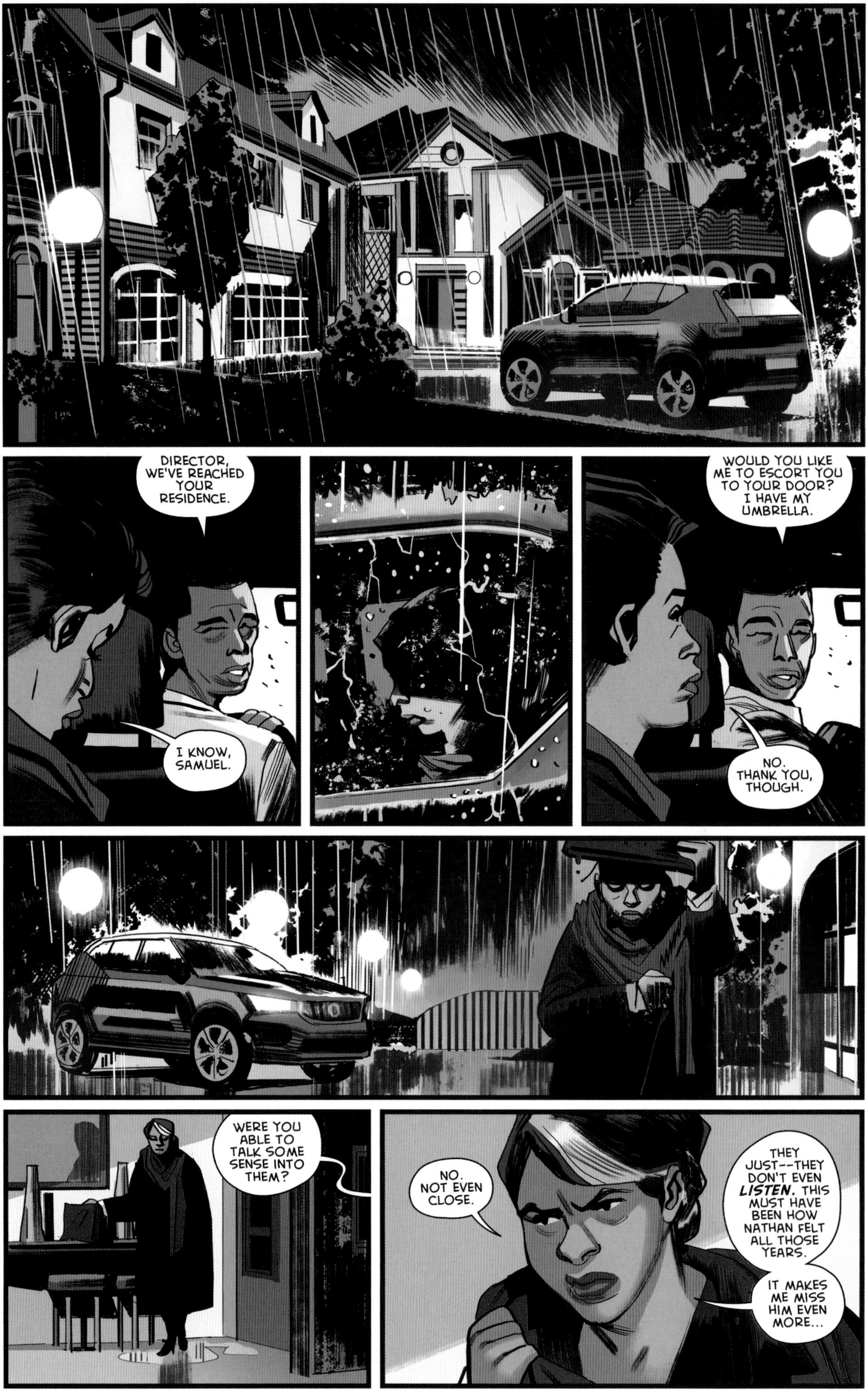
DIRECTOR, WE'VE REACHED YOUR RESIDENCE.
I KNOW, SAMUEL.
WOULD YOU LIKE ME TO ESCORT YOU TO YOUR DOOR? I HAVE MY UMBRELLA.
NO. THANK YOU, THOUGH.
WERE YOU ABLE TO TALK SOME SENSE INTO THEM?
NO. NOT EVEN CLOSE.
THEY JUST--THEY DON'T EVEN LISTEN. THIS MUST HAVE BEEN HOW NATHAN FELT ALL THOSE YEARS.
IT MAKES ME MISS HIM EVEN MORE...

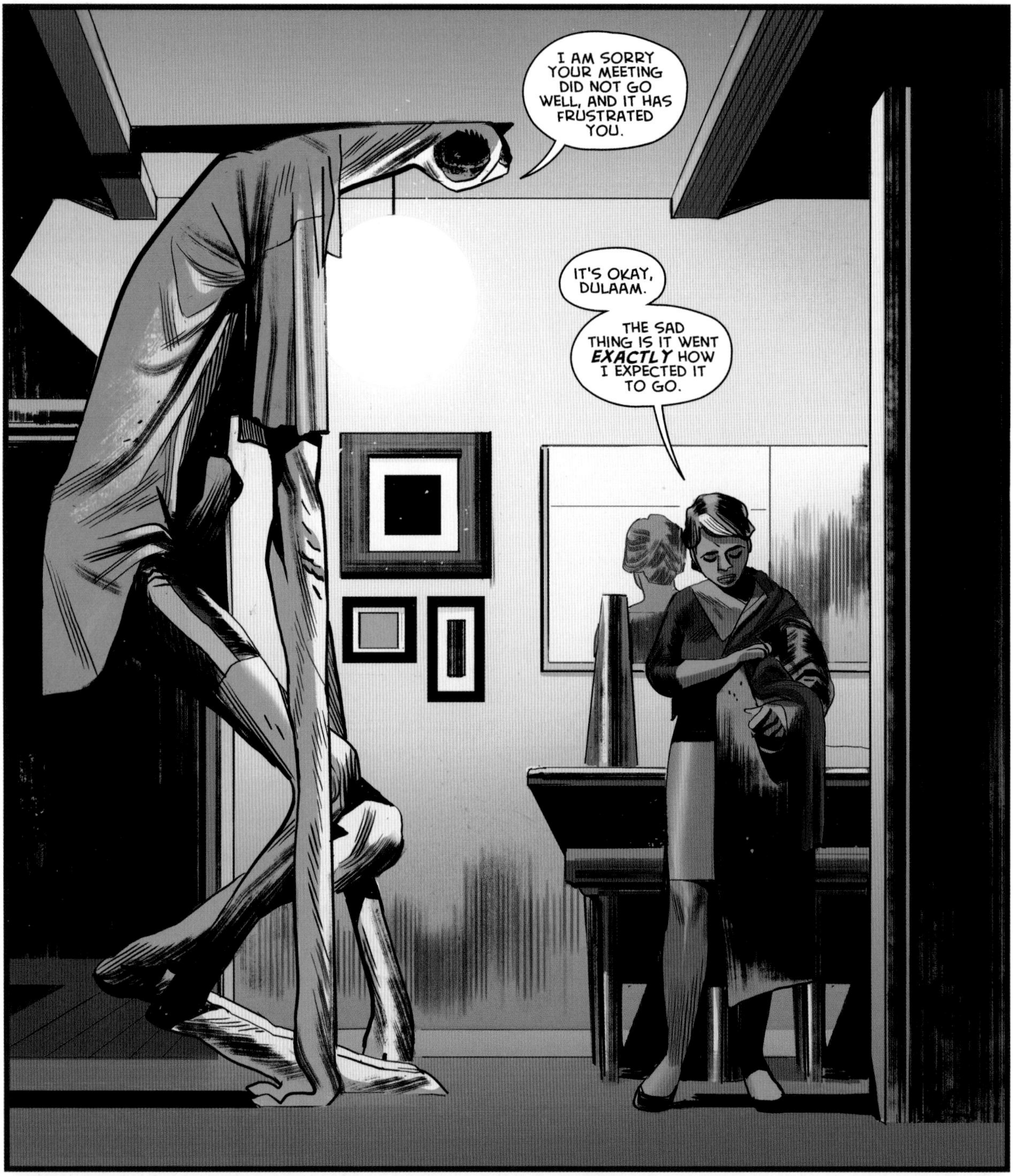
I AM SORRY YOUR MEETING DID NOT GO WELL, AND IT HAS FRUSTRATED YOU.
IT'S OKAY, DULAAM.
THE SAD THING IS IT WENT EXACTLY HOW I EXPECTED IT TO GO.

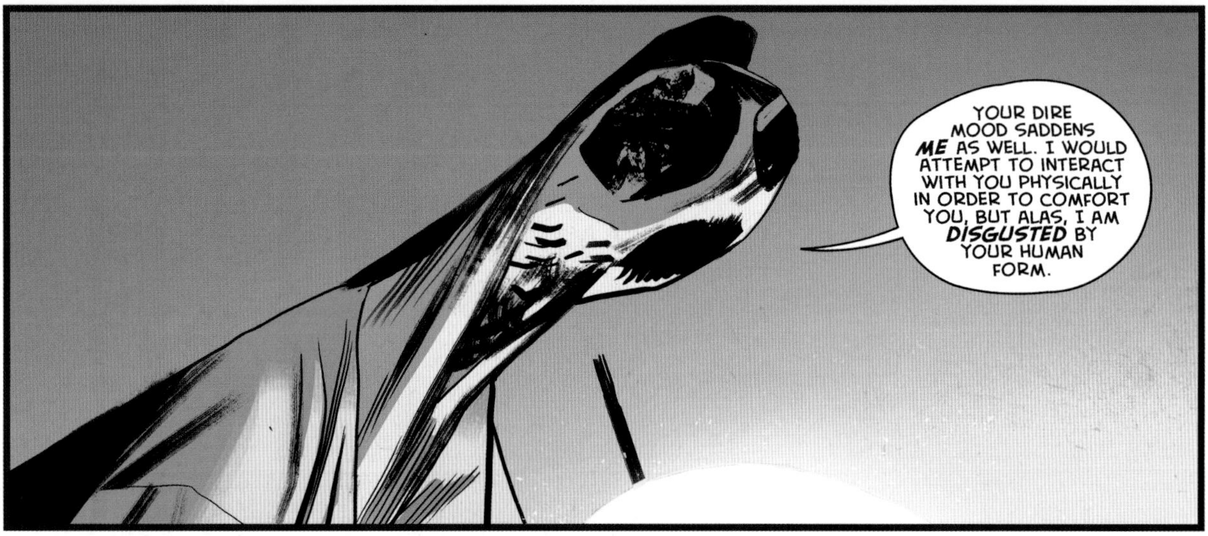
YOUR DIRE MOOD SADDENS ME AS WELL. I WOULD ATTEMPT TO INTERACT WITH YOU PHYSICALLY IN ORDER TO COMFORT YOU, BUT ALAS, I AM DISGUSTED BY YOUR HUMAN FORM.

DID MY ATTEMPT AT EARTH HUMOR AMUSE YOU?

A LITTLE BIT. *YEAH.*

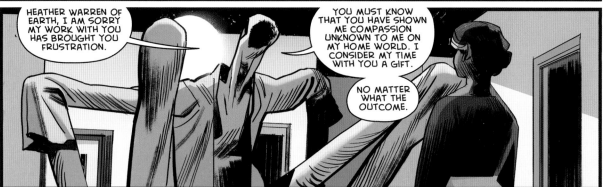

HEATHER WARREN OF EARTH, I AM SORRY MY WORK WITH YOU HAS BROUGHT YOU FRUSTRATION.

YOU MUST KNOW THAT YOU HAVE SHOWN ME COMPASSION UNKNOWN TO ME ON MY HOME WORLD. I CONSIDER MY TIME WITH YOU A GIFT.

NO MATTER WHAT THE OUTCOME.

AND YOU, DULAAM, HAVE TAUGHT ME MORE THAN I COULD HAVE LEARNED IN A LIFETIME ON MY OWN.

THIS IS A SETBACK, NOT THE END. OUR WORK WILL SAVE *BOTH* OUR WORLDS.

YOU SPEAK ALMOST AS WELL AS ONE OF MY KIND NOW. *VERY* IMPRESSIVE.

I WOULD VERY MUCH LIKE TO WATCH THE HOUSEWIVES IN THE TELEVISION NOW.

SAME.

I'LL MAKE POPCORN.

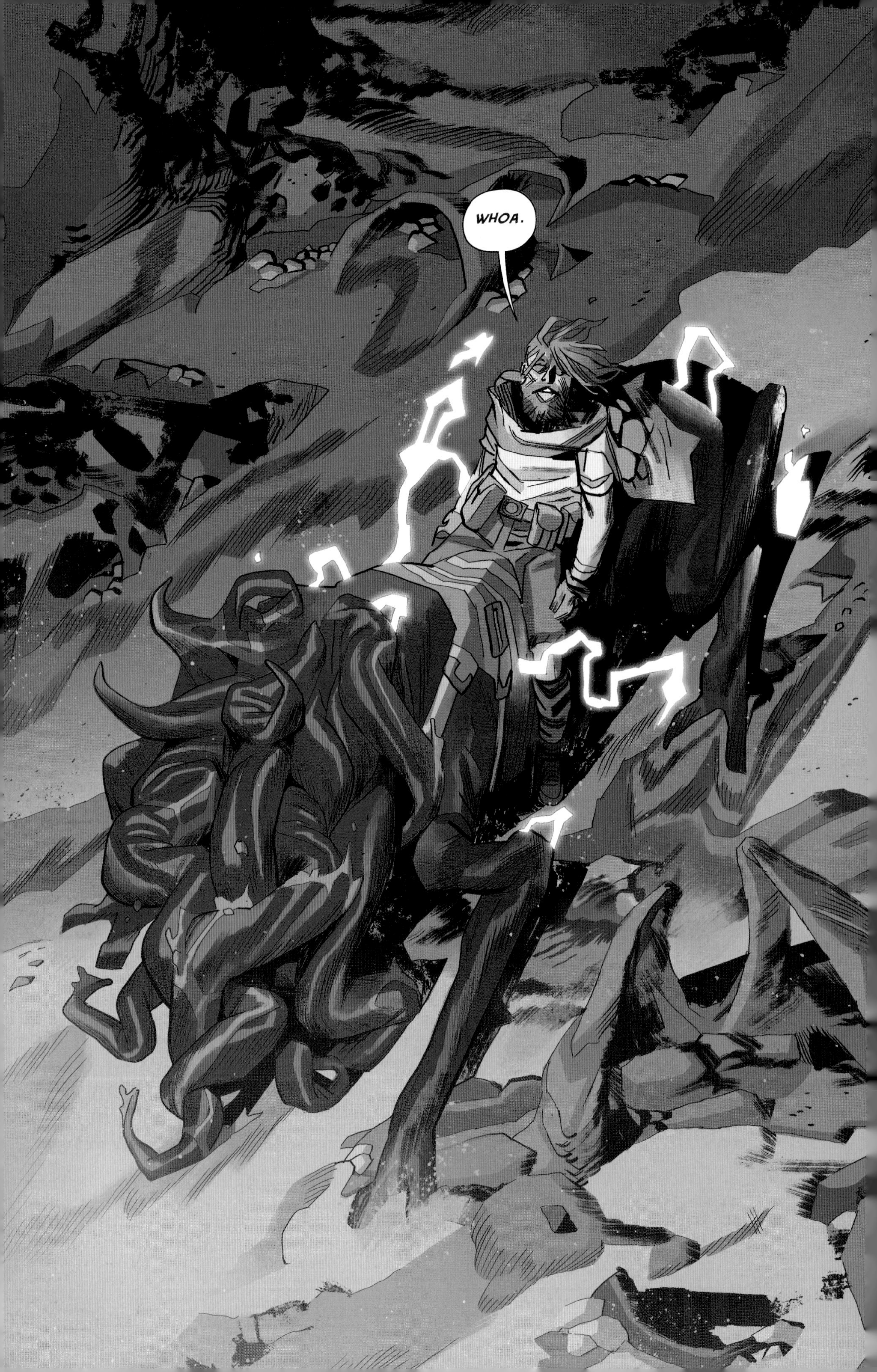
WHOA.

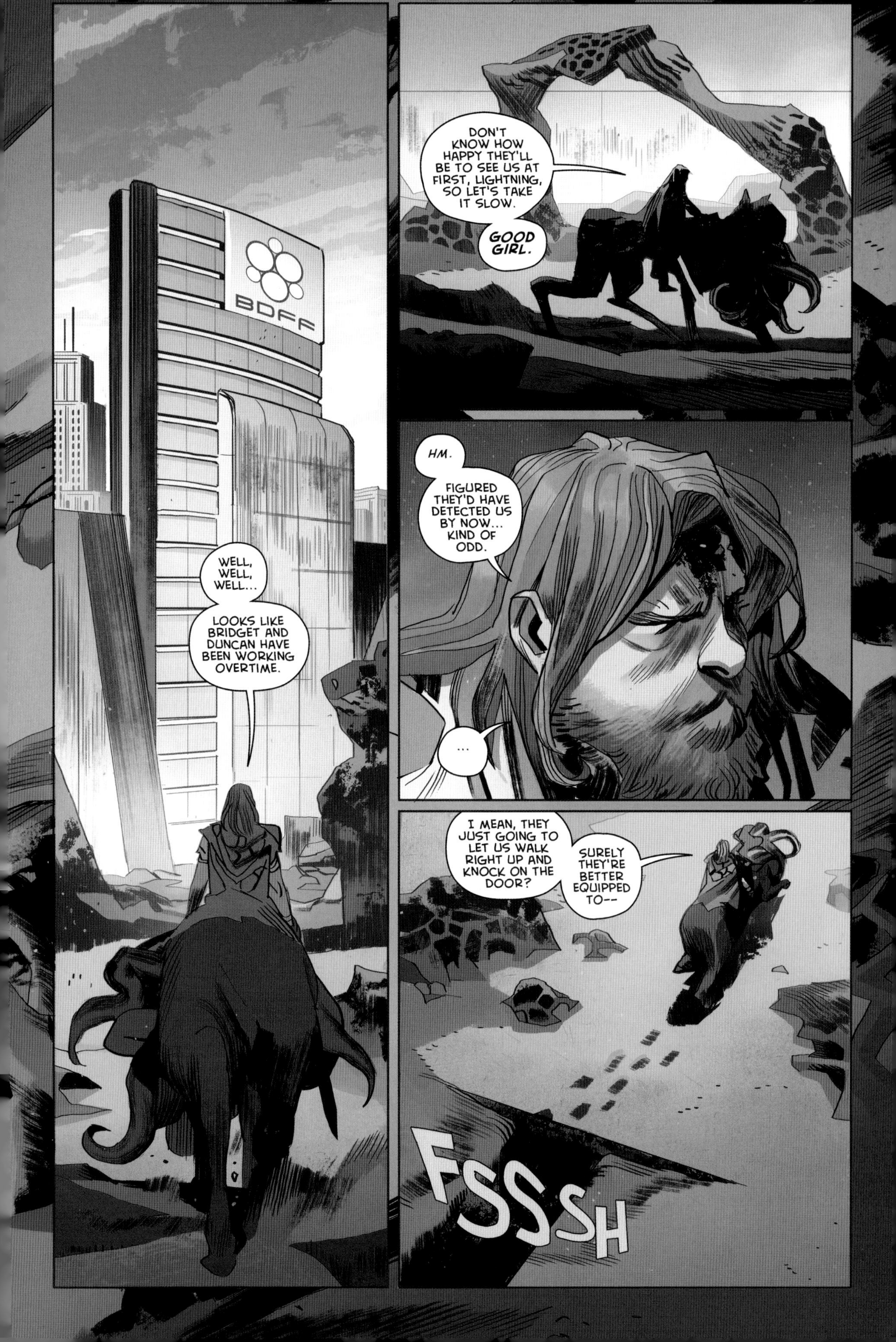
BDFF
WELL, WELL, WELL...
LOOKS LIKE BRIDGET AND DUNCAN HAVE BEEN WORKING OVERTIME.
DON'T KNOW HOW HAPPY THEY'LL BE TO SEE US AT FIRST, LIGHTNING, SO LET'S TAKE IT SLOW.
GOOD GIRL.
HM.
FIGURED THEY'D HAVE DETECTED US BY NOW... KIND OF ODD.
...
I MEAN, THEY JUST GOING TO LET US WALK RIGHT UP AND KNOCK ON THE DOOR?
SURELY THEY'RE BETTER EQUIPPED TO--
FSSSH

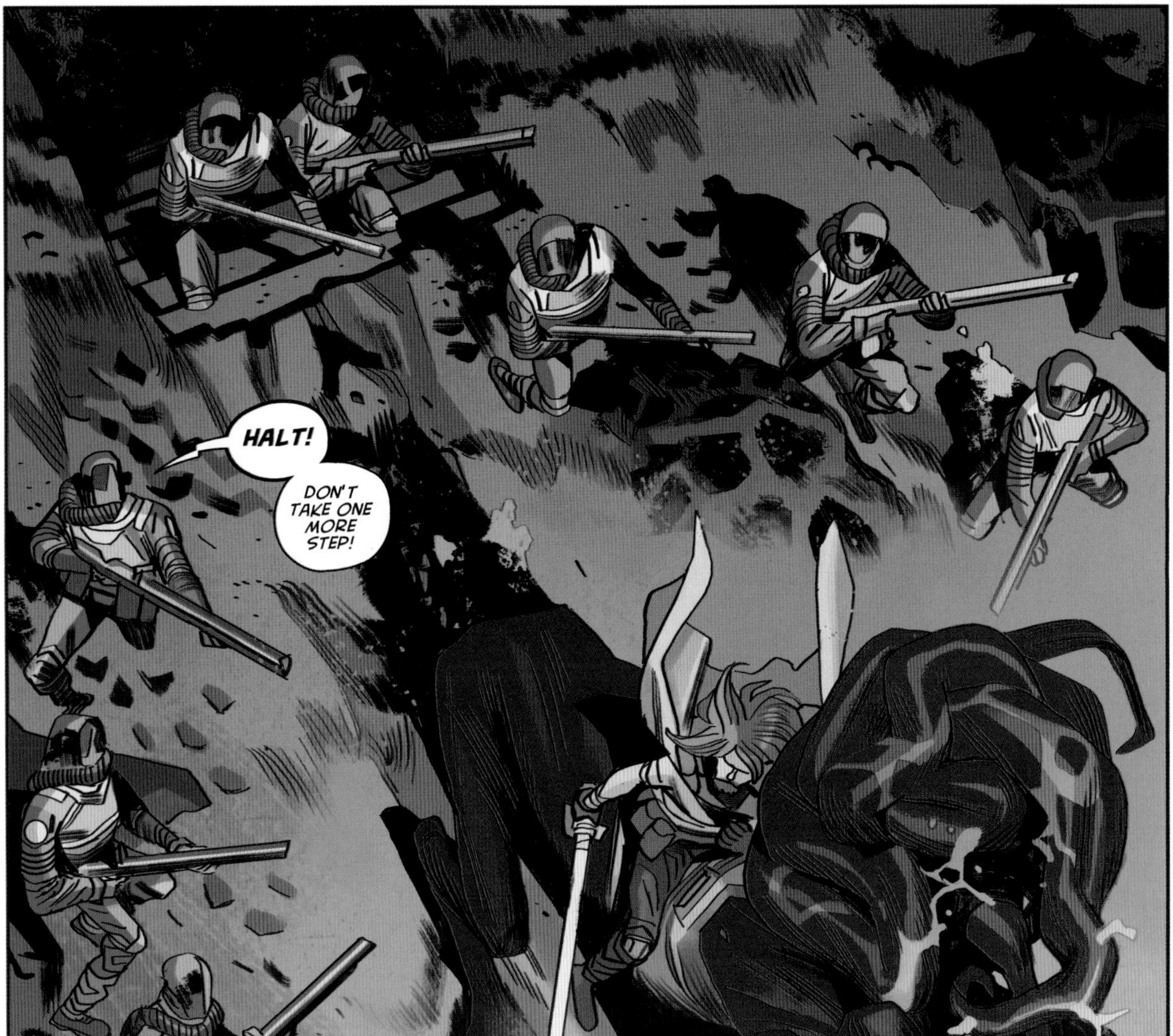
HALT!
DON'T TAKE ONE MORE STEP!

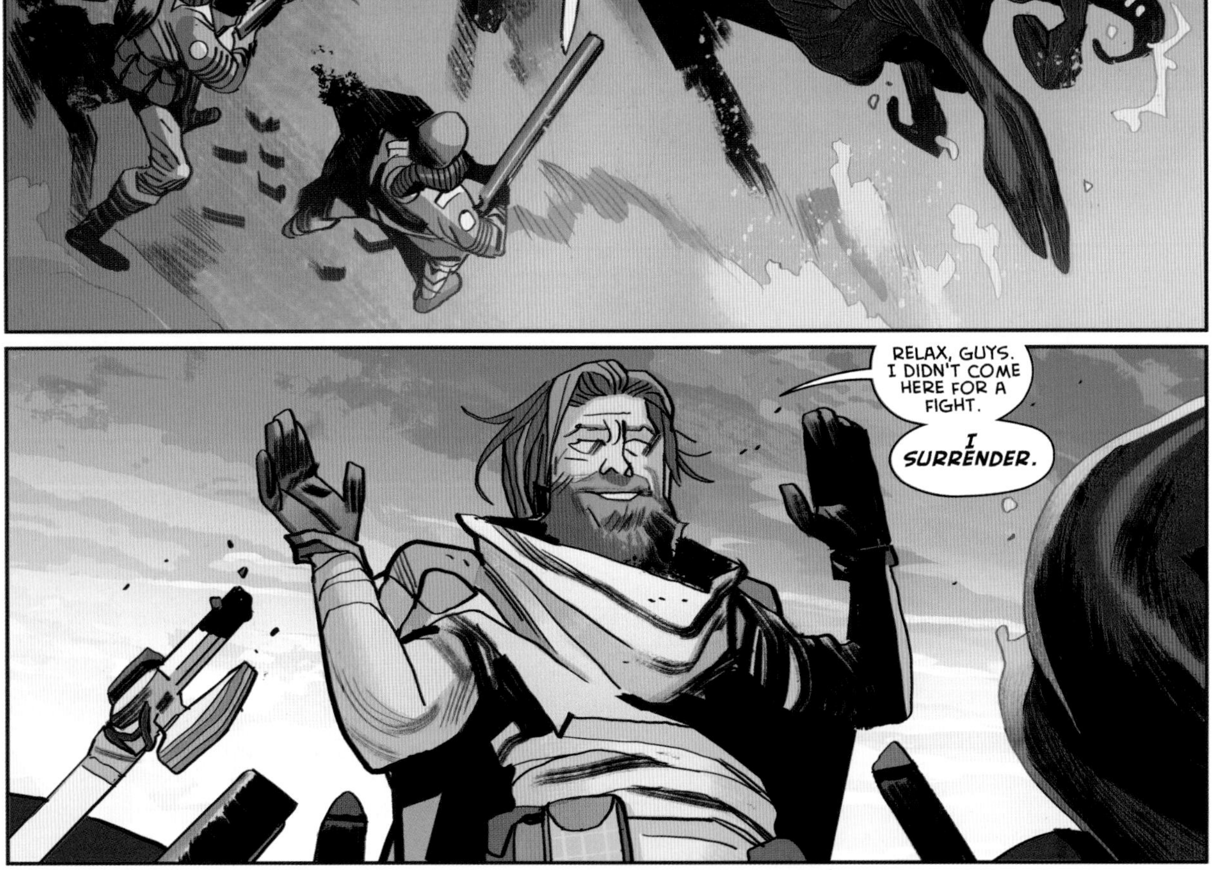
RELAX, GUYS. I DIDN'T COME HERE FOR A FIGHT.
I SURRENDER.

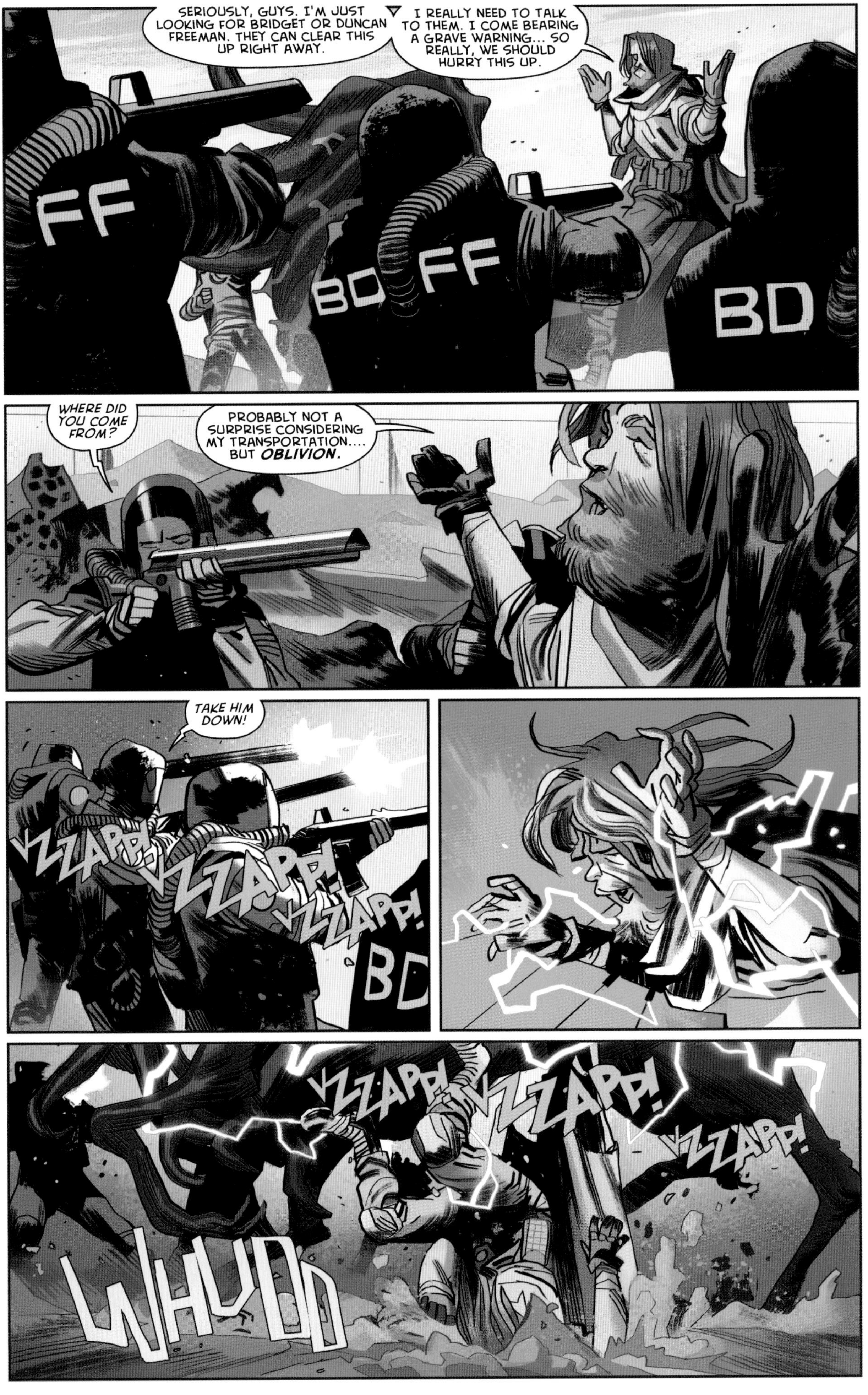
SERIOUSLY, GUYS. I'M JUST LOOKING FOR BRIDGET OR DUNCAN FREEMAN. THEY CAN CLEAR THIS UP RIGHT AWAY.
I REALLY NEED TO TALK TO THEM. I COME BEARING A GRAVE WARNING... SO REALLY, WE SHOULD HURRY THIS UP.
FF
BD
FF
BD
WHERE DID YOU COME FROM?
PROBABLY NOT A SURPRISE CONSIDERING MY TRANSPORTATION.... BUT OBLIVION.
TAKE HIM DOWN!
VZZAPP!
VZZAPP!
VZZAPP!
BD
VZZAPP!
VZZAPP!
VZZAPP!
WHUDD

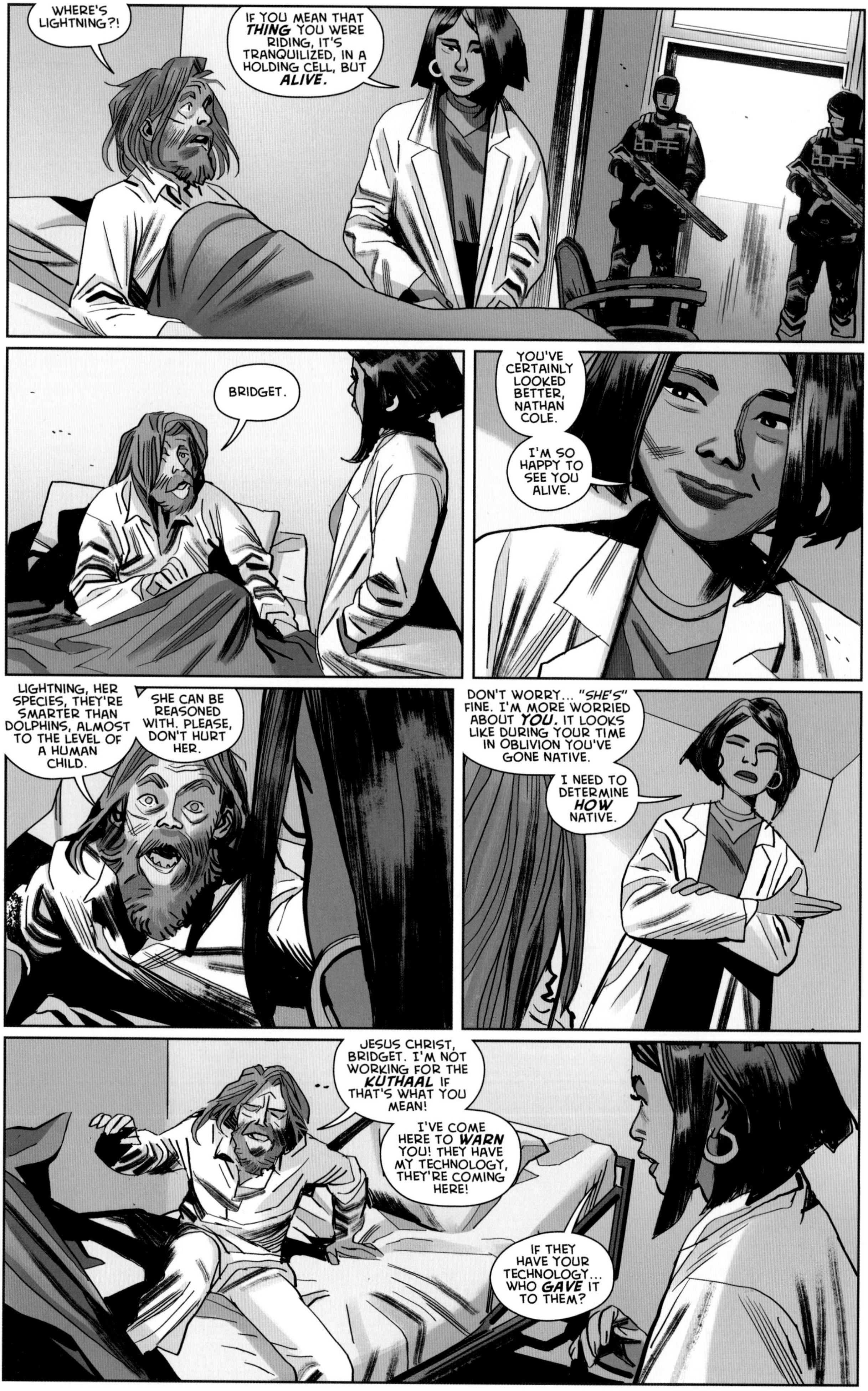
WHERE'S LIGHTNING?!
IF YOU MEAN THAT *THING* YOU WERE RIDING, IT'S TRANQUILIZED, IN A HOLDING CELL, BUT *ALIVE.*
BDFF
BDFF
...
BRIDGET.
YOU'VE CERTAINLY LOOKED BETTER, NATHAN COLE.
I'M SO HAPPY TO SEE YOU ALIVE.
LIGHTNING, HER SPECIES, THEY'RE SMARTER THAN DOLPHINS, ALMOST TO THE LEVEL OF A HUMAN CHILD.
SHE CAN BE REASONED WITH. PLEASE, DON'T HURT HER.
DON'T WORRY... *"SHE'S"* FINE. I'M MORE WORRIED ABOUT *YOU.* IT LOOKS LIKE DURING YOUR TIME IN OBLIVION YOU'VE GONE NATIVE.
I NEED TO DETERMINE *HOW* NATIVE.
..
JESUS CHRIST, BRIDGET. I'M NOT WORKING FOR THE *KUTHAAL* IF THAT'S WHAT YOU MEAN!
I'VE COME HERE TO *WARN* YOU! THEY HAVE MY TECHNOLOGY, THEY'RE COMING HERE!
IF THEY HAVE YOUR TECHNOLOGY... WHO *GAVE* IT TO THEM?

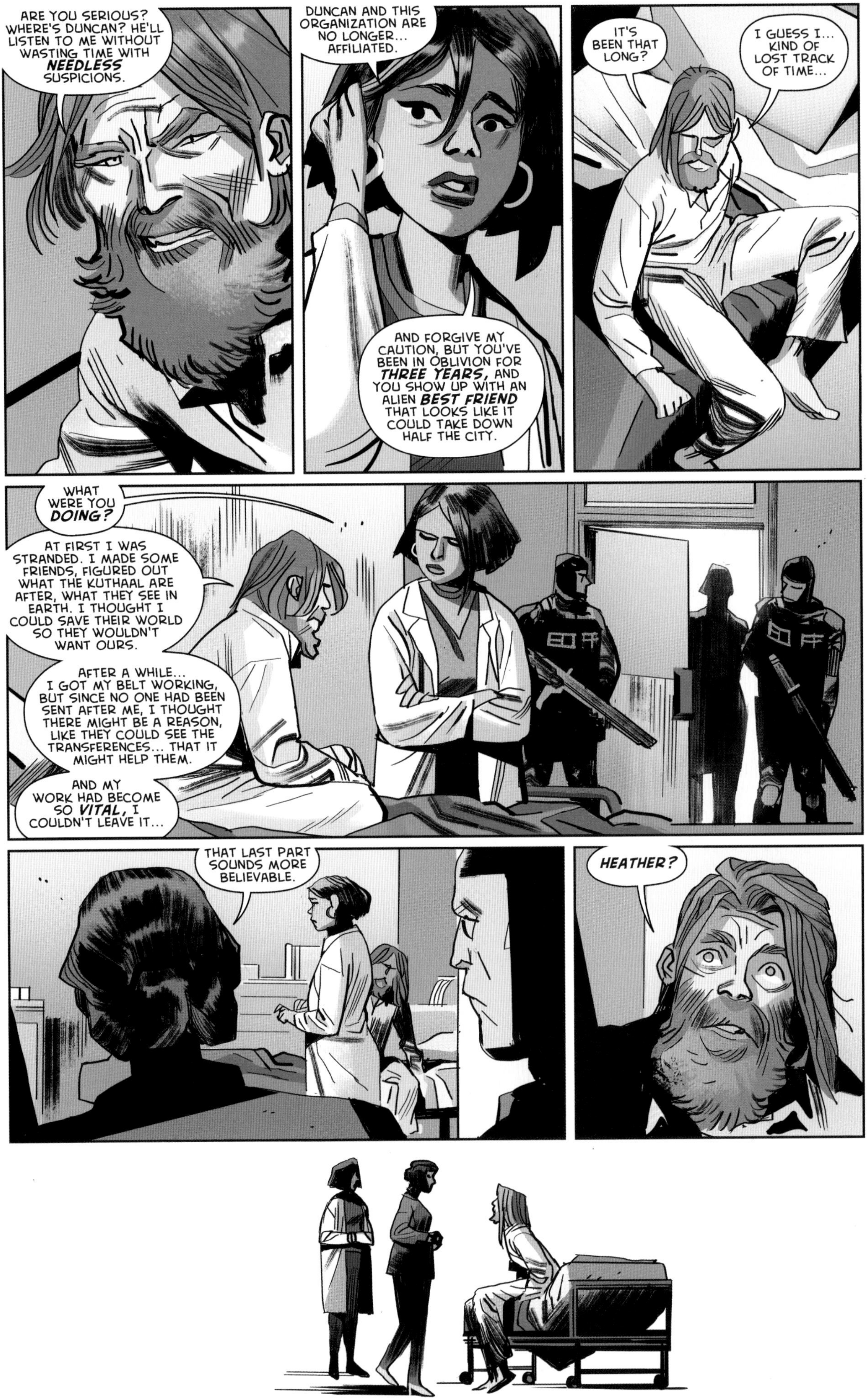
ARE YOU SERIOUS? WHERE'S DUNCAN? HE'LL LISTEN TO ME WITHOUT WASTING TIME WITH NEEDLESS SUSPICIONS.
DUNCAN AND THIS ORGANIZATION ARE NO LONGER... AFFILIATED.
AND FORGIVE MY CAUTION, BUT YOU'VE BEEN IN OBLIVION FOR THREE YEARS, AND YOU SHOW UP WITH AN ALIEN BEST FRIEND THAT LOOKS LIKE IT COULD TAKE DOWN HALF THE CITY.
IT'S BEEN THAT LONG?
I GUESS I... KIND OF LOST TRACK OF TIME...
WHAT WERE YOU DOING?
AT FIRST I WAS STRANDED. I MADE SOME FRIENDS, FIGURED OUT WHAT THE KUTHAAL ARE AFTER, WHAT THEY SEE IN EARTH. I THOUGHT I COULD SAVE THEIR WORLD SO THEY WOULDN'T WANT OURS.
AFTER A WHILE... I GOT MY BELT WORKING, BUT SINCE NO ONE HAD BEEN SENT AFTER ME, I THOUGHT THERE MIGHT BE A REASON, LIKE THEY COULD SEE THE TRANSFERENCES... THAT IT MIGHT HELP THEM.
AND MY WORK HAD BECOME SO VITAL, I COULDN'T LEAVE IT...
THAT LAST PART SOUNDS MORE BELIEVABLE.
HEATHER?

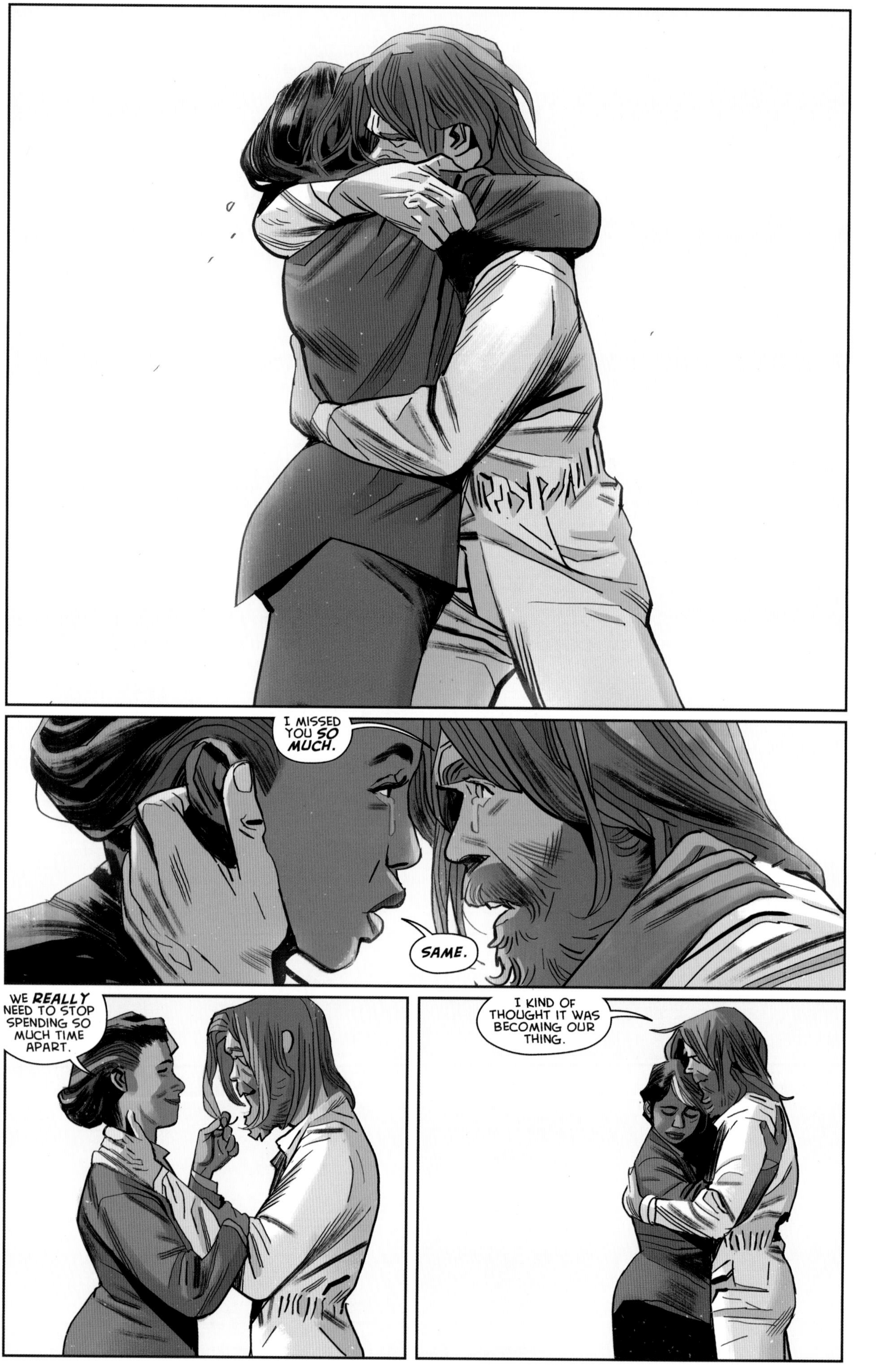
I MISSED YOU *SO MUCH.*
SAME.
WE ***REALLY*** NEED TO STOP SPENDING SO MUCH TIME APART.
I KIND OF THOUGHT IT WAS BECOMING OUR THING.

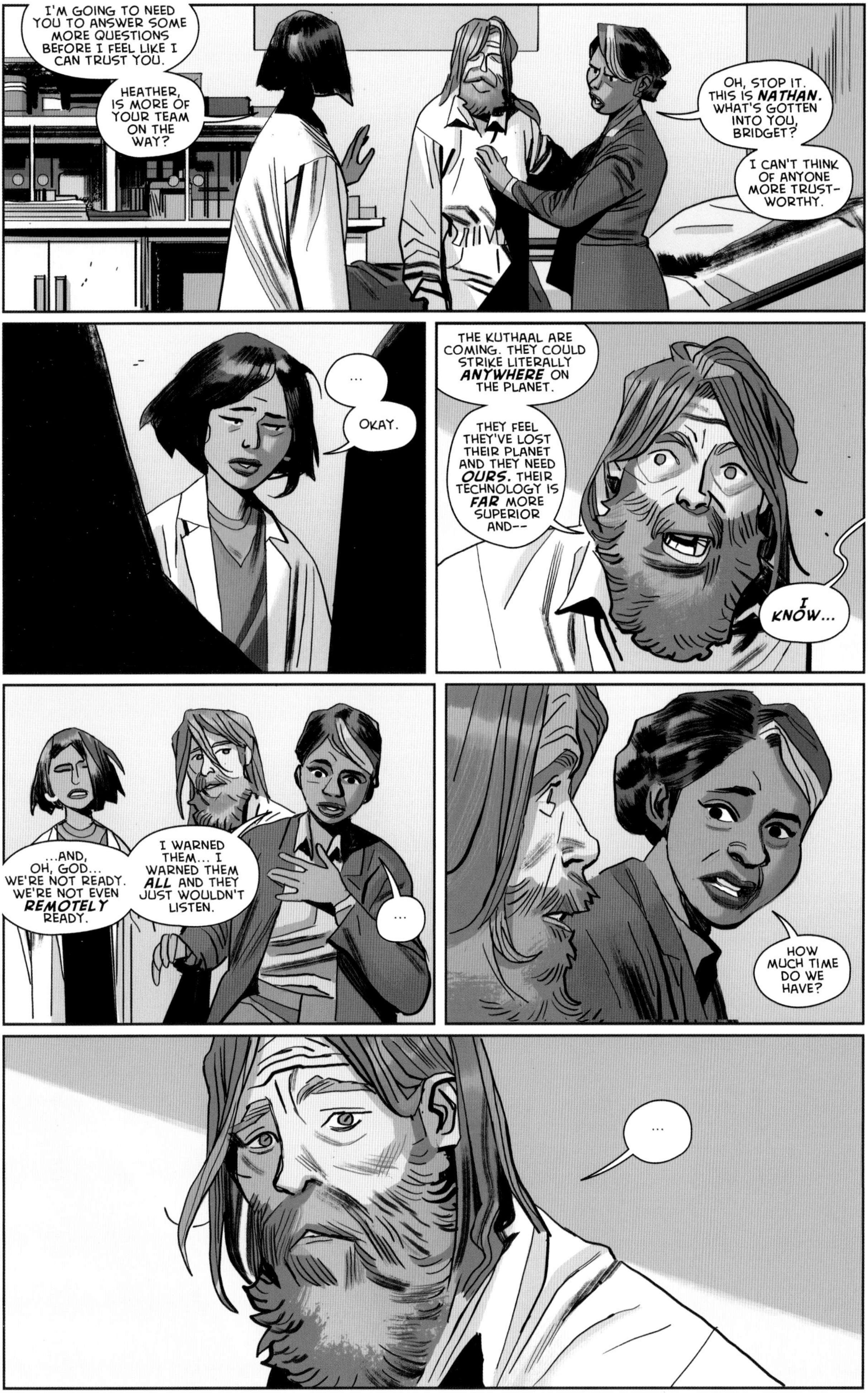
I'M GOING TO NEED YOU TO ANSWER SOME MORE QUESTIONS BEFORE I FEEL LIKE I CAN TRUST YOU.
HEATHER, IS MORE OF YOUR TEAM ON THE WAY?
OH, STOP IT. THIS IS NATHAN. WHAT'S GOTTEN INTO YOU, BRIDGET?
I CAN'T THINK OF ANYONE MORE TRUST-WORTHY.
...
OKAY.
THE KUTHAAL ARE COMING. THEY COULD STRIKE LITERALLY ANYWHERE ON THE PLANET.
THEY FEEL THEY'VE LOST THEIR PLANET AND THEY NEED OURS. THEIR TECHNOLOGY IS FAR MORE SUPERIOR AND--
I KNOW...
...AND, OH, GOD... WE'RE NOT READY. WE'RE NOT EVEN REMOTELY READY.
I WARNED THEM... I WARNED THEM ALL AND THEY JUST WOULDN'T LISTEN.
...
HOW MUCH TIME DO WE HAVE?
...

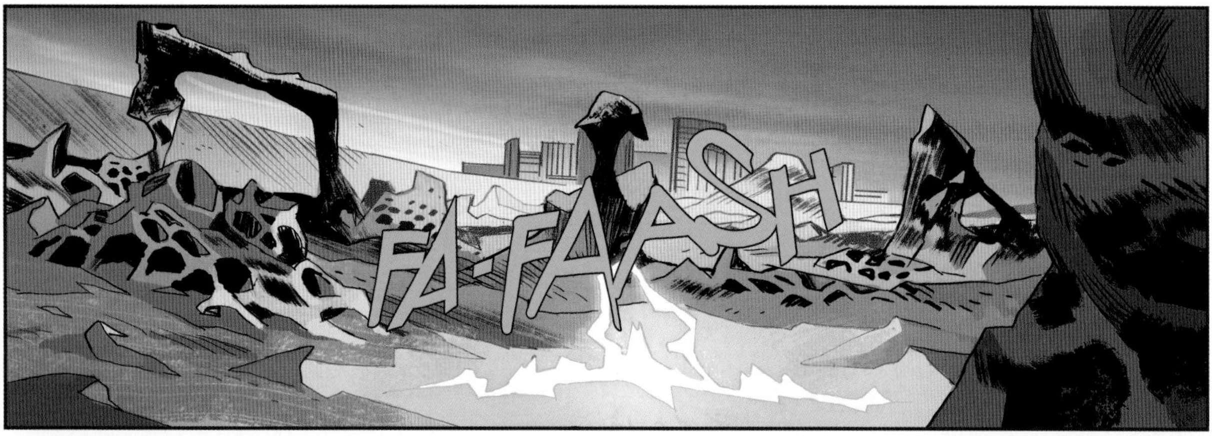
FA-FAASH

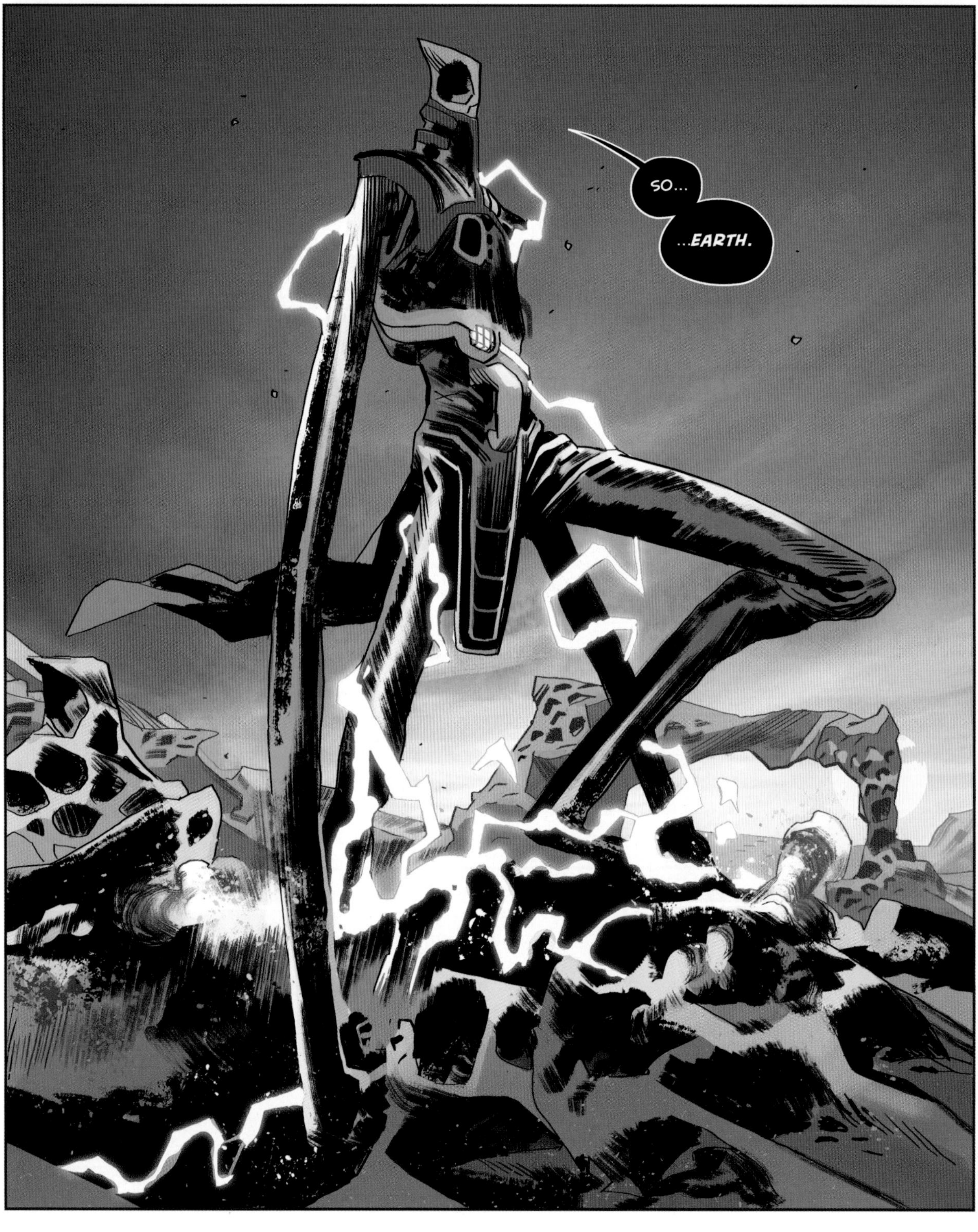
SO...
...EARTH.

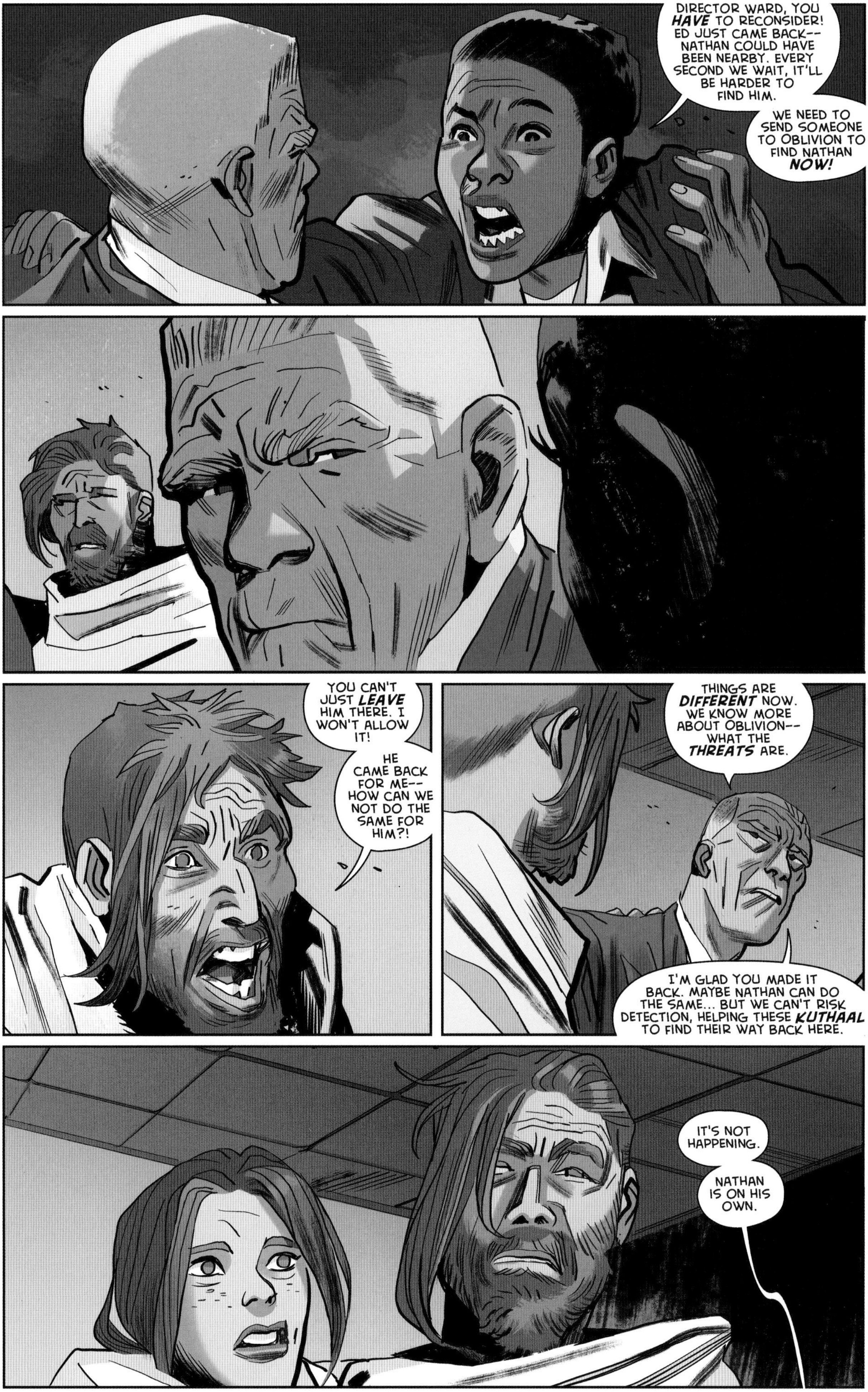
DIRECTOR WARD, YOU HAVE TO RECONSIDER! ED JUST CAME BACK-- NATHAN COULD HAVE BEEN NEARBY. EVERY SECOND WE WAIT, IT'LL BE HARDER TO FIND HIM.
WE NEED TO SEND SOMEONE TO OBLIVION TO FIND NATHAN NOW!
YOU CAN'T JUST LEAVE HIM THERE. I WON'T ALLOW IT!
HE CAME BACK FOR ME-- HOW CAN WE NOT DO THE SAME FOR HIM?!
THINGS ARE DIFFERENT NOW. WE KNOW MORE ABOUT OBLIVION-- WHAT THE THREATS ARE.
I'M GLAD YOU MADE IT BACK. MAYBE NATHAN CAN DO THE SAME... BUT WE CAN'T RISK DETECTION, HELPING THESE KUTHAAL TO FIND THEIR WAY BACK HERE.
IT'S NOT HAPPENING.
NATHAN IS ON HIS OWN.

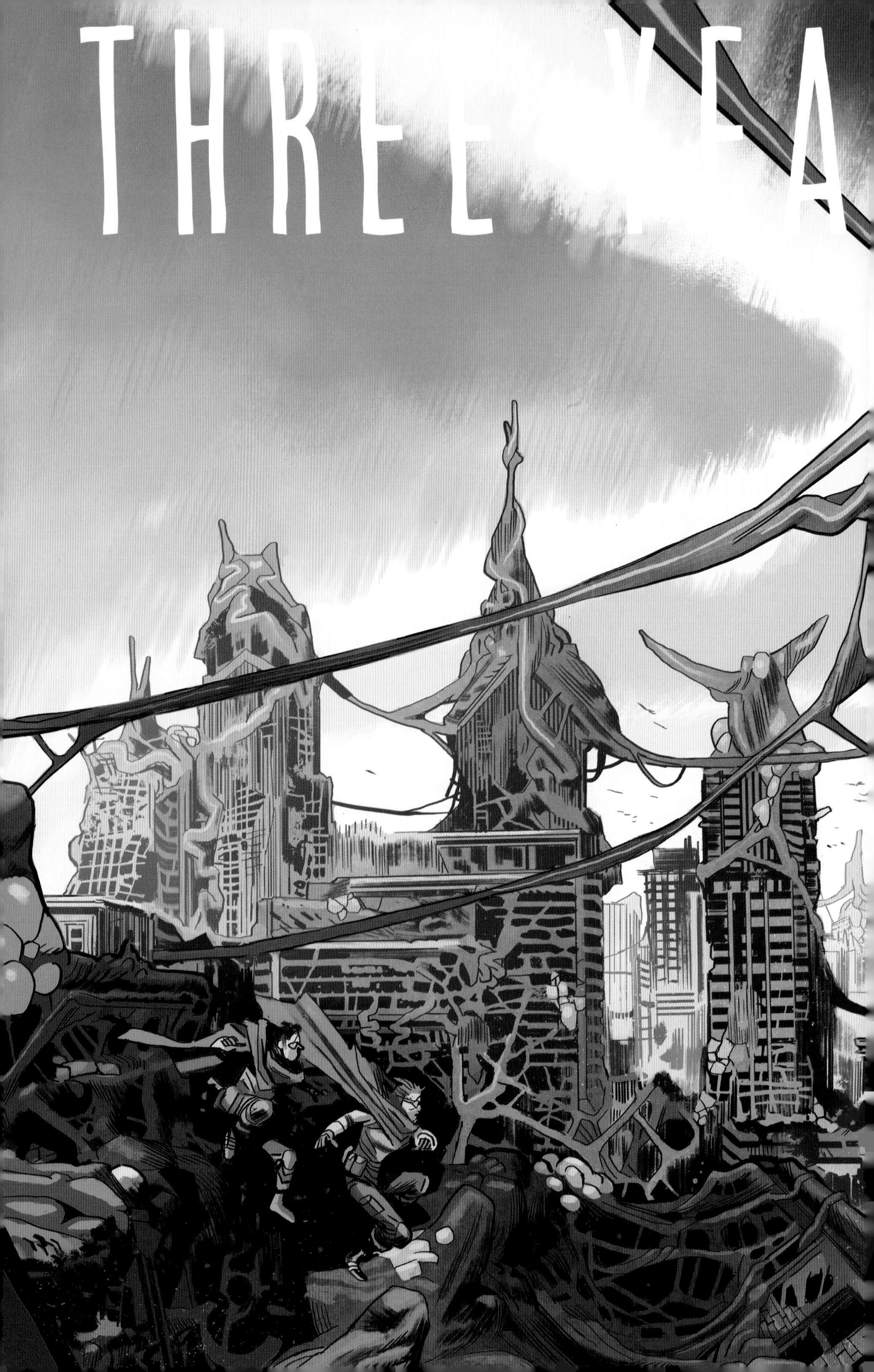
THREE YEA

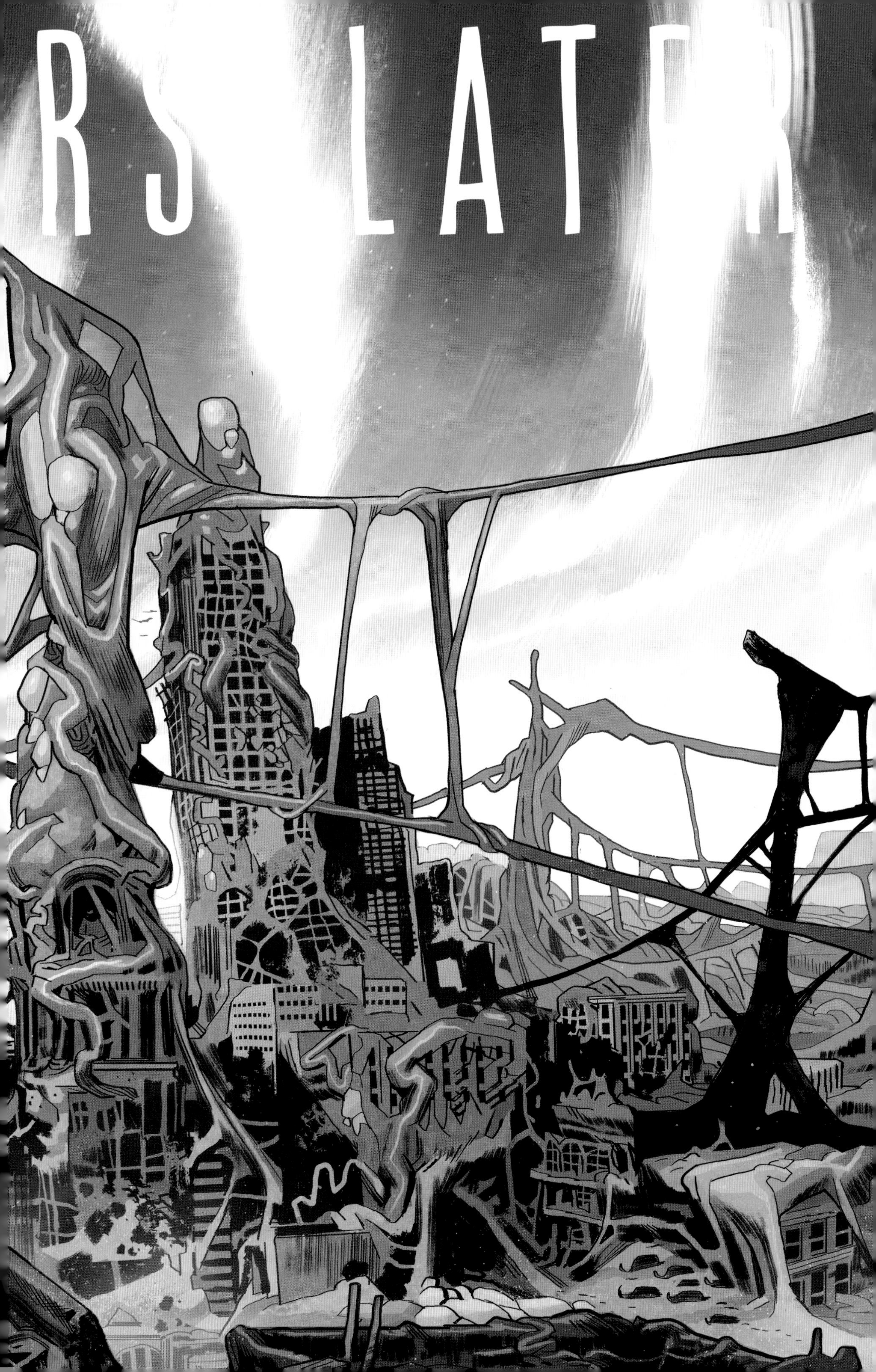
RS LATER

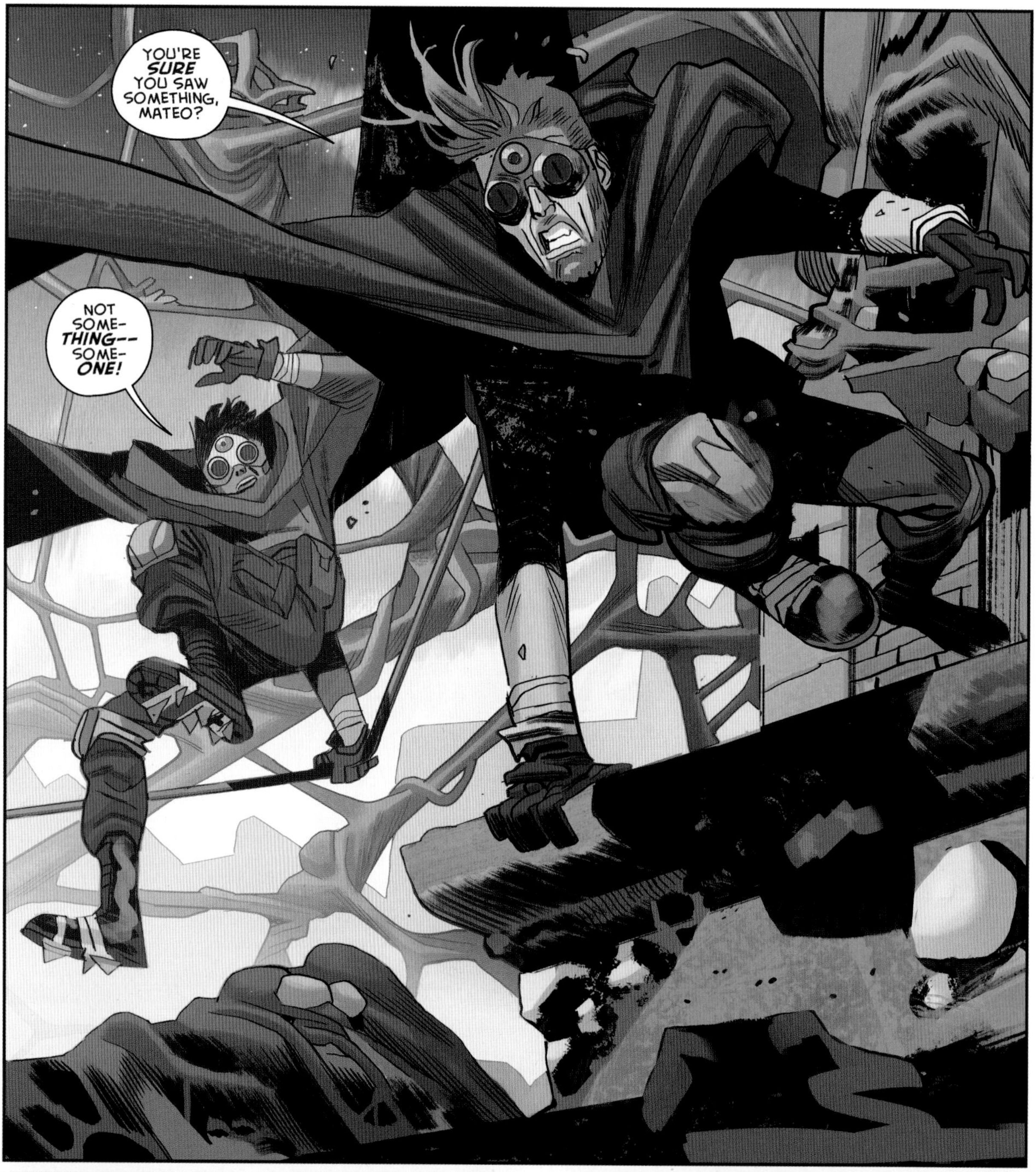
YOU'RE SURE YOU SAW SOMETHING, MATEO?
NOT SOME-THING-- SOME-ONE!
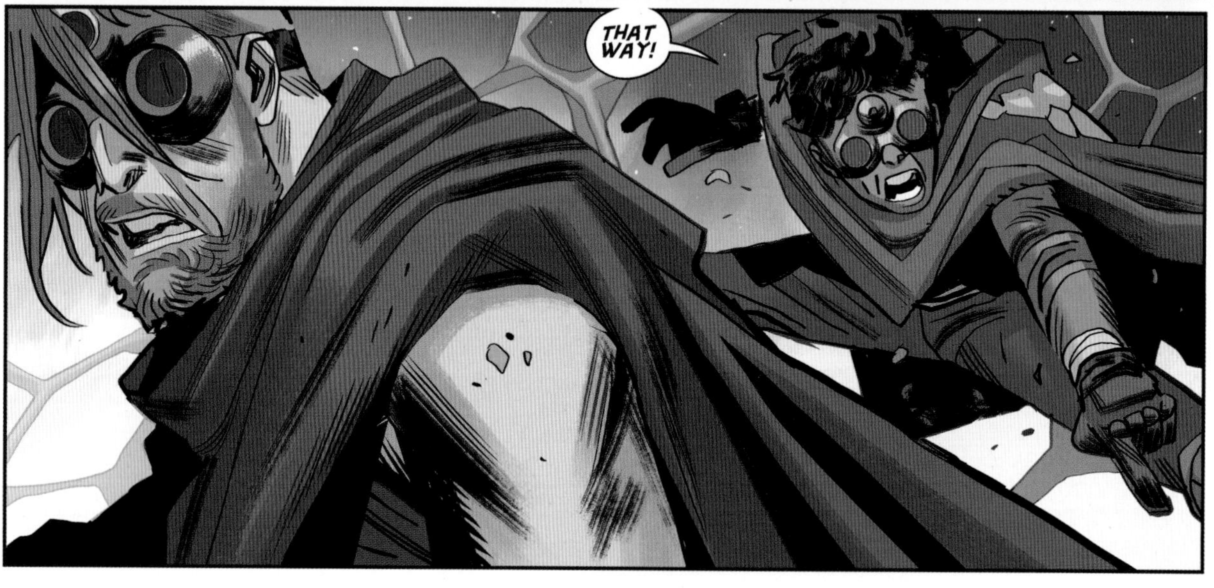
THAT WAY!

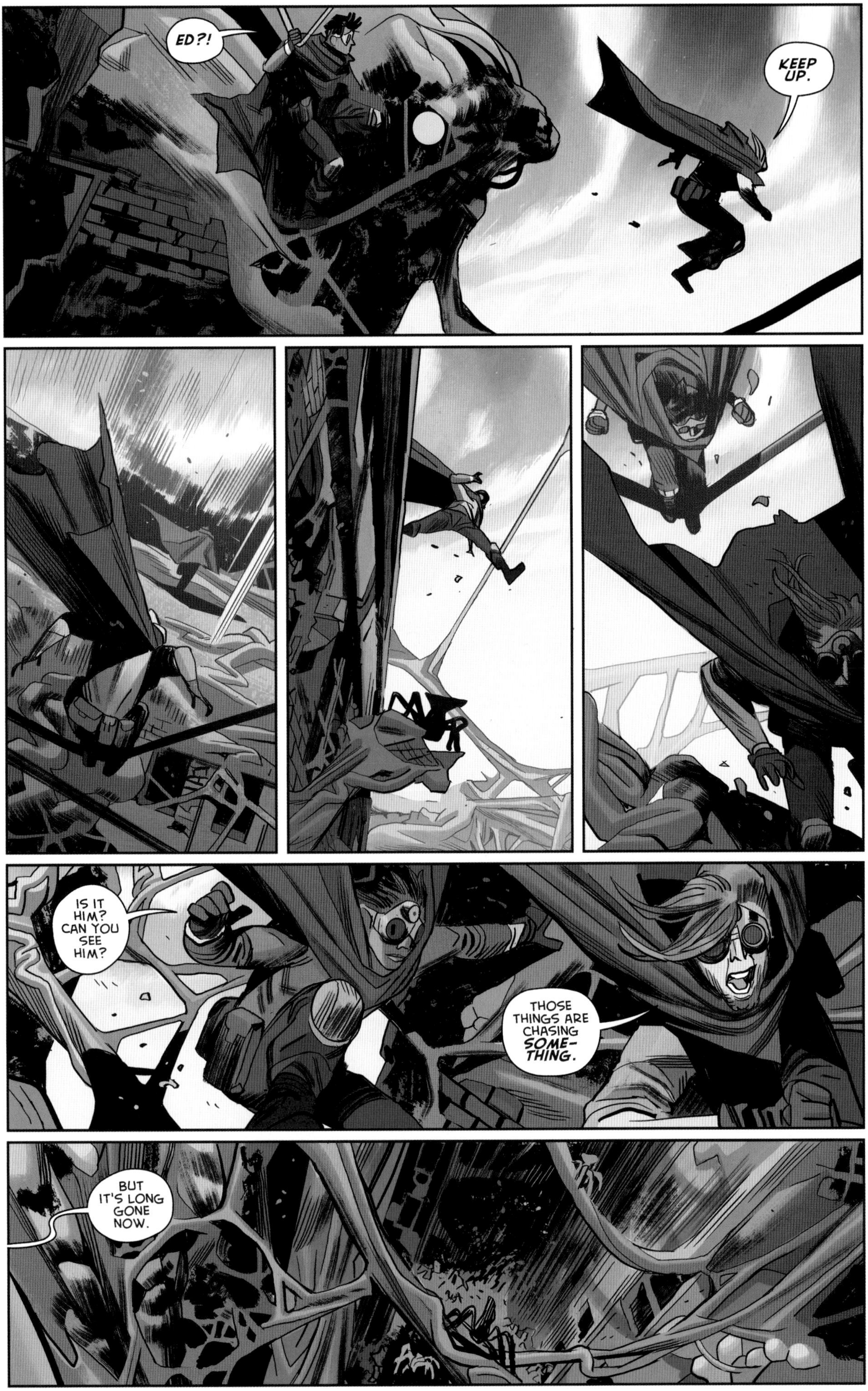
ED?!
KEEP UP.
IS IT HIM? CAN YOU SEE HIM?
THOSE THINGS ARE CHASING SOME-THING.
BUT IT'S LONG GONE NOW.

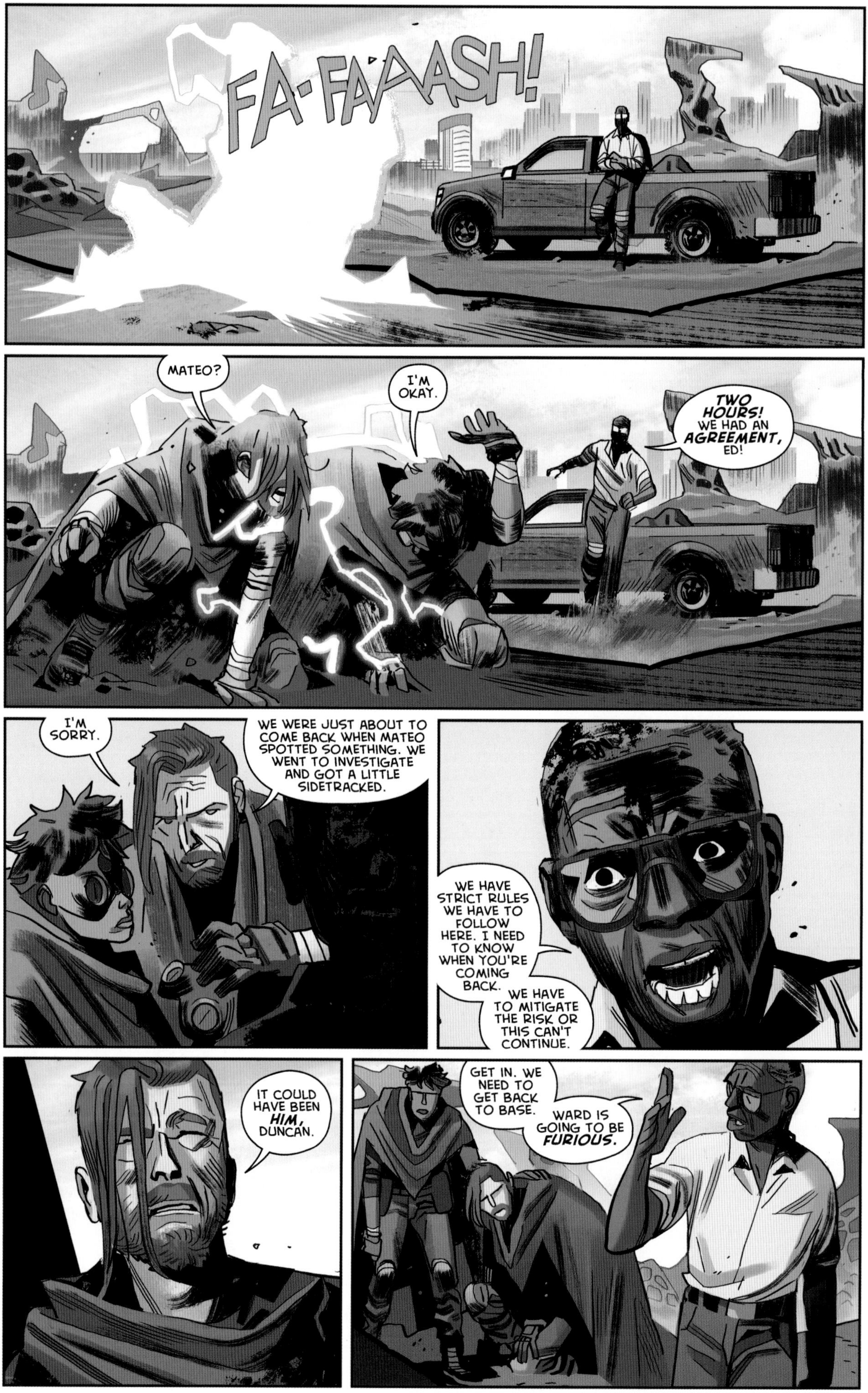
FA-FAAAASH!
MATEO?
I'M OKAY.
TWO HOURS! WE HAD AN AGREEMENT, ED!
I'M SORRY.
WE WERE JUST ABOUT TO COME BACK WHEN MATEO SPOTTED SOMETHING. WE WENT TO INVESTIGATE AND GOT A LITTLE SIDETRACKED.
WE HAVE STRICT RULES WE HAVE TO FOLLOW HERE. I NEED TO KNOW WHEN YOU'RE COMING BACK.
WE HAVE TO MITIGATE THE RISK OR THIS CAN'T CONTINUE.
IT COULD HAVE BEEN HIM, DUNCAN.
GET IN. WE NEED TO GET BACK TO BASE.
WARD IS GOING TO BE FURIOUS.

YOU BROKE PROTOCOL-- *AGAIN?!*

TOLD YOU.

LAST TIME IT WAS ONLY A COUPLE MINUTES. I'M SORRY, I *KNOW* WE HAVE TO KEEP OUR WINDOWS SHORT, I *KNOW* WE'RE TRYING TO AVOID DETECTION. I KNOW *ALL* THESE THINGS.

I THOUGHT WE WERE CLOSE. I THOUGHT WE FOUND *NATHAN.*

I WANT TO FIND HIM AS MUCH AS ANYONE. I HONESTLY DO. WE KNOW THE B.D.F.F. MONITORS THE DEAD ZONE. WE HAVE THEIR SCHEDULE. YOU CAN'T KEEP PUTTING DUNCAN AT RISK LIKE THIS.

YOUR MISSION IS RETRIEVING SAMPLES SO DUNCAN CAN CONTINUE HIS WORK... FOR THE GOOD OF MANKIND. LOOKING FOR NATHAN ALONG THE WAY IS A FAVOR TO *YOU.*

YOU KNOW AS WELL AS I DO HOW SLIM THE CHANCES ARE THAT HE'S STILL--

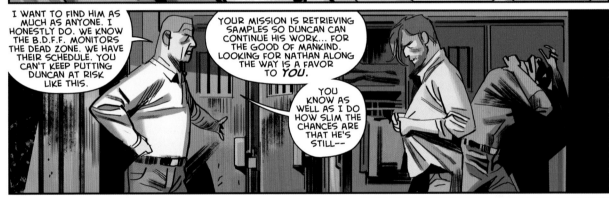

...

I'M JUST TRYING TO BE REALISTIC.

I KNOW IT. STILL DON'T LIKE IT.

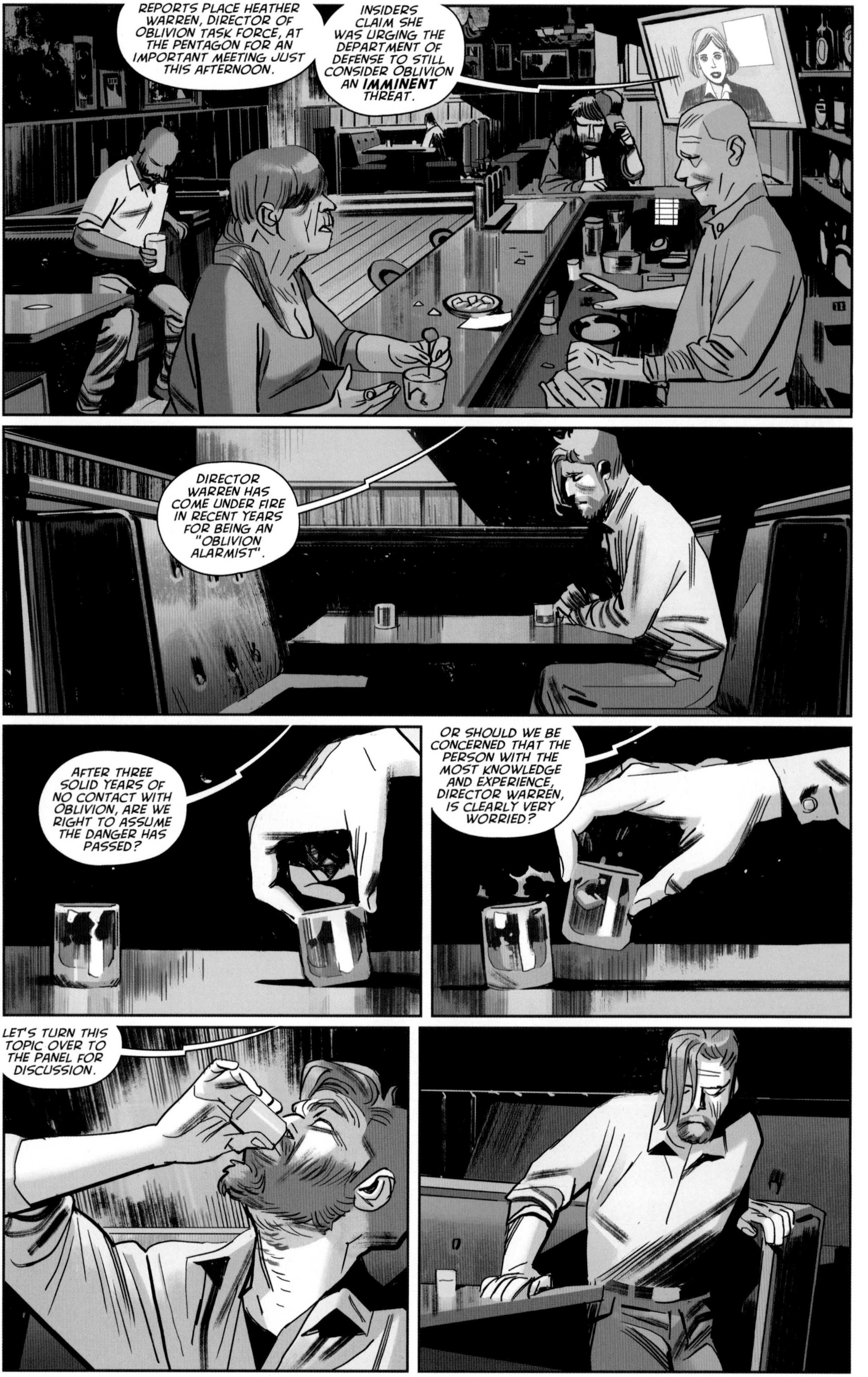
REPORTS PLACE HEATHER WARREN, DIRECTOR OF OBLIVION TASK FORCE, AT THE PENTAGON FOR AN IMPORTANT MEETING JUST THIS AFTERNOON.
INSIDERS CLAIM SHE WAS URGING THE DEPARTMENT OF DEFENSE TO STILL CONSIDER OBLIVION AN IMMINENT THREAT.
DIRECTOR WARREN HAS COME UNDER FIRE IN RECENT YEARS FOR BEING AN "OBLIVION ALARMIST".
AFTER THREE SOLID YEARS OF NO CONTACT WITH OBLIVION, ARE WE RIGHT TO ASSUME THE DANGER HAS PASSED?
OR SHOULD WE BE CONCERNED THAT THE PERSON WITH THE MOST KNOWLEDGE AND EXPERIENCE, DIRECTOR WARREN, IS CLEARLY VERY WORRIED?
LET'S TURN THIS TOPIC OVER TO THE PANEL FOR DISCUSSION.

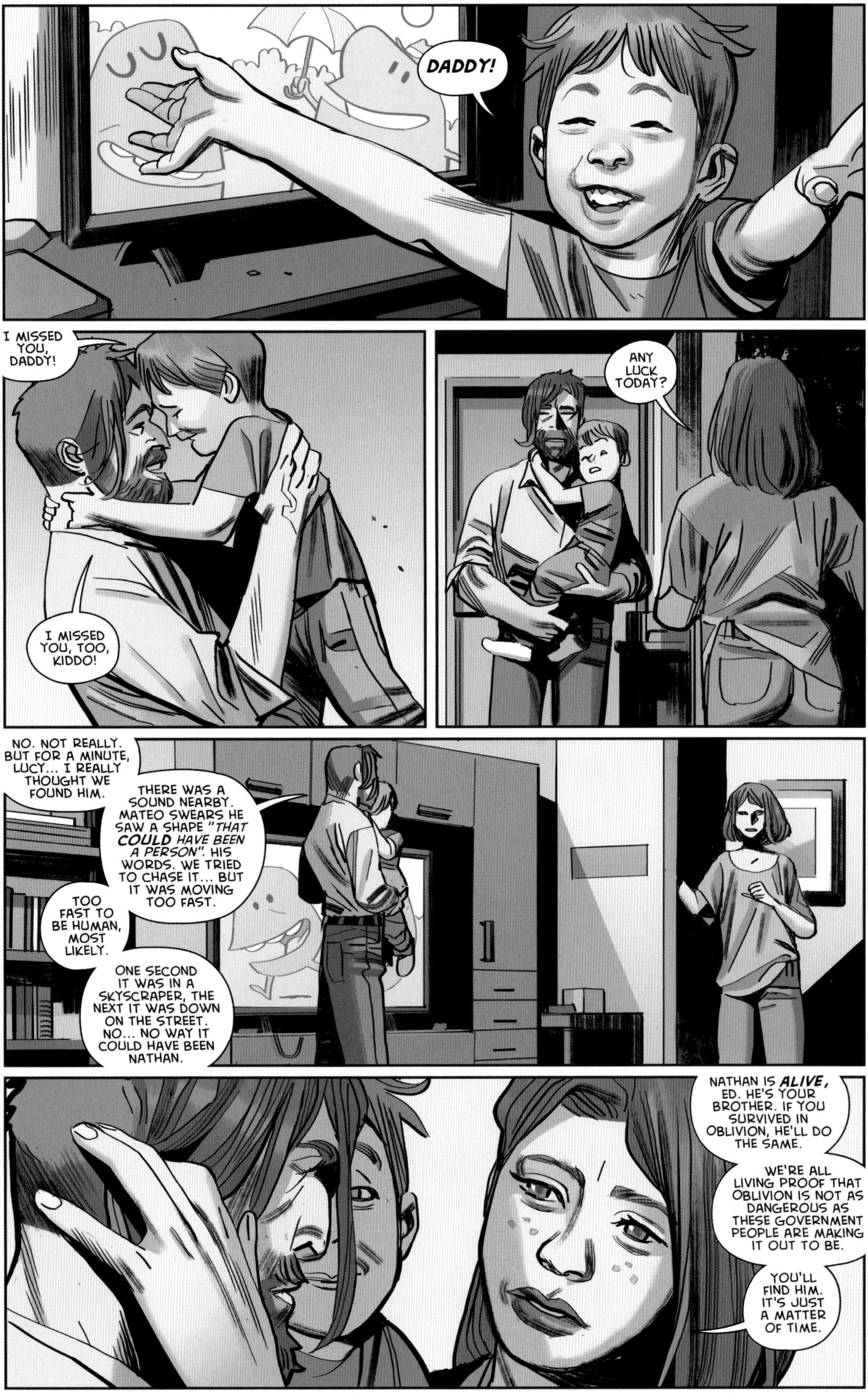
DADDY!
I MISSED YOU, DADDY!
I MISSED YOU, TOO, KIDDO!
ANY LUCK TODAY?
NO. NOT REALLY. BUT FOR A MINUTE, LUCY... I REALLY THOUGHT WE FOUND HIM.
THERE WAS A SOUND NEARBY. MATEO SWEARS HE SAW A SHAPE *"THAT **COULD** HAVE BEEN A PERSON"*. HIS WORDS. WE TRIED TO CHASE IT... BUT IT WAS MOVING TOO FAST.
TOO FAST TO BE HUMAN, MOST LIKELY.
ONE SECOND IT WAS IN A SKYSCRAPER, THE NEXT IT WAS DOWN ON THE STREET. NO... NO WAY IT COULD HAVE BEEN NATHAN.
NATHAN IS ***ALIVE,*** ED. HE'S YOUR BROTHER. IF YOU SURVIVED IN OBLIVION, HE'LL DO THE SAME.
WE'RE ALL LIVING PROOF THAT OBLIVION IS NOT AS DANGEROUS AS THESE GOVERNMENT PEOPLE ARE MAKING IT OUT TO BE.
YOU'LL FIND HIM. IT'S JUST A MATTER OF TIME.

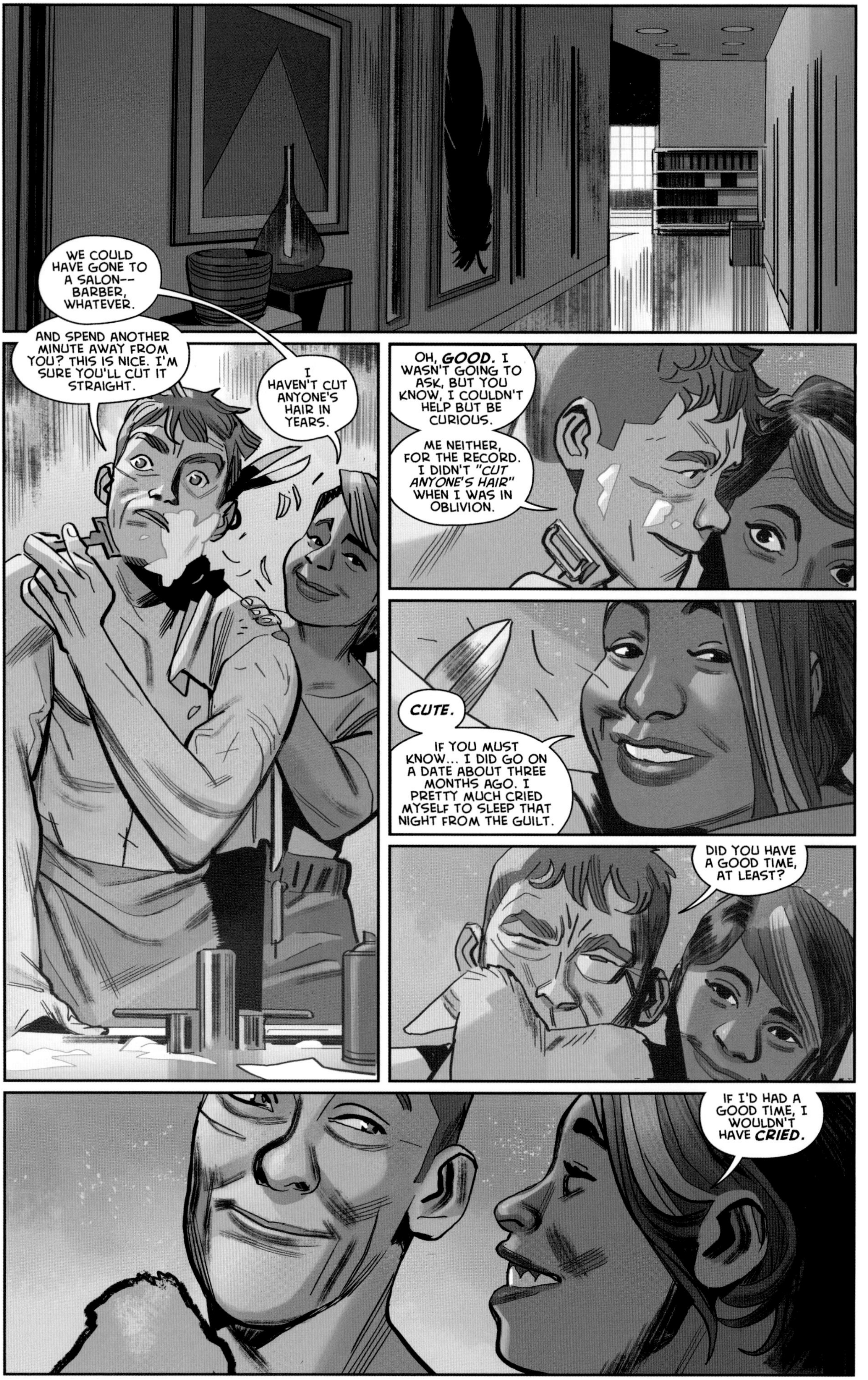
WE COULD HAVE GONE TO A SALON-- BARBER, WHATEVER.
AND SPEND ANOTHER MINUTE AWAY FROM YOU? THIS IS NICE. I'M SURE YOU'LL CUT IT STRAIGHT.
I HAVEN'T CUT ANYONE'S HAIR IN YEARS.
OH, GOOD. I WASN'T GOING TO ASK, BUT YOU KNOW, I COULDN'T HELP BUT BE CURIOUS.
ME NEITHER, FOR THE RECORD. I DIDN'T "CUT ANYONE'S HAIR" WHEN I WAS IN OBLIVION.
CUTE.
IF YOU MUST KNOW... I DID GO ON A DATE ABOUT THREE MONTHS AGO. I PRETTY MUCH CRIED MYSELF TO SLEEP THAT NIGHT FROM THE GUILT.
DID YOU HAVE A GOOD TIME, AT LEAST?
IF I'D HAD A GOOD TIME, I WOULDN'T HAVE CRIED.

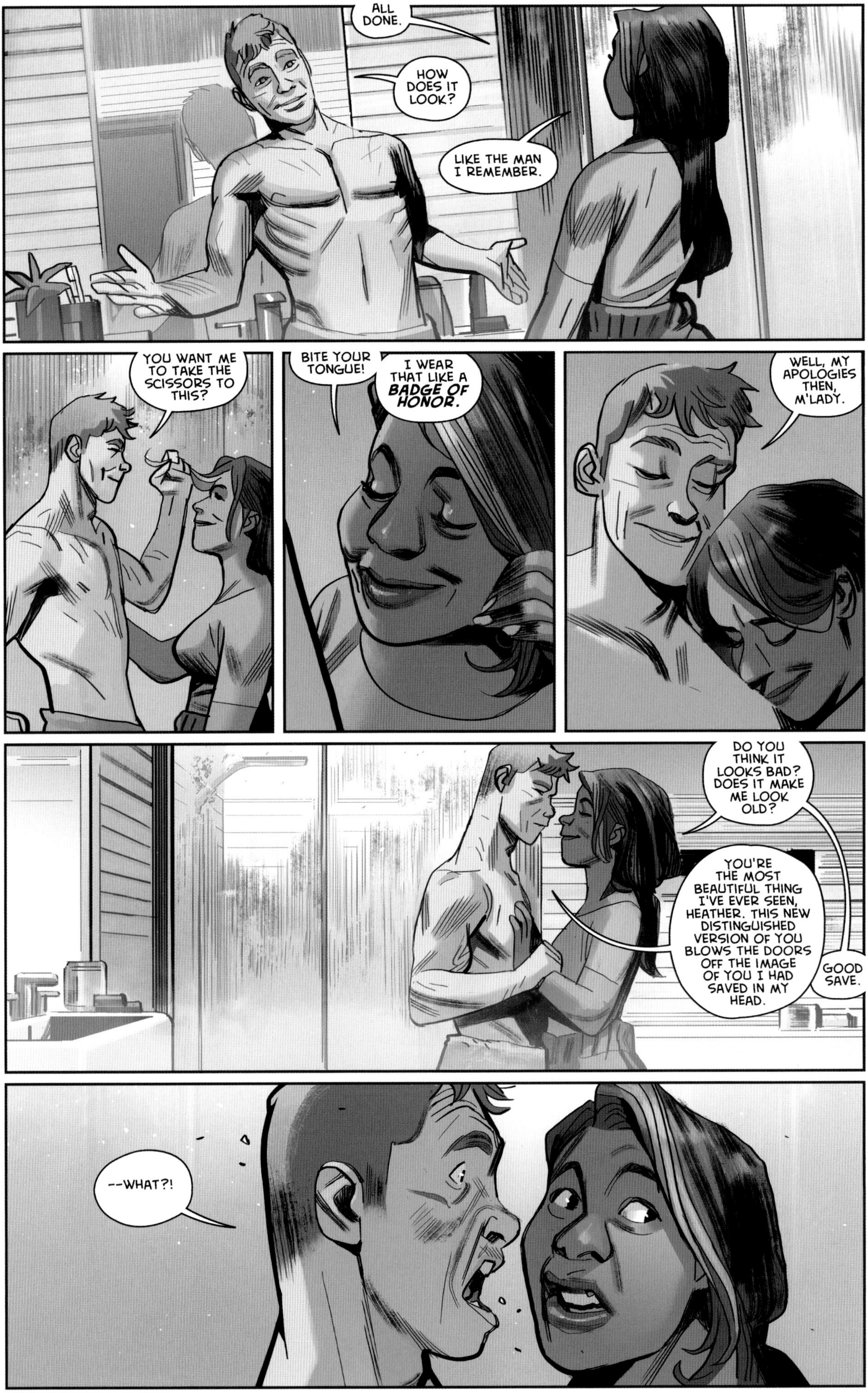
ALL DONE.
HOW DOES IT LOOK?
LIKE THE MAN I REMEMBER.
YOU WANT ME TO TAKE THE SCISSORS TO THIS?
BITE YOUR TONGUE!
I WEAR THAT LIKE A BADGE OF HONOR.
WELL, MY APOLOGIES THEN, M'LADY.
DO YOU THINK IT LOOKS BAD? DOES IT MAKE ME LOOK OLD?
YOU'RE THE MOST BEAUTIFUL THING I'VE EVER SEEN, HEATHER. THIS NEW DISTINGUISHED VERSION OF YOU BLOWS THE DOORS OFF THE IMAGE OF YOU I HAD SAVED IN MY HEAD.
GOOD SAVE.
--WHAT?!

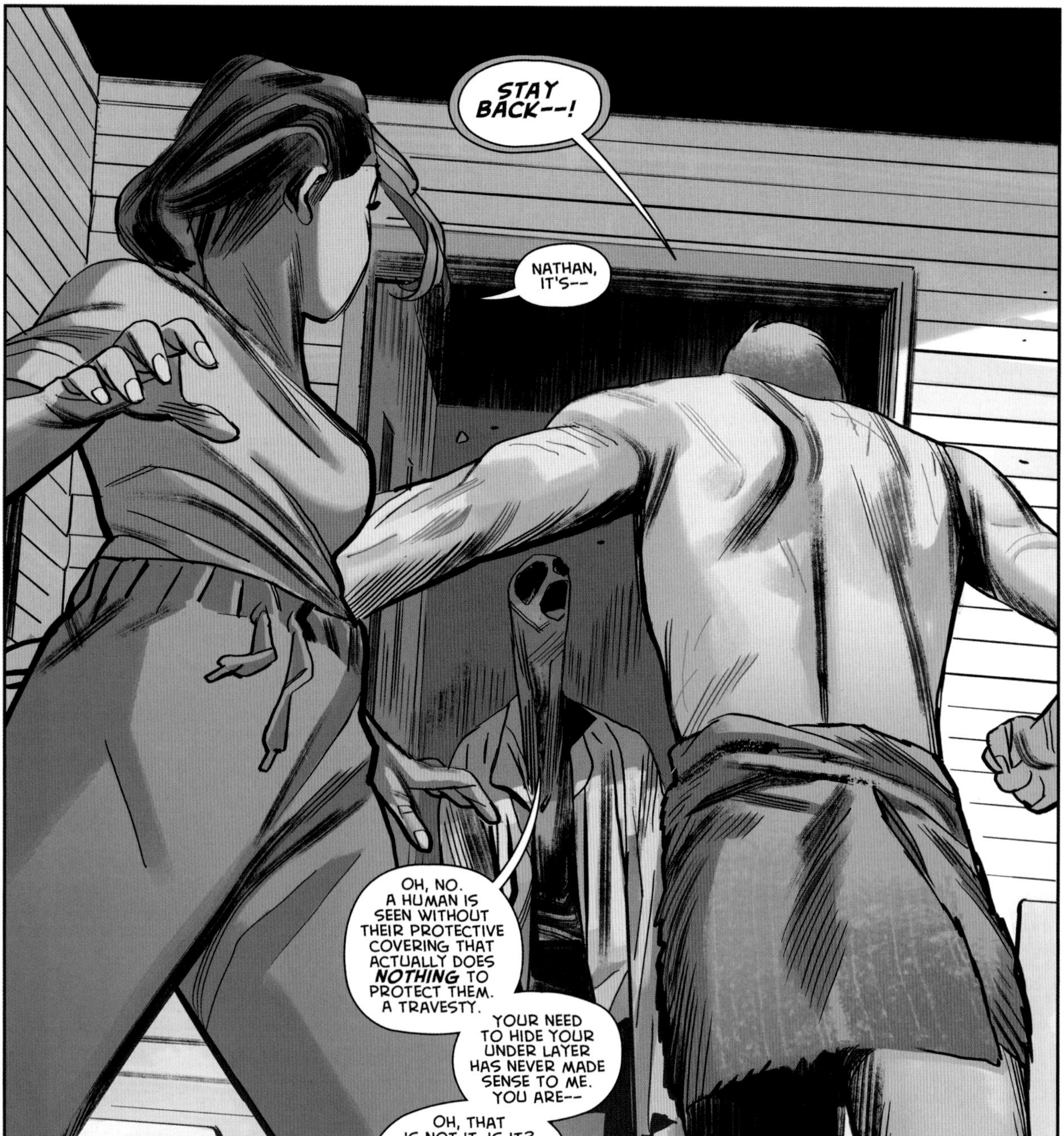
STAY BACK--!
NATHAN, IT'S--
OH, NO. A HUMAN IS SEEN WITHOUT THEIR PROTECTIVE COVERING THAT ACTUALLY DOES ***NOTHING*** TO PROTECT THEM. A TRAVESTY.
YOUR NEED TO HIDE YOUR UNDER LAYER HAS NEVER MADE SENSE TO ME. YOU ARE--
OH, THAT IS NOT IT, IS IT? YOU WERE NOT EXPECTING TO SEE A ***KUTHAAL*** HERE. I AM BIG, STRINGY, ALIEN MONSTER TO YOU. I FORGET AND AM SORRY.

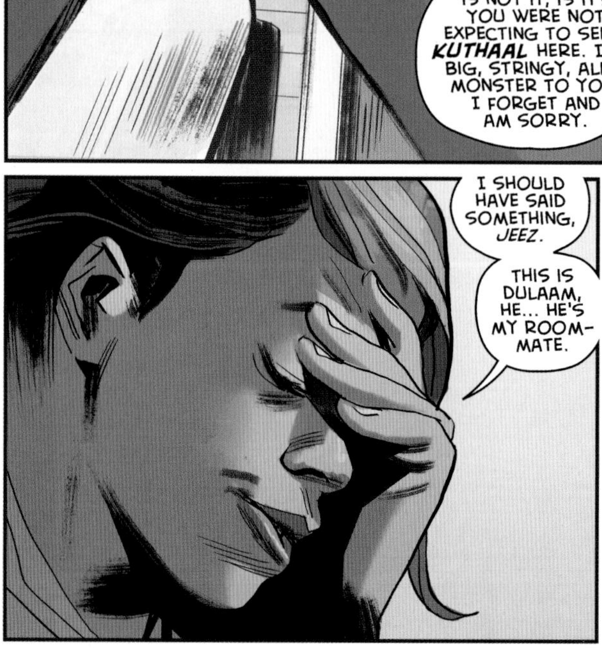
I SHOULD HAVE SAID SOMETHING, *JEEZ.*
THIS IS DULAAM, HE... HE'S MY ROOM-MATE.

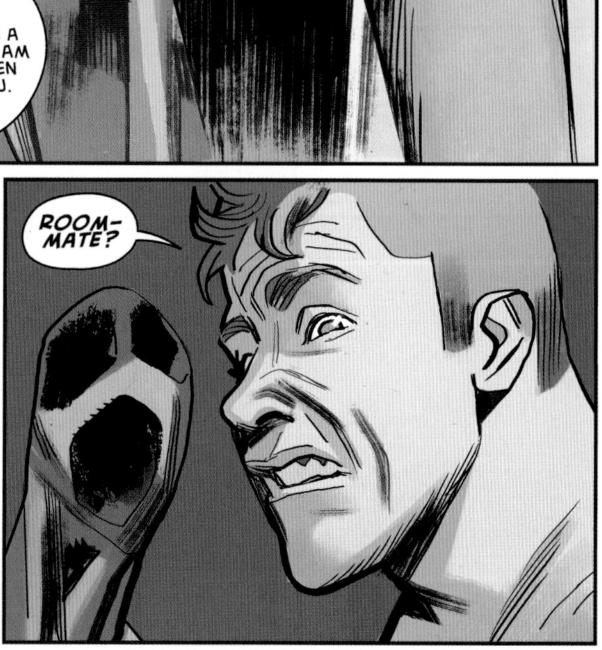
ROOM-MATE?

DULAAM WAS ONE OF THE KUTHAAL WHO WERE STRANDED HERE DURING THE RESCUE OF ED'S PEOPLE. WE ORIGINALLY THOUGHT HE FELL TO HIS DEATH.

WARD AND I WERE PRETTY MUCH THE ONLY PEOPLE WHO KNEW DULAAM SURVIVED. WE KEPT HIM HIDDEN, TRYING TO GET AS MUCH INFORMATION FROM HIM AS WE COULD.

HE WENT FROM COOPERATIVE TO FRIENDLY AND EVENTUALLY... LONG STORY... I HAD TO HIDE HIM HERE.

WE WATCH THE HOUSEWIVES TOGETHER. THEIR FIGHTING BRINGS US JOY. IT IS *WEIRD.*

I MADE MY OWN KUTHAAL FRIENDS, IN OBLIVION.

GAKAAL AND HIS OFFSPRING, NANU--

GAKAAL THE GHOZAN COMMANDER?!

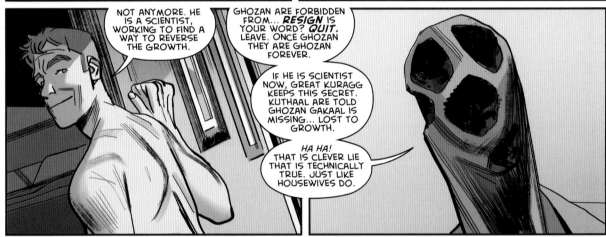

NOT ANYMORE. HE IS A SCIENTIST, WORKING TO FIND A WAY TO REVERSE THE GROWTH.

GHOZAN ARE FORBIDDEN FROM... *RESIGN* IS YOUR WORD? *QUIT.* LEAVE. ONCE GHOZAN THEY ARE GHOZAN FOREVER.

IF HE IS SCIENTIST NOW, GREAT KURAGG KEEPS THIS SECRET. KUTHAAL ARE TOLD GHOZAN GAKAAL IS MISSING... LOST TO GROWTH.

HA HA! THAT IS CLEVER LIE THAT IS TECHNICALLY TRUE. JUST LIKE HOUSEWIVES DO.

YOU ARE AN UNUSUAL KUTHAAL, DULAAM.

HE GROWS ON YOU.

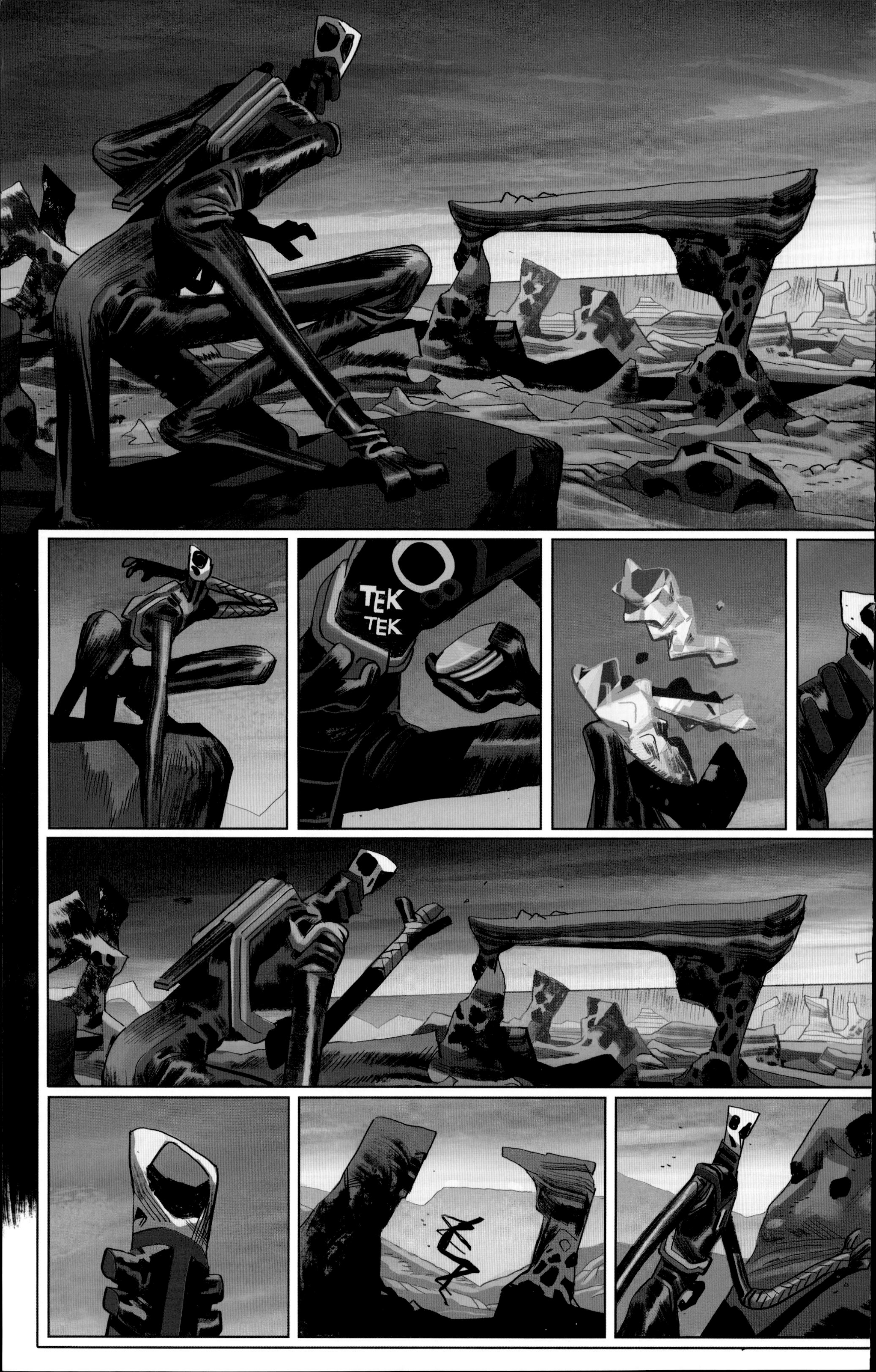
TEK
TEK

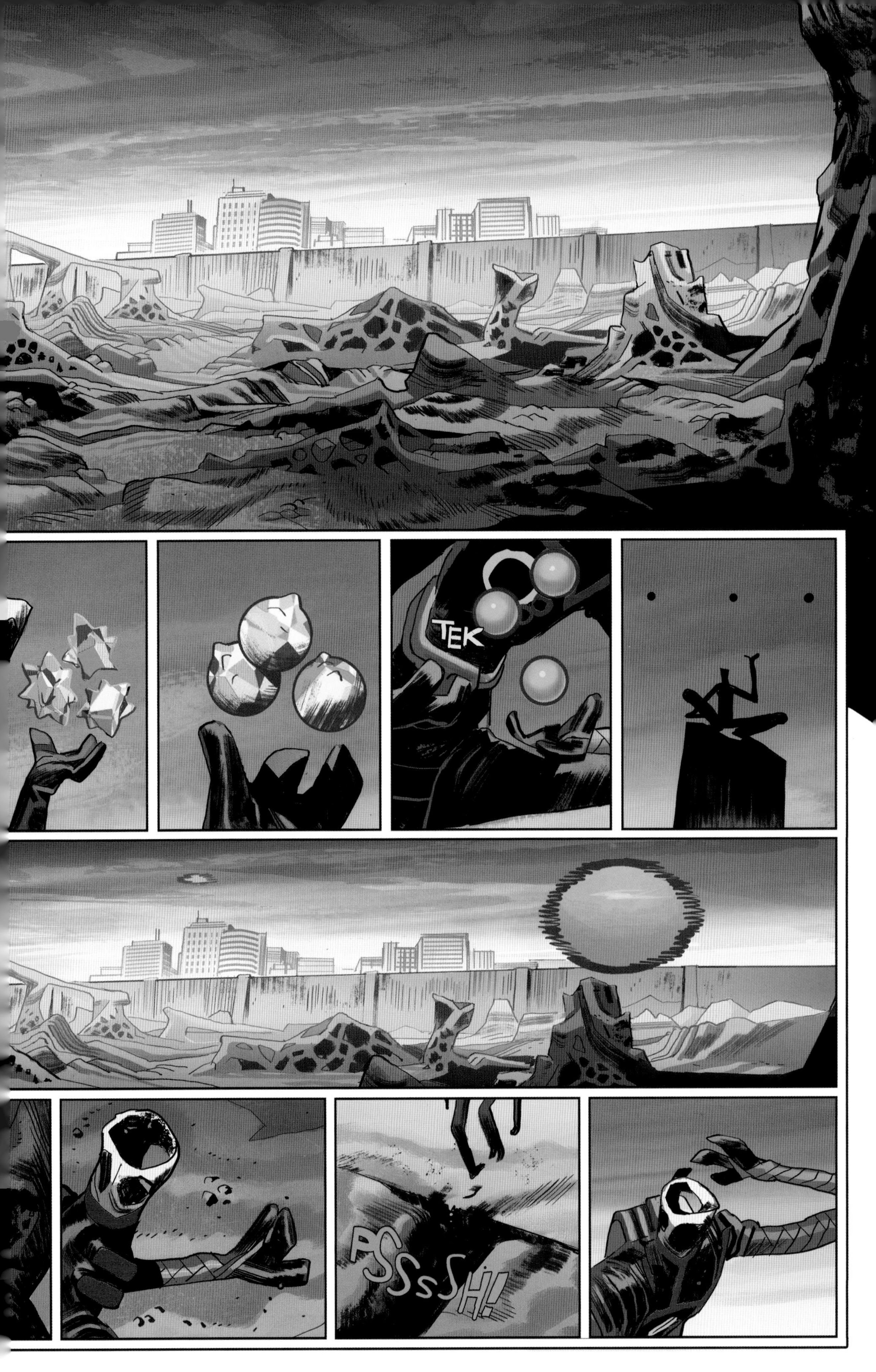
TEK
PSSsSH!!

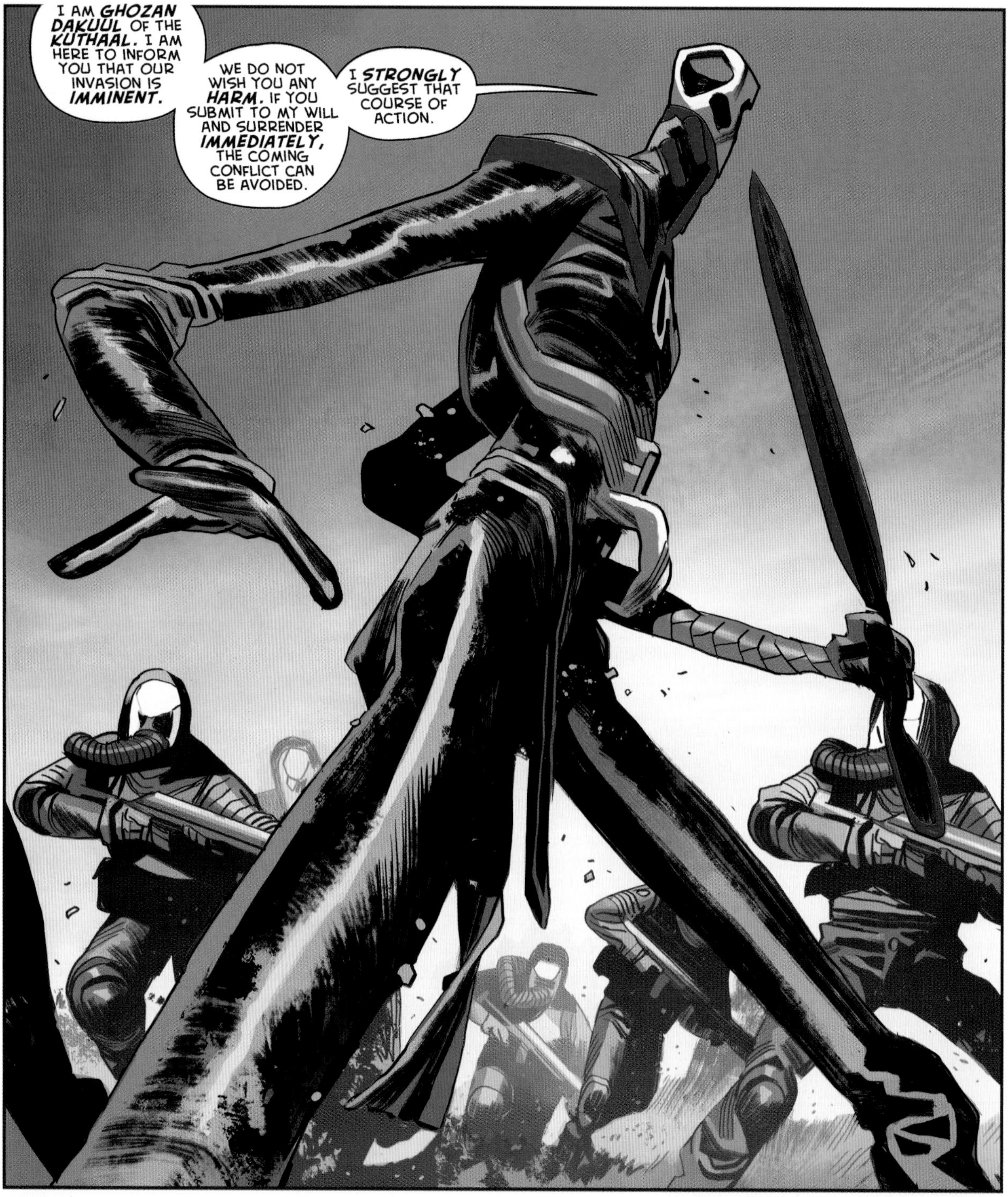
I AM GHOZAN DAKUUL OF THE KUTHAAL. I AM HERE TO INFORM YOU THAT OUR INVASION IS IMMINENT.
WE DO NOT WISH YOU ANY HARM. IF YOU SUBMIT TO MY WILL AND SURRENDER IMMEDIATELY, THE COMING CONFLICT CAN BE AVOIDED.
I STRONGLY SUGGEST THAT COURSE OF ACTION.

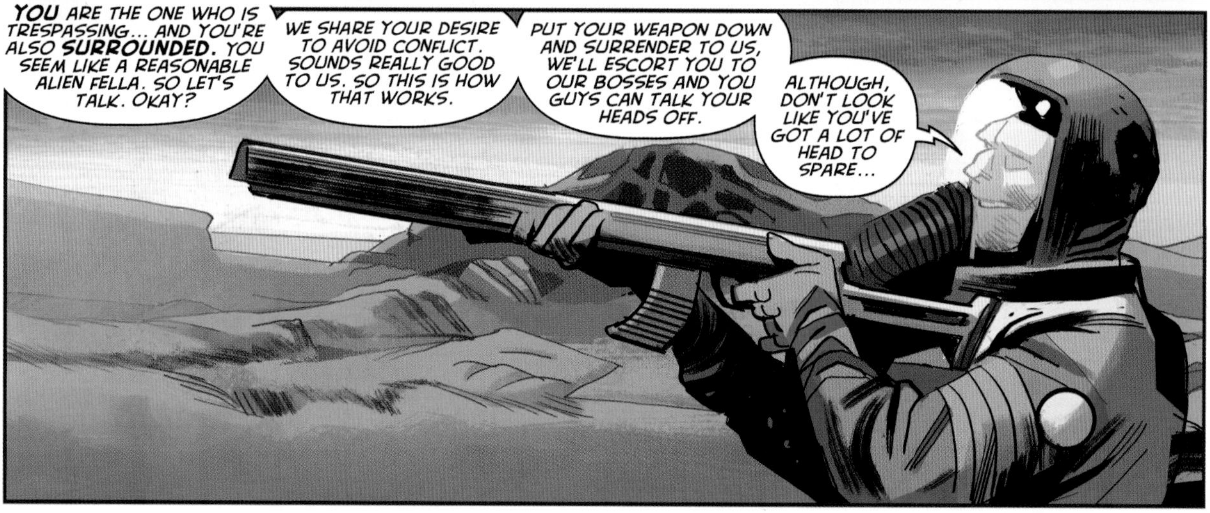
YOU ARE THE ONE WHO IS TRESPASSING... AND YOU'RE ALSO SURROUNDED. YOU SEEM LIKE A REASONABLE ALIEN FELLA. SO LET'S TALK. OKAY?
WE SHARE YOUR DESIRE TO AVOID CONFLICT. SOUNDS REALLY GOOD TO US. SO THIS IS HOW THAT WORKS.
PUT YOUR WEAPON DOWN AND SURRENDER TO US, WE'LL ESCORT YOU TO OUR BOSSES AND YOU GUYS CAN TALK YOUR HEADS OFF.
ALTHOUGH, DON'T LOOK LIKE YOU'VE GOT A LOT OF HEAD TO SPARE...

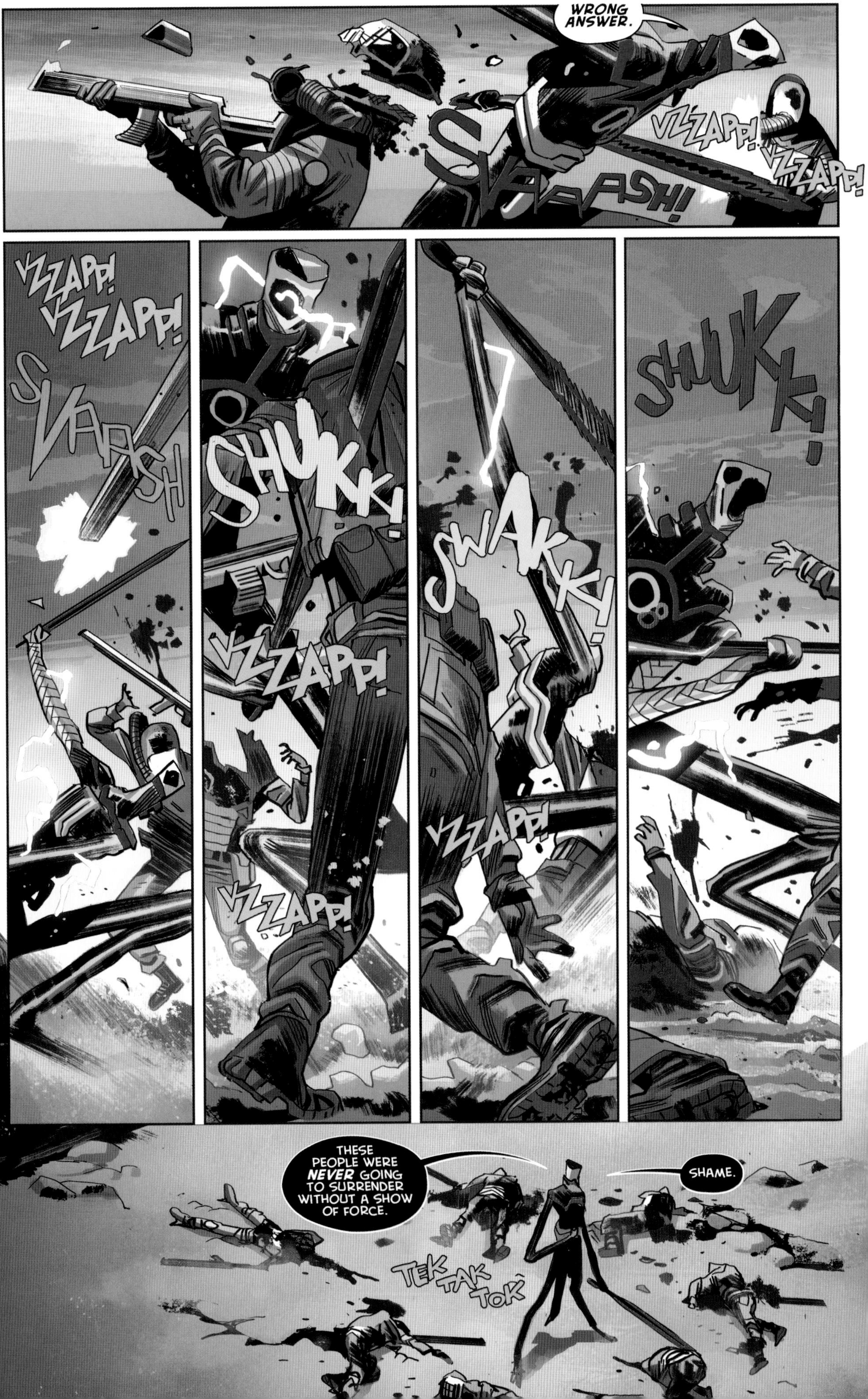
WRONG ANSWER.
SVAAASH!
VZZAPP!
VZZAPP!
VZZAPP!
VZZAPP!
SVARSH
SHUKKK!
VZZAPP!
VZZAPP!
SWAKKK!
VZZAPP!
SHUUKK!
THESE PEOPLE WERE NEVER GOING TO SURRENDER WITHOUT A SHOW OF FORCE.
SHAME.
TEK TAK TOK

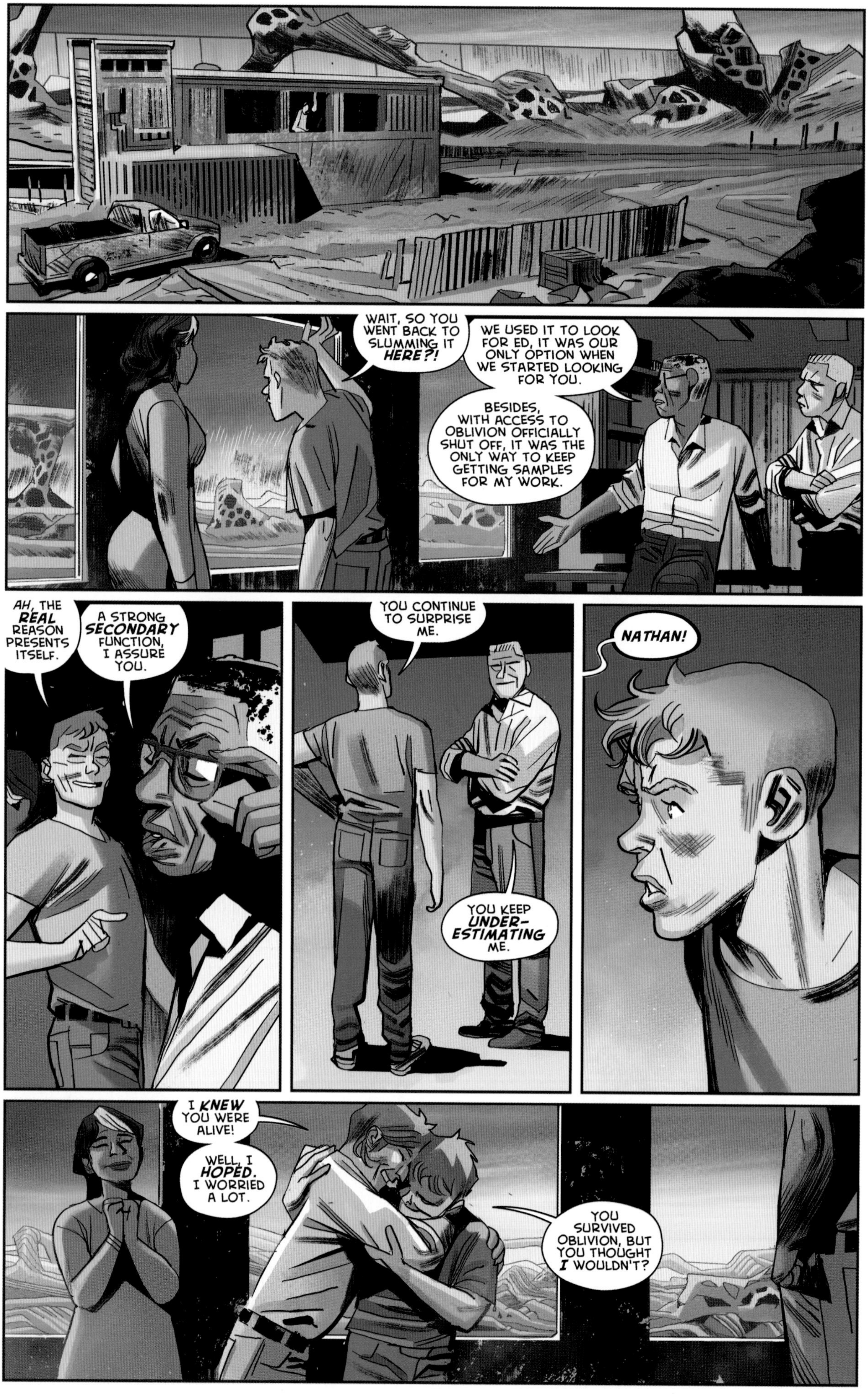

WAIT, SO YOU WENT BACK TO SLUMMING IT HERE?!
WE USED IT TO LOOK FOR ED, IT WAS OUR ONLY OPTION WHEN WE STARTED LOOKING FOR YOU.
BESIDES, WITH ACCESS TO OBLIVION OFFICIALLY SHUT OFF, IT WAS THE ONLY WAY TO KEEP GETTING SAMPLES FOR MY WORK.
AH, THE REAL REASON PRESENTS ITSELF.
A STRONG SECONDARY FUNCTION, I ASSURE YOU.
YOU CONTINUE TO SURPRISE ME.
YOU KEEP UNDER-ESTIMATING ME.
NATHAN!
I KNEW YOU WERE ALIVE!
WELL, I HOPED. I WORRIED A LOT.
YOU SURVIVED OBLIVION, BUT YOU THOUGHT I WOULDN'T?

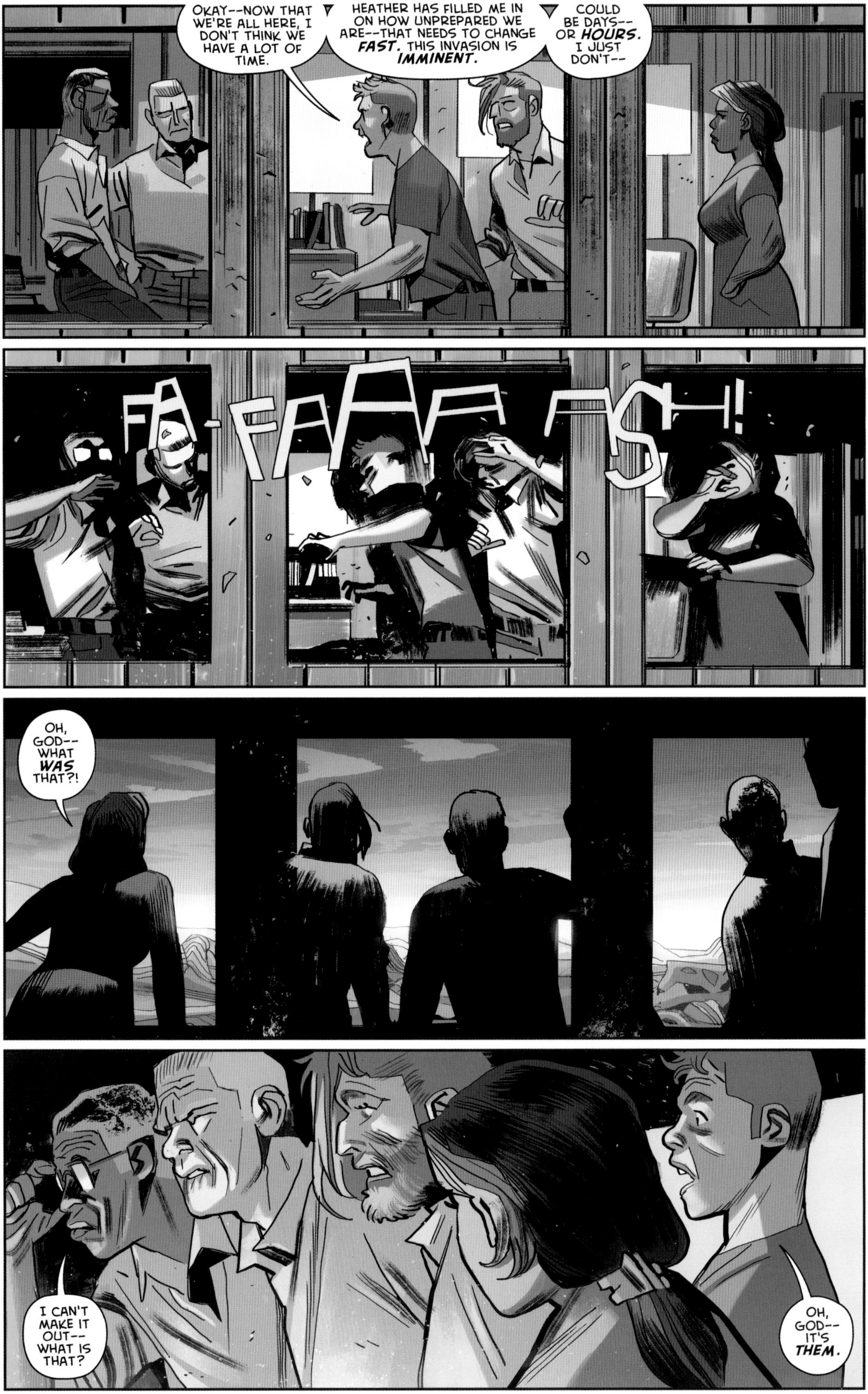
OKAY--NOW THAT WE'RE ALL HERE, I DON'T THINK WE HAVE A LOT OF TIME.
HEATHER HAS FILLED ME IN ON HOW UNPREPARED WE ARE--THAT NEEDS TO CHANGE FAST. THIS INVASION IS IMMINENT.
COULD BE DAYS-- OR HOURS. I JUST DON'T--
FA-FAAAA-ASH!
OH, GOD-- WHAT WAS THAT?!
I CAN'T MAKE IT OUT-- WHAT IS THAT?
OH, GOD-- IT'S THEM.

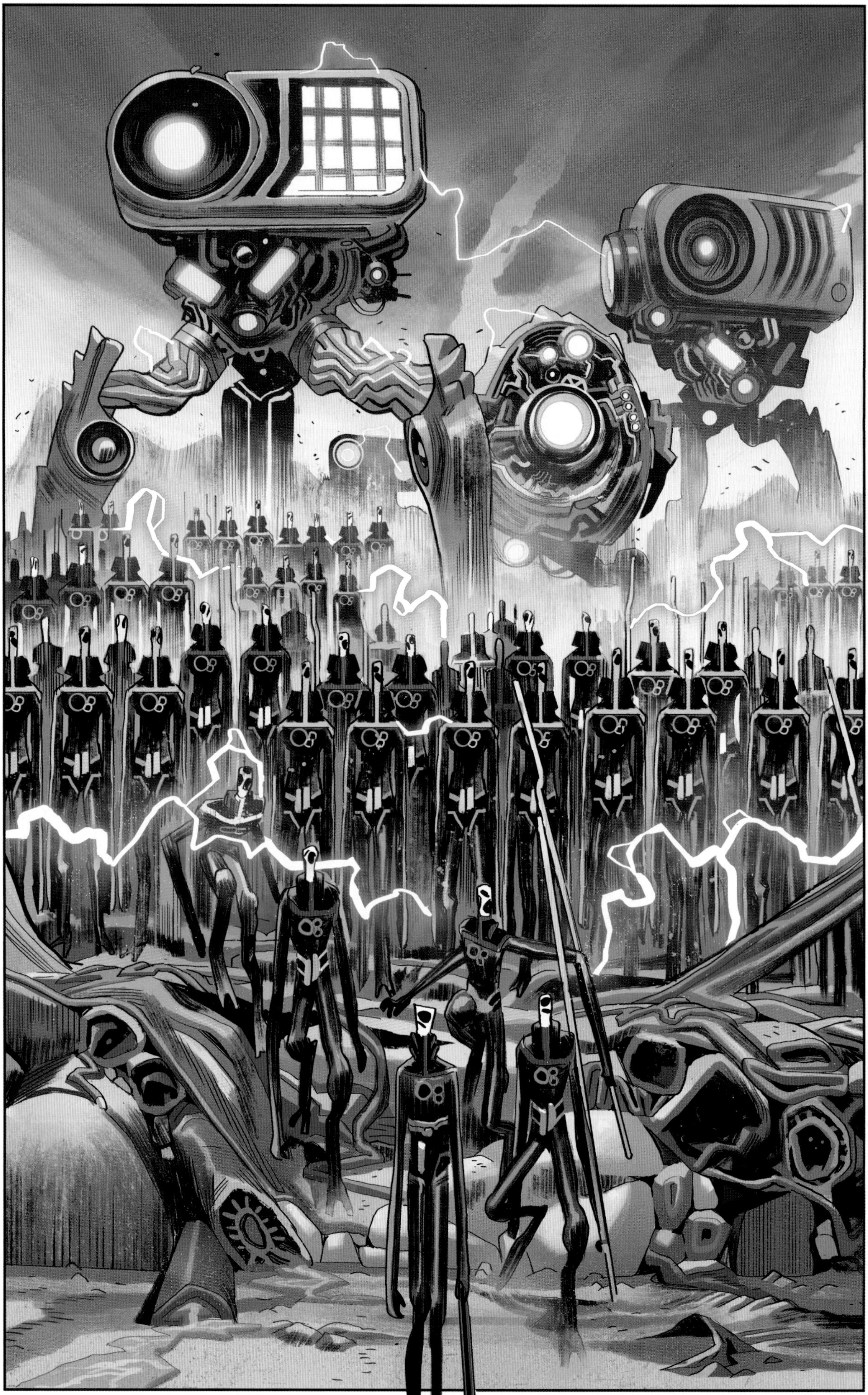

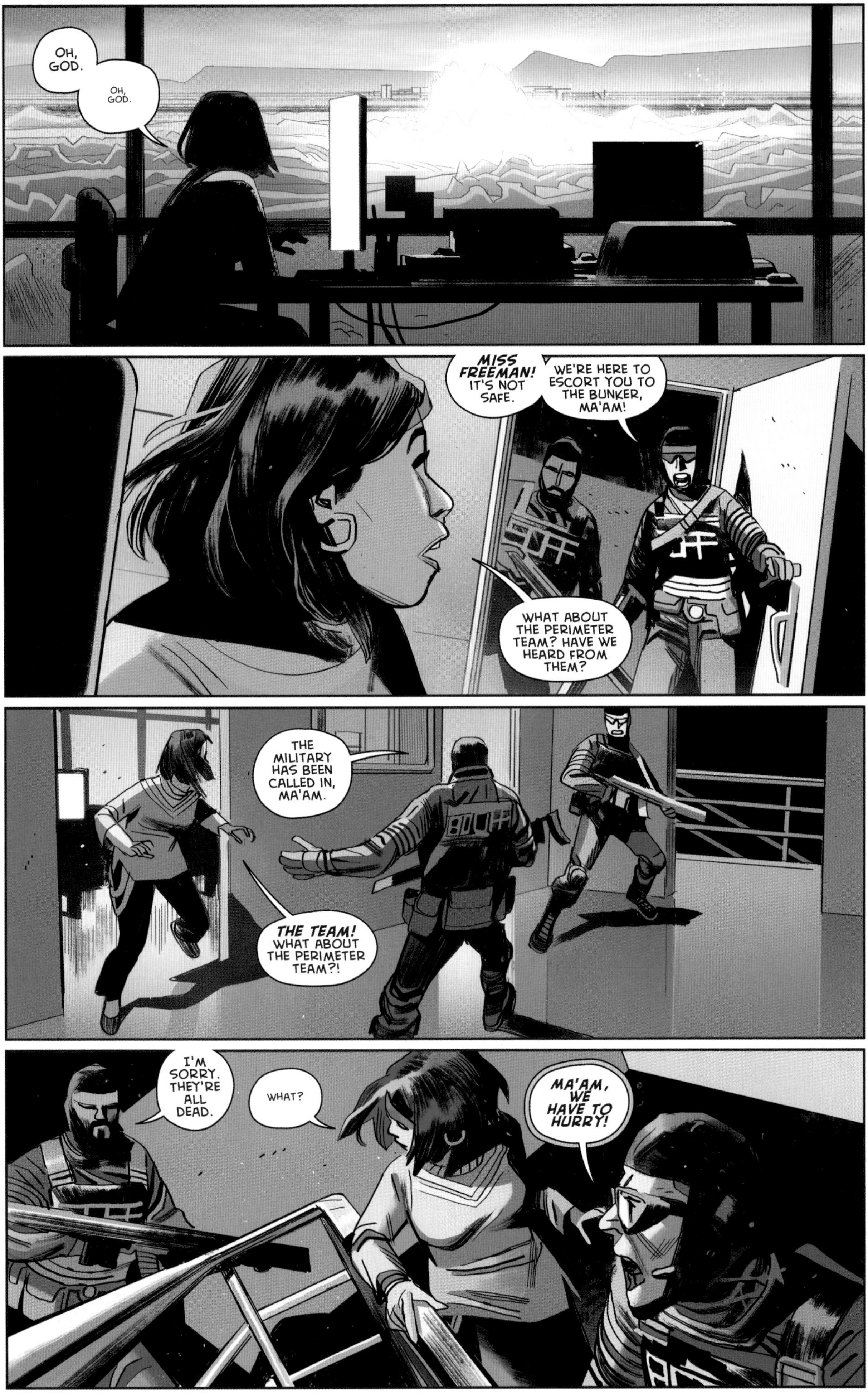
OH, GOD.
OH, GOD.
MISS FREEMAN! IT'S NOT SAFE.
WE'RE HERE TO ESCORT YOU TO THE BUNKER, MA'AM!
WHAT ABOUT THE PERIMETER TEAM? HAVE WE HEARD FROM THEM?
THE MILITARY HAS BEEN CALLED IN, MA'AM.
THE TEAM! WHAT ABOUT THE PERIMETER TEAM?!
I'M SORRY. THEY'RE ALL DEAD.
WHAT?
MA'AM, WE HAVE TO HURRY!

DEAR GOD. NATHAN, DO YOU HAVE ANY IDEA WHAT THEY *WANT?*

OUR PLANET. THEIRS IS OVERRUN. THEY WANT TO EVACUATE HERE.

MY GOD--I'VE BEEN WARNING THE MILITARY ABOUT THIS FOR *YEARS.* THE GROWTH--IT'S TAKING OVER THEIR PLANET. THEY COULDN'T FIND A WAY TO STOP IT.

ONCE THEY FOUND OUT ABOUT EARTH--IT WAS ONLY A MATTER OF TIME BEFORE THEY RECOGNIZED IT AS AN ALTERNATIVE.

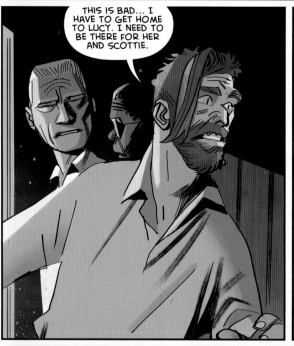

THIS IS BAD... I HAVE TO GET HOME TO LUCY. I NEED TO BE THERE FOR HER AND SCOTTIE.

NO. WE DON'T HAVE *TIME* FOR THAT. WE HAVE TO ACT *NOW*-- WE HAVE TO CONTAIN THEM.

IF THEY GET OUT INTO THE CITY, IT WILL BE *CHAOS.*

WE'VE FACED THEM, ED--WE KNOW WHAT WE'RE UP AGAINST.

DO WE?

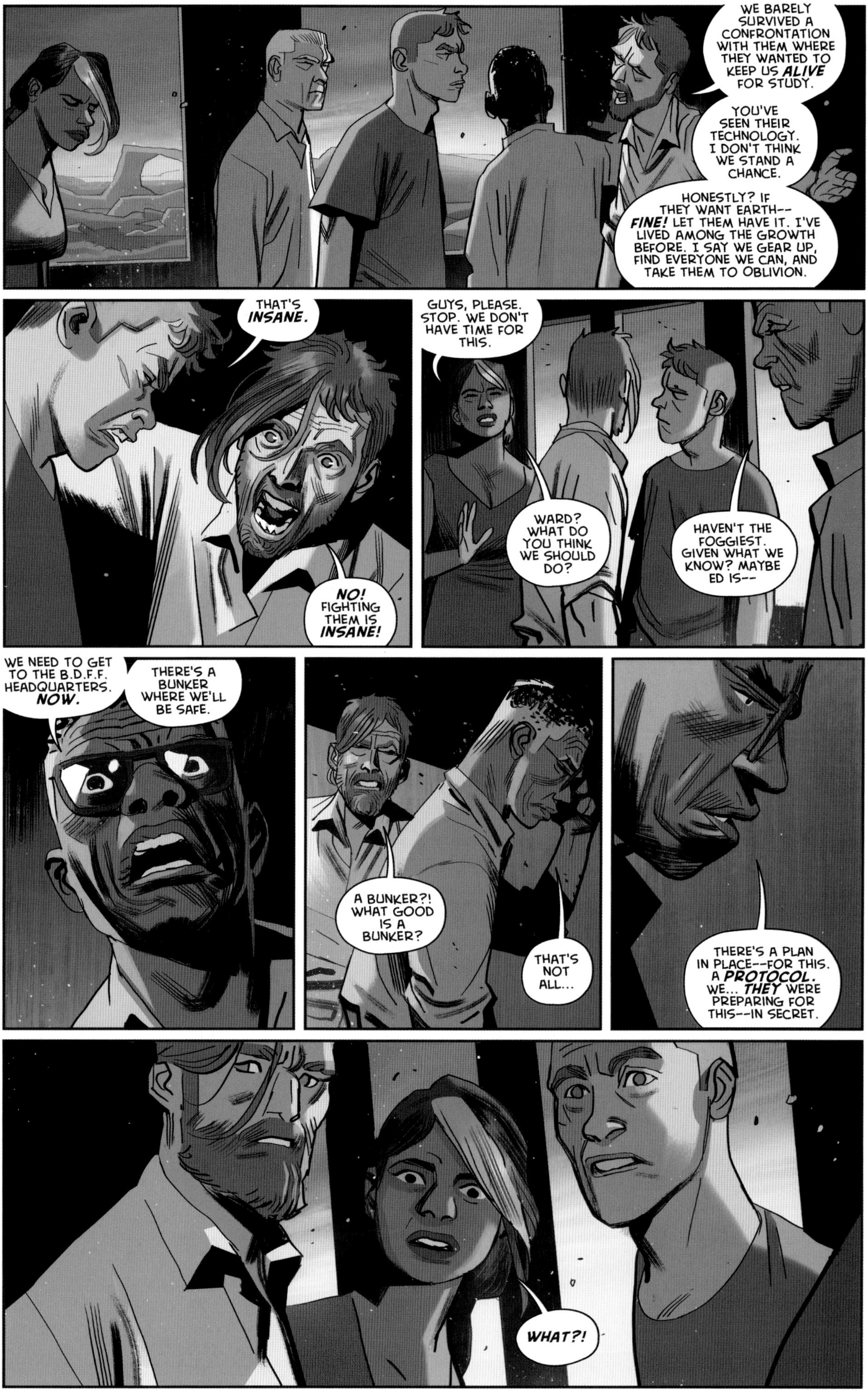
WE BARELY SURVIVED A CONFRONTATION WITH THEM WHERE THEY WANTED TO KEEP US ALIVE FOR STUDY.
YOU'VE SEEN THEIR TECHNOLOGY. I DON'T THINK WE STAND A CHANCE.
HONESTLY? IF THEY WANT EARTH-- FINE! LET THEM HAVE IT. I'VE LIVED AMONG THE GROWTH BEFORE. I SAY WE GEAR UP, FIND EVERYONE WE CAN, AND TAKE THEM TO OBLIVION.
THAT'S INSANE.
NO! FIGHTING THEM IS INSANE!
GUYS, PLEASE. STOP. WE DON'T HAVE TIME FOR THIS.
WARD? WHAT DO YOU THINK WE SHOULD DO?
HAVEN'T THE FOGGIEST. GIVEN WHAT WE KNOW? MAYBE ED IS--
WE NEED TO GET TO THE B.D.F.F. HEADQUARTERS. NOW.
THERE'S A BUNKER WHERE WE'LL BE SAFE.
A BUNKER?! WHAT GOOD IS A BUNKER?
THAT'S NOT ALL...
THERE'S A PLAN IN PLACE--FOR THIS. A PROTOCOL. WE... THEY WERE PREPARING FOR THIS--IN SECRET.
WHAT?!

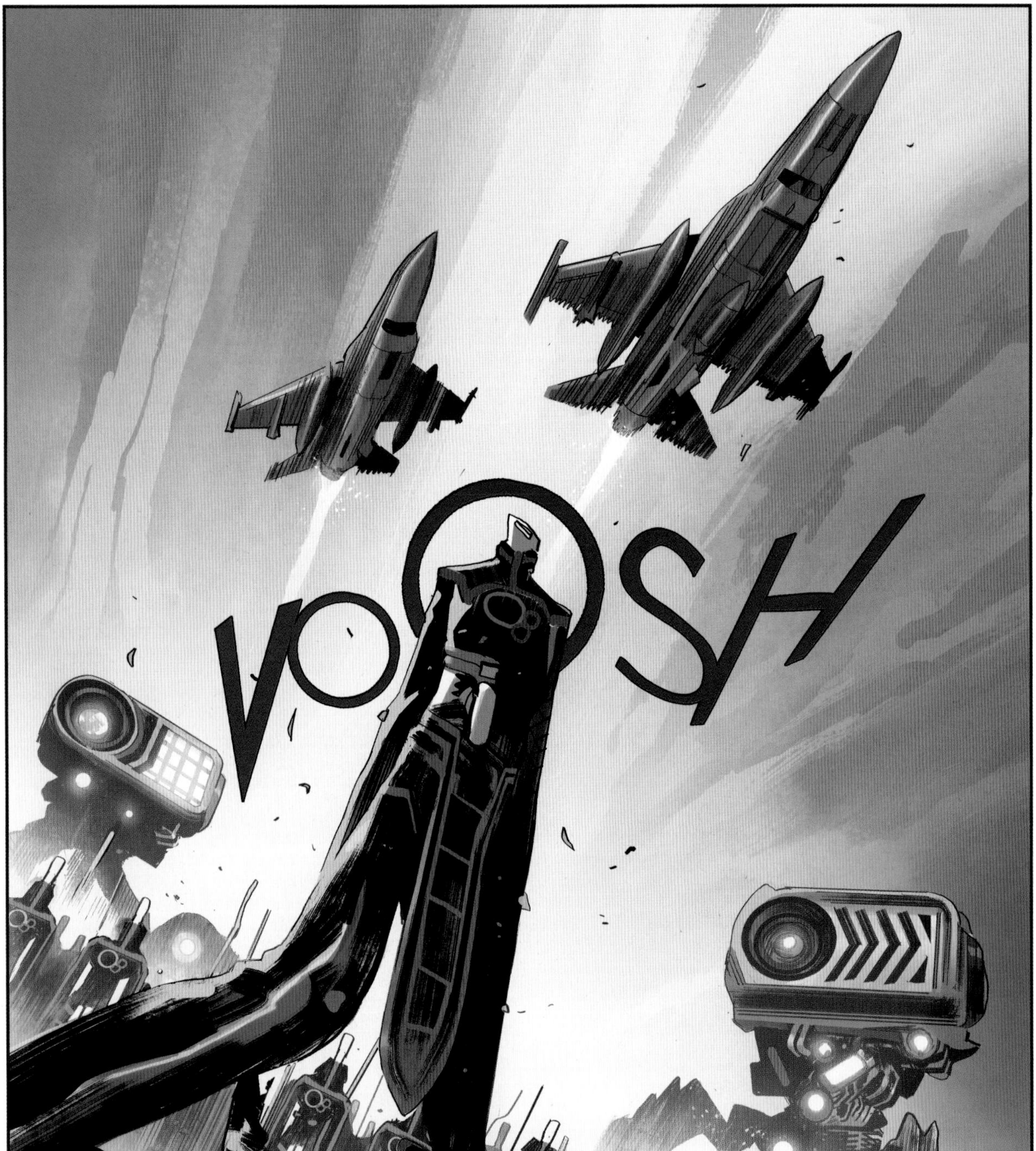
VOOSH

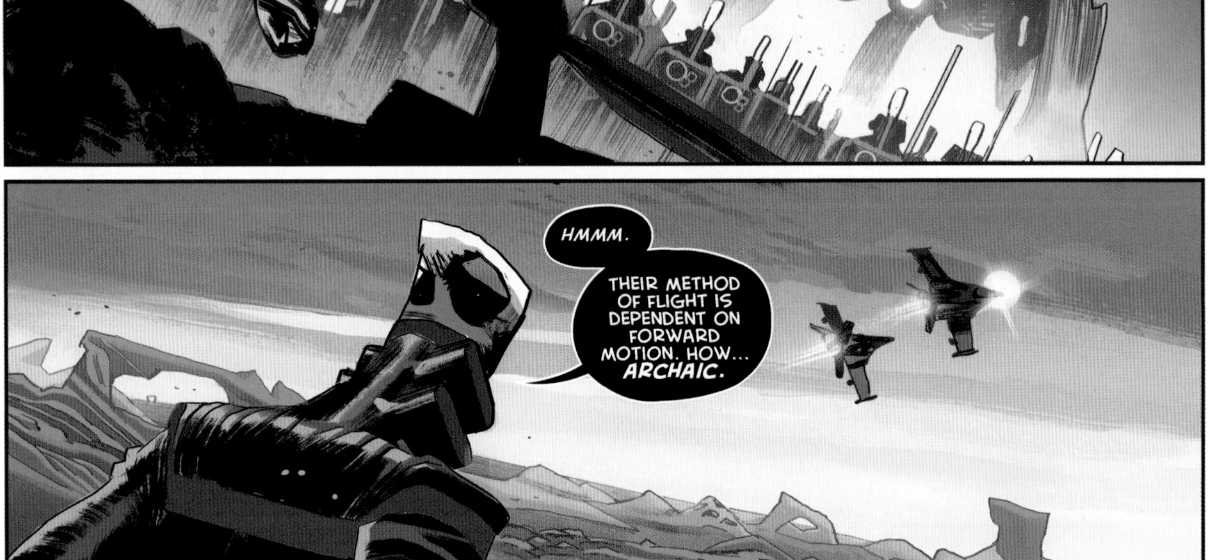
HMMM.
THEIR METHOD OF FLIGHT IS DEPENDENT ON FORWARD MOTION. HOW... ARCHAIC.

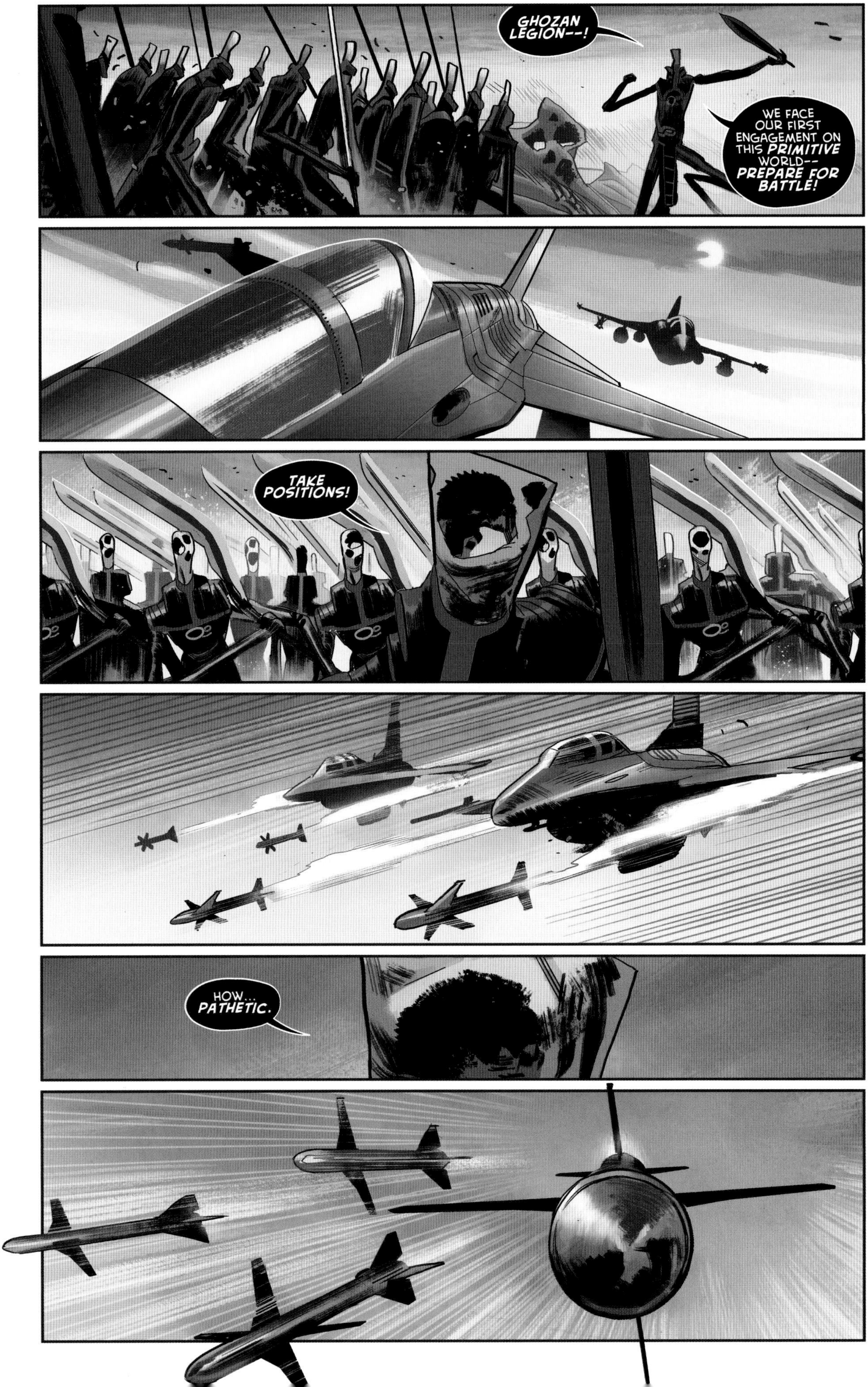
GHOZAN LEGION--!
WE FACE OUR FIRST ENGAGEMENT ON THIS PRIMITIVE WORLD-- PREPARE FOR BATTLE!
TAKE POSITIONS!
HOW... PATHETIC.

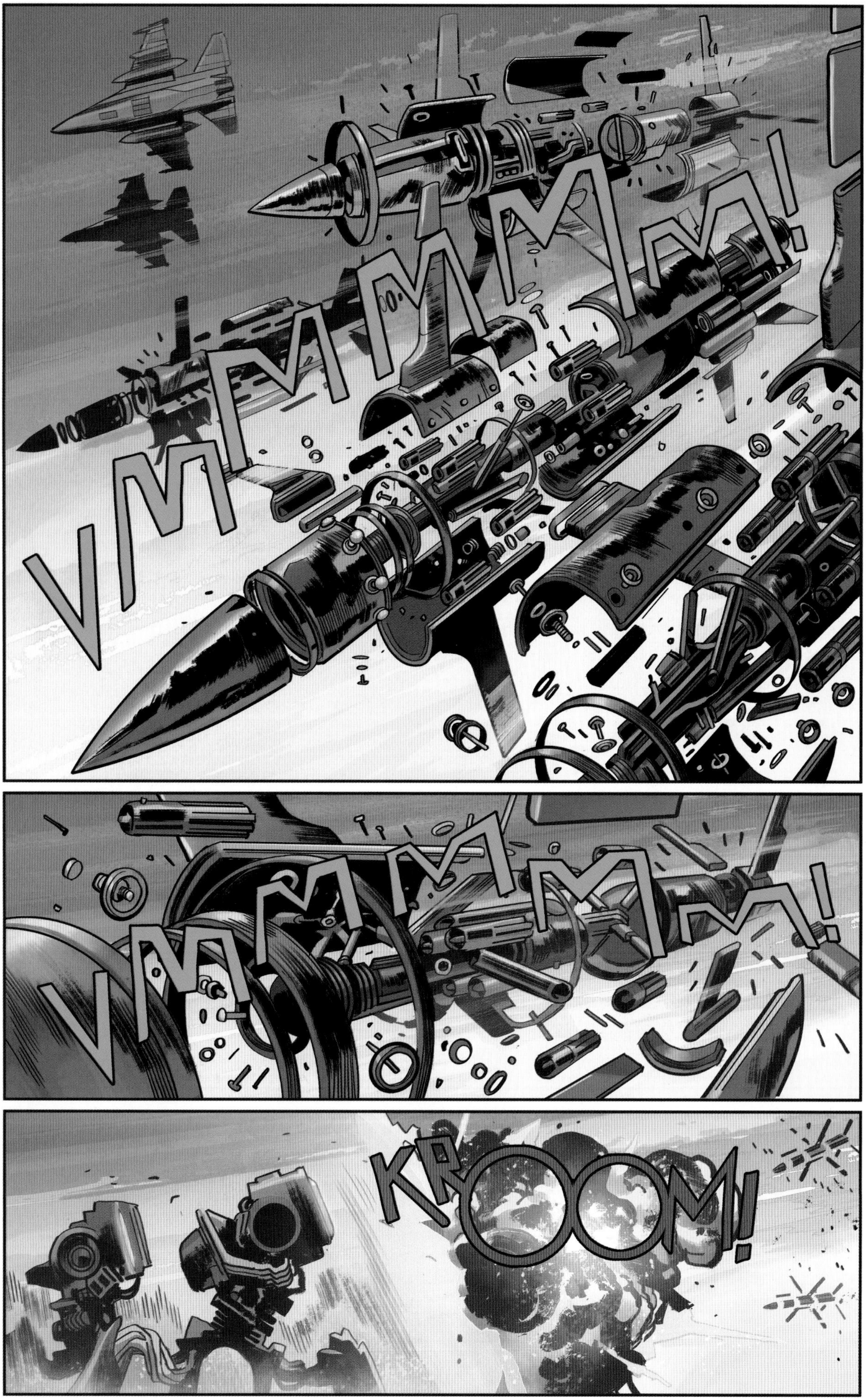
VMMMMM!
VMMMMM!
KROOOM!

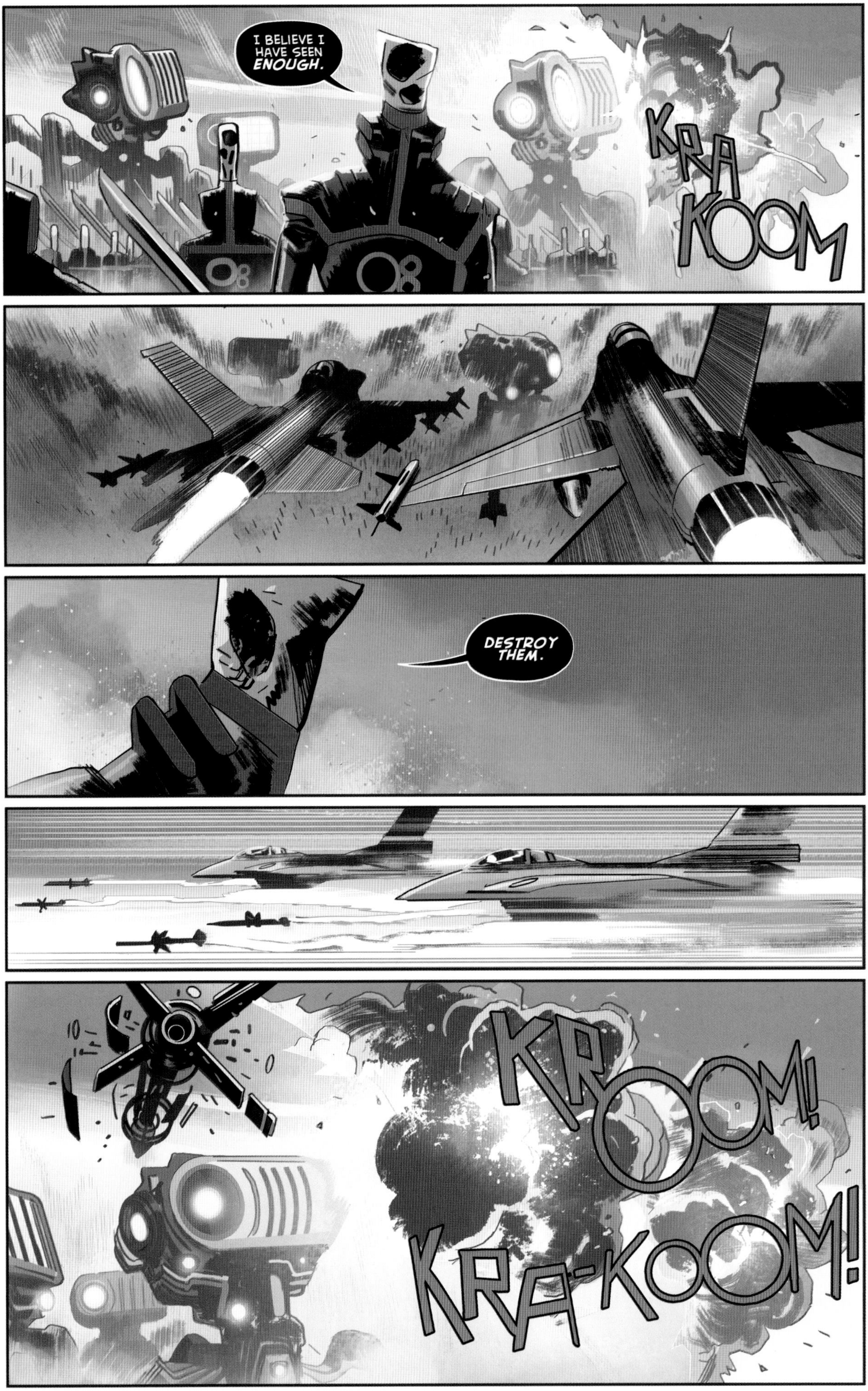
I BELIEVE I HAVE SEEN *ENOUGH*.
KRA KOOM
DESTROY THEM.
KROOOM!
KRA-KOOOM!

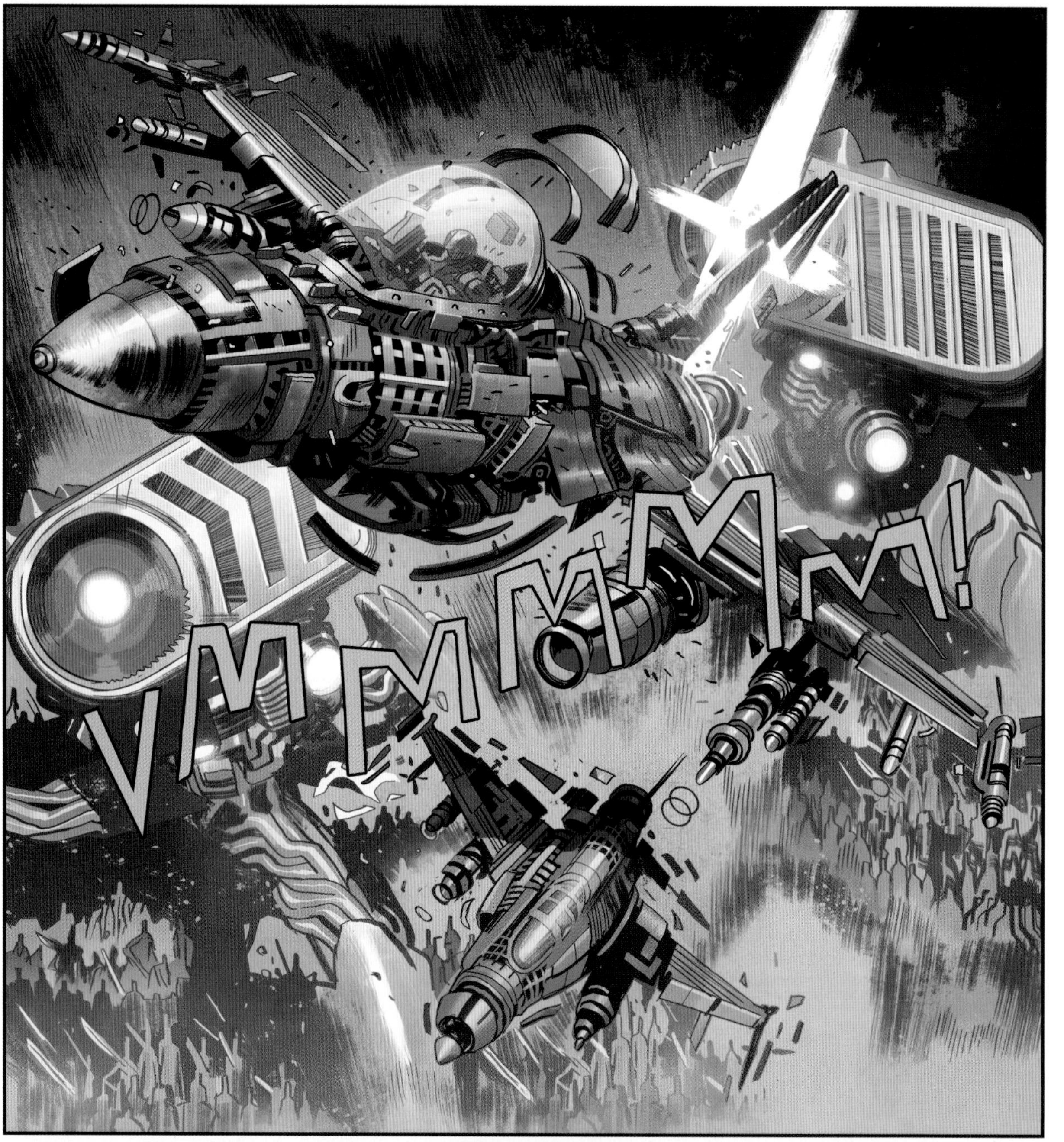
VMMMMMM!

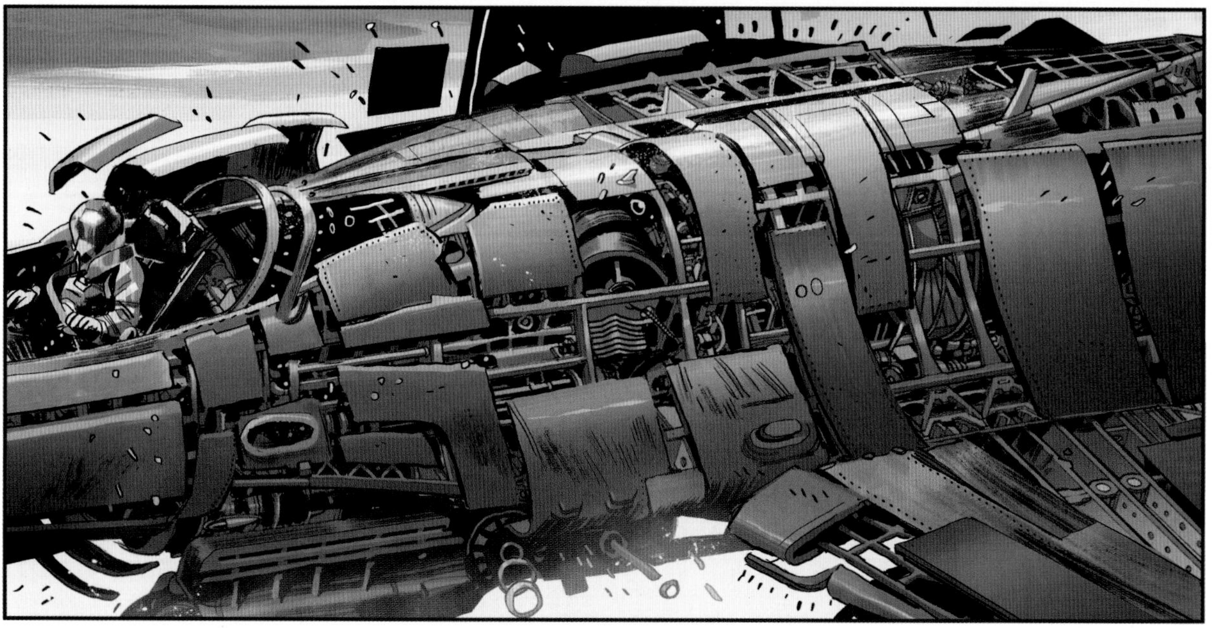

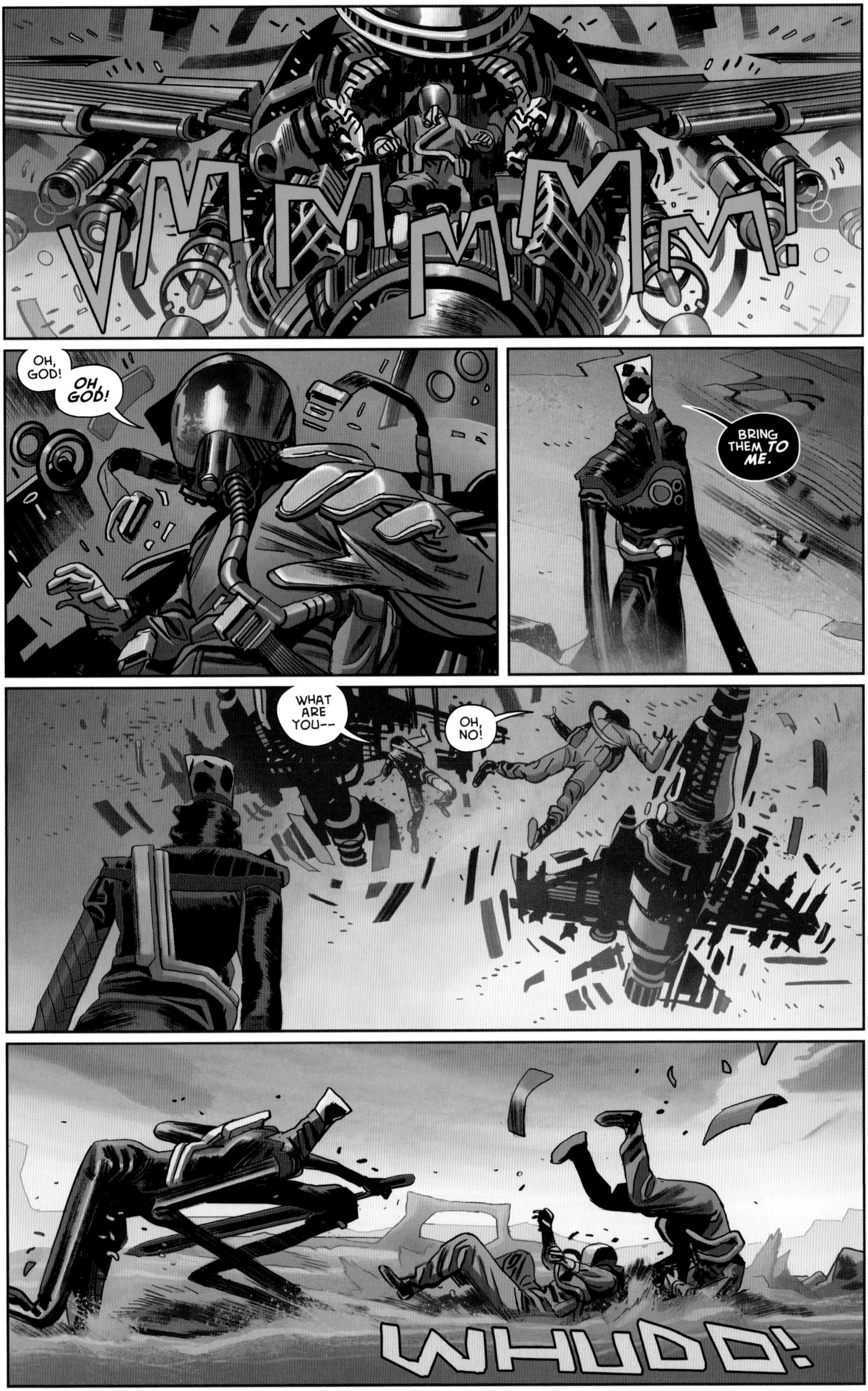
VMMMMMM!
OH, GOD!
OH, GOD!
BRING THEM TO ME.
WHAT ARE YOU--
OH, NO!
WHUDD!

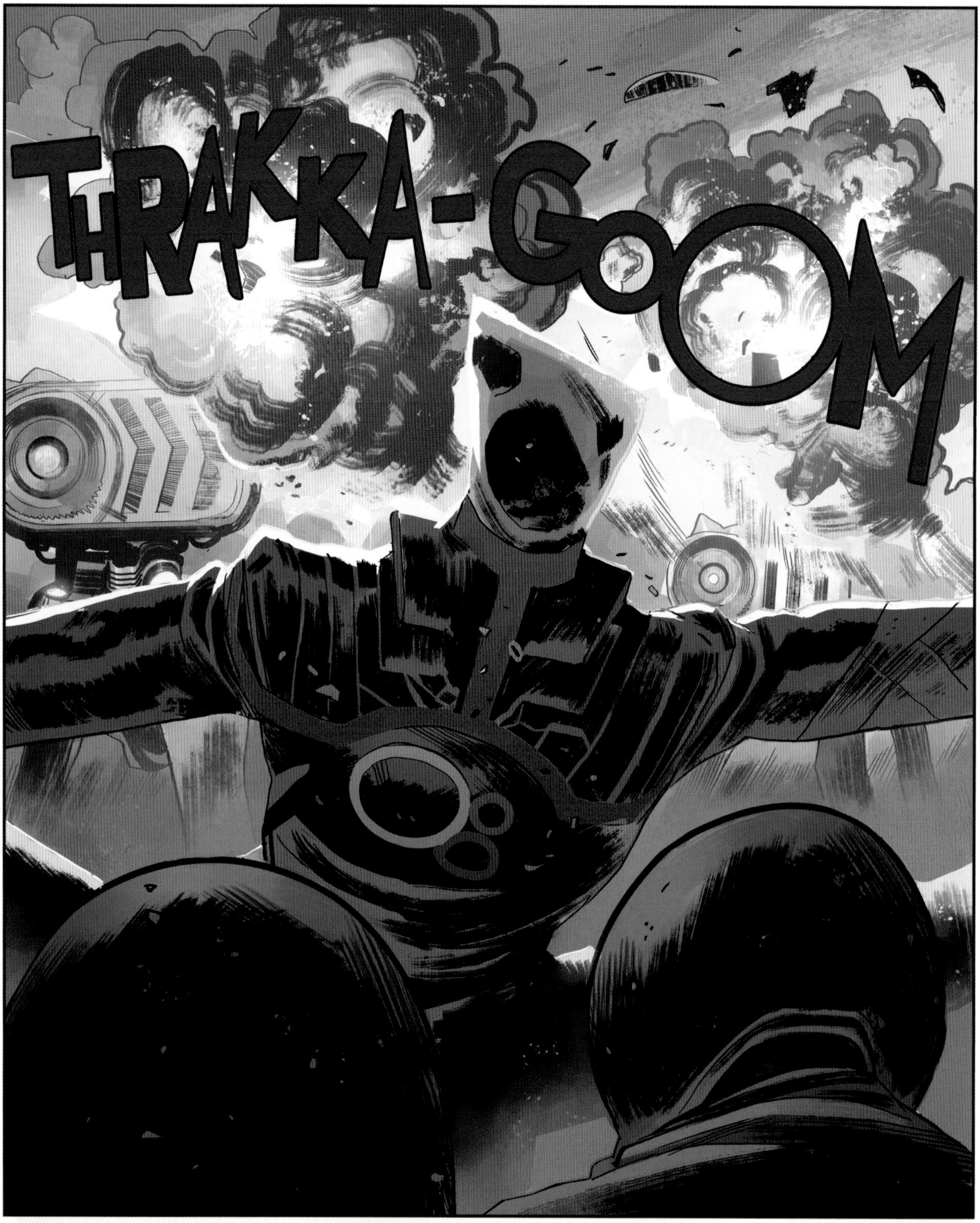
THRAKKA-GOOM

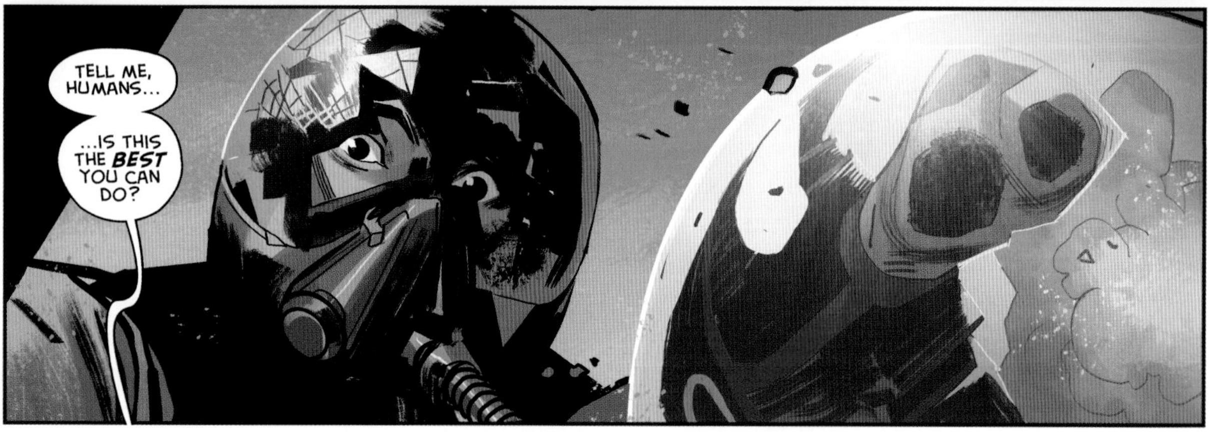
TELL ME, HUMANS...
...IS THIS THE BEST YOU CAN DO?

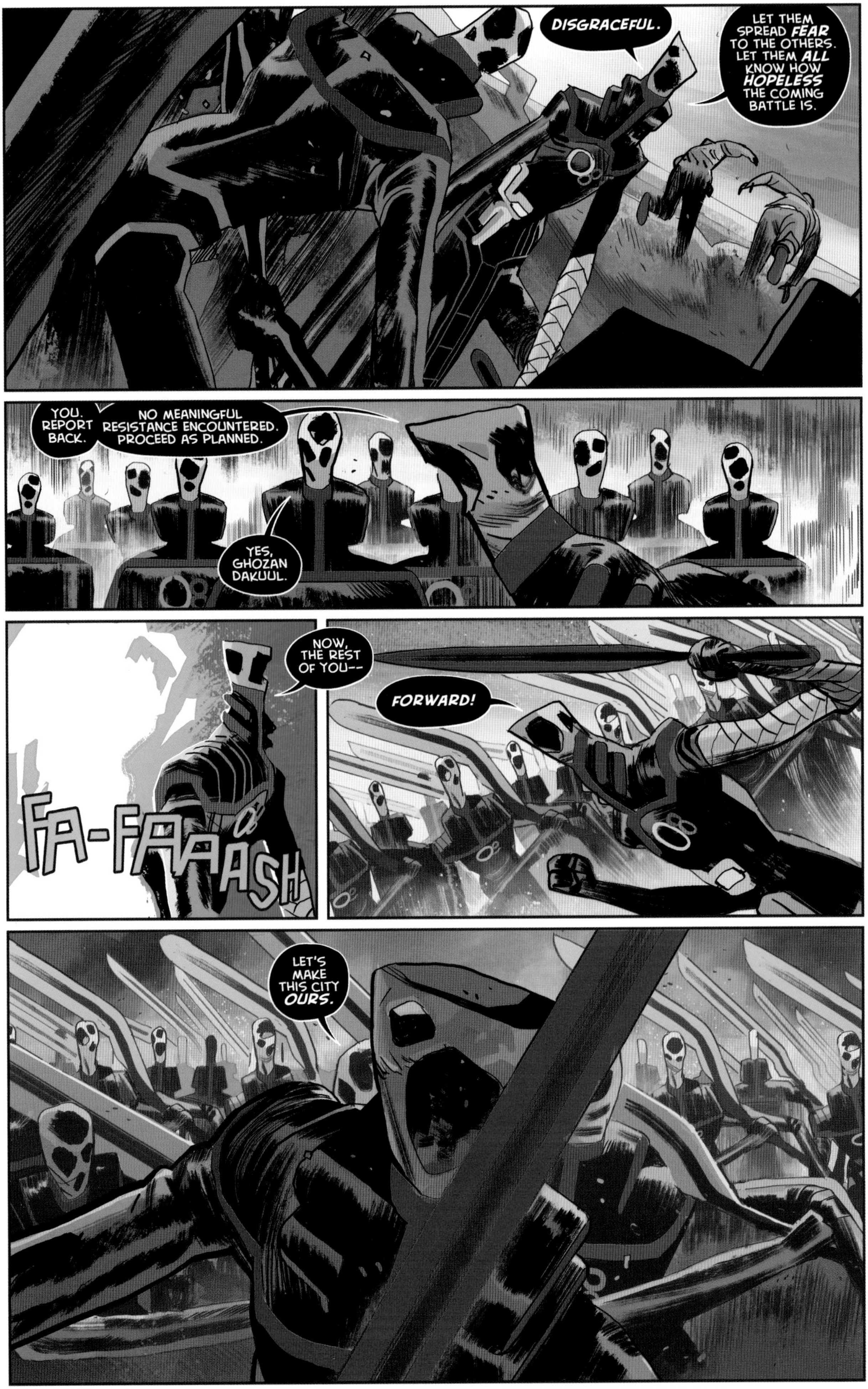
DISGRACEFUL.
LET THEM SPREAD FEAR TO THE OTHERS. LET THEM ALL KNOW HOW HOPELESS THE COMING BATTLE IS.
YOU. REPORT BACK.
NO MEANINGFUL RESISTANCE ENCOUNTERED. PROCEED AS PLANNED.
YES, GHOZAN DAKUUL.
NOW, THE REST OF YOU--
FA-FAAAASH
FORWARD!
LET'S MAKE THIS CITY OURS.

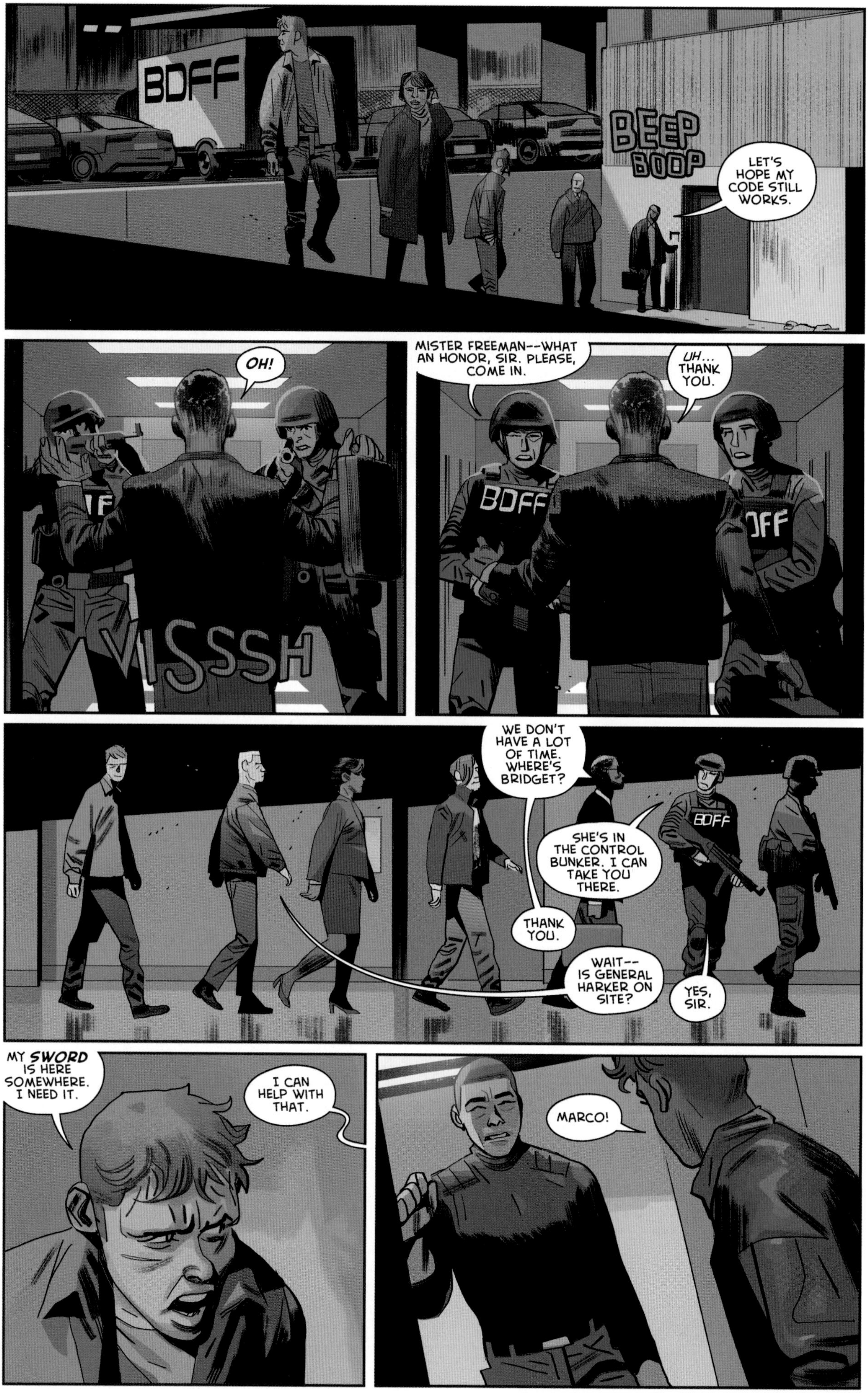
BDFF
BEEP BOOP
LET'S HOPE MY CODE STILL WORKS.
OH!
VISSSH
MISTER FREEMAN--WHAT AN HONOR, SIR. PLEASE, COME IN.
UH... THANK YOU.
BDFF
WE DON'T HAVE A LOT OF TIME. WHERE'S BRIDGET?
SHE'S IN THE CONTROL BUNKER. I CAN TAKE YOU THERE.
THANK YOU.
WAIT-- IS GENERAL HARKER ON SITE?
YES, SIR.
MY SWORD IS HERE SOMEWHERE. I NEED IT.
I CAN HELP WITH THAT.
MARCO!

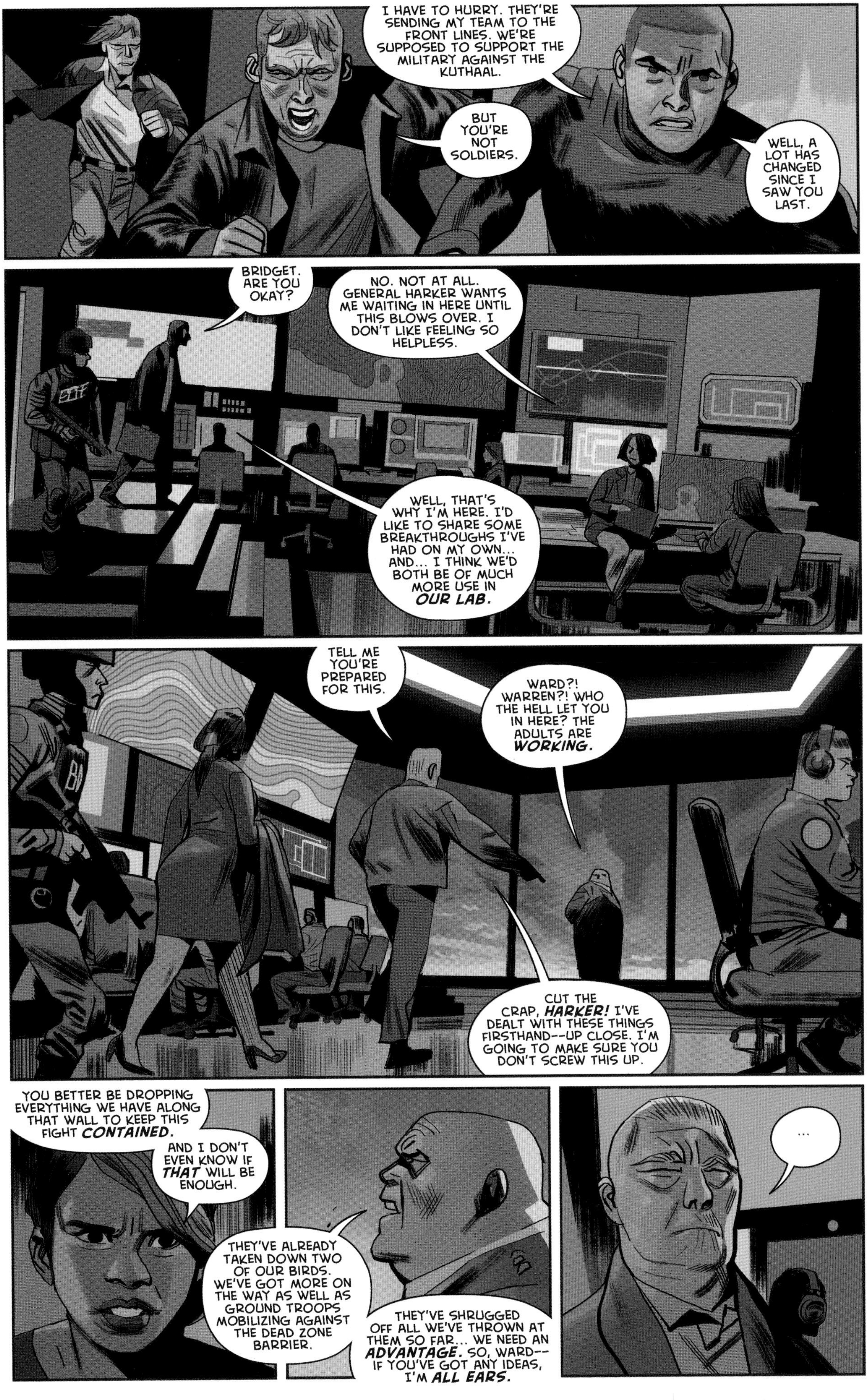
I HAVE TO HURRY. THEY'RE SENDING MY TEAM TO THE FRONT LINES. WE'RE SUPPOSED TO SUPPORT THE MILITARY AGAINST THE KUTHAAL.
BUT YOU'RE NOT SOLDIERS.
WELL, A LOT HAS CHANGED SINCE I SAW YOU LAST.
BRIDGET. ARE YOU OKAY?
NO. NOT AT ALL. GENERAL HARKER WANTS ME WAITING IN HERE UNTIL THIS BLOWS OVER. I DON'T LIKE FEELING SO HELPLESS.
WELL, THAT'S WHY I'M HERE. I'D LIKE TO SHARE SOME BREAKTHROUGHS I'VE HAD ON MY OWN... AND... I THINK WE'D BOTH BE OF MUCH MORE USE IN OUR LAB.
TELL ME YOU'RE PREPARED FOR THIS.
WARD?! WARREN?! WHO THE HELL LET YOU IN HERE? THE ADULTS ARE WORKING.
CUT THE CRAP, HARKER! I'VE DEALT WITH THESE THINGS FIRSTHAND--UP CLOSE. I'M GOING TO MAKE SURE YOU DON'T SCREW THIS UP.
YOU BETTER BE DROPPING EVERYTHING WE HAVE ALONG THAT WALL TO KEEP THIS FIGHT CONTAINED.
AND I DON'T EVEN KNOW IF THAT WILL BE ENOUGH.
THEY'VE ALREADY TAKEN DOWN TWO OF OUR BIRDS. WE'VE GOT MORE ON THE WAY AS WELL AS GROUND TROOPS MOBILIZING AGAINST THE DEAD ZONE BARRIER.
THEY'VE SHRUGGED OFF ALL WE'VE THROWN AT THEM SO FAR... WE NEED AN ADVANTAGE. SO, WARD-- IF YOU'VE GOT ANY IDEAS, I'M ALL EARS.
...

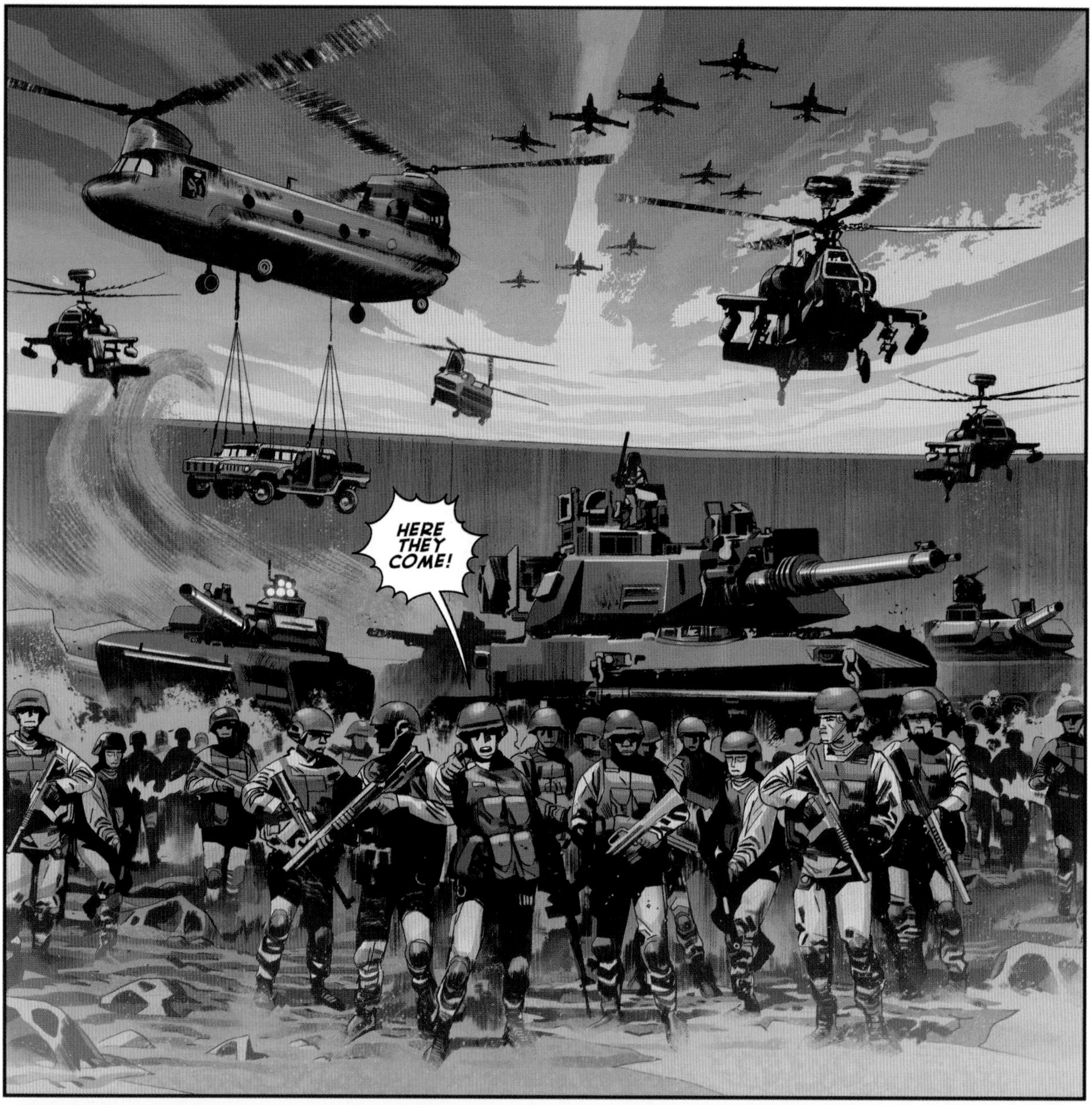
HERE THEY COME!

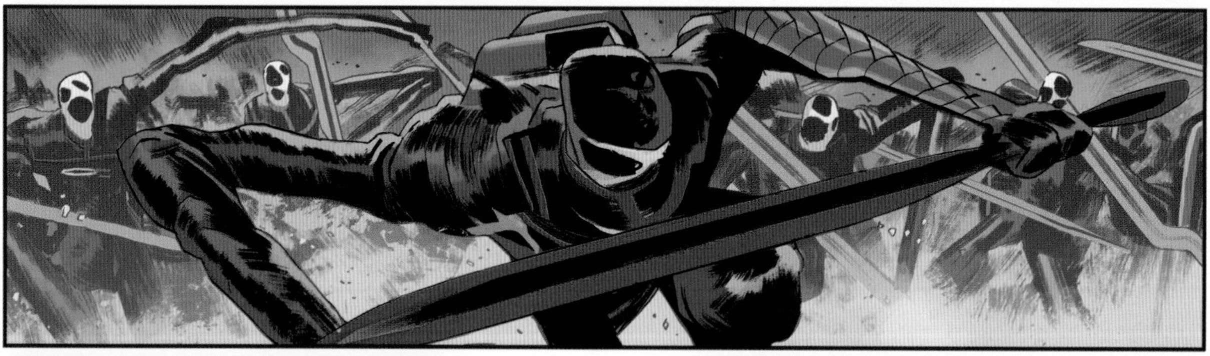

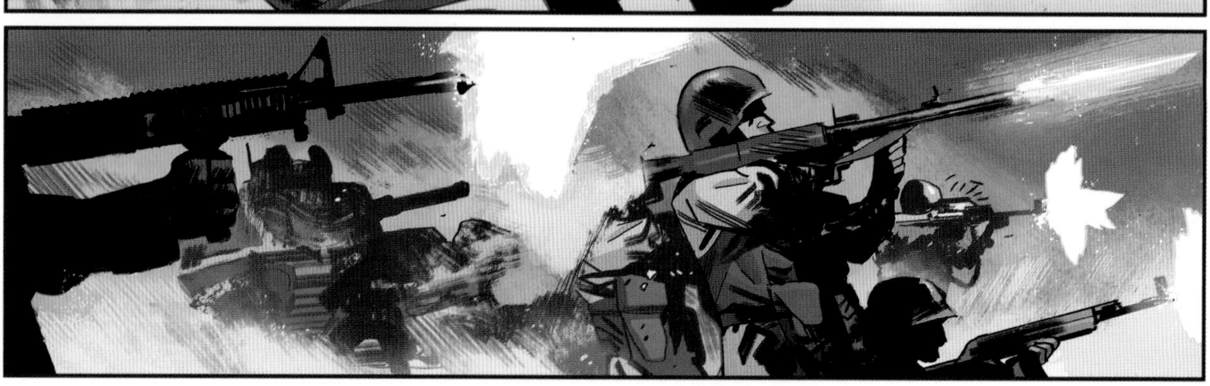

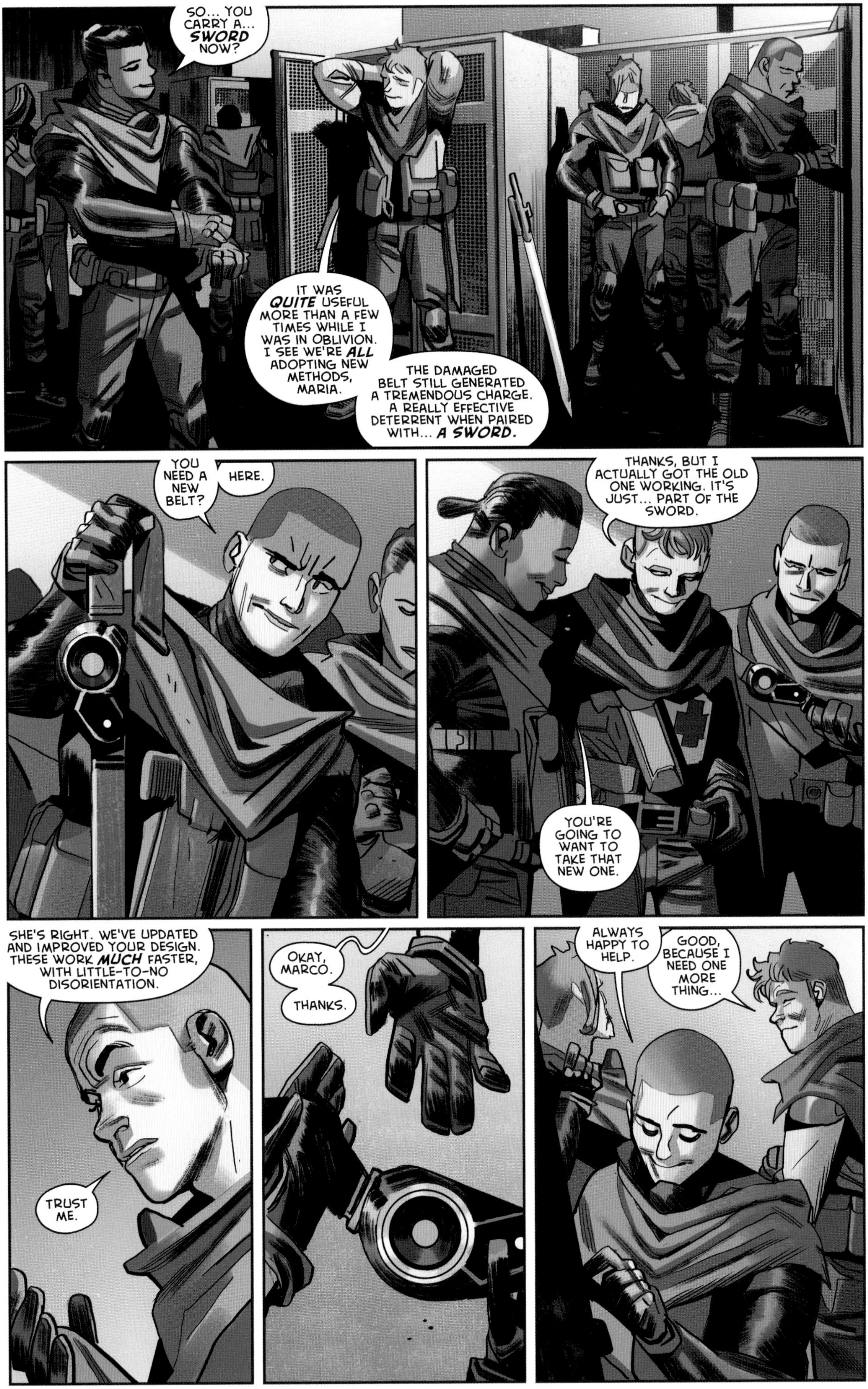
SO... YOU CARRY A... SWORD NOW?
IT WAS QUITE USEFUL MORE THAN A FEW TIMES WHILE I WAS IN OBLIVION. I SEE WE'RE ALL ADOPTING NEW METHODS, MARIA.
THE DAMAGED BELT STILL GENERATED A TREMENDOUS CHARGE. A REALLY EFFECTIVE DETERRENT WHEN PAIRED WITH... A SWORD.
YOU NEED A NEW BELT?
HERE.
THANKS, BUT I ACTUALLY GOT THE OLD ONE WORKING. IT'S JUST... PART OF THE SWORD.
YOU'RE GOING TO WANT TO TAKE THAT NEW ONE.
SHE'S RIGHT. WE'VE UPDATED AND IMPROVED YOUR DESIGN. THESE WORK MUCH FASTER, WITH LITTLE-TO-NO DISORIENTATION.
TRUST ME.
OKAY, MARCO.
THANKS.
ALWAYS HAPPY TO HELP.
GOOD, BECAUSE I NEED ONE MORE THING...

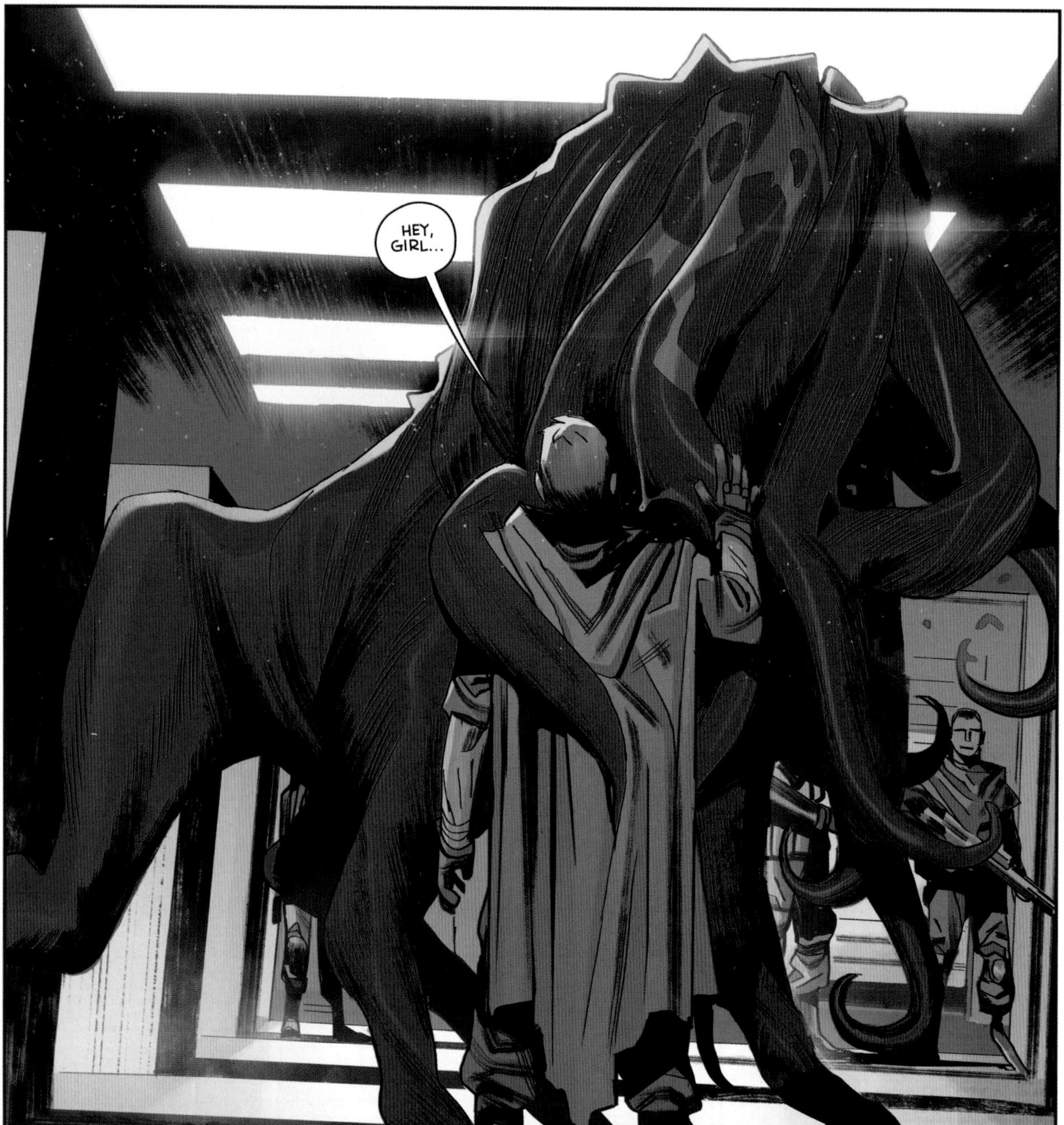
HEY, GIRL...

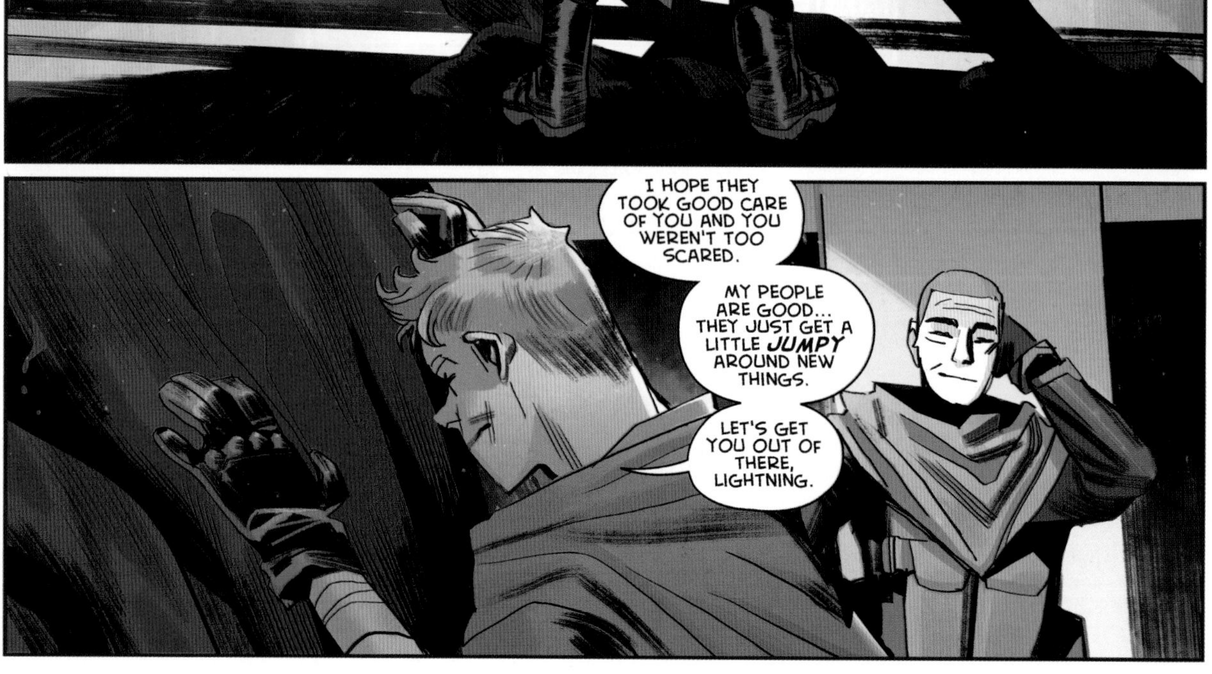
I HOPE THEY TOOK GOOD CARE OF YOU AND YOU WEREN'T TOO SCARED.
MY PEOPLE ARE GOOD... THEY JUST GET A LITTLE *JUMPY* AROUND NEW THINGS.
LET'S GET YOU OUT OF THERE, LIGHTNING.

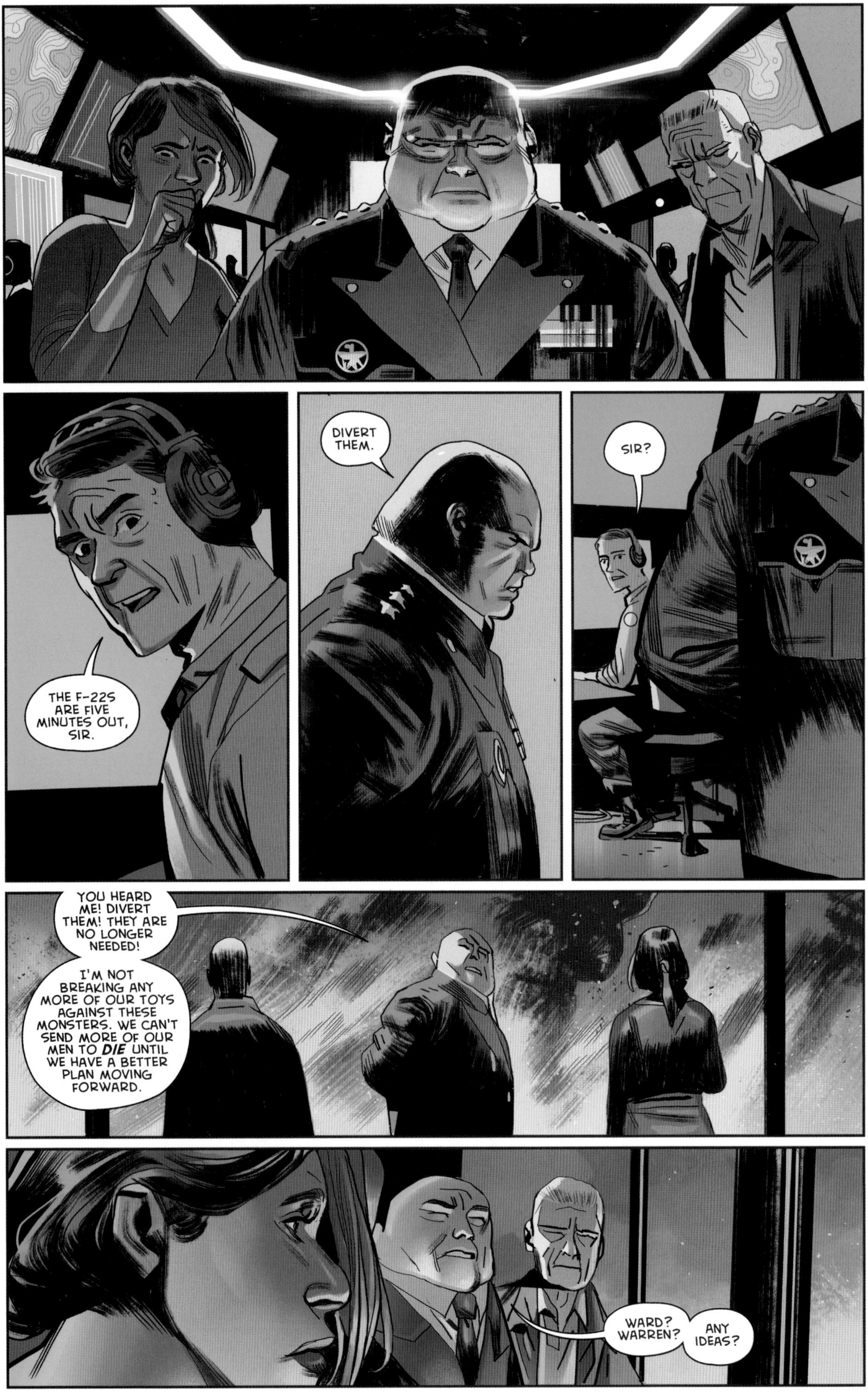
THE F-22S ARE FIVE MINUTES OUT, SIR.
DIVERT THEM.
SIR?
YOU HEARD ME! DIVERT THEM! THEY ARE NO LONGER NEEDED!
I'M NOT BREAKING ANY MORE OF OUR TOYS AGAINST THESE MONSTERS. WE CAN'T SEND MORE OF OUR MEN TO ***DIE*** UNTIL WE HAVE A BETTER PLAN MOVING FORWARD.
WARD? WARREN?
ANY IDEAS?

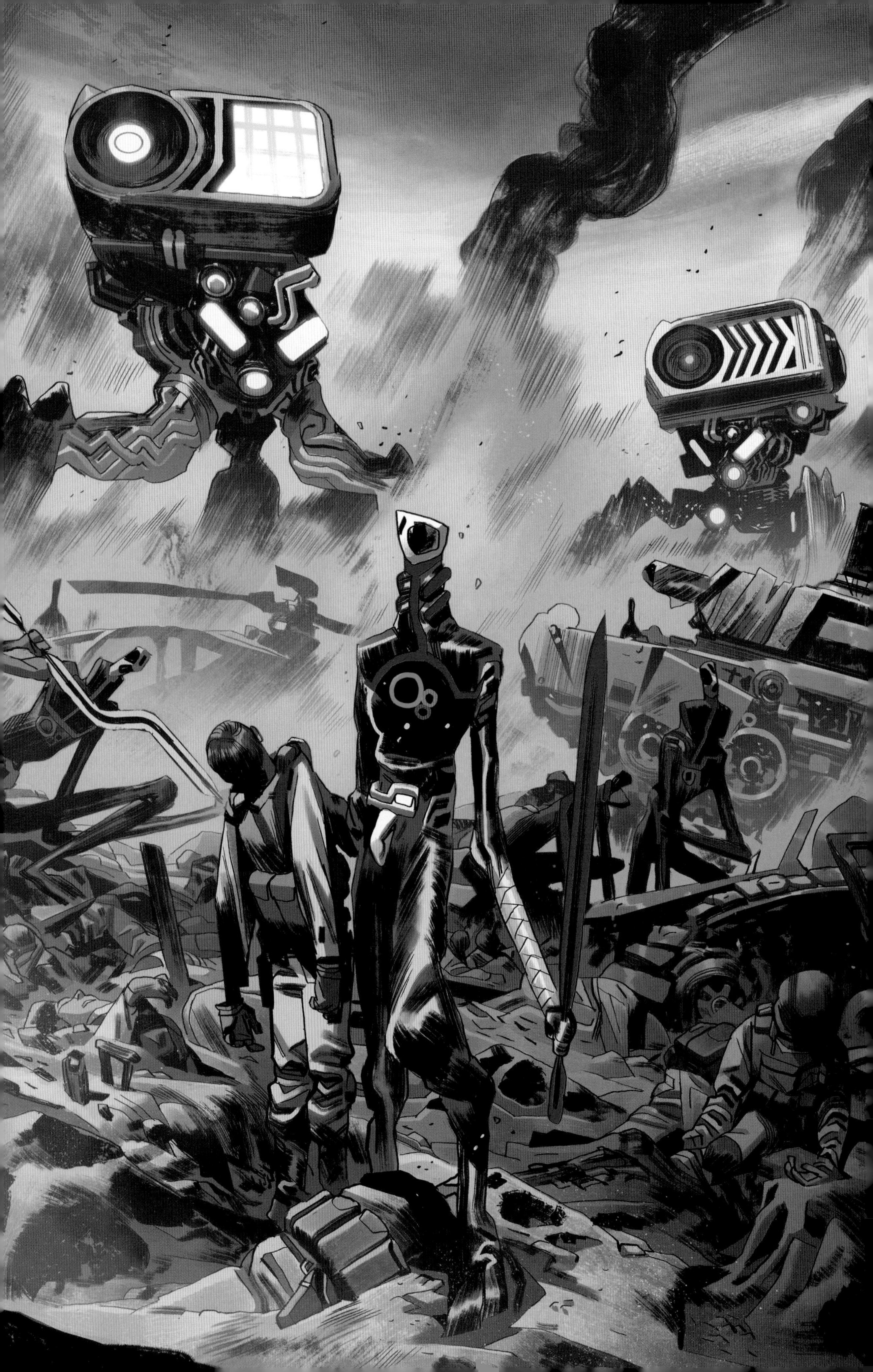

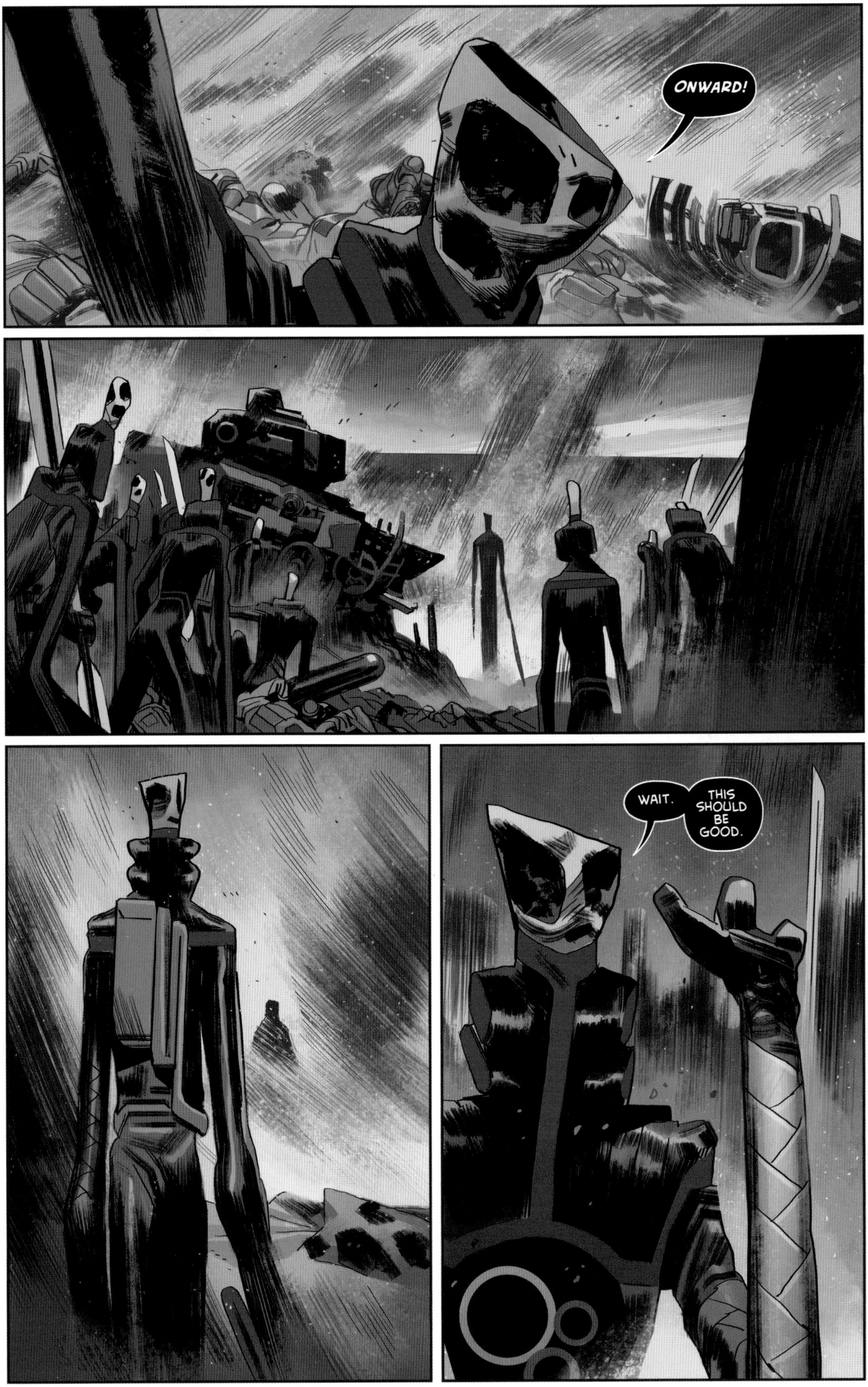
ONWARD!
WAIT.
THIS SHOULD BE GOOD.

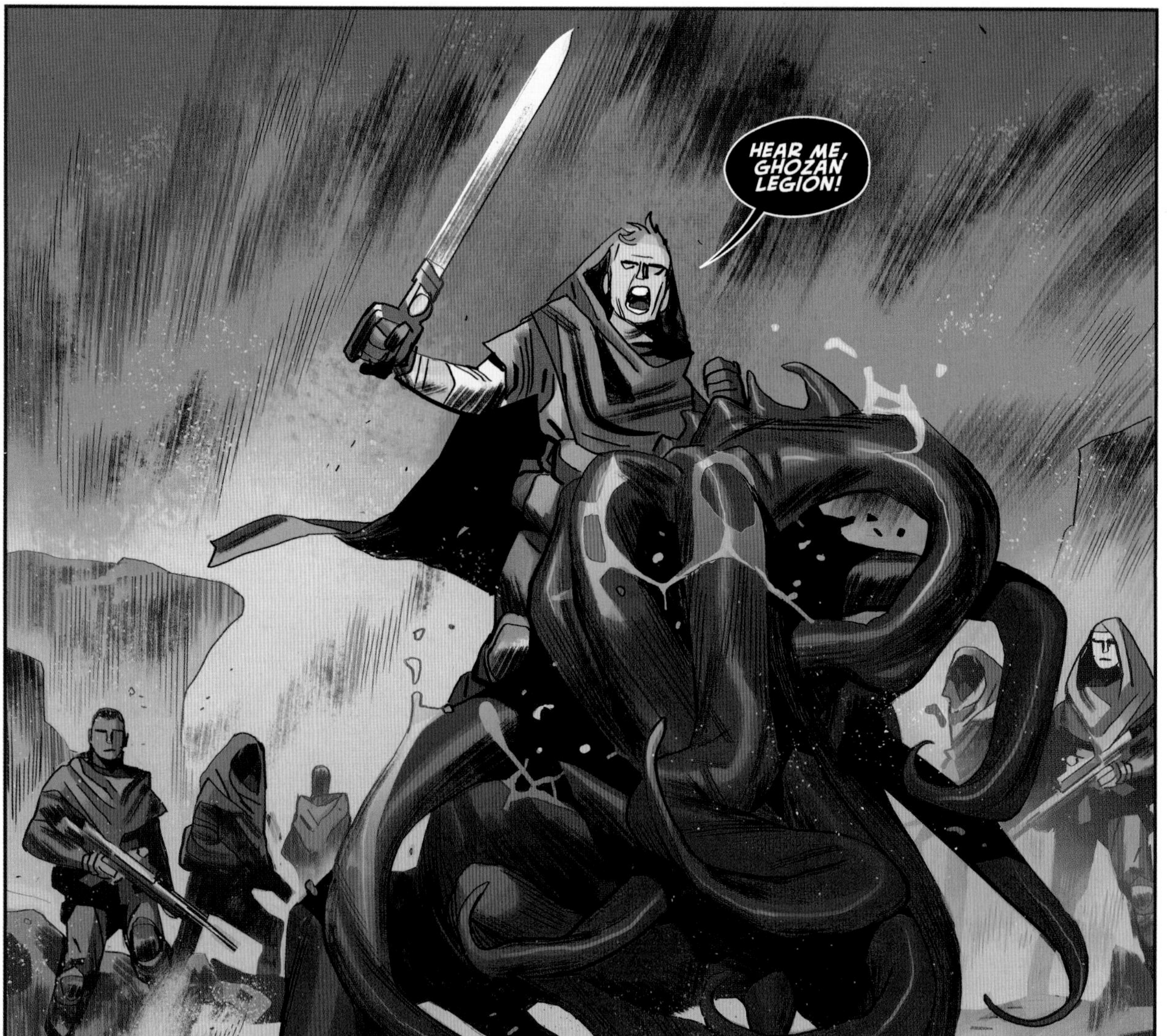
HEAR ME, GHOZAN LEGION!

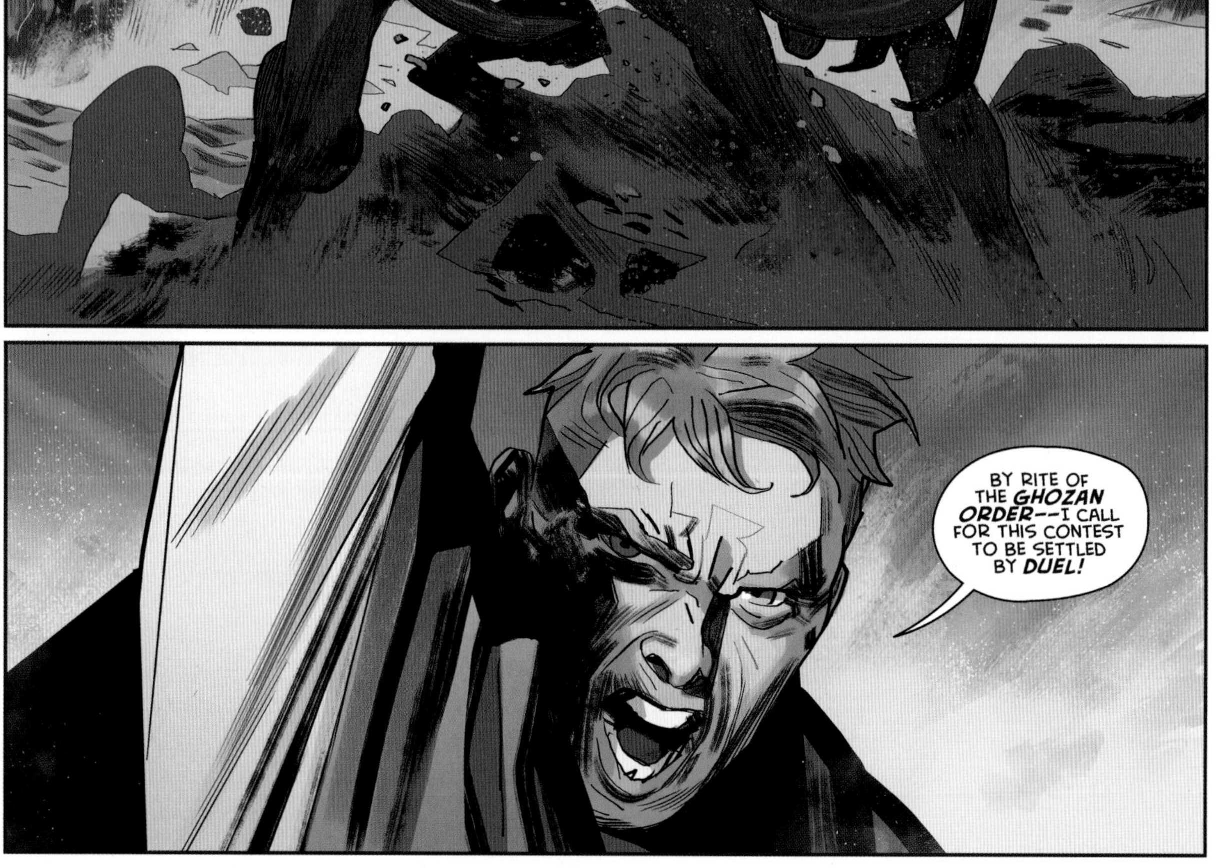
BY RITE OF THE GHOZAN ORDER--I CALL FOR THIS CONTEST TO BE SETTLED BY DUEL!

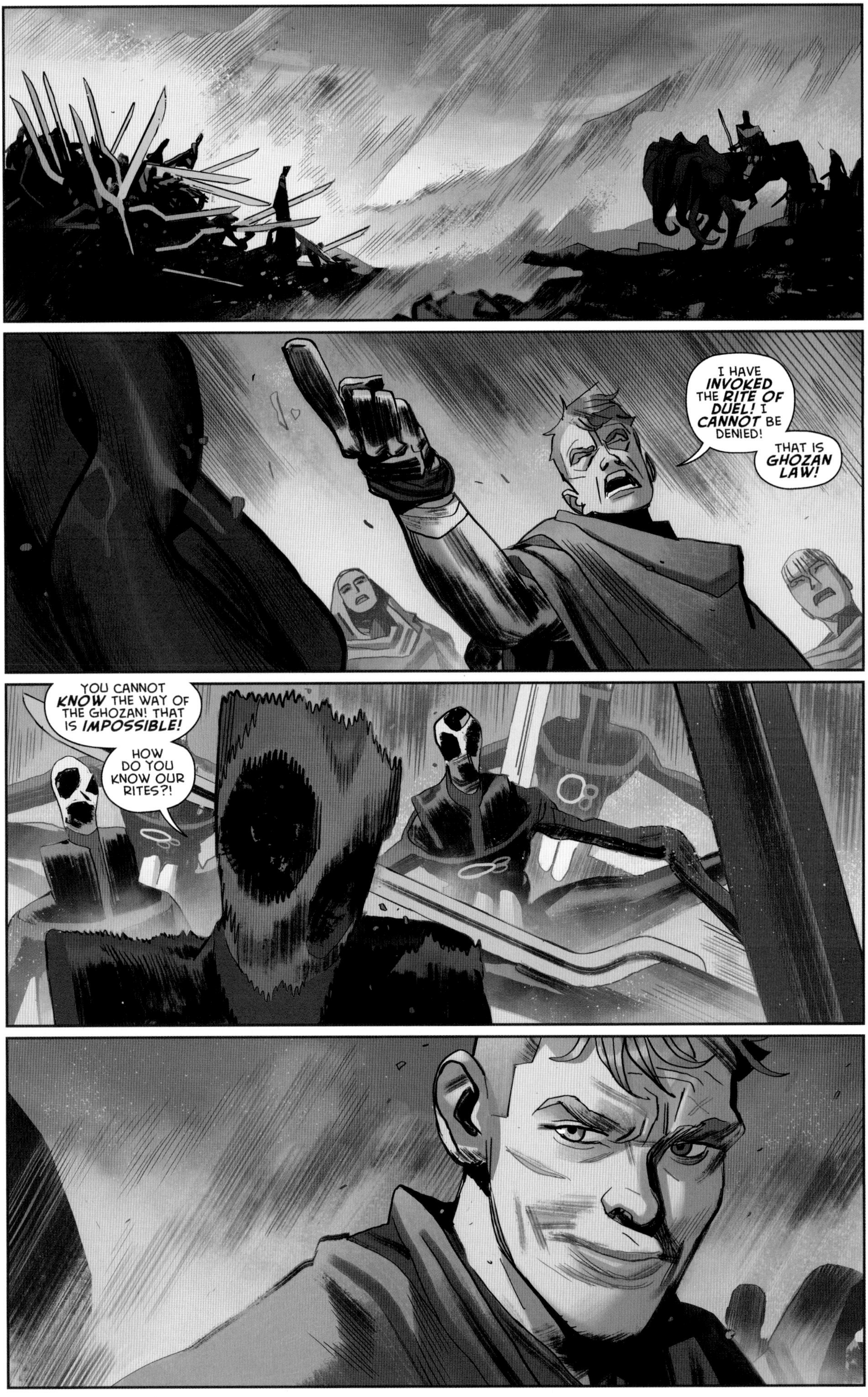
I HAVE INVOKED THE RITE OF DUEL! I CANNOT BE DENIED!
THAT IS GHOZAN LAW!
YOU CANNOT KNOW THE WAY OF THE GHOZAN! THAT IS IMPOSSIBLE!
HOW DO YOU KNOW OUR RITES?!

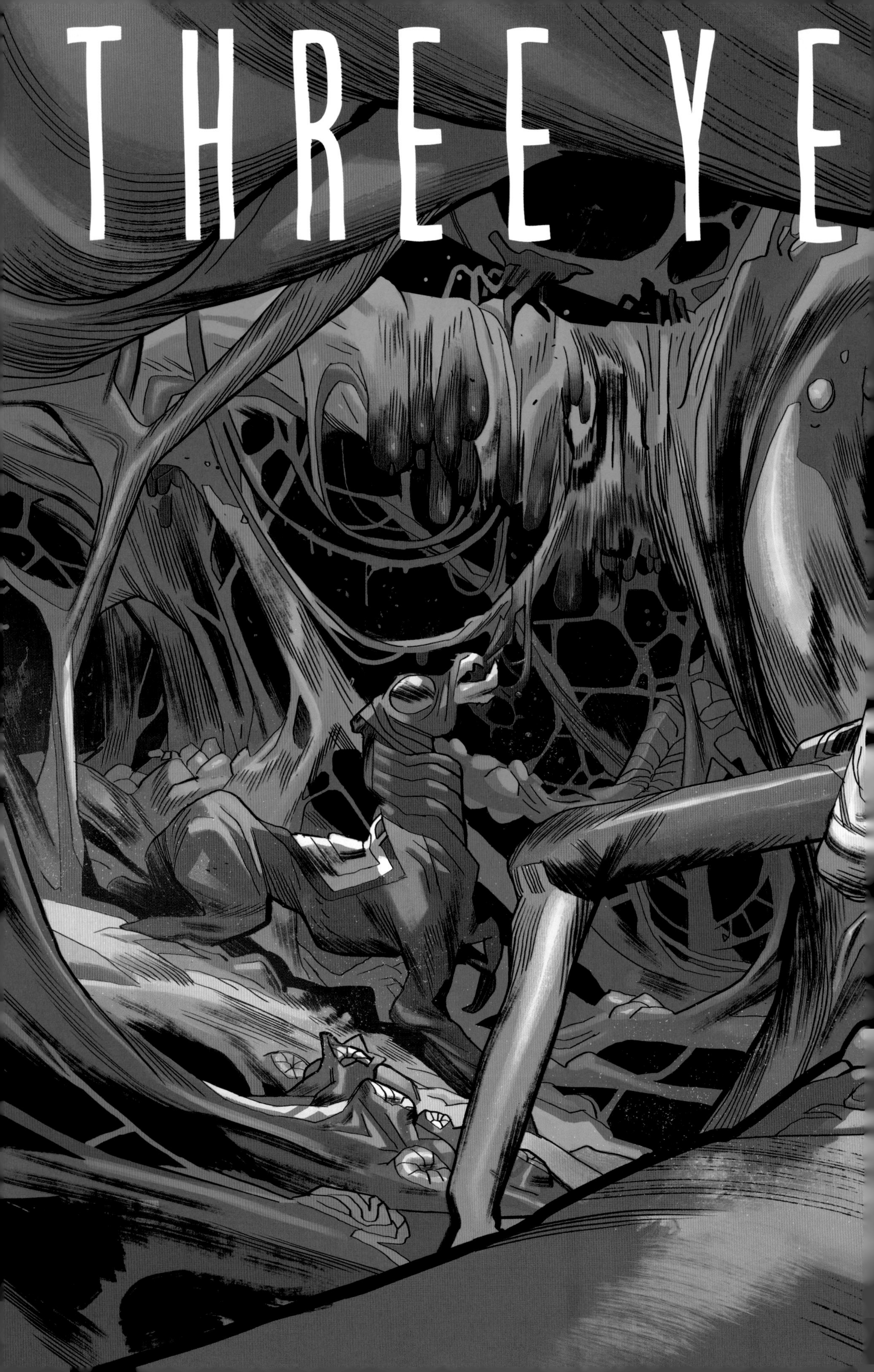
THREE YE

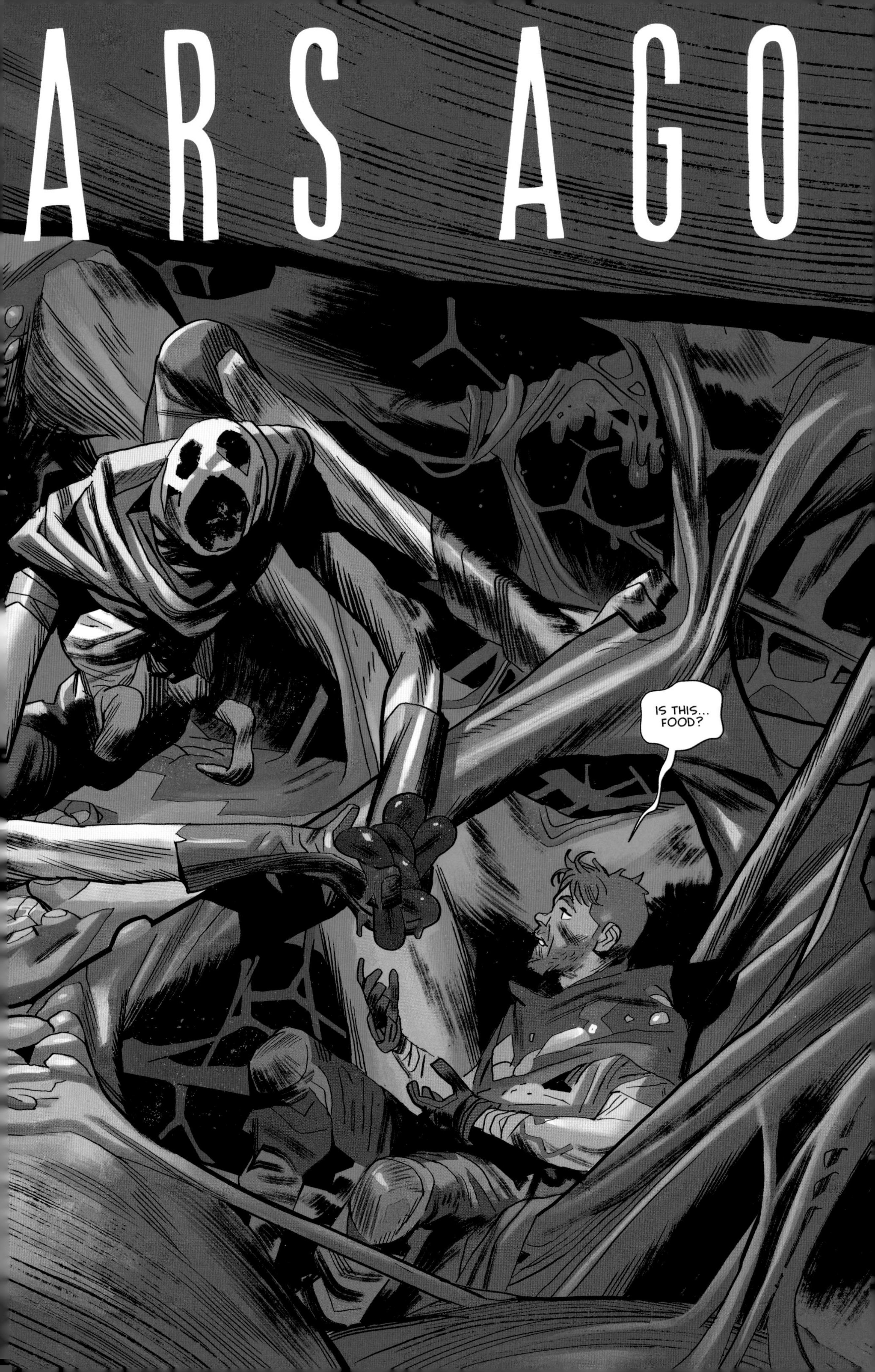
ARS AGO
IS THIS...
FOOD?

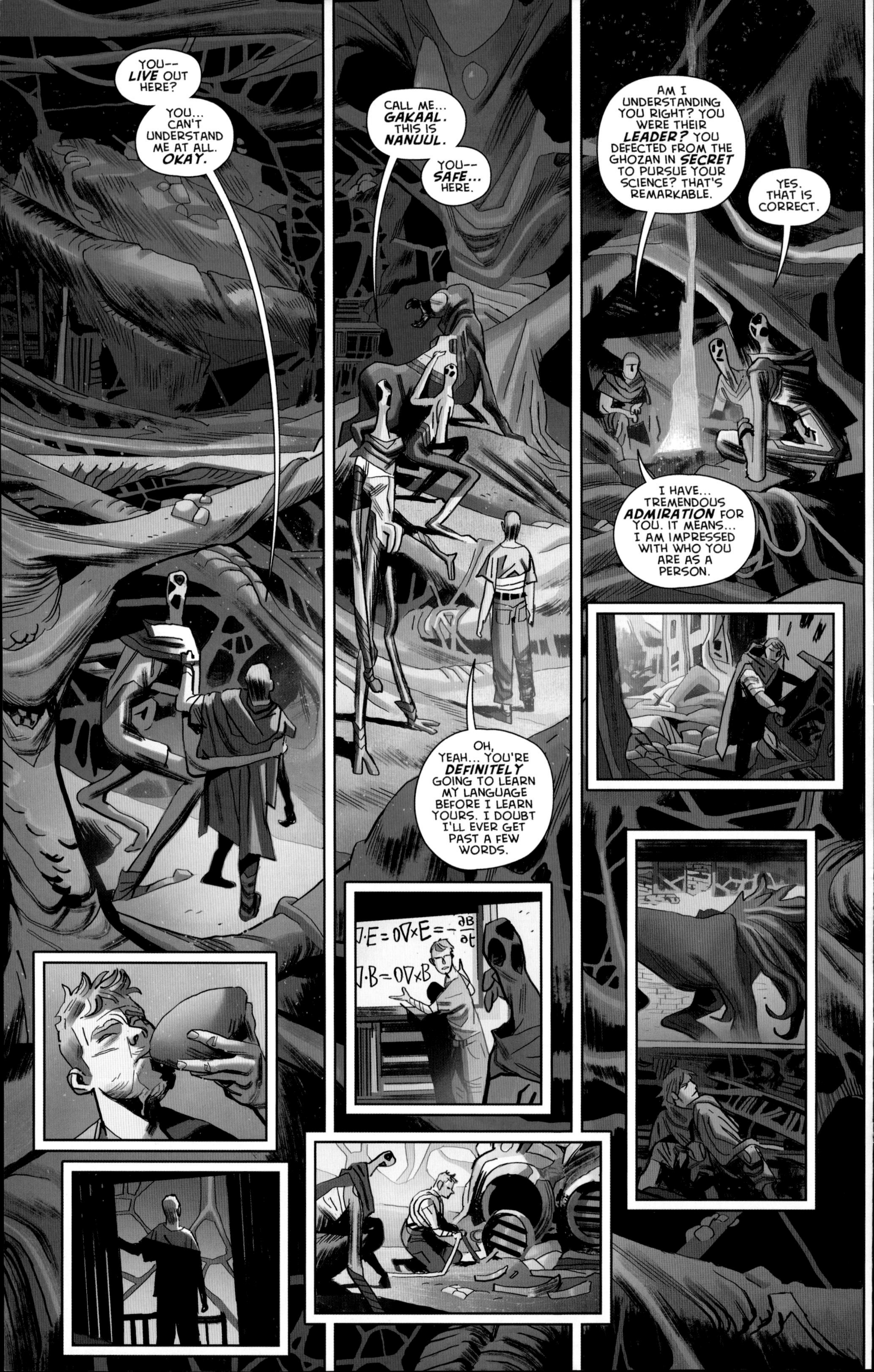
YOU-- LIVE OUT HERE?
YOU... CAN'T UNDERSTAND ME AT ALL. OKAY.
CALL ME... GAKAAL. THIS IS NANUUL.
YOU-- SAFE... HERE.
OH, YEAH... YOU'RE DEFINITELY GOING TO LEARN MY LANGUAGE BEFORE I LEARN YOURS. I DOUBT I'LL EVER GET PAST A FEW WORDS.
AM I UNDERSTANDING YOU RIGHT? YOU WERE THEIR LEADER? YOU DEFECTED FROM THE GHOZAN IN SECRET TO PURSUE YOUR SCIENCE? THAT'S REMARKABLE.
YES. THAT IS CORRECT.
I HAVE... TREMENDOUS ADMIRATION FOR YOU. IT MEANS... I AM IMPRESSED WITH WHO YOU ARE AS A PERSON.

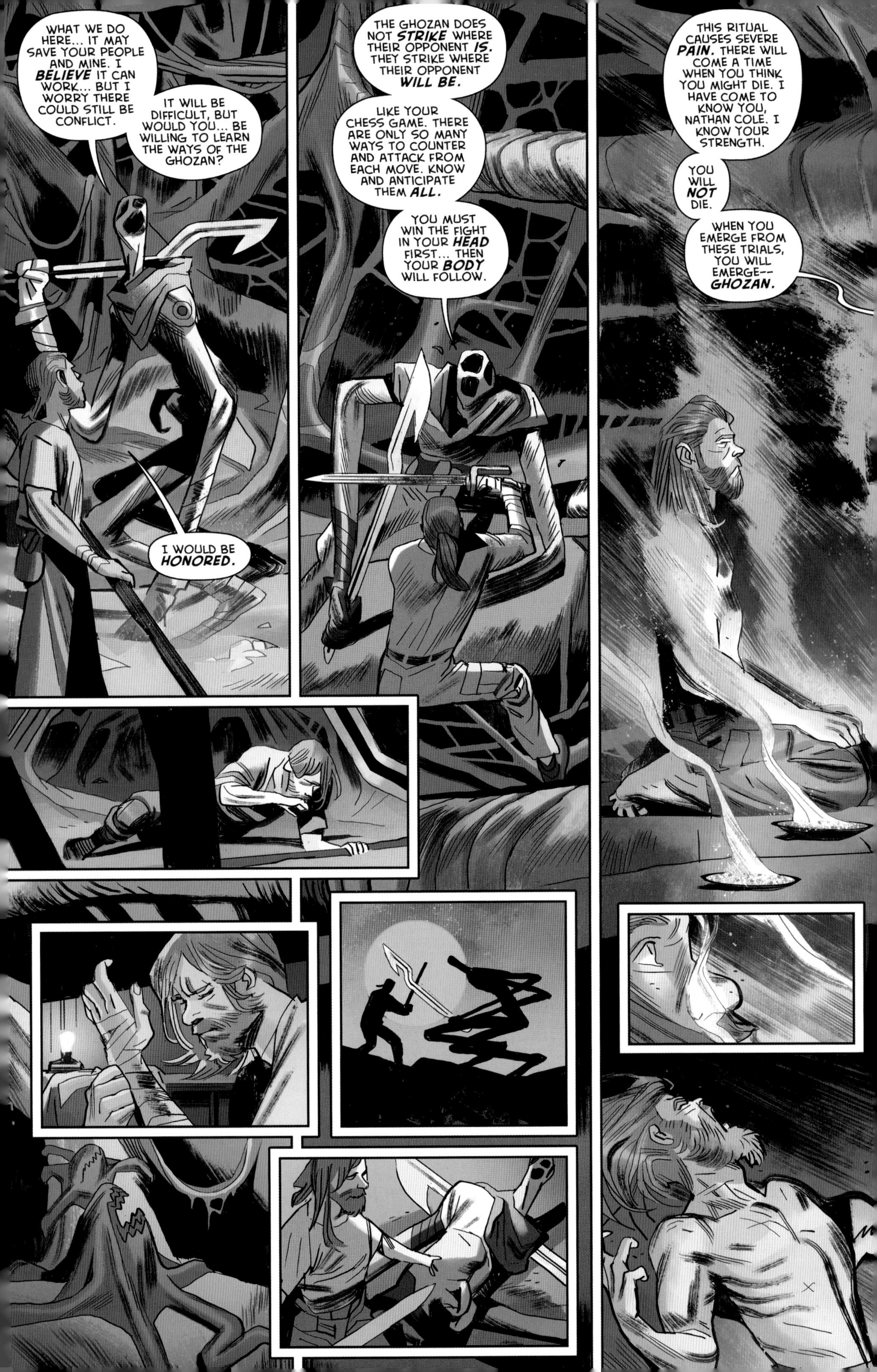
WHAT WE DO HERE... IT MAY SAVE YOUR PEOPLE AND MINE. I BELIEVE IT CAN WORK... BUT I WORRY THERE COULD STILL BE CONFLICT.
IT WILL BE DIFFICULT, BUT WOULD YOU... BE WILLING TO LEARN THE WAYS OF THE GHOZAN?
I WOULD BE HONORED.
THE GHOZAN DOES NOT STRIKE WHERE THEIR OPPONENT IS. THEY STRIKE WHERE THEIR OPPONENT WILL BE.
LIKE YOUR CHESS GAME. THERE ARE ONLY SO MANY WAYS TO COUNTER AND ATTACK FROM EACH MOVE. KNOW AND ANTICIPATE THEM ALL.
YOU MUST WIN THE FIGHT IN YOUR HEAD FIRST... THEN YOUR BODY WILL FOLLOW.
THIS RITUAL CAUSES SEVERE PAIN. THERE WILL COME A TIME WHEN YOU THINK YOU MIGHT DIE. I HAVE COME TO KNOW YOU, NATHAN COLE. I KNOW YOUR STRENGTH.
YOU WILL NOT DIE.
WHEN YOU EMERGE FROM THESE TRIALS, YOU WILL EMERGE-- GHOZAN.

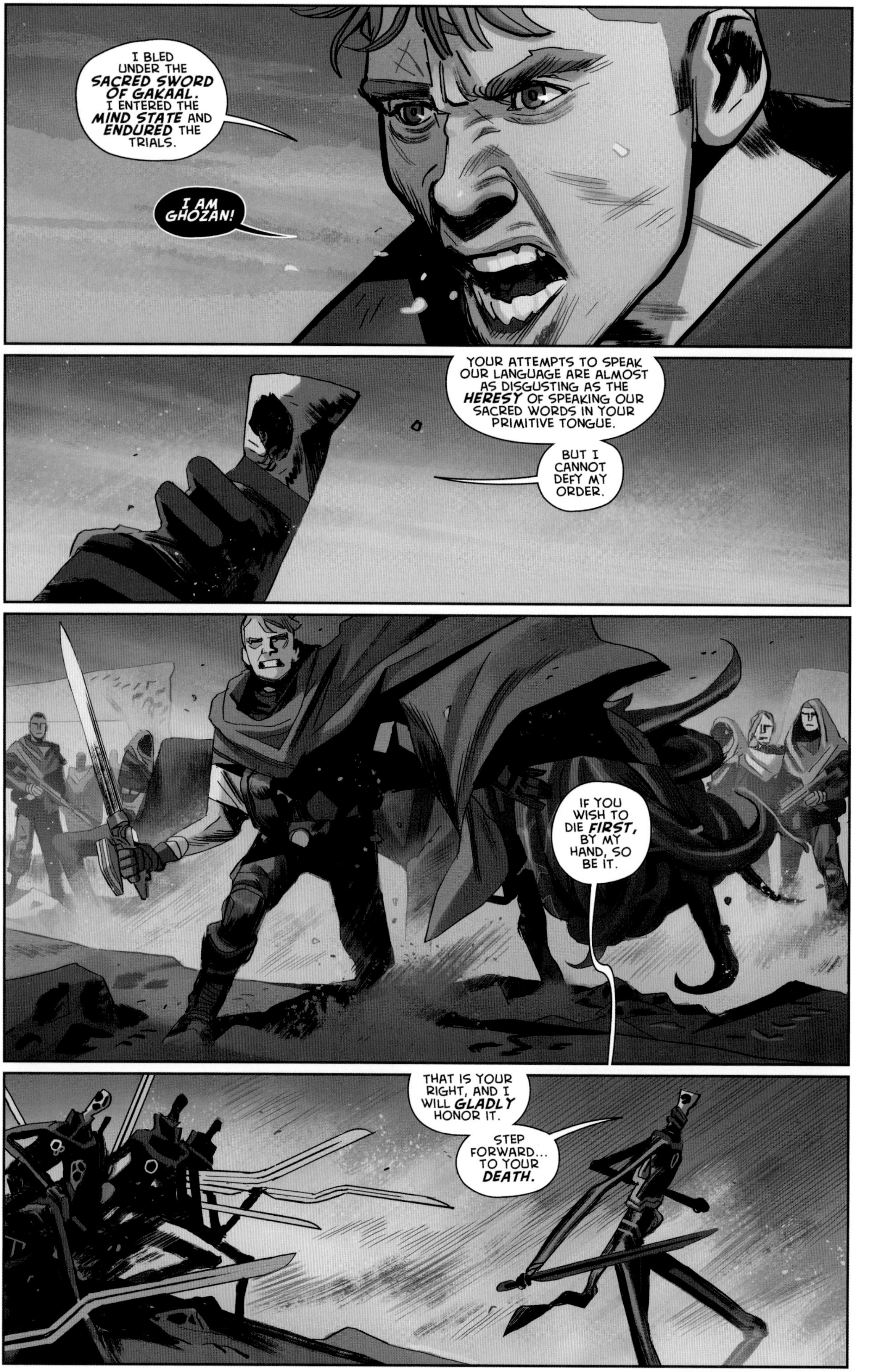
I BLED UNDER THE SACRED SWORD OF GAKAAL. I ENTERED THE MIND STATE AND ENDURED THE TRIALS.
I AM GHOZAN!
YOUR ATTEMPTS TO SPEAK OUR LANGUAGE ARE ALMOST AS DISGUSTING AS THE HERESY OF SPEAKING OUR SACRED WORDS IN YOUR PRIMITIVE TONGUE.
BUT I CANNOT DEFY MY ORDER.
IF YOU WISH TO DIE FIRST, BY MY HAND, SO BE IT.
THAT IS YOUR RIGHT, AND I WILL GLADLY HONOR IT.
STEP FORWARD... TO YOUR DEATH.

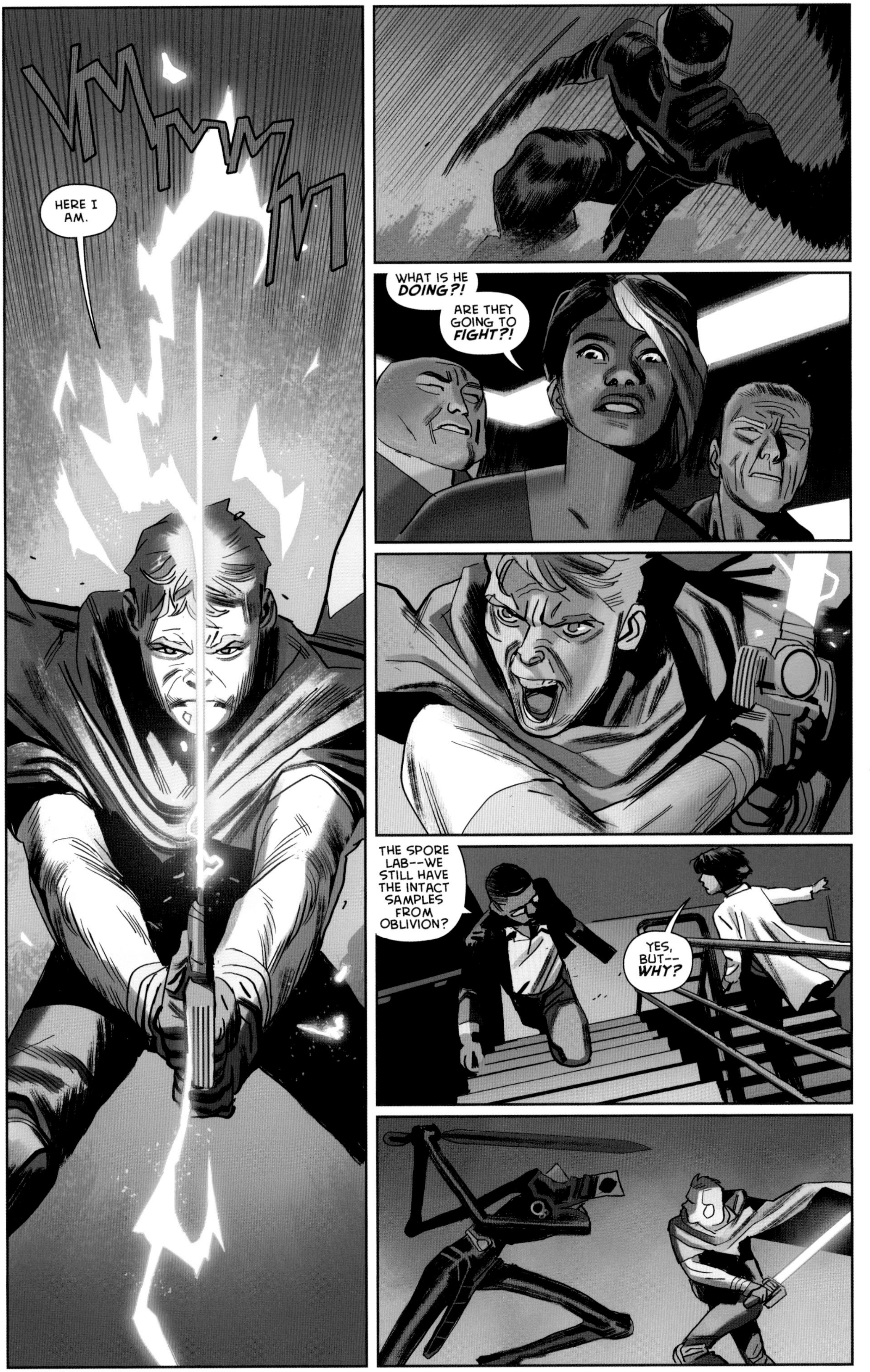
VMMMMM
HERE I AM.
WHAT IS HE DOING?!
ARE THEY GOING TO FIGHT?!
THE SPORE LAB--WE STILL HAVE THE INTACT SAMPLES FROM OBLIVION?
YES, BUT-- WHY?

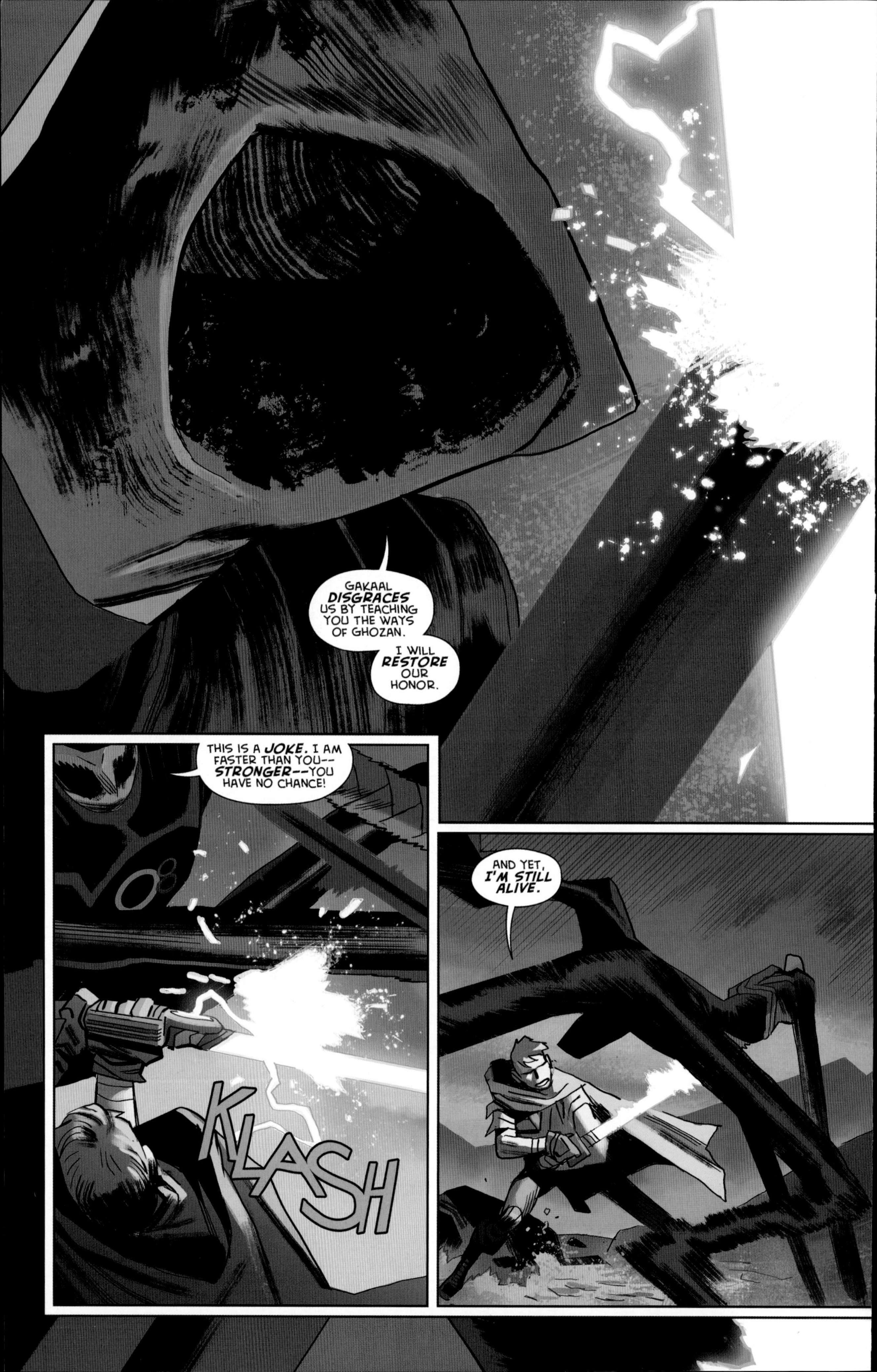
GAKAAL DISGRACES US BY TEACHING YOU THE WAYS OF GHOZAN.
I WILL RESTORE OUR HONOR.
THIS IS A JOKE. I AM FASTER THAN YOU-- STRONGER--YOU HAVE NO CHANCE!
KLASH
AND YET, I'M STILL ALIVE.

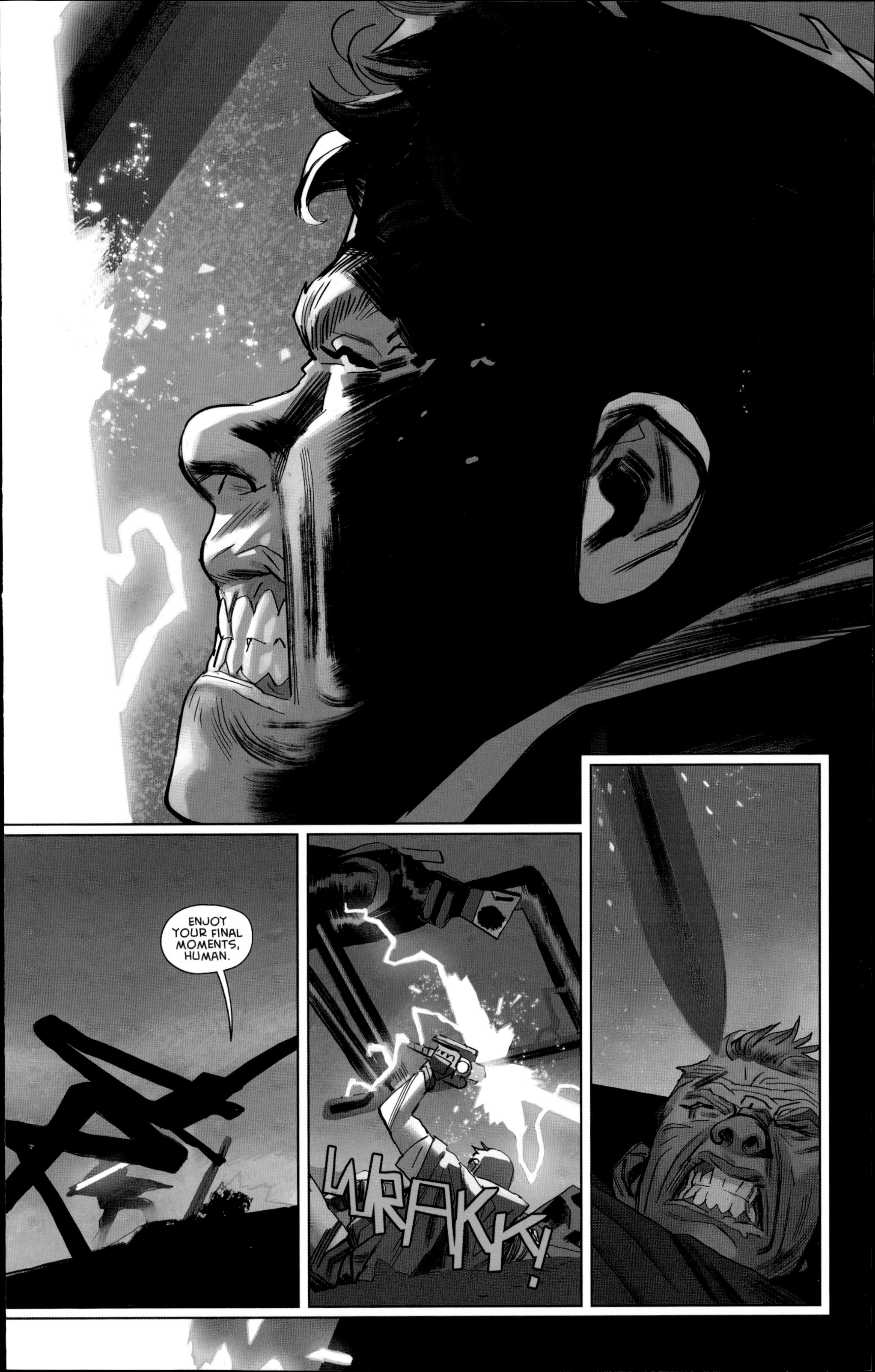
ENJOY YOUR FINAL MOMENTS, HUMAN.
WRAKK!

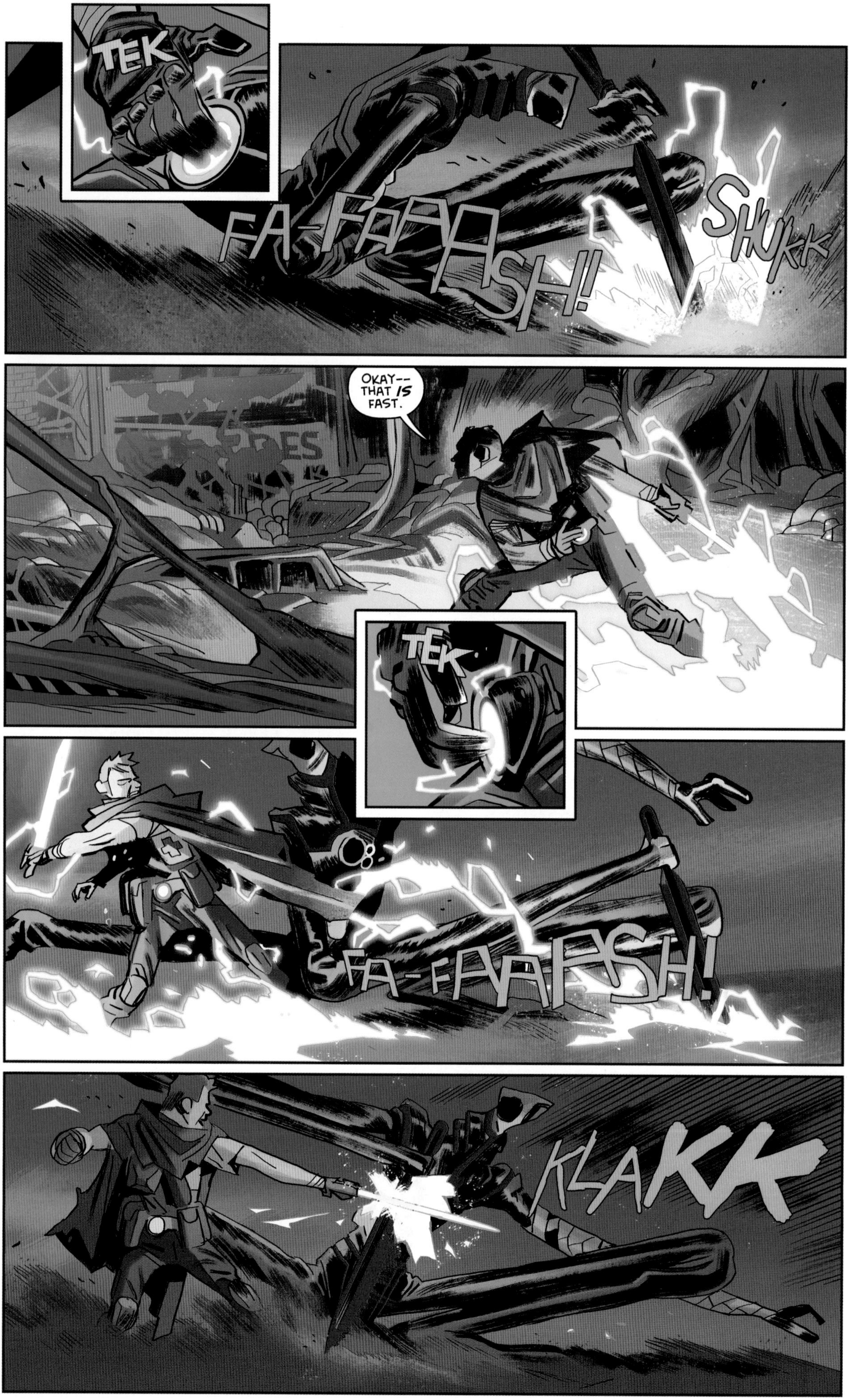
TEK
FA-FAAASH!
SHUKK
OKAY--
THAT IS
FAST.
TEK
FA-FAAASH!
KLAKK

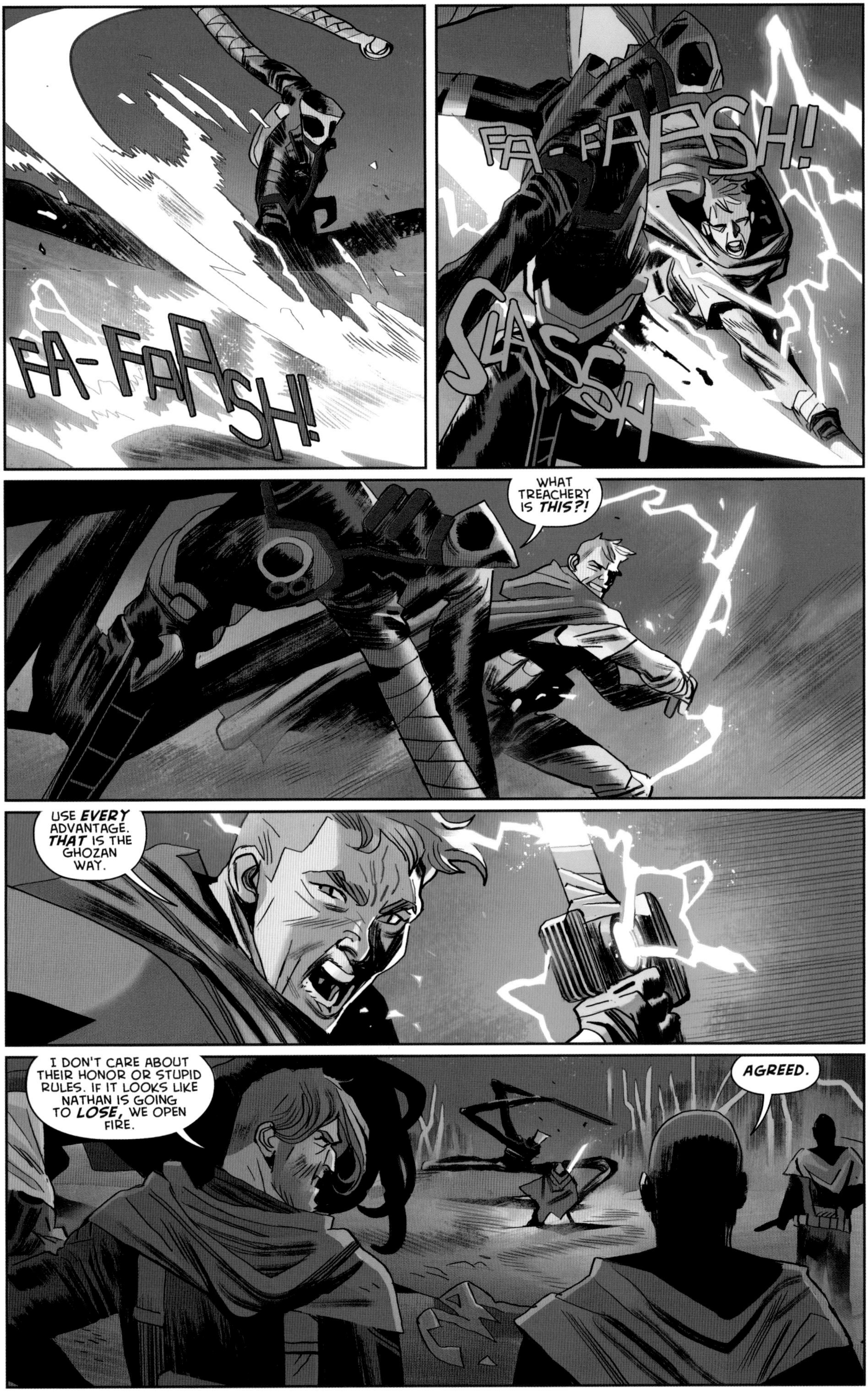
FA-FAASH!
FA-FAASH!
SLASSSH
WHAT TREACHERY IS *THIS?!*
USE *EVERY* ADVANTAGE. *THAT* IS THE GHOZAN WAY.
I DON'T CARE ABOUT THEIR HONOR OR STUPID RULES. IF IT LOOKS LIKE NATHAN IS GOING TO *LOSE,* WE OPEN FIRE.
AGREED.

WHAT BREAK-THROUGHS? WHAT ARE WE **DOING** HERE, DUNCAN?

HOLD ON--IT'S... GOOD TO BE BACK IN THIS LAB, **TOGETHER**.

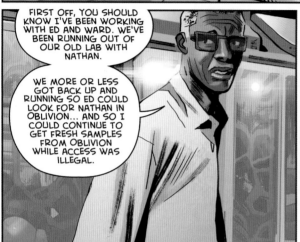

FIRST OFF, YOU SHOULD KNOW I'VE BEEN WORKING WITH ED AND WARD. WE'VE BEEN RUNNING OUT OF OUR OLD LAB WITH NATHAN.

WE MORE OR LESS GOT BACK UP AND RUNNING SO ED COULD LOOK FOR NATHAN IN OBLIVION... AND SO I COULD CONTINUE TO GET FRESH SAMPLES FROM OBLIVION WHILE ACCESS WAS ILLEGAL.

I KNOW.

YOU DID?

LOOK, WE'VE HAD OUR DIFFERENCES IN THE PAST, BUT I THINK WE BOTH AGREE NO ONE KNOWS US BETTER THAN WE KNOW EACH OTHER.

THE TIMING OF YOUR EXIT WAS PRETTY **OBVIOUS**, DUNCAN.

I GUESS IT WAS.

OKAY, I'M PULLING THE DATA FROM MY RECENT STUDIES OFF THE CLOUD.

I SPOKE TO NATHAN, HE SPENT **YEARS** IN OBLIVION WORKING WITH A KUTHAAL SCIENTIST TRYING TO **STOP** THE GROWTH OVERTAKING THEIR WORLD.

APPARENTLY, THERE WAS A TWO-TRACK PLAN. OPTION ONE WAS STOP THE GROWTH. OPTION TWO WAS INVADE EARTH. THEY GAINED THE MEANS TO INVADE FIRST-- HENCE WHERE WE CURRENTLY ARE.

SO THEY DON'T NECESSARILY *WANT* TO INVADE...

EXACTLY.

THEY'RE SIMPLY TRYING TO ESCAPE. WE TAKE AWAY THE *NEED* FOR ESCAPE-- *INVASION OVER.*

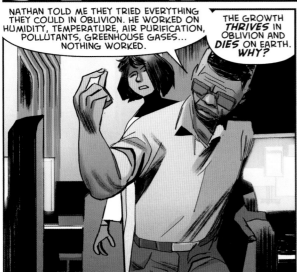

NATHAN TOLD ME THEY TRIED EVERYTHING THEY COULD IN OBLIVION. HE WORKED ON HUMIDITY, TEMPERATURE, AIR PURIFICATION, POLLUTANTS, GREENHOUSE GASES... NOTHING WORKED.

THE GROWTH *THRIVES* IN OBLIVION AND *DIES* ON EARTH. *WHY?*

NATHAN HAD TO *CREATE* ASPECTS OF EARTH'S ENVIRONMENTS IN OBLIVION... ALL WE HAVE TO DO IS... *BLOCK THEM* UNTIL WE FIND THE RIGHT ONE.

YES!

AND WE HAVE *LIVING SAMPLES* HERE IN THE LAB! SO WHATEVER IT IS THAT KEEPS THEM ALIVE... WE'RE *ALREADY DOING IT.*

WE'RE FACING A SUPERIOR MILITARY FORCE THAT WE HAVE *NO HOPE* OF DEFEATING.

YOU AND ME, WE'RE THE ONLY ONES WHO CAN SOLVE THIS PROBLEM... AND SOLVING THIS PROBLEM IS THE ONLY WAY TO SAVE *EARTH.*

LET'S GET TO WORK.

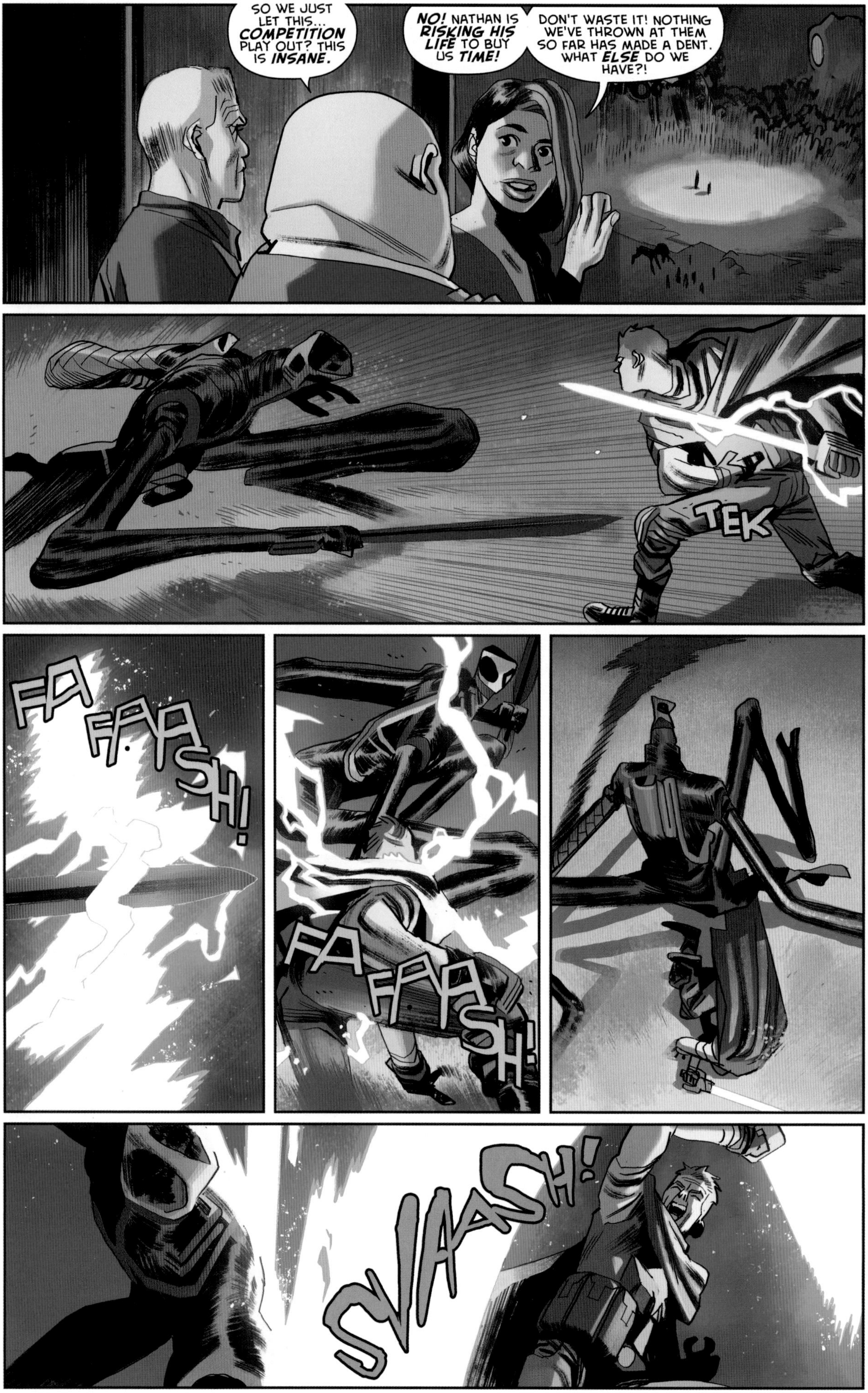

SO WE JUST LET THIS... COMPETITION PLAY OUT? THIS IS INSANE.
NO! NATHAN IS RISKING HIS LIFE TO BUY US TIME!
DON'T WASTE IT! NOTHING WE'VE THROWN AT THEM SO FAR HAS MADE A DENT. WHAT ELSE DO WE HAVE?!
TEK
FA FAAASH!
FA FAAASH!
SVAASH!

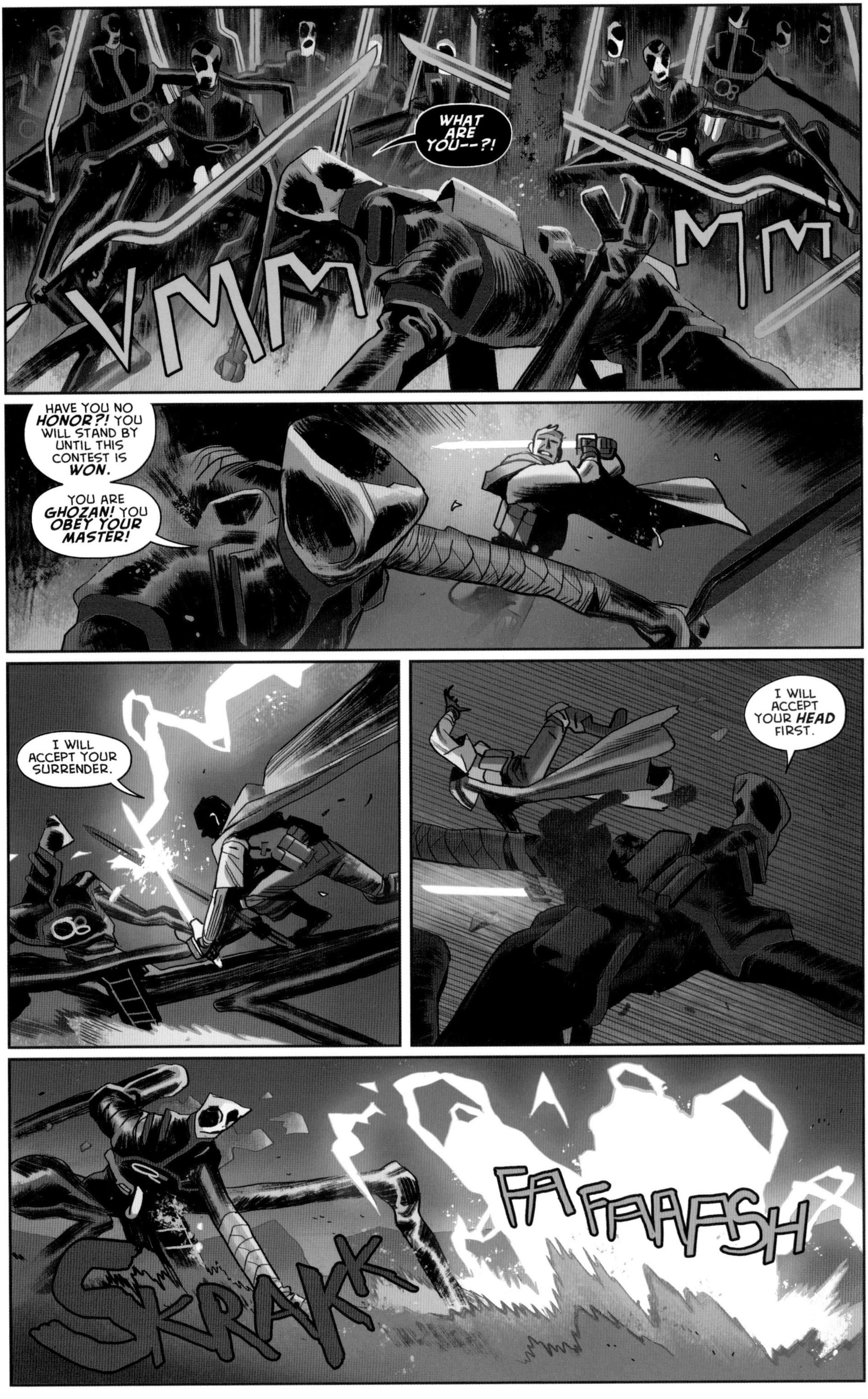
WHAT ARE YOU--?!
VMM
MM
HAVE YOU NO HONOR?! YOU WILL STAND BY UNTIL THIS CONTEST IS WON.
YOU ARE GHOZAN! YOU OBEY YOUR MASTER!
I WILL ACCEPT YOUR SURRENDER.
I WILL ACCEPT YOUR HEAD FIRST.
SKRAKK
FA FAAASH

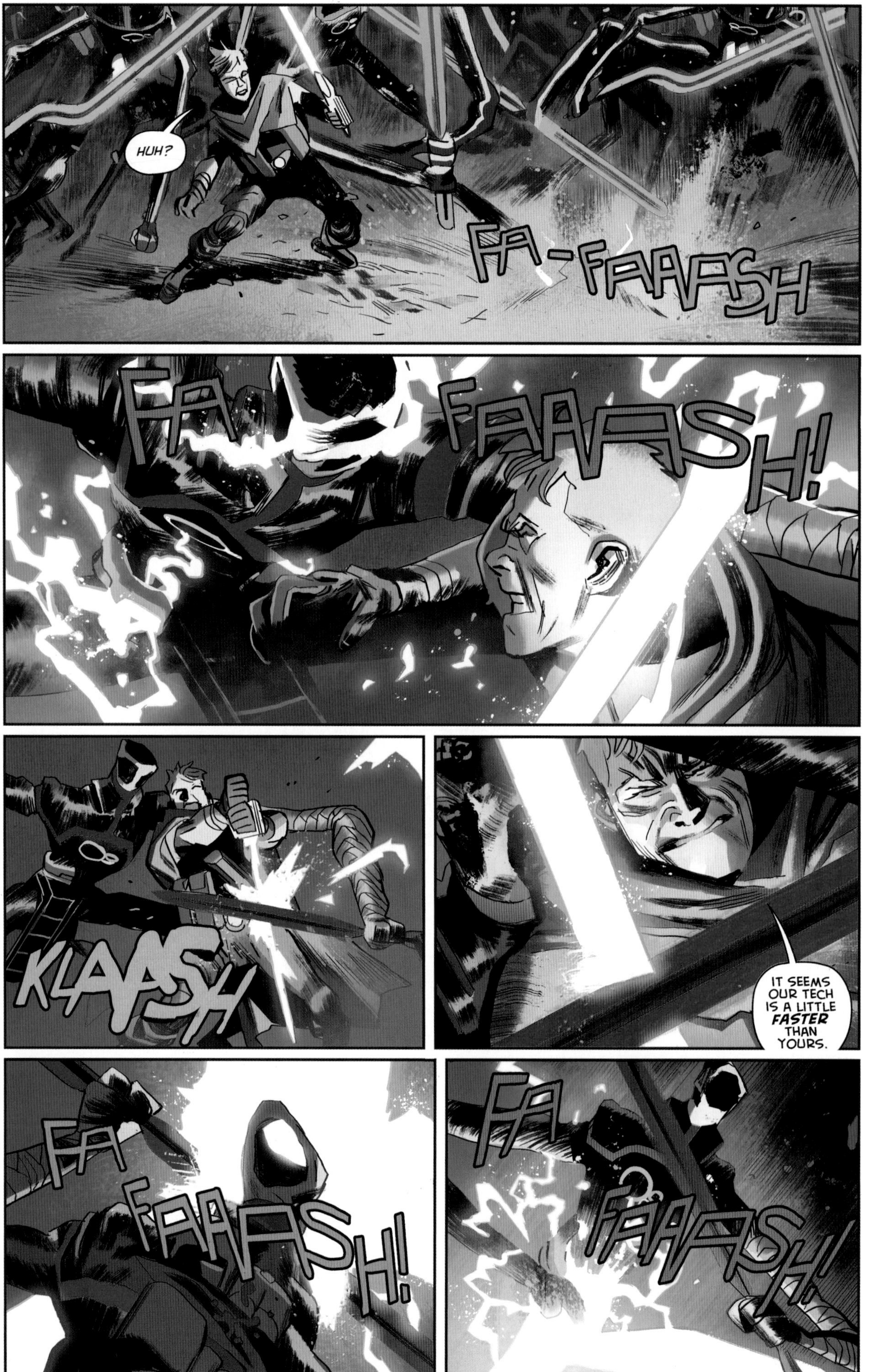
HUH?
FA-FAAASH
FA FAAASH!
KLAASH
IT SEEMS OUR TECH IS A LITTLE FASTER THAN YOURS.
FA FAAASH!
FA FAAASH!

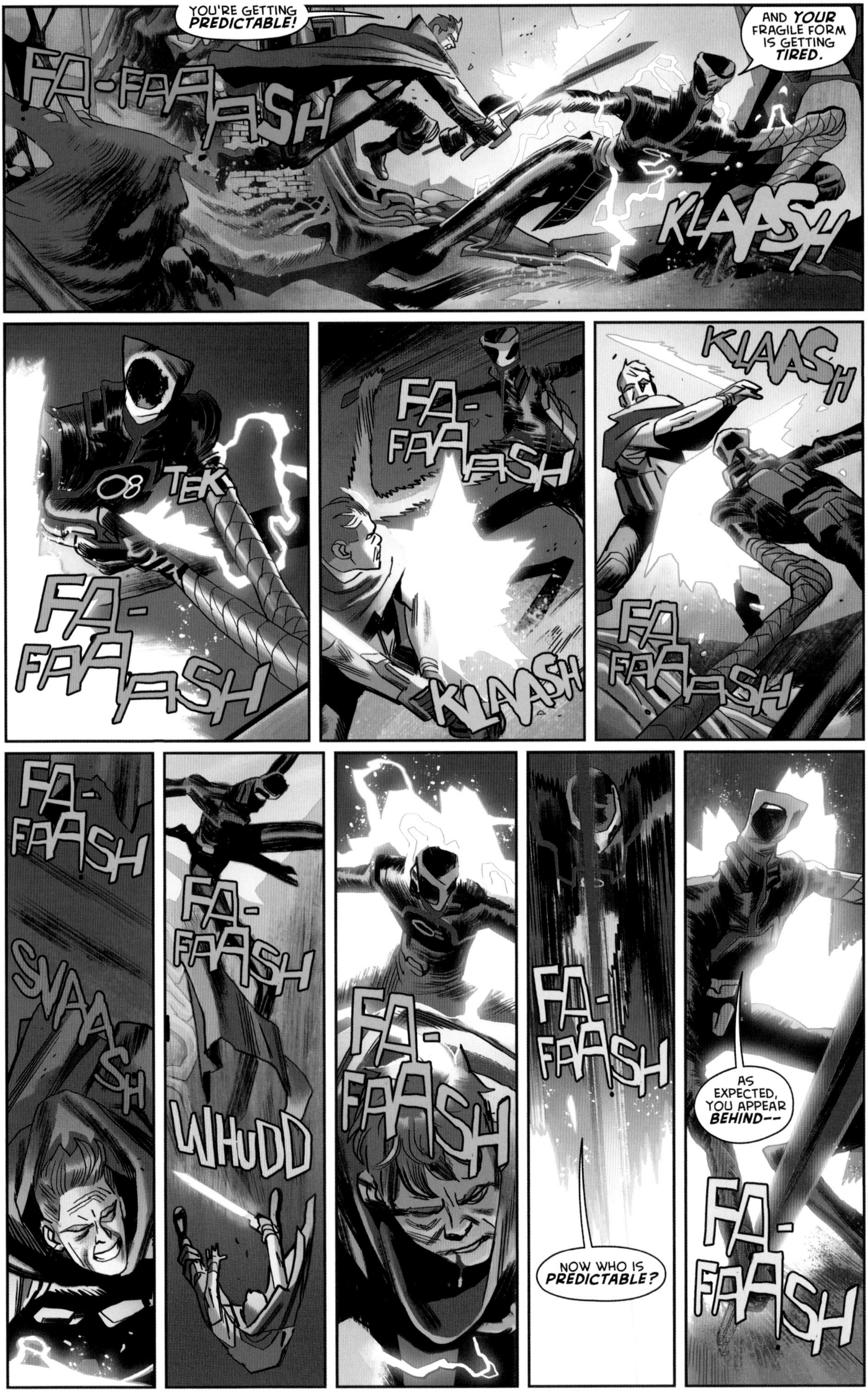
YOU'RE GETTING PREDICTABLE!
FA-FAAAASH
AND YOUR FRAGILE FORM IS GETTING TIRED.
KLAASH
TEK
FA-FAAAASH
FA-FAAAASH
KLAASH
KLAASH
FA-FAAAASH
FA-FAASH
SWAASH
FA-FAASH
WHUDD
FA-FAASH
FA-FAASH
NOW WHO IS PREDICTABLE?
AS EXPECTED, YOU APPEAR BEHIND--
FA-FAASH

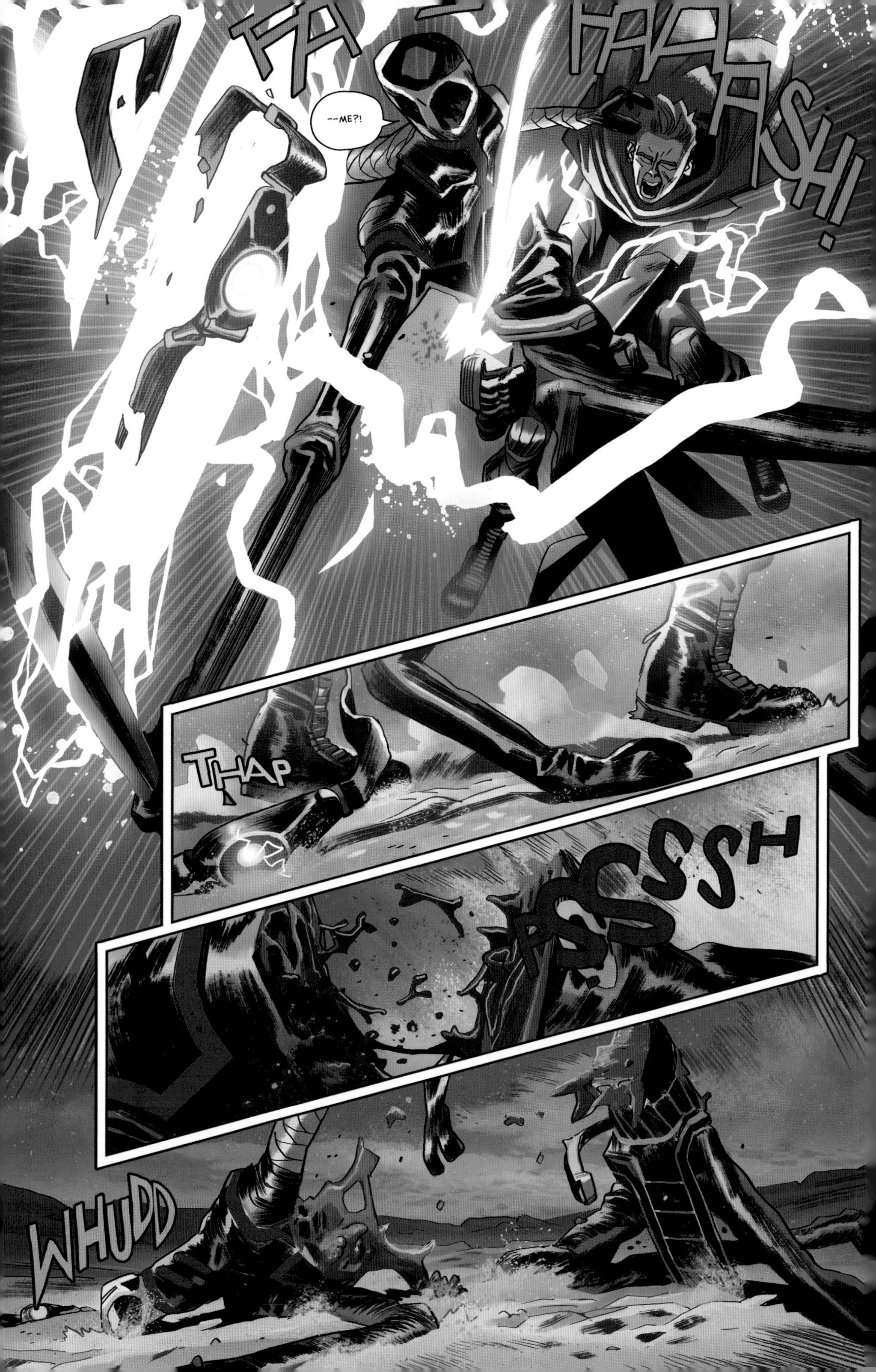
FA--
--ME?!
FRAAAASH!
THAP
PSSSSH
WHUDD

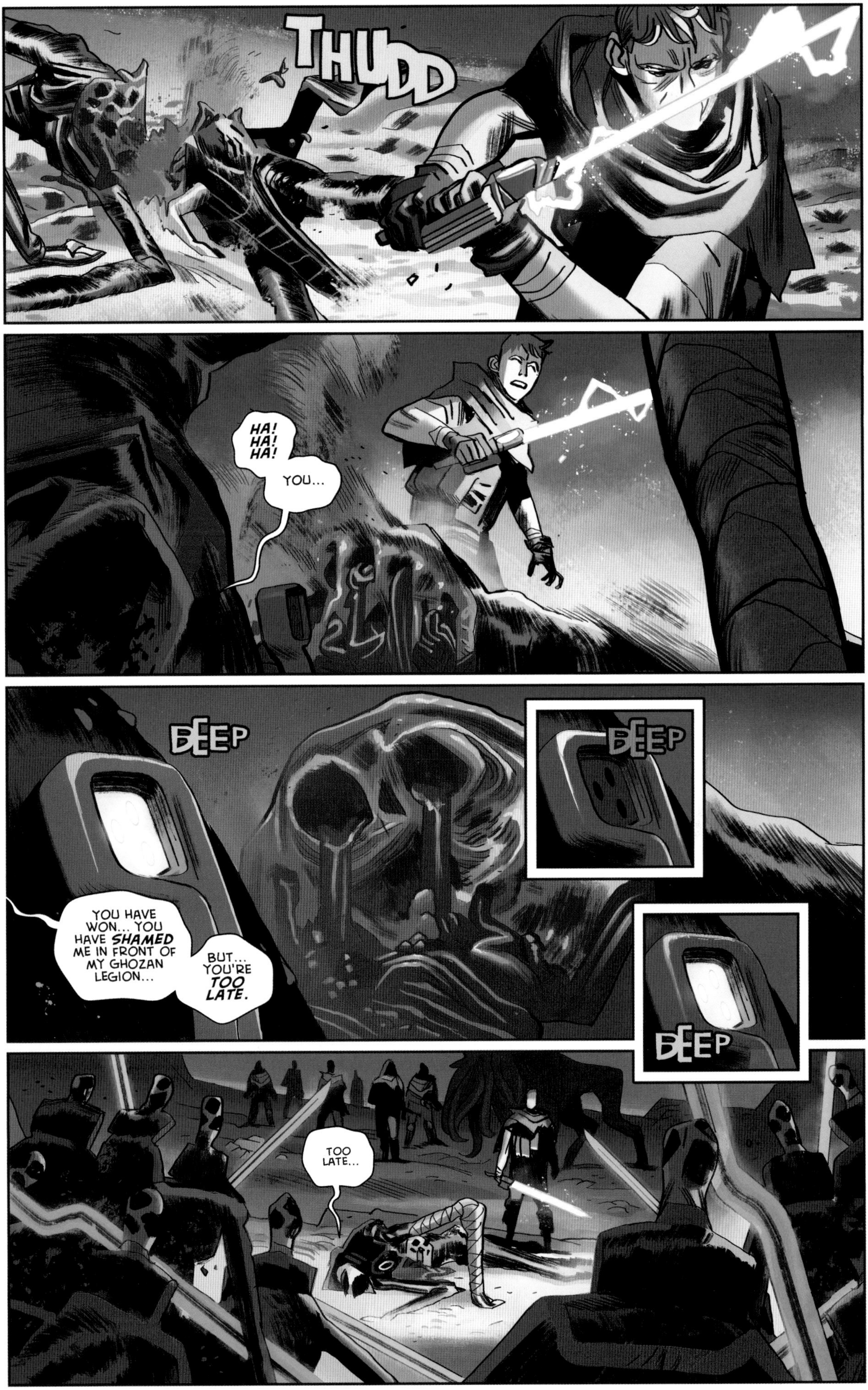
THUDD
HA! HA! HA!
YOU...
BEEP
BEEP
YOU HAVE WON... YOU HAVE SHAMED ME IN FRONT OF MY GHOZAN LEGION...
BUT... YOU'RE TOO LATE.
BEEP
TOO LATE...

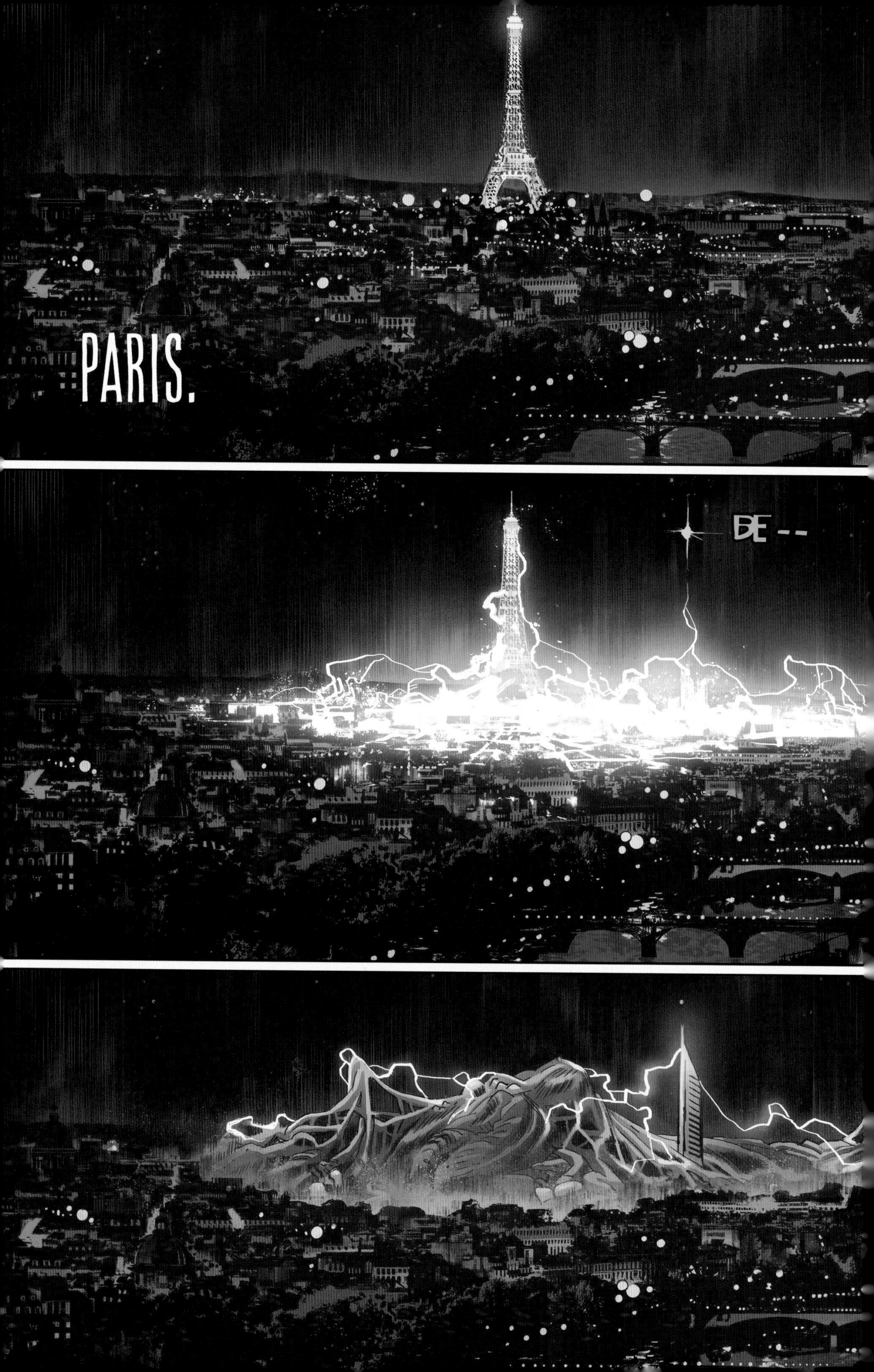
PARIS.
BE--

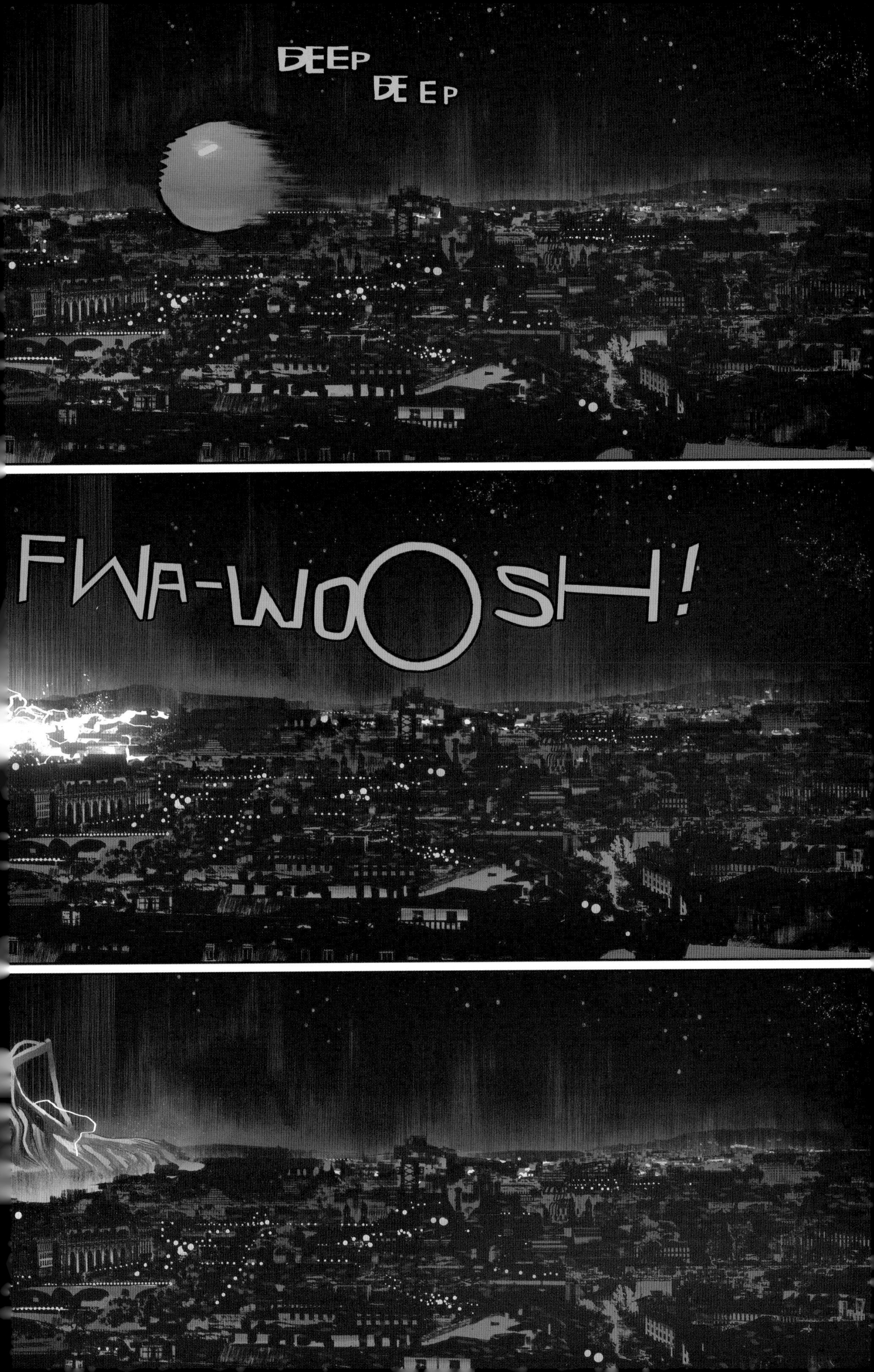
BEEP
BEEP
FWA-WOOSH!

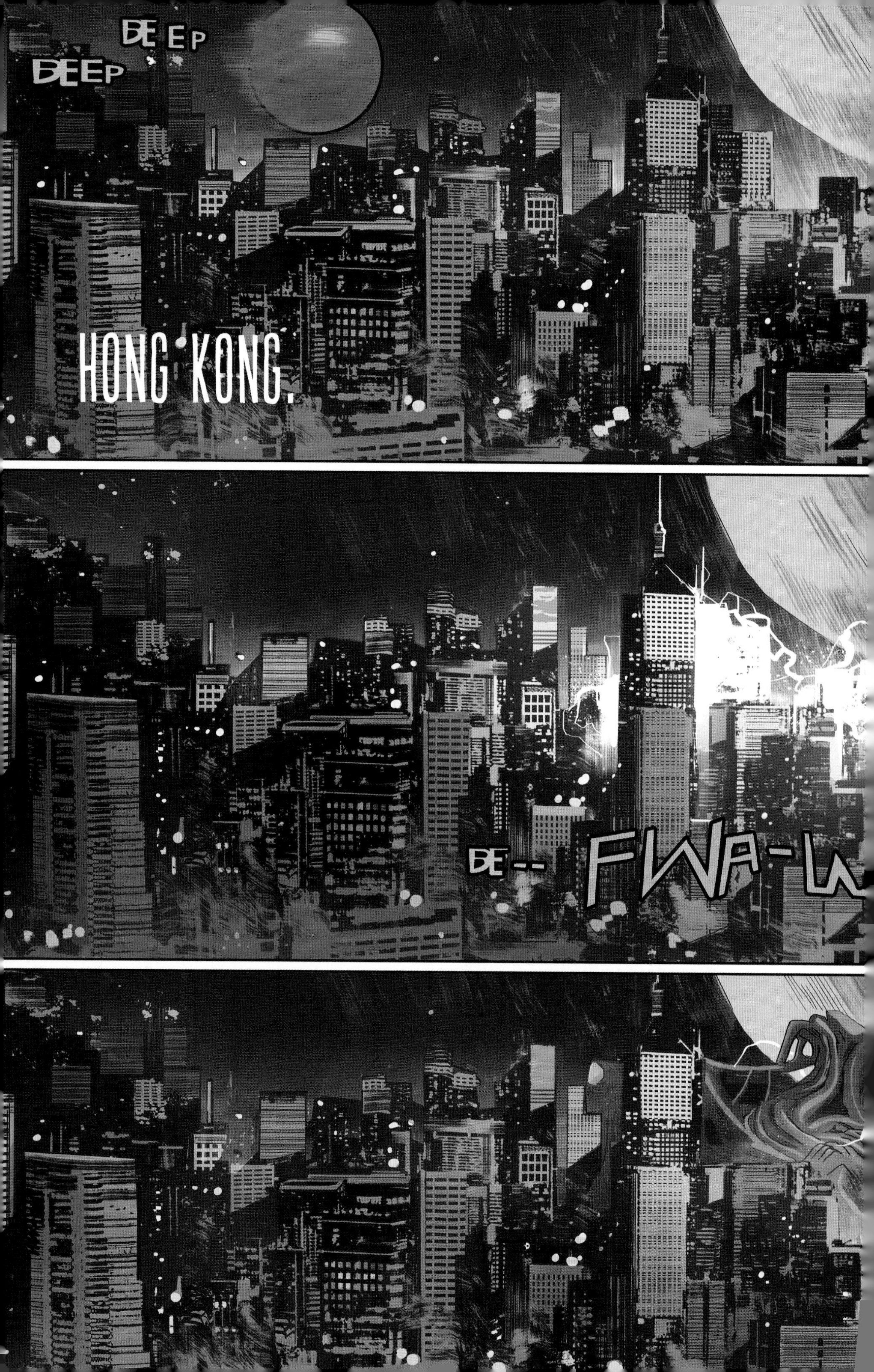
BEEP
BEEP
HONG KONG.
BE--
FWA-LA

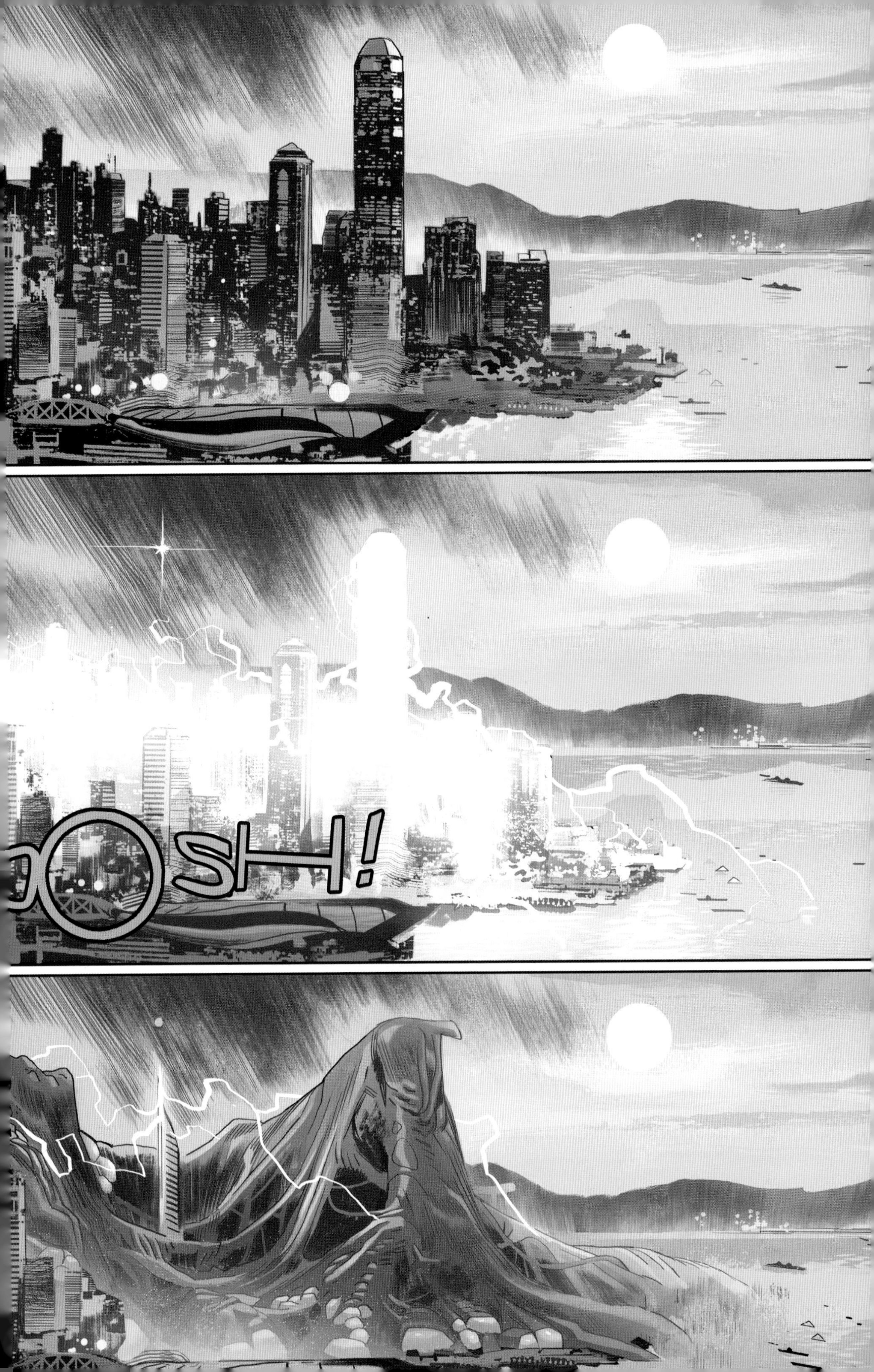
OSH!

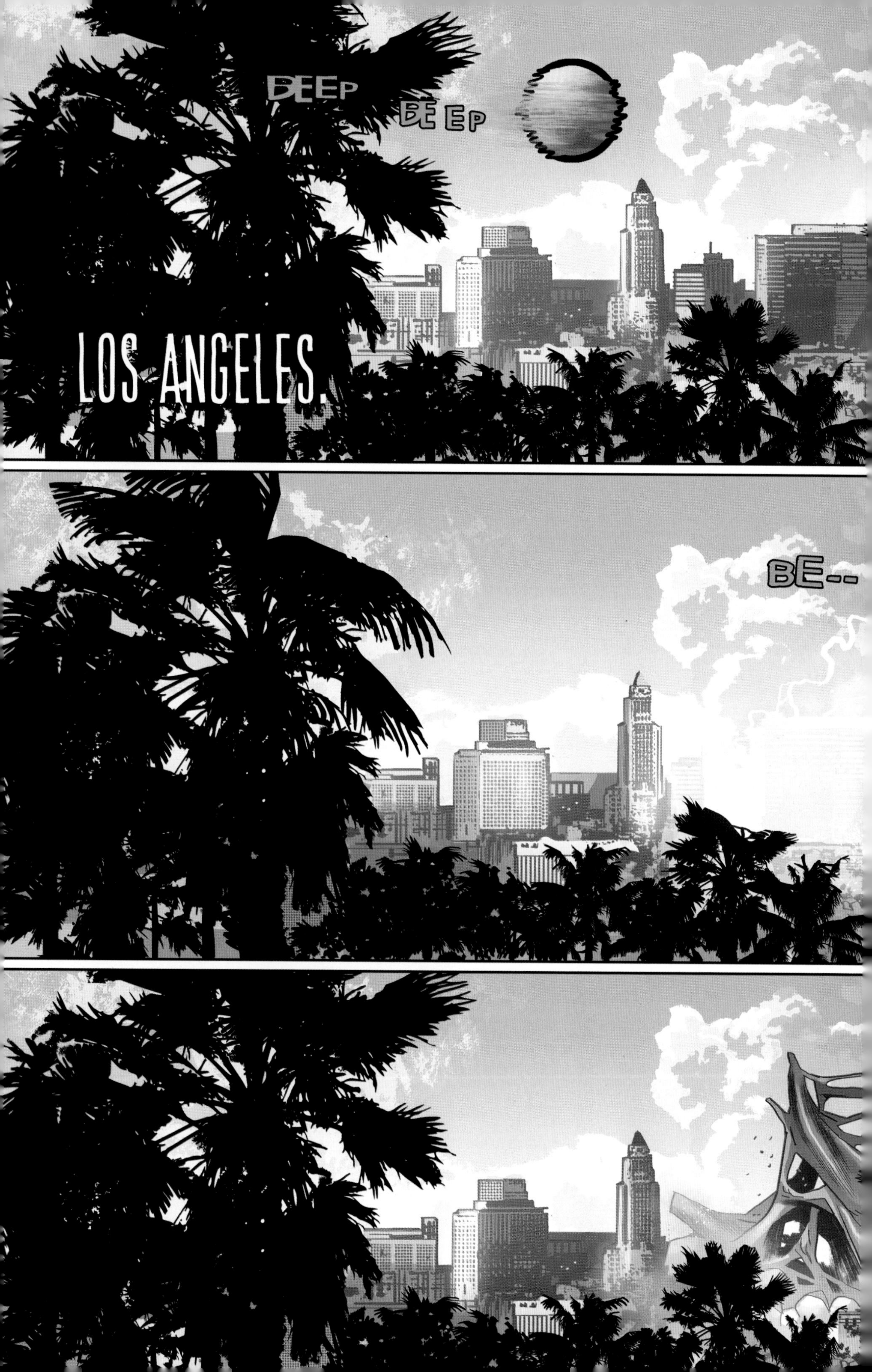
BEEP
BEEP
LOS ANGELES.
BE--

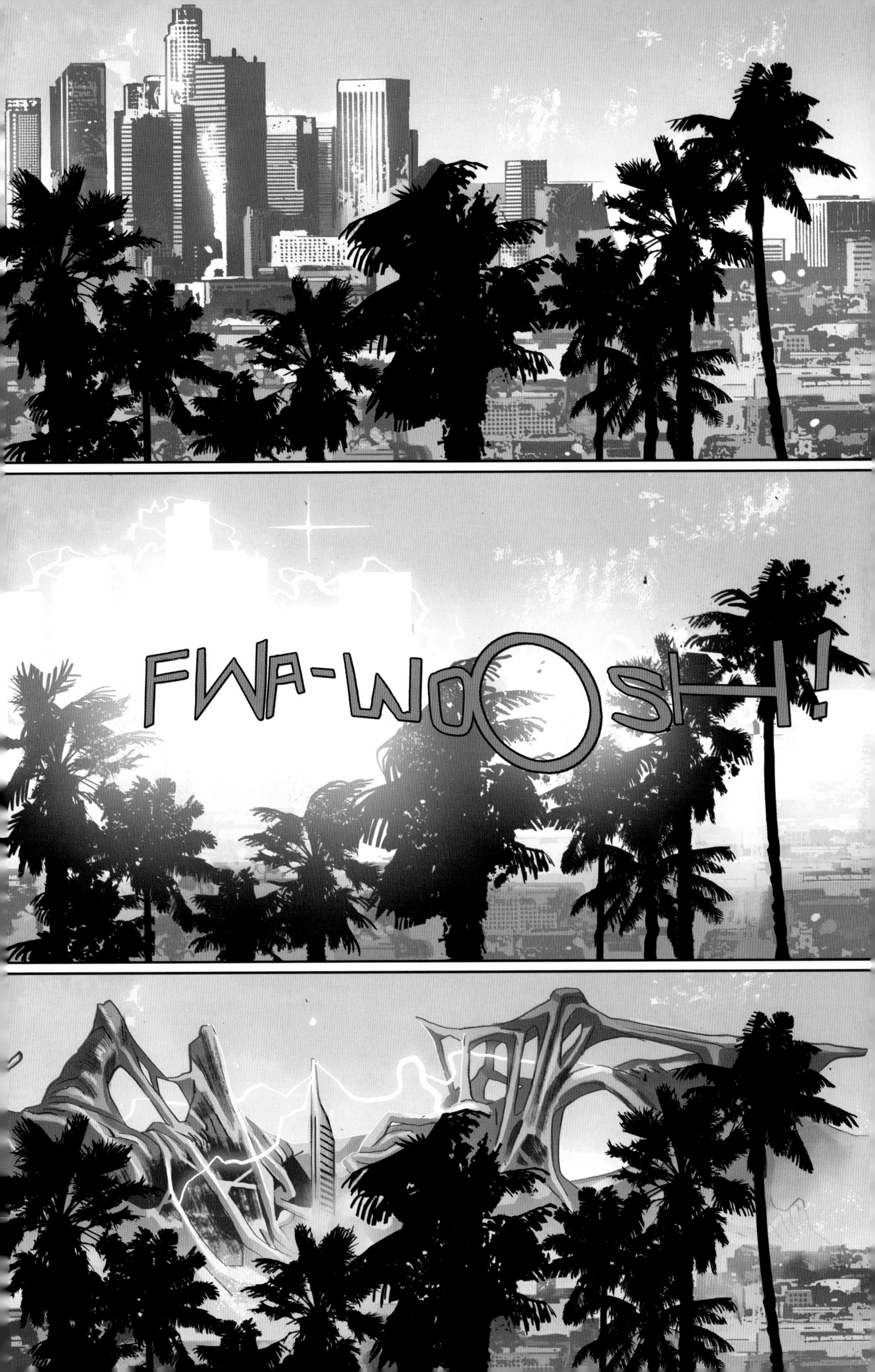
FWA-WOOSH!

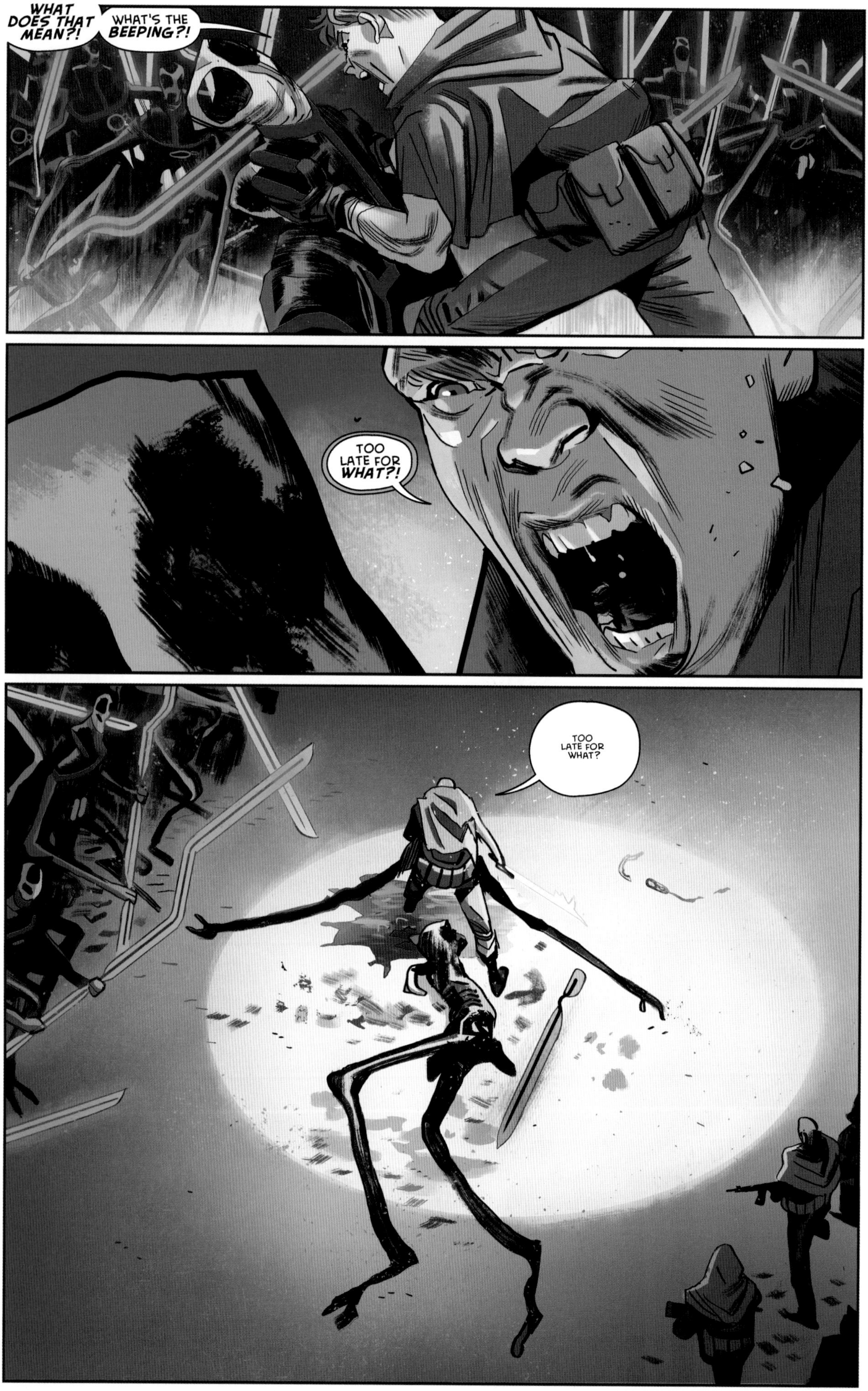
WHAT DOES THAT MEAN?!
WHAT'S THE BEEPING?!
TOO LATE FOR WHAT?!
TOO LATE FOR WHAT?

BONUS

STORY

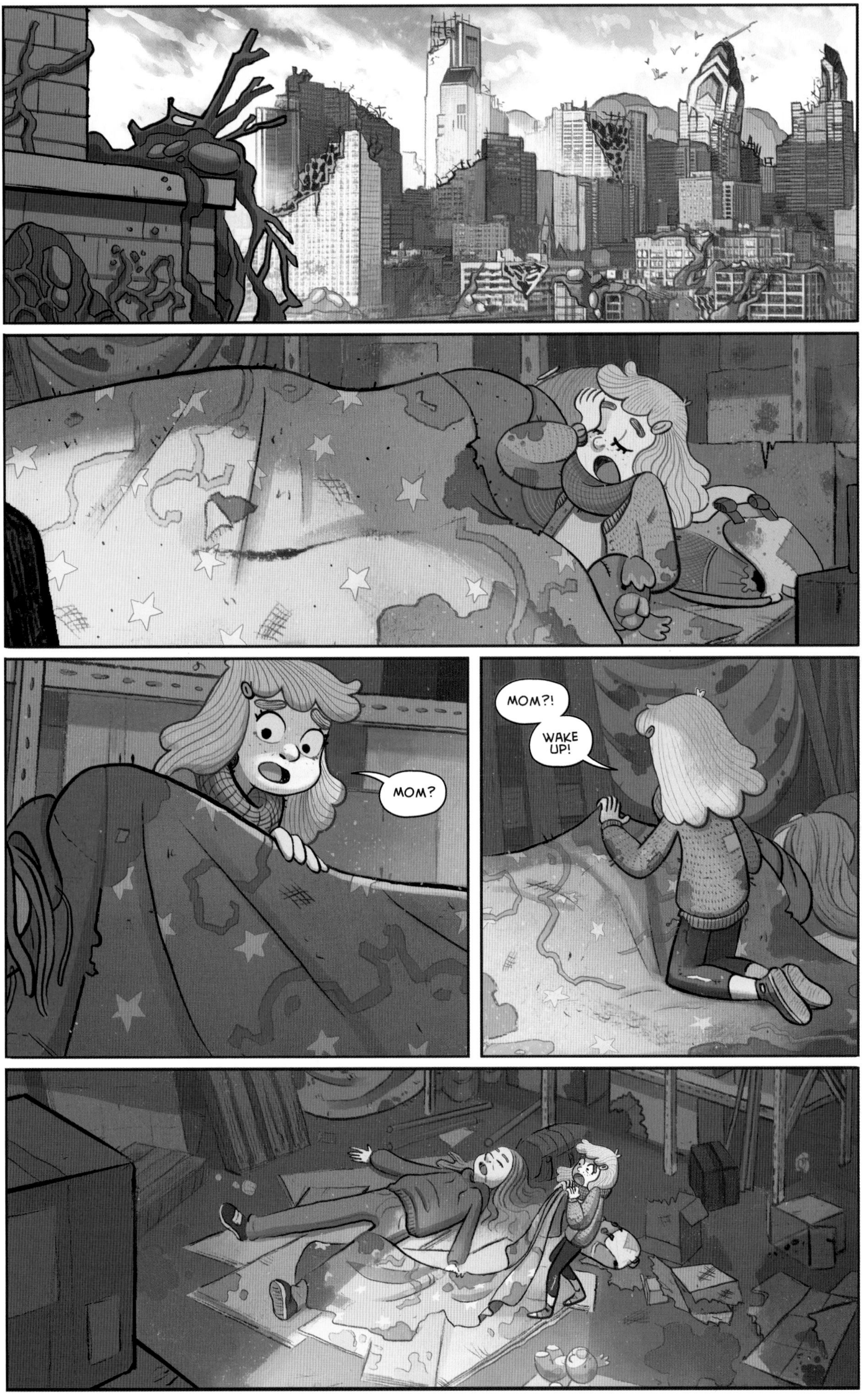
MOM?
MOM?!
WAKE UP!

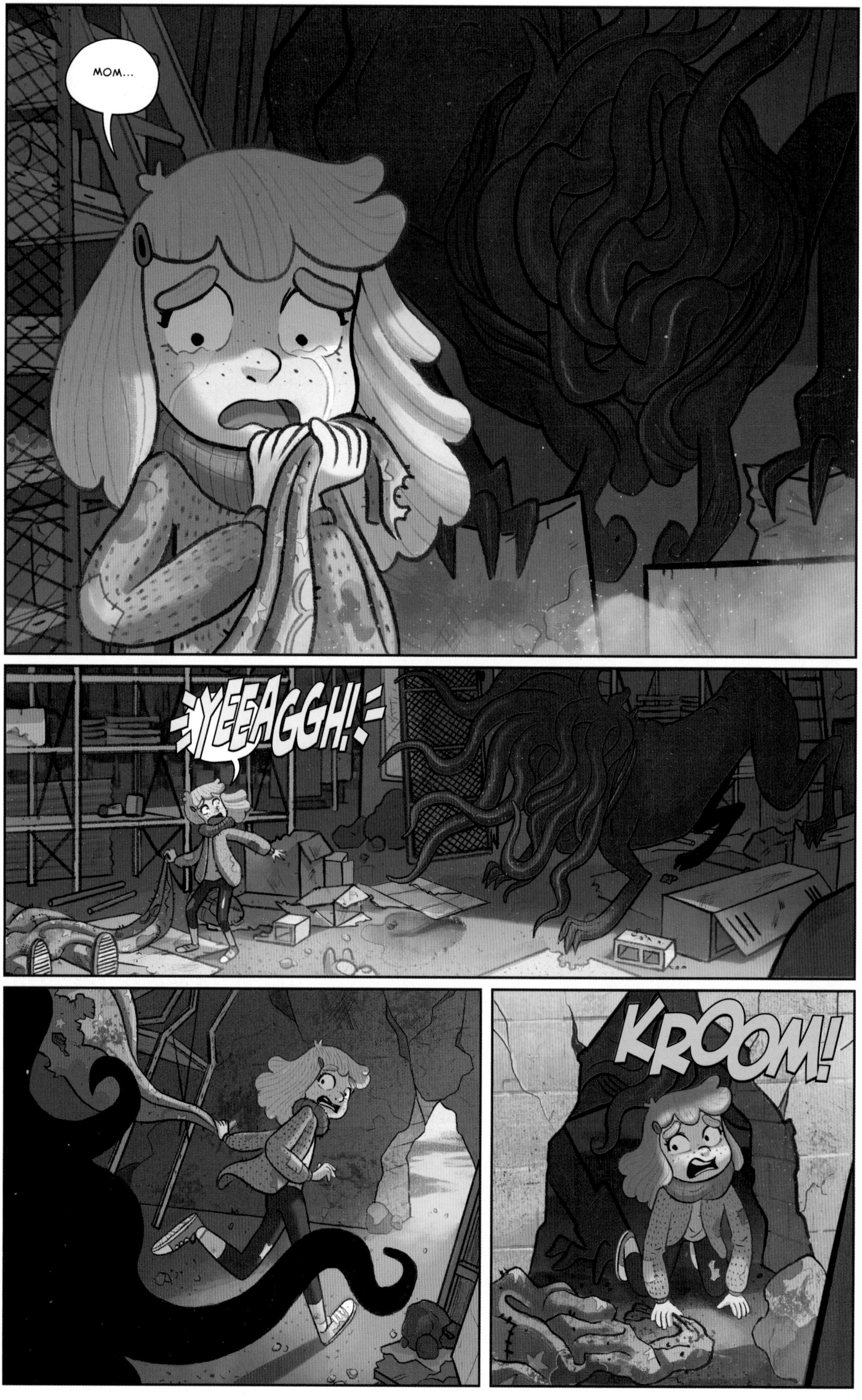
MOM...
YEEAGGH!
KROOM!

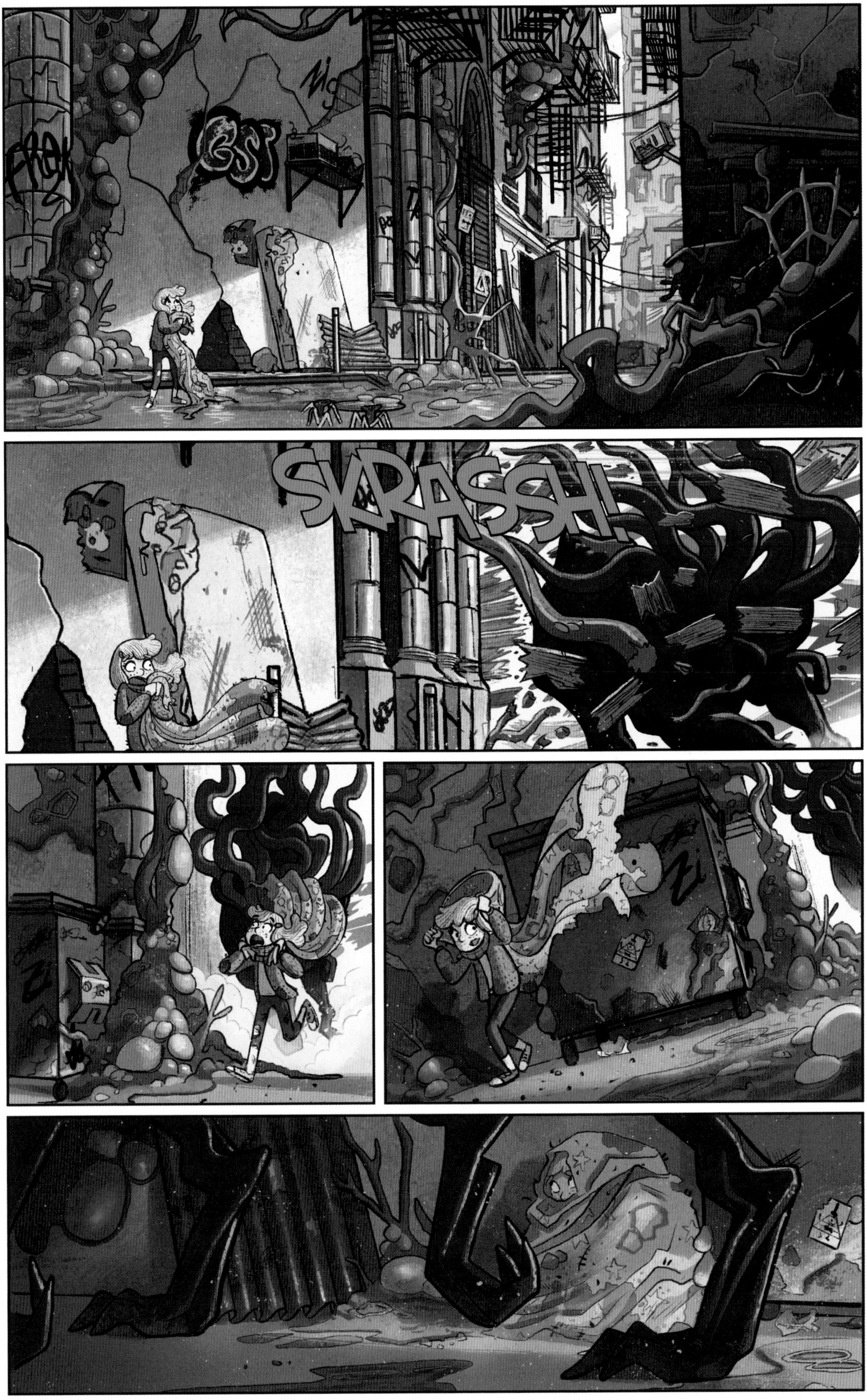
SKRASSH!

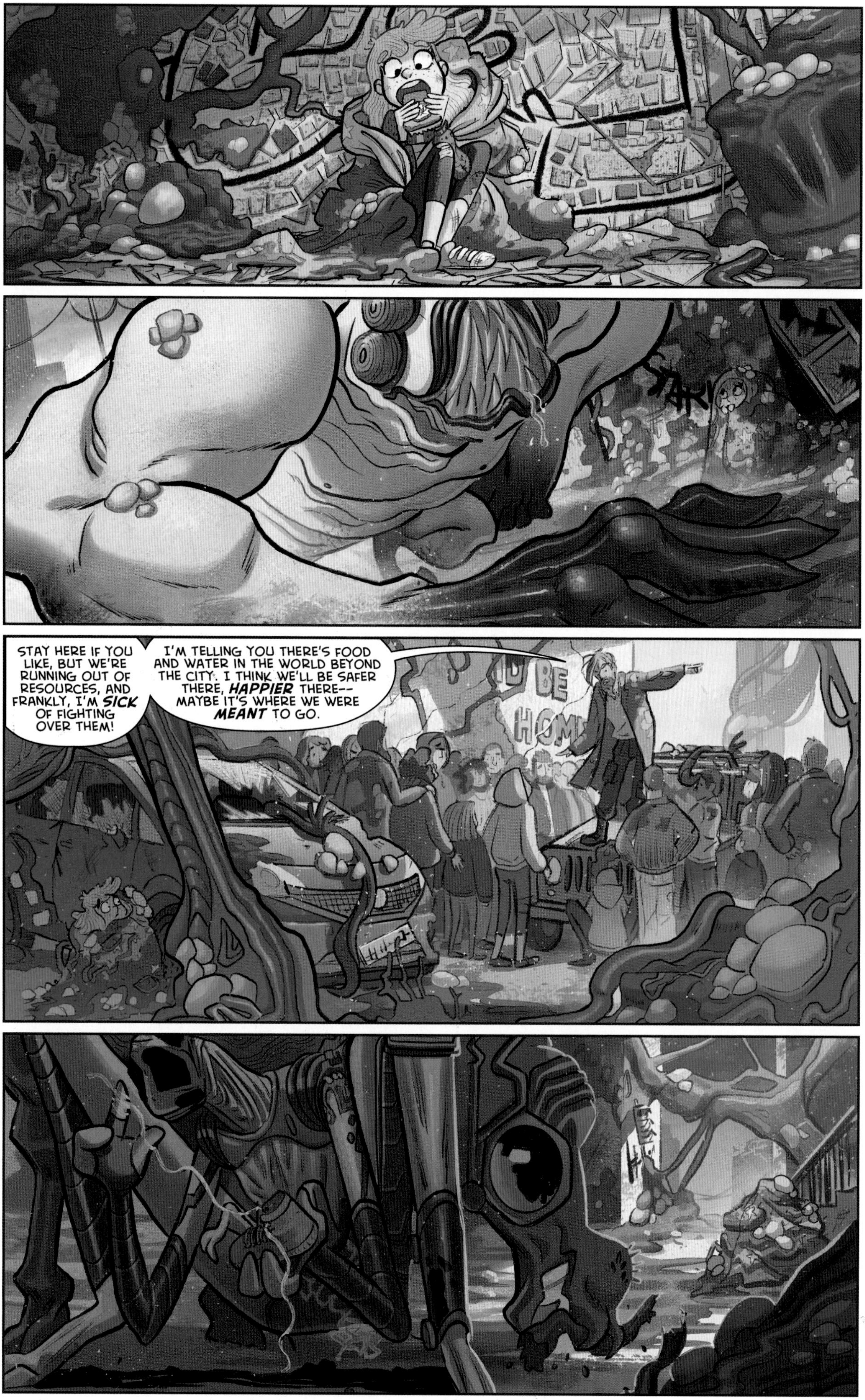
STAY HERE IF YOU LIKE, BUT WE'RE RUNNING OUT OF RESOURCES, AND FRANKLY, I'M SICK OF FIGHTING OVER THEM!
I'M TELLING YOU THERE'S FOOD AND WATER IN THE WORLD BEYOND THE CITY. I THINK WE'LL BE SAFER THERE, HAPPIER THERE-- MAYBE IT'S WHERE WE WERE MEANT TO GO.

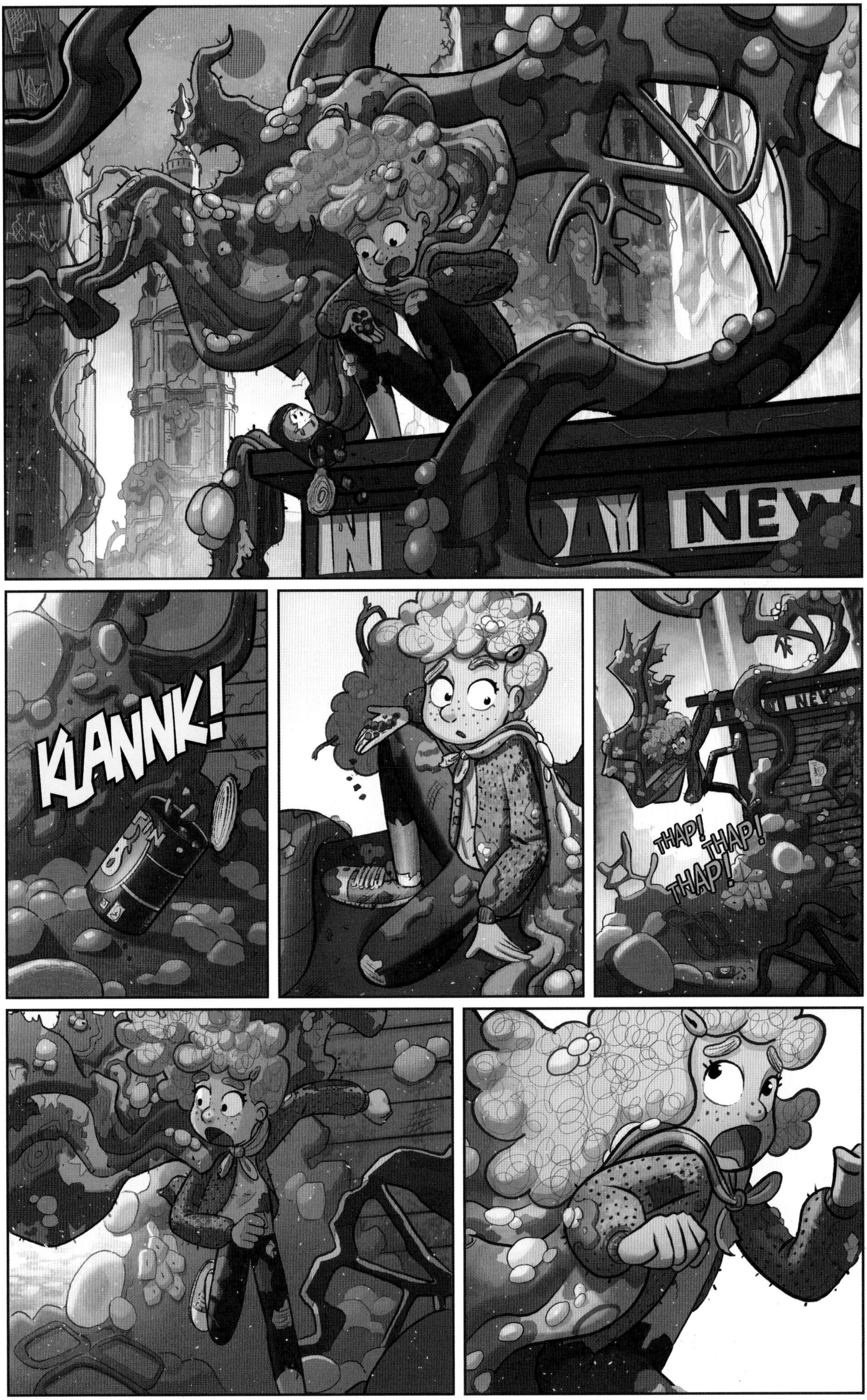
KLANNK!
THAP! THAP! THAP!

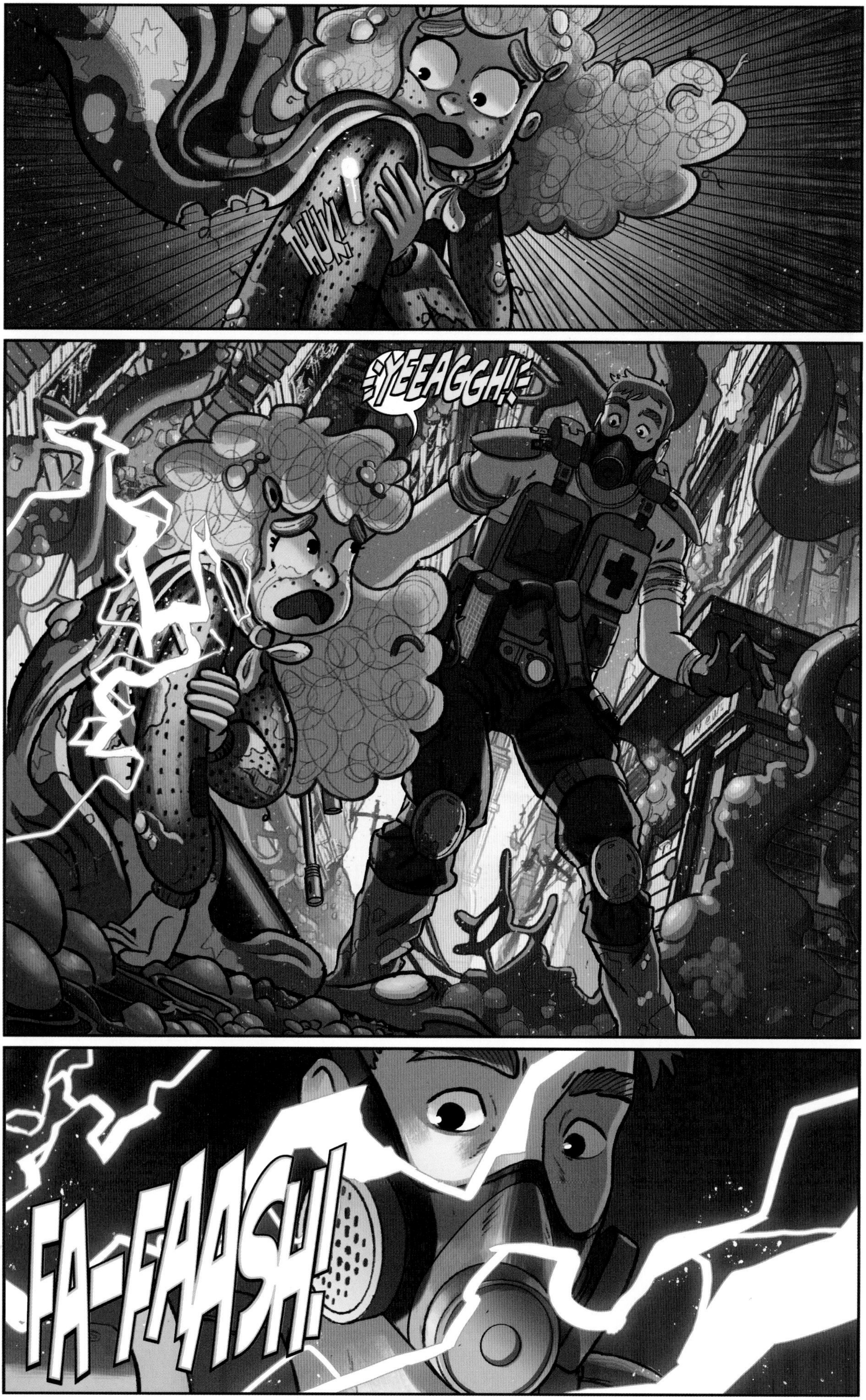
THUK!
YEEAGGH!
FA-FAASH!

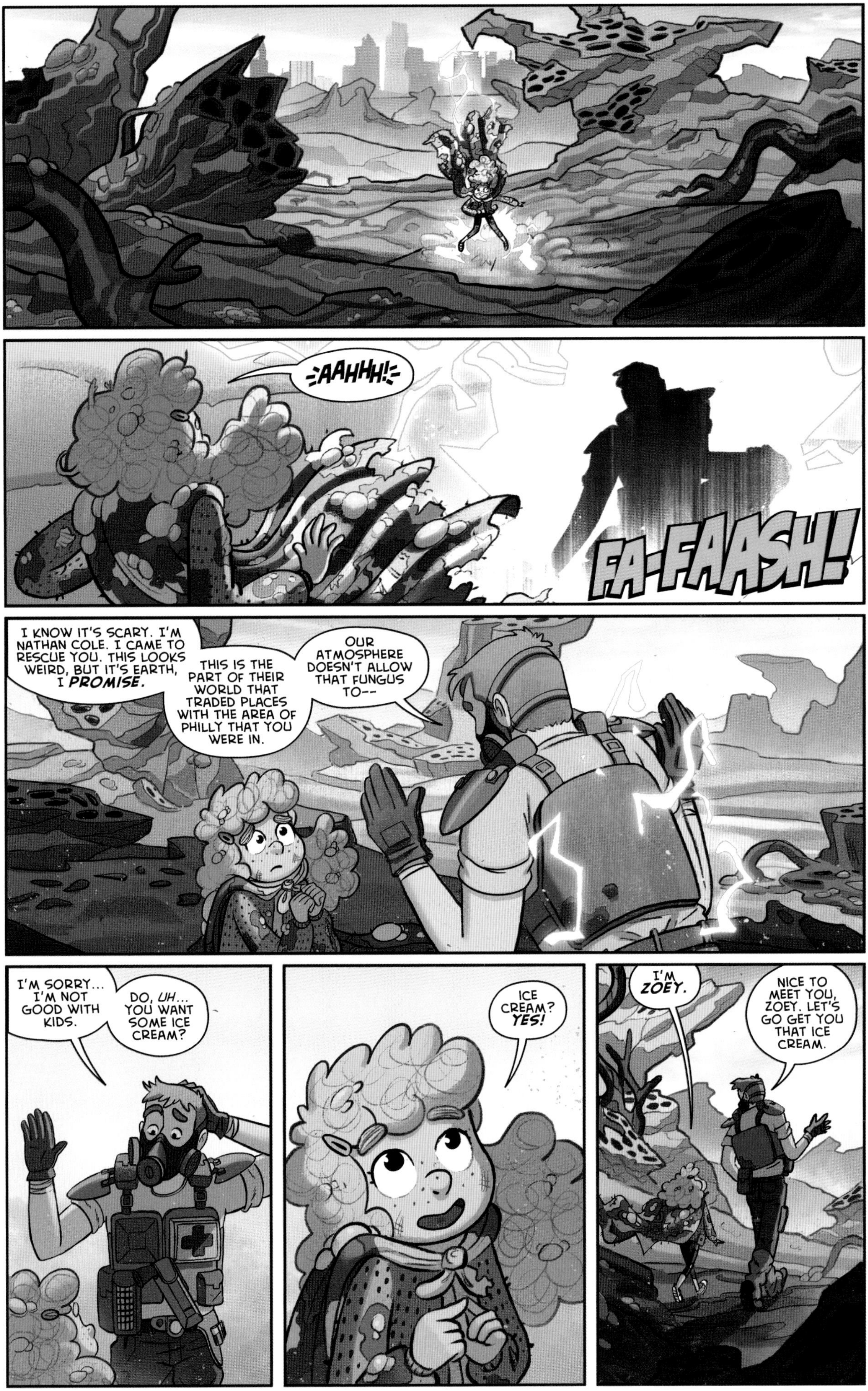

-AAHHH!-
FA-FAASH!
I KNOW IT'S SCARY. I'M NATHAN COLE. I CAME TO RESCUE YOU. THIS LOOKS WEIRD, BUT IT'S EARTH, I PROMISE.
THIS IS THE PART OF THEIR WORLD THAT TRADED PLACES WITH THE AREA OF PHILLY THAT YOU WERE IN.
OUR ATMOSPHERE DOESN'T ALLOW THAT FUNGUS TO--
I'M SORRY... I'M NOT GOOD WITH KIDS.
DO, UH... YOU WANT SOME ICE CREAM?
ICE CREAM? YES!
I'M ZOEY.
NICE TO MEET YOU, ZOEY. LET'S GO GET YOU THAT ICE CREAM.

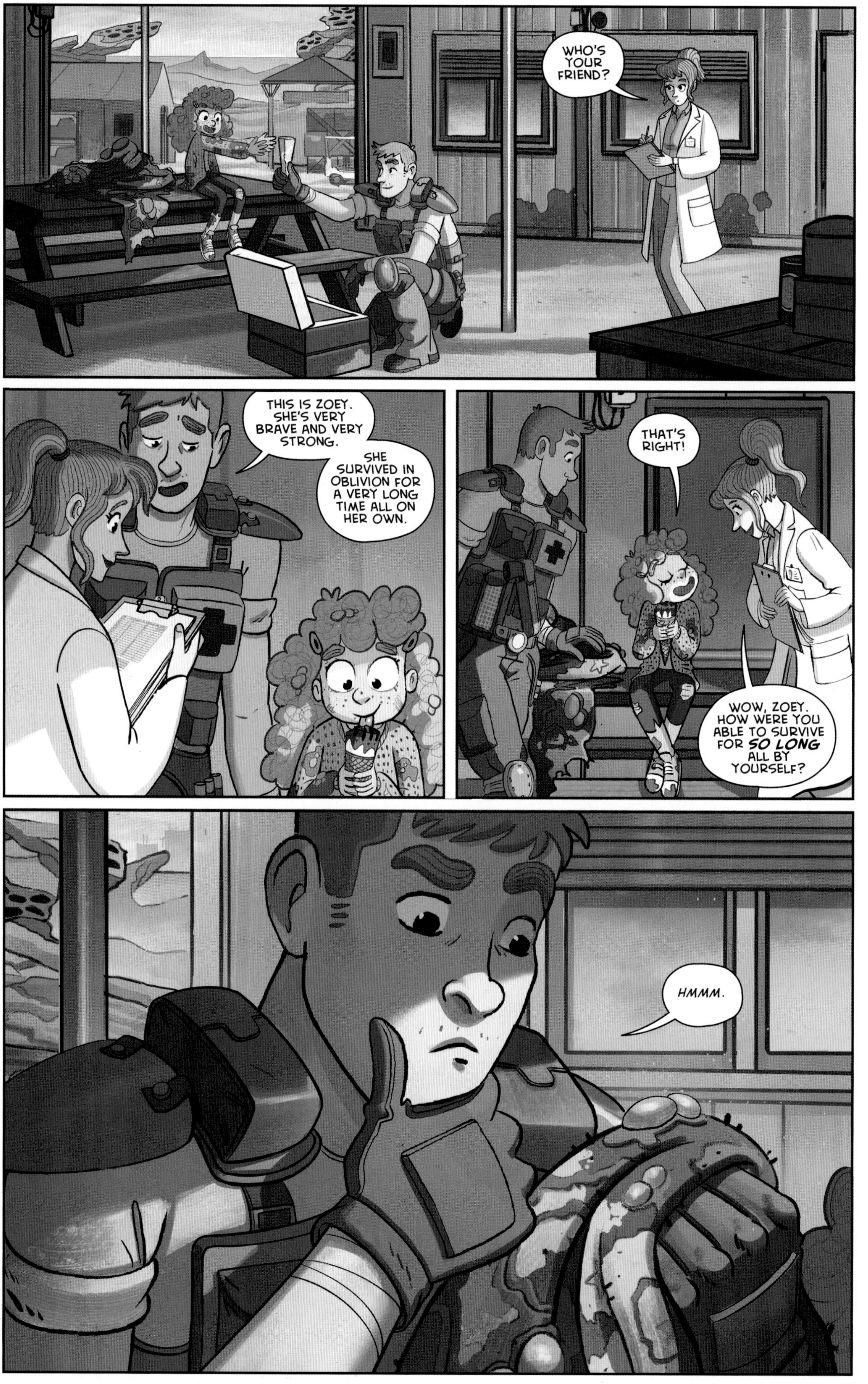
WHO'S YOUR FRIEND?
THIS IS ZOEY. SHE'S VERY BRAVE AND VERY STRONG.
SHE SURVIVED IN OBLIVION FOR A VERY LONG TIME ALL ON HER OWN.
THAT'S RIGHT!
WOW, ZOEY. HOW WERE YOU ABLE TO SURVIVE FOR **SO LONG** ALL BY YOURSELF?
HMMM.

CHAPTER

SIX

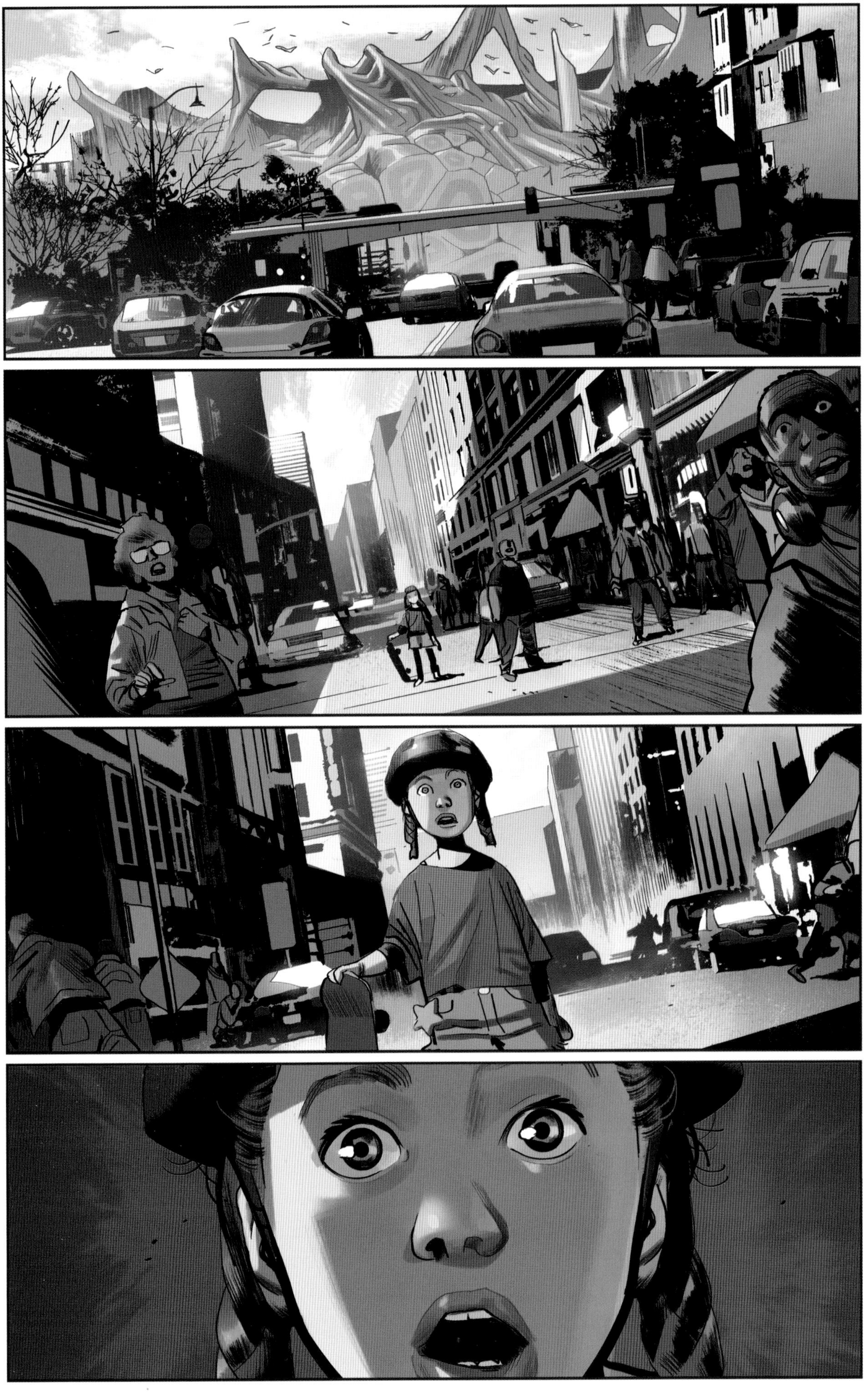

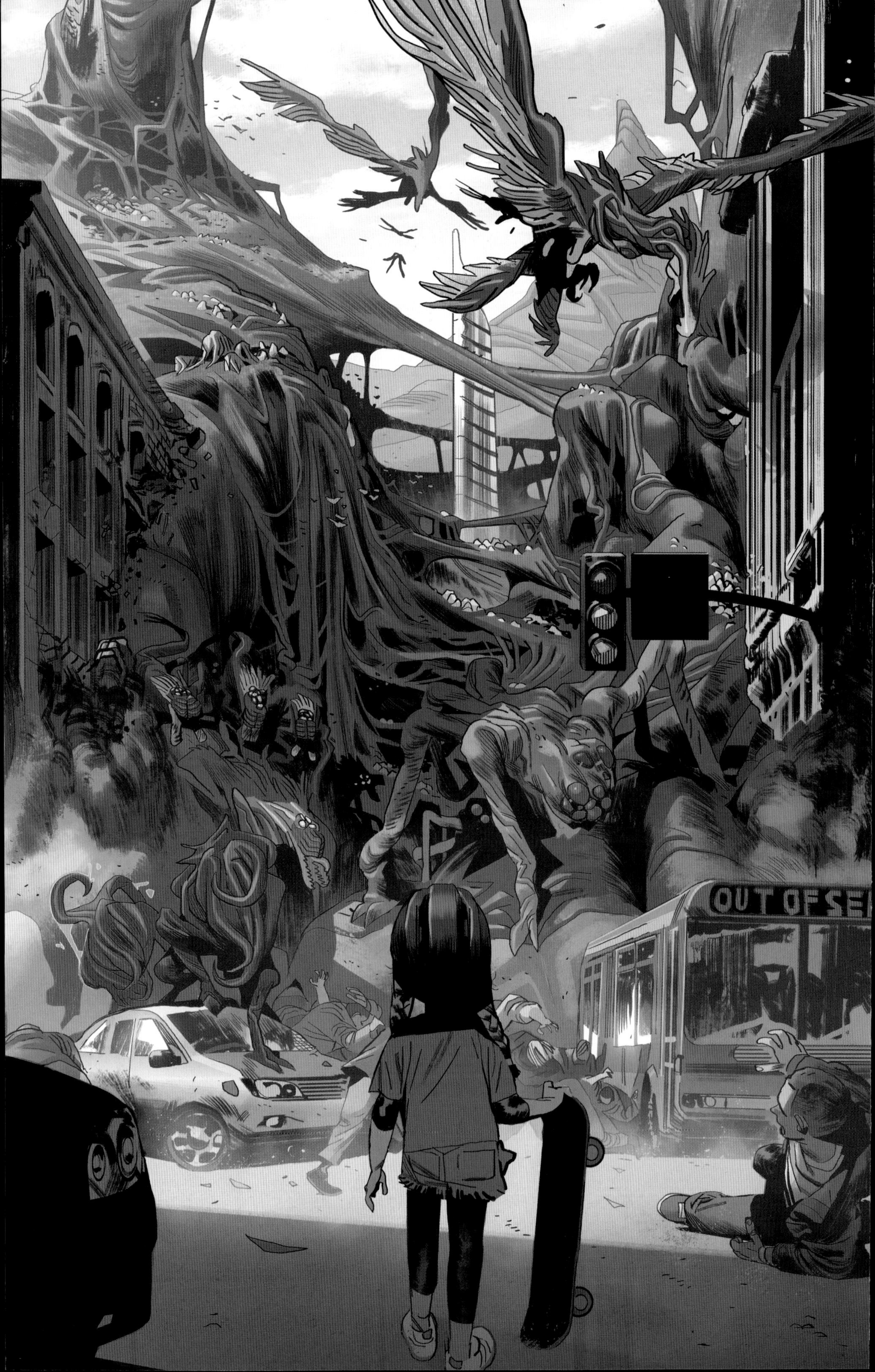

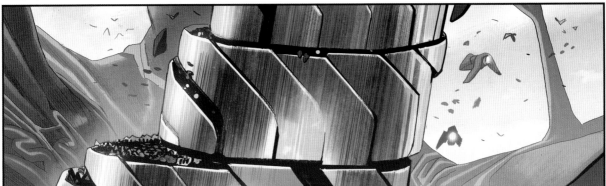

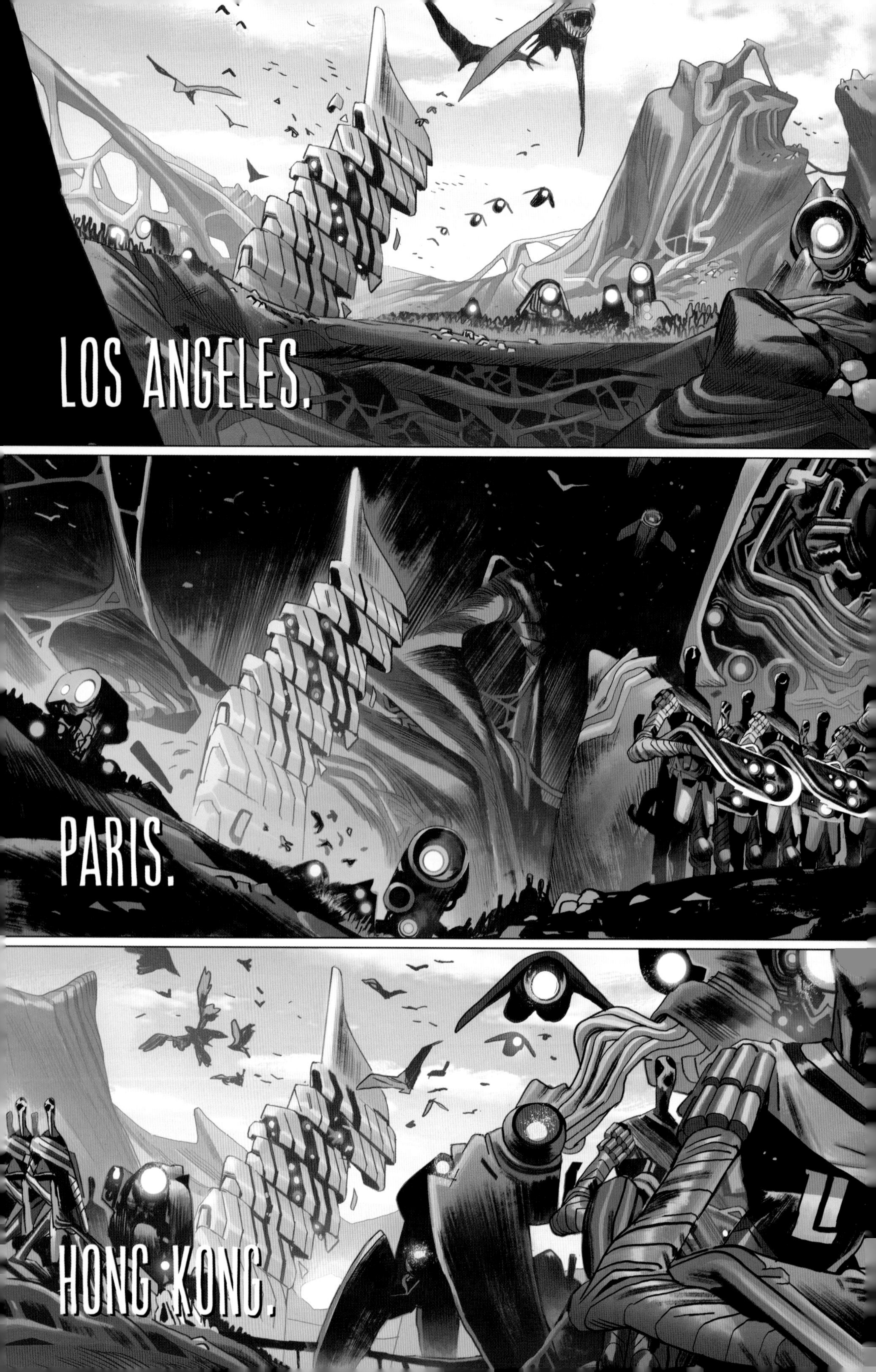
LOS ANGELES.
PARIS.
HONG KONG.

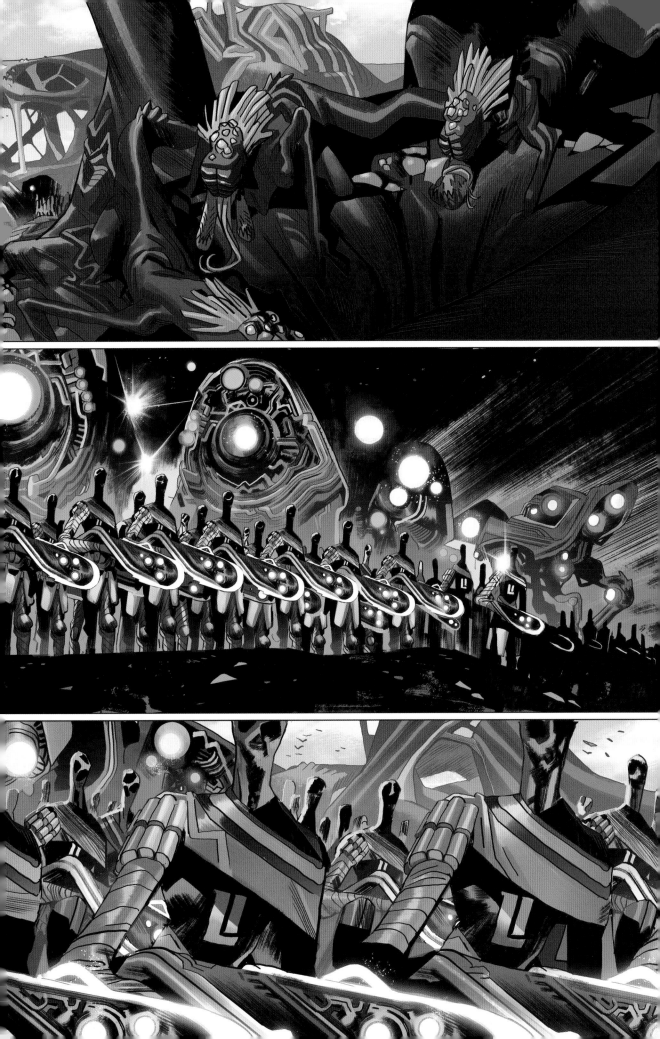

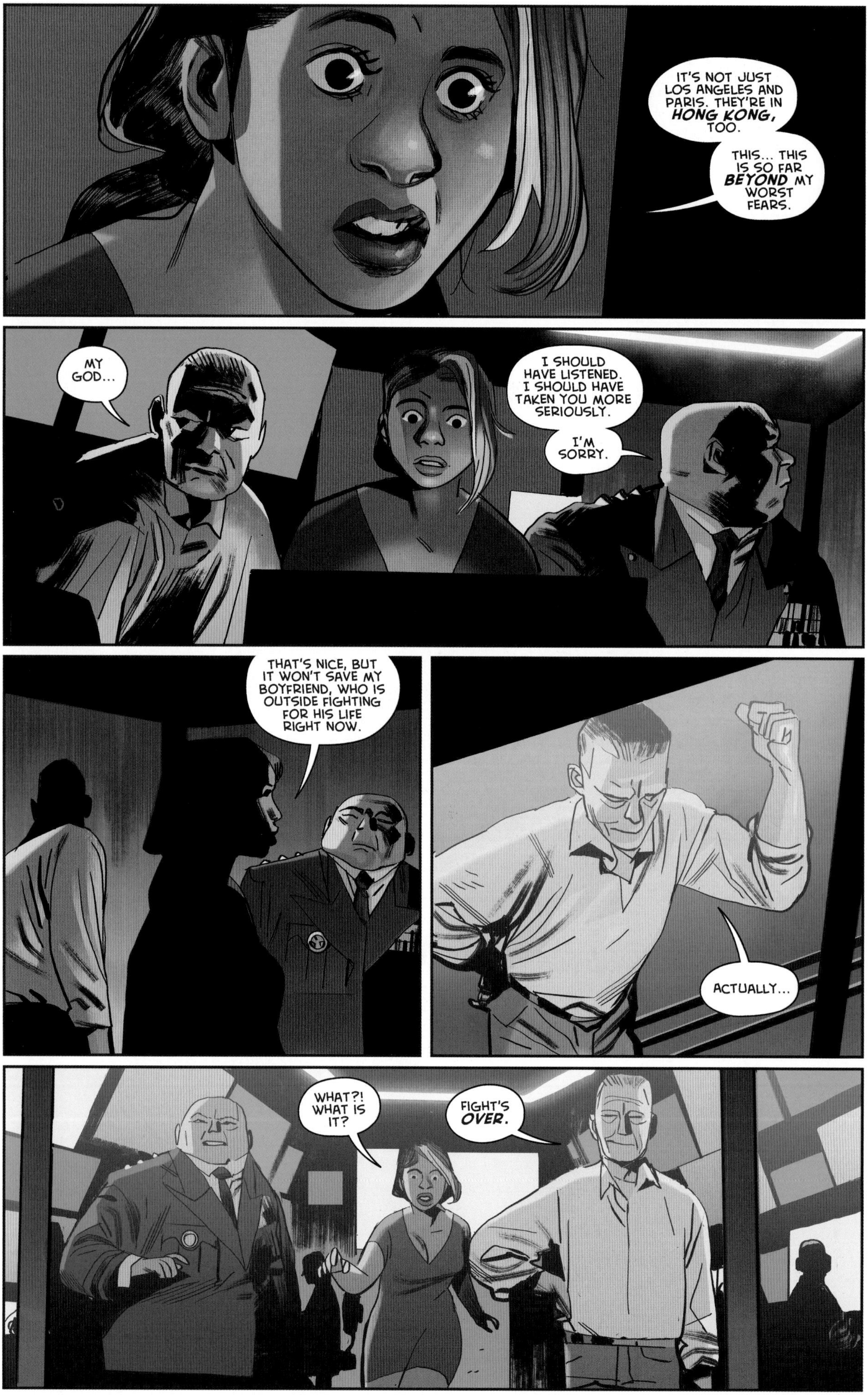
IT'S NOT JUST LOS ANGELES AND PARIS. THEY'RE IN HONG KONG, TOO.
THIS... THIS IS SO FAR BEYOND MY WORST FEARS.
MY GOD...
I SHOULD HAVE LISTENED. I SHOULD HAVE TAKEN YOU MORE SERIOUSLY.
I'M SORRY.
THAT'S NICE, BUT IT WON'T SAVE MY BOYFRIEND, WHO IS OUTSIDE FIGHTING FOR HIS LIFE RIGHT NOW.
ACTUALLY...
WHAT?! WHAT IS IT?
FIGHT'S OVER.

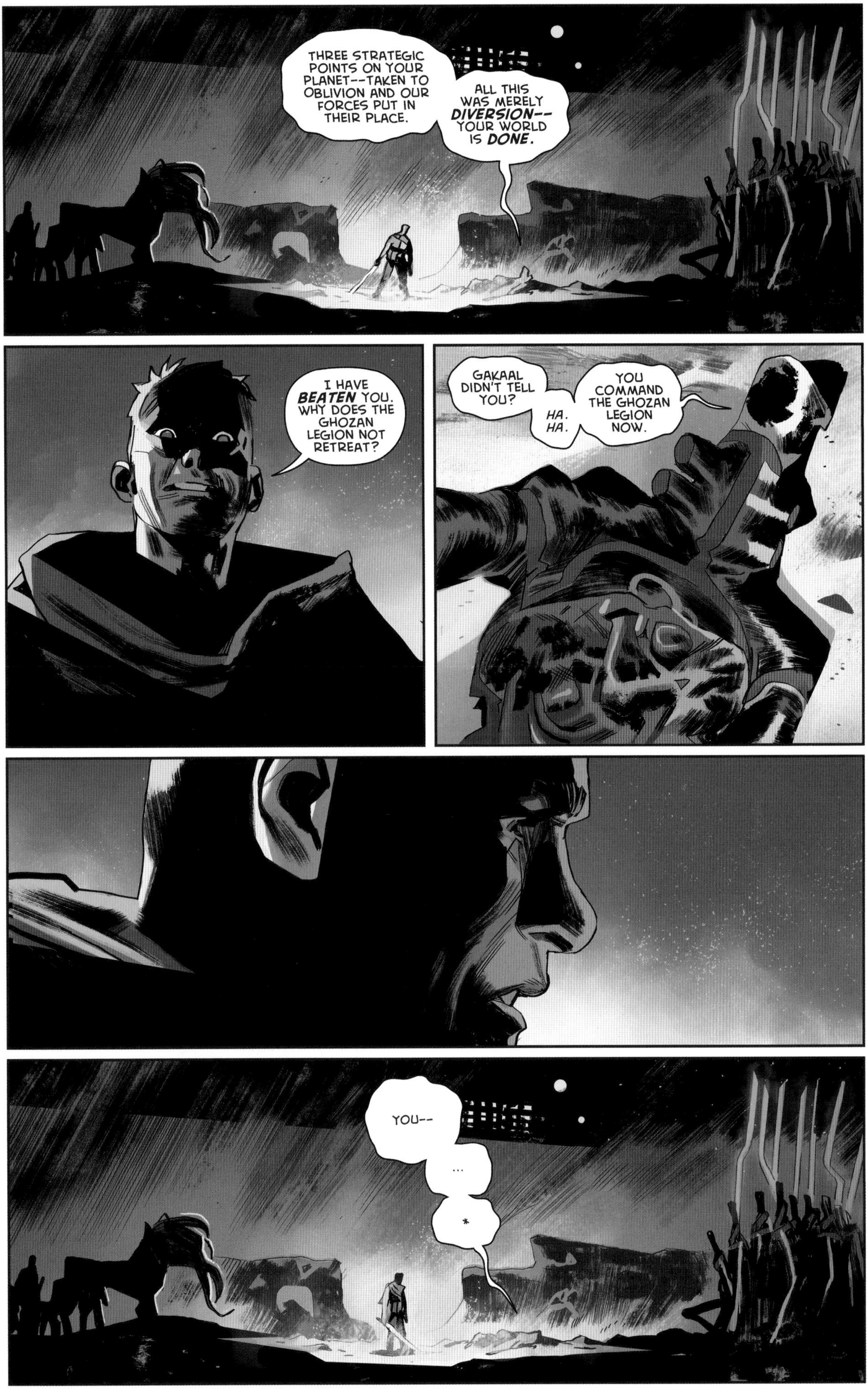
THREE STRATEGIC POINTS ON YOUR PLANET--TAKEN TO OBLIVION AND OUR FORCES PUT IN THEIR PLACE.
ALL THIS WAS MERELY **DIVERSION--** YOUR WORLD IS **DONE.**
I HAVE **BEATEN** YOU. WHY DOES THE GHOZAN LEGION NOT RETREAT?
GAKAAL DIDN'T TELL YOU?
HA. HA.
YOU COMMAND THE GHOZAN LEGION NOW.
YOU--
...
*

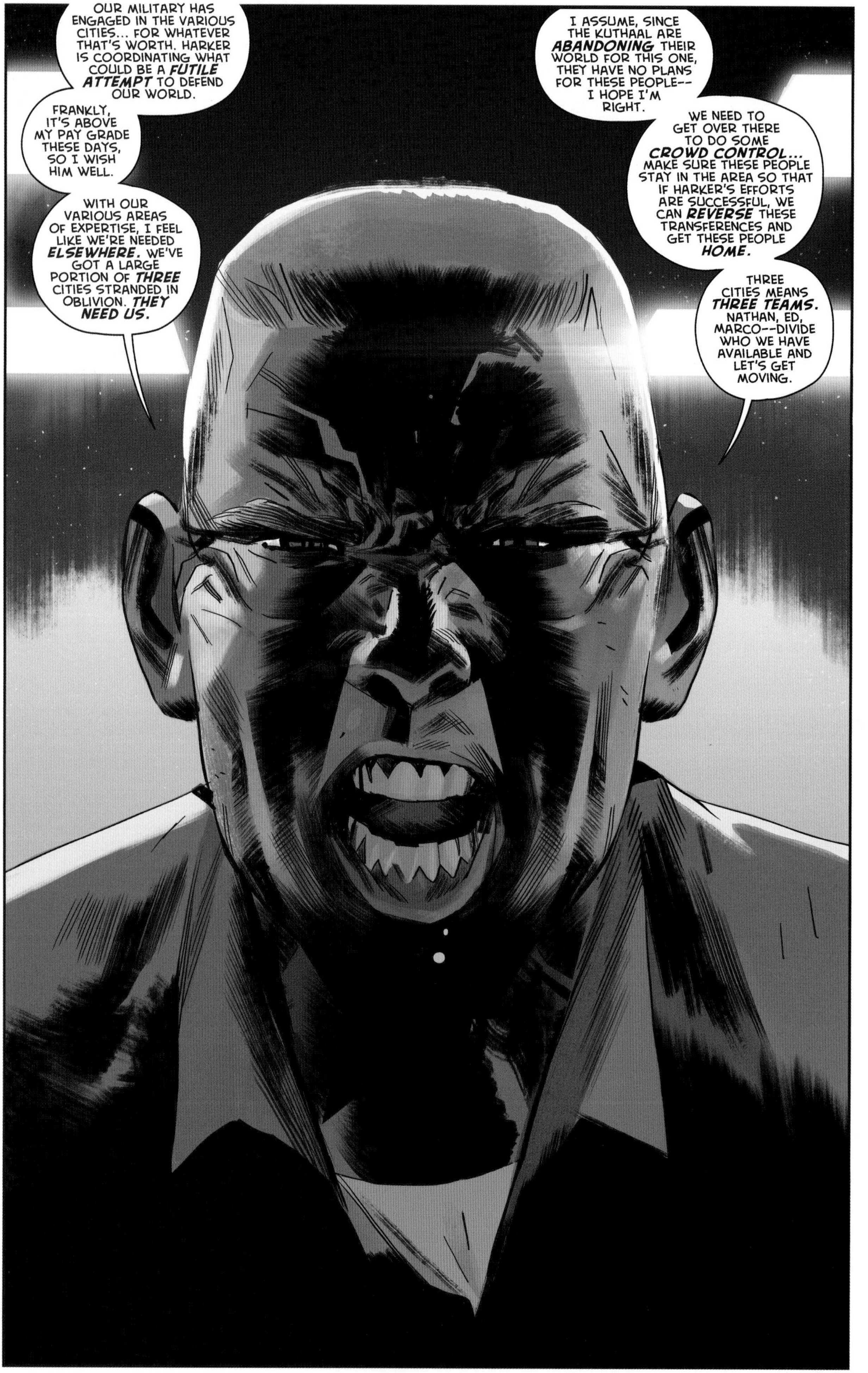
OUR MILITARY HAS ENGAGED IN THE VARIOUS CITIES... FOR WHATEVER THAT'S WORTH. HARKER IS COORDINATING WHAT COULD BE A FUTILE ATTEMPT TO DEFEND OUR WORLD.
FRANKLY, IT'S ABOVE MY PAY GRADE THESE DAYS, SO I WISH HIM WELL.
WITH OUR VARIOUS AREAS OF EXPERTISE, I FEEL LIKE WE'RE NEEDED ELSEWHERE. WE'VE GOT A LARGE PORTION OF THREE CITIES STRANDED IN OBLIVION. THEY NEED US.
I ASSUME, SINCE THE KUTHAAL ARE ABANDONING THEIR WORLD FOR THIS ONE, THEY HAVE NO PLANS FOR THESE PEOPLE-- I HOPE I'M RIGHT.
WE NEED TO GET OVER THERE TO DO SOME CROWD CONTROL... MAKE SURE THESE PEOPLE STAY IN THE AREA SO THAT IF HARKER'S EFFORTS ARE SUCCESSFUL, WE CAN REVERSE THESE TRANSFERENCES AND GET THESE PEOPLE HOME.
THREE CITIES MEANS THREE TEAMS. NATHAN, ED, MARCO--DIVIDE WHO WE HAVE AVAILABLE AND LET'S GET MOVING.

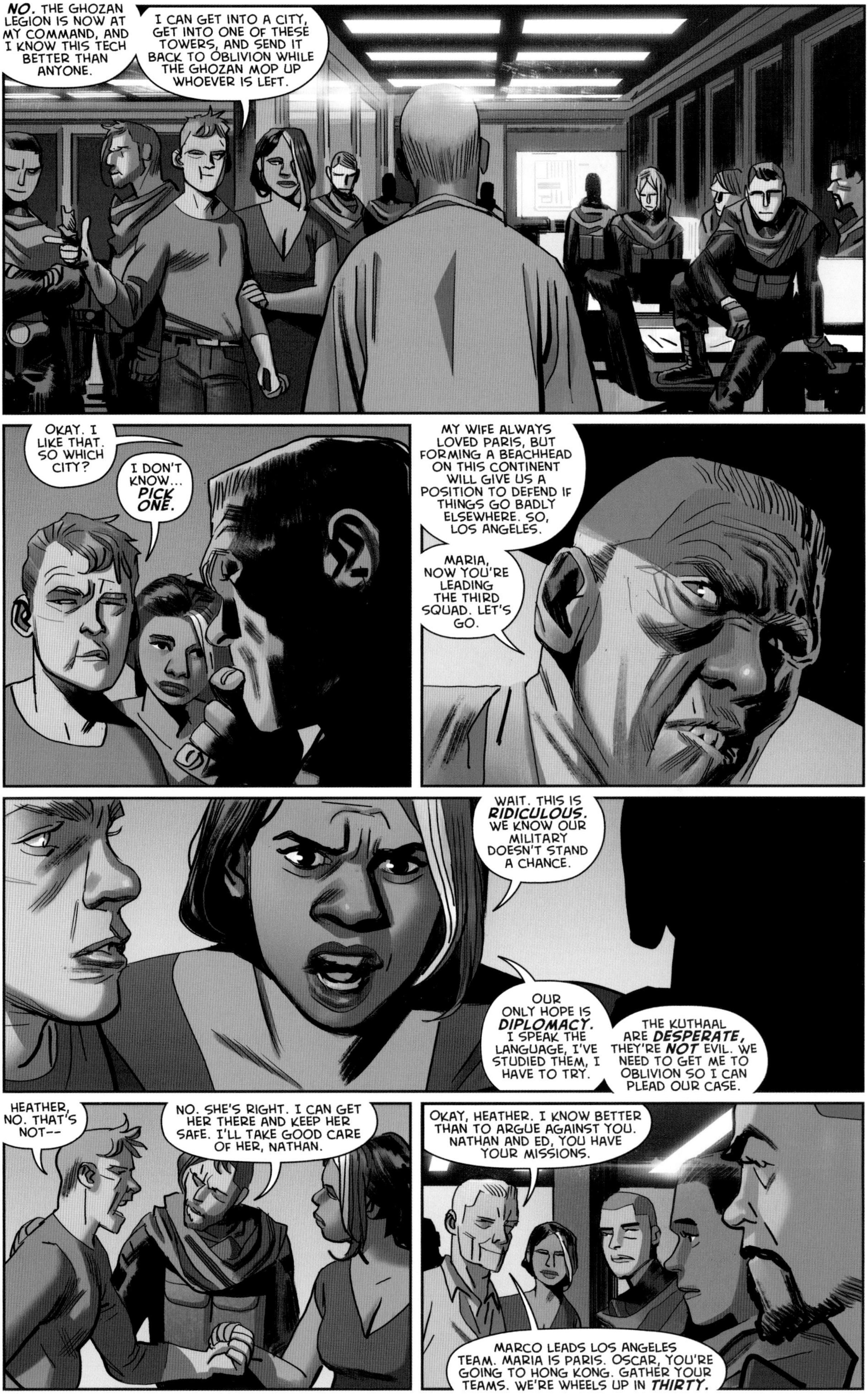
NO. THE GHOZAN LEGION IS NOW AT MY COMMAND, AND I KNOW THIS TECH BETTER THAN ANYONE.
I CAN GET INTO A CITY, GET INTO ONE OF THESE TOWERS, AND SEND IT BACK TO OBLIVION WHILE THE GHOZAN MOP UP WHOEVER IS LEFT.
OKAY. I LIKE THAT. SO WHICH CITY?
I DON'T KNOW... PICK ONE.
MY WIFE ALWAYS LOVED PARIS, BUT FORMING A BEACHHEAD ON THIS CONTINENT WILL GIVE US A POSITION TO DEFEND IF THINGS GO BADLY ELSEWHERE. SO, LOS ANGELES.
MARIA, NOW YOU'RE LEADING THE THIRD SQUAD. LET'S GO.
WAIT. THIS IS RIDICULOUS. WE KNOW OUR MILITARY DOESN'T STAND A CHANCE.
OUR ONLY HOPE IS DIPLOMACY. I SPEAK THE LANGUAGE, I'VE STUDIED THEM, I HAVE TO TRY.
THE KUTHAAL ARE DESPERATE, THEY'RE NOT EVIL. WE NEED TO GET ME TO OBLIVION SO I CAN PLEAD OUR CASE.
HEATHER, NO. THAT'S NOT--
NO. SHE'S RIGHT. I CAN GET HER THERE AND KEEP HER SAFE. I'LL TAKE GOOD CARE OF HER, NATHAN.
OKAY, HEATHER. I KNOW BETTER THAN TO ARGUE AGAINST YOU. NATHAN AND ED, YOU HAVE YOUR MISSIONS.
MARCO LEADS LOS ANGELES TEAM. MARIA IS PARIS. OSCAR, YOU'RE GOING TO HONG KONG. GATHER YOUR TEAMS. WE'RE WHEELS UP IN THIRTY.

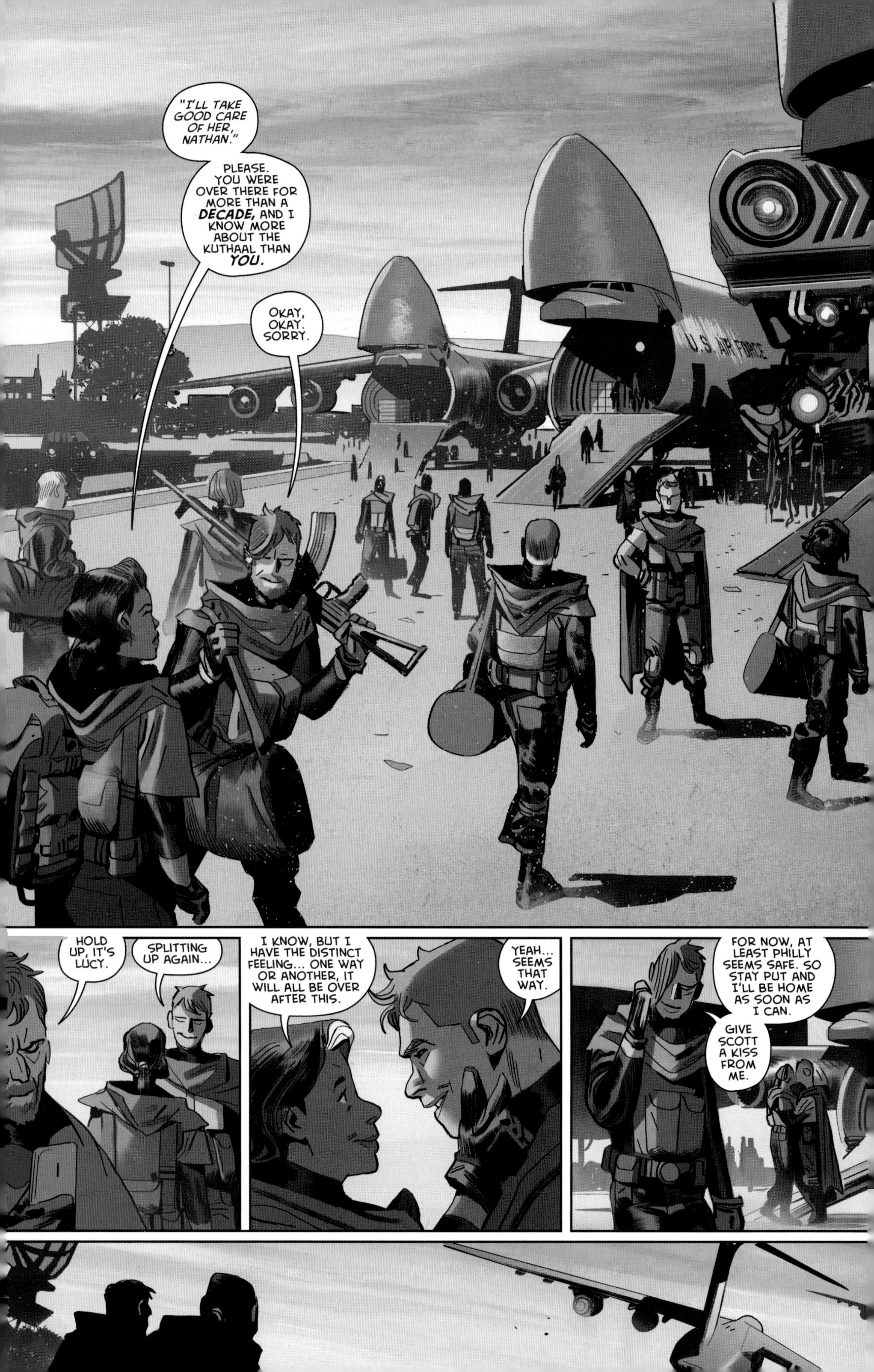
"I'LL TAKE GOOD CARE OF HER, NATHAN."
PLEASE. YOU WERE OVER THERE FOR MORE THAN A **DECADE,** AND I KNOW MORE ABOUT THE KUTHAAL THAN **YOU.**
OKAY, OKAY. SORRY.
U.S. AIR FORCE
HOLD UP, IT'S LUCY.
SPLITTING UP AGAIN...
I KNOW, BUT I HAVE THE DISTINCT FEELING... ONE WAY OR ANOTHER, IT WILL ALL BE OVER AFTER THIS.
YEAH... SEEMS THAT WAY.
FOR NOW, AT LEAST PHILLY SEEMS SAFE. SO STAY PUT AND I'LL BE HOME AS SOON AS I CAN.
GIVE SCOTT A KISS FROM ME.

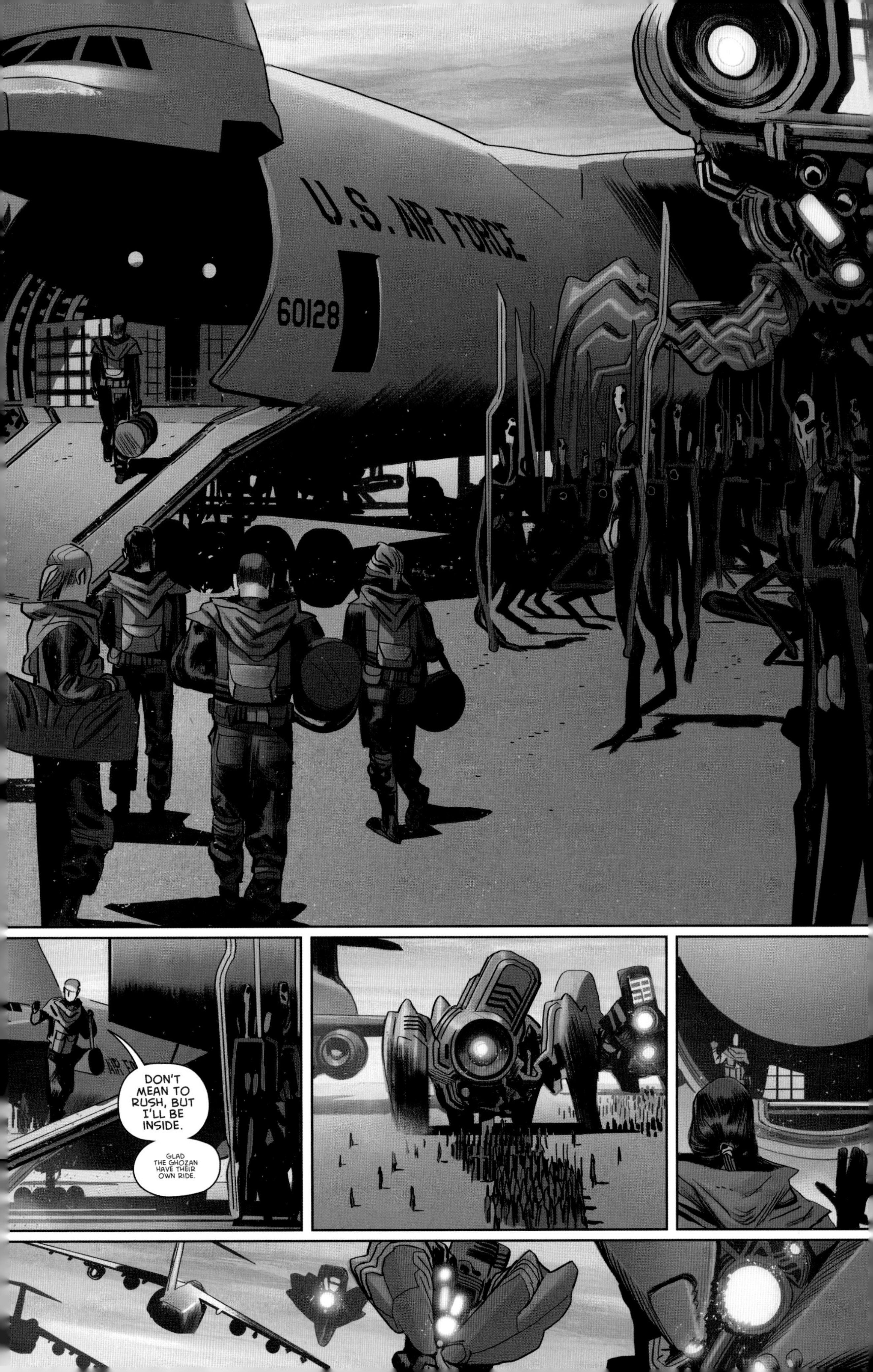
U.S. AIR FORCE
60128
DON'T MEAN TO RUSH, BUT I'LL BE INSIDE.
GLAD THE GHOZAN HAVE THEIR OWN RIDE.

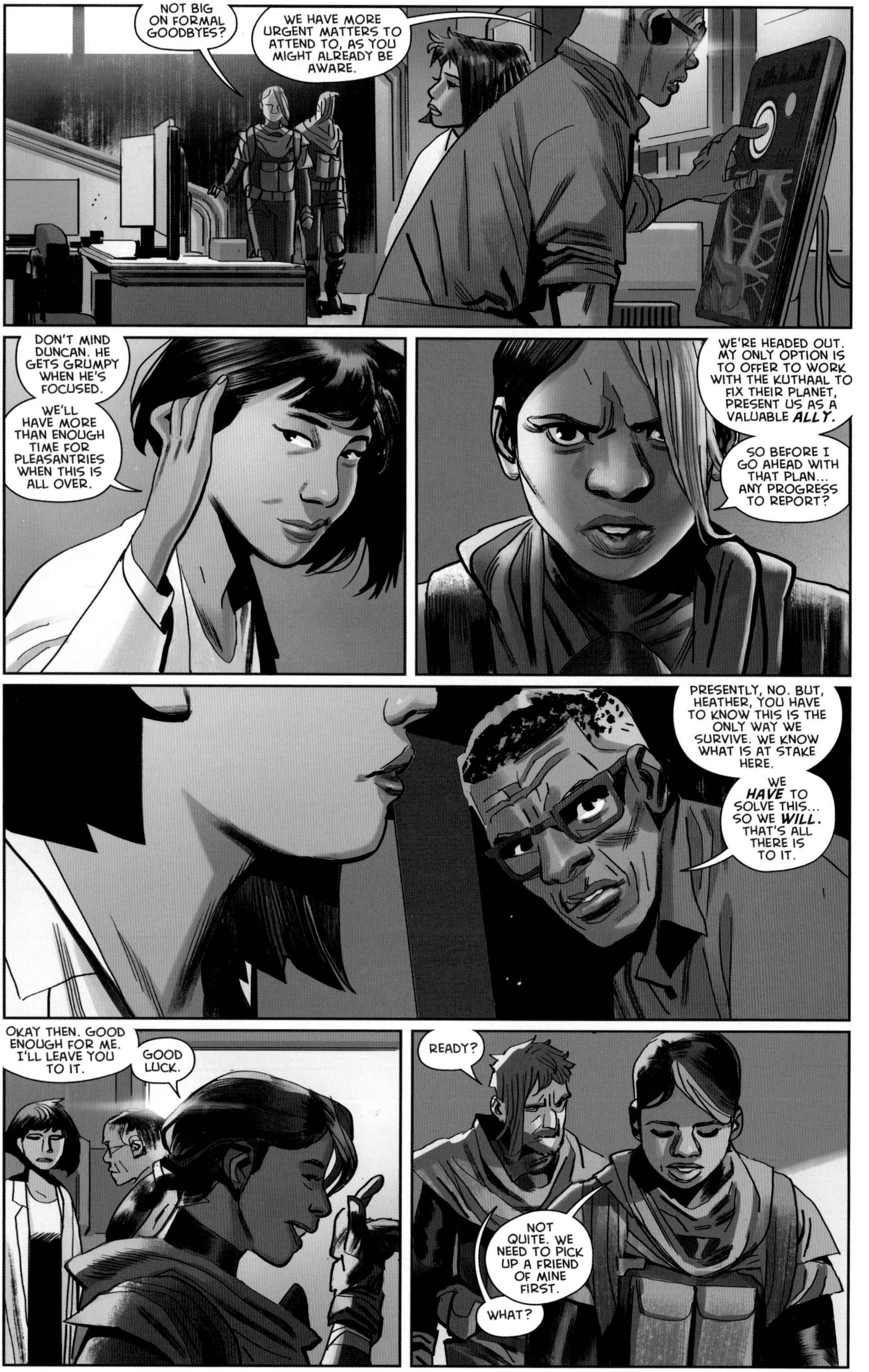
NOT BIG ON FORMAL GOODBYES?
WE HAVE MORE URGENT MATTERS TO ATTEND TO, AS YOU MIGHT ALREADY BE AWARE.
DON'T MIND DUNCAN. HE GETS GRUMPY WHEN HE'S FOCUSED.
WE'LL HAVE MORE THAN ENOUGH TIME FOR PLEASANTRIES WHEN THIS IS ALL OVER.
WE'RE HEADED OUT. MY ONLY OPTION IS TO OFFER TO WORK WITH THE KUTHAAL TO FIX THEIR PLANET, PRESENT US AS A VALUABLE ALLY.
SO BEFORE I GO AHEAD WITH THAT PLAN... ANY PROGRESS TO REPORT?
PRESENTLY, NO. BUT, HEATHER, YOU HAVE TO KNOW THIS IS THE ONLY WAY WE SURVIVE. WE KNOW WHAT IS AT STAKE HERE.
WE HAVE TO SOLVE THIS... SO WE WILL. THAT'S ALL THERE IS TO IT.
OKAY THEN. GOOD ENOUGH FOR ME. I'LL LEAVE YOU TO IT.
GOOD LUCK.
READY?
NOT QUITE. WE NEED TO PICK UP A FRIEND OF MINE FIRST.
WHAT?

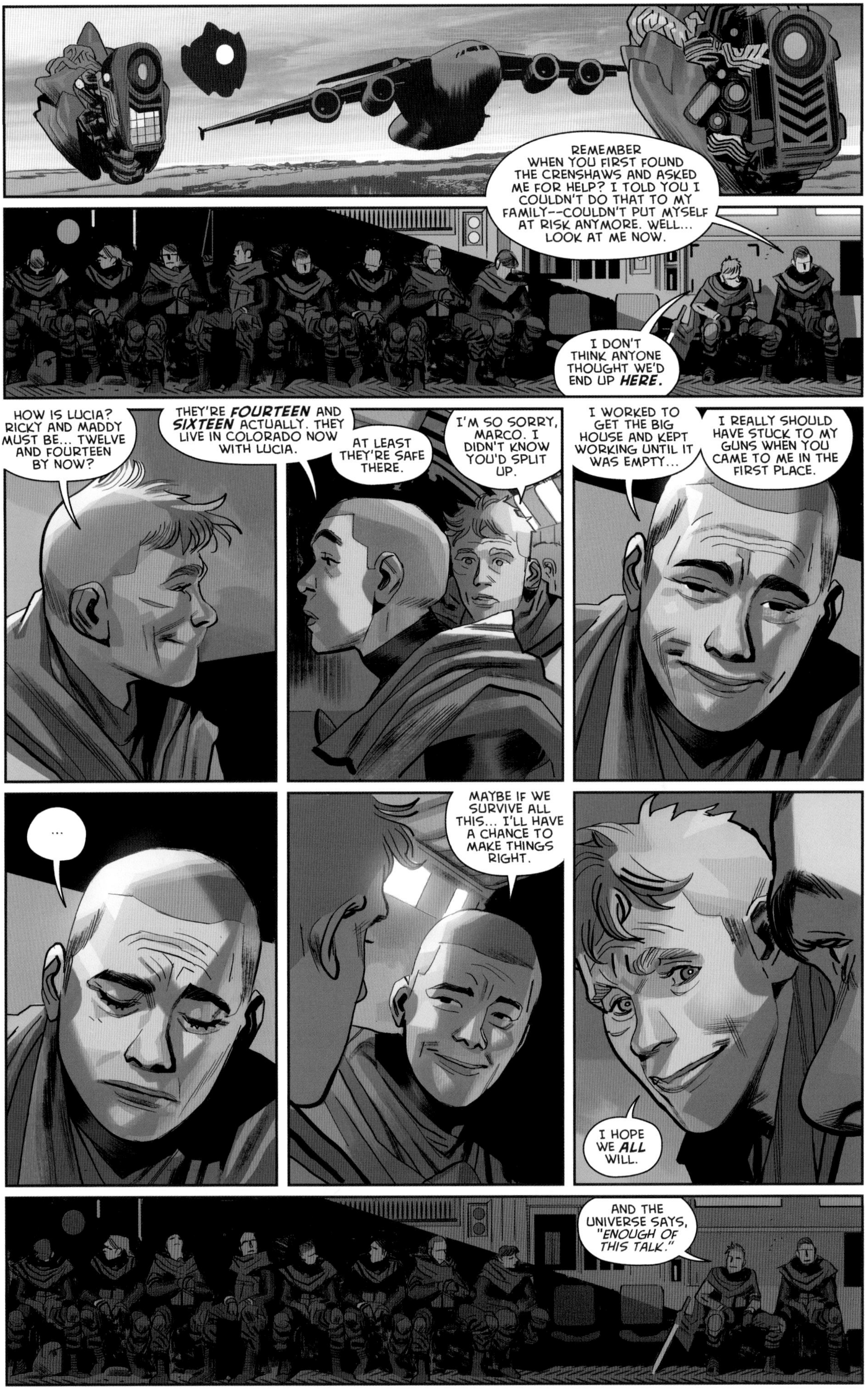
REMEMBER WHEN YOU FIRST FOUND THE CRENSHAWS AND ASKED ME FOR HELP? I TOLD YOU I COULDN'T DO THAT TO MY FAMILY--COULDN'T PUT MYSELF AT RISK ANYMORE. WELL... LOOK AT ME NOW.
I DON'T THINK ANYONE THOUGHT WE'D END UP *HERE*.
HOW IS LUCIA? RICKY AND MADDY MUST BE... TWELVE AND FOURTEEN BY NOW?
THEY'RE *FOURTEEN* AND *SIXTEEN* ACTUALLY. THEY LIVE IN COLORADO NOW WITH LUCIA.
AT LEAST THEY'RE SAFE THERE.
I'M SO SORRY, MARCO. I DIDN'T KNOW YOU'D SPLIT UP.
I WORKED TO GET THE BIG HOUSE AND KEPT WORKING UNTIL IT WAS EMPTY...
I REALLY SHOULD HAVE STUCK TO MY GUNS WHEN YOU CAME TO ME IN THE FIRST PLACE.
...
MAYBE IF WE SURVIVE ALL THIS... I'LL HAVE A CHANCE TO MAKE THINGS RIGHT.
I HOPE WE *ALL* WILL.
AND THE UNIVERSE SAYS, *"ENOUGH OF THIS TALK."*

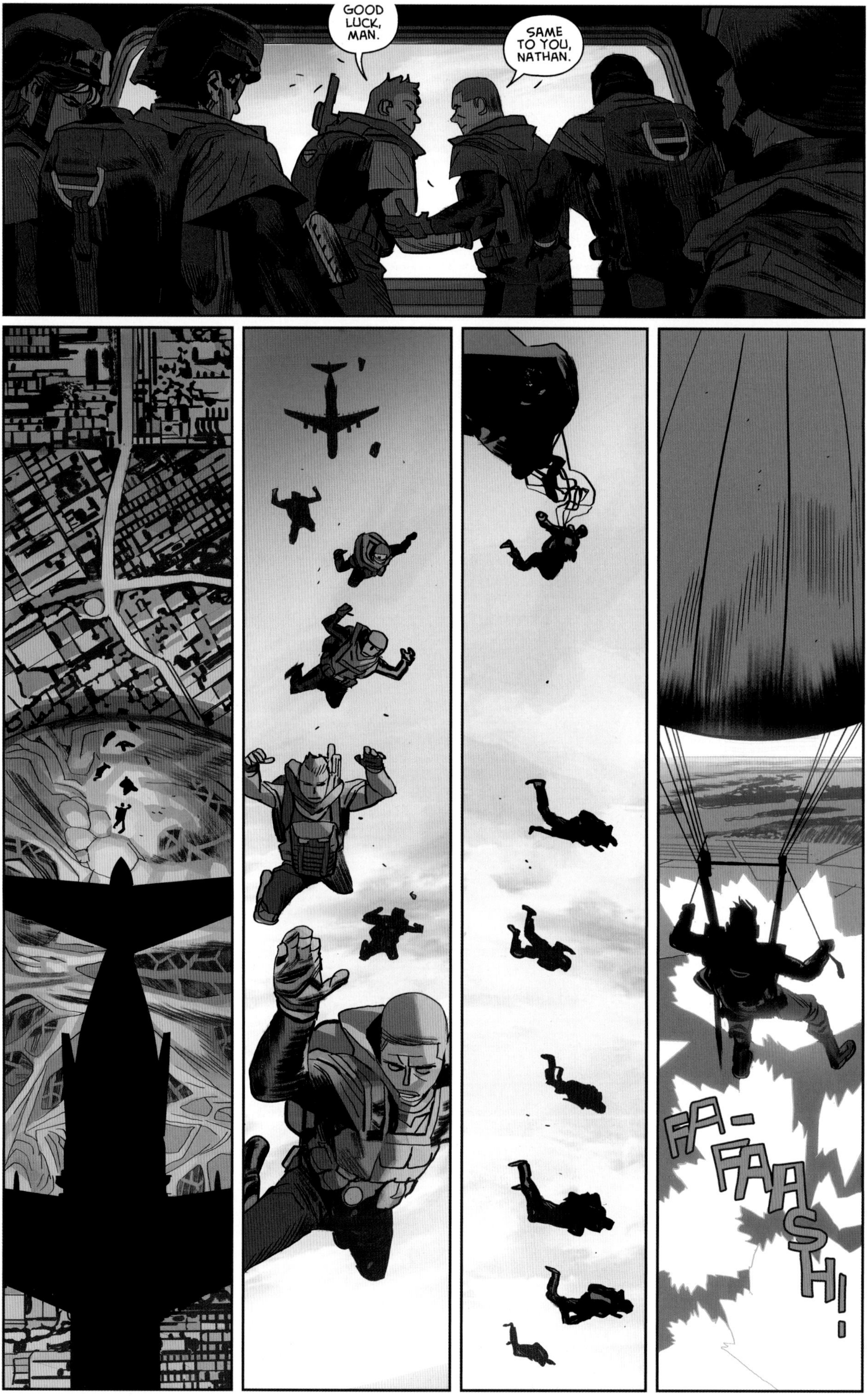
GOOD LUCK, MAN.
SAME TO YOU, NATHAN.
FA-FAAASH!!

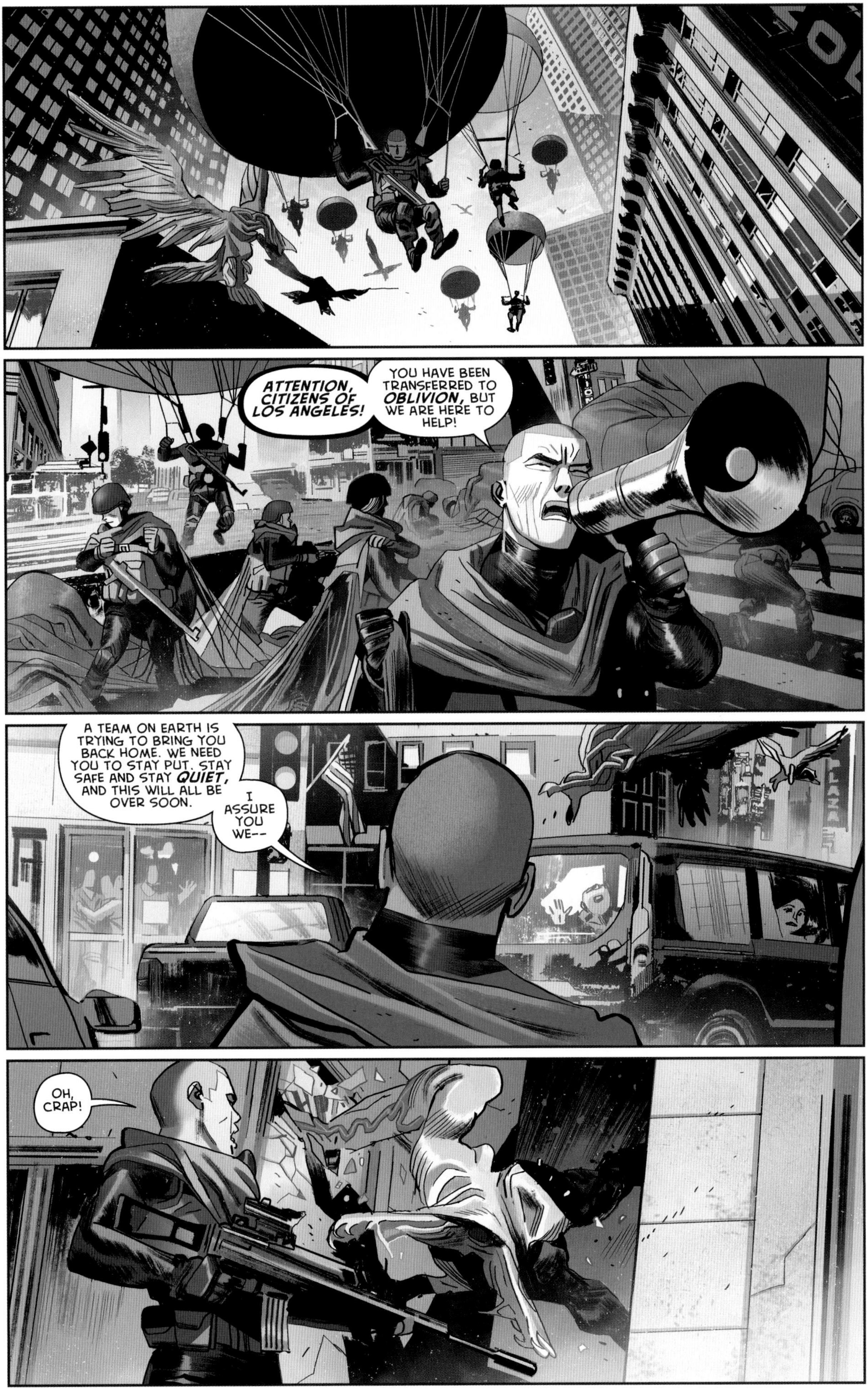
ATTENTION, CITIZENS OF LOS ANGELES!
YOU HAVE BEEN TRANSFERRED TO OBLIVION, BUT WE ARE HERE TO HELP!
A TEAM ON EARTH IS TRYING TO BRING YOU BACK HOME. WE NEED YOU TO STAY PUT. STAY SAFE AND STAY QUIET, AND THIS WILL ALL BE OVER SOON.
I ASSURE YOU WE--
OH, CRAP!

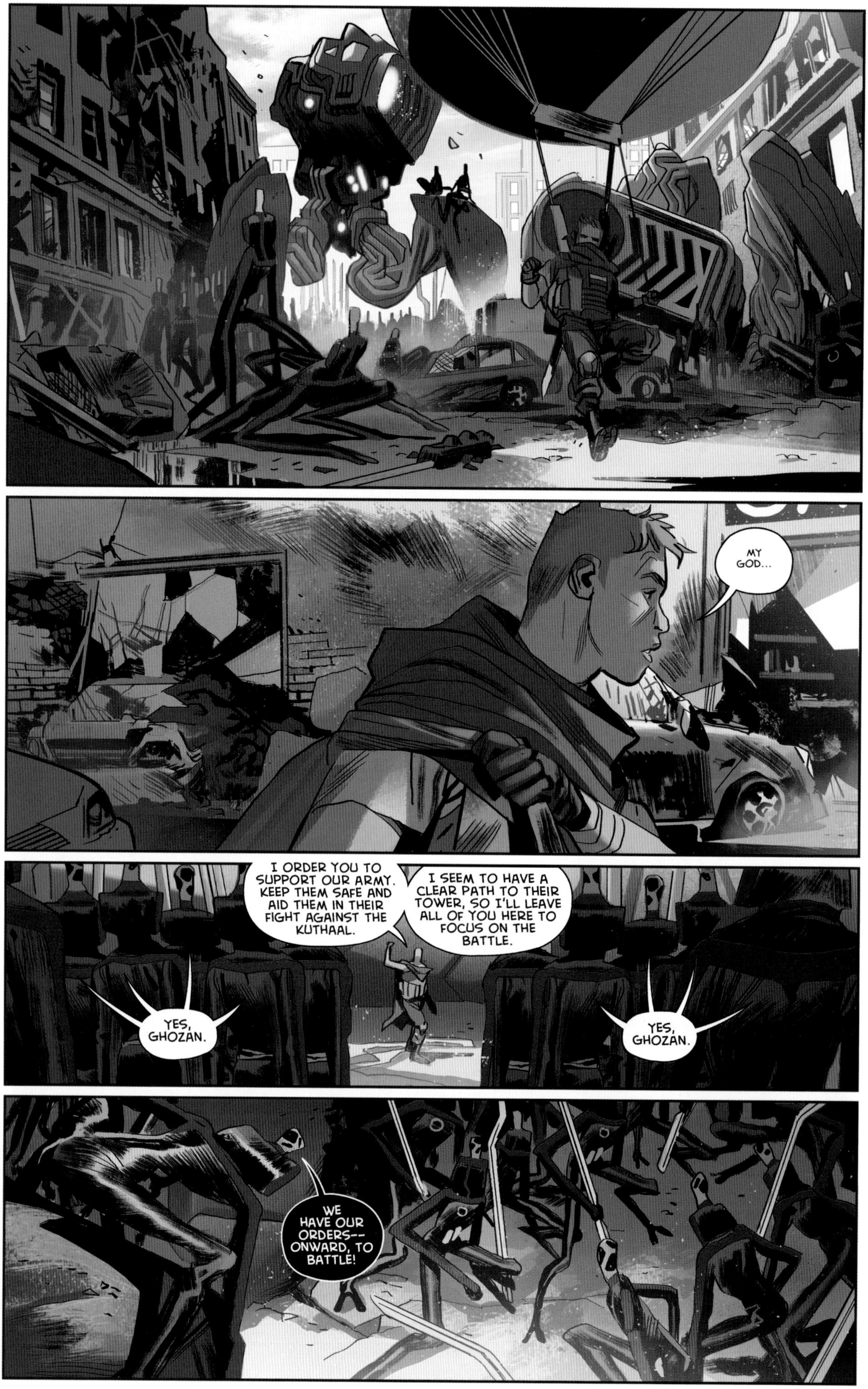

MY GOD...
I ORDER YOU TO SUPPORT OUR ARMY. KEEP THEM SAFE AND AID THEM IN THEIR FIGHT AGAINST THE KUTHAAL.
I SEEM TO HAVE A CLEAR PATH TO THEIR TOWER, SO I'LL LEAVE ALL OF YOU HERE TO FOCUS ON THE BATTLE.
YES, GHOZAN.
YES, GHOZAN.
WE HAVE OUR ORDERS-- ONWARD, TO BATTLE!

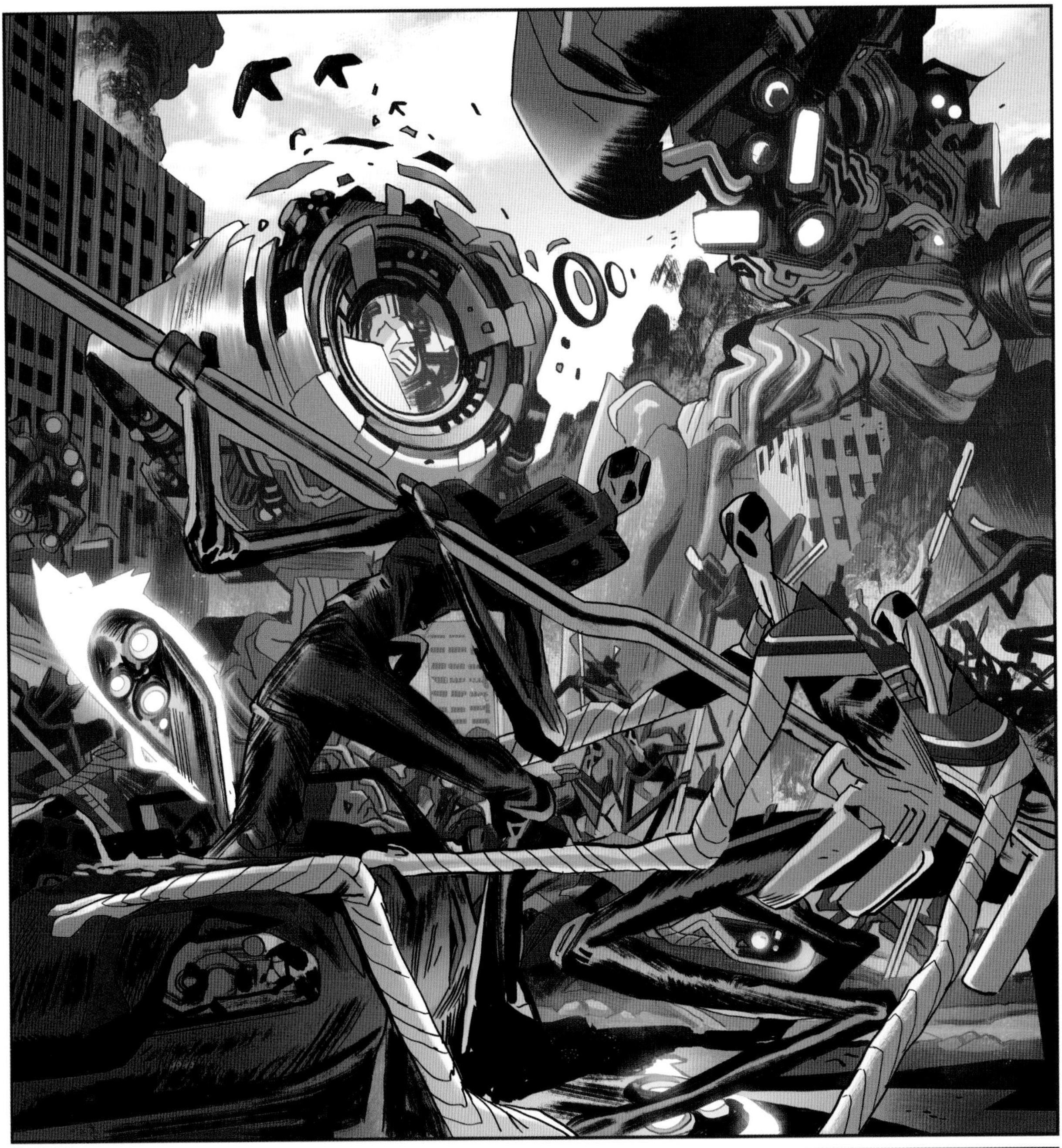

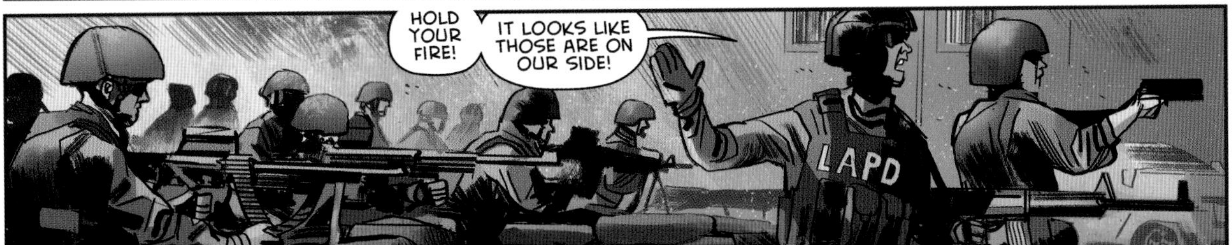
HOLD YOUR FIRE!
IT LOOKS LIKE THOSE ARE ON OUR SIDE!
LAPD

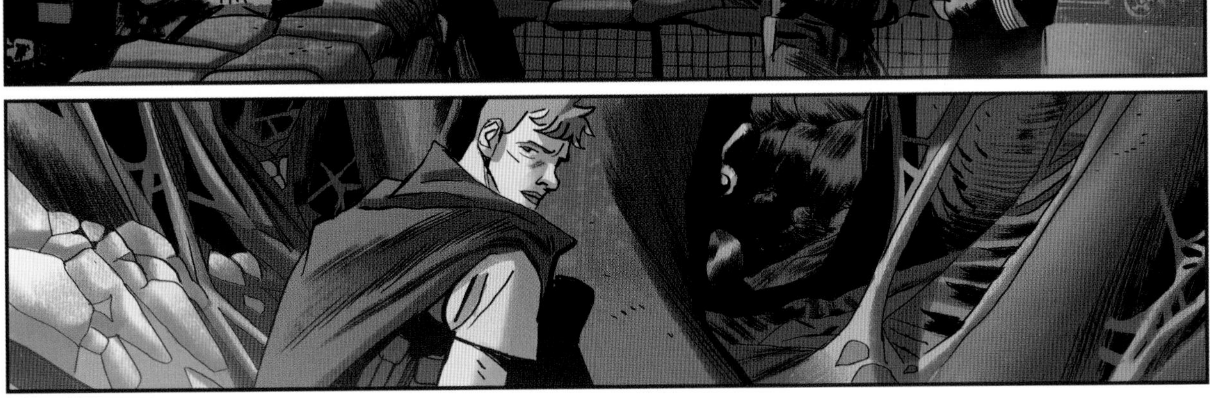

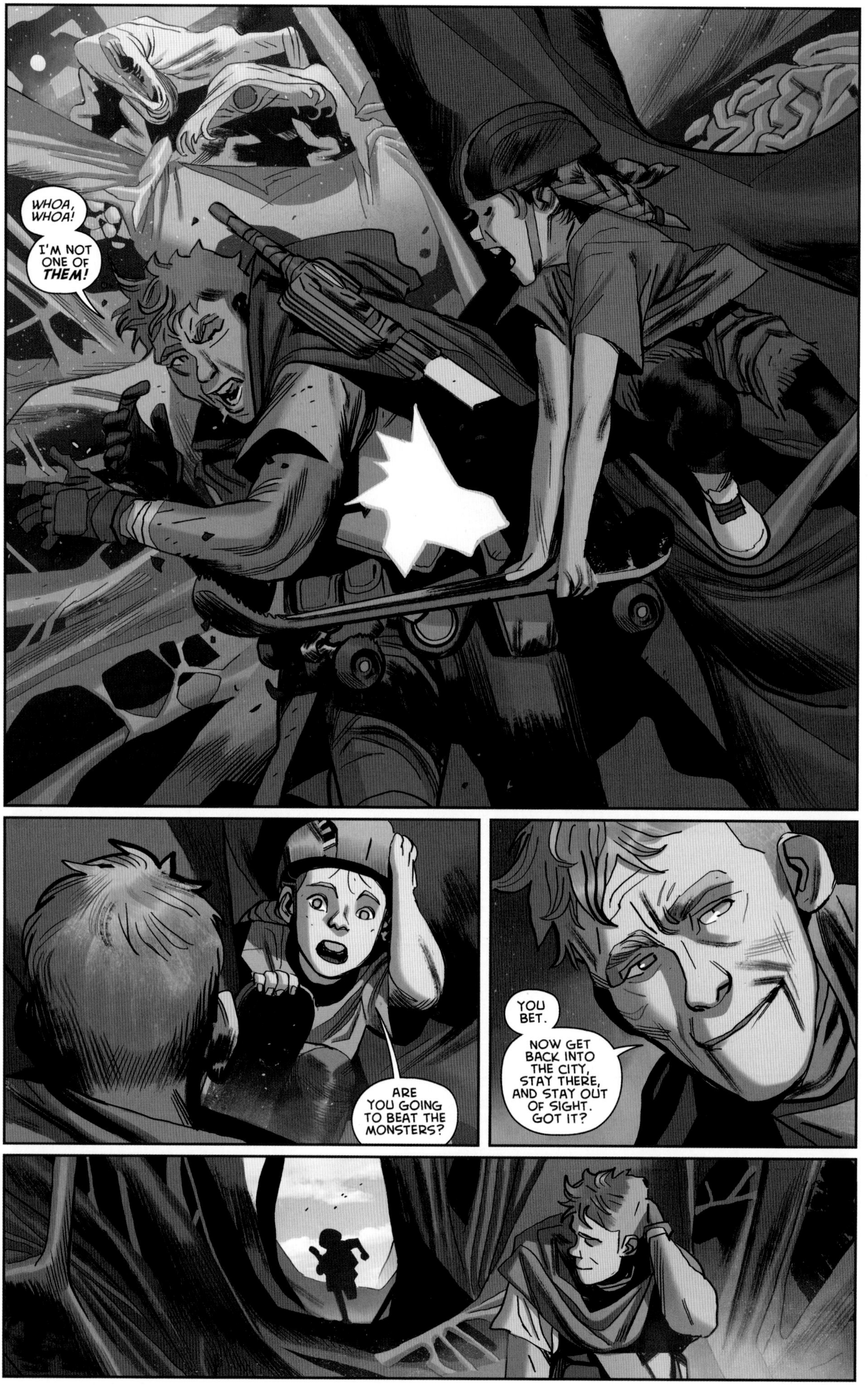
WHOA, WHOA!
I'M NOT ONE OF **THEM!**
ARE YOU GOING TO BEAT THE MONSTERS?
YOU BET.
NOW GET BACK INTO THE CITY, STAY THERE, AND STAY OUT OF SIGHT. GOT IT?

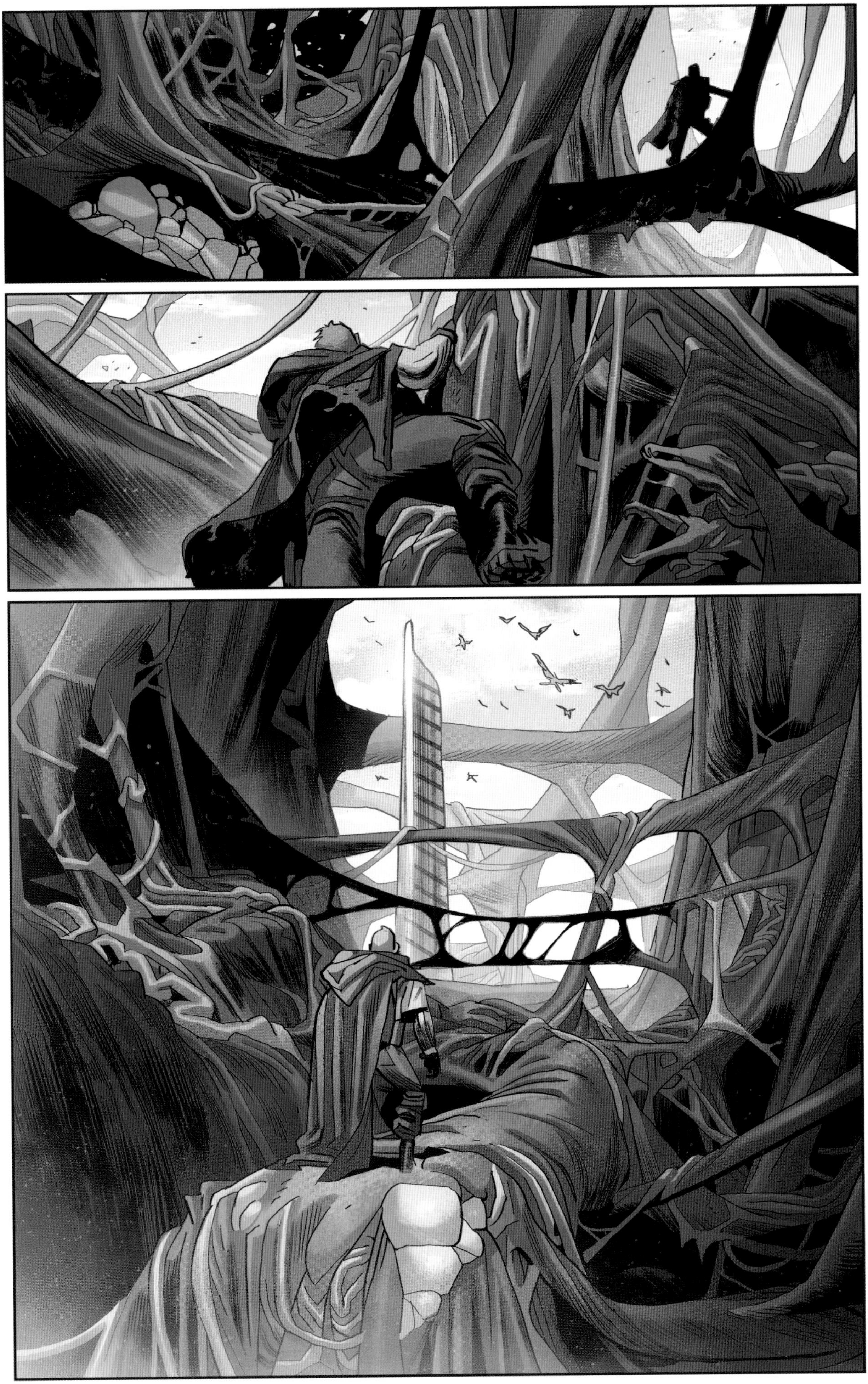

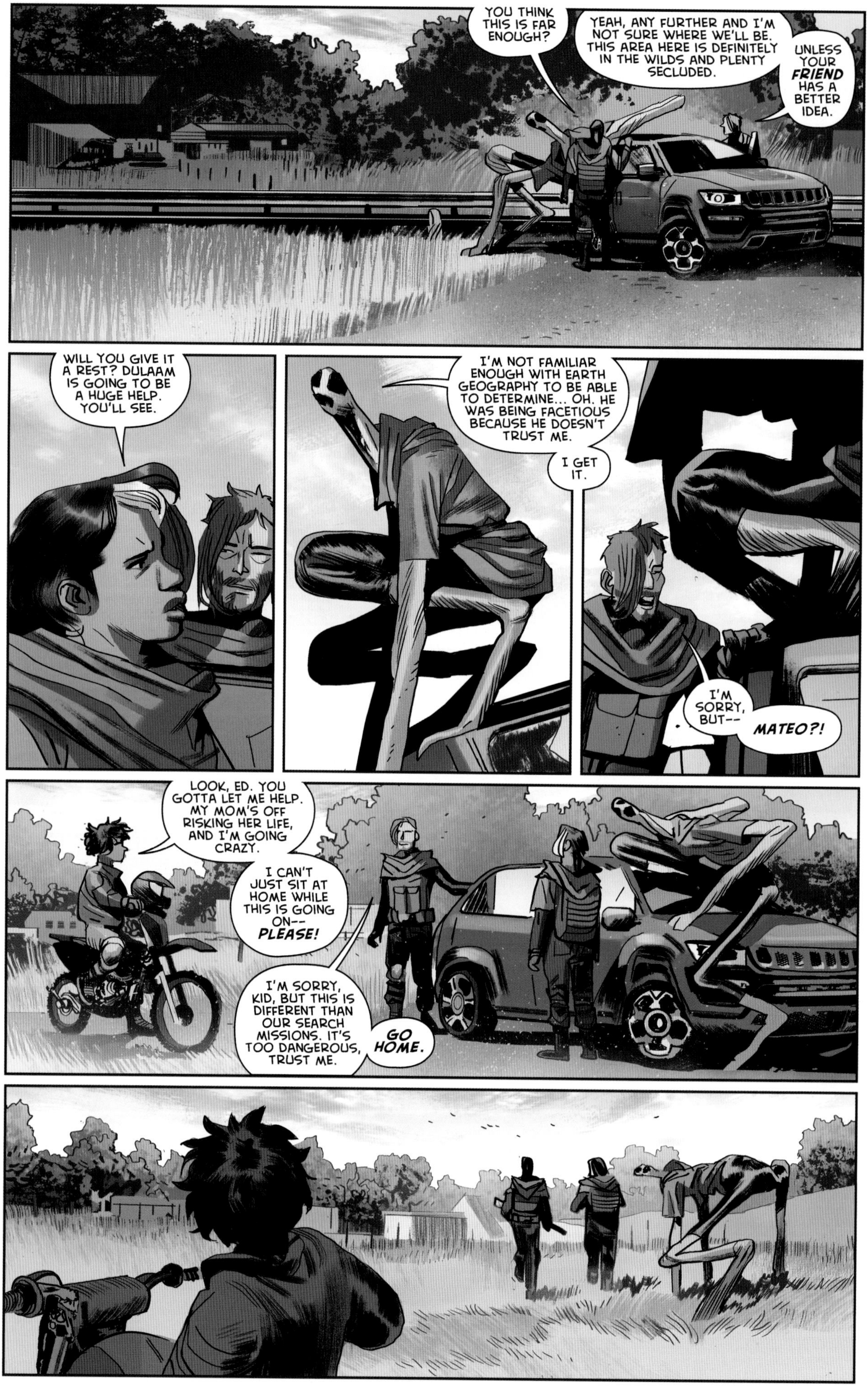
YOU THINK THIS IS FAR ENOUGH?
YEAH, ANY FURTHER AND I'M NOT SURE WHERE WE'LL BE. THIS AREA HERE IS DEFINITELY IN THE WILDS AND PLENTY SECLUDED.
UNLESS YOUR FRIEND HAS A BETTER IDEA.
WILL YOU GIVE IT A REST? DULAAM IS GOING TO BE A HUGE HELP. YOU'LL SEE.
I'M NOT FAMILIAR ENOUGH WITH EARTH GEOGRAPHY TO BE ABLE TO DETERMINE... OH. HE WAS BEING FACETIOUS BECAUSE HE DOESN'T TRUST ME.
I GET IT.
I'M SORRY, BUT--
MATEO?!
LOOK, ED. YOU GOTTA LET ME HELP. MY MOM'S OFF RISKING HER LIFE, AND I'M GOING CRAZY.
I CAN'T JUST SIT AT HOME WHILE THIS IS GOING ON-- PLEASE!
I'M SORRY, KID, BUT THIS IS DIFFERENT THAN OUR SEARCH MISSIONS. IT'S TOO DANGEROUS, TRUST ME.
GO HOME.

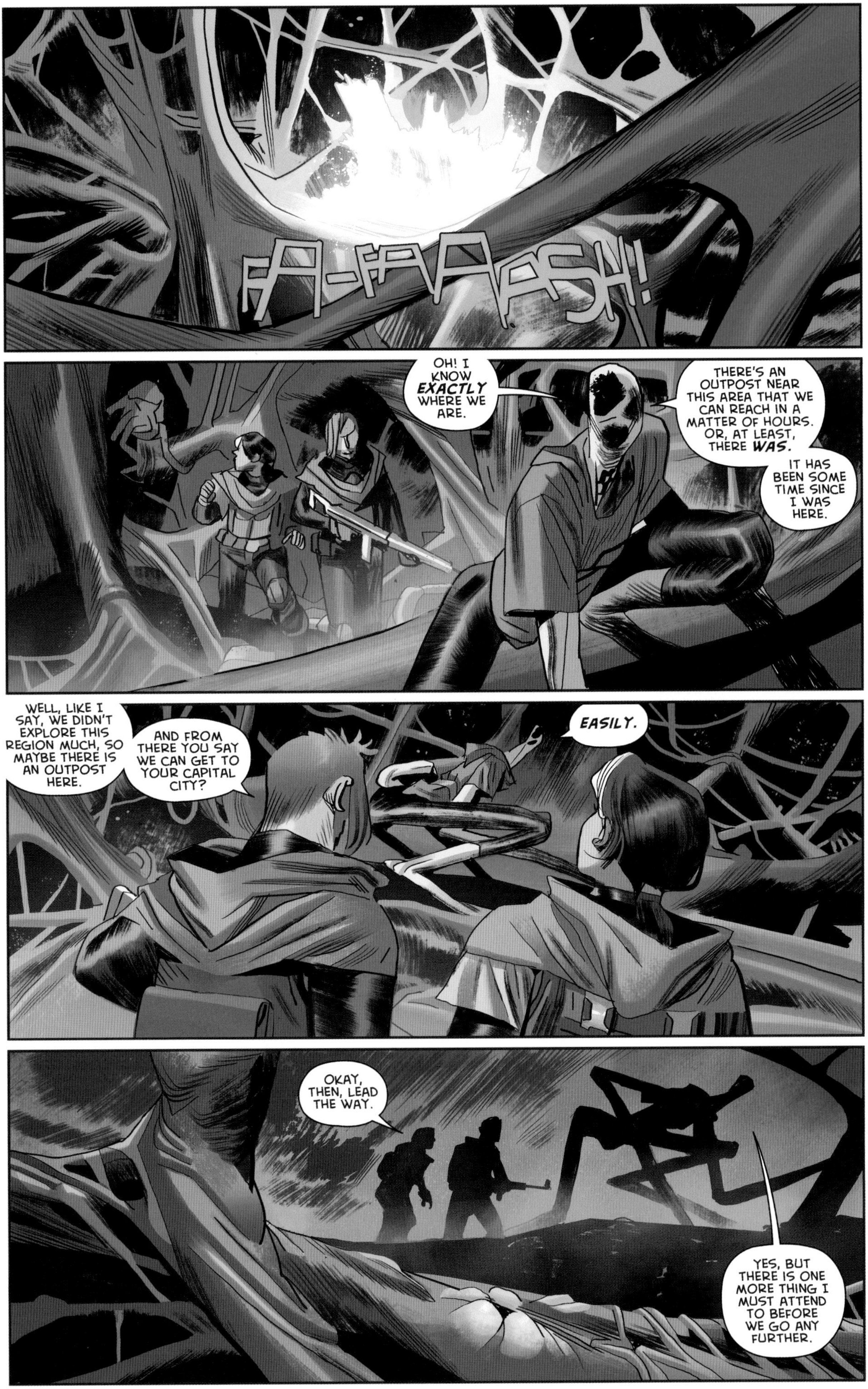
FA-FAAASH!
OH! I KNOW EXACTLY WHERE WE ARE.
THERE'S AN OUTPOST NEAR THIS AREA THAT WE CAN REACH IN A MATTER OF HOURS. OR, AT LEAST, THERE WAS.
IT HAS BEEN SOME TIME SINCE I WAS HERE.
WELL, LIKE I SAY, WE DIDN'T EXPLORE THIS REGION MUCH, SO MAYBE THERE IS AN OUTPOST HERE.
AND FROM THERE YOU SAY WE CAN GET TO YOUR CAPITAL CITY?
EASILY.
OKAY, THEN, LEAD THE WAY.
YES, BUT THERE IS ONE MORE THING I MUST ATTEND TO BEFORE WE GO ANY FURTHER.

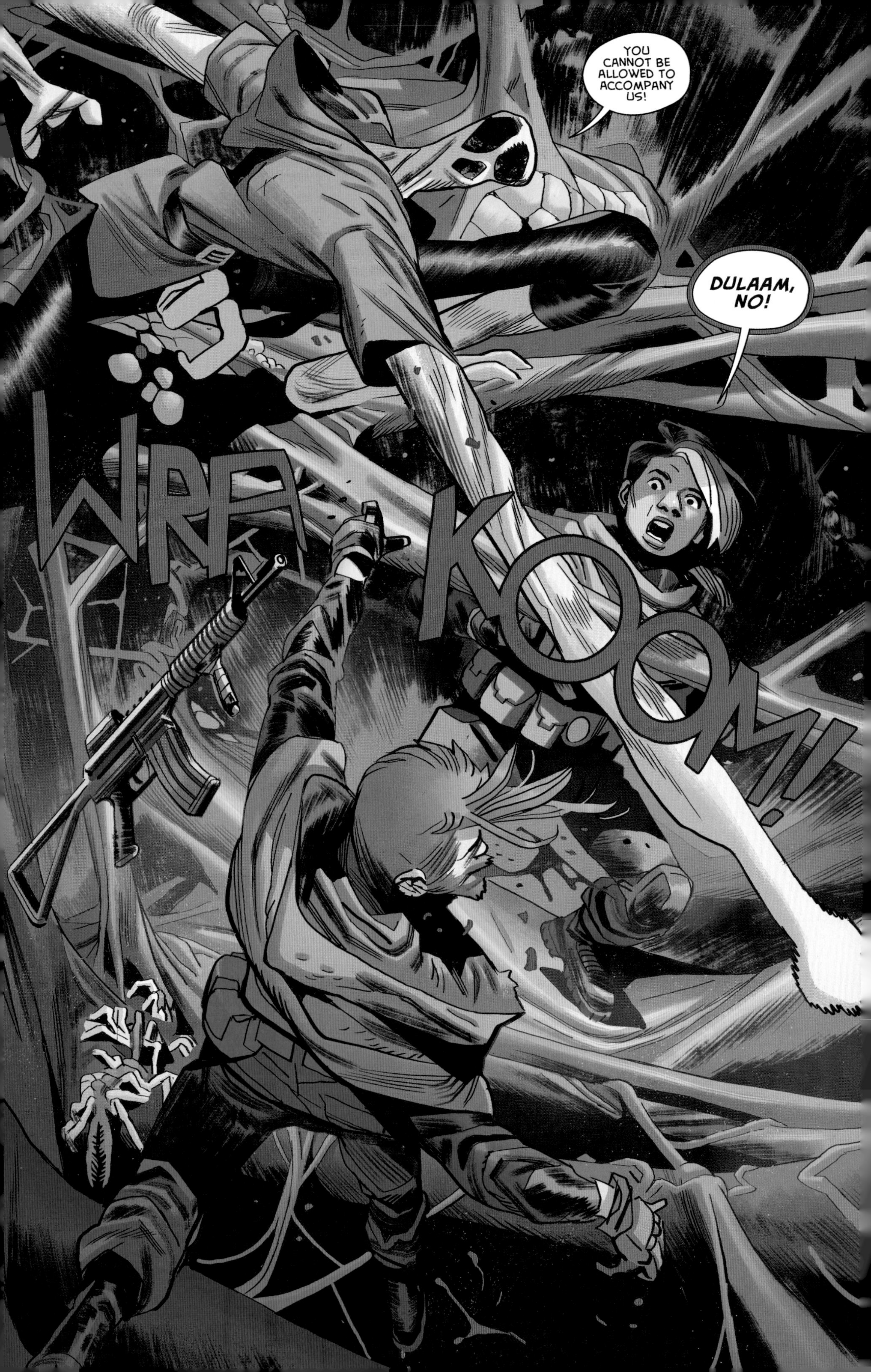
YOU CANNOT BE ALLOWED TO ACCOMPANY US!
DULAAM, NO!
WRAA
KOOOM!!

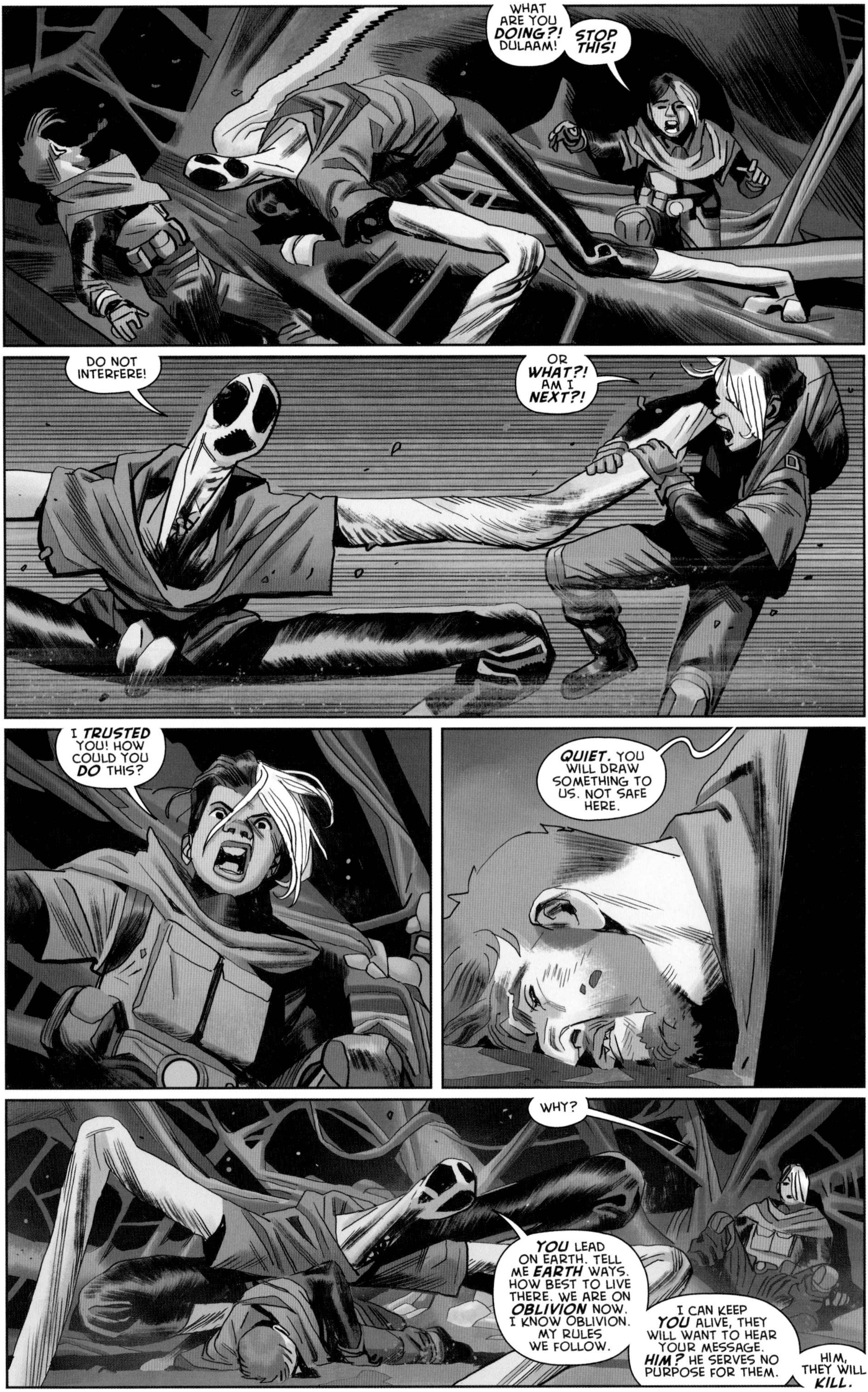
WHAT ARE YOU DOING?! DULAAM!
STOP THIS!
DO NOT INTERFERE!
OR WHAT?! AM I NEXT?!
I TRUSTED YOU! HOW COULD YOU DO THIS?
QUIET. YOU WILL DRAW SOMETHING TO US. NOT SAFE HERE.
WHY?
YOU LEAD ON EARTH. TELL ME EARTH WAYS. HOW BEST TO LIVE THERE. WE ARE ON OBLIVION NOW. I KNOW OBLIVION. MY RULES WE FOLLOW.
I CAN KEEP YOU ALIVE, THEY WILL WANT TO HEAR YOUR MESSAGE. HIM? HE SERVES NO PURPOSE FOR THEM.
HIM, THEY WILL KILL.

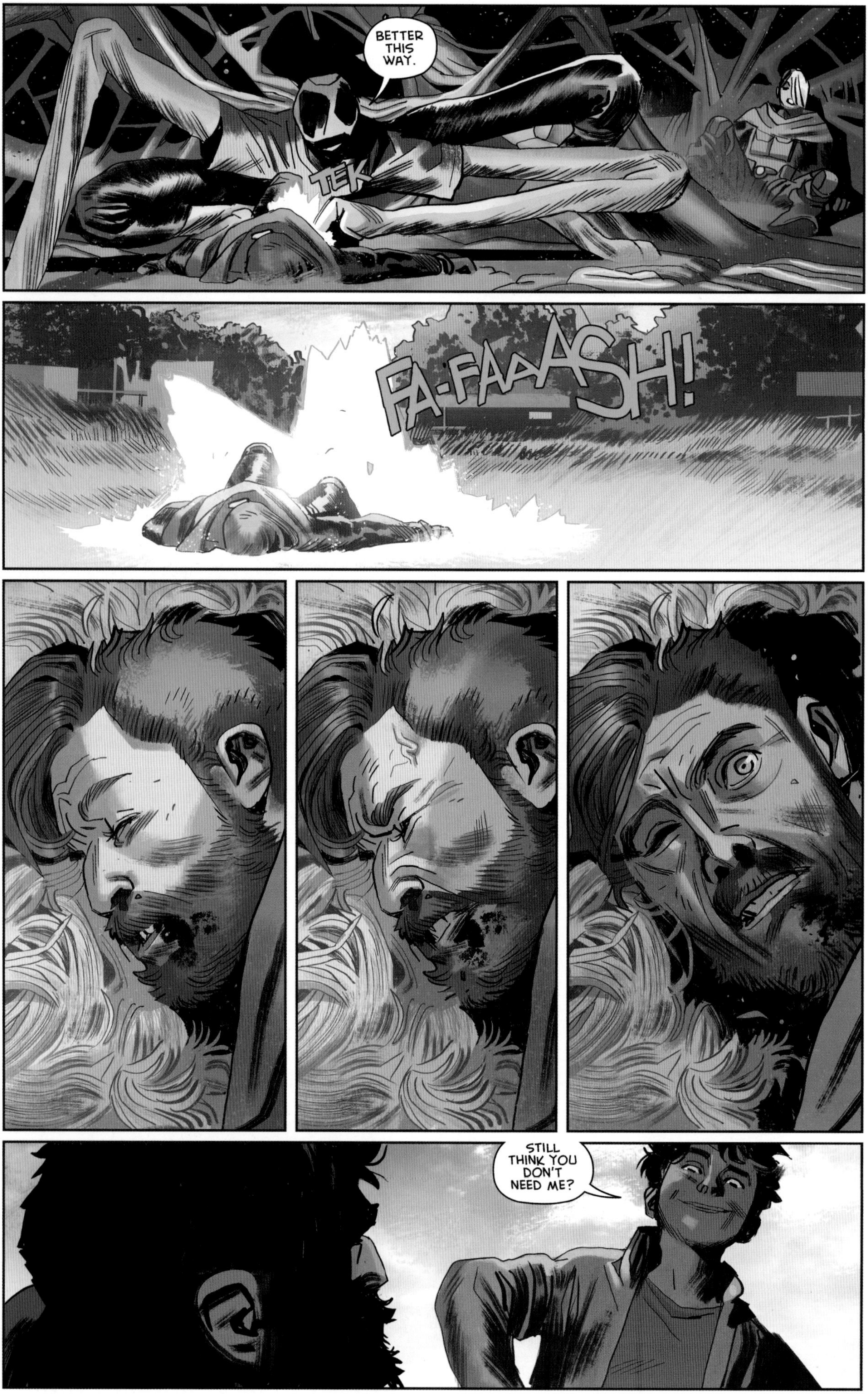
BETTER THIS WAY.
TEK
FA-FAAASH!
STILL THINK YOU DON'T NEED ME?

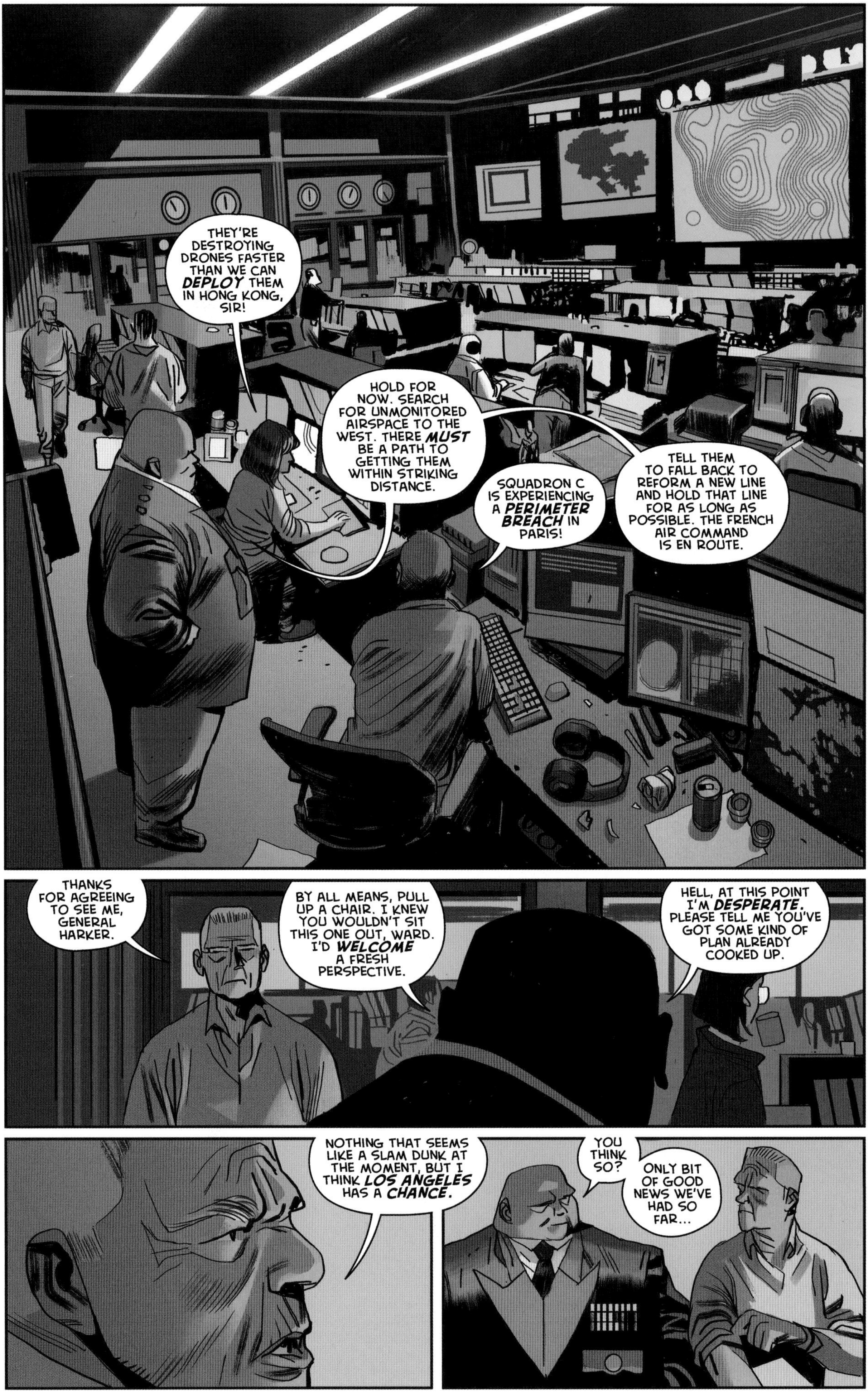
THEY'RE DESTROYING DRONES FASTER THAN WE CAN DEPLOY THEM IN HONG KONG, SIR!
HOLD FOR NOW. SEARCH FOR UNMONITORED AIRSPACE TO THE WEST. THERE MUST BE A PATH TO GETTING THEM WITHIN STRIKING DISTANCE.
SQUADRON C IS EXPERIENCING A PERIMETER BREACH IN PARIS!
TELL THEM TO FALL BACK TO REFORM A NEW LINE AND HOLD THAT LINE FOR AS LONG AS POSSIBLE. THE FRENCH AIR COMMAND IS EN ROUTE.
THANKS FOR AGREEING TO SEE ME, GENERAL HARKER.
BY ALL MEANS, PULL UP A CHAIR. I KNEW YOU WOULDN'T SIT THIS ONE OUT, WARD. I'D WELCOME A FRESH PERSPECTIVE.
HELL, AT THIS POINT I'M DESPERATE. PLEASE TELL ME YOU'VE GOT SOME KIND OF PLAN ALREADY COOKED UP.
NOTHING THAT SEEMS LIKE A SLAM DUNK AT THE MOMENT, BUT I THINK LOS ANGELES HAS A CHANCE.
YOU THINK SO?
ONLY BIT OF GOOD NEWS WE'VE HAD SO FAR...

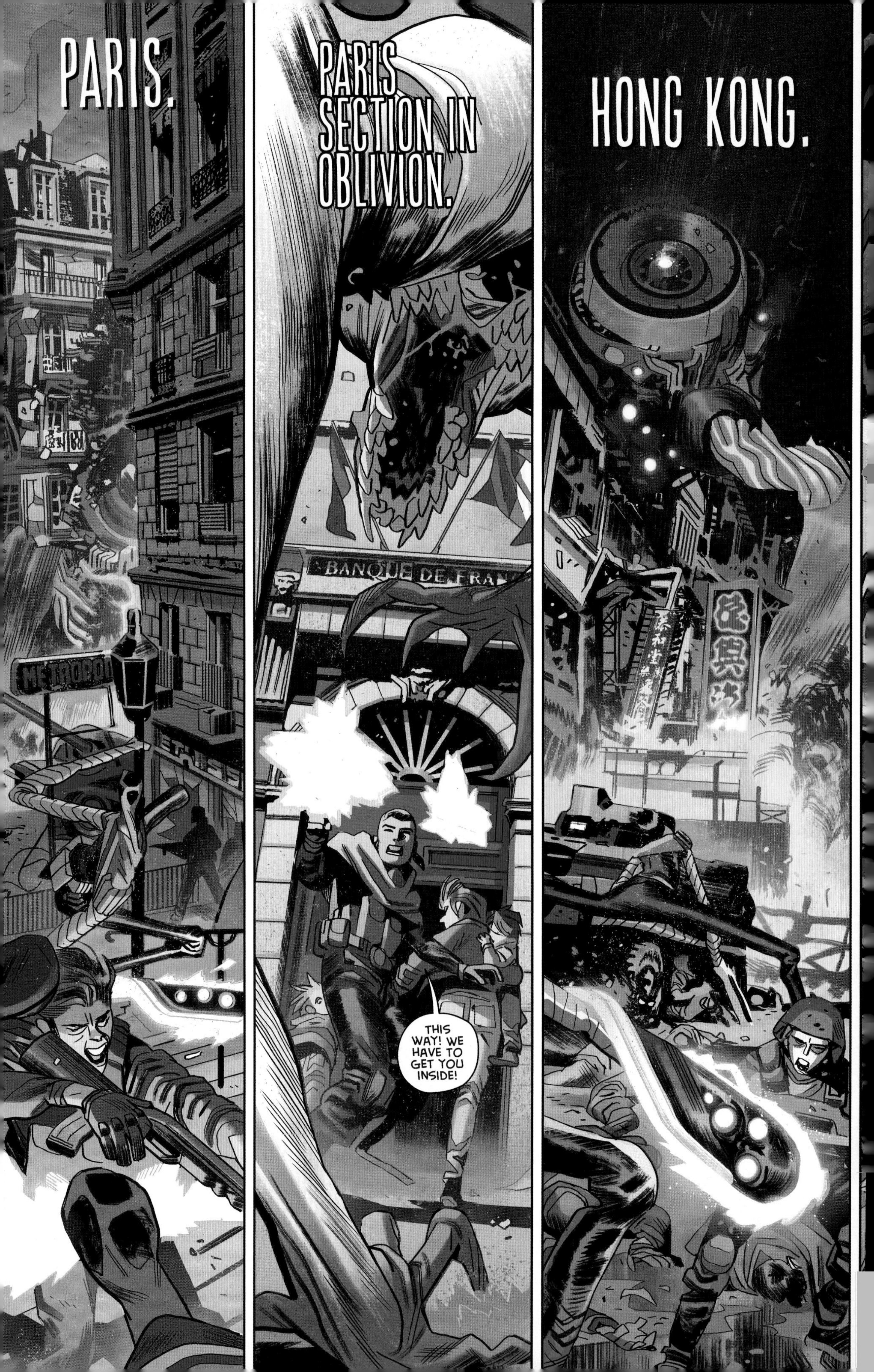
PARIS.
PARIS SECTION IN OBLIVION.
THIS WAY! WE HAVE TO GET YOU INSIDE!
HONG KONG.

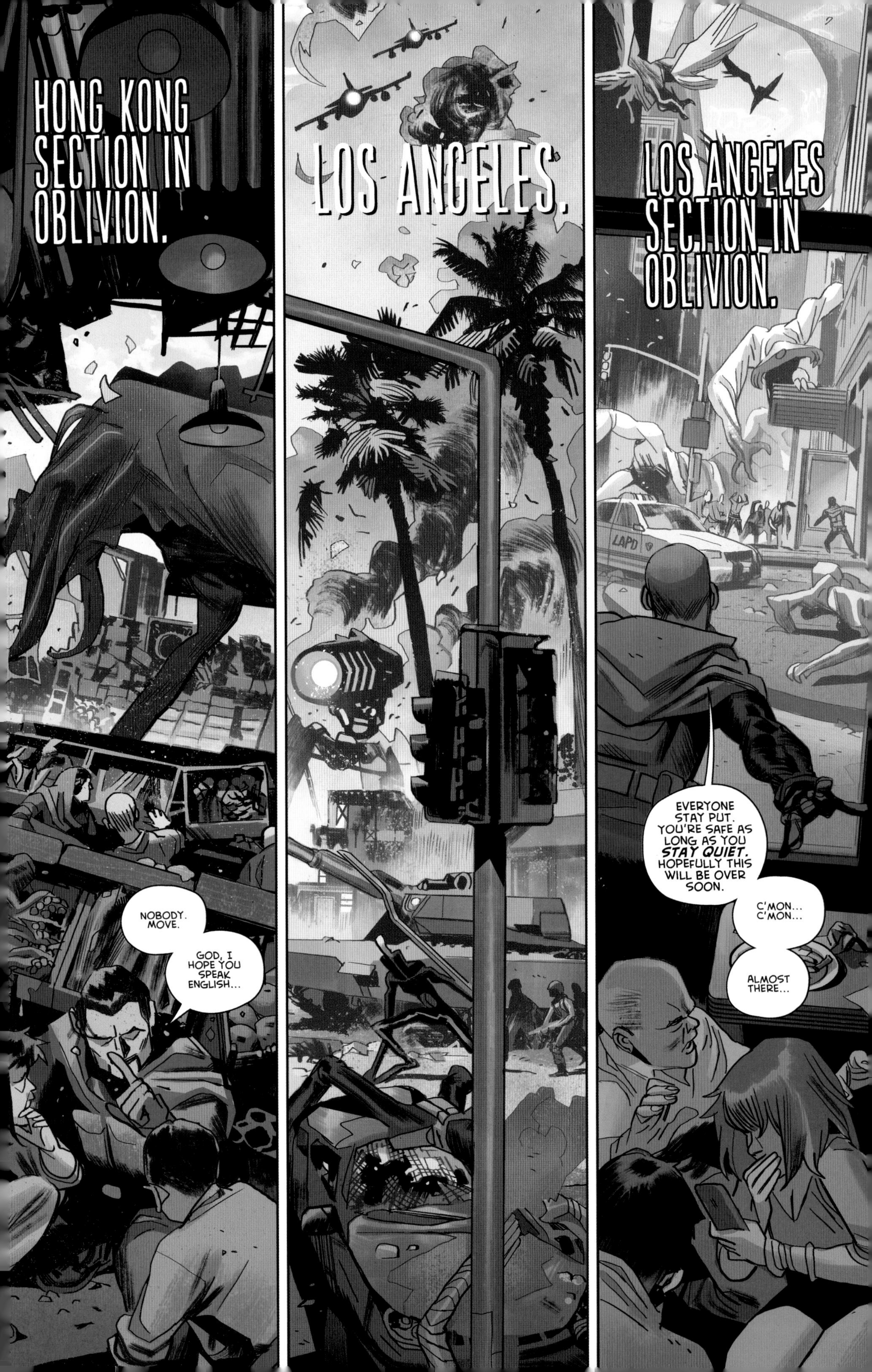
HONG KONG SECTION IN OBLIVION.
NOBODY. MOVE.
GOD, I HOPE YOU SPEAK ENGLISH...
LOS ANGELES.
LOS ANGELES SECTION IN OBLIVION.
LAPD
EVERYONE STAY PUT. YOU'RE SAFE AS LONG AS YOU STAY QUIET. HOPEFULLY THIS WILL BE OVER SOON.
C'MON... C'MON...
ALMOST THERE...

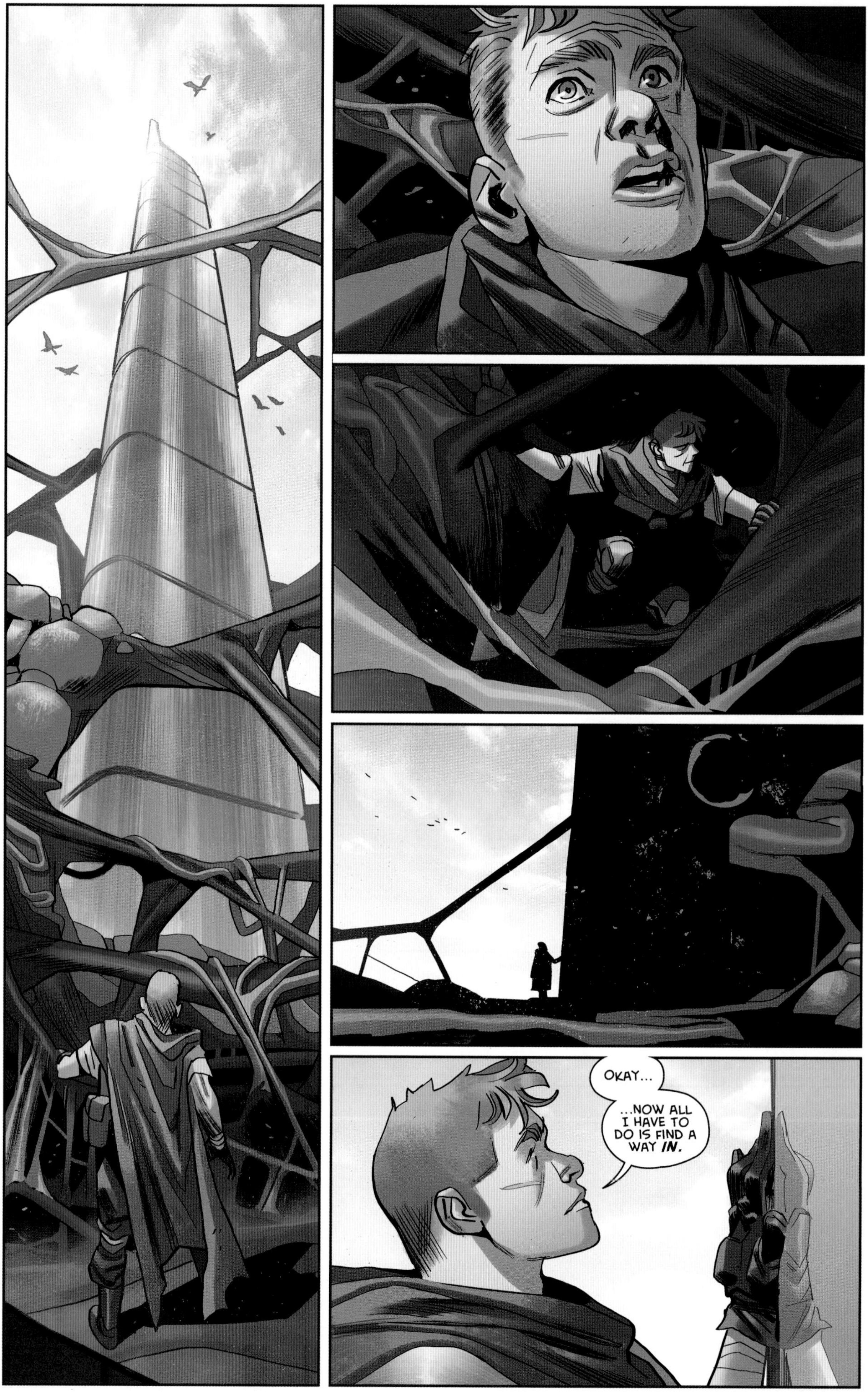
OKAY...
...NOW ALL I HAVE TO DO IS FIND A WAY *IN.*

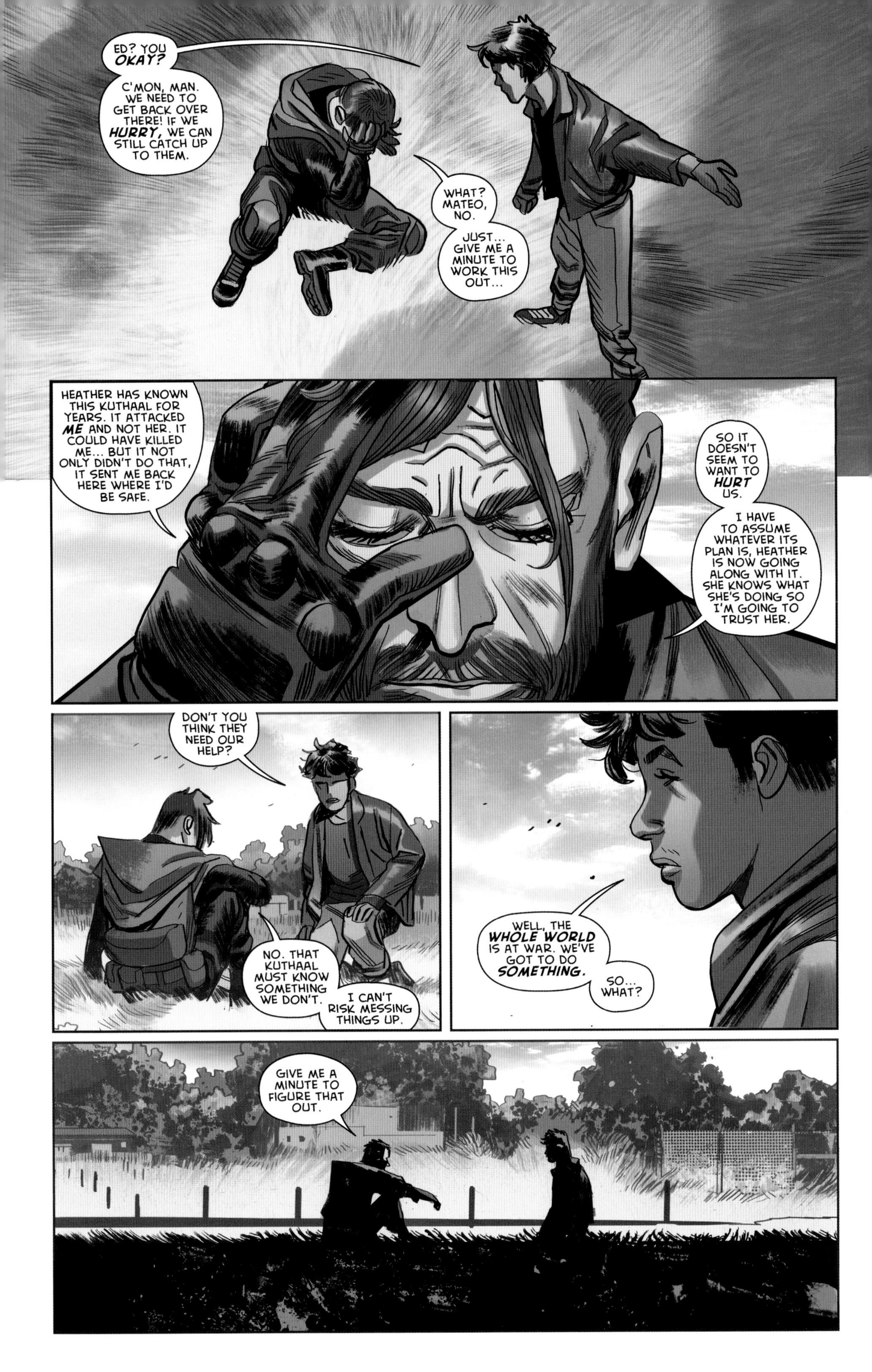
ED? YOU OKAY?
C'MON, MAN. WE NEED TO GET BACK OVER THERE! IF WE HURRY, WE CAN STILL CATCH UP TO THEM.
WHAT? MATEO, NO.
JUST... GIVE ME A MINUTE TO WORK THIS OUT...
HEATHER HAS KNOWN THIS KUTHAAL FOR YEARS. IT ATTACKED ME AND NOT HER. IT COULD HAVE KILLED ME... BUT IT NOT ONLY DIDN'T DO THAT, IT SENT ME BACK HERE WHERE I'D BE SAFE.
SO IT DOESN'T SEEM TO WANT TO HURT US.
I HAVE TO ASSUME WHATEVER ITS PLAN IS, HEATHER IS NOW GOING ALONG WITH IT. SHE KNOWS WHAT SHE'S DOING SO I'M GOING TO TRUST HER.
DON'T YOU THINK THEY NEED OUR HELP?
NO. THAT KUTHAAL MUST KNOW SOMETHING WE DON'T.
I CAN'T RISK MESSING THINGS UP.
WELL, THE WHOLE WORLD IS AT WAR. WE'VE GOT TO DO SOMETHING.
SO... WHAT?
GIVE ME A MINUTE TO FIGURE THAT OUT.

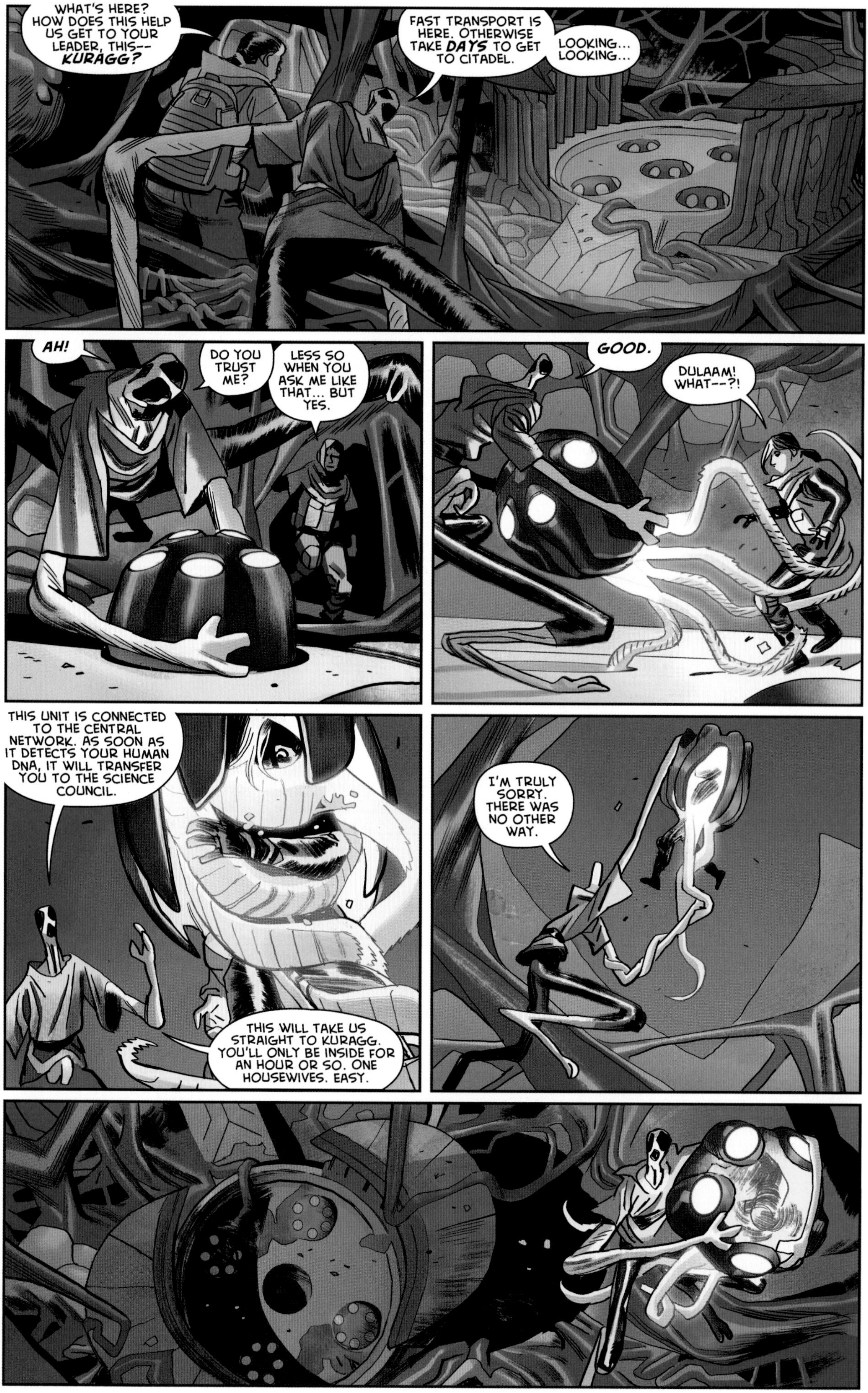
WHAT'S HERE? HOW DOES THIS HELP US GET TO YOUR LEADER, THIS-- KURAGG?
FAST TRANSPORT IS HERE. OTHERWISE TAKE DAYS TO GET TO CITADEL.
LOOKING... LOOKING...
AH!
DO YOU TRUST ME?
LESS SO WHEN YOU ASK ME LIKE THAT... BUT YES.
GOOD.
DULAAM! WHAT--?!
THIS UNIT IS CONNECTED TO THE CENTRAL NETWORK. AS SOON AS IT DETECTS YOUR HUMAN DNA, IT WILL TRANSFER YOU TO THE SCIENCE COUNCIL.
THIS WILL TAKE US STRAIGHT TO KURAGG. YOU'LL ONLY BE INSIDE FOR AN HOUR OR SO. ONE HOUSEWIVES. EASY.
I'M TRULY SORRY. THERE WAS NO OTHER WAY.

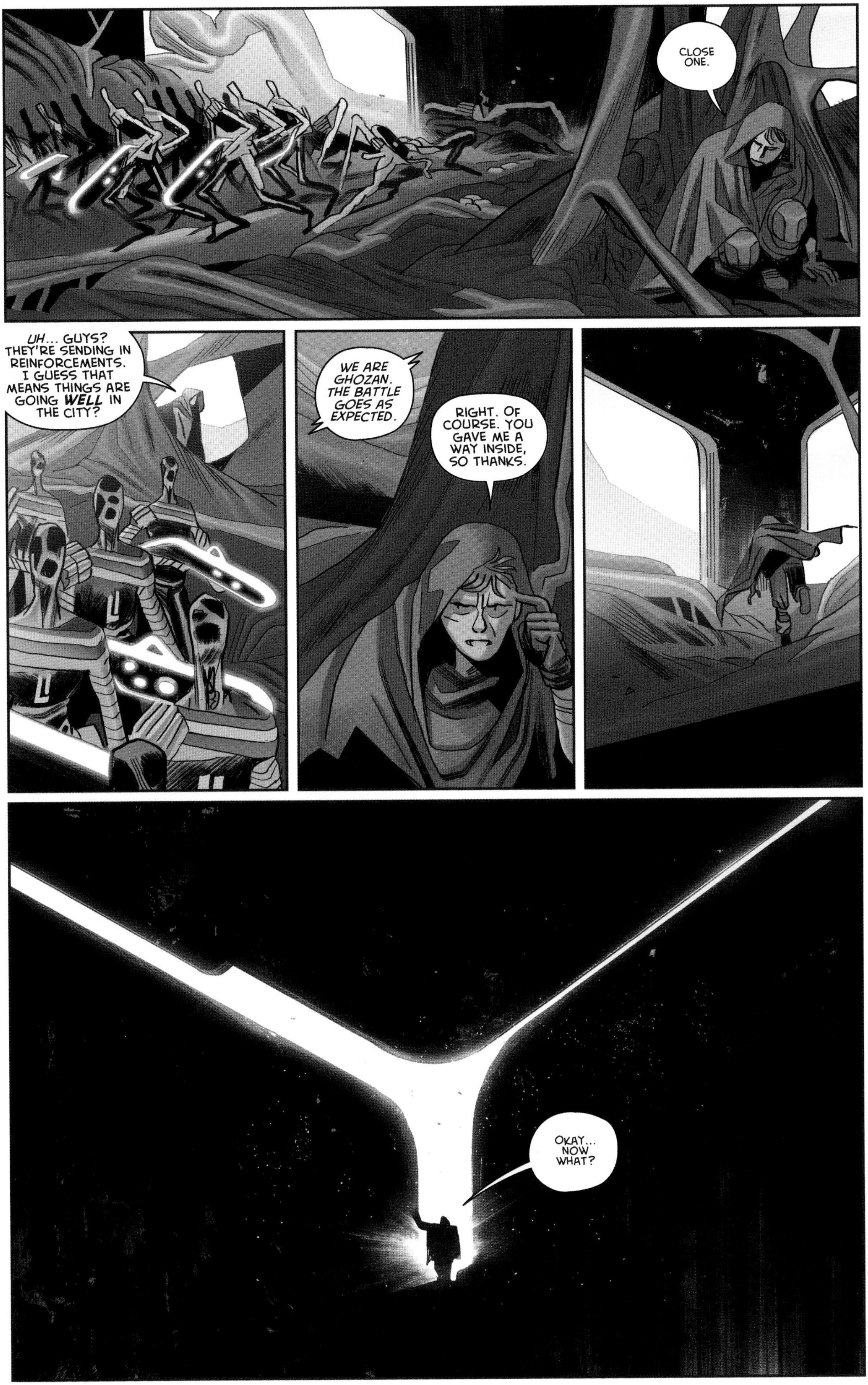
CLOSE ONE.
UH... GUYS? THEY'RE SENDING IN REINFORCEMENTS. I GUESS THAT MEANS THINGS ARE GOING **WELL** IN THE CITY?
WE ARE GHOZAN. THE BATTLE GOES AS EXPECTED.
RIGHT. OF COURSE. YOU GAVE ME A WAY INSIDE, SO THANKS.
OKAY... NOW WHAT?

DAMN IT!

CALM DOWN BEFORE YOU LET YOUR FRAGILE MALE EGO DESTROY ANOTHER SAMPLE.

THAT WAS AN ACCIDENT.

SURE.

WE'RE RUNNING OUT OF TIME.

I KNOW.

WE HAVEN'T MADE ANY PROGRESS...

I KNOW.

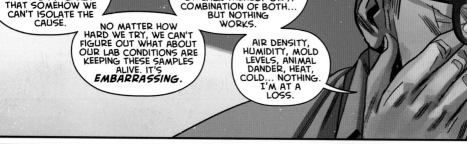

THIS GROWTH... IT DIES OUT IMMEDIATELY ON EARTH IN OPEN AIR... IN SUNLIGHT. IT'S DRIVING ME CRAZY THAT SOMEHOW WE CAN'T ISOLATE THE CAUSE.

NO MATTER HOW HARD WE TRY, WE CAN'T FIGURE OUT WHAT ABOUT OUR LAB CONDITIONS ARE KEEPING THESE SAMPLES ALIVE. IT'S *EMBARRASSING*.

ALL THIS TIME WE JUST ASSUMED IT WAS OUR SUNLIGHT, OUR HUMIDITY... OR LACK THEREOF OR A COMBINATION OF BOTH... BUT NOTHING WORKS.

AIR DENSITY, HUMIDITY, MOLD LEVELS, ANIMAL DANDER, HEAT, COLD... NOTHING. I'M AT A LOSS.

MAYBE WE'RE ADDING WHEN WE SHOULD BE SUBTRACTING?

WAIT... WHAT?

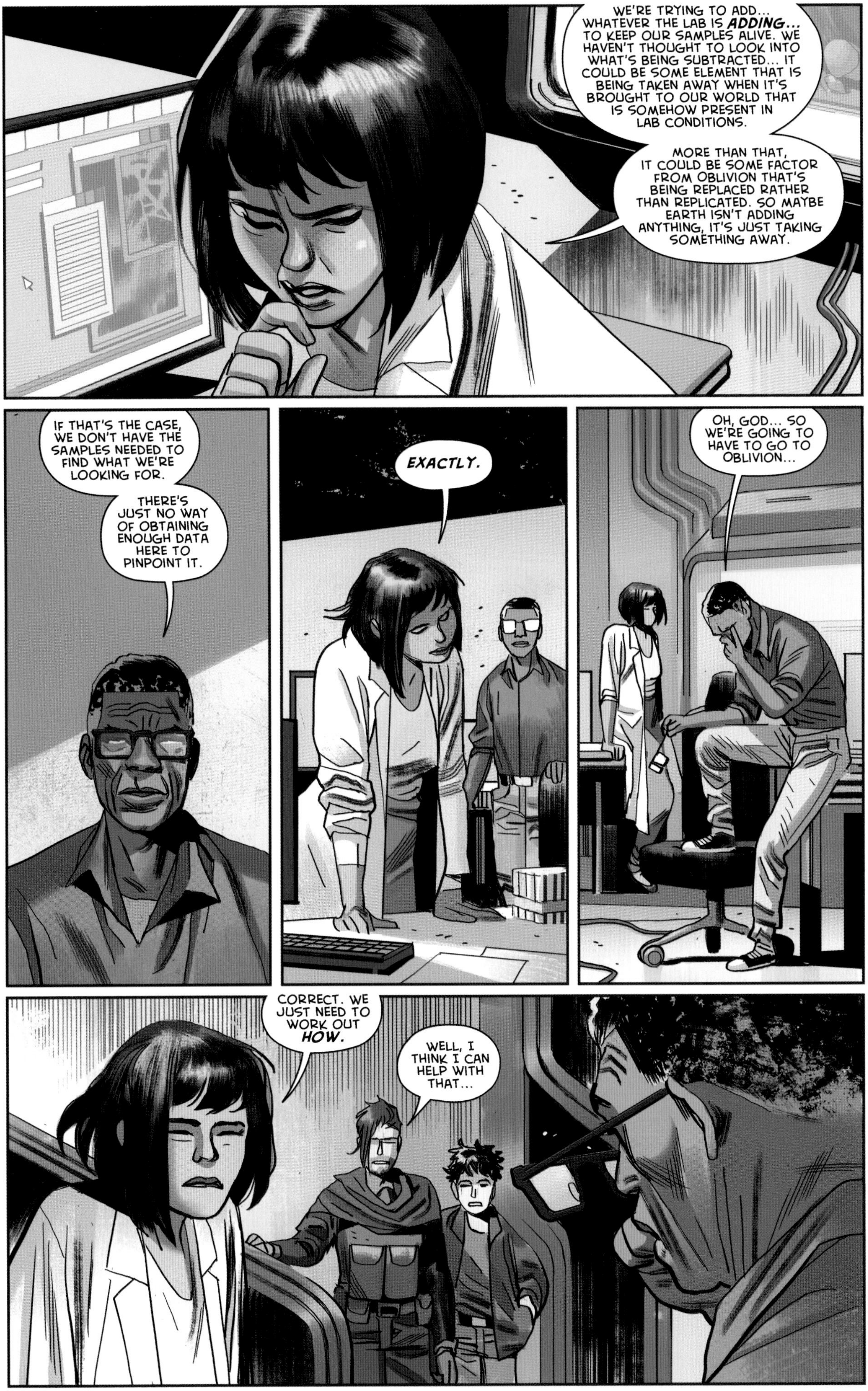
WE'RE TRYING TO ADD... WHATEVER THE LAB IS ADDING... TO KEEP OUR SAMPLES ALIVE. WE HAVEN'T THOUGHT TO LOOK INTO WHAT'S BEING SUBTRACTED... IT COULD BE SOME ELEMENT THAT IS BEING TAKEN AWAY WHEN IT'S BROUGHT TO OUR WORLD THAT IS SOMEHOW PRESENT IN LAB CONDITIONS.
MORE THAN THAT, IT COULD BE SOME FACTOR FROM OBLIVION THAT'S BEING REPLACED RATHER THAN REPLICATED. SO MAYBE EARTH ISN'T ADDING ANYTHING, IT'S JUST TAKING SOMETHING AWAY.
IF THAT'S THE CASE, WE DON'T HAVE THE SAMPLES NEEDED TO FIND WHAT WE'RE LOOKING FOR.
THERE'S JUST NO WAY OF OBTAINING ENOUGH DATA HERE TO PINPOINT IT.
EXACTLY.
OH, GOD... SO WE'RE GOING TO HAVE TO GO TO OBLIVION...
CORRECT. WE JUST NEED TO WORK OUT HOW.
WELL, I THINK I CAN HELP WITH THAT...

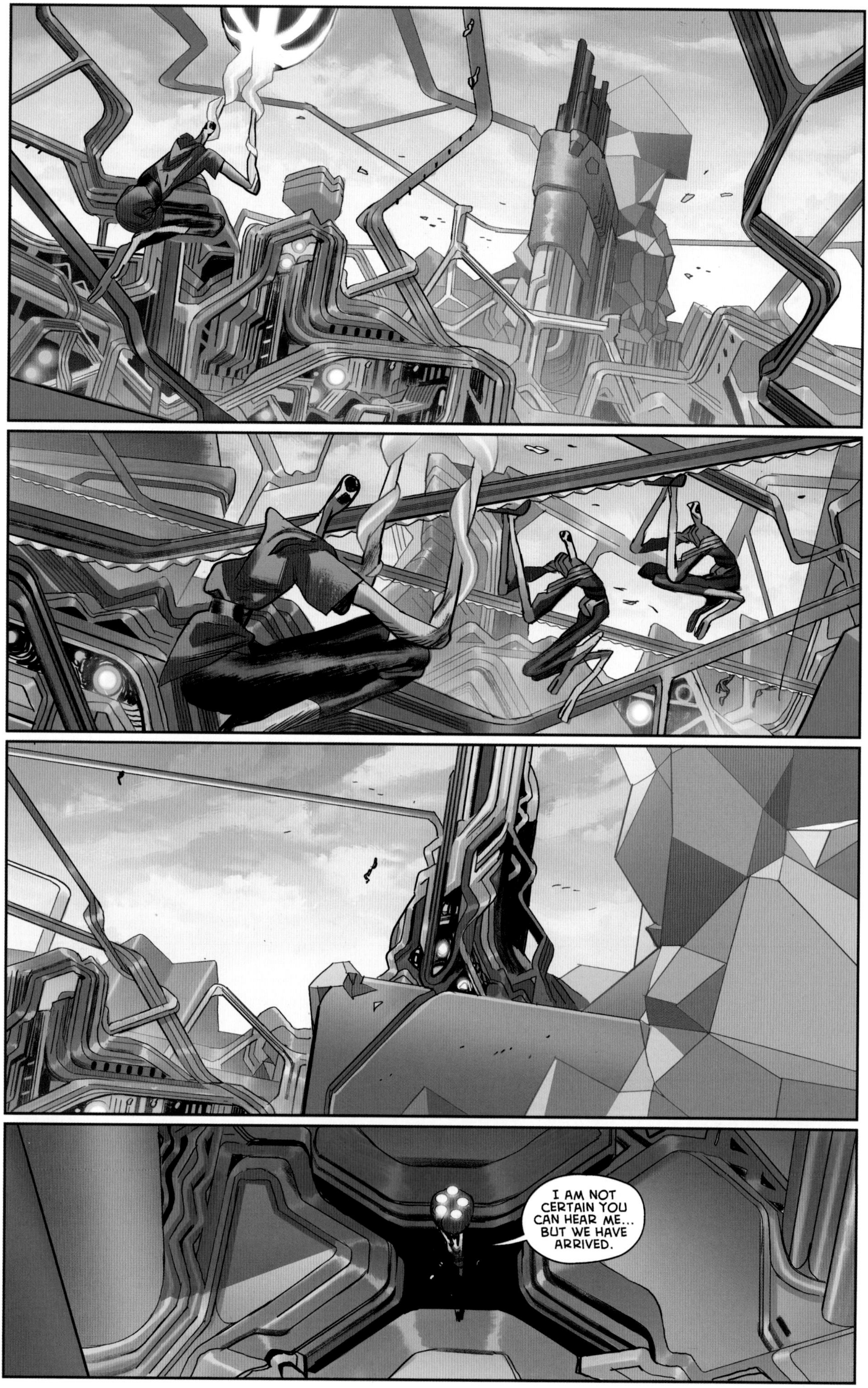
I AM NOT CERTAIN YOU CAN HEAR ME... BUT WE HAVE ARRIVED.

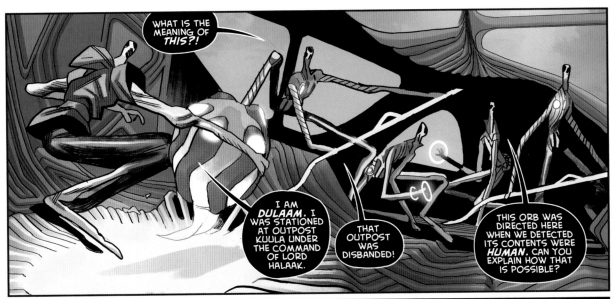

WHAT IS THE MEANING OF *THIS?!*

I AM *DULAAM.* I WAS STATIONED AT OUTPOST KUULA UNDER THE COMMAND OF LORD HALAAK.

THAT OUTPOST WAS DISBANDED!

THIS ORB WAS DIRECTED HERE WHEN WE DETECTED ITS CONTENTS WERE *HUMAN.* CAN YOU EXPLAIN HOW THAT IS POSSIBLE?

WHAT THE *HELL* IS--?!

UH...

IT *IS* HUMAN!

I HAVE BEEN STRANDED ON EARTH FOR THREE YEARS. THIS HUMAN BECAME MY ALLY. I BELIEVE *ALL* HUMANS COULD BECOME OUR ALLIES.

I AM AWARE OF THE GROWING CONFLICT WITH THEIR WORLD. IT MUST BE ENDED SWIFTLY. I BELIEVE WE KNOW A WAY.

I DEMAND WE BE BROUGHT BEFORE THE *GREAT KURAGG....*

AT ONCE!

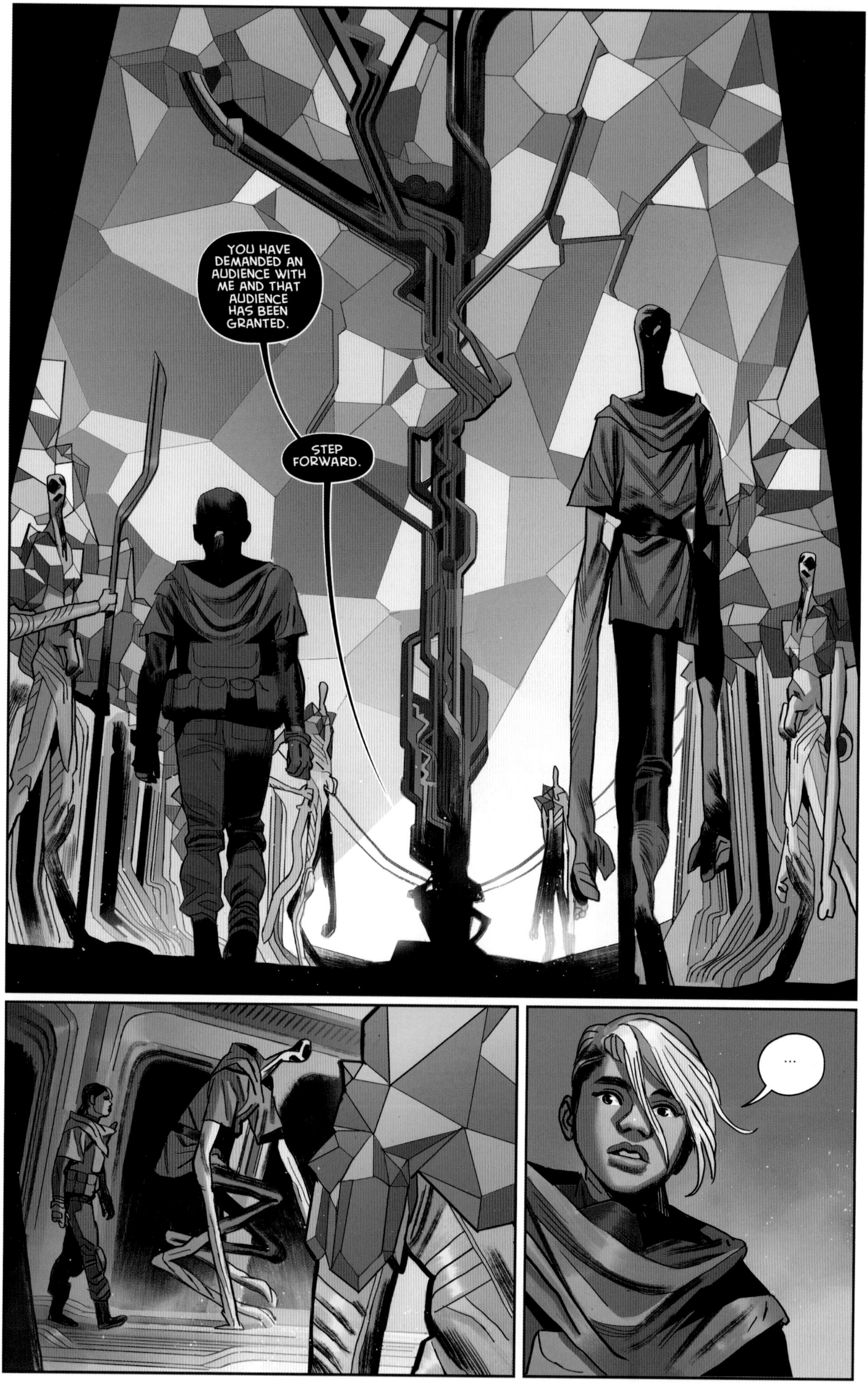
YOU HAVE DEMANDED AN AUDIENCE WITH ME AND THAT AUDIENCE HAS BEEN GRANTED.
STEP FORWARD.
...

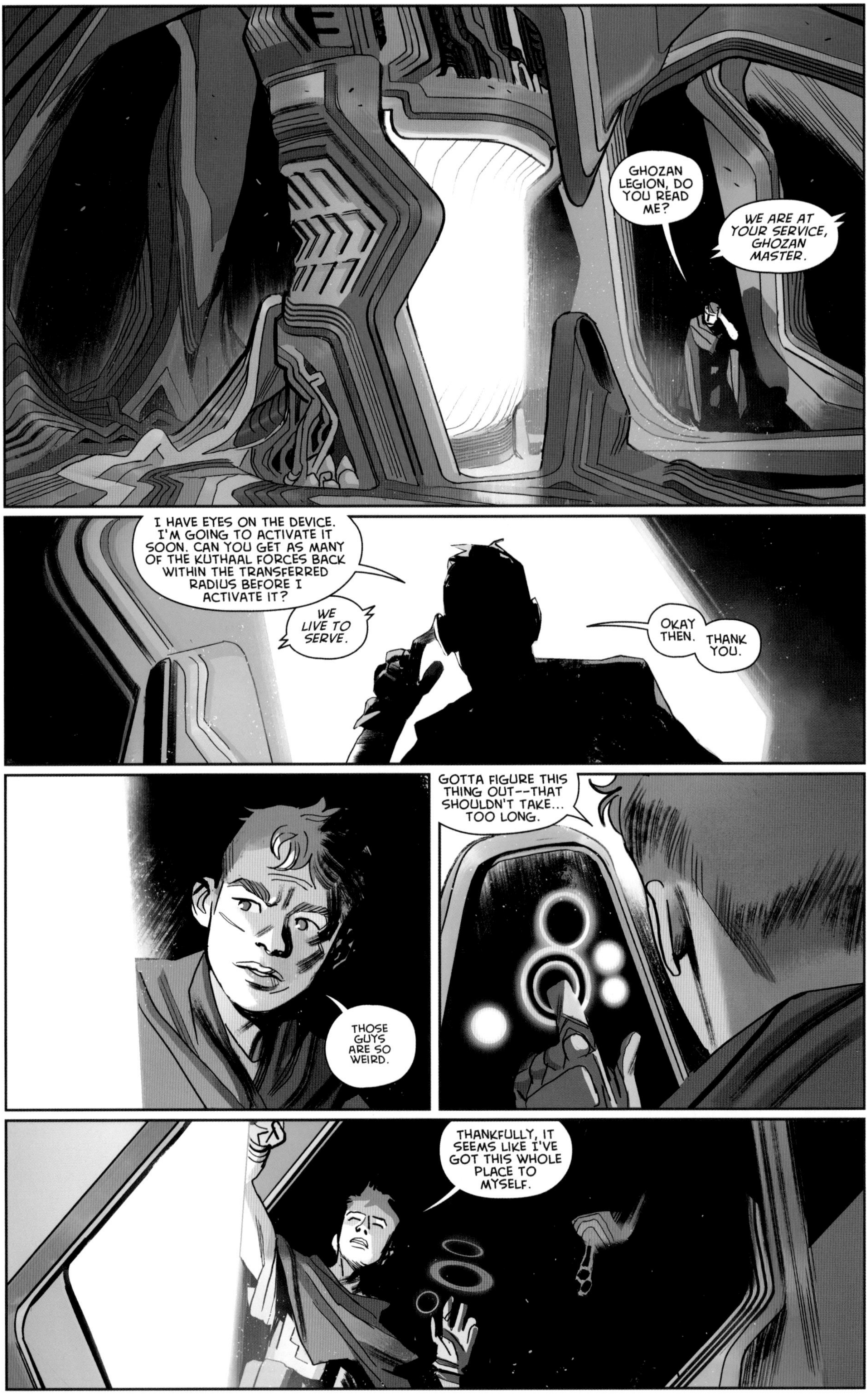
GHOZAN LEGION, DO YOU READ ME?
WE ARE AT YOUR SERVICE, GHOZAN MASTER.
I HAVE EYES ON THE DEVICE. I'M GOING TO ACTIVATE IT SOON. CAN YOU GET AS MANY OF THE KUTHAAL FORCES BACK WITHIN THE TRANSFERRED RADIUS BEFORE I ACTIVATE IT?
WE LIVE TO SERVE.
OKAY THEN.
THANK YOU.
THOSE GUYS ARE SO WEIRD.
GOTTA FIGURE THIS THING OUT--THAT SHOULDN'T TAKE... TOO LONG.
THANKFULLY, IT SEEMS LIKE I'VE GOT THIS WHOLE PLACE TO MYSELF.

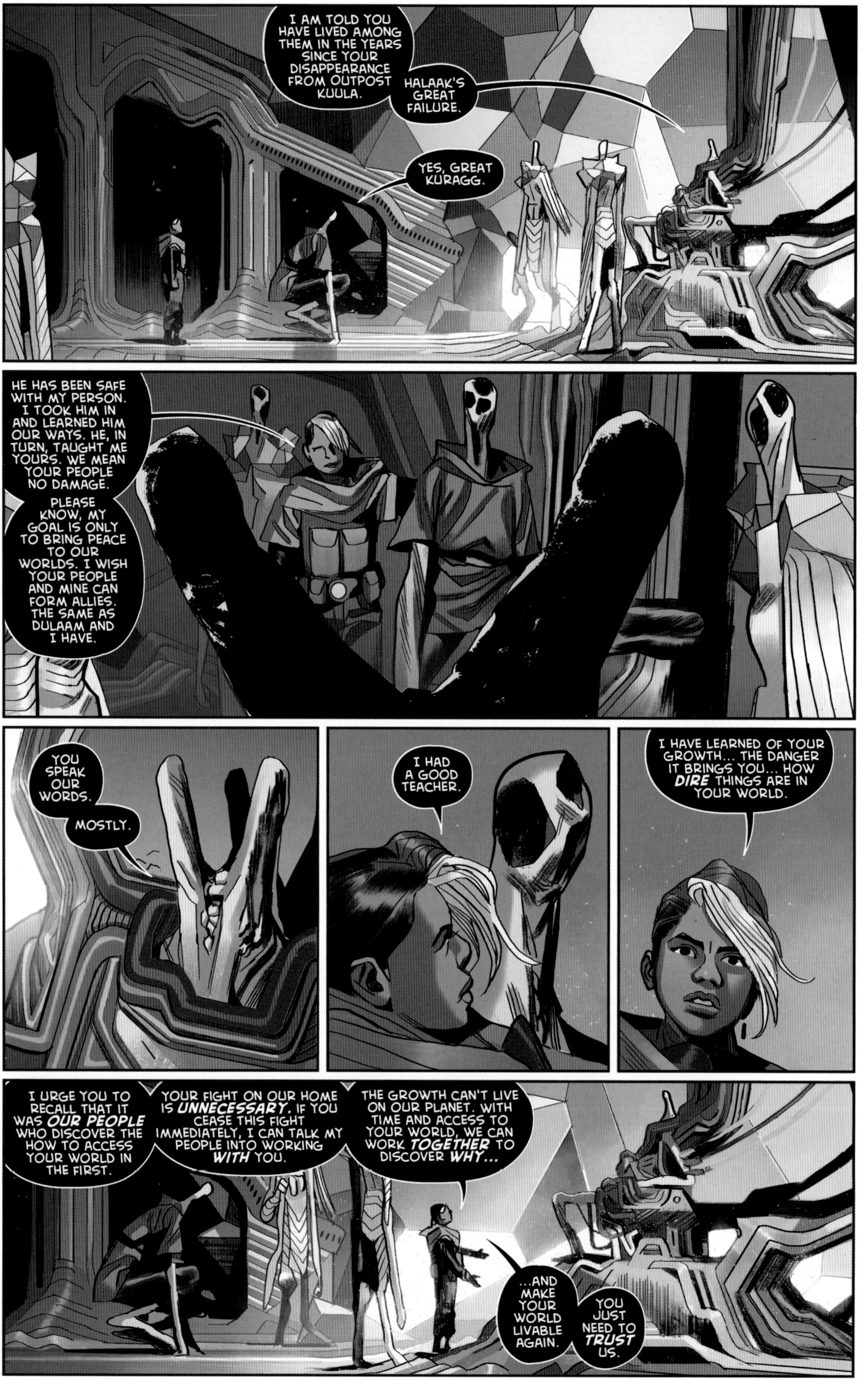
I AM TOLD YOU HAVE LIVED AMONG THEM IN THE YEARS SINCE YOUR DISAPPEARANCE FROM OUTPOST KUULA.
HALAAK'S GREAT FAILURE.
YES, GREAT KURAGG.
HE HAS BEEN SAFE WITH MY PERSON. I TOOK HIM IN AND LEARNED HIM OUR WAYS. HE, IN TURN, TAUGHT ME YOURS. WE MEAN YOUR PEOPLE NO DAMAGE.
PLEASE KNOW, MY GOAL IS ONLY TO BRING PEACE TO OUR WORLDS. I WISH YOUR PEOPLE AND MINE CAN FORM ALLIES. THE SAME AS DULAAM AND I HAVE.
YOU SPEAK OUR WORDS.
MOSTLY.
I HAD A GOOD TEACHER.
I HAVE LEARNED OF YOUR GROWTH... THE DANGER IT BRINGS YOU... HOW DIRE THINGS ARE IN YOUR WORLD.
I URGE YOU TO RECALL THAT IT WAS OUR PEOPLE WHO DISCOVER THE HOW TO ACCESS YOUR WORLD IN THE FIRST.
YOUR FIGHT ON OUR HOME IS UNNECESSARY. IF YOU CEASE THIS FIGHT IMMEDIATELY, I CAN TALK MY PEOPLE INTO WORKING WITH YOU.
THE GROWTH CAN'T LIVE ON OUR PLANET. WITH TIME AND ACCESS TO YOUR WORLD, WE CAN WORK TOGETHER TO DISCOVER WHY...
...AND MAKE YOUR WORLD LIVABLE AGAIN.
YOU JUST NEED TO TRUST US.

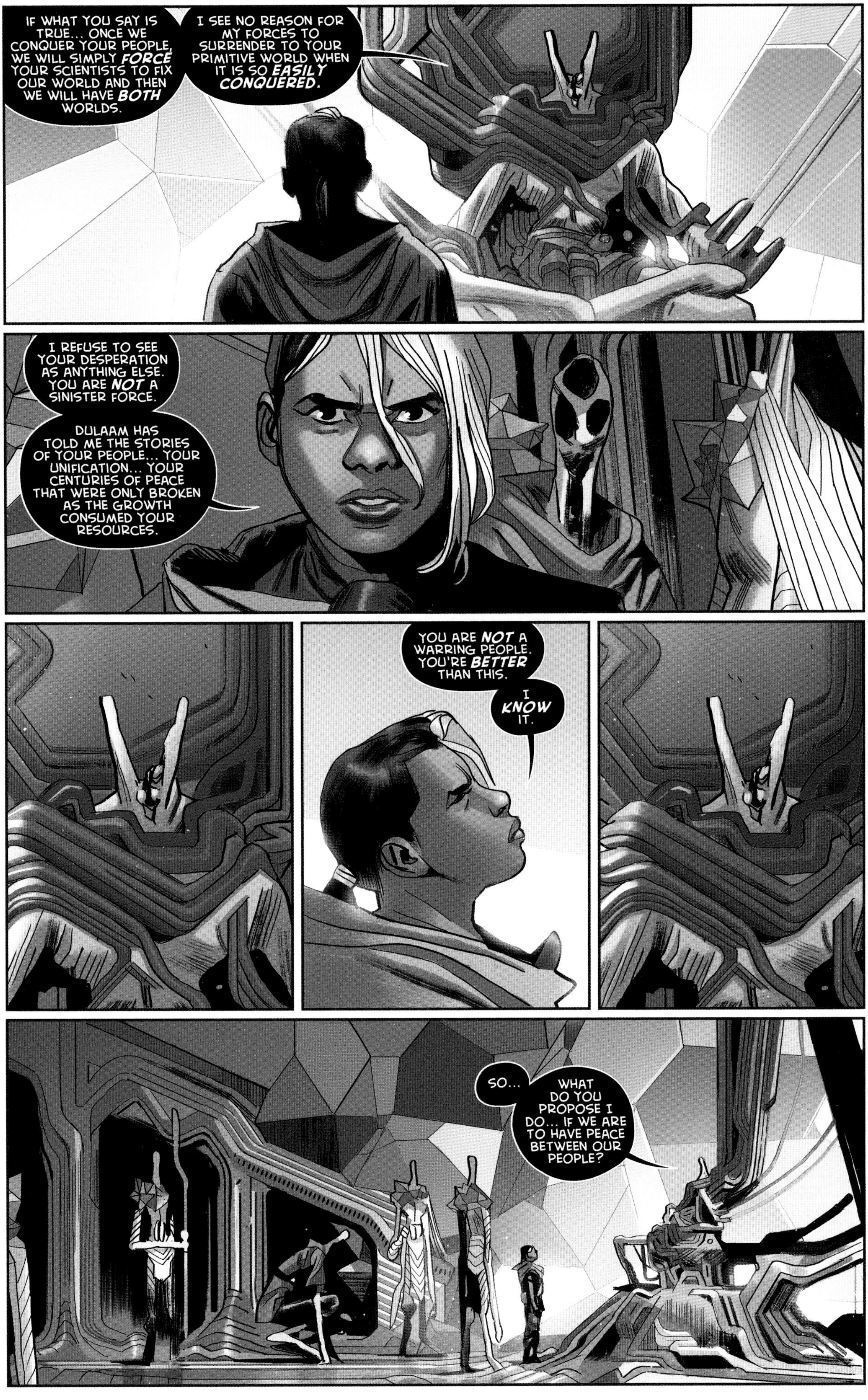
IF WHAT YOU SAY IS TRUE... ONCE WE CONQUER YOUR PEOPLE, WE WILL SIMPLY FORCE YOUR SCIENTISTS TO FIX OUR WORLD AND THEN WE WILL HAVE BOTH WORLDS.
I SEE NO REASON FOR MY FORCES TO SURRENDER TO YOUR PRIMITIVE WORLD WHEN IT IS SO EASILY CONQUERED.
I REFUSE TO SEE YOUR DESPERATION AS ANYTHING ELSE. YOU ARE NOT A SINISTER FORCE.
DULAAM HAS TOLD ME THE STORIES OF YOUR PEOPLE... YOUR UNIFICATION... YOUR CENTURIES OF PEACE THAT WERE ONLY BROKEN AS THE GROWTH CONSUMED YOUR RESOURCES.
YOU ARE NOT A WARRING PEOPLE. YOU'RE BETTER THAN THIS.
I KNOW IT.
SO...
WHAT DO YOU PROPOSE I DO... IF WE ARE TO HAVE PEACE BETWEEN OUR PEOPLE?

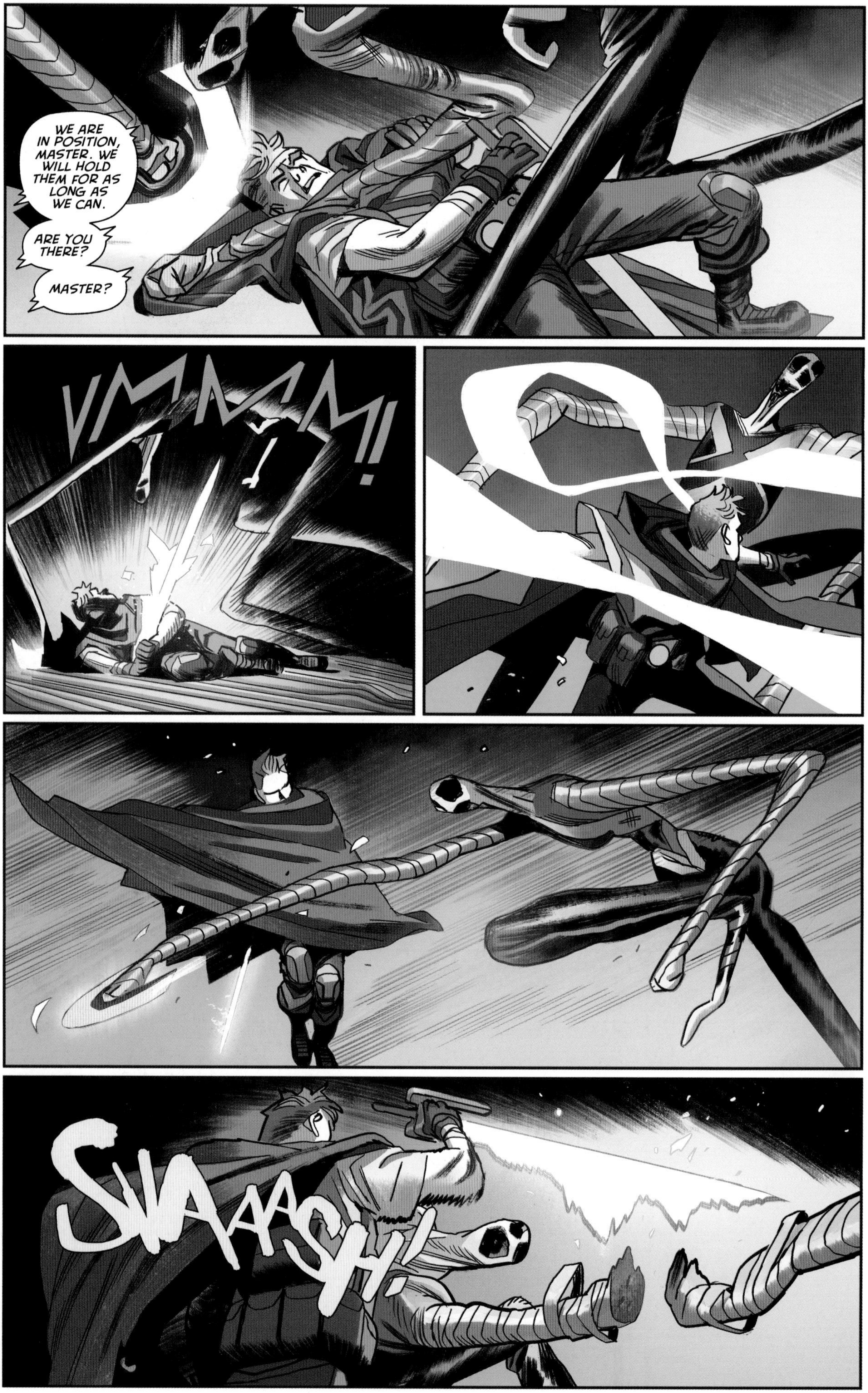
WE ARE IN POSITION, MASTER. WE WILL HOLD THEM FOR AS LONG AS WE CAN.
ARE YOU THERE?
MASTER?
VMMM!!
SHAAASH!

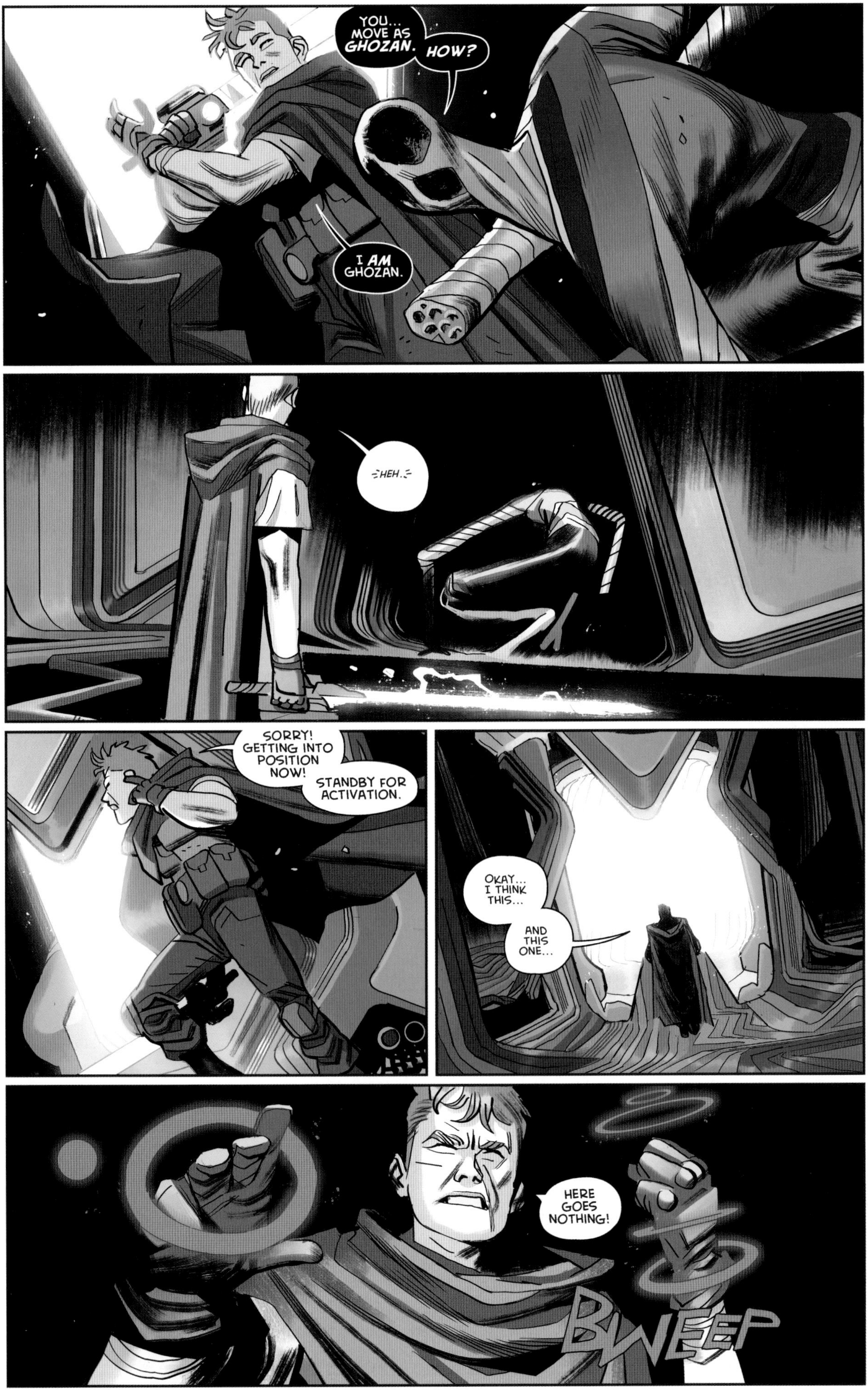
YOU... MOVE AS GHOZAN.
HOW?
I AM GHOZAN.
HEH.
SORRY! GETTING INTO POSITION NOW!
STANDBY FOR ACTIVATION.
OKAY... I THINK THIS...
AND THIS ONE...
HERE GOES NOTHING!
BWEEP

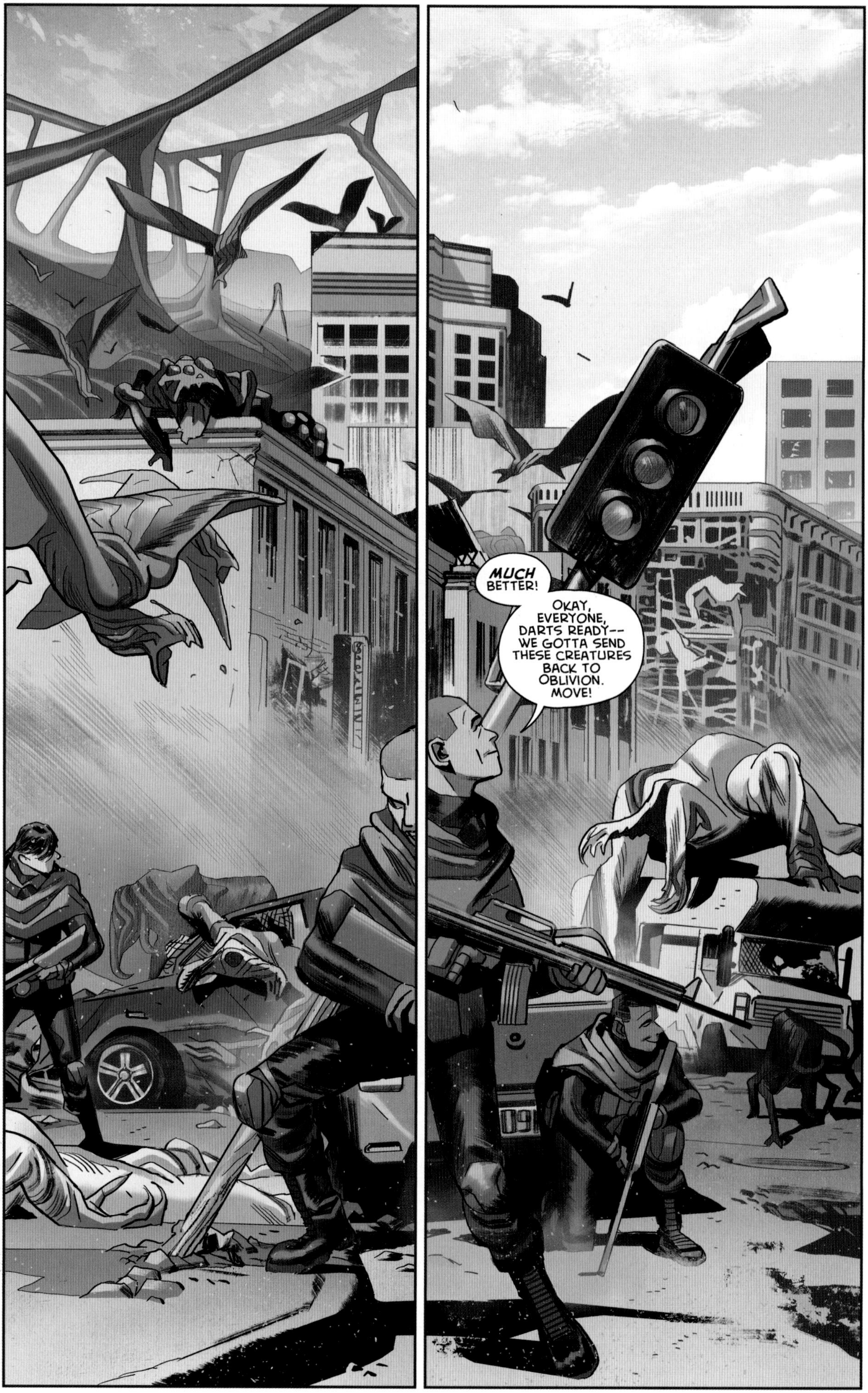
MUCH BETTER!
OKAY, EVERYONE, DARTS READY--WE GOTTA SEND THESE CREATURES BACK TO OBLIVION. MOVE!

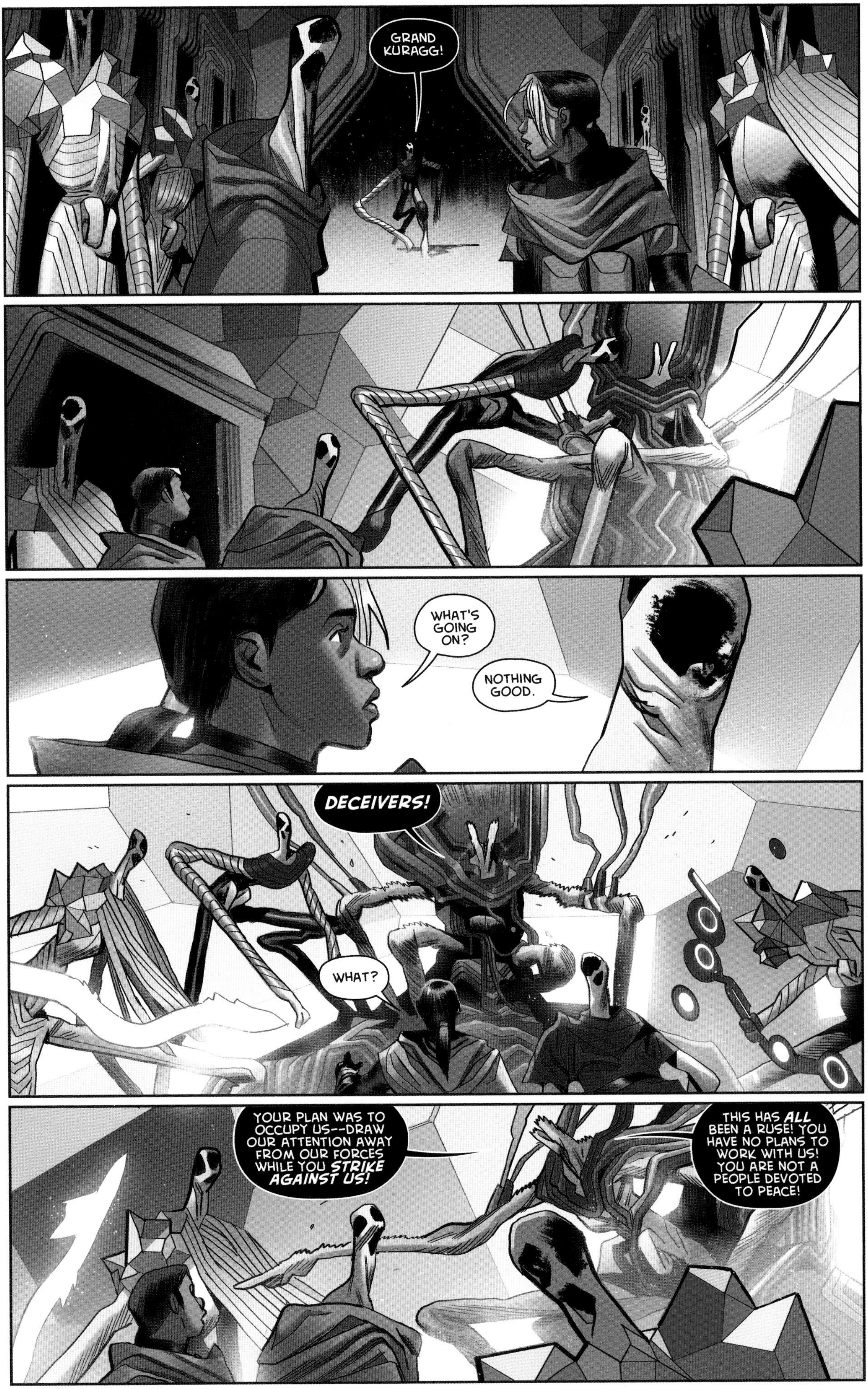
GRAND KURAGG!
WHAT'S GOING ON?
NOTHING GOOD.
DECEIVERS!
WHAT?
YOUR PLAN WAS TO OCCUPY US--DRAW OUR ATTENTION AWAY FROM OUR FORCES WHILE YOU STRIKE AGAINST US!
THIS HAS ALL BEEN A RUSE! YOU HAVE NO PLANS TO WORK WITH US! YOU ARE NOT A PEOPLE DEVOTED TO PEACE!

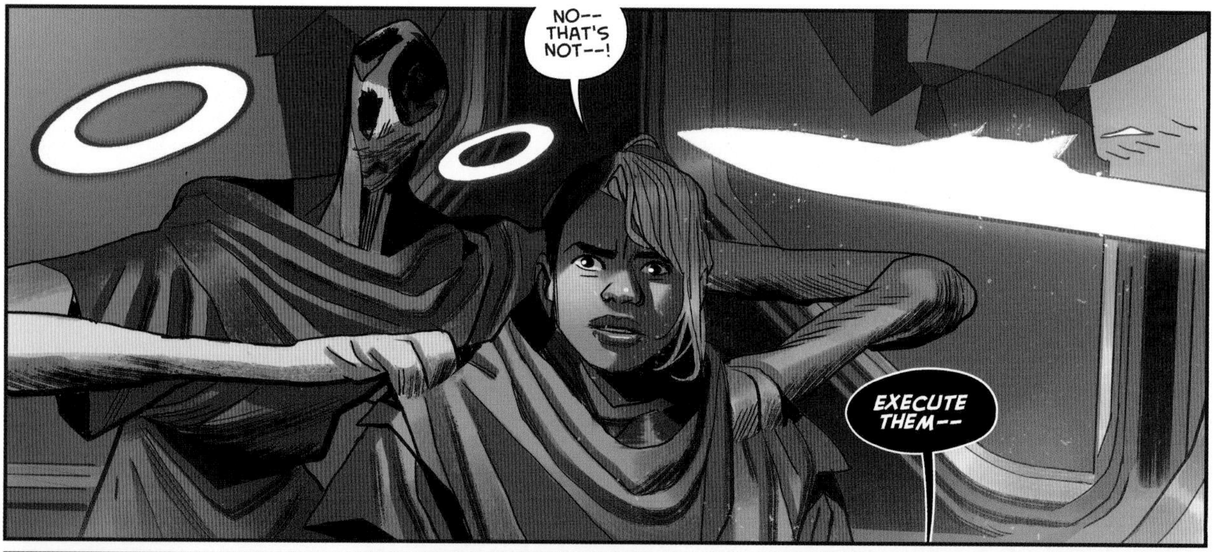
NO-- THAT'S NOT--!
EXECUTE THEM--
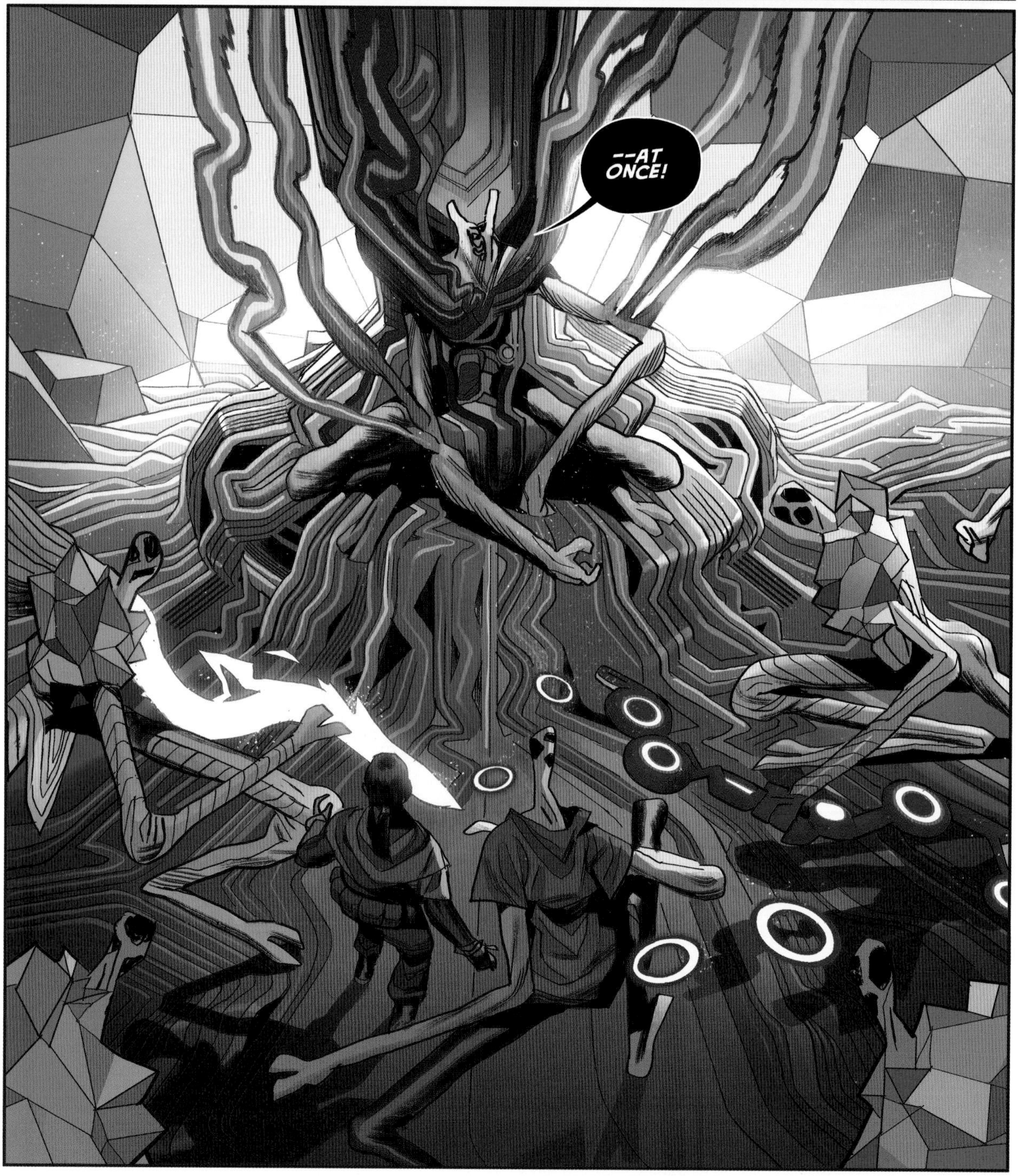
--AT ONCE!

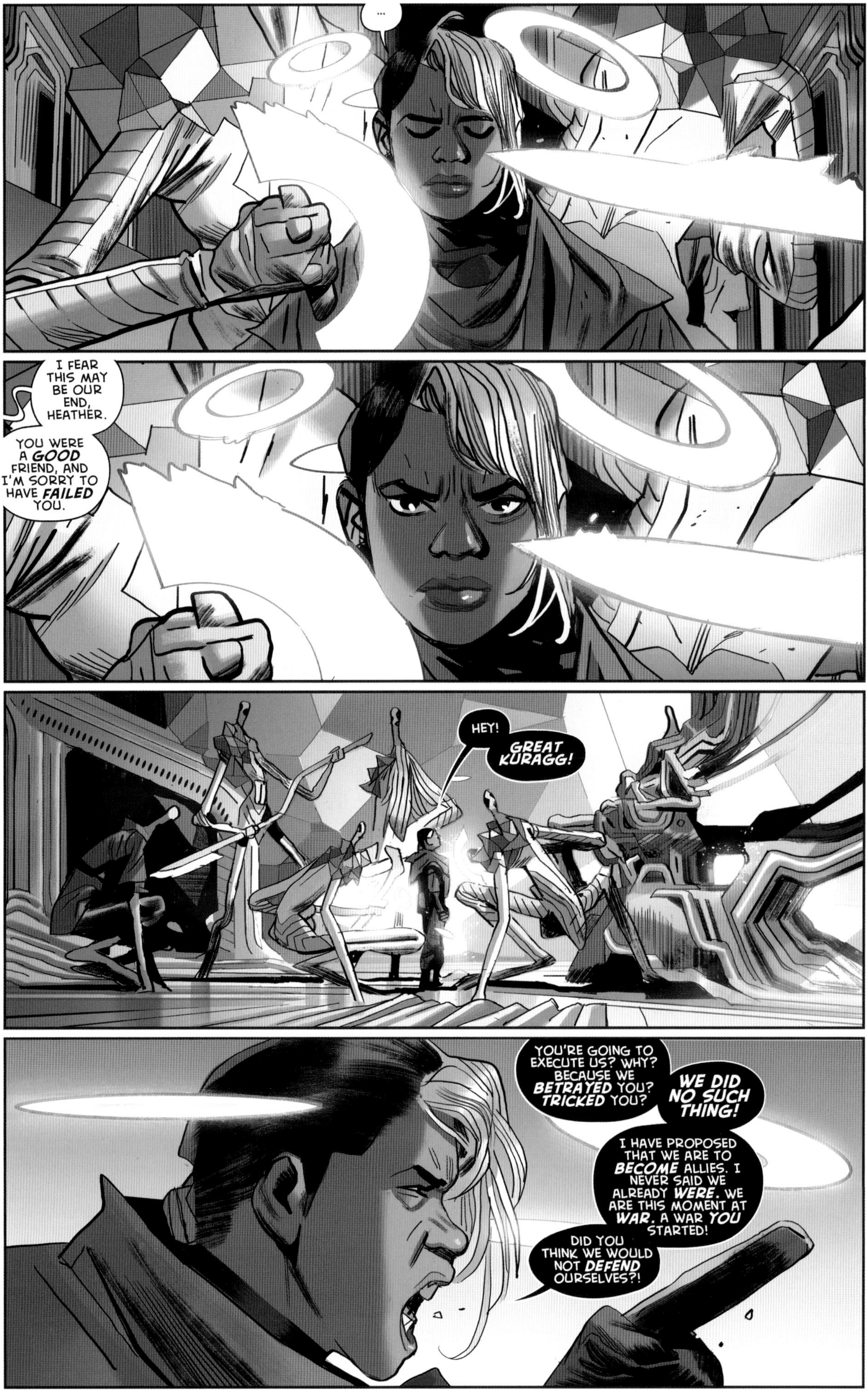
...
I FEAR THIS MAY BE OUR END, HEATHER.
YOU WERE A GOOD FRIEND, AND I'M SORRY TO HAVE FAILED YOU.
HEY! GREAT KURAGG!
YOU'RE GOING TO EXECUTE US? WHY? BECAUSE WE BETRAYED YOU? TRICKED YOU?
WE DID NO SUCH THING!
I HAVE PROPOSED THAT WE ARE TO BECOME ALLIES. I NEVER SAID WE ALREADY WERE. WE ARE THIS MOMENT AT WAR. A WAR YOU STARTED!
DID YOU THINK WE WOULD NOT DEFEND OURSELVES?!

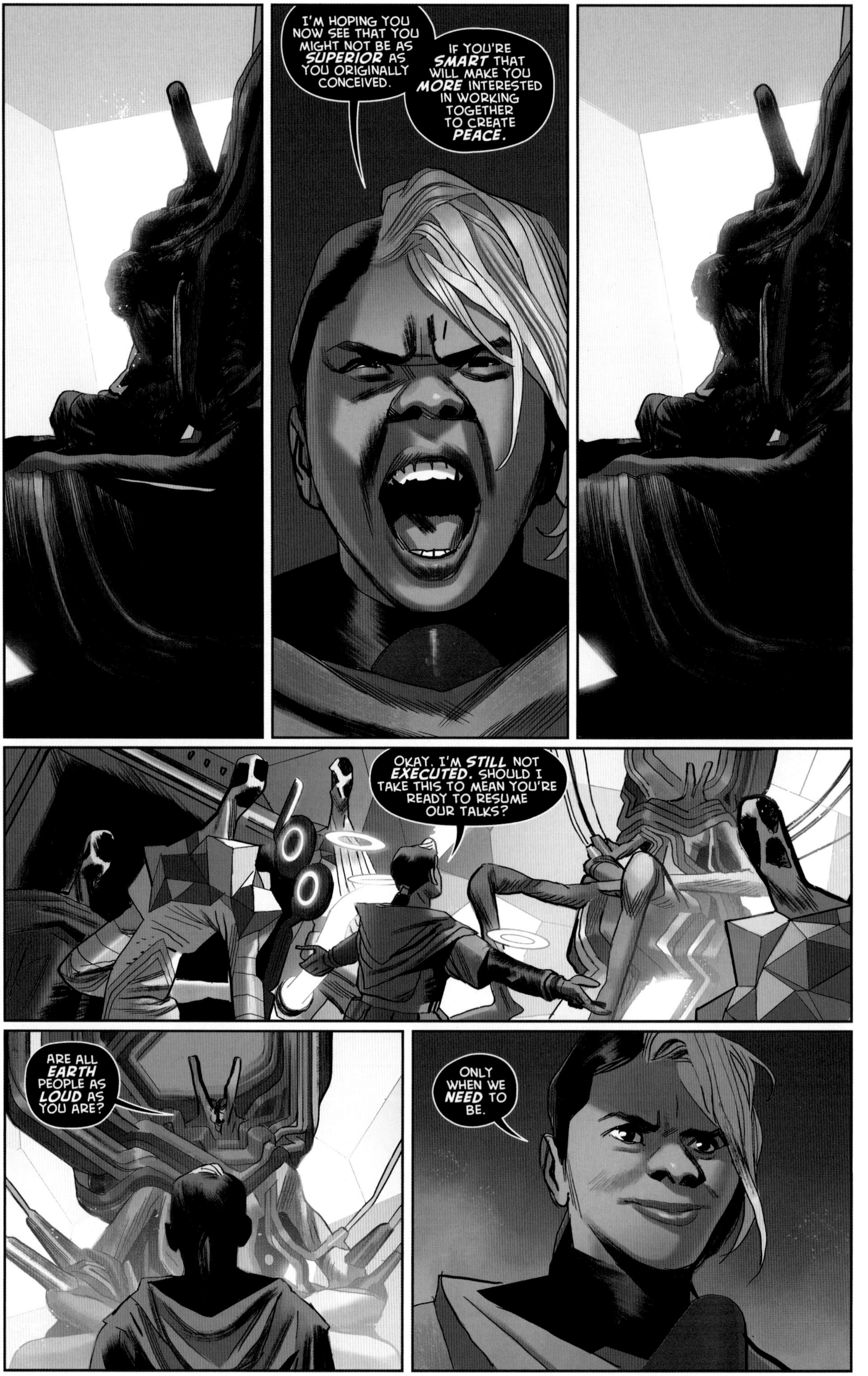
I'M HOPING YOU NOW SEE THAT YOU MIGHT NOT BE AS SUPERIOR AS YOU ORIGINALLY CONCEIVED.
IF YOU'RE SMART THAT WILL MAKE YOU MORE INTERESTED IN WORKING TOGETHER TO CREATE PEACE.
OKAY. I'M STILL NOT EXECUTED. SHOULD I TAKE THIS TO MEAN YOU'RE READY TO RESUME OUR TALKS?
ARE ALL EARTH PEOPLE AS LOUD AS YOU ARE?
ONLY WHEN WE NEED TO BE.

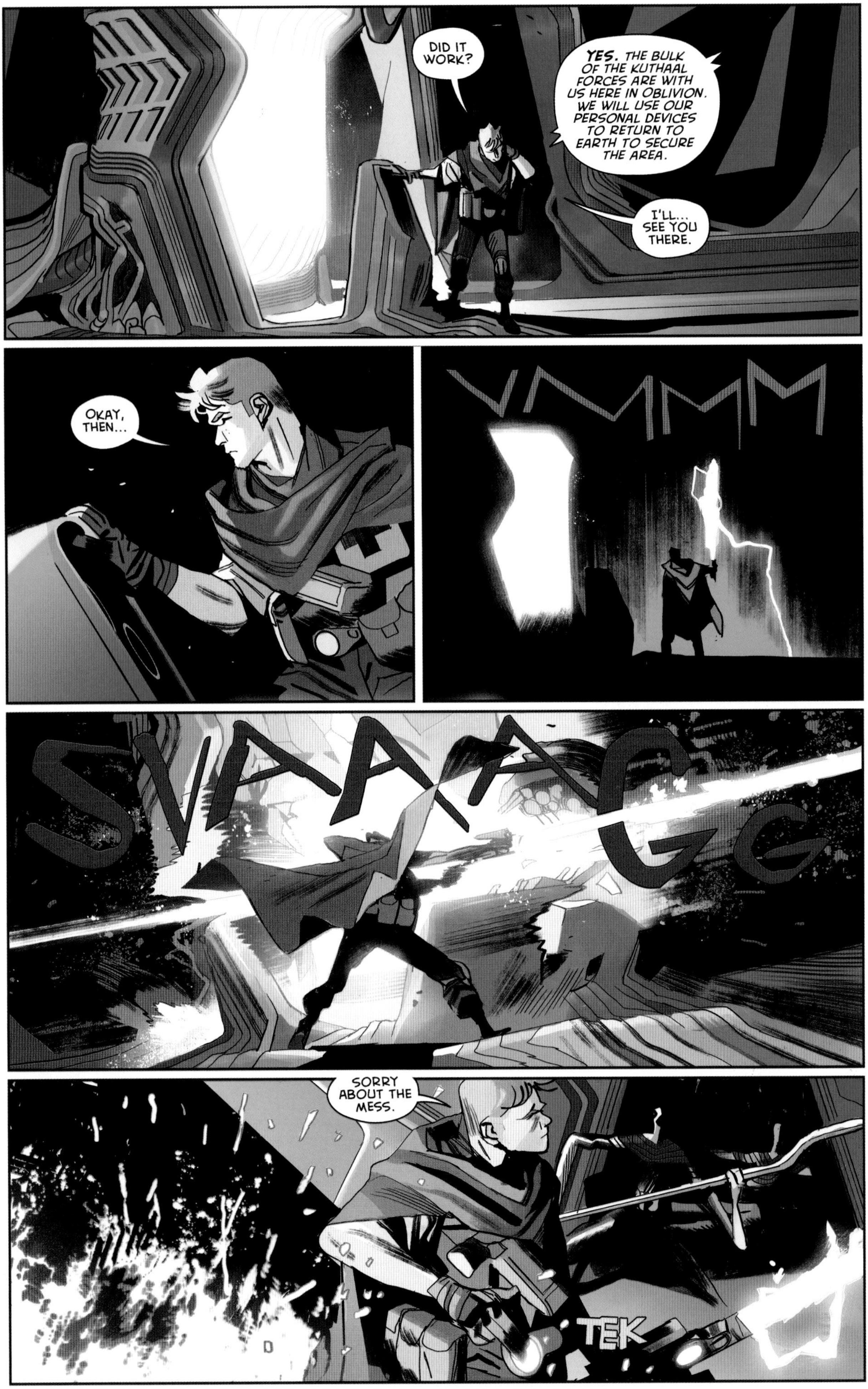
DID IT WORK?
YES. THE BULK OF THE KUTHAAL FORCES ARE WITH US HERE IN OBLIVION. WE WILL USE OUR PERSONAL DEVICES TO RETURN TO EARTH TO SECURE THE AREA.
I'LL... SEE YOU THERE.
OKAY, THEN...
VMMM
SVAAAGG
SORRY ABOUT THE MESS.
TEK

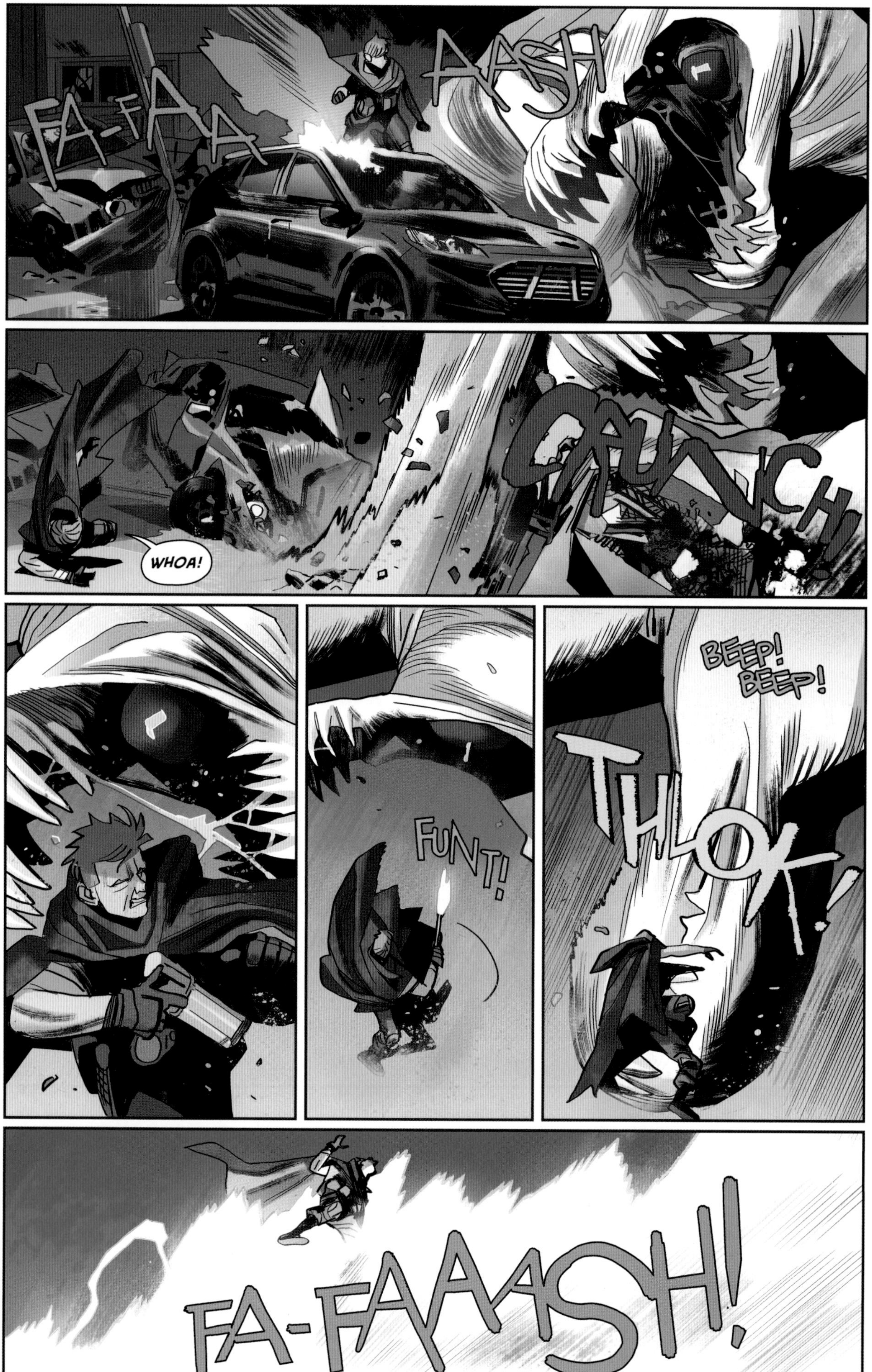
FA-FAA
AASH
CRUNCH!
WHOA!
FUNT!
BEEP! BEEP!
THLOK!
FA-FAAASH!

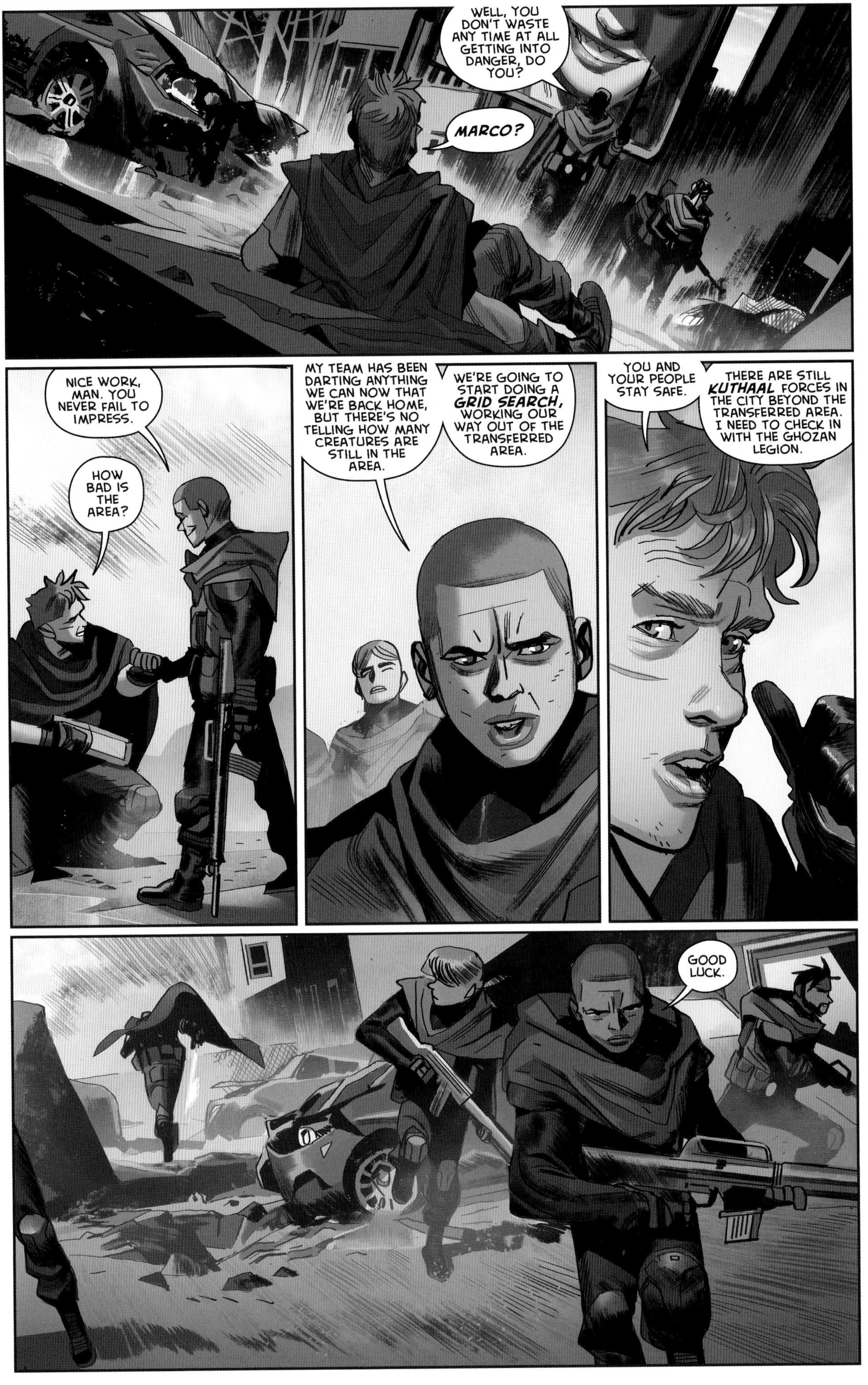
WELL, YOU DON'T WASTE ANY TIME AT ALL GETTING INTO DANGER, DO YOU?
MARCO?
NICE WORK, MAN. YOU NEVER FAIL TO IMPRESS.
HOW BAD IS THE AREA?
MY TEAM HAS BEEN DARTING ANYTHING WE CAN NOW THAT WE'RE BACK HOME, BUT THERE'S NO TELLING HOW MANY CREATURES ARE STILL IN THE AREA.
WE'RE GOING TO START DOING A GRID SEARCH, WORKING OUR WAY OUT OF THE TRANSFERRED AREA.
YOU AND YOUR PEOPLE STAY SAFE.
THERE ARE STILL KUTHAAL FORCES IN THE CITY BEYOND THE TRANSFERRED AREA. I NEED TO CHECK IN WITH THE GHOZAN LEGION.
GOOD LUCK.

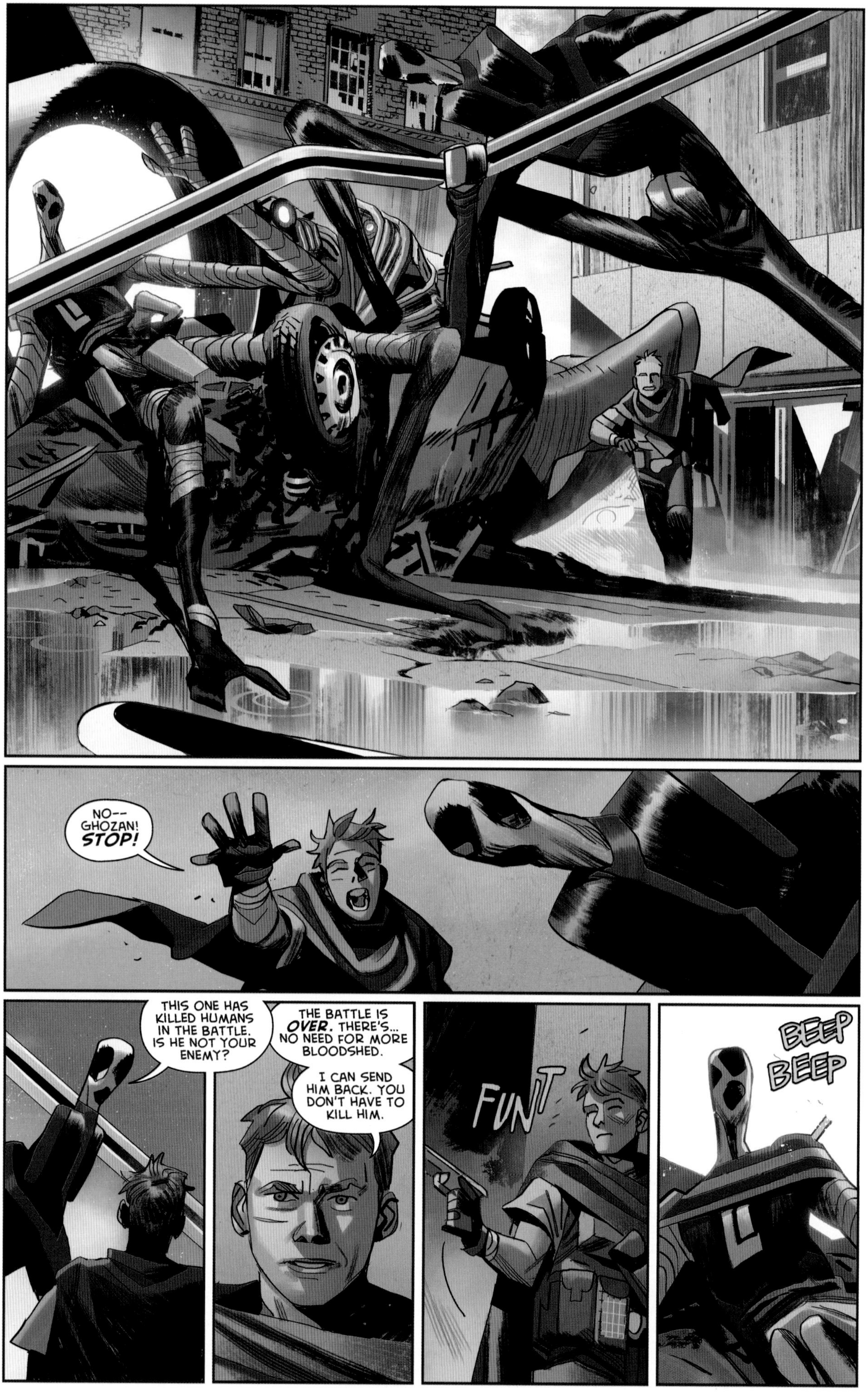
NO--
GHOZAN!
STOP!
THIS ONE HAS KILLED HUMANS IN THE BATTLE. IS HE NOT YOUR ENEMY?
THE BATTLE IS OVER. THERE'S... NO NEED FOR MORE BLOODSHED.
I CAN SEND HIM BACK. YOU DON'T HAVE TO KILL HIM.
FUNT
BEEP
BEEP

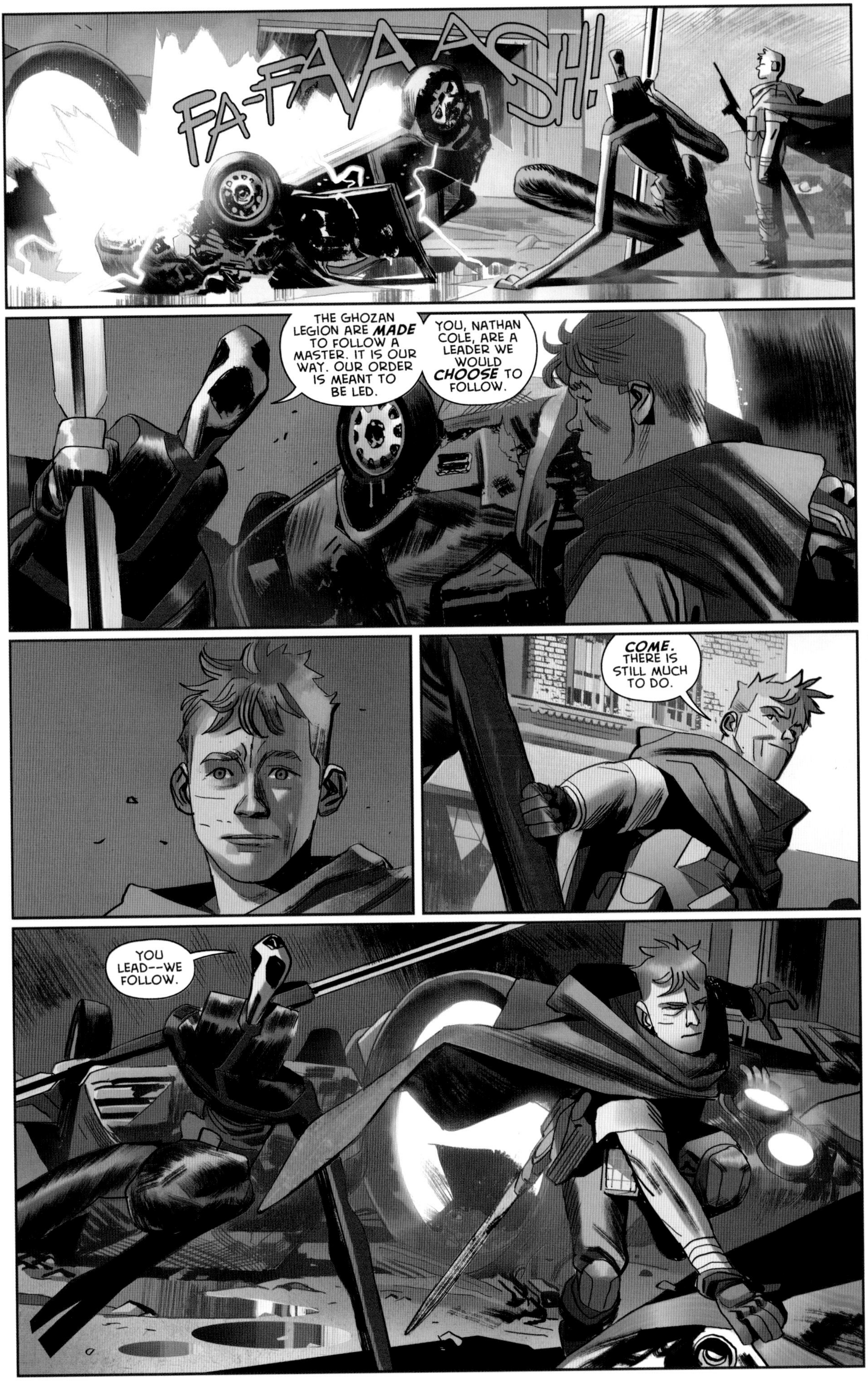
FA-FAAASH!
THE GHOZAN LEGION ARE MADE TO FOLLOW A MASTER. IT IS OUR WAY. OUR ORDER IS MEANT TO BE LED.
YOU, NATHAN COLE, ARE A LEADER WE WOULD CHOOSE TO FOLLOW.
COME. THERE IS STILL MUCH TO DO.
YOU LEAD--WE FOLLOW.

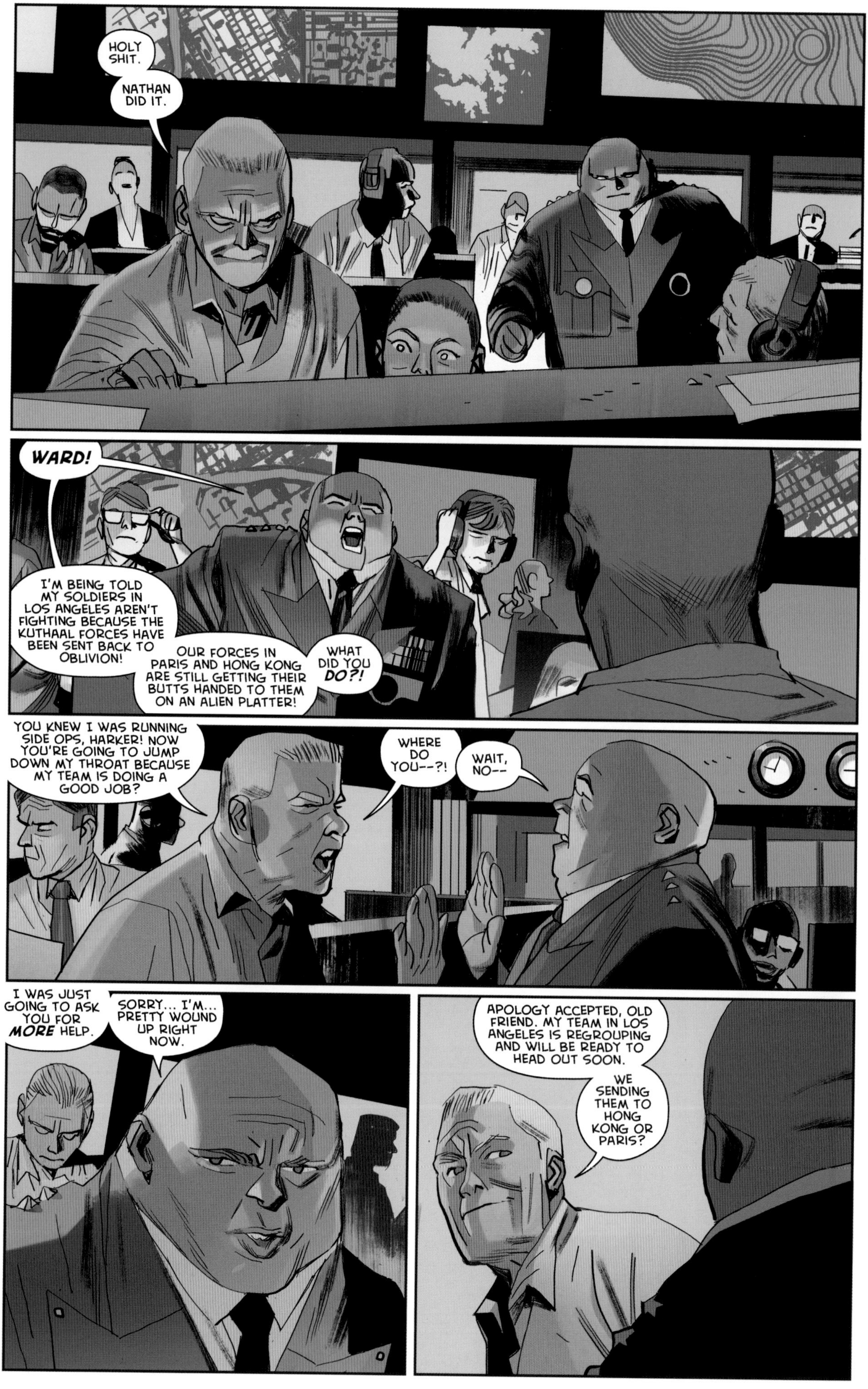
HOLY SHIT.
NATHAN DID IT.
WARD!
I'M BEING TOLD MY SOLDIERS IN LOS ANGELES AREN'T FIGHTING BECAUSE THE KUTHAAL FORCES HAVE BEEN SENT BACK TO OBLIVION!
OUR FORCES IN PARIS AND HONG KONG ARE STILL GETTING THEIR BUTTS HANDED TO THEM ON AN ALIEN PLATTER!
WHAT DID YOU *DO?!*
YOU KNEW I WAS RUNNING SIDE OPS, HARKER! NOW YOU'RE GOING TO JUMP DOWN MY THROAT BECAUSE MY TEAM IS DOING A GOOD JOB?
WHERE DO YOU--?!
WAIT, NO--
I WAS JUST GOING TO ASK YOU FOR *MORE* HELP.
SORRY... I'M... PRETTY WOUND UP RIGHT NOW.
APOLOGY ACCEPTED, OLD FRIEND. MY TEAM IN LOS ANGELES IS REGROUPING AND WILL BE READY TO HEAD OUT SOON.
WE SENDING THEM TO HONG KONG OR PARIS?

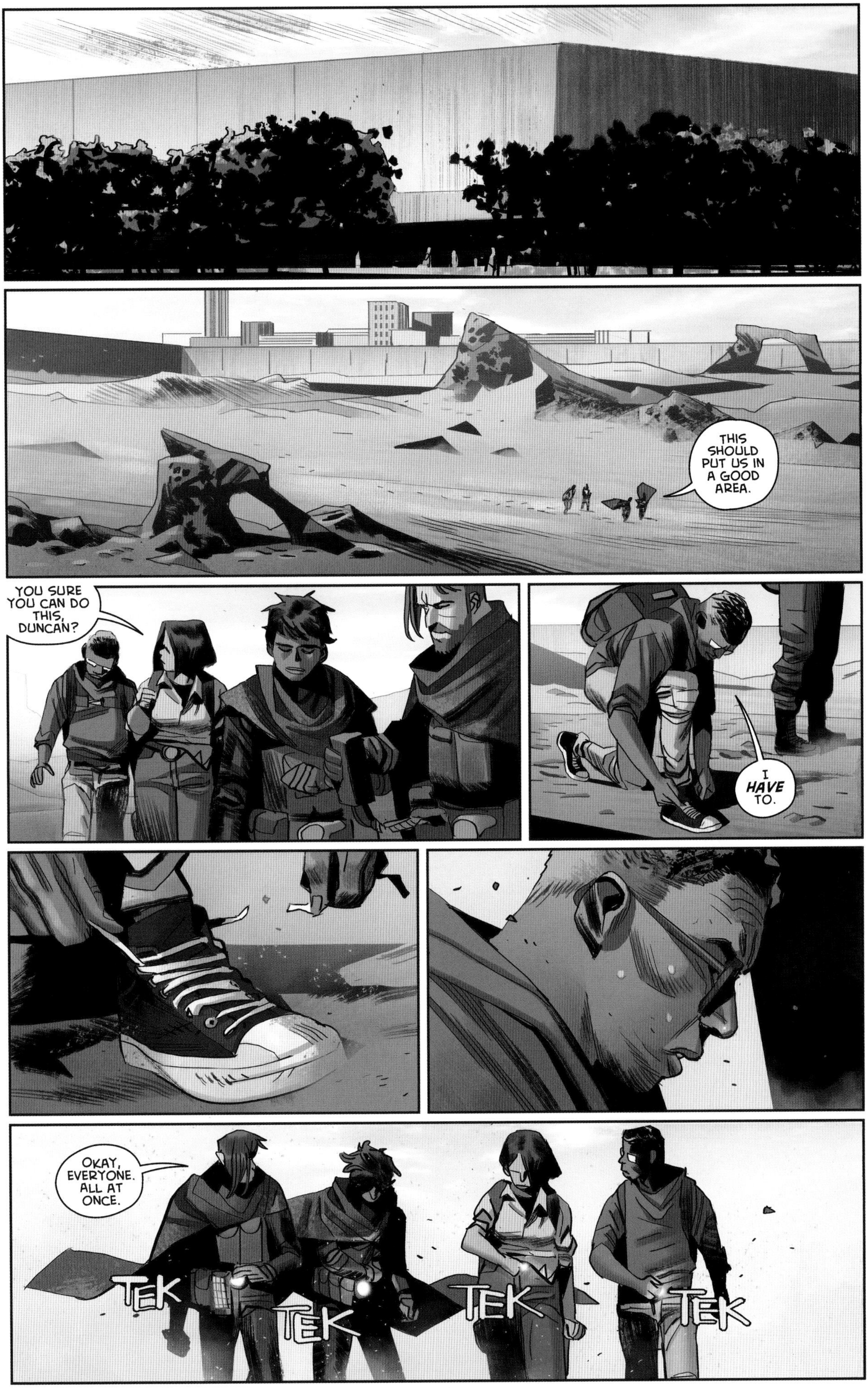
THIS SHOULD PUT US IN A GOOD AREA.
YOU SURE YOU CAN DO THIS, DUNCAN?
I *HAVE* TO.
OKAY, EVERYONE. ALL AT ONCE.
TEK
TEK
TEK
TEK

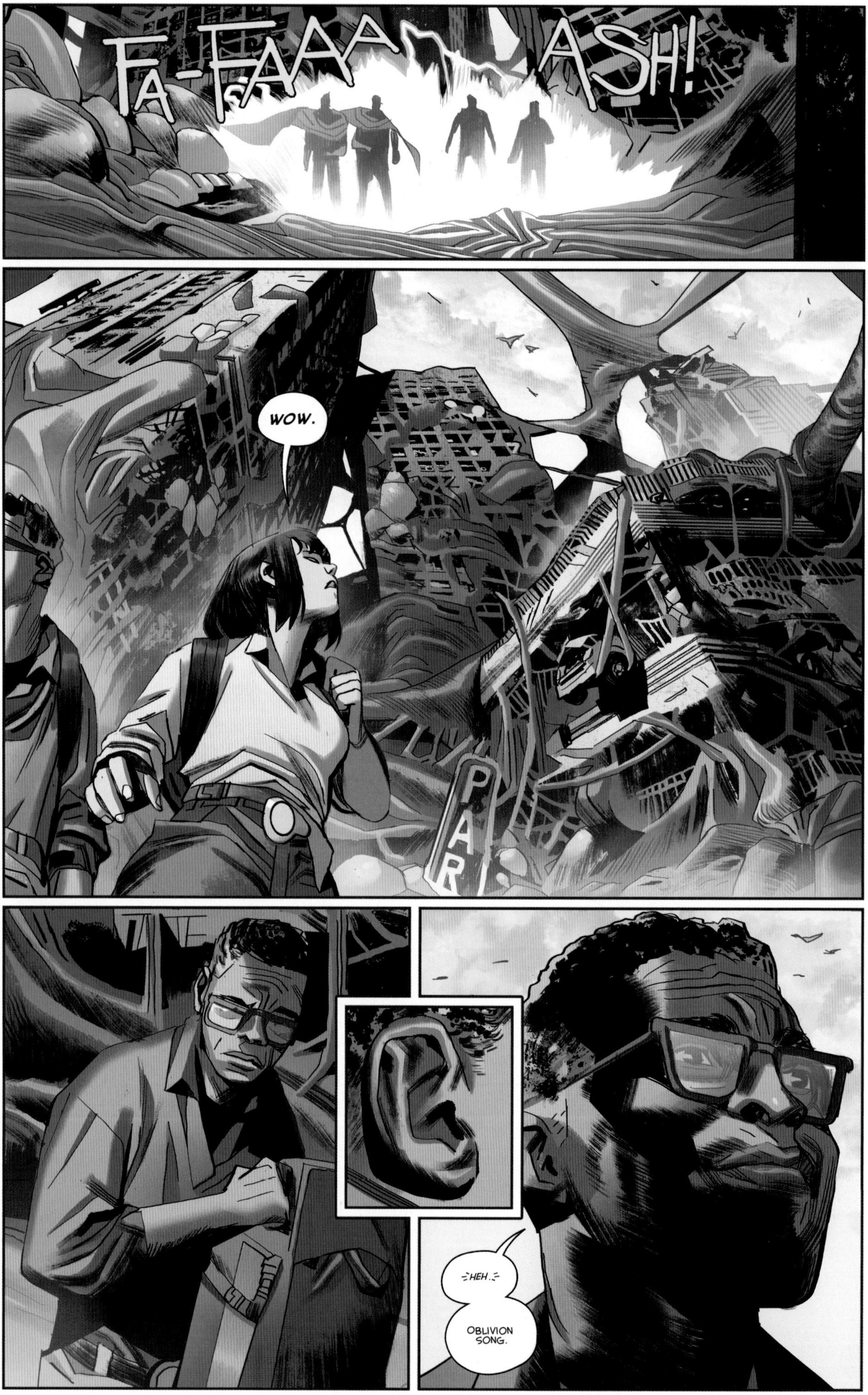
FA-FAAA ASH!
WOW.
HEH.
OBLIVION SONG.

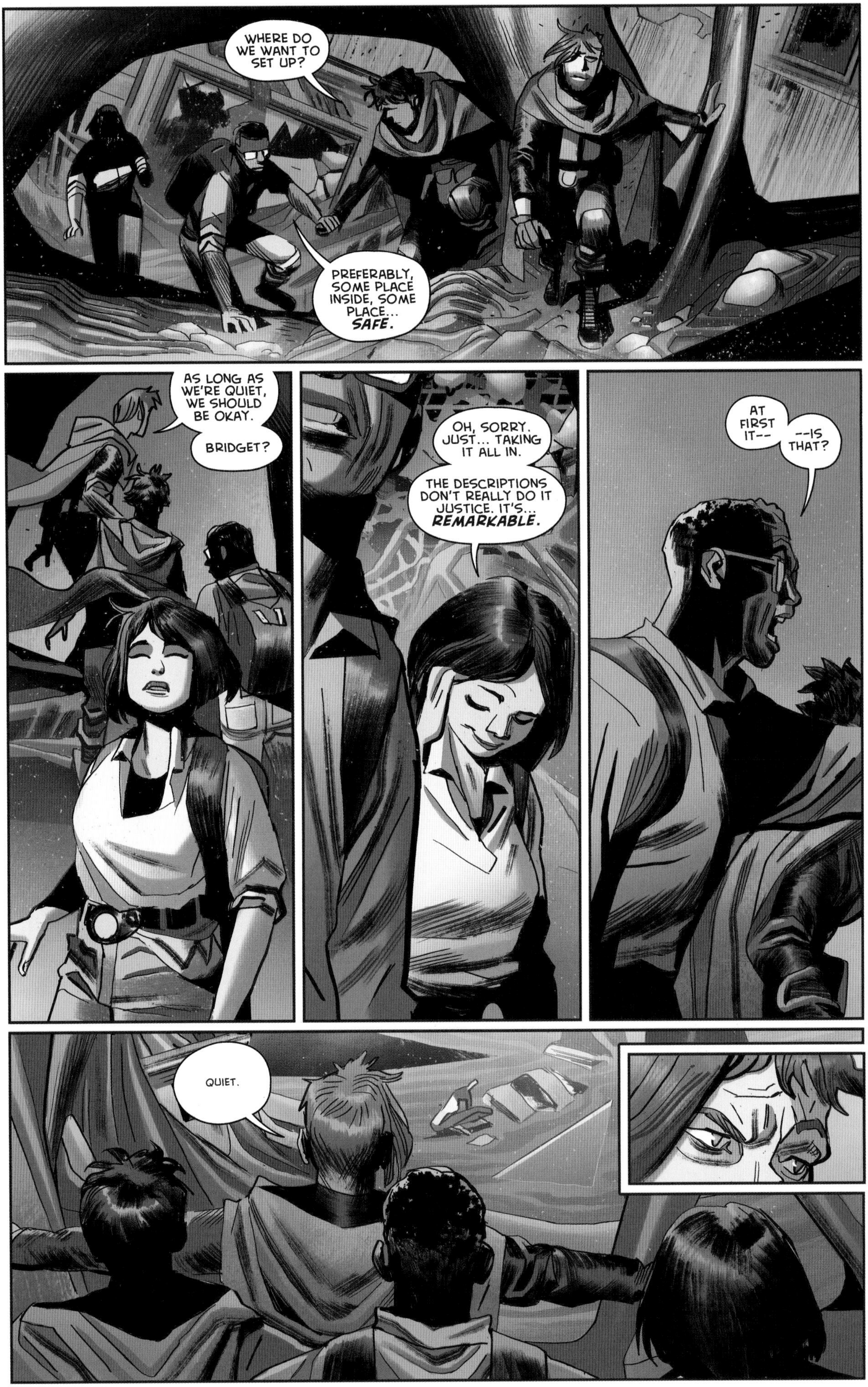
WHERE DO WE WANT TO SET UP?
PREFERABLY, SOME PLACE INSIDE, SOME PLACE... SAFE.
AS LONG AS WE'RE QUIET, WE SHOULD BE OKAY.
BRIDGET?
OH, SORRY. JUST... TAKING IT ALL IN.
THE DESCRIPTIONS DON'T REALLY DO IT JUSTICE. IT'S... REMARKABLE.
AT FIRST IT--
--IS THAT?
QUIET.

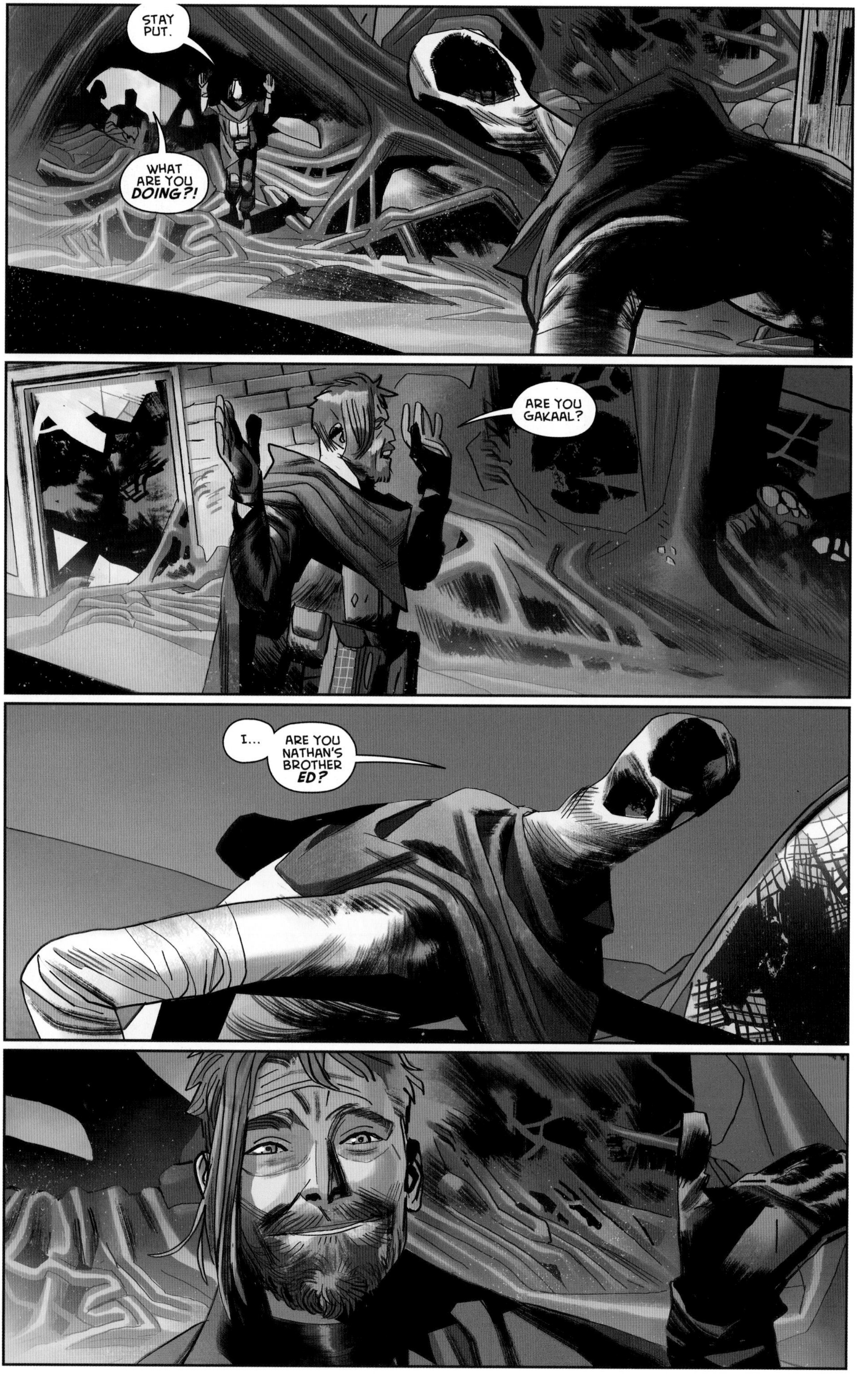
STAY PUT.
WHAT ARE YOU DOING?!
ARE YOU GAKAAL?
I...
ARE YOU NATHAN'S BROTHER ED?

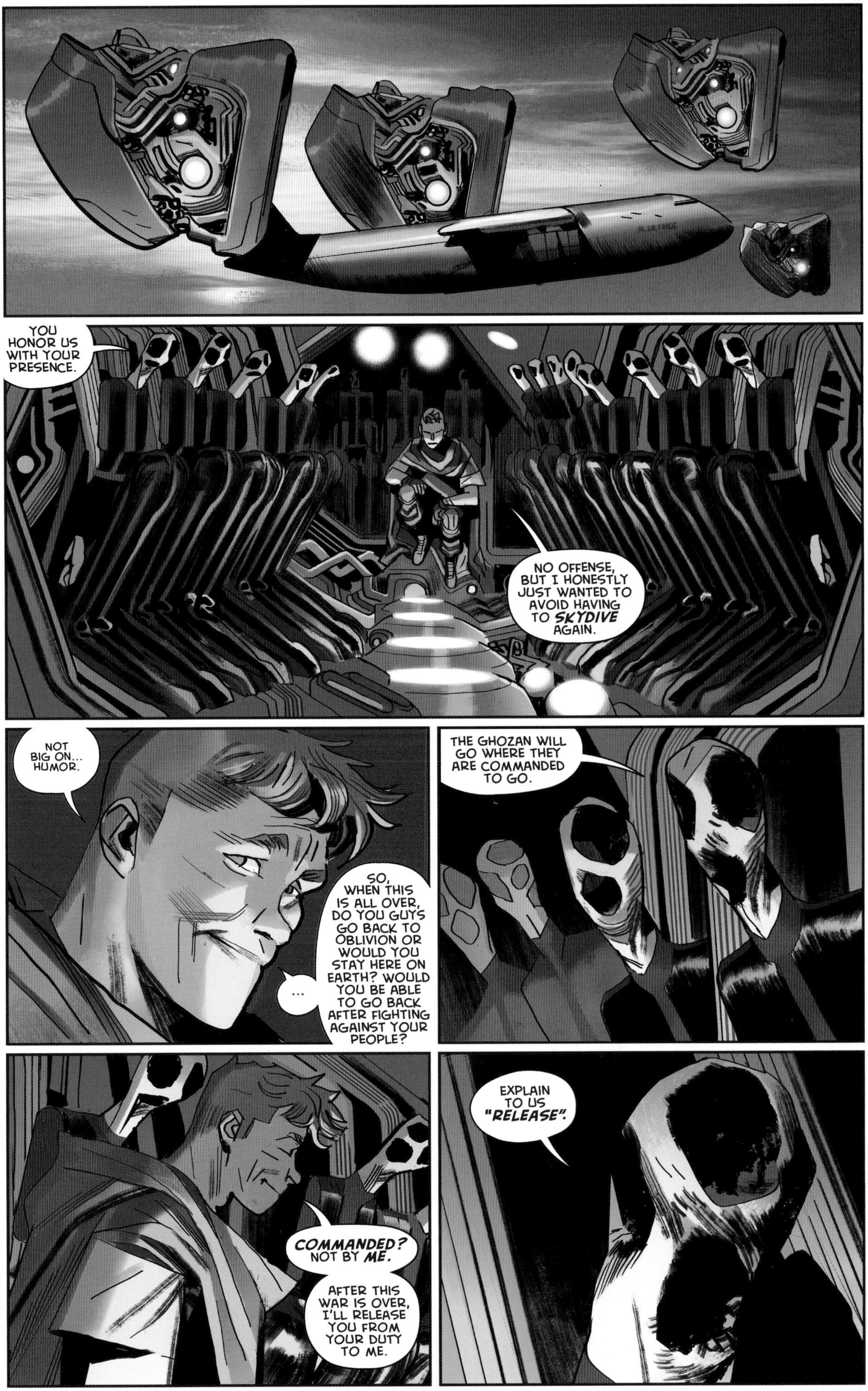
YOU HONOR US WITH YOUR PRESENCE.
NO OFFENSE, BUT I HONESTLY JUST WANTED TO AVOID HAVING TO SKYDIVE AGAIN.
NOT BIG ON... HUMOR.
...
SO, WHEN THIS IS ALL OVER, DO YOU GUYS GO BACK TO OBLIVION OR WOULD YOU STAY HERE ON EARTH? WOULD YOU BE ABLE TO GO BACK AFTER FIGHTING AGAINST YOUR PEOPLE?
THE GHOZAN WILL GO WHERE THEY ARE COMMANDED TO GO.
COMMANDED? NOT BY ME.
AFTER THIS WAR IS OVER, I'LL RELEASE YOU FROM YOUR DUTY TO ME.
EXPLAIN TO US "RELEASE".

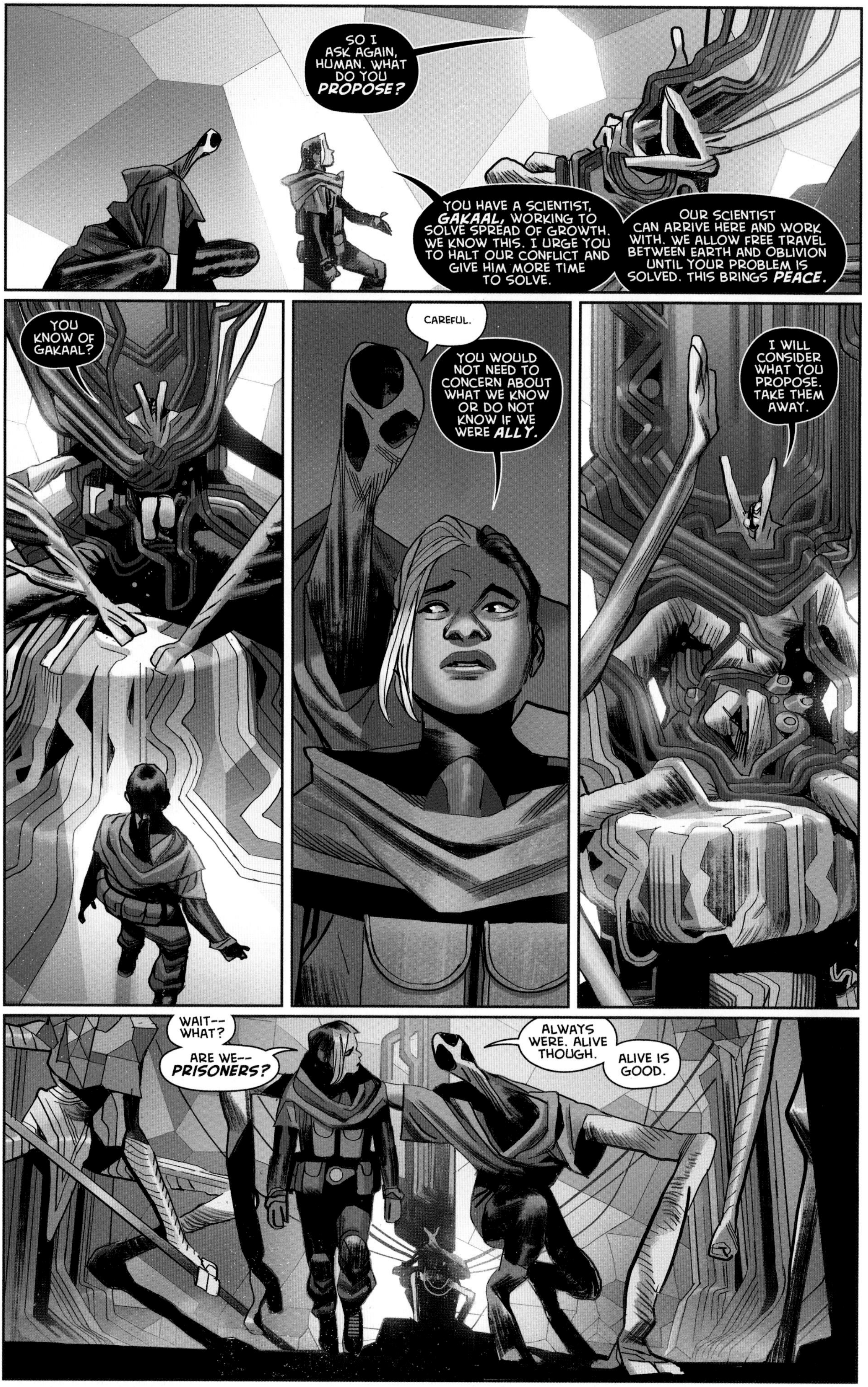

SO I ASK AGAIN, HUMAN. WHAT DO YOU PROPOSE?
YOU HAVE A SCIENTIST, GAKAAL, WORKING TO SOLVE SPREAD OF GROWTH. WE KNOW THIS. I URGE YOU TO HALT OUR CONFLICT AND GIVE HIM MORE TIME TO SOLVE.
OUR SCIENTIST CAN ARRIVE HERE AND WORK WITH. WE ALLOW FREE TRAVEL BETWEEN EARTH AND OBLIVION UNTIL YOUR PROBLEM IS SOLVED. THIS BRINGS PEACE.
YOU KNOW OF GAKAAL?
CAREFUL.
YOU WOULD NOT NEED TO CONCERN ABOUT WHAT WE KNOW OR DO NOT KNOW IF WE WERE ALLY.
I WILL CONSIDER WHAT YOU PROPOSE. TAKE THEM AWAY.
WAIT-- WHAT?
ARE WE-- PRISONERS?
ALWAYS WERE. ALIVE THOUGH.
ALIVE IS GOOD.

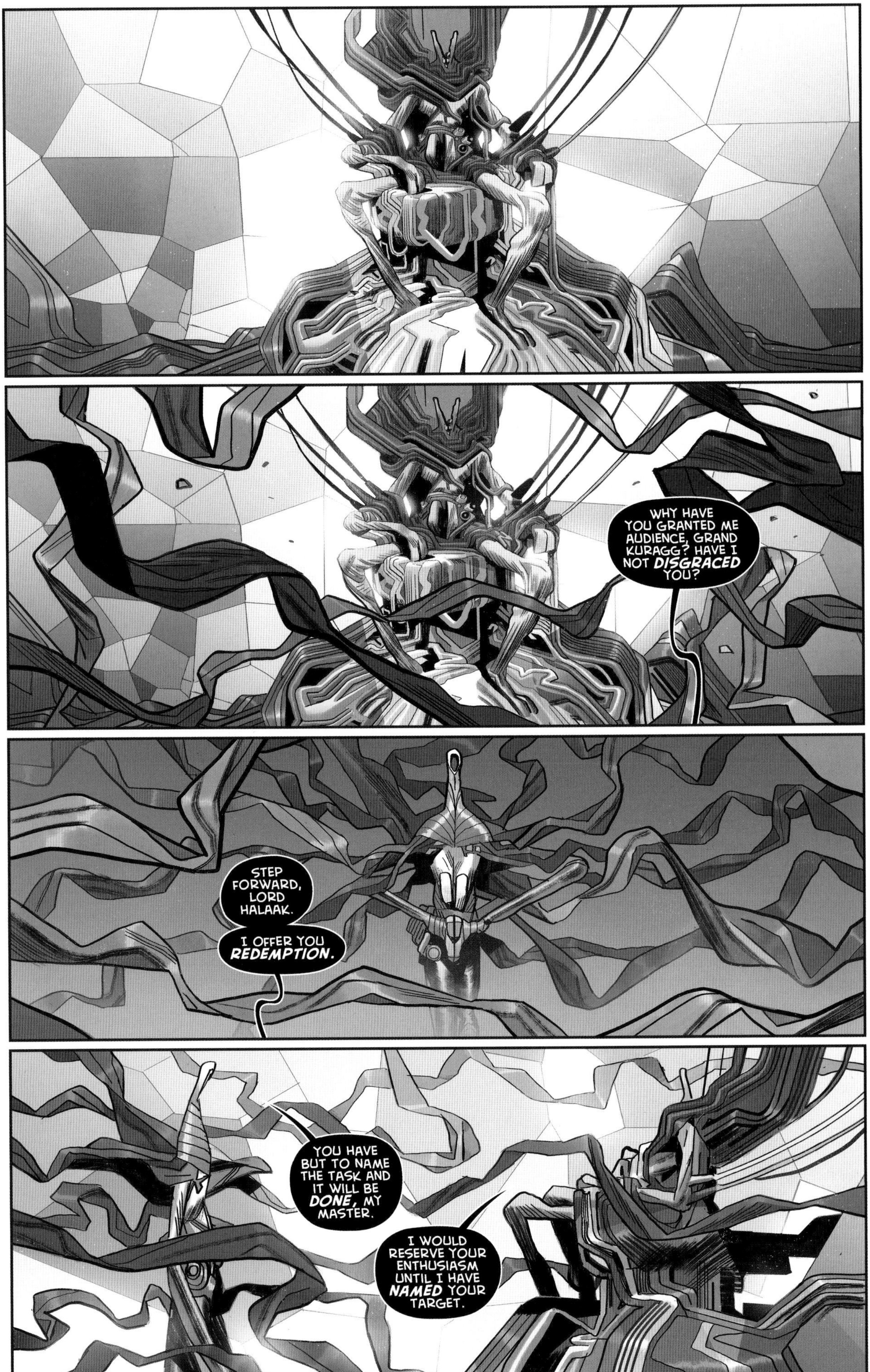
WHY HAVE YOU GRANTED ME AUDIENCE, GRAND KURAGG? HAVE I NOT DISGRACED YOU?
STEP FORWARD, LORD HALAAK.
I OFFER YOU REDEMPTION.
YOU HAVE BUT TO NAME THE TASK AND IT WILL BE DONE, MY MASTER.
I WOULD RESERVE YOUR ENTHUSIASM UNTIL I HAVE NAMED YOUR TARGET.

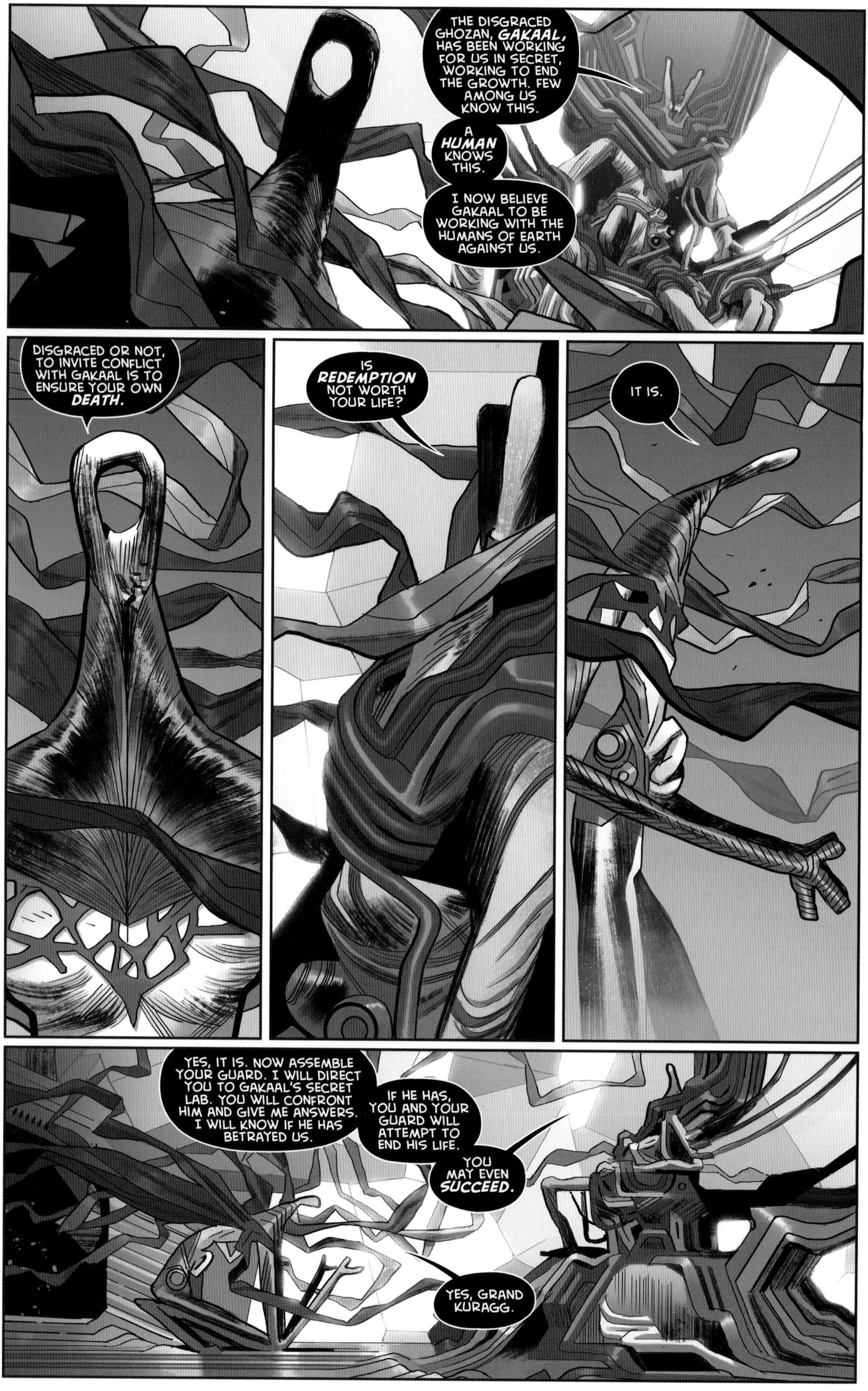
THE DISGRACED GHOZAN, GAKAAL, HAS BEEN WORKING FOR US IN SECRET, WORKING TO END THE GROWTH. FEW AMONG US KNOW THIS.
A HUMAN KNOWS THIS.
I NOW BELIEVE GAKAAL TO BE WORKING WITH THE HUMANS OF EARTH AGAINST US.
DISGRACED OR NOT, TO INVITE CONFLICT WITH GAKAAL IS TO ENSURE YOUR OWN DEATH.
IS REDEMPTION NOT WORTH YOUR LIFE?
IT IS.
YES, IT IS. NOW ASSEMBLE YOUR GUARD. I WILL DIRECT YOU TO GAKAAL'S SECRET LAB. YOU WILL CONFRONT HIM AND GIVE ME ANSWERS. I WILL KNOW IF HE HAS BETRAYED US.
IF HE HAS, YOU AND YOUR GUARD WILL ATTEMPT TO END HIS LIFE.
YOU MAY EVEN SUCCEED.
YES, GRAND KURAGG.

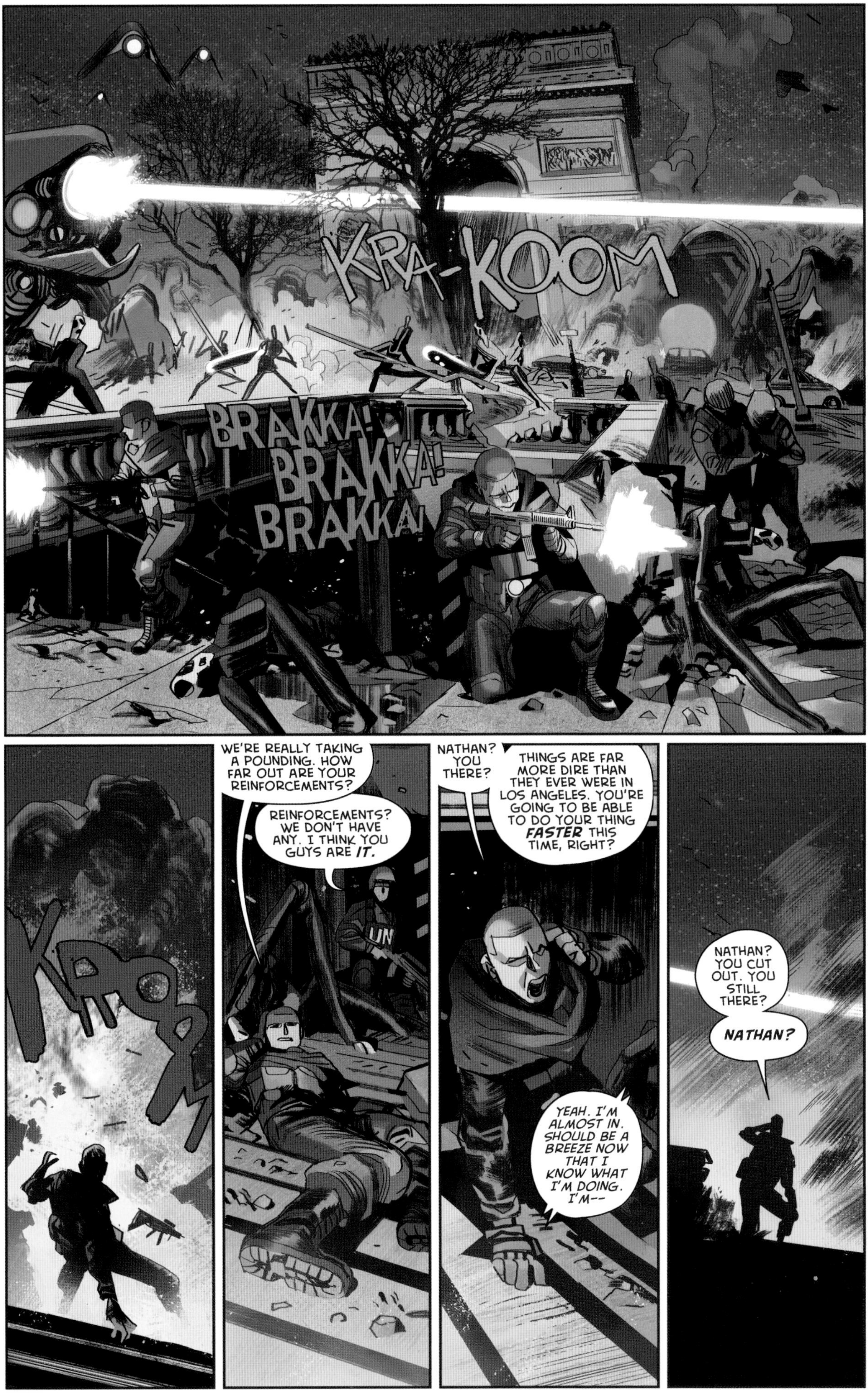
KRA-KOOM
BRAKKA! BRAKKA! BRAKKA!
KROOM
WE'RE REALLY TAKING A POUNDING. HOW FAR OUT ARE YOUR REINFORCEMENTS?
REINFORCEMENTS? WE DON'T HAVE ANY. I THINK YOU GUYS ARE IT.
UN
NATHAN? YOU THERE?
THINGS ARE FAR MORE DIRE THAN THEY EVER WERE IN LOS ANGELES. YOU'RE GOING TO BE ABLE TO DO YOUR THING FASTER THIS TIME, RIGHT?
YEAH. I'M ALMOST IN. SHOULD BE A BREEZE NOW THAT I KNOW WHAT I'M DOING. I'M--
NATHAN? YOU CUT OUT. YOU STILL THERE?
NATHAN?

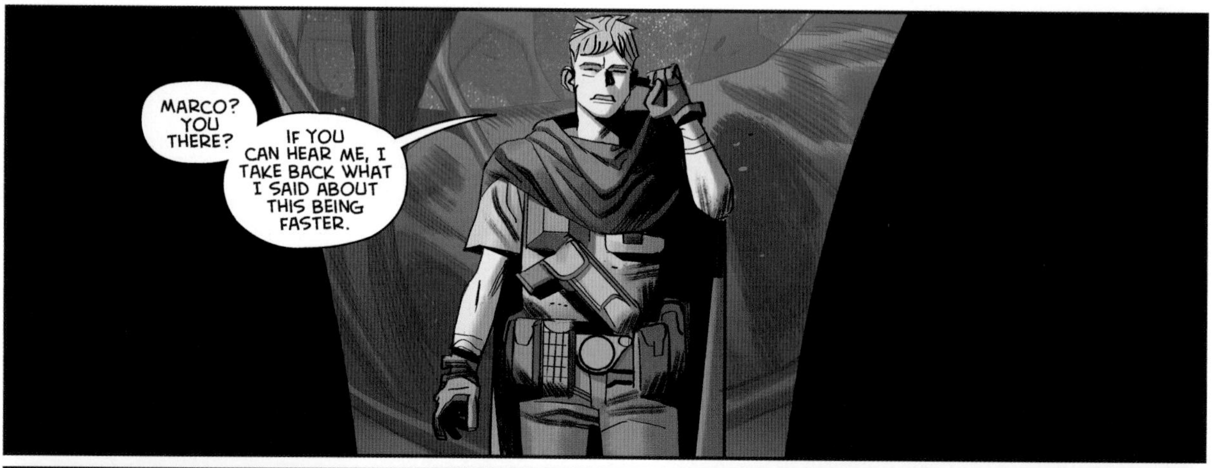
MARCO? YOU THERE?
IF YOU CAN HEAR ME, I TAKE BACK WHAT I SAID ABOUT THIS BEING FASTER.
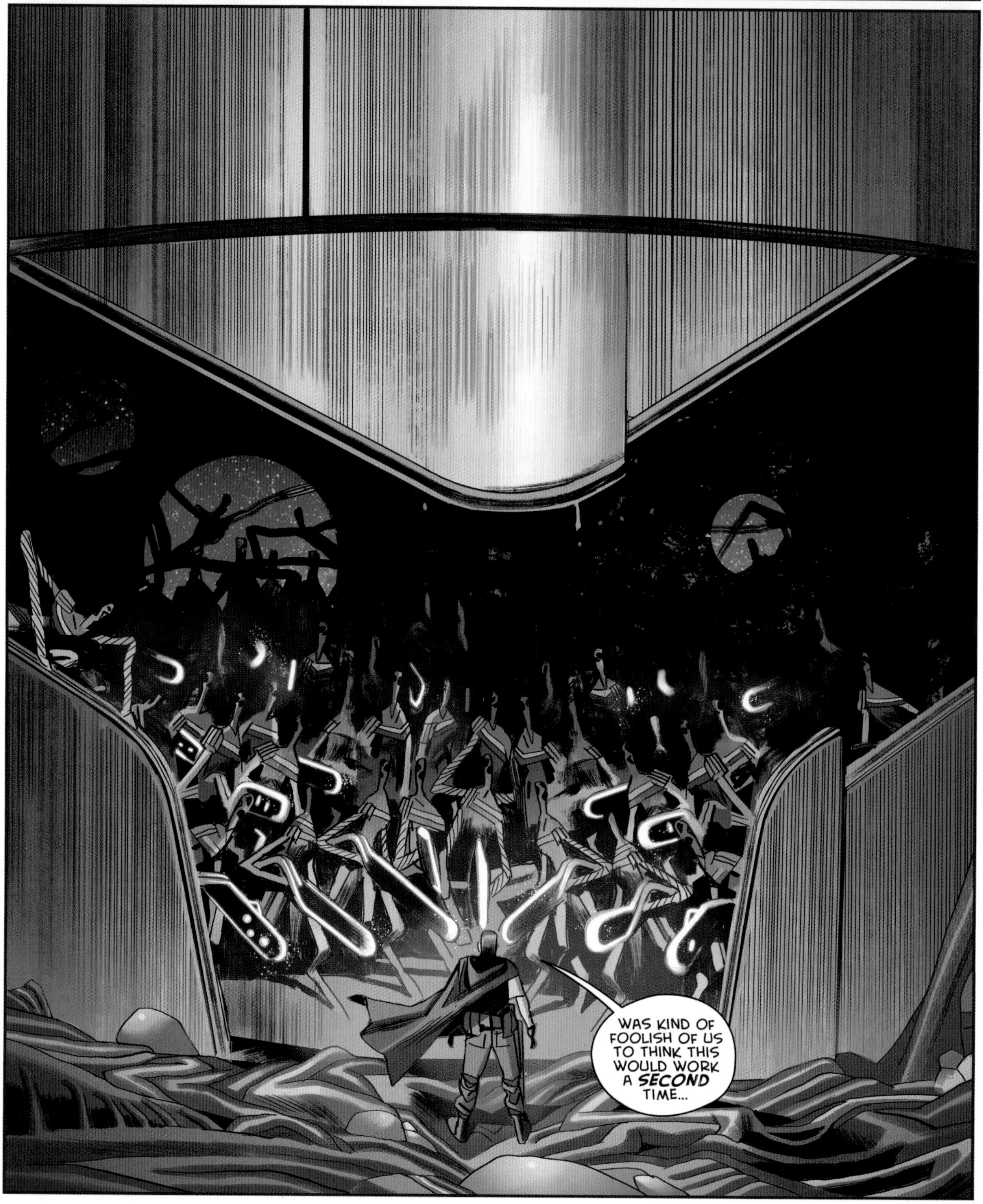
WAS KIND OF FOOLISH OF US TO THINK THIS WOULD WORK A SECOND TIME...

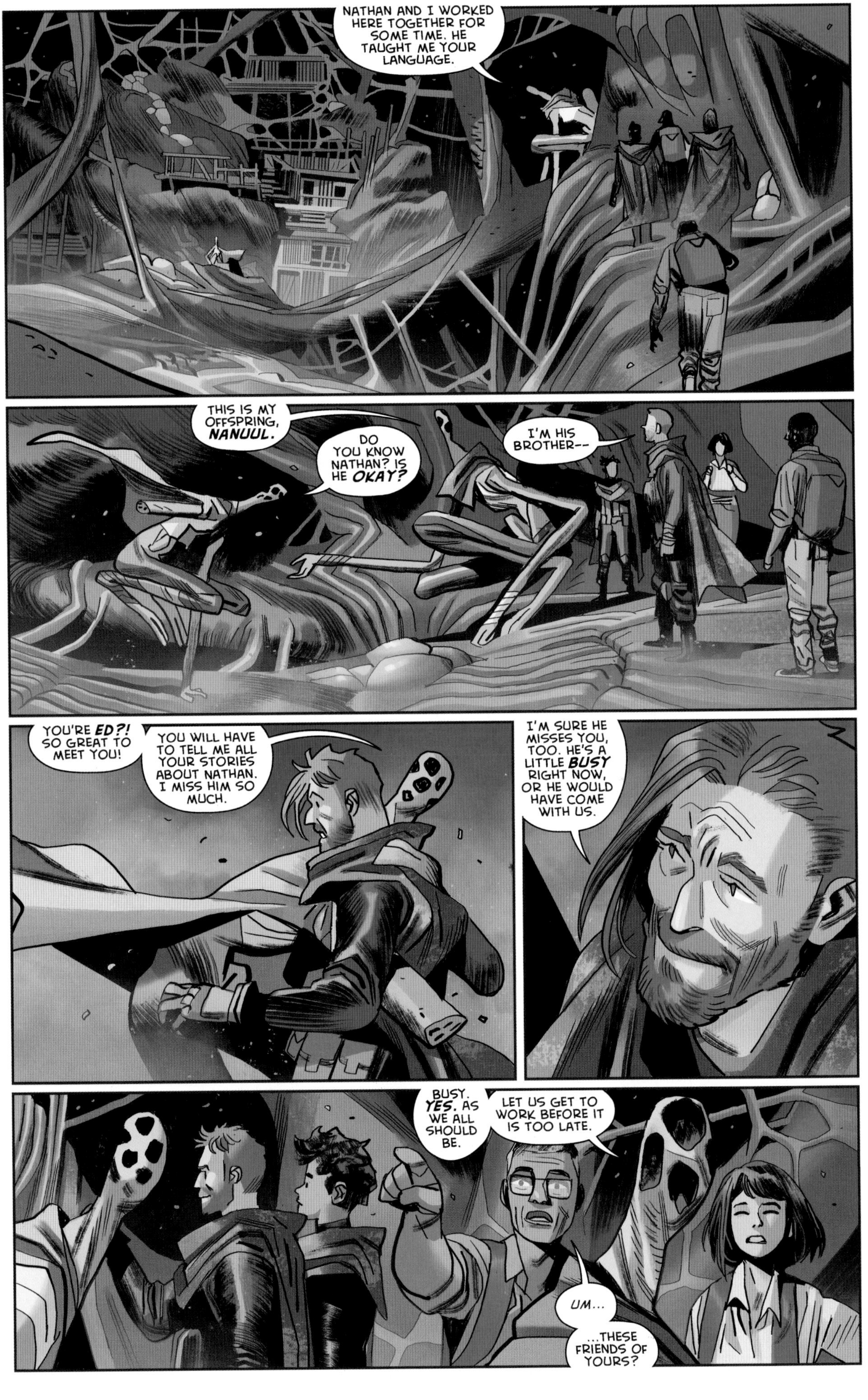
NATHAN AND I WORKED HERE TOGETHER FOR SOME TIME. HE TAUGHT ME YOUR LANGUAGE.
THIS IS MY OFFSPRING, NANUUL.
DO YOU KNOW NATHAN? IS HE OKAY?
I'M HIS BROTHER--
YOU'RE ED?! SO GREAT TO MEET YOU!
YOU WILL HAVE TO TELL ME ALL YOUR STORIES ABOUT NATHAN. I MISS HIM SO MUCH.
I'M SURE HE MISSES YOU, TOO. HE'S A LITTLE BUSY RIGHT NOW, OR HE WOULD HAVE COME WITH US.
BUSY. YES. AS WE ALL SHOULD BE.
LET US GET TO WORK BEFORE IT IS TOO LATE.
UM...
...THESE FRIENDS OF YOURS?

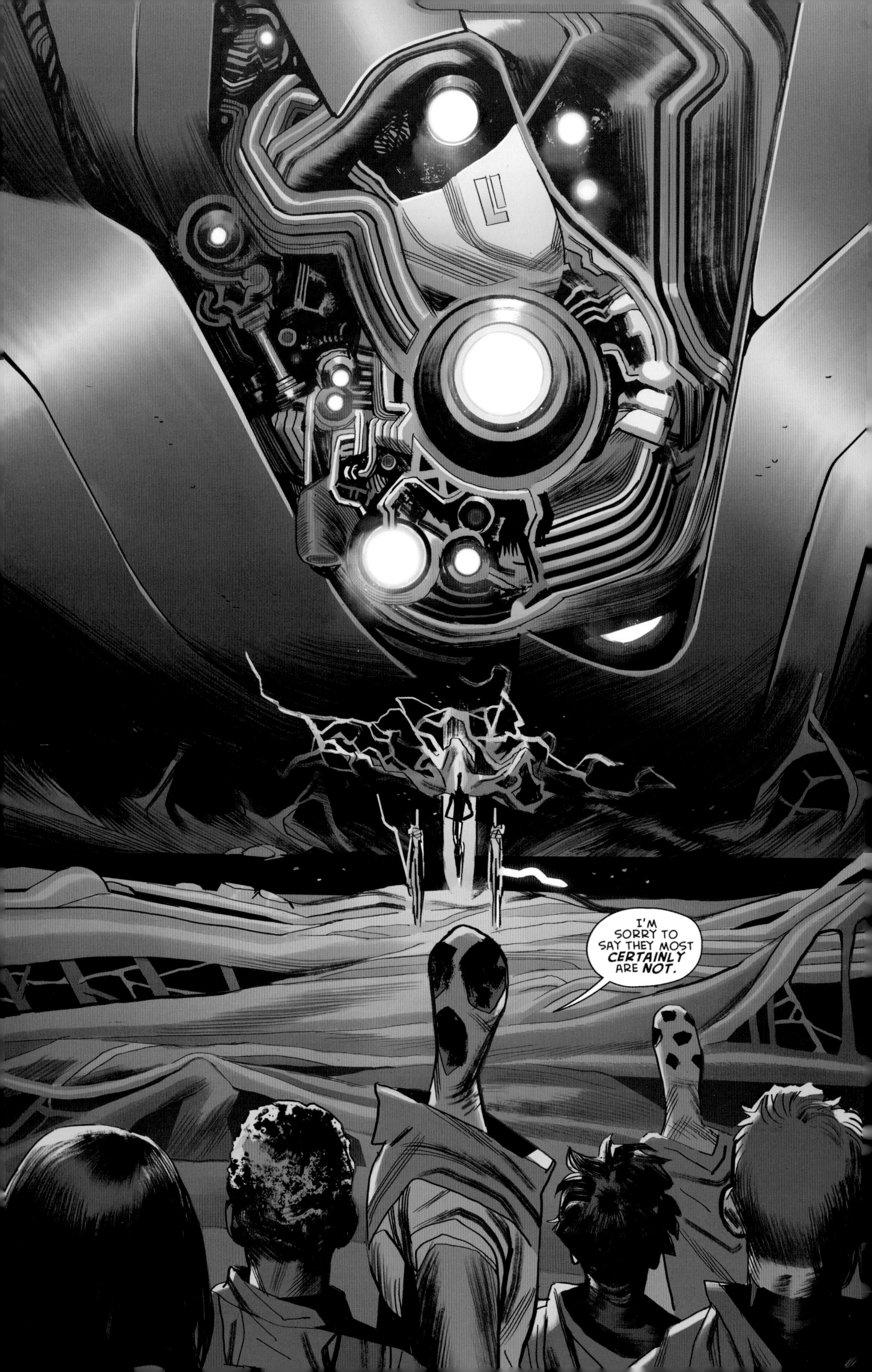
I'M SORRY TO SAY THEY MOST CERTAINLY ARE NOT.

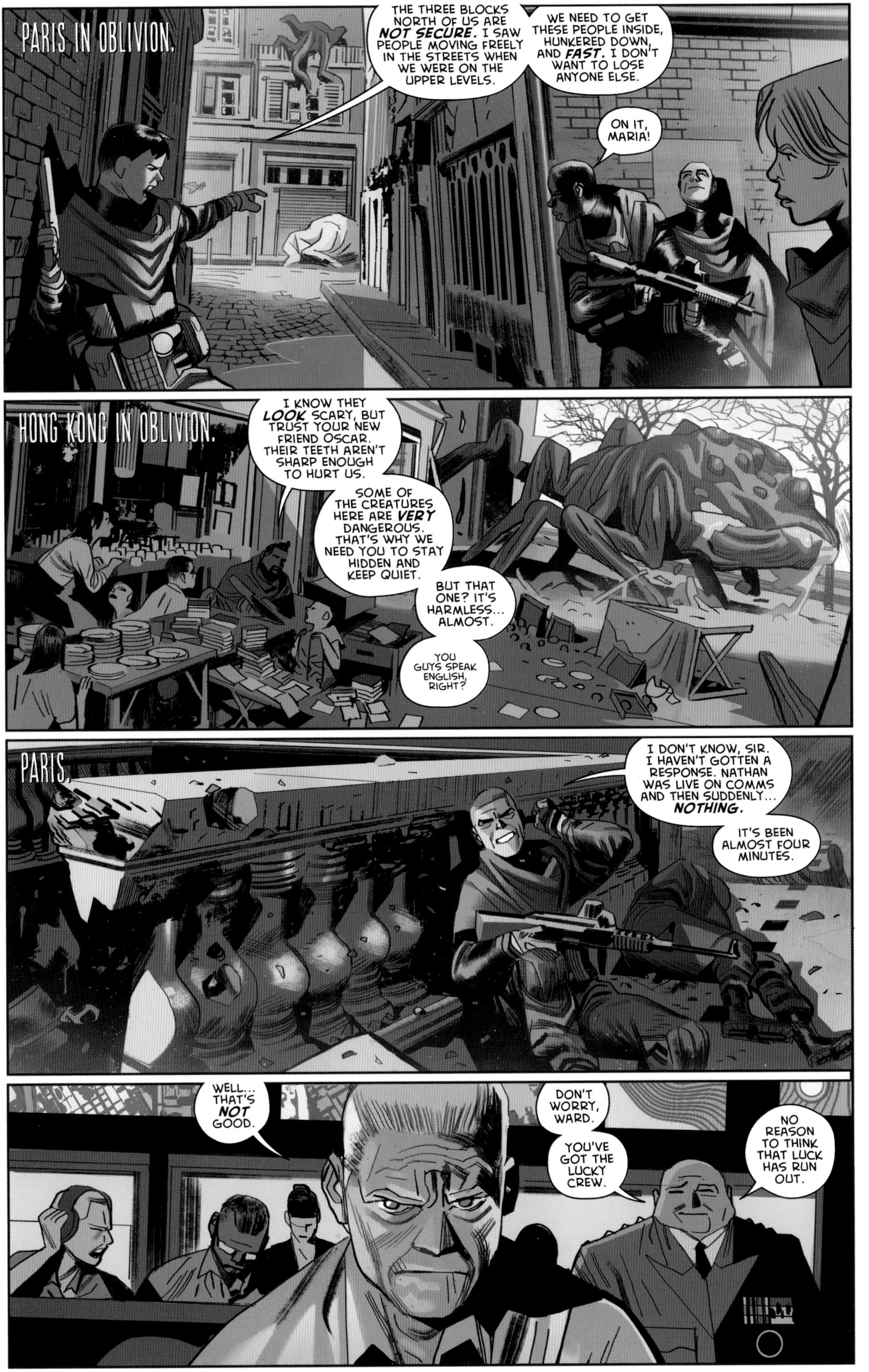
PARIS IN OBLIVION.
THE THREE BLOCKS NORTH OF US ARE NOT SECURE. I SAW PEOPLE MOVING FREELY IN THE STREETS WHEN WE WERE ON THE UPPER LEVELS.
WE NEED TO GET THESE PEOPLE INSIDE, HUNKERED DOWN, AND FAST. I DON'T WANT TO LOSE ANYONE ELSE.
ON IT, MARIA!
HONG KONG IN OBLIVION.
I KNOW THEY LOOK SCARY, BUT TRUST YOUR NEW FRIEND OSCAR. THEIR TEETH AREN'T SHARP ENOUGH TO HURT US.
SOME OF THE CREATURES HERE ARE VERY DANGEROUS. THAT'S WHY WE NEED YOU TO STAY HIDDEN AND KEEP QUIET.
BUT THAT ONE? IT'S HARMLESS... ALMOST.
YOU GUYS SPEAK ENGLISH, RIGHT?
PARIS.
I DON'T KNOW, SIR. I HAVEN'T GOTTEN A RESPONSE. NATHAN WAS LIVE ON COMMS AND THEN SUDDENLY... NOTHING.
IT'S BEEN ALMOST FOUR MINUTES.
WELL... THAT'S NOT GOOD.
DON'T WORRY, WARD.
YOU'VE GOT THE LUCKY CREW.
NO REASON TO THINK THAT LUCK HAS RUN OUT.

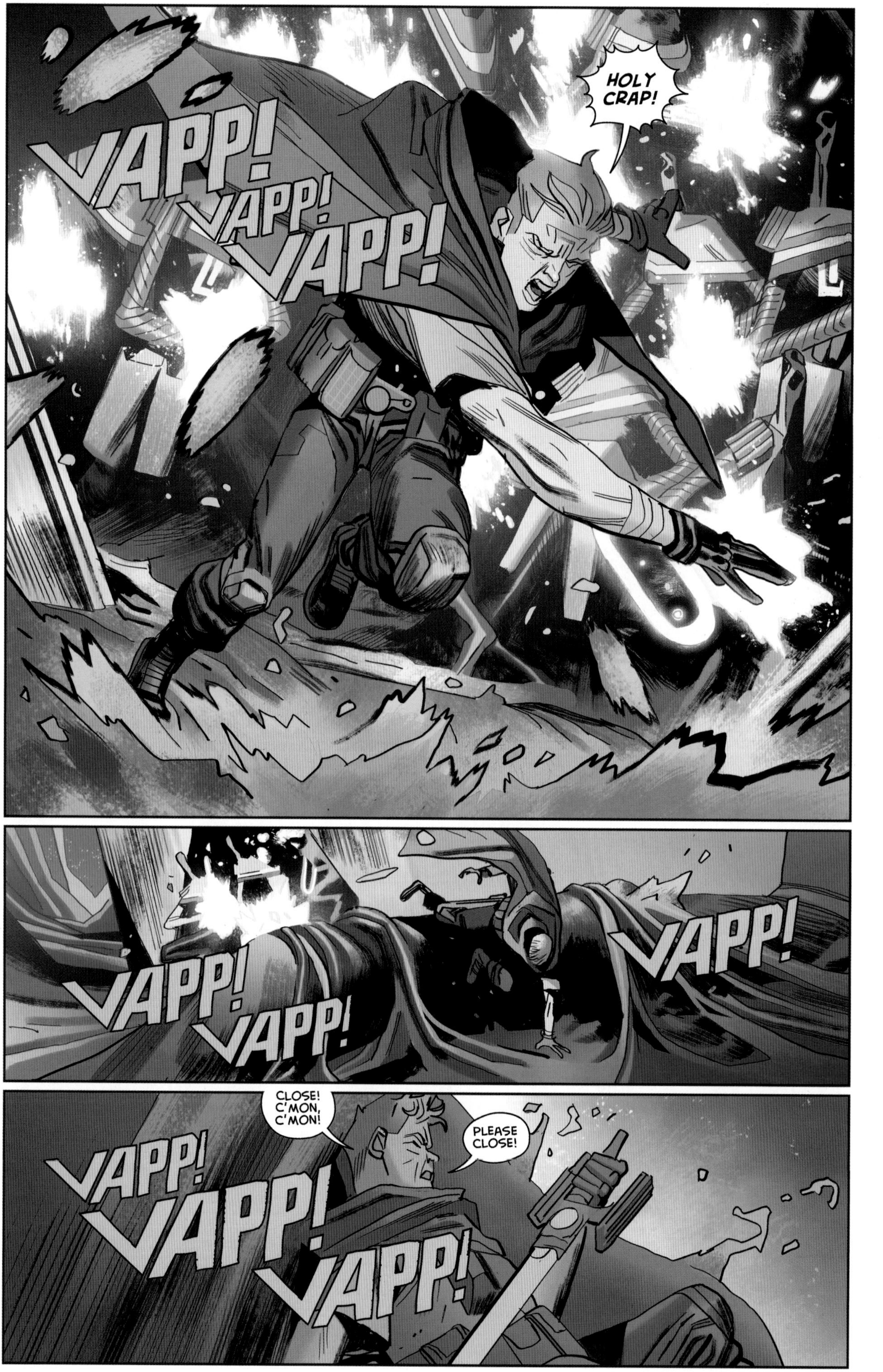
HOLY CRAP!
VAPP!
VAPP!
VAPP!
VAPP!
VAPP!
VAPP!
CLOSE! C'MON, C'MON!
PLEASE CLOSE!
VAPP!
VAPP!
VAPP!

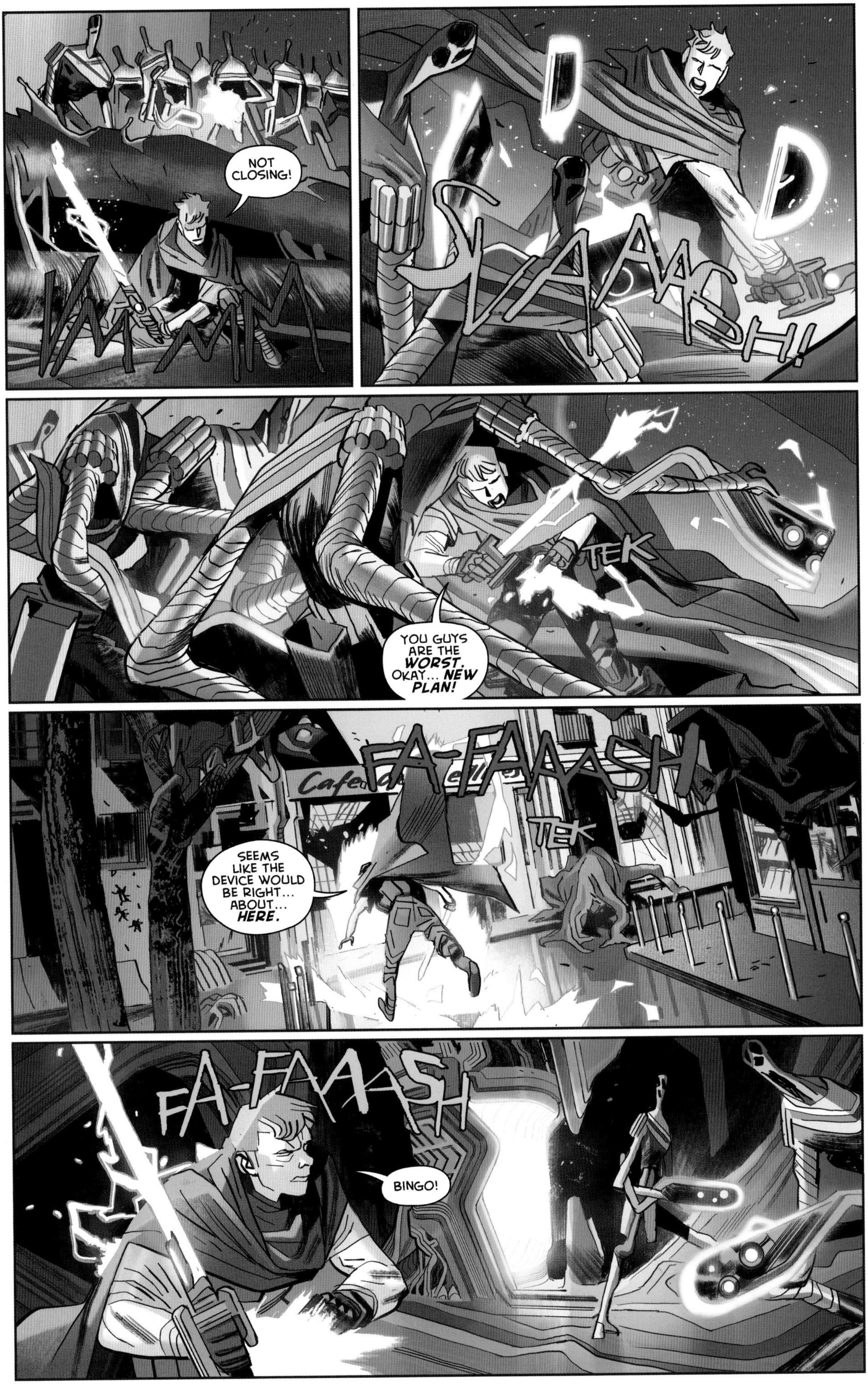
NOT CLOSING!
VMMM
SVAAASH!
TEK
YOU GUYS ARE THE WORST. OKAY... NEW PLAN!
FA-FAAASH
Cafe
TEK
SEEMS LIKE THE DEVICE WOULD BE RIGHT... ABOUT... HERE.
FA-FAAASH
BINGO!

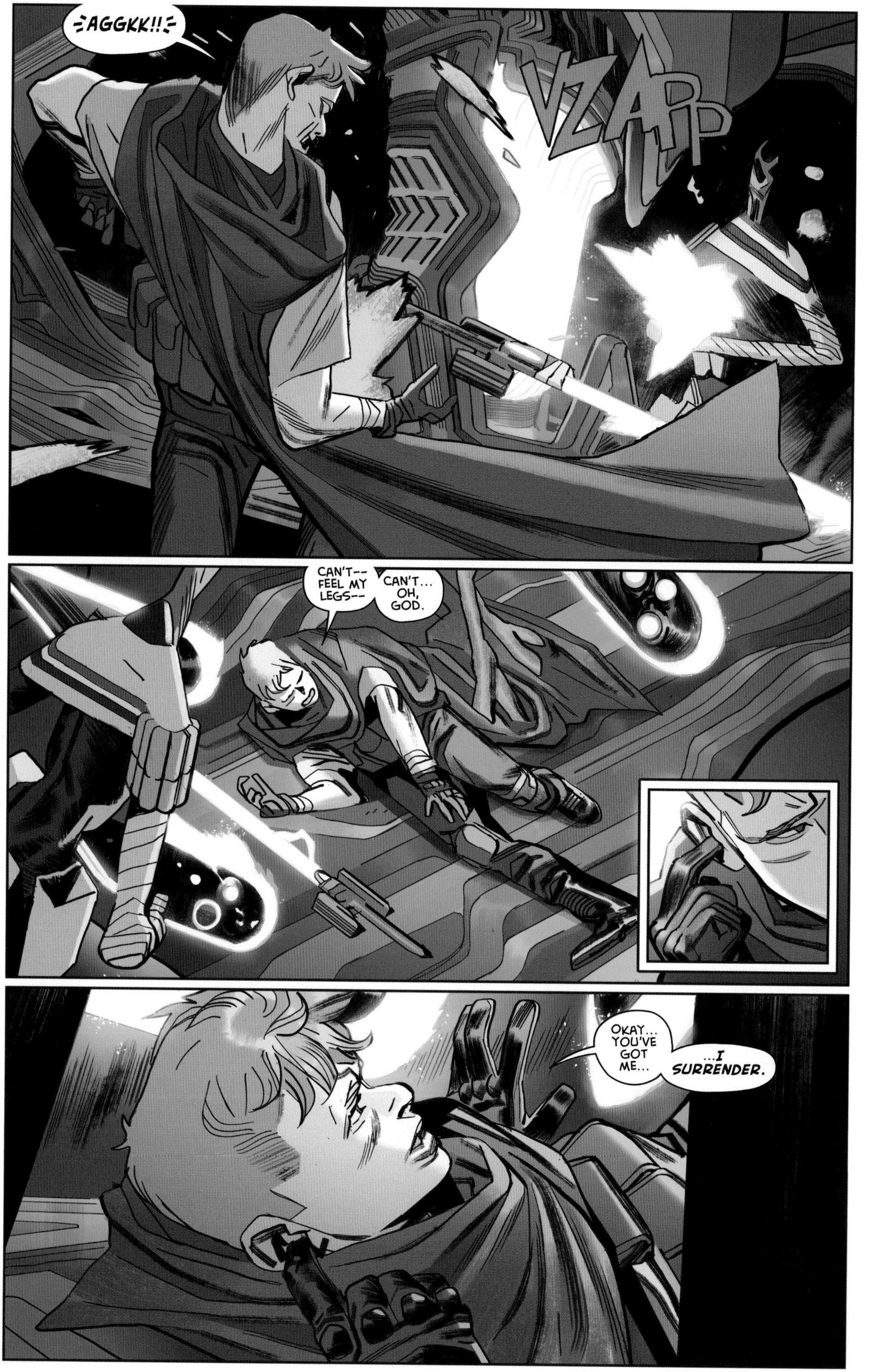

AGGKK!!
VZARRP
CAN'T-- FEEL MY LEGS--
CAN'T... OH, GOD.
OKAY... YOU'VE GOT ME...
...I SURRENDER.

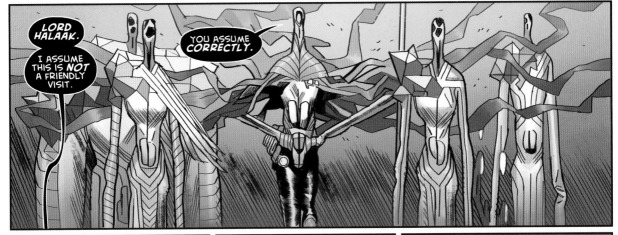

LORD HALAAK. I ASSUME THIS IS *NOT* A FRIENDLY VISIT.

YOU ASSUME *CORRECTLY.*

YOU KNOW WHO I AM?

GAKAAL. FORMER *MASTER* OF THE *GHOZAN LEGION.*

SO YOU KNOW WHAT I AM CAPABLE OF.

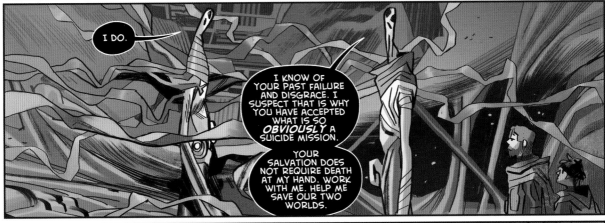

I DO.

I KNOW OF YOUR PAST FAILURE AND DISGRACE. I SUSPECT THAT IS WHY YOU HAVE ACCEPTED WHAT IS SO *OBVIOUSLY* A SUICIDE MISSION.

YOUR SALVATION DOES NOT REQUIRE DEATH AT MY HAND. WORK WITH ME. HELP ME SAVE OUR TWO WORLDS.

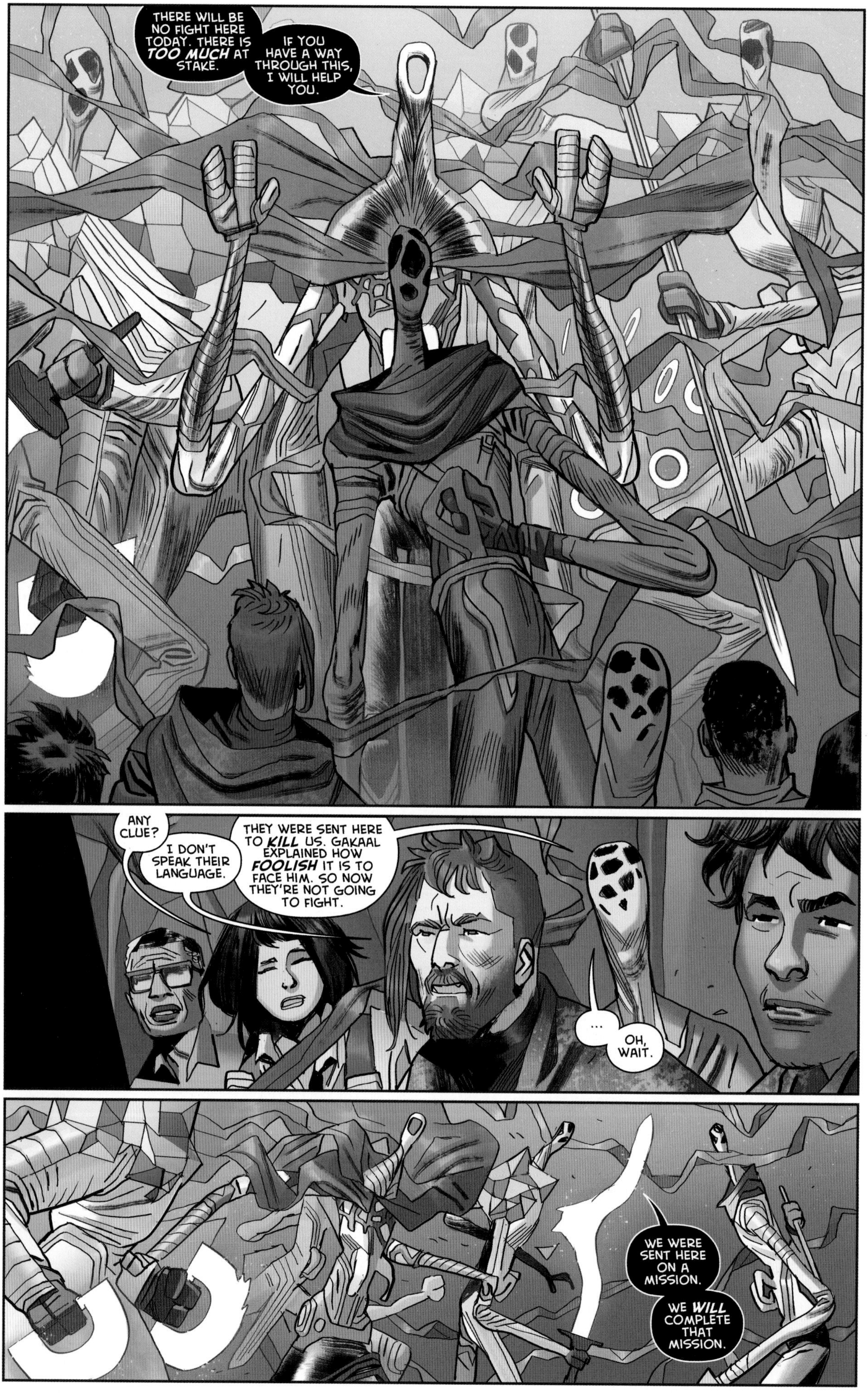
THERE WILL BE NO FIGHT HERE TODAY. THERE IS TOO MUCH AT STAKE.
IF YOU HAVE A WAY THROUGH THIS, I WILL HELP YOU.
ANY CLUE?
I DON'T SPEAK THEIR LANGUAGE.
THEY WERE SENT HERE TO KILL US. GAKAAL EXPLAINED HOW FOOLISH IT IS TO FACE HIM. SO NOW THEY'RE NOT GOING TO FIGHT.
...
OH, WAIT.
WE WERE SENT HERE ON A MISSION.
WE WILL COMPLETE THAT MISSION.

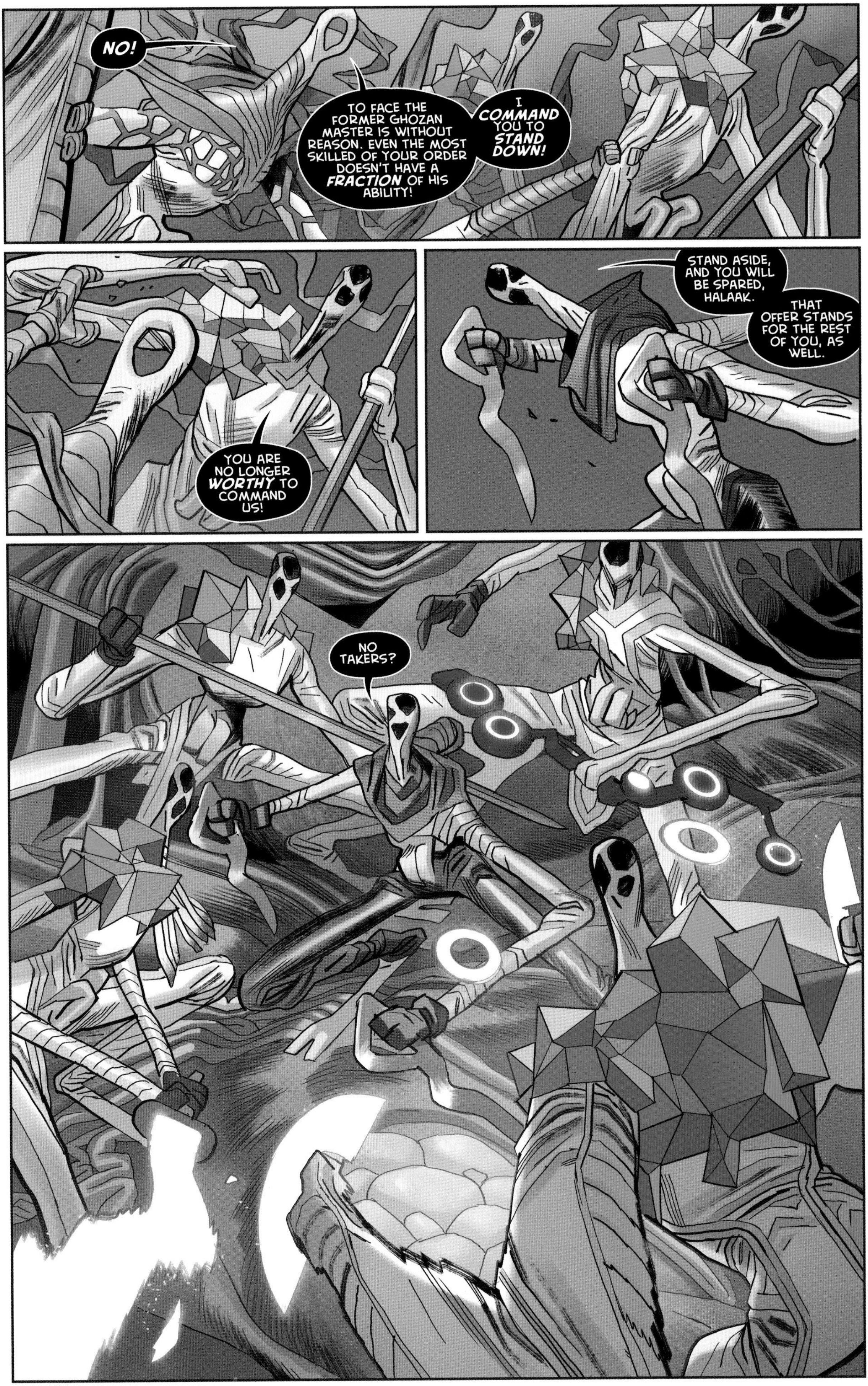
NO!
TO FACE THE FORMER GHOZAN MASTER IS WITHOUT REASON. EVEN THE MOST SKILLED OF YOUR ORDER DOESN'T HAVE A FRACTION OF HIS ABILITY!
I COMMAND YOU TO STAND DOWN!
YOU ARE NO LONGER WORTHY TO COMMAND US!
STAND ASIDE, AND YOU WILL BE SPARED, HALAAK.
THAT OFFER STANDS FOR THE REST OF YOU, AS WELL.
NO TAKERS?

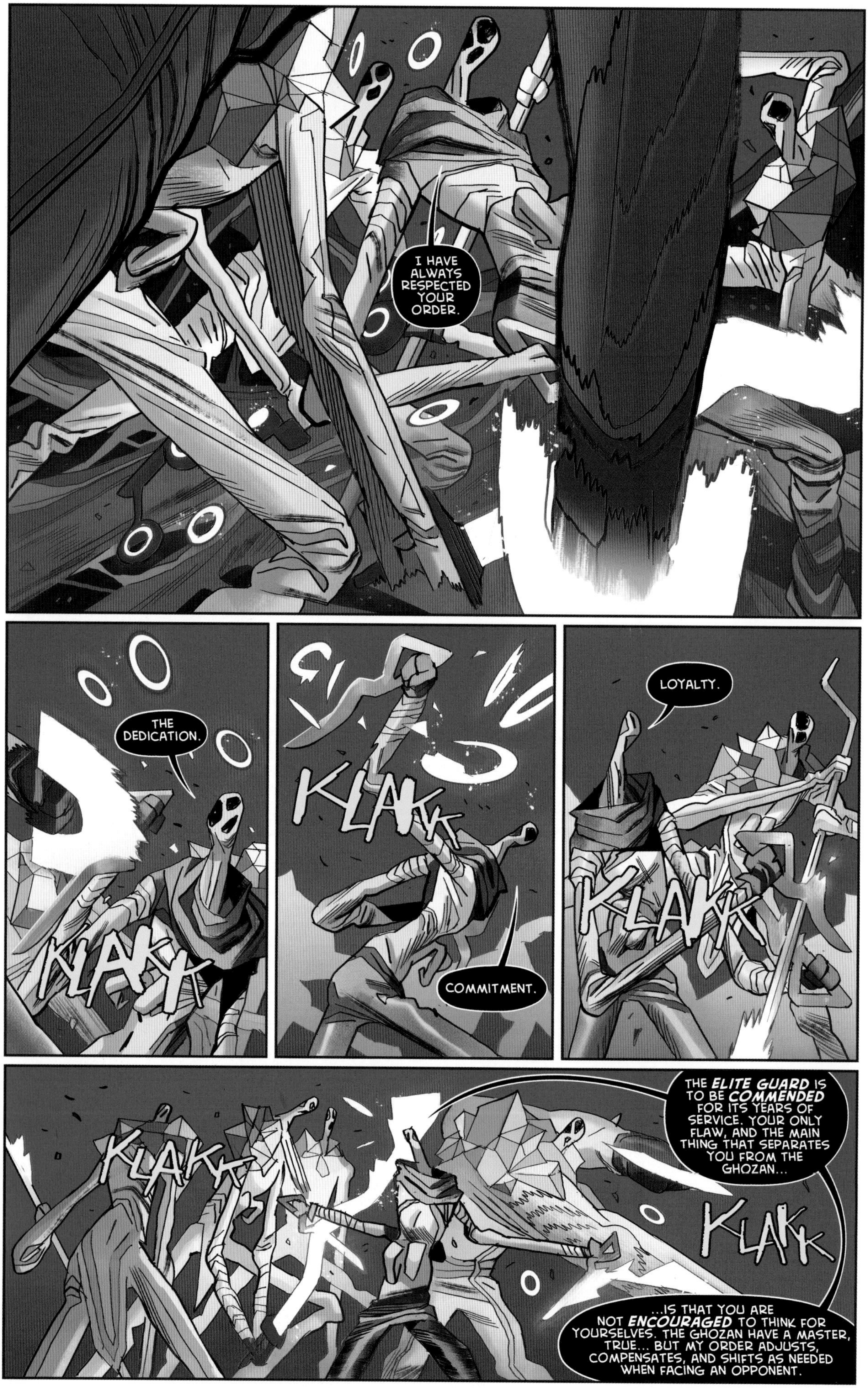
I HAVE ALWAYS RESPECTED YOUR ORDER.
THE DEDICATION.
KLAKK
KLAKK
COMMITMENT.
LOYALTY.
KLAKK
THE ELITE GUARD IS TO BE COMMENDED FOR ITS YEARS OF SERVICE. YOUR ONLY FLAW, AND THE MAIN THING THAT SEPARATES YOU FROM THE GHOZAN...
KLAKK
KLAKK
...IS THAT YOU ARE NOT ENCOURAGED TO THINK FOR YOURSELVES. THE GHOZAN HAVE A MASTER, TRUE... BUT MY ORDER ADJUSTS, COMPENSATES, AND SHIFTS AS NEEDED WHEN FACING AN OPPONENT.

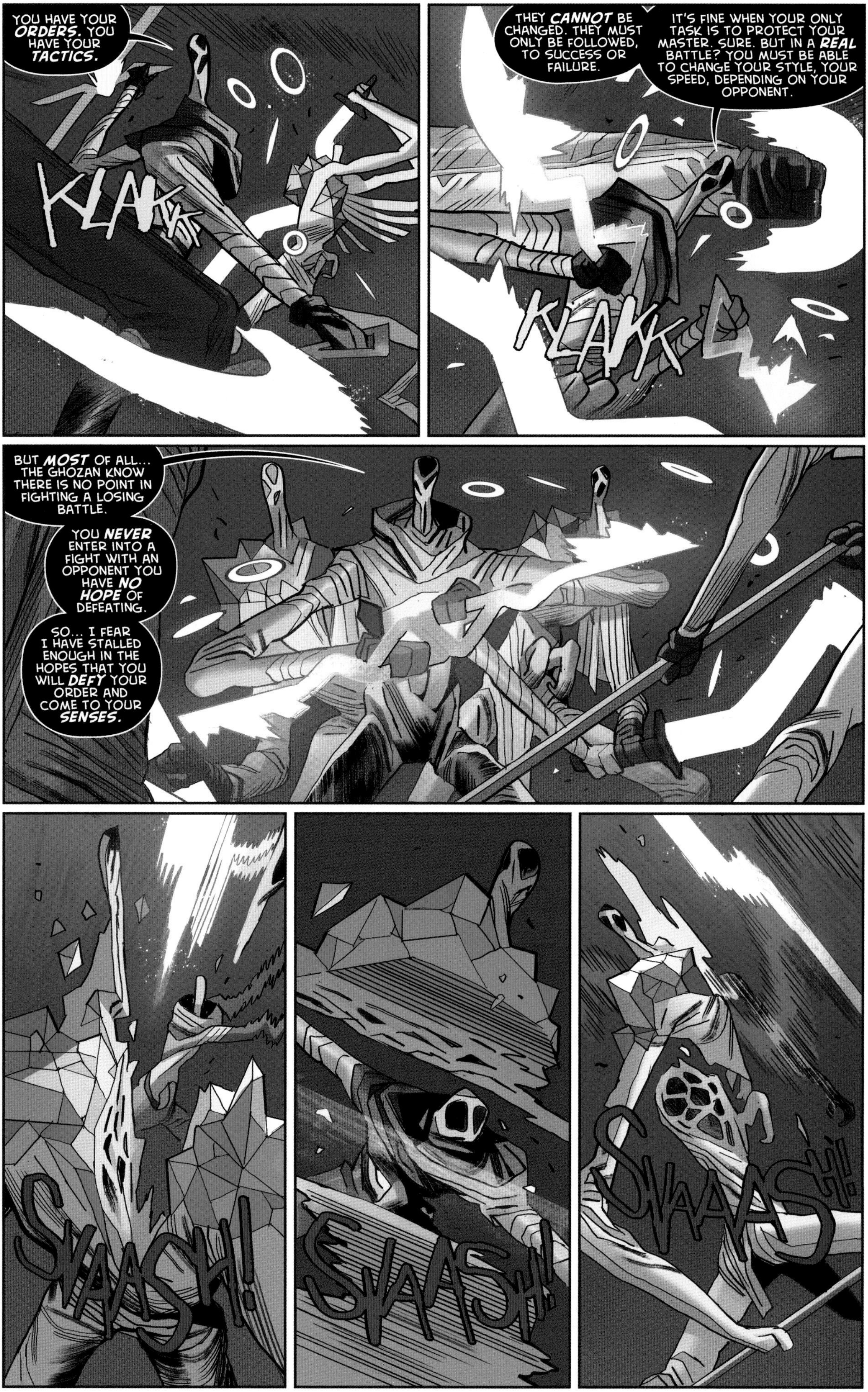
YOU HAVE YOUR ORDERS. YOU HAVE YOUR TACTICS.
KLAKK
THEY CANNOT BE CHANGED. THEY MUST ONLY BE FOLLOWED, TO SUCCESS OR FAILURE.
IT'S FINE WHEN YOUR ONLY TASK IS TO PROTECT YOUR MASTER. SURE. BUT IN A REAL BATTLE? YOU MUST BE ABLE TO CHANGE YOUR STYLE, YOUR SPEED, DEPENDING ON YOUR OPPONENT.
KLAKK
BUT MOST OF ALL... THE GHOZAN KNOW THERE IS NO POINT IN FIGHTING A LOSING BATTLE.
YOU NEVER ENTER INTO A FIGHT WITH AN OPPONENT YOU HAVE NO HOPE OF DEFEATING.
SO... I FEAR I HAVE STALLED ENOUGH IN THE HOPES THAT YOU WILL DEFY YOUR ORDER AND COME TO YOUR SENSES.
SWASH!
SWASH!
SWAASH!

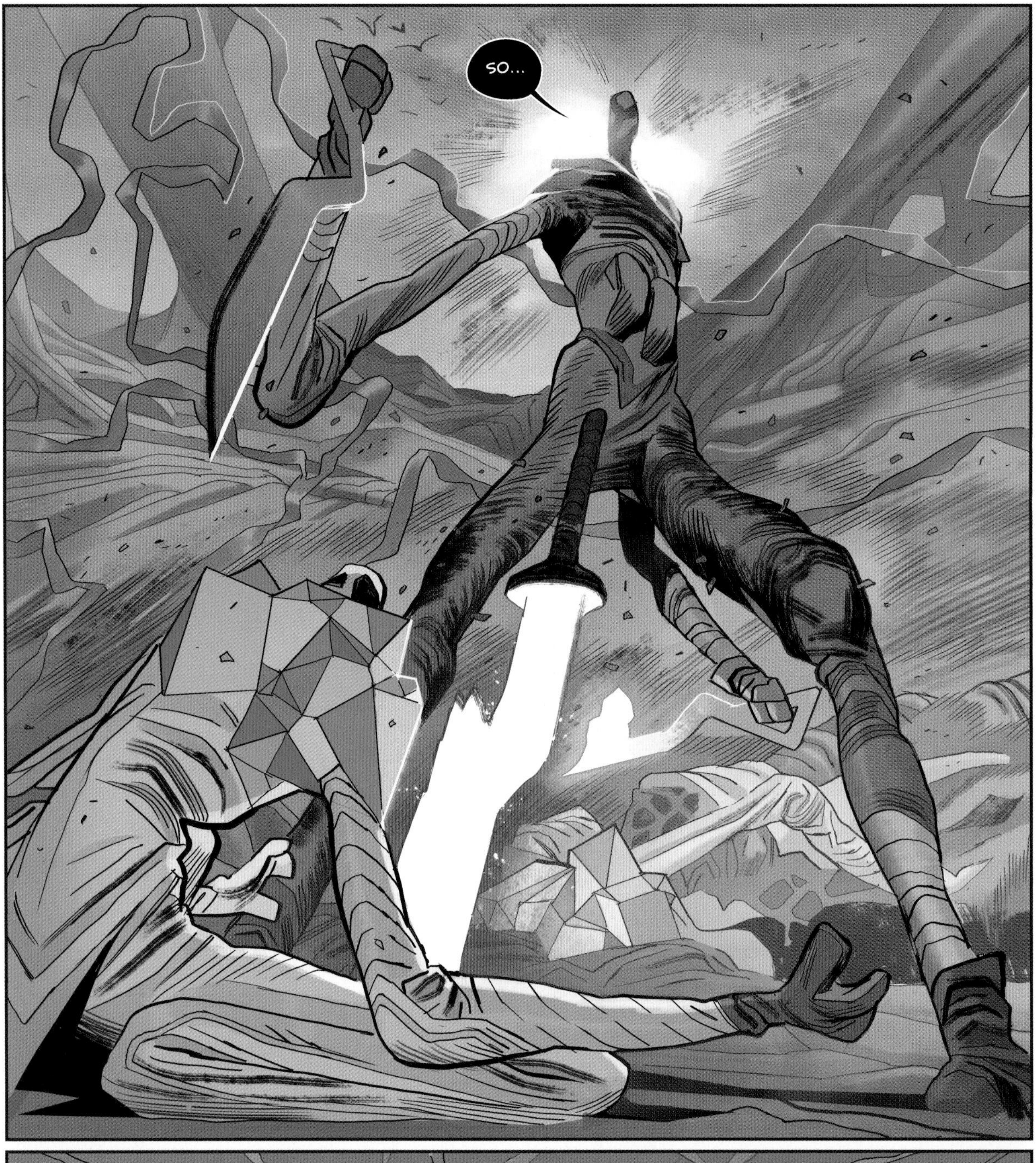
SO...
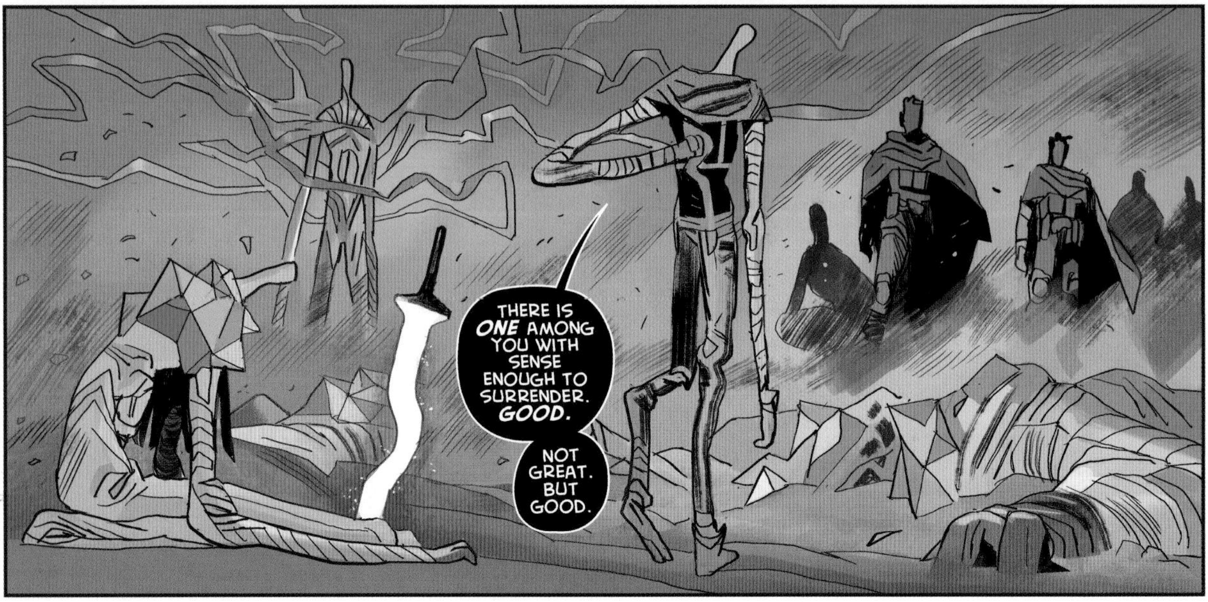
THERE IS ONE AMONG YOU WITH SENSE ENOUGH TO SURRENDER. GOOD.
NOT GREAT. BUT GOOD.

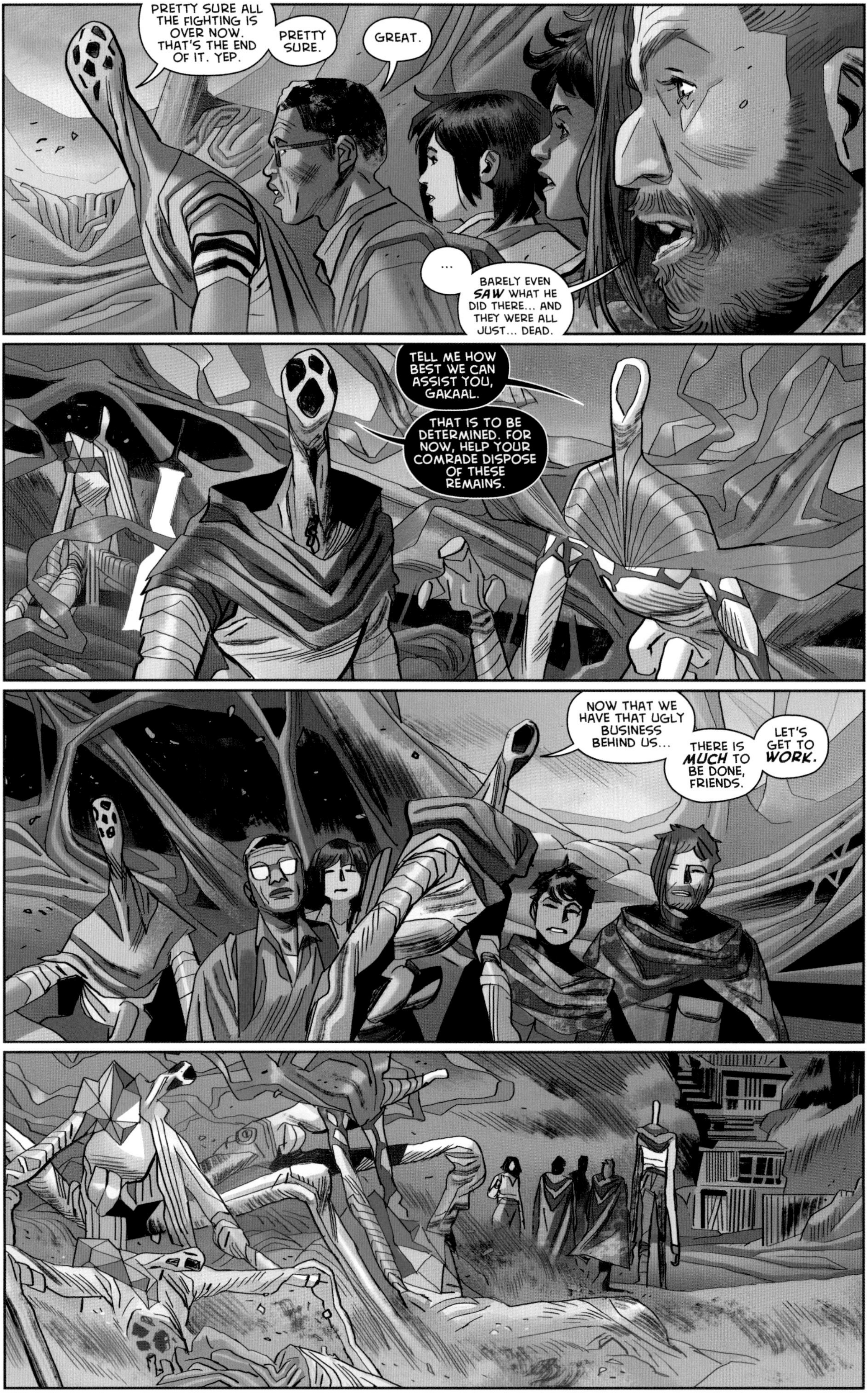
PRETTY SURE ALL THE FIGHTING IS OVER NOW. THAT'S THE END OF IT. YEP.
PRETTY SURE.
GREAT.
...
BARELY EVEN SAW WHAT HE DID THERE... AND THEY WERE ALL JUST... DEAD.
TELL ME HOW BEST WE CAN ASSIST YOU, GAKAAL.
THAT IS TO BE DETERMINED. FOR NOW, HELP YOUR COMRADE DISPOSE OF THESE REMAINS.
NOW THAT WE HAVE THAT UGLY BUSINESS BEHIND US...
THERE IS MUCH TO BE DONE, FRIENDS.
LET'S GET TO WORK.

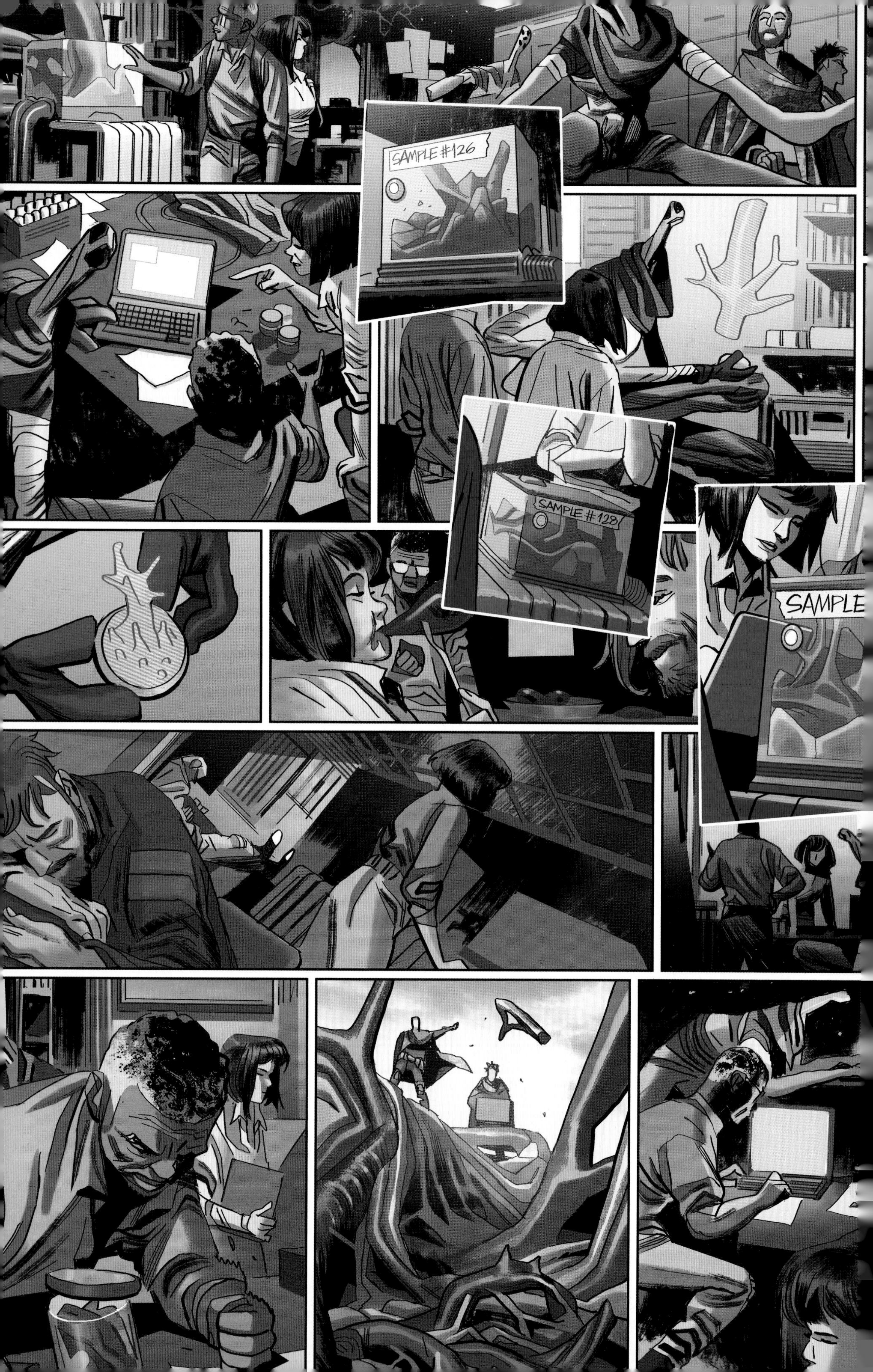
SAMPLE #126
SAMPLE #128
SAMPLE

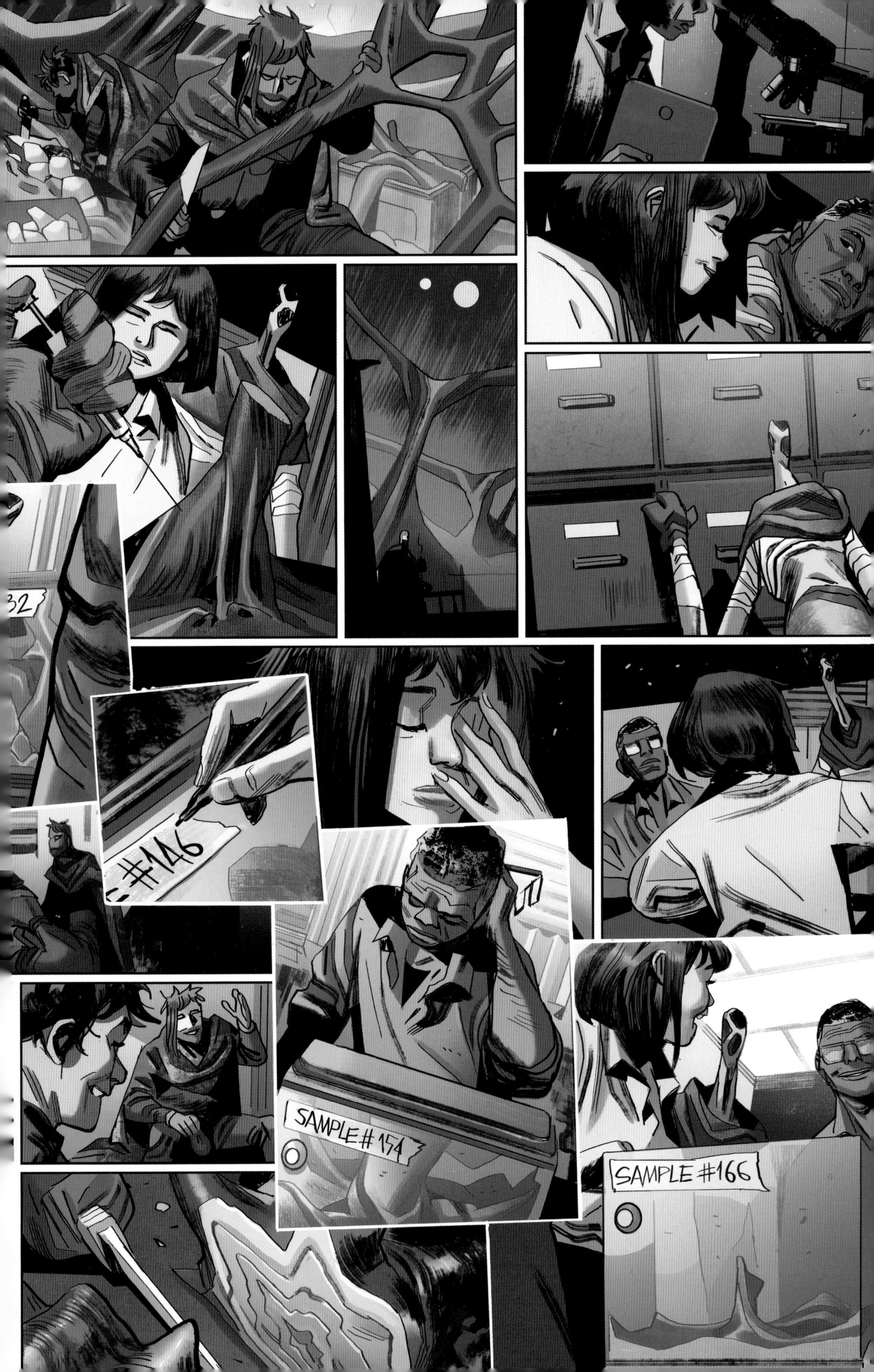

32
#146
SAMPLE #154
SAMPLE #166

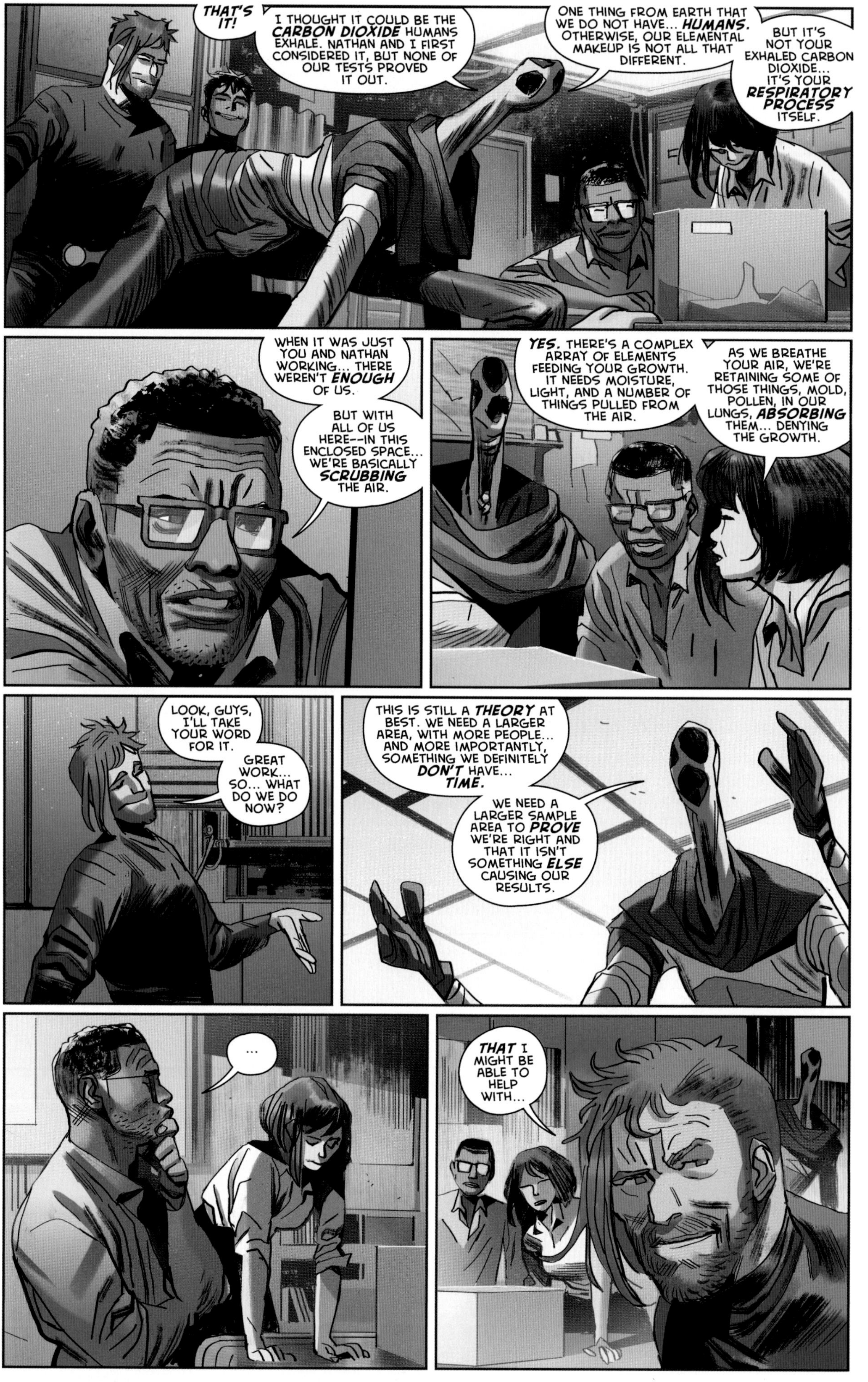
THAT'S IT!
I THOUGHT IT COULD BE THE CARBON DIOXIDE HUMANS EXHALE. NATHAN AND I FIRST CONSIDERED IT, BUT NONE OF OUR TESTS PROVED IT OUT.
ONE THING FROM EARTH THAT WE DO NOT HAVE... HUMANS. OTHERWISE, OUR ELEMENTAL MAKEUP IS NOT ALL THAT DIFFERENT.
BUT IT'S NOT YOUR EXHALED CARBON DIOXIDE... IT'S YOUR RESPIRATORY PROCESS ITSELF.
WHEN IT WAS JUST YOU AND NATHAN WORKING... THERE WEREN'T ENOUGH OF US.
BUT WITH ALL OF US HERE--IN THIS ENCLOSED SPACE... WE'RE BASICALLY SCRUBBING THE AIR.
YES. THERE'S A COMPLEX ARRAY OF ELEMENTS FEEDING YOUR GROWTH. IT NEEDS MOISTURE, LIGHT, AND A NUMBER OF THINGS PULLED FROM THE AIR.
AS WE BREATHE YOUR AIR, WE'RE RETAINING SOME OF THOSE THINGS, MOLD, POLLEN, IN OUR LUNGS, ABSORBING THEM... DENYING THE GROWTH.
LOOK, GUYS, I'LL TAKE YOUR WORD FOR IT.
GREAT WORK... SO... WHAT DO WE DO NOW?
THIS IS STILL A THEORY AT BEST. WE NEED A LARGER AREA, WITH MORE PEOPLE... AND MORE IMPORTANTLY, SOMETHING WE DEFINITELY DON'T HAVE... TIME.
WE NEED A LARGER SAMPLE AREA TO PROVE WE'RE RIGHT AND THAT IT ISN'T SOMETHING ELSE CAUSING OUR RESULTS.
...
THAT I MIGHT BE ABLE TO HELP WITH...

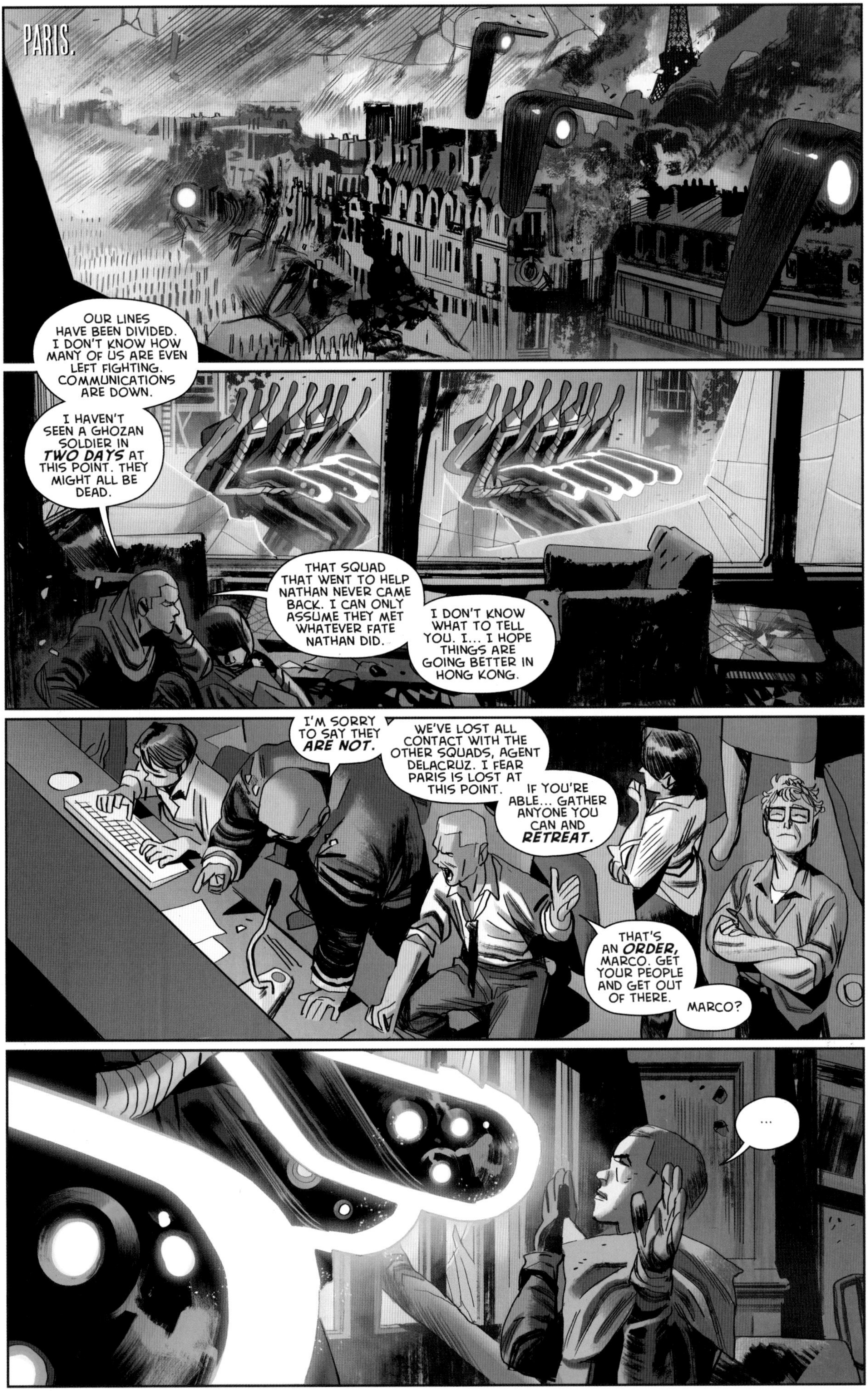
PARIS.
OUR LINES HAVE BEEN DIVIDED. I DON'T KNOW HOW MANY OF US ARE EVEN LEFT FIGHTING. COMMUNICATIONS ARE DOWN.
I HAVEN'T SEEN A GHOZAN SOLDIER IN TWO DAYS AT THIS POINT. THEY MIGHT ALL BE DEAD.
THAT SQUAD THAT WENT TO HELP NATHAN NEVER CAME BACK. I CAN ONLY ASSUME THEY MET WHATEVER FATE NATHAN DID.
I DON'T KNOW WHAT TO TELL YOU. I... I HOPE THINGS ARE GOING BETTER IN HONG KONG.
I'M SORRY TO SAY THEY ARE NOT.
WE'VE LOST ALL CONTACT WITH THE OTHER SQUADS, AGENT DELACRUZ. I FEAR PARIS IS LOST AT THIS POINT.
IF YOU'RE ABLE... GATHER ANYONE YOU CAN AND RETREAT.
THAT'S AN ORDER, MARCO. GET YOUR PEOPLE AND GET OUT OF THERE.
MARCO?
...

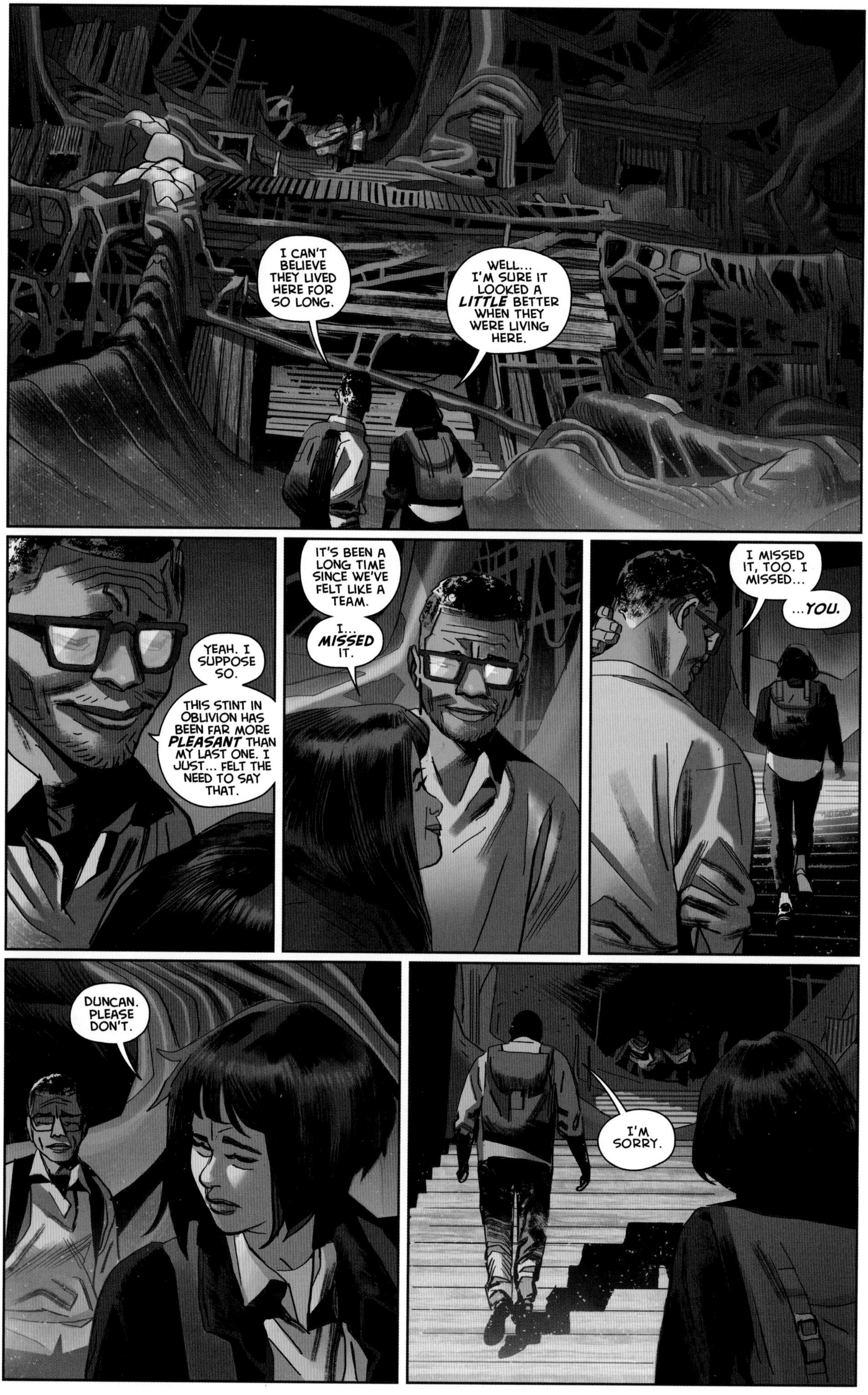
I CAN'T BELIEVE THEY LIVED HERE FOR SO LONG.
WELL... I'M SURE IT LOOKED A LITTLE BETTER WHEN THEY WERE LIVING HERE.
YEAH. I SUPPOSE SO.
THIS STINT IN OBLIVION HAS BEEN FAR MORE PLEASANT THAN MY LAST ONE. I JUST... FELT THE NEED TO SAY THAT.
IT'S BEEN A LONG TIME SINCE WE'VE FELT LIKE A TEAM.
I... MISSED IT.
I MISSED IT, TOO. I MISSED...
...YOU.
DUNCAN. PLEASE DON'T.
I'M SORRY.

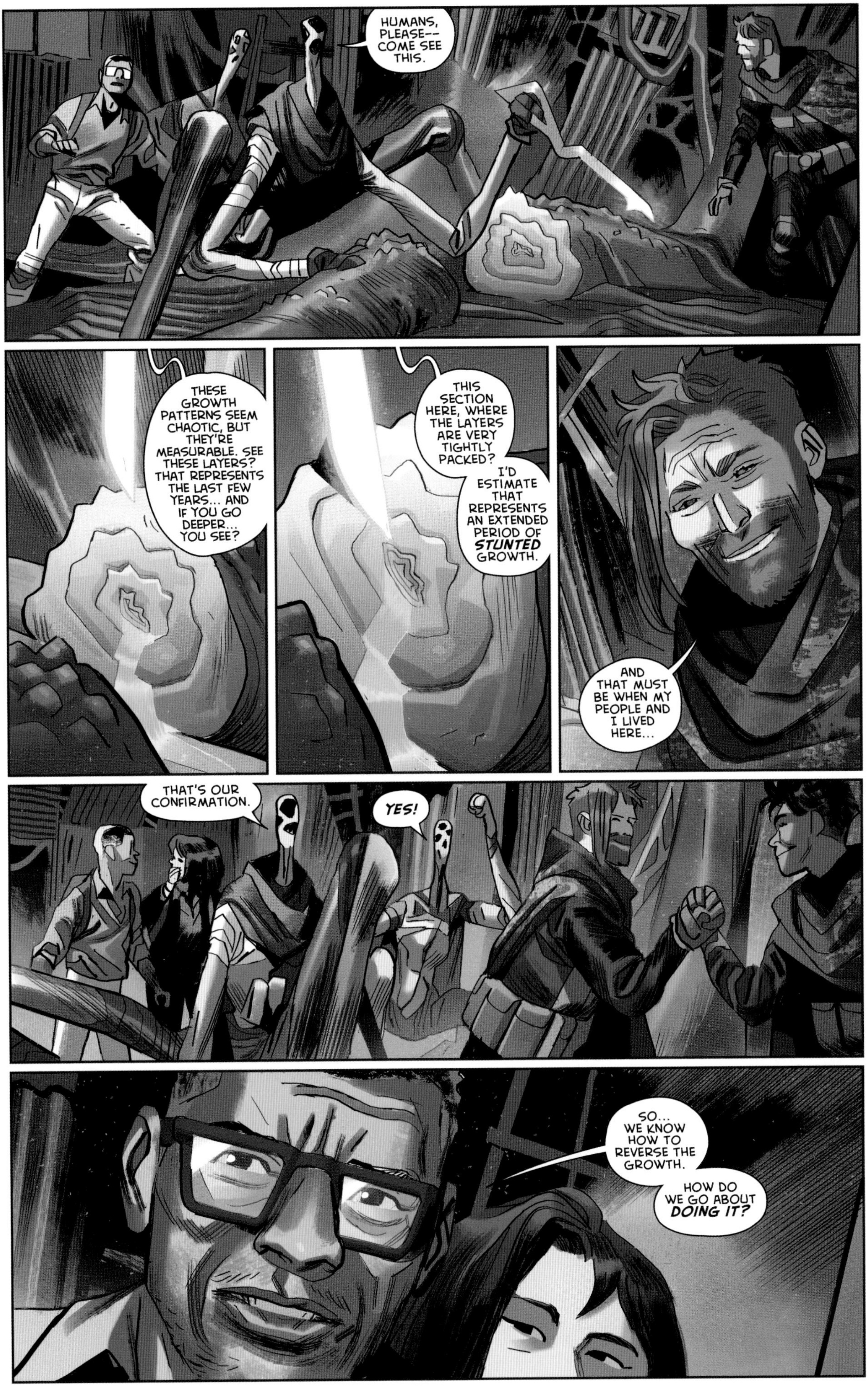
HUMANS, PLEASE-- COME SEE THIS.
THESE GROWTH PATTERNS SEEM CHAOTIC, BUT THEY'RE MEASURABLE. SEE THESE LAYERS? THAT REPRESENTS THE LAST FEW YEARS... AND IF YOU GO DEEPER... YOU SEE?
THIS SECTION HERE, WHERE THE LAYERS ARE VERY TIGHTLY PACKED?
I'D ESTIMATE THAT REPRESENTS AN EXTENDED PERIOD OF ***STUNTED*** GROWTH.
AND THAT MUST BE WHEN MY PEOPLE AND I LIVED HERE...
THAT'S OUR CONFIRMATION.
YES!
SO... WE KNOW HOW TO REVERSE THE GROWTH.
HOW DO WE GO ABOUT ***DOING IT?***

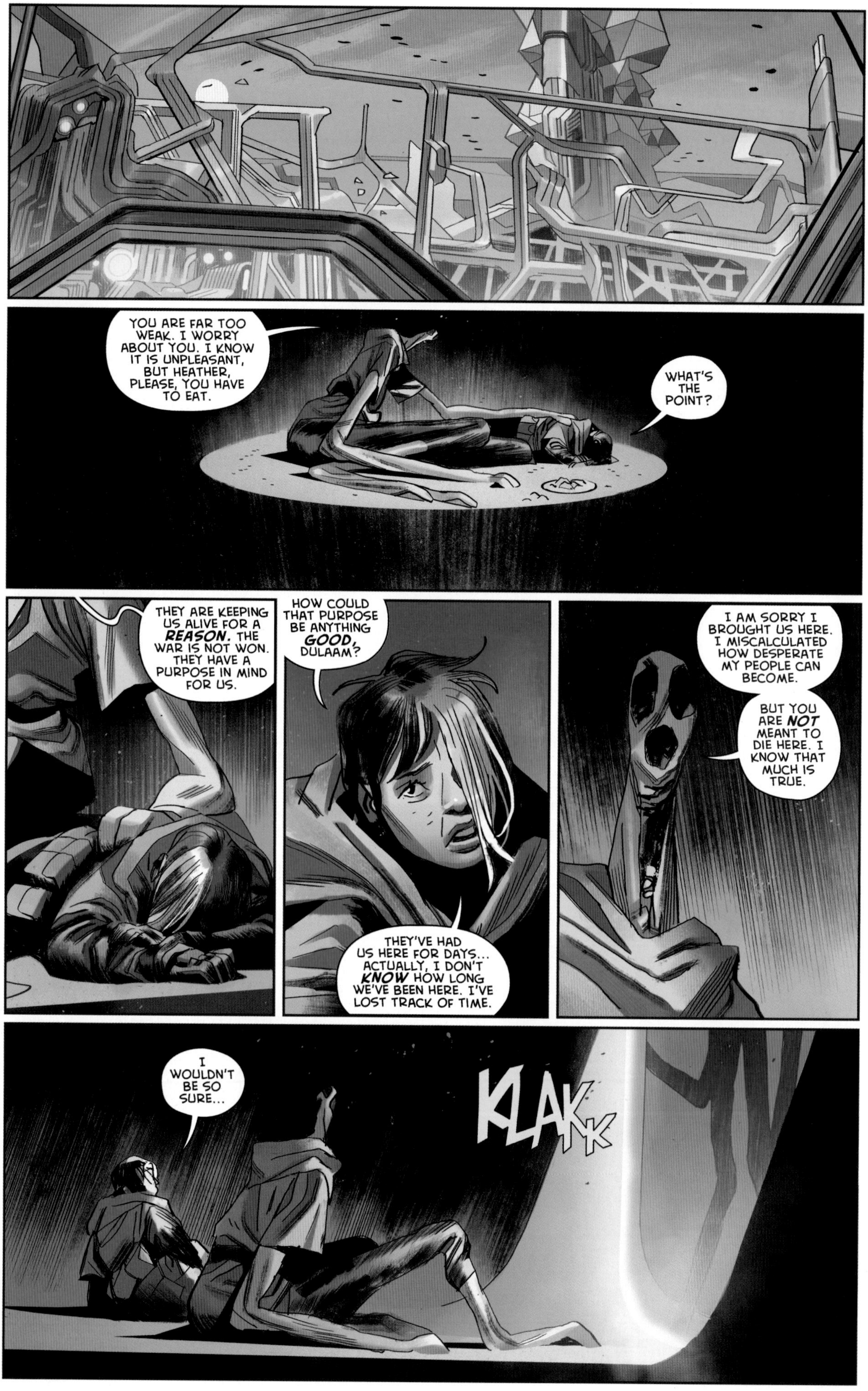

YOU ARE FAR TOO WEAK. I WORRY ABOUT YOU. I KNOW IT IS UNPLEASANT, BUT HEATHER, PLEASE, YOU HAVE TO EAT.
WHAT'S THE POINT?
THEY ARE KEEPING US ALIVE FOR A **REASON.** THE WAR IS NOT WON. THEY HAVE A PURPOSE IN MIND FOR US.
HOW COULD THAT PURPOSE BE ANYTHING **GOOD,** DULAAM?
THEY'VE HAD US HERE FOR DAYS... ACTUALLY, I DON'T **KNOW** HOW LONG WE'VE BEEN HERE. I'VE LOST TRACK OF TIME.
I AM SORRY I BROUGHT US HERE. I MISCALCULATED HOW DESPERATE MY PEOPLE CAN BECOME.
BUT YOU ARE **NOT** MEANT TO DIE HERE. I KNOW THAT MUCH IS TRUE.
I WOULDN'T BE SO SURE...
KLAKKK

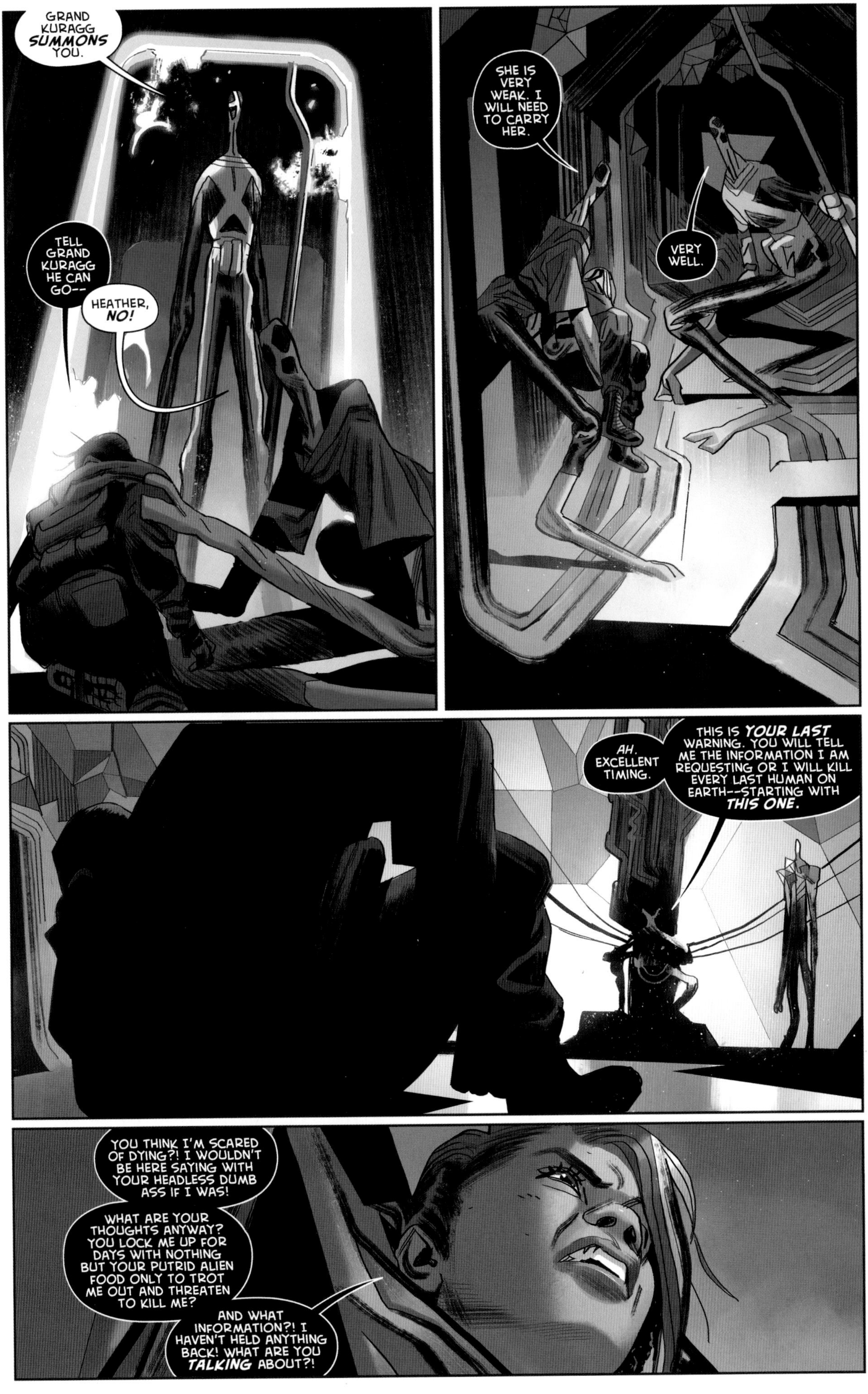
GRAND KURAGG SUMMONS YOU.
TELL GRAND KURAGG HE CAN GO--
HEATHER, NO!
SHE IS VERY WEAK. I WILL NEED TO CARRY HER.
VERY WELL.
AH. EXCELLENT TIMING.
THIS IS YOUR LAST WARNING. YOU WILL TELL ME THE INFORMATION I AM REQUESTING OR I WILL KILL EVERY LAST HUMAN ON EARTH--STARTING WITH THIS ONE.
YOU THINK I'M SCARED OF DYING?! I WOULDN'T BE HERE SAYING WITH YOUR HEADLESS DUMB ASS IF I WAS!
WHAT ARE YOUR THOUGHTS ANYWAY? YOU LOCK ME UP FOR DAYS WITH NOTHING BUT YOUR PUTRID ALIEN FOOD ONLY TO TROT ME OUT AND THREATEN TO KILL ME?
AND WHAT INFORMATION?! I HAVEN'T HELD ANYTHING BACK! WHAT ARE YOU TALKING ABOUT?!

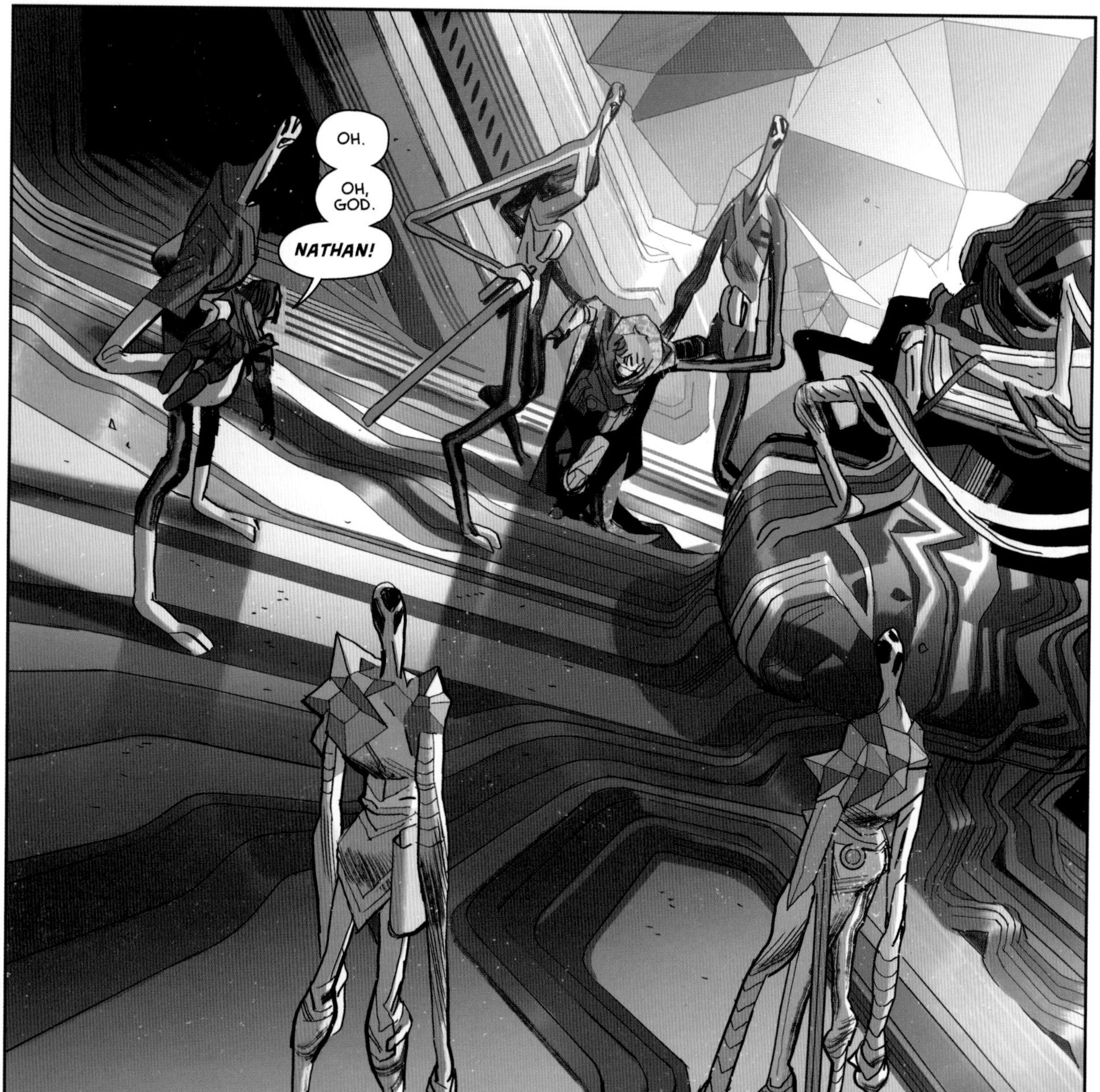
OH.
OH, GOD.
NATHAN!

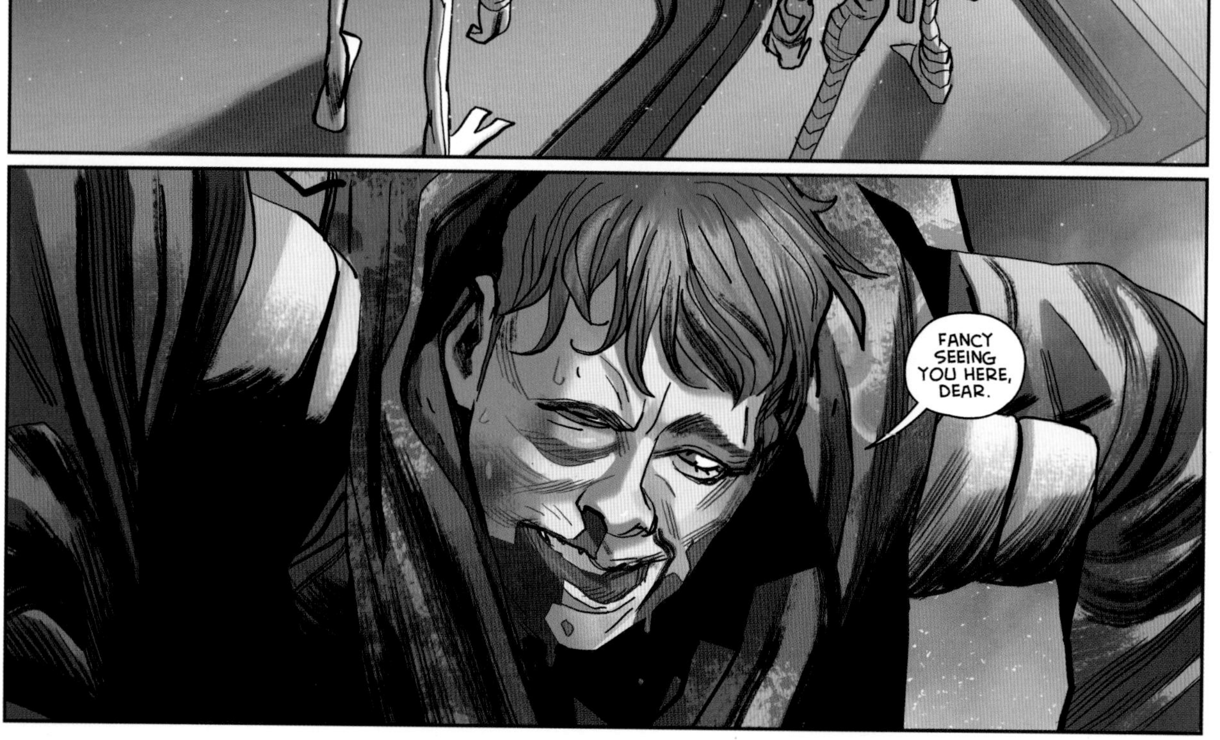
FANCY SEEING YOU HERE, DEAR.

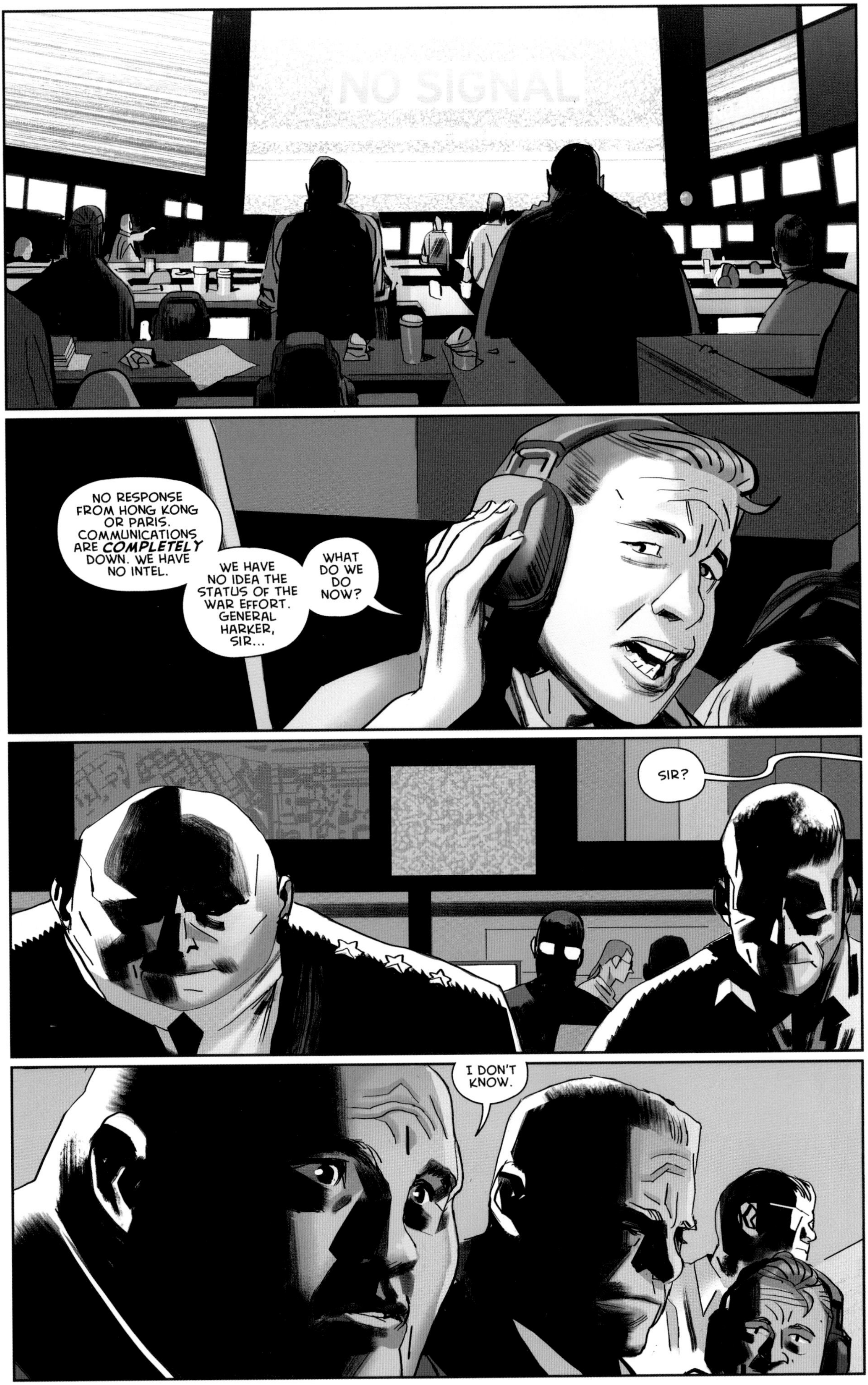
NO SIGNAL
NO RESPONSE FROM HONG KONG OR PARIS. COMMUNICATIONS ARE COMPLETELY DOWN. WE HAVE NO INTEL.
WE HAVE NO IDEA THE STATUS OF THE WAR EFFORT. GENERAL HARKER, SIR...
WHAT DO WE DO NOW?
SIR?
I DON'T KNOW.

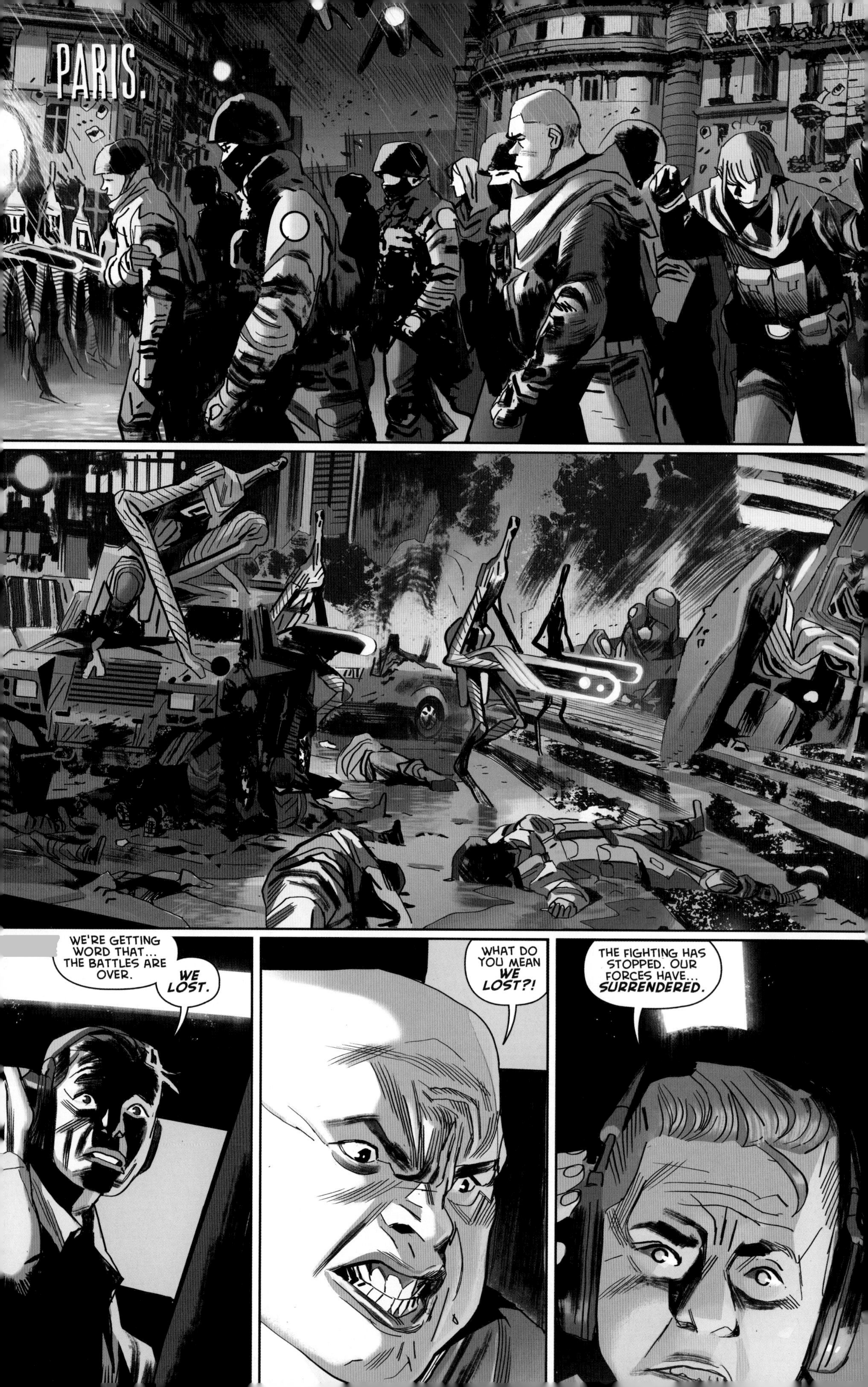
PARIS.
WE'RE GETTING WORD THAT... THE BATTLES ARE OVER.
WE LOST.
WHAT DO YOU MEAN WE LOST?!
THE FIGHTING HAS STOPPED. OUR FORCES HAVE... SURRENDERED.

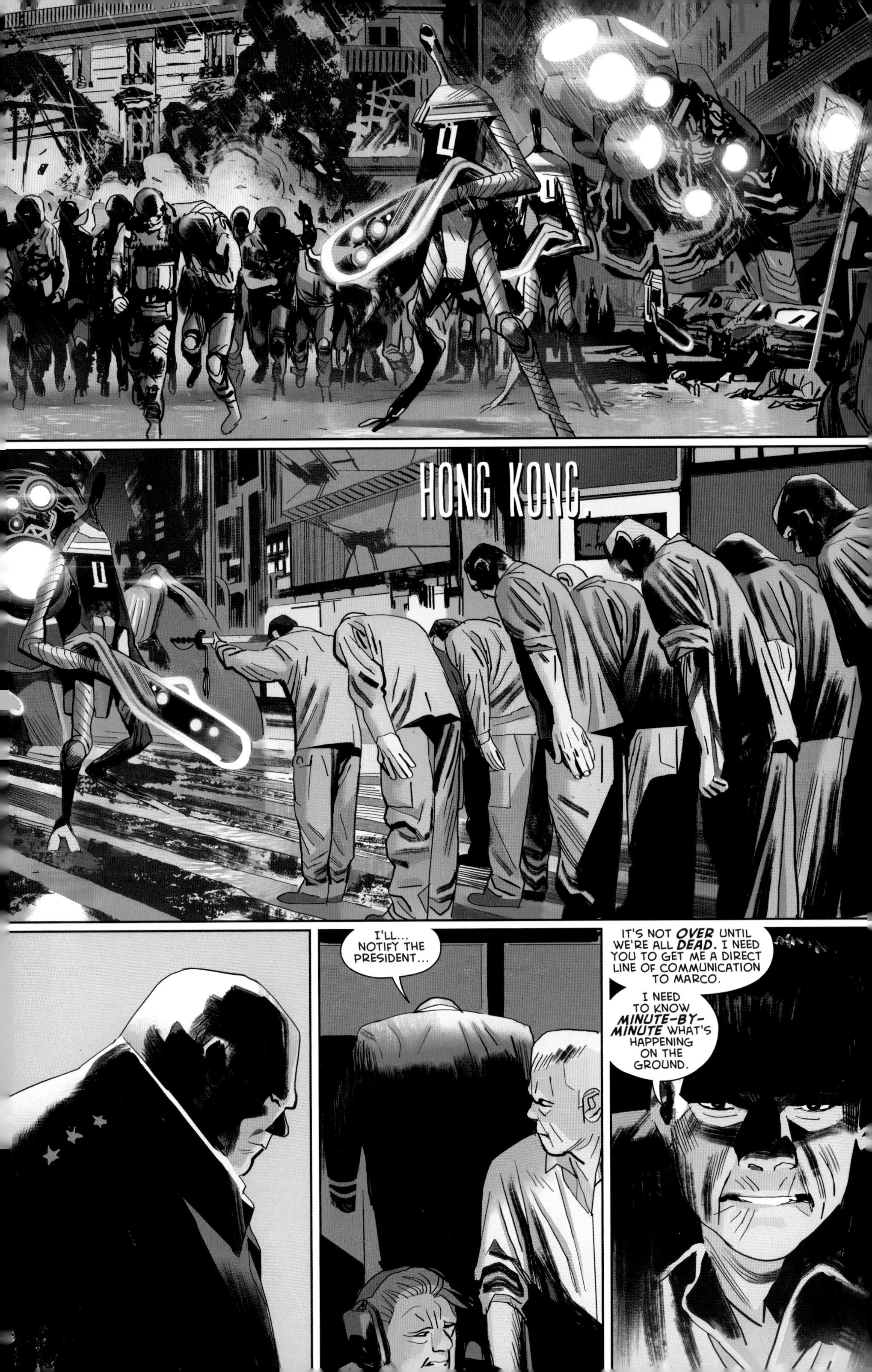
HONG KONG.
I'LL... NOTIFY THE PRESIDENT...
IT'S NOT OVER UNTIL WE'RE ALL DEAD. I NEED YOU TO GET ME A DIRECT LINE OF COMMUNICATION TO MARCO.
I NEED TO KNOW MINUTE-BY-MINUTE WHAT'S HAPPENING ON THE GROUND.

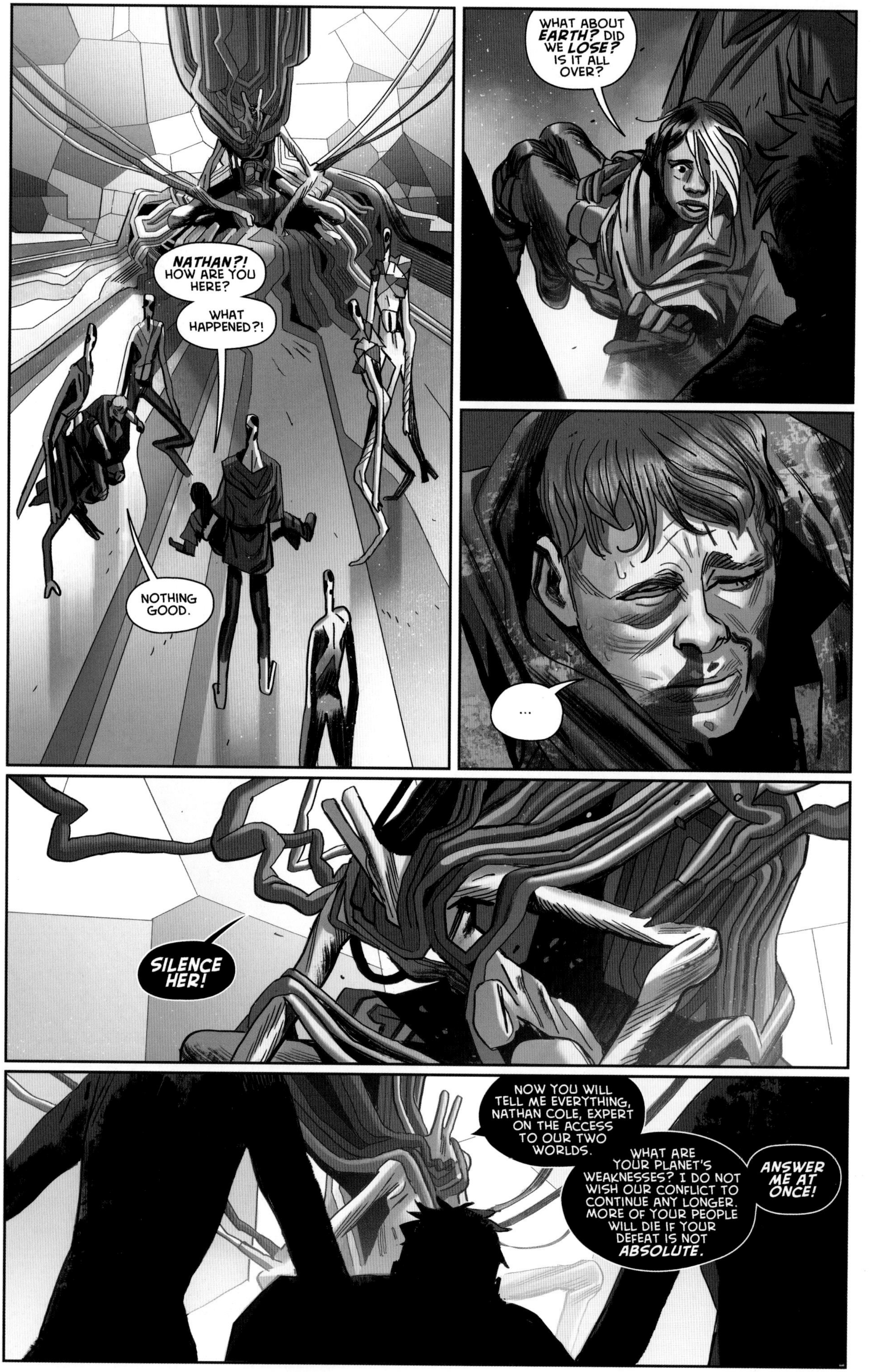
NATHAN?! HOW ARE YOU HERE?
WHAT HAPPENED?!
NOTHING GOOD.
WHAT ABOUT EARTH? DID WE LOSE? IS IT ALL OVER?
...
SILENCE HER!
NOW YOU WILL TELL ME EVERYTHING, NATHAN COLE, EXPERT ON THE ACCESS TO OUR TWO WORLDS.
WHAT ARE YOUR PLANET'S WEAKNESSES? I DO NOT WISH OUR CONFLICT TO CONTINUE ANY LONGER. MORE OF YOUR PEOPLE WILL DIE IF YOUR DEFEAT IS NOT ABSOLUTE.
ANSWER ME AT ONCE!

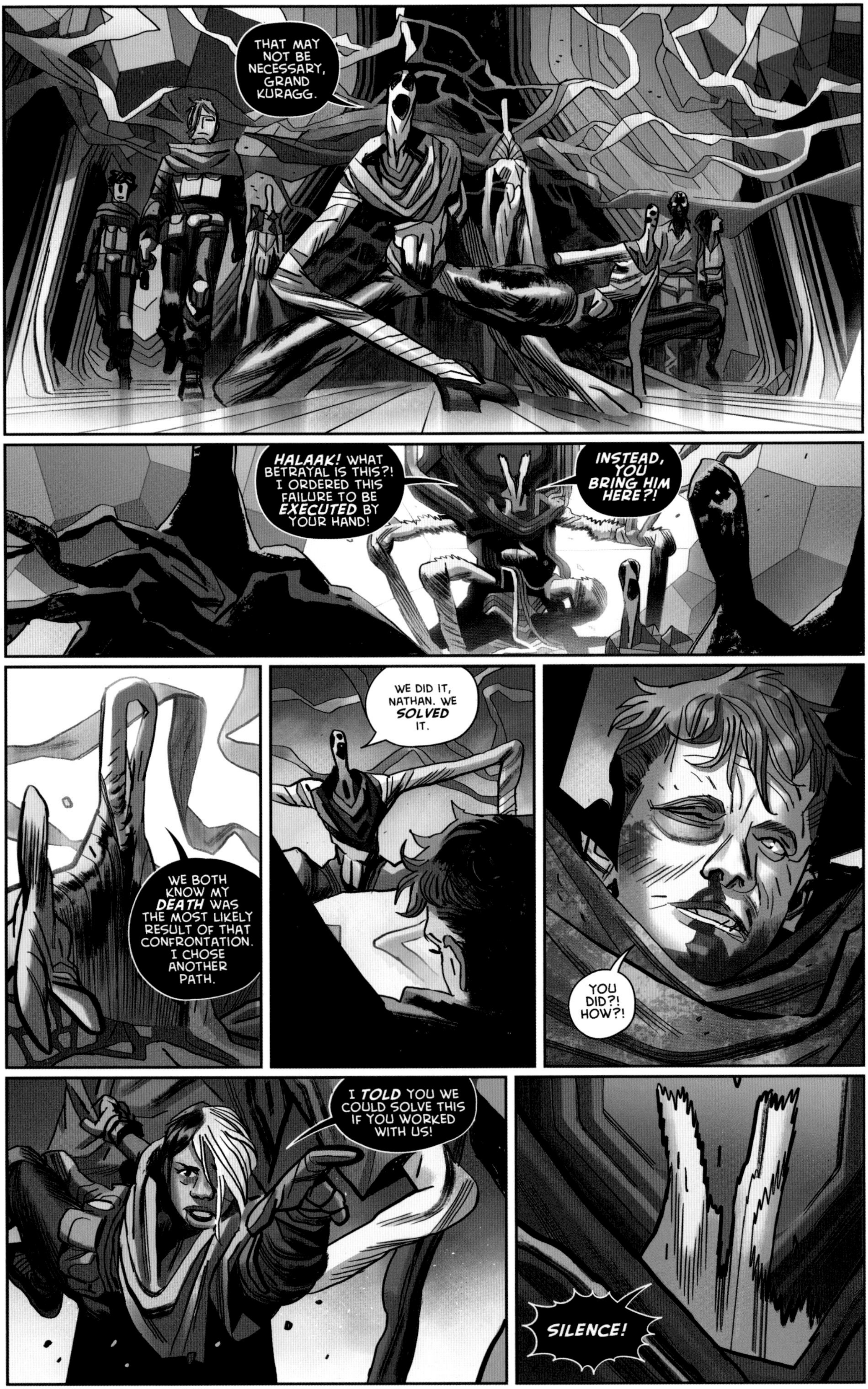
THAT MAY NOT BE NECESSARY, GRAND KURAGG.
HALAAK! WHAT BETRAYAL IS THIS?! I ORDERED THIS FAILURE TO BE EXECUTED BY YOUR HAND!
INSTEAD, YOU BRING HIM HERE?!
WE BOTH KNOW MY DEATH WAS THE MOST LIKELY RESULT OF THAT CONFRONTATION. I CHOSE ANOTHER PATH.
WE DID IT, NATHAN. WE SOLVED IT.
YOU DID?! HOW?!
I TOLD YOU WE COULD SOLVE THIS IF YOU WORKED WITH US!
SILENCE!

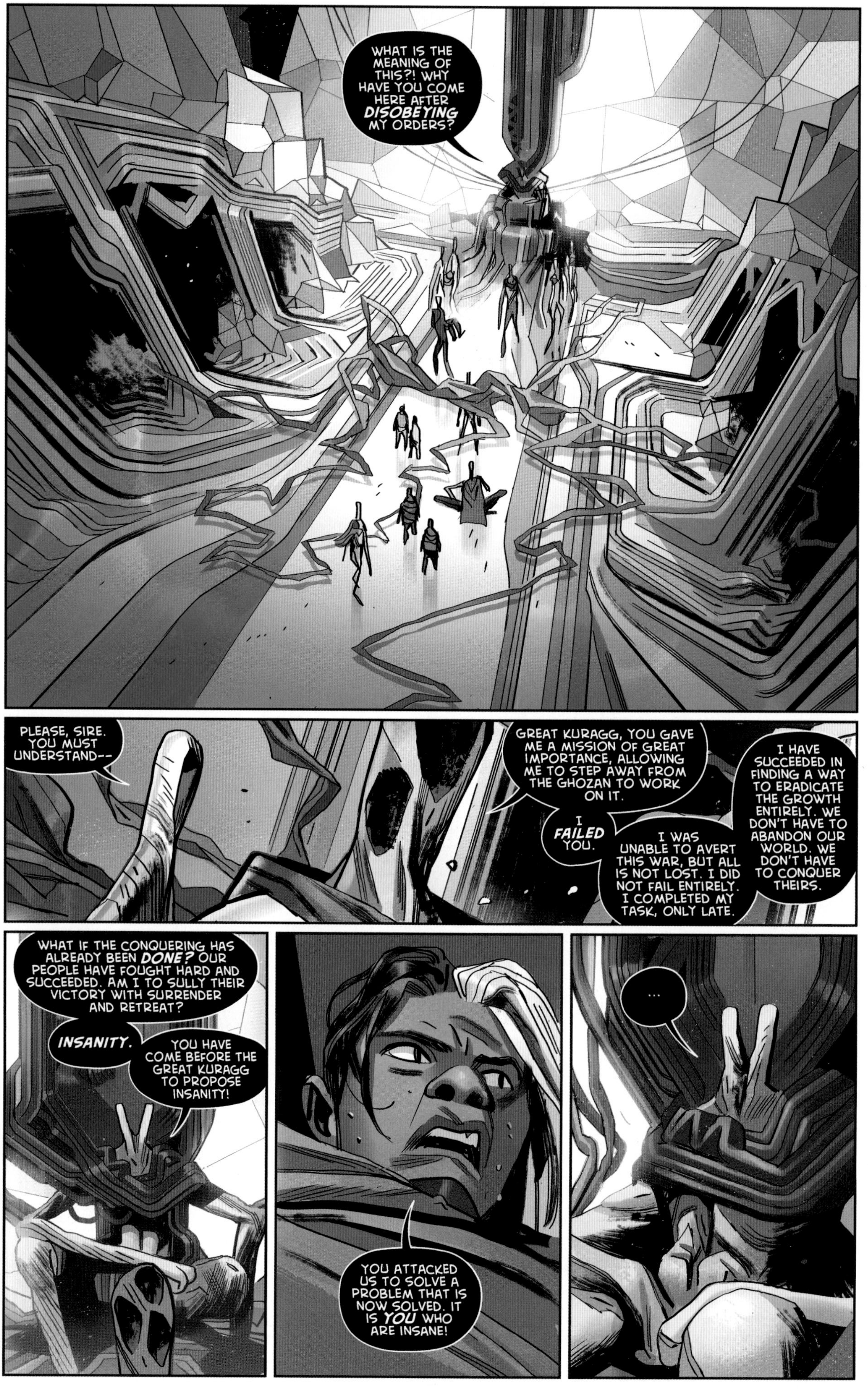
WHAT IS THE MEANING OF THIS?! WHY HAVE YOU COME HERE AFTER *DISOBEYING* MY ORDERS?
PLEASE, SIRE. YOU MUST UNDERSTAND--
GREAT KURAGG, YOU GAVE ME A MISSION OF GREAT IMPORTANCE, ALLOWING ME TO STEP AWAY FROM THE GHOZAN TO WORK ON IT.
I *FAILED* YOU.
I WAS UNABLE TO AVERT THIS WAR, BUT ALL IS NOT LOST. I DID NOT FAIL ENTIRELY. I COMPLETED MY TASK, ONLY LATE.
I HAVE SUCCEEDED IN FINDING A WAY TO ERADICATE THE GROWTH ENTIRELY. WE DON'T HAVE TO ABANDON OUR WORLD. WE DON'T HAVE TO CONQUER THEIRS.
WHAT IF THE CONQUERING HAS ALREADY BEEN *DONE?* OUR PEOPLE HAVE FOUGHT HARD AND SUCCEEDED. AM I TO SULLY THEIR VICTORY WITH SURRENDER AND RETREAT?
INSANITY.
YOU HAVE COME BEFORE THE GREAT KURAGG TO PROPOSE INSANITY!
YOU ATTACKED US TO SOLVE A PROBLEM THAT IS NOW SOLVED. IT IS *YOU* WHO ARE INSANE!
...

I HAVE TOLERATED YOUR PRESENCE LONG ENOUGH!
ELITE GUARD! KILL ALL THE HUMANS IN THIS ROOM IMMEDIATELY!
WHAT?! NO!
NO! YOU CAN'T!
GRAND KURAGG, PLEASE, YOU MUSTN'T!
OH, GOD! OH, GOD!
NOW, GUYS--

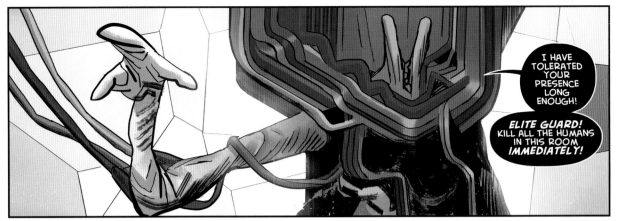

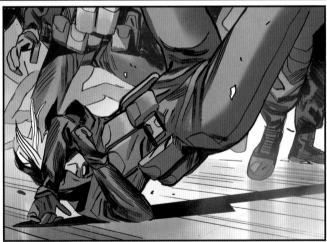

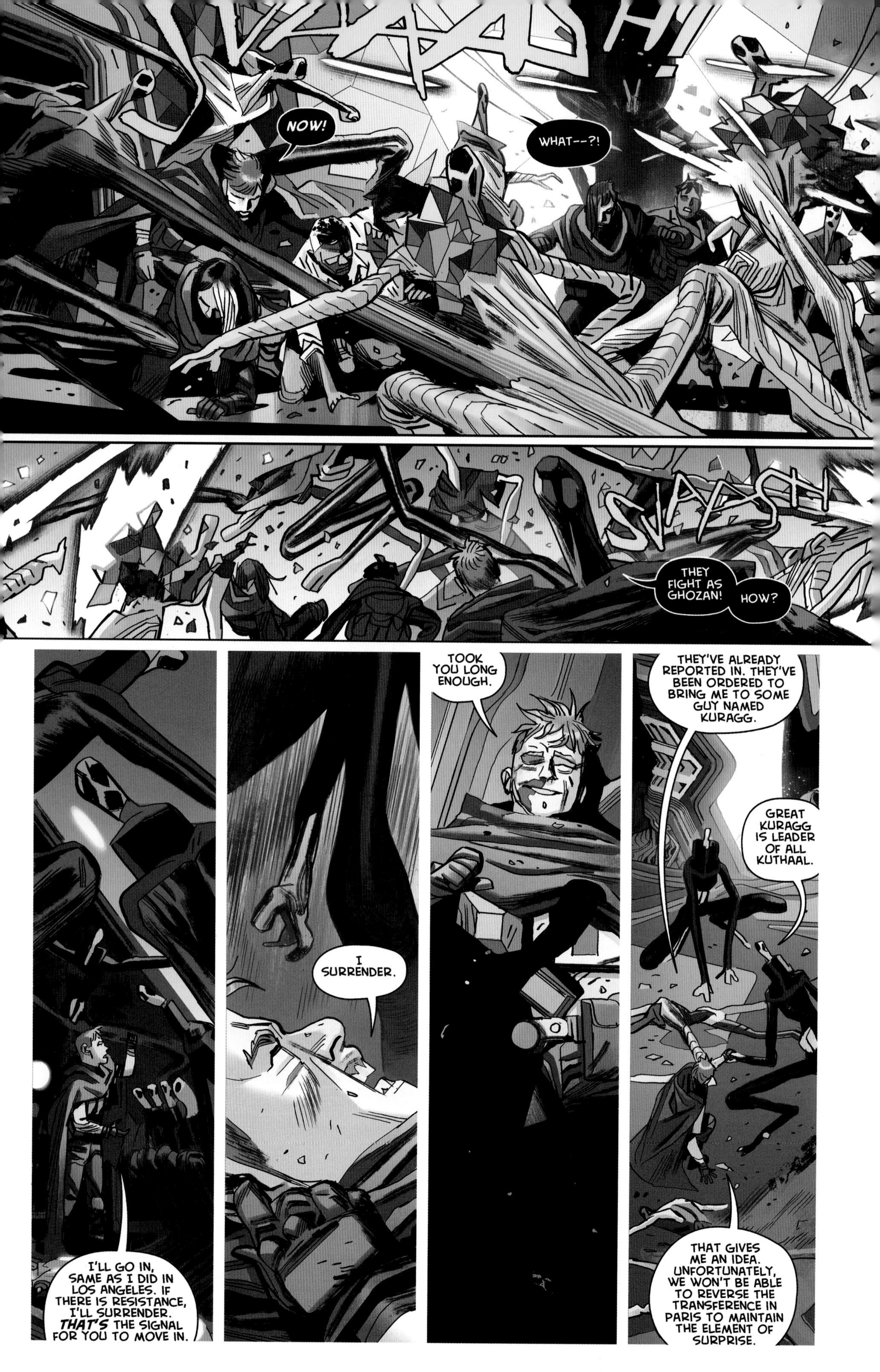

NOW!
WHAT--?!
SWASH
THEY FIGHT AS GHOZAN!
HOW?
I'LL GO IN, SAME AS I DID IN LOS ANGELES. IF THERE IS RESISTANCE, I'LL SURRENDER. *THAT'S* THE SIGNAL FOR YOU TO MOVE IN.
I SURRENDER.
TOOK YOU LONG ENOUGH.
THEY'VE ALREADY REPORTED IN. THEY'VE BEEN ORDERED TO BRING ME TO SOME GUY NAMED KURAGG.
GREAT KURAGG IS LEADER OF ALL KUTHAAL.
THAT GIVES ME AN IDEA. UNFORTUNATELY, WE WON'T BE ABLE TO REVERSE THE TRANSFERENCE IN PARIS TO MAINTAIN THE ELEMENT OF SURPRISE.

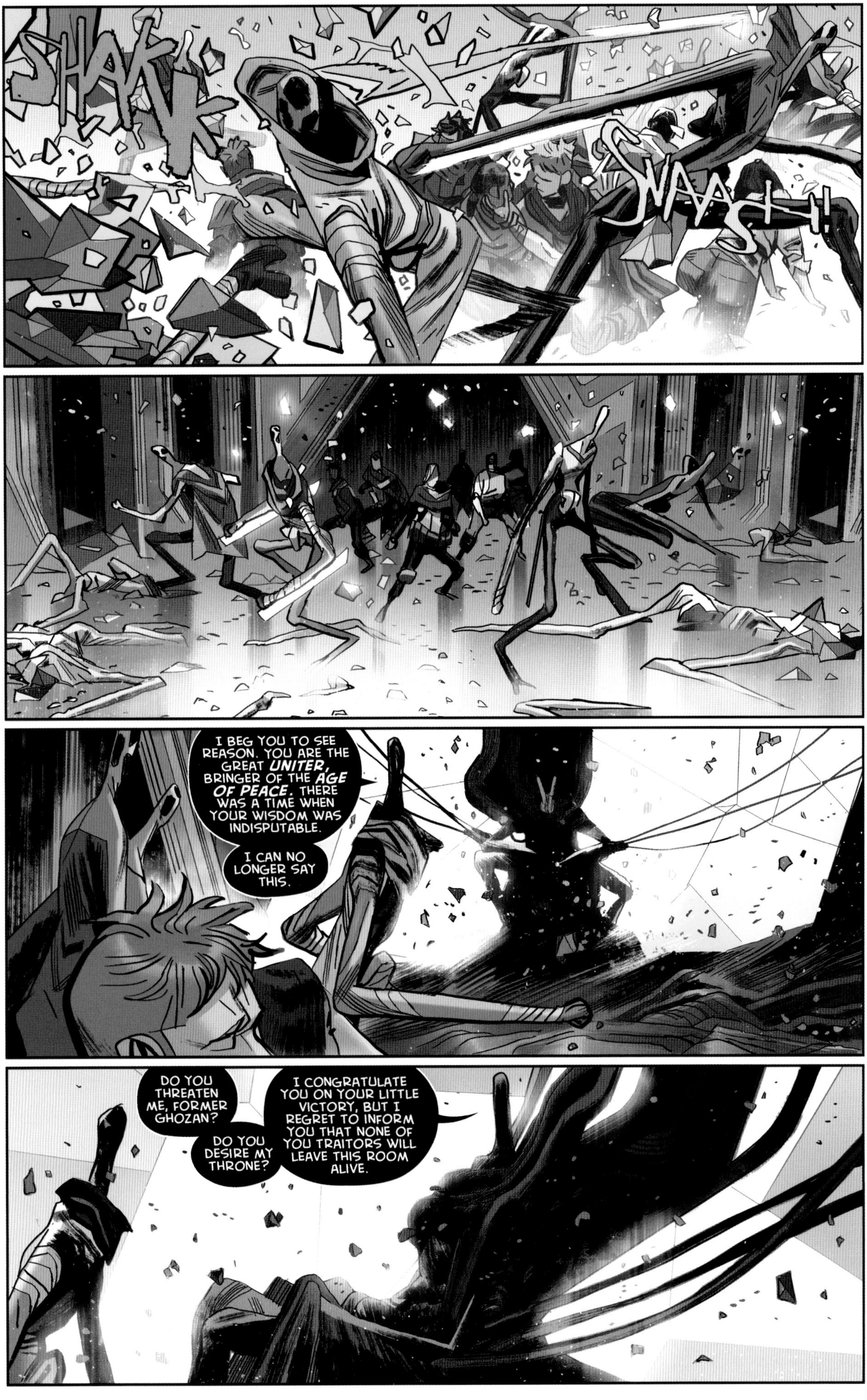
SHAKK
SWAASHH
I BEG YOU TO SEE REASON. YOU ARE THE GREAT UNITER, BRINGER OF THE AGE OF PEACE. THERE WAS A TIME WHEN YOUR WISDOM WAS INDISPUTABLE.
I CAN NO LONGER SAY THIS.
DO YOU THREATEN ME, FORMER GHOZAN?
DO YOU DESIRE MY THRONE?
I CONGRATULATE YOU ON YOUR LITTLE VICTORY, BUT I REGRET TO INFORM YOU THAT NONE OF YOU TRAITORS WILL LEAVE THIS ROOM ALIVE.

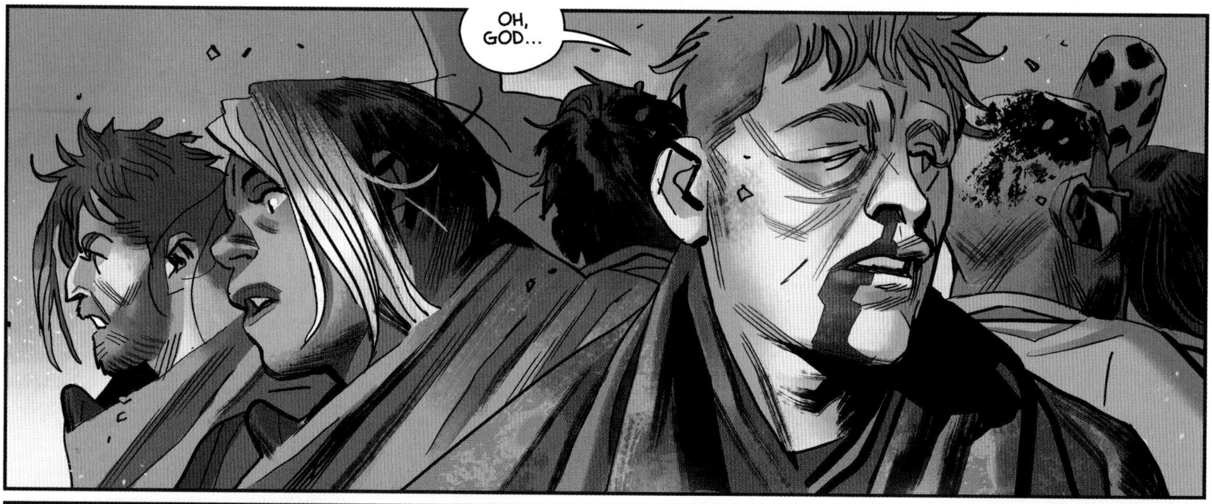
OH, GOD...
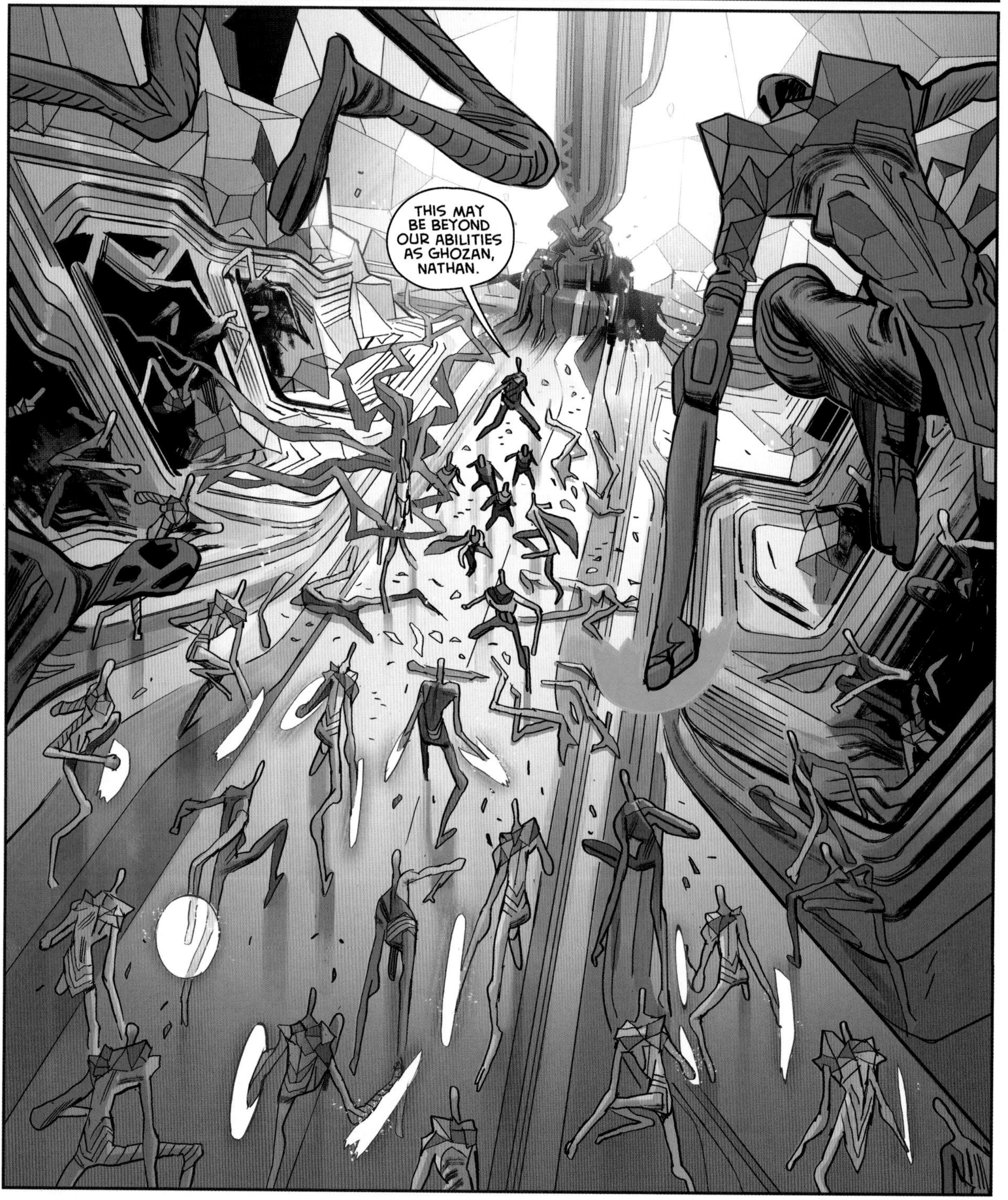
THIS MAY BE BEYOND OUR ABILITIES AS GHOZAN, NATHAN.

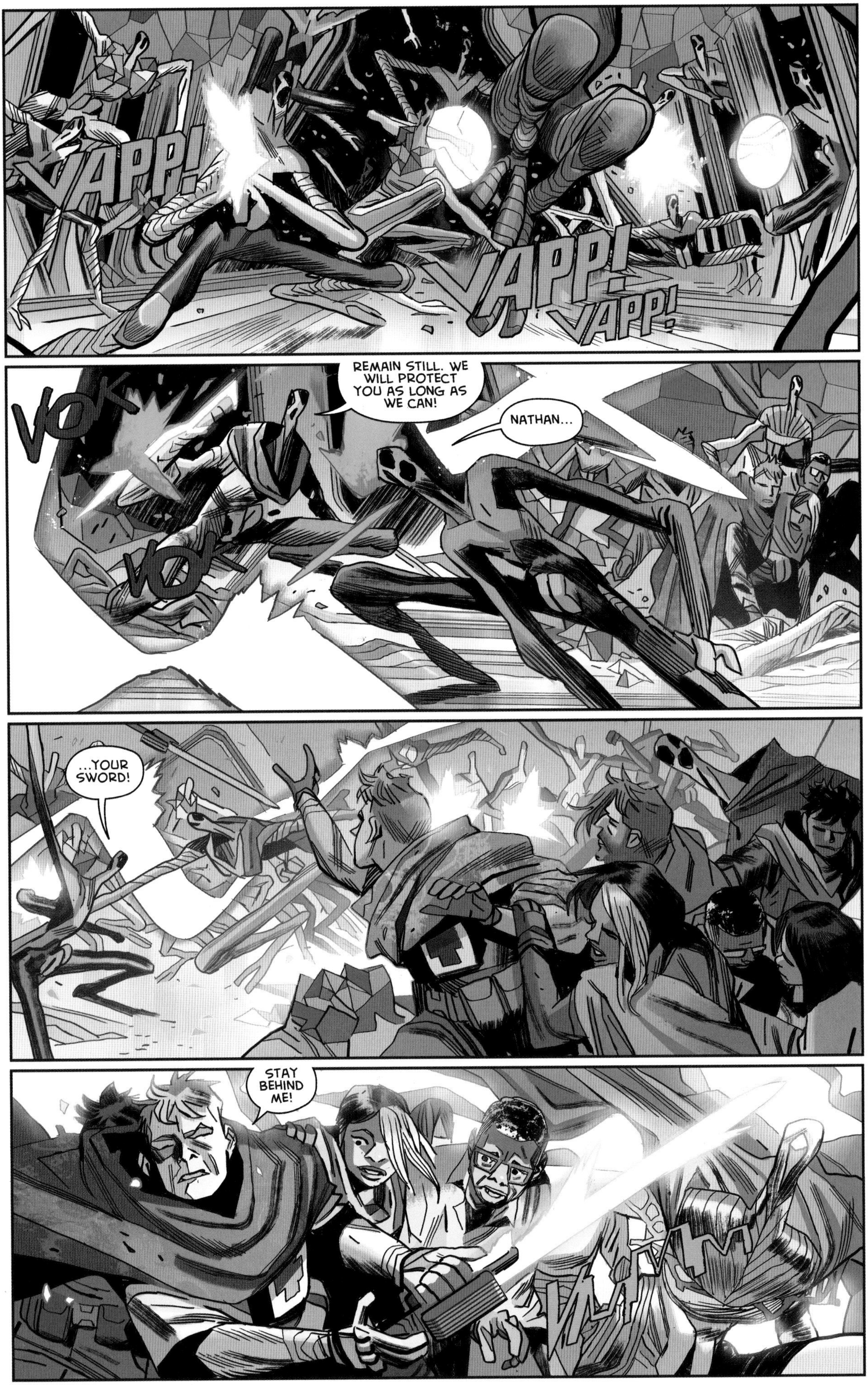
VAPP!
VAPP!
VAPP!
VOK
VOK
REMAIN STILL. WE WILL PROTECT YOU AS LONG AS WE CAN!
NATHAN...
...YOUR SWORD!
STAY BEHIND ME!

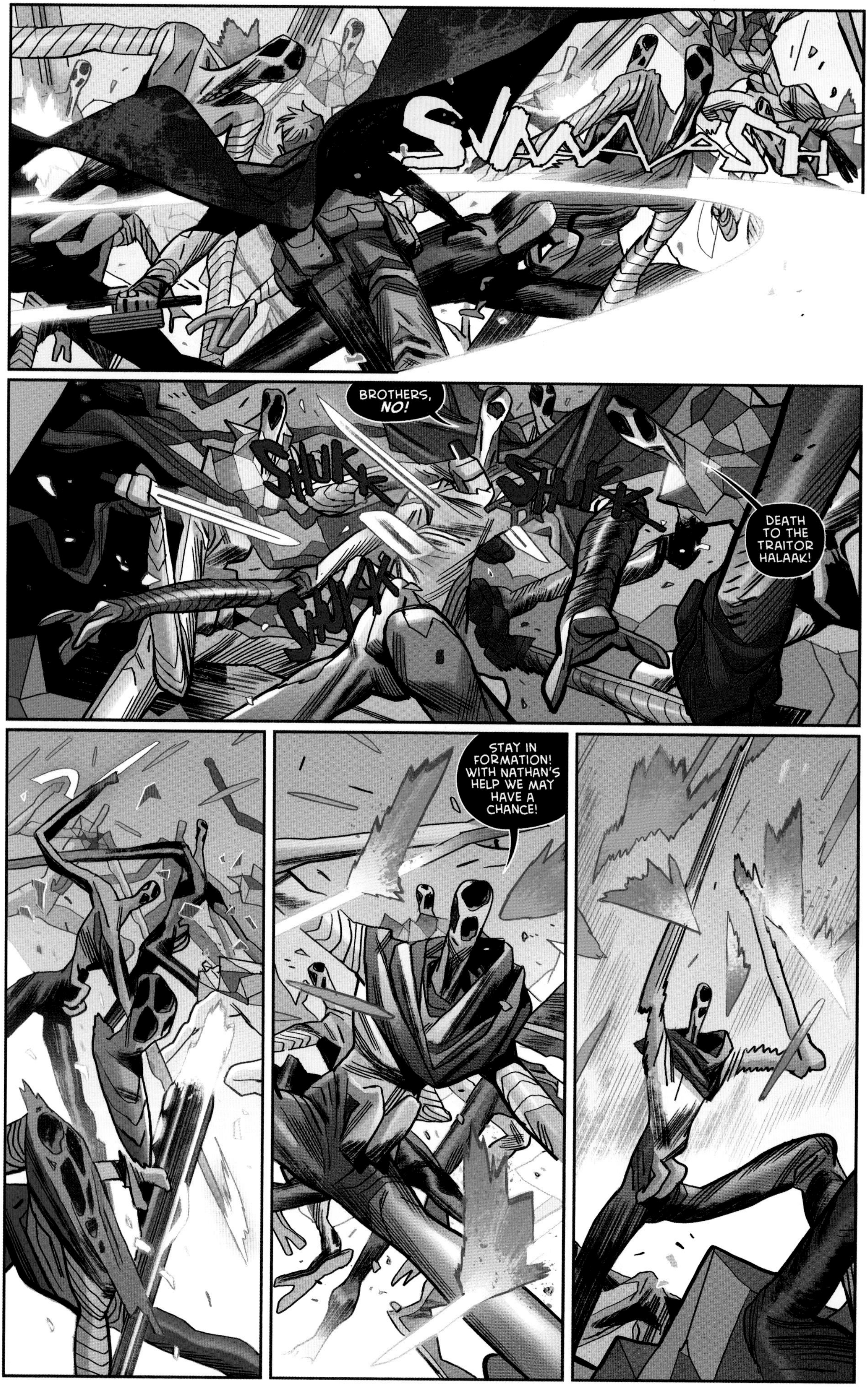
SWAASH
BROTHERS, NO!
SHUKK
SHUKK
SHUKK
DEATH TO THE TRAITOR HALAAK!
STAY IN FORMATION! WITH NATHAN'S HELP WE MAY HAVE A CHANCE!

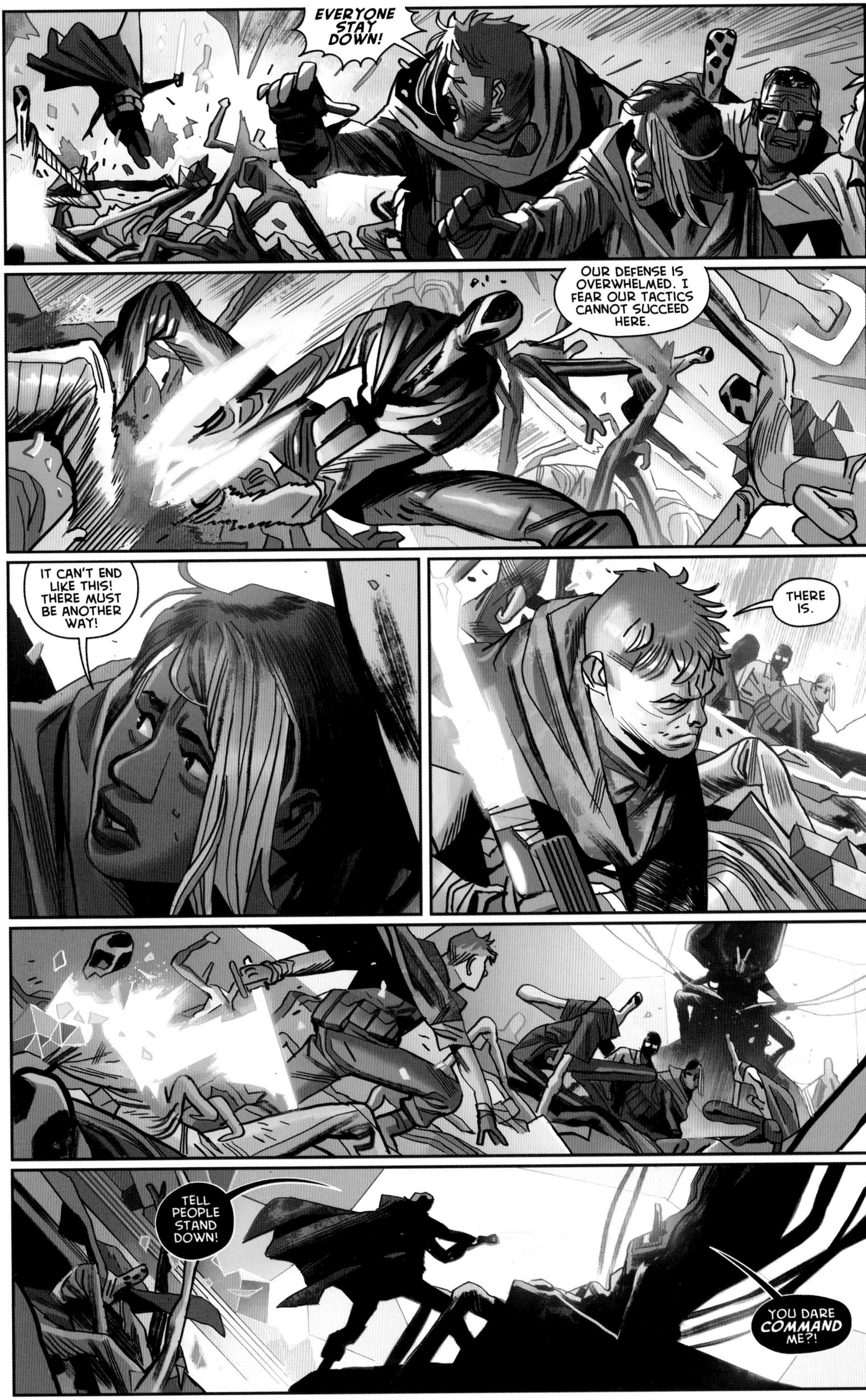
EVERYONE STAY DOWN!
OUR DEFENSE IS OVERWHELMED. I FEAR OUR TACTICS CANNOT SUCCEED HERE.
IT CAN'T END LIKE THIS! THERE MUST BE ANOTHER WAY!
THERE IS.
TELL PEOPLE STAND DOWN!
YOU DARE COMMAND ME?!

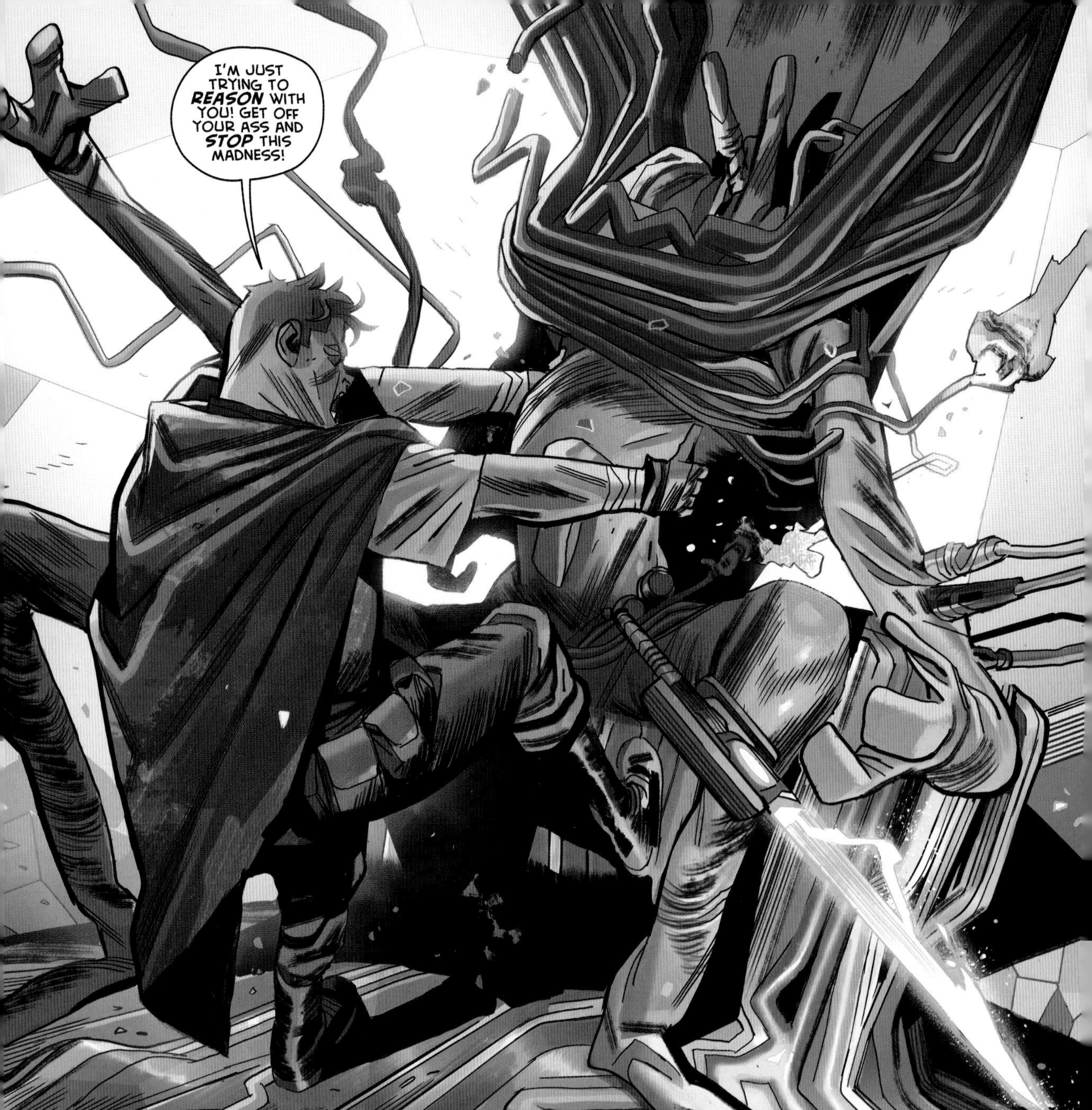
I'M JUST TRYING TO REASON WITH YOU! GET OFF YOUR ASS AND STOP THIS MADNESS!

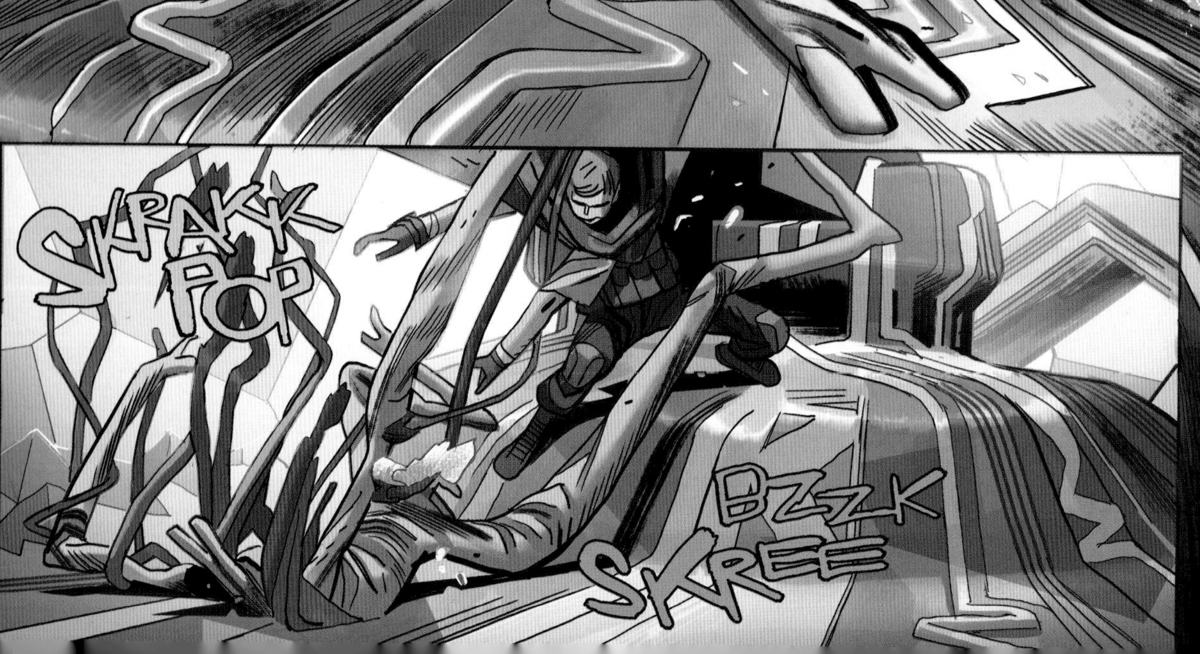
SKRAKK
POP
BZZK
SKREE

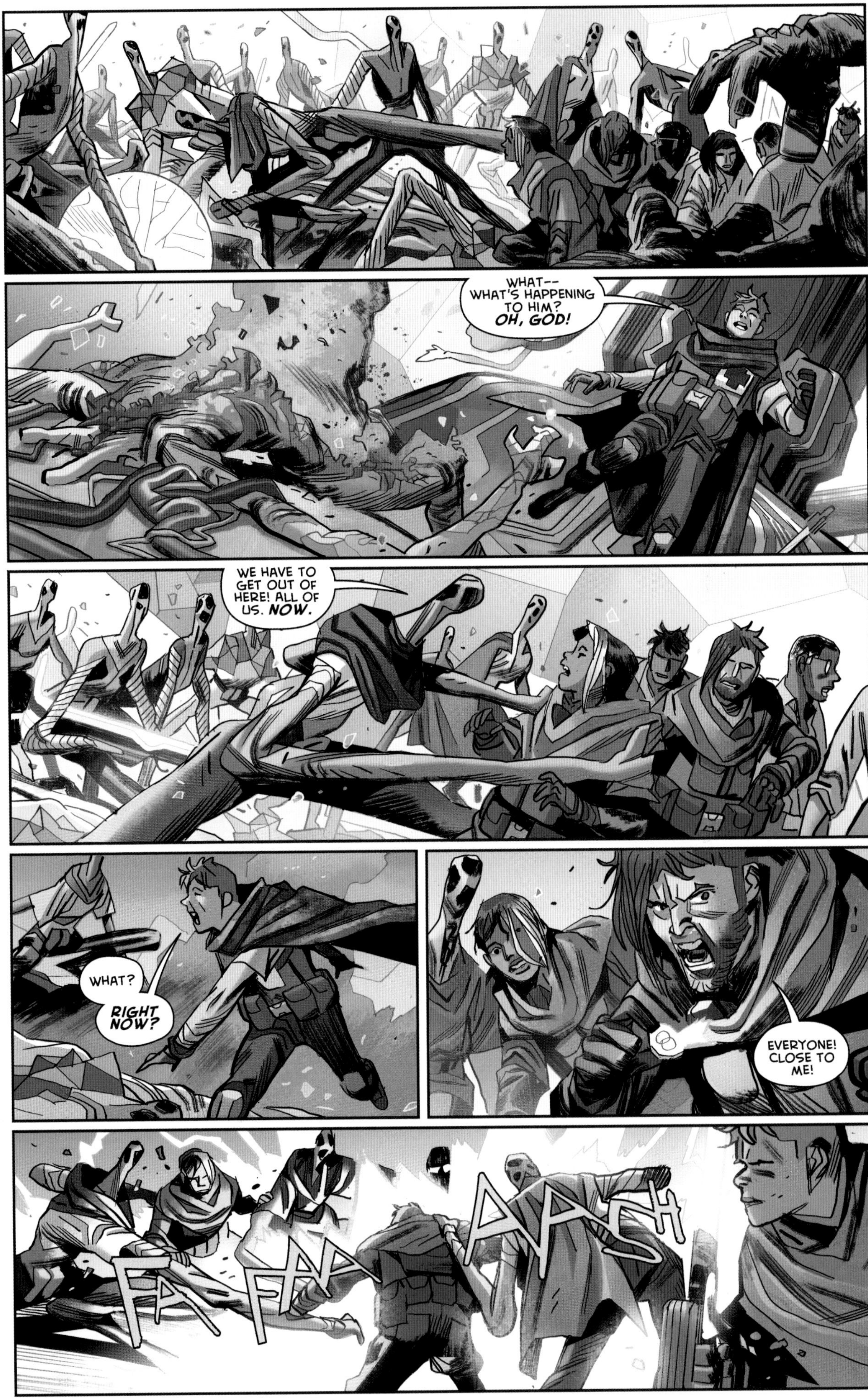
WHAT-- WHAT'S HAPPENING TO HIM? OH, GOD!
WE HAVE TO GET OUT OF HERE! ALL OF US. NOW.
WHAT? RIGHT NOW?
EVERYONE! CLOSE TO ME!
FA FAA AACH

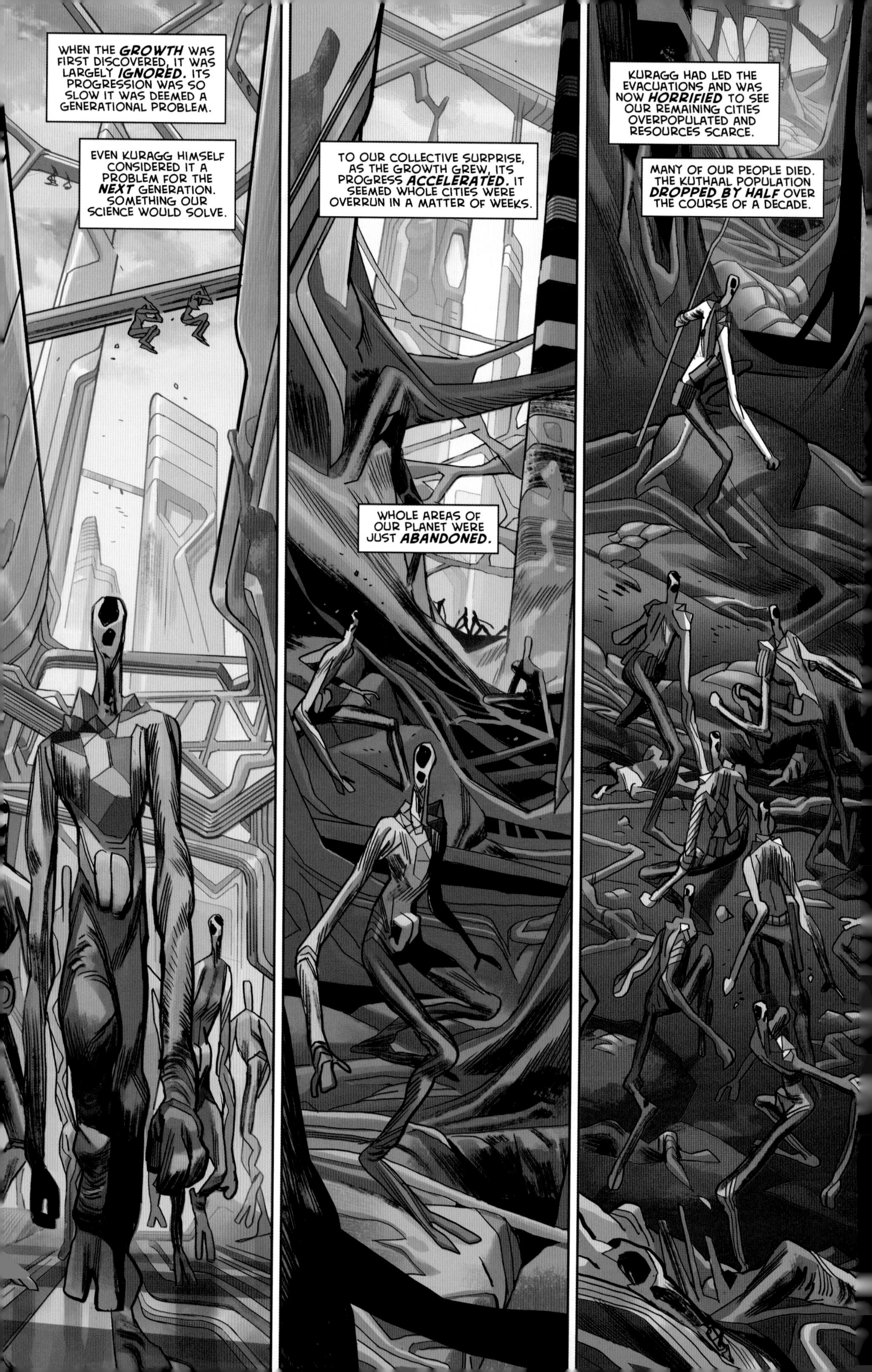
WHEN THE GROWTH WAS FIRST DISCOVERED, IT WAS LARGELY IGNORED. ITS PROGRESSION WAS SO SLOW IT WAS DEEMED A GENERATIONAL PROBLEM.
EVEN KURAGG HIMSELF CONSIDERED IT A PROBLEM FOR THE NEXT GENERATION. SOMETHING OUR SCIENCE WOULD SOLVE.
TO OUR COLLECTIVE SURPRISE, AS THE GROWTH GREW, ITS PROGRESS ACCELERATED. IT SEEMED WHOLE CITIES WERE OVERRUN IN A MATTER OF WEEKS.
WHOLE AREAS OF OUR PLANET WERE JUST ABANDONED.
KURAGG HAD LED THE EVACUATIONS AND WAS NOW HORRIFIED TO SEE OUR REMAINING CITIES OVERPOPULATED AND RESOURCES SCARCE.
MANY OF OUR PEOPLE DIED. THE KUTHAAL POPULATION DROPPED BY HALF OVER THE COURSE OF A DECADE.

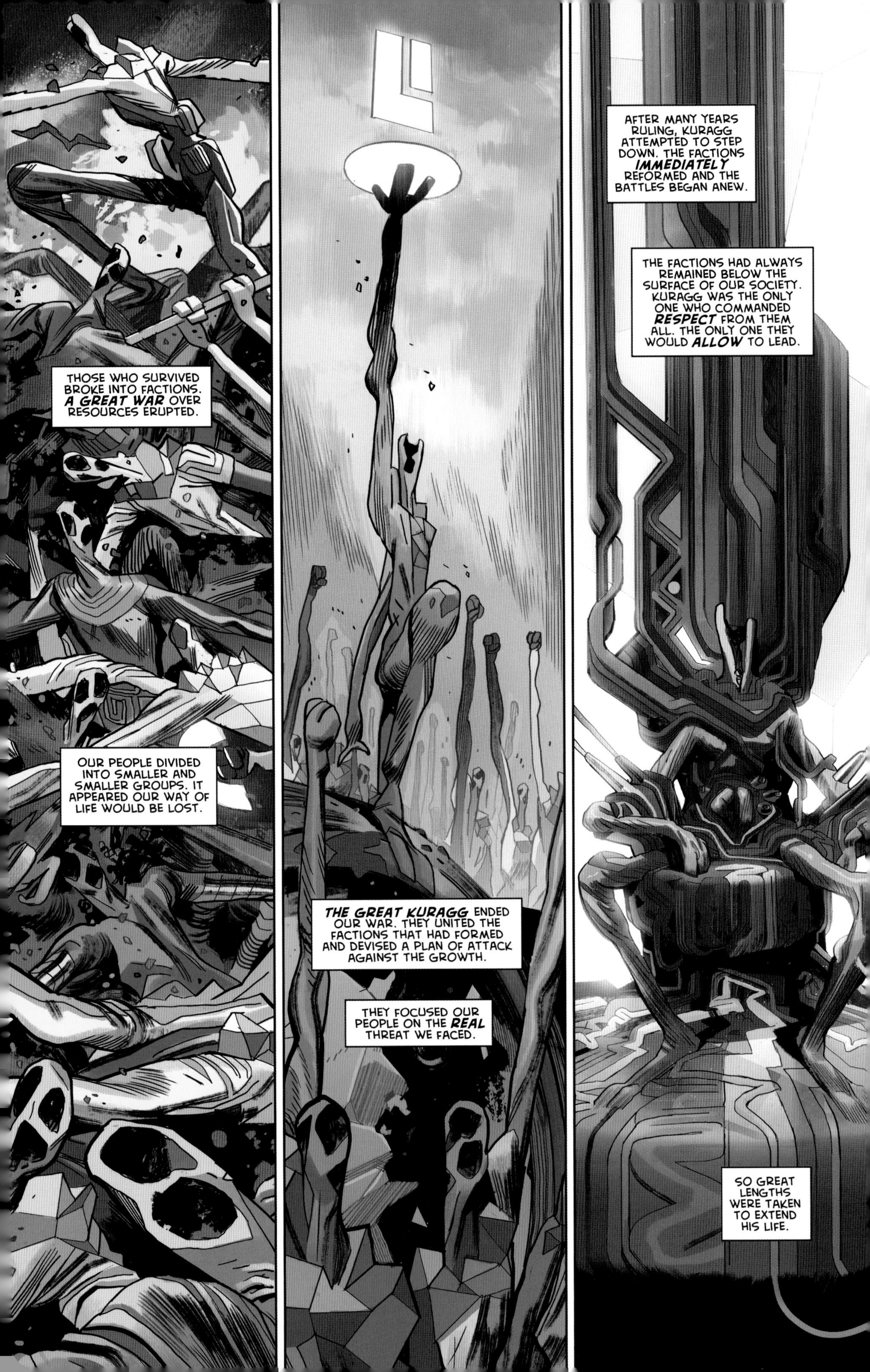
THOSE WHO SURVIVED BROKE INTO FACTIONS. A GREAT WAR OVER RESOURCES ERUPTED.
OUR PEOPLE DIVIDED INTO SMALLER AND SMALLER GROUPS. IT APPEARED OUR WAY OF LIFE WOULD BE LOST.
THE GREAT KURAGG ENDED OUR WAR. THEY UNITED THE FACTIONS THAT HAD FORMED AND DEVISED A PLAN OF ATTACK AGAINST THE GROWTH.
THEY FOCUSED OUR PEOPLE ON THE REAL THREAT WE FACED.
AFTER MANY YEARS RULING, KURAGG ATTEMPTED TO STEP DOWN. THE FACTIONS IMMEDIATELY REFORMED AND THE BATTLES BEGAN ANEW.
THE FACTIONS HAD ALWAYS REMAINED BELOW THE SURFACE OF OUR SOCIETY. KURAGG WAS THE ONLY ONE WHO COMMANDED RESPECT FROM THEM ALL. THE ONLY ONE THEY WOULD ALLOW TO LEAD.
SO GREAT LENGTHS WERE TAKEN TO EXTEND HIS LIFE.

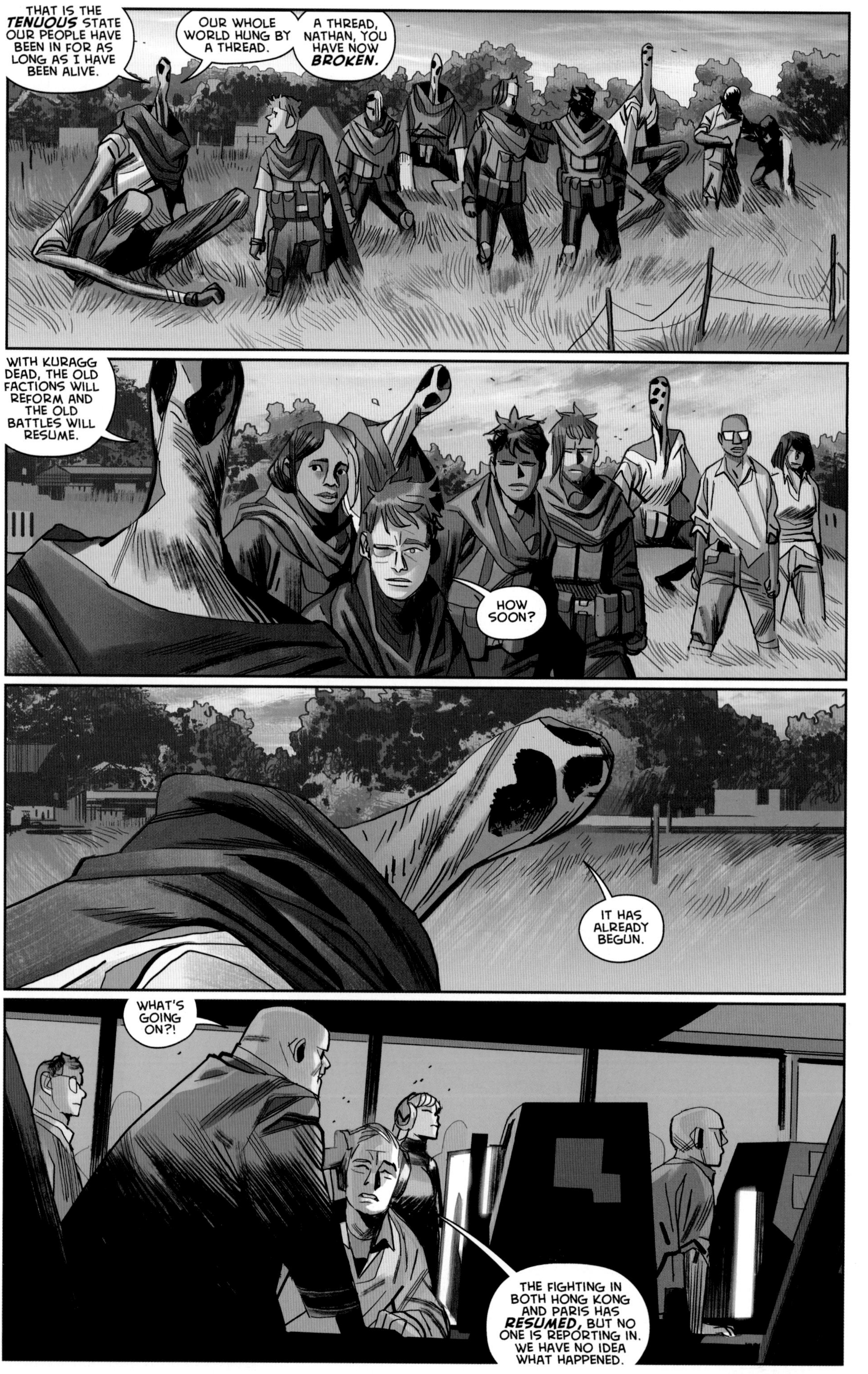
THAT IS THE TENUOUS STATE OUR PEOPLE HAVE BEEN IN FOR AS LONG AS I HAVE BEEN ALIVE.
OUR WHOLE WORLD HUNG BY A THREAD.
A THREAD, NATHAN, YOU HAVE NOW BROKEN.
WITH KURAGG DEAD, THE OLD FACTIONS WILL REFORM AND THE OLD BATTLES WILL RESUME.
HOW SOON?
IT HAS ALREADY BEGUN.
WHAT'S GOING ON?!
THE FIGHTING IN BOTH HONG KONG AND PARIS HAS RESUMED, BUT NO ONE IS REPORTING IN. WE HAVE NO IDEA WHAT HAPPENED.

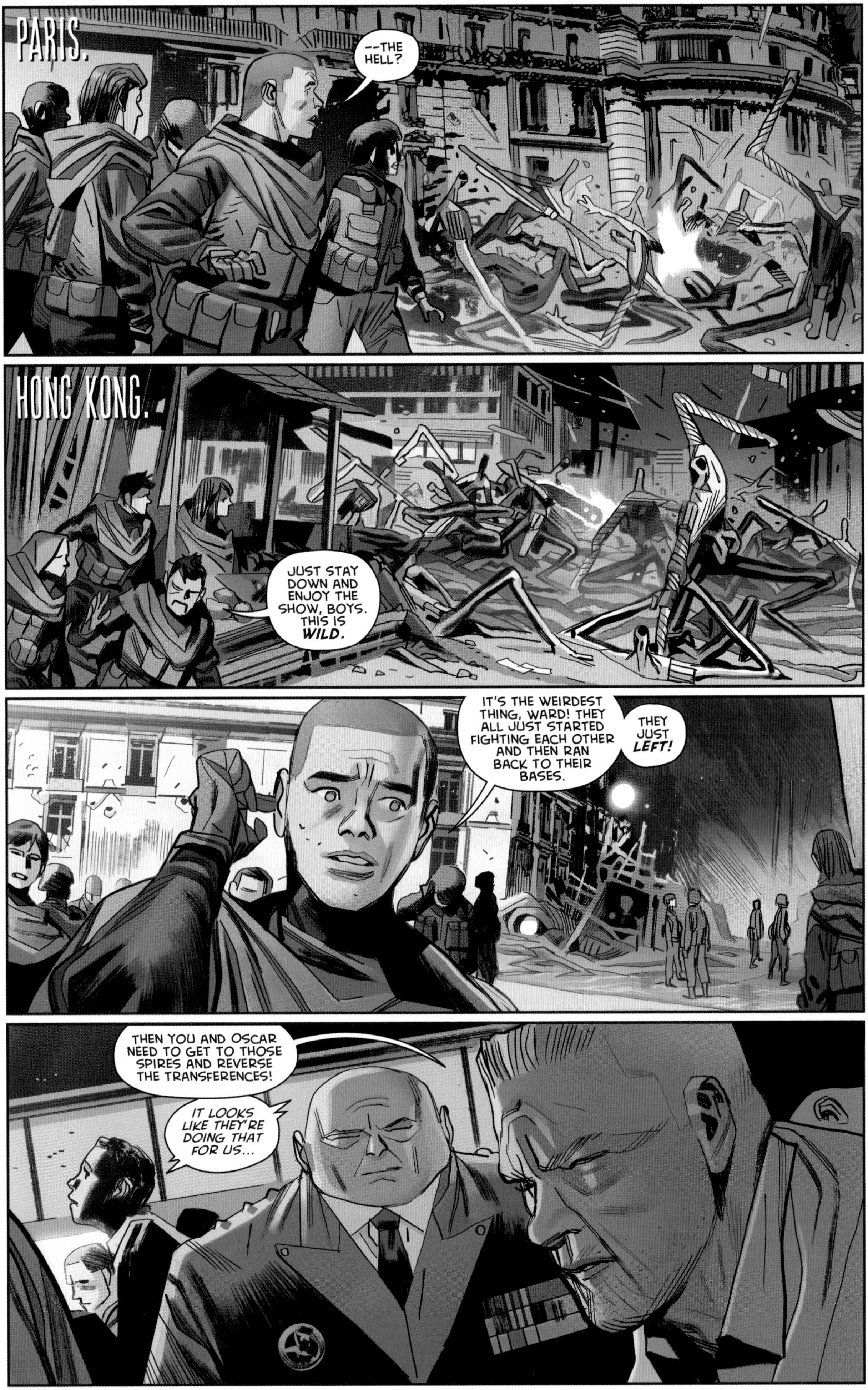
PARIS.
--THE HELL?
HONG KONG.
JUST STAY DOWN AND ENJOY THE SHOW, BOYS. THIS IS WILD.
IT'S THE WEIRDEST THING, WARD! THEY ALL JUST STARTED FIGHTING EACH OTHER AND THEN RAN BACK TO THEIR BASES.
THEY JUST LEFT!
THEN YOU AND OSCAR NEED TO GET TO THOSE SPIRES AND REVERSE THE TRANSFERENCES!
IT LOOKS LIKE THEY'RE DOING THAT FOR US...

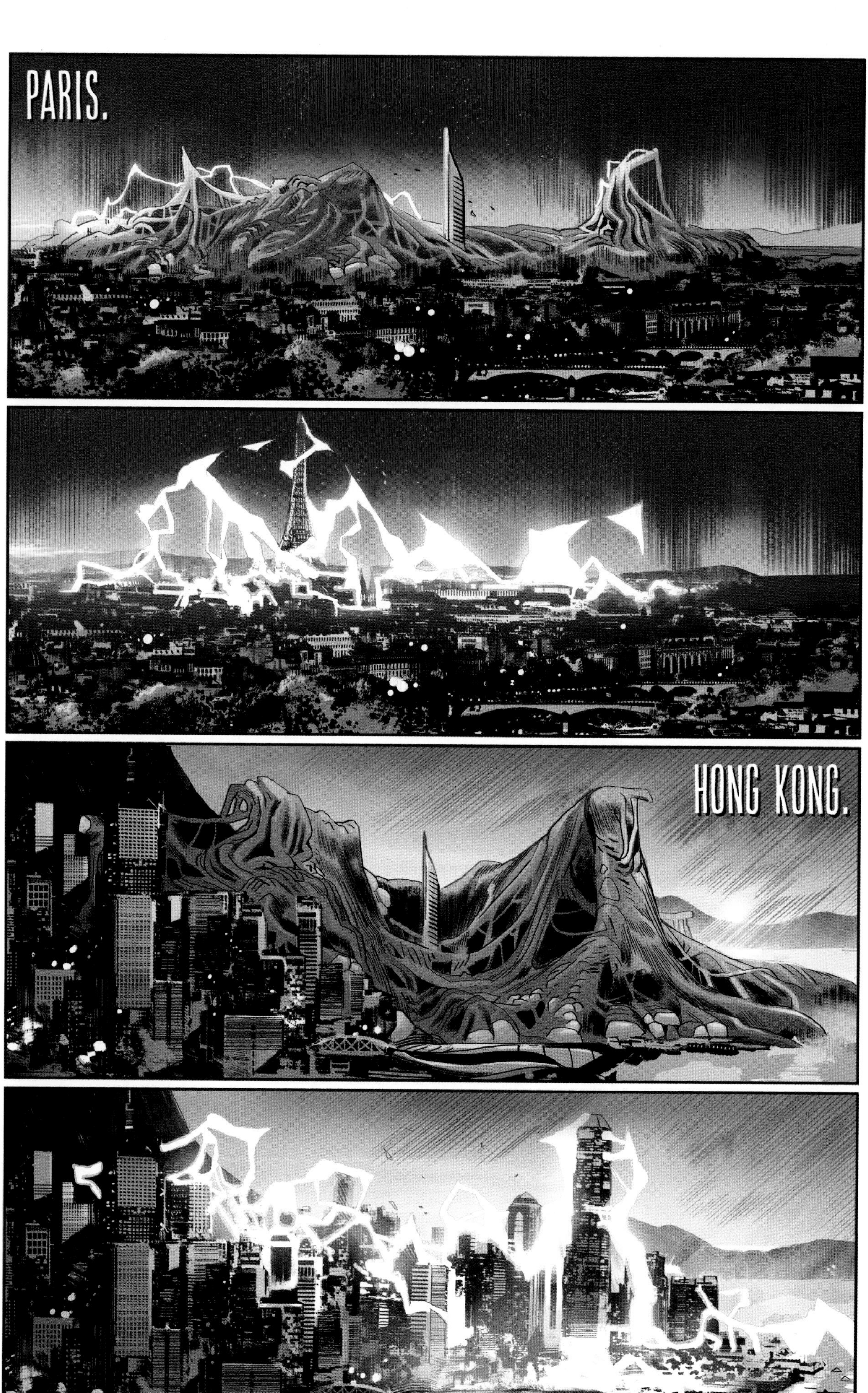
PARIS.
HONG KONG.

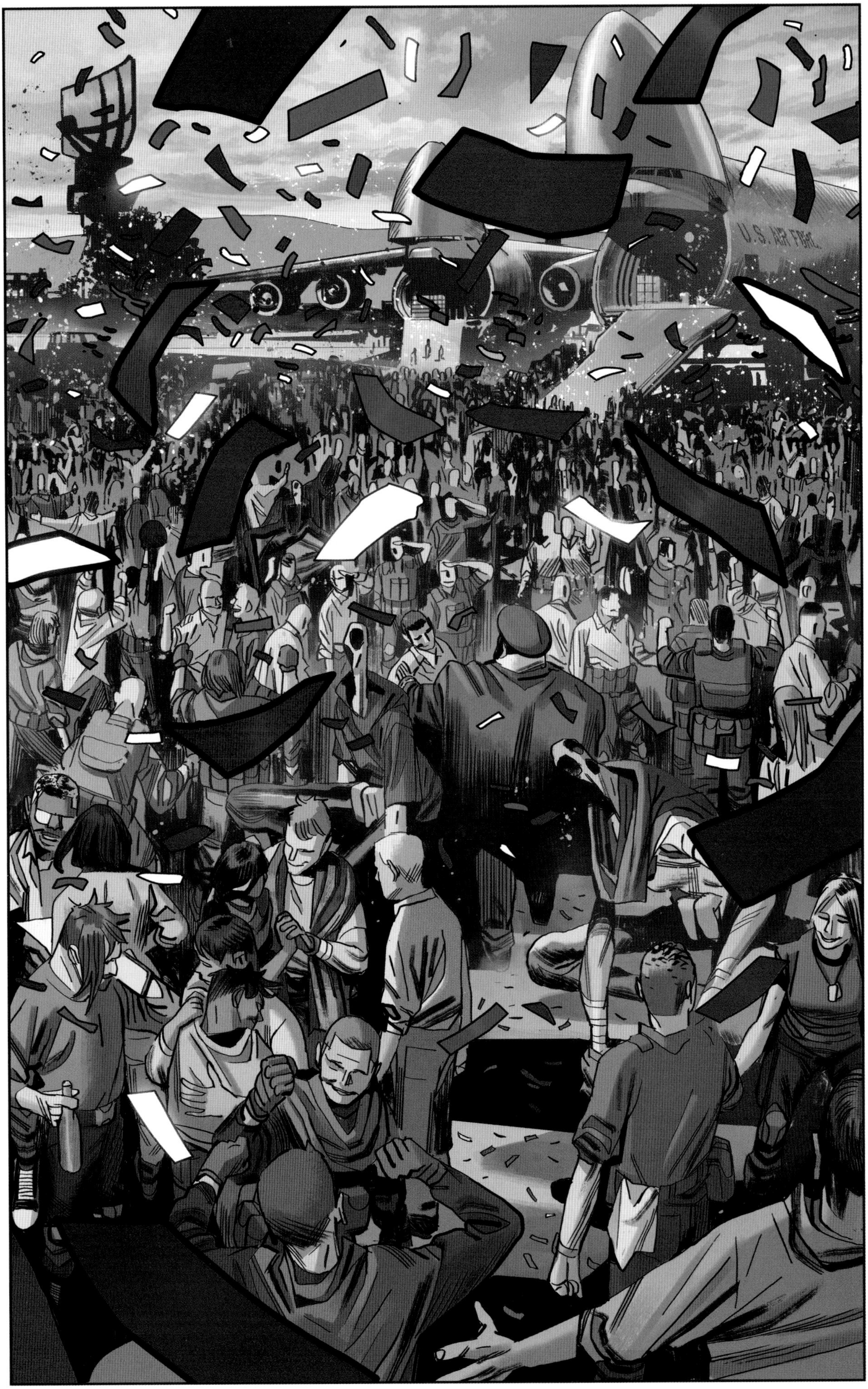

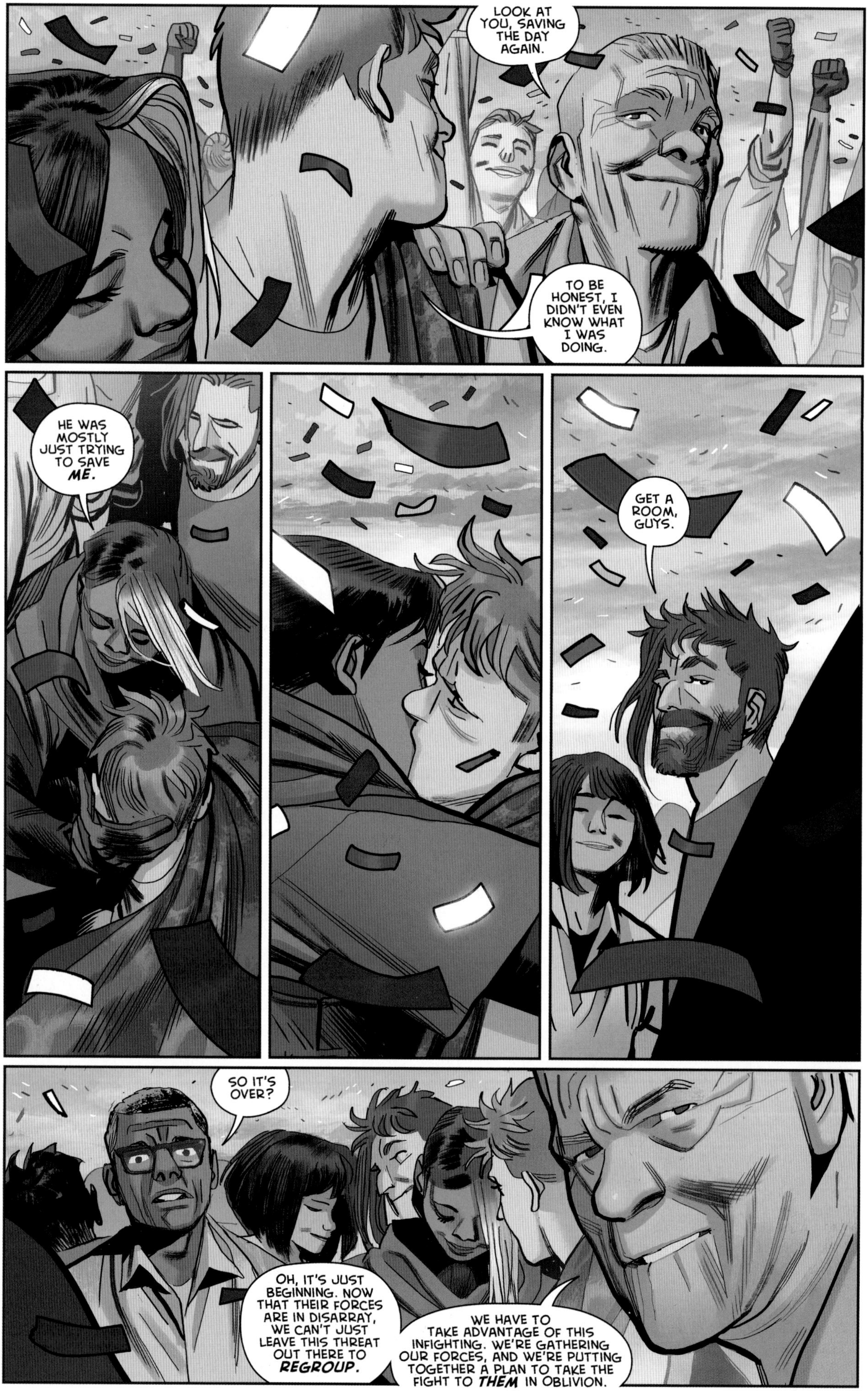
LOOK AT YOU, SAVING THE DAY AGAIN.
TO BE HONEST, I DIDN'T EVEN KNOW WHAT I WAS DOING.
HE WAS MOSTLY JUST TRYING TO SAVE *ME*.
GET A ROOM, GUYS.
SO IT'S OVER?
OH, IT'S JUST BEGINNING. NOW THAT THEIR FORCES ARE IN DISARRAY, WE CAN'T JUST LEAVE THIS THREAT OUT THERE TO *REGROUP*.
WE HAVE TO TAKE ADVANTAGE OF THIS INFIGHTING. WE'RE GATHERING OUR FORCES, AND WE'RE PUTTING TOGETHER A PLAN TO TAKE THE FIGHT TO *THEM* IN OBLIVION.

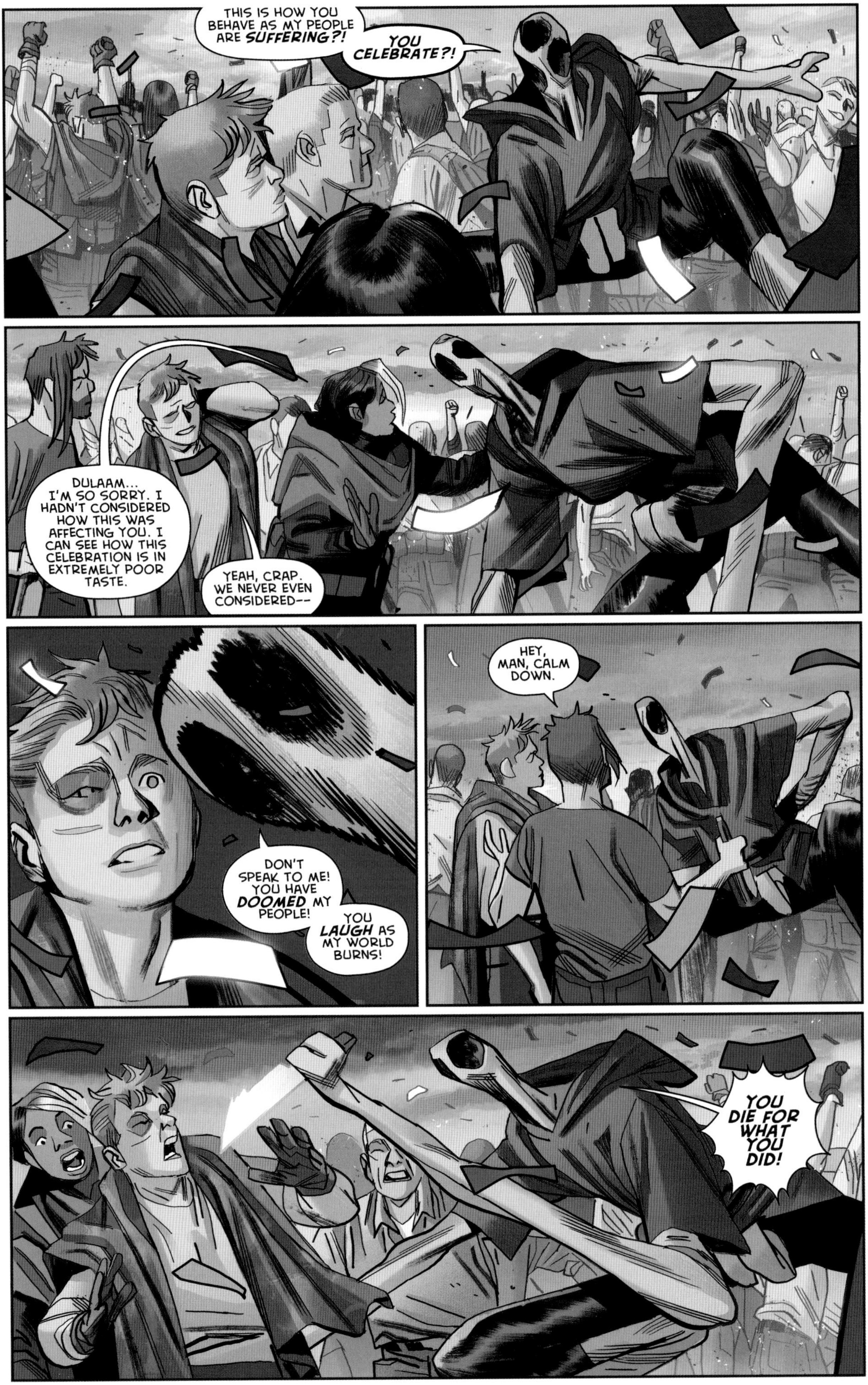

THIS IS HOW YOU BEHAVE AS MY PEOPLE ARE SUFFERING?!
YOU CELEBRATE?!
DULAAM... I'M SO SORRY. I HADN'T CONSIDERED HOW THIS WAS AFFECTING YOU. I CAN SEE HOW THIS CELEBRATION IS IN EXTREMELY POOR TASTE.
YEAH, CRAP. WE NEVER EVEN CONSIDERED--
DON'T SPEAK TO ME! YOU HAVE DOOMED MY PEOPLE!
YOU LAUGH AS MY WORLD BURNS!
HEY, MAN, CALM DOWN.
YOU DIE FOR WHAT YOU DID!

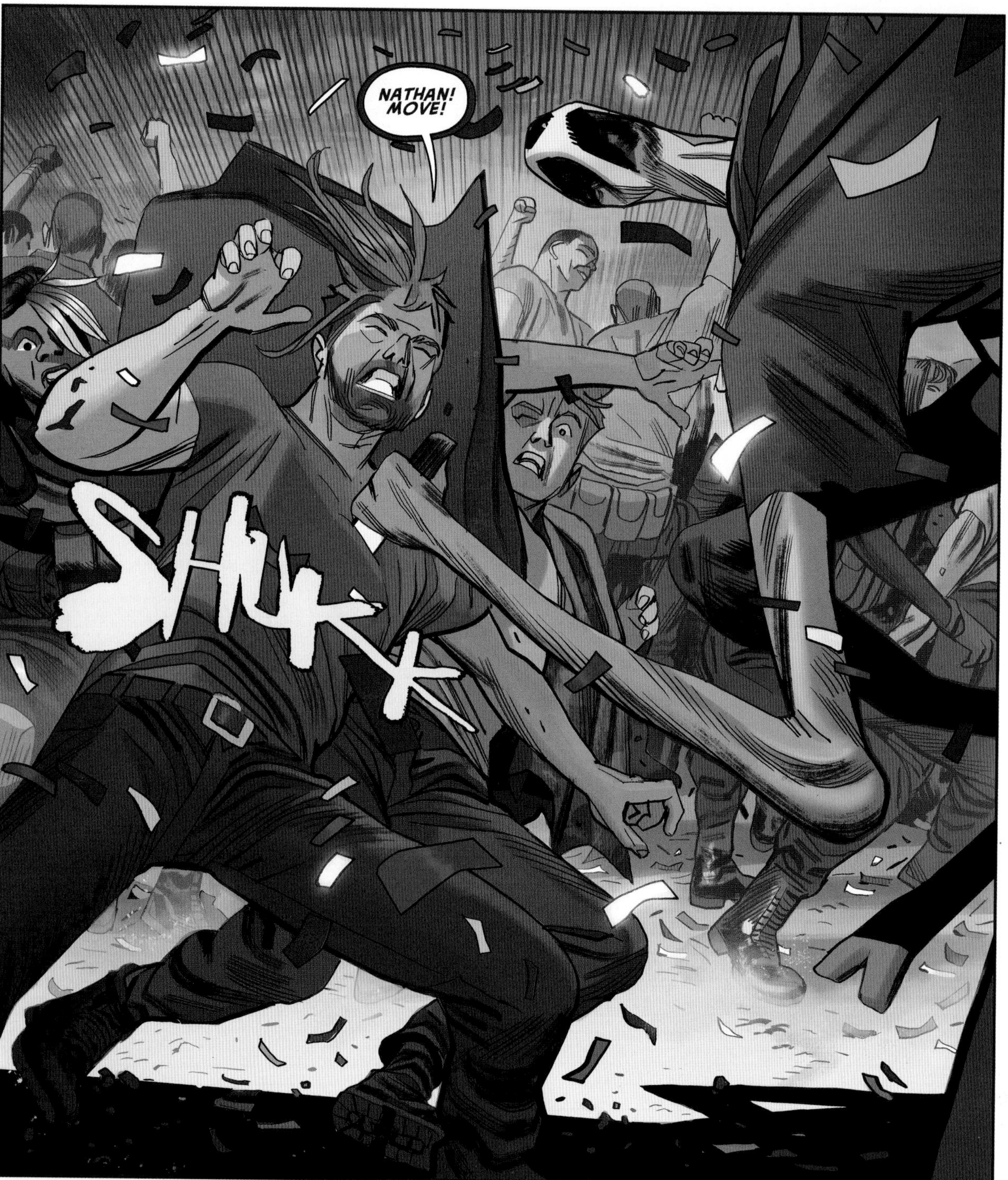
NATHAN! MOVE!
SHUK
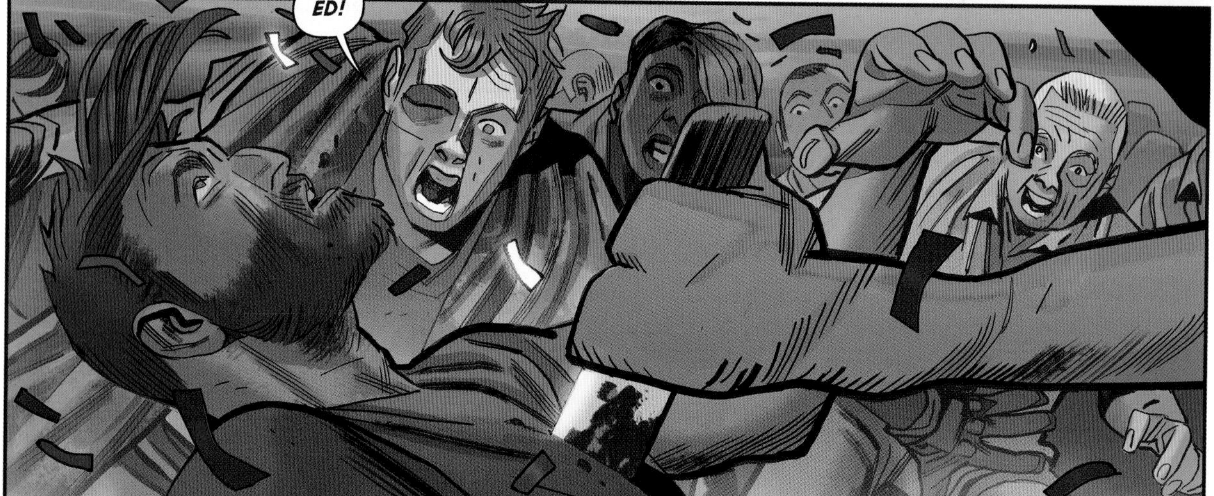
ED!

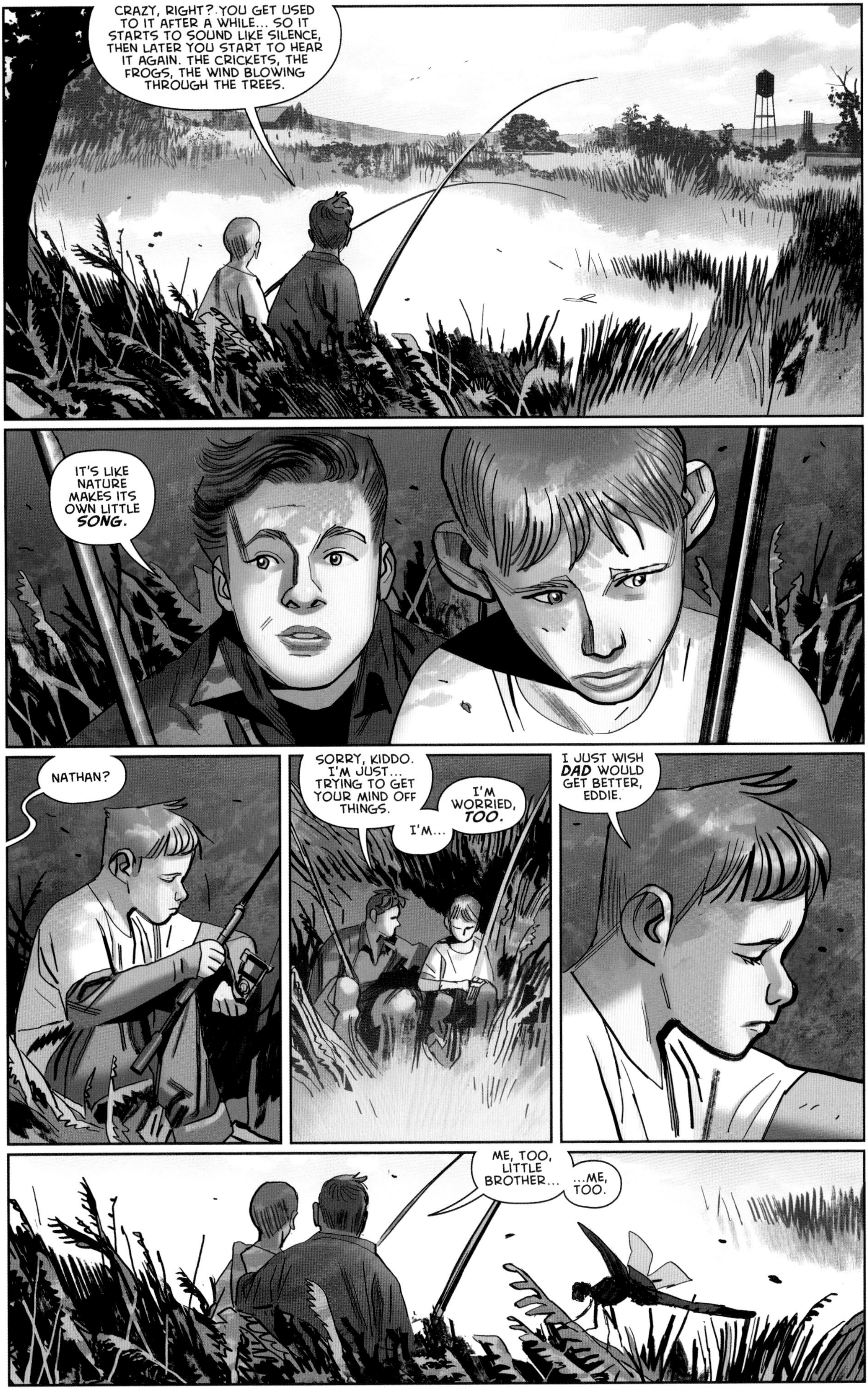
CRAZY, RIGHT? YOU GET USED TO IT AFTER A WHILE... SO IT STARTS TO SOUND LIKE SILENCE, THEN LATER YOU START TO HEAR IT AGAIN. THE CRICKETS, THE FROGS, THE WIND BLOWING THROUGH THE TREES.
IT'S LIKE NATURE MAKES ITS OWN LITTLE SONG.
NATHAN?
SORRY, KIDDO. I'M JUST... TRYING TO GET YOUR MIND OFF THINGS.
I'M...
I'M WORRIED, TOO.
I JUST WISH DAD WOULD GET BETTER, EDDIE.
ME, TOO, LITTLE BROTHER...
...ME, TOO.

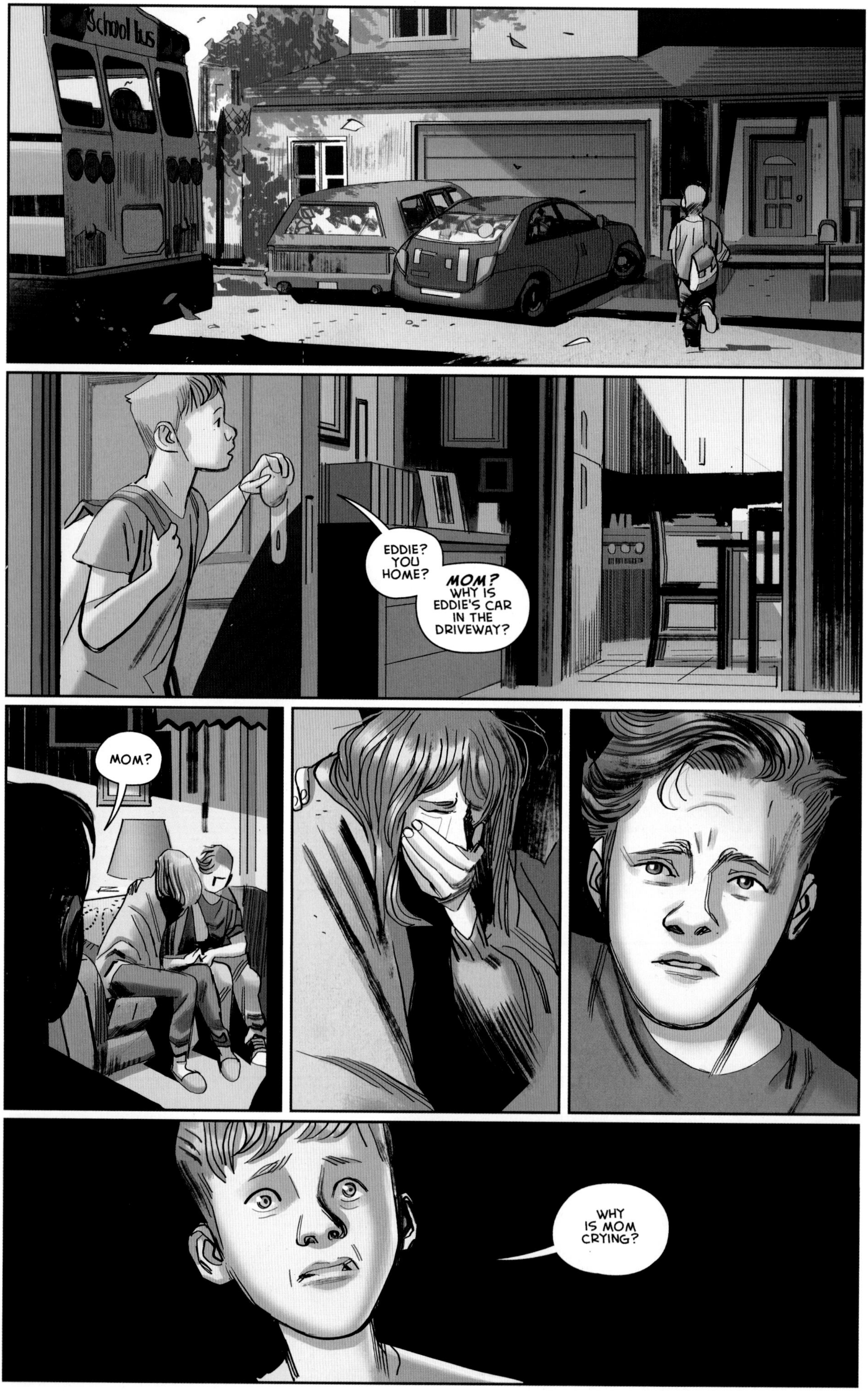

School bus
EDDIE? YOU HOME?
MOM? WHY IS EDDIE'S CAR IN THE DRIVEWAY?
MOM?
WHY IS MOM CRYING?

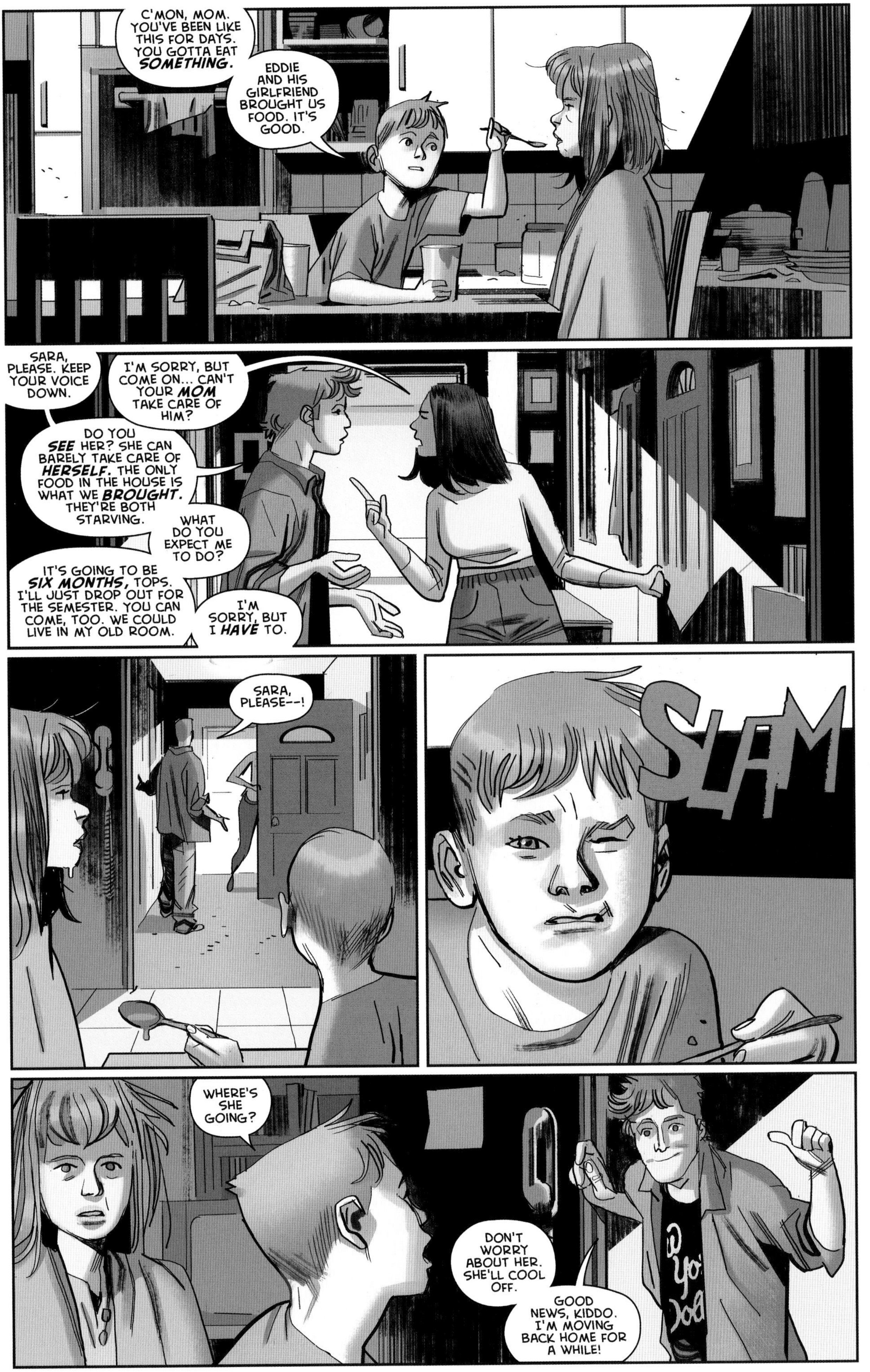
C'MON, MOM. YOU'VE BEEN LIKE THIS FOR DAYS. YOU GOTTA EAT SOMETHING.
EDDIE AND HIS GIRLFRIEND BROUGHT US FOOD. IT'S GOOD.
SARA, PLEASE. KEEP YOUR VOICE DOWN.
I'M SORRY, BUT COME ON... CAN'T YOUR MOM TAKE CARE OF HIM?
DO YOU SEE HER? SHE CAN BARELY TAKE CARE OF HERSELF. THE ONLY FOOD IN THE HOUSE IS WHAT WE BROUGHT. THEY'RE BOTH STARVING.
WHAT DO YOU EXPECT ME TO DO?
IT'S GOING TO BE SIX MONTHS, TOPS. I'LL JUST DROP OUT FOR THE SEMESTER. YOU CAN COME, TOO. WE COULD LIVE IN MY OLD ROOM.
I'M SORRY, BUT I HAVE TO.
SARA, PLEASE--!
SLAM
WHERE'S SHE GOING?
DON'T WORRY ABOUT HER. SHE'LL COOL OFF.
GOOD NEWS, KIDDO. I'M MOVING BACK HOME FOR A WHILE!

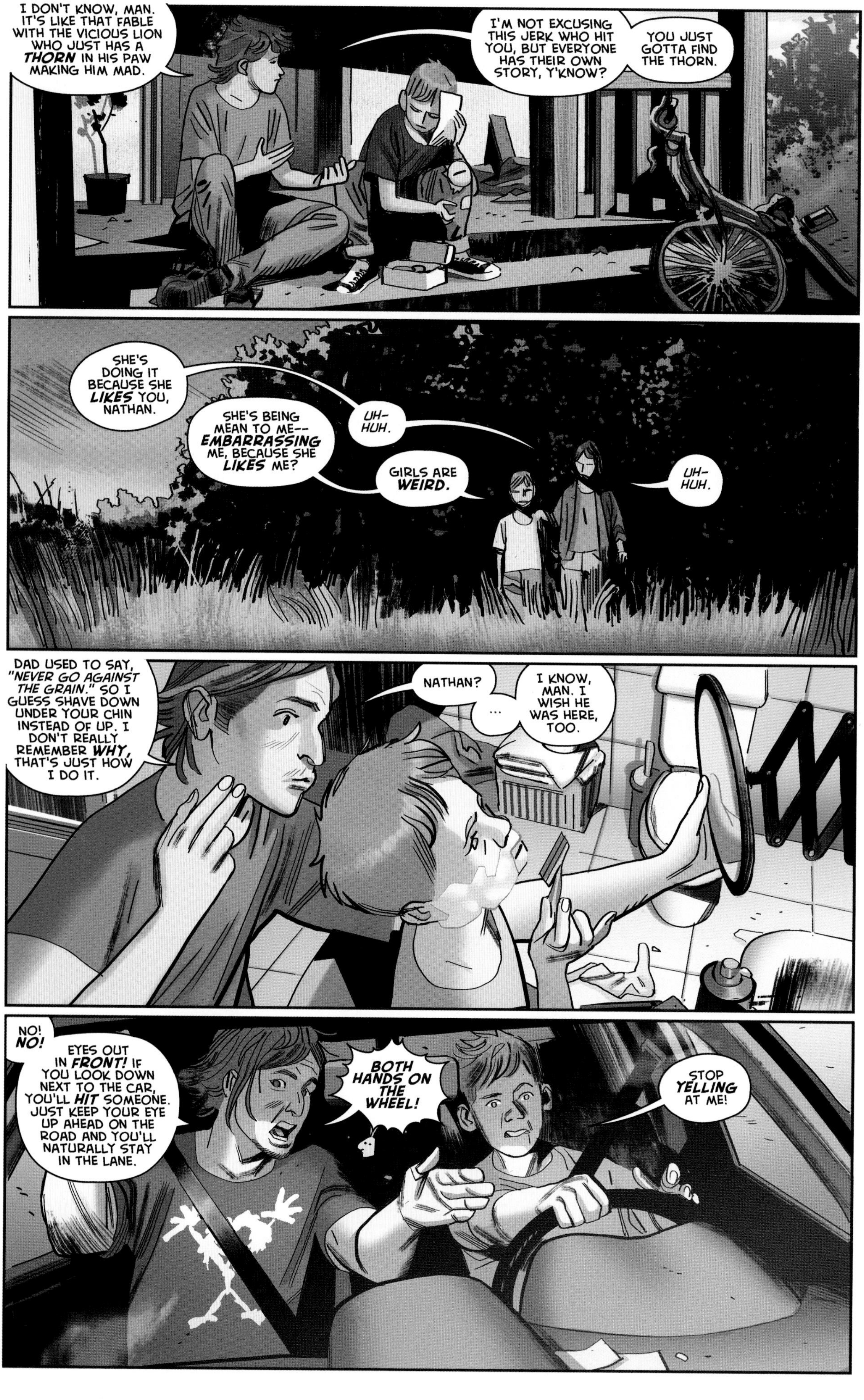
I DON'T KNOW, MAN. IT'S LIKE THAT FABLE WITH THE VICIOUS LION WHO JUST HAS A *THORN* IN HIS PAW MAKING HIM MAD.
I'M NOT EXCUSING THIS JERK WHO HIT YOU, BUT EVERYONE HAS THEIR OWN STORY, Y'KNOW?
YOU JUST GOTTA FIND THE THORN.
SHE'S DOING IT BECAUSE SHE *LIKES* YOU, NATHAN.
UH-HUH.
SHE'S BEING MEAN TO ME-- *EMBARRASSING* ME, BECAUSE SHE *LIKES* ME?
UH-HUH.
GIRLS ARE *WEIRD.*
DAD USED TO SAY, *"NEVER GO AGAINST THE GRAIN."* SO I GUESS SHAVE DOWN UNDER YOUR CHIN INSTEAD OF UP. I DON'T REALLY REMEMBER *WHY*, THAT'S JUST HOW I DO IT.
NATHAN?
...
I KNOW, MAN. I WISH HE WAS HERE, TOO.
NO! *NO!*
EYES OUT IN *FRONT!* IF YOU LOOK DOWN NEXT TO THE CAR, YOU'LL *HIT* SOMEONE. JUST KEEP YOUR EYE UP AHEAD ON THE ROAD AND YOU'LL NATURALLY STAY IN THE LANE.
BOTH HANDS ON THE WHEEL!
STOP *YELLING* AT ME!

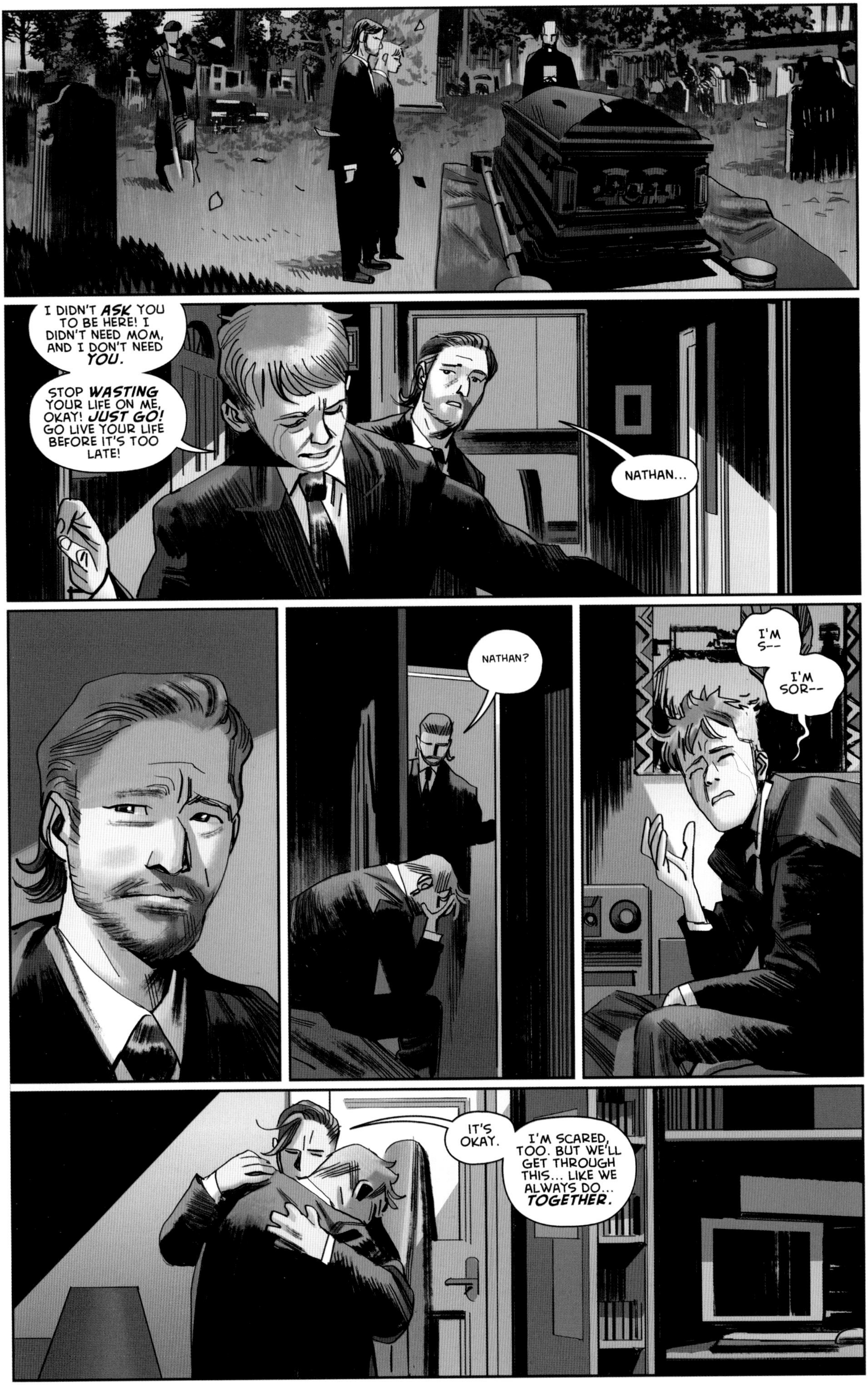
I DIDN'T ASK YOU TO BE HERE! I DIDN'T NEED MOM, AND I DON'T NEED YOU.
STOP WASTING YOUR LIFE ON ME, OKAY! JUST GO! GO LIVE YOUR LIFE BEFORE IT'S TOO LATE!
NATHAN...
NATHAN?
I'M S--
I'M SOR--
IT'S OKAY.
I'M SCARED, TOO. BUT WE'LL GET THROUGH THIS... LIKE WE ALWAYS DO... TOGETHER.

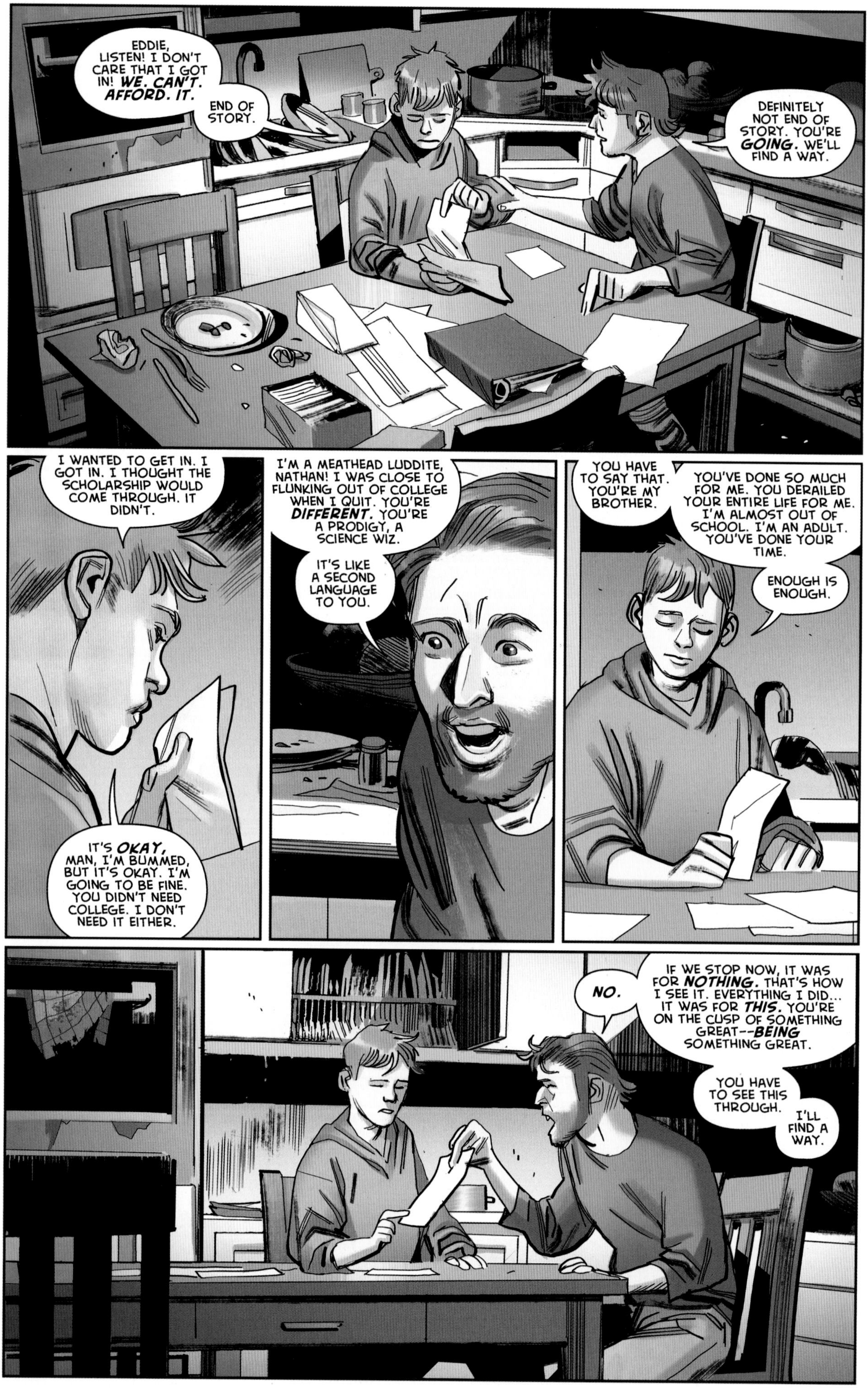
EDDIE, LISTEN! I DON'T CARE THAT I GOT IN! WE. CAN'T. AFFORD. IT.
END OF STORY.
DEFINITELY NOT END OF STORY. YOU'RE GOING. WE'LL FIND A WAY.
I WANTED TO GET IN. I GOT IN. I THOUGHT THE SCHOLARSHIP WOULD COME THROUGH. IT DIDN'T.
IT'S OKAY, MAN, I'M BUMMED, BUT IT'S OKAY. I'M GOING TO BE FINE. YOU DIDN'T NEED COLLEGE. I DON'T NEED IT EITHER.
I'M A MEATHEAD LUDDITE, NATHAN! I WAS CLOSE TO FLUNKING OUT OF COLLEGE WHEN I QUIT. YOU'RE DIFFERENT. YOU'RE A PRODIGY, A SCIENCE WIZ.
IT'S LIKE A SECOND LANGUAGE TO YOU.
YOU HAVE TO SAY THAT. YOU'RE MY BROTHER.
YOU'VE DONE SO MUCH FOR ME. YOU DERAILED YOUR ENTIRE LIFE FOR ME. I'M ALMOST OUT OF SCHOOL. I'M AN ADULT. YOU'VE DONE YOUR TIME.
ENOUGH IS ENOUGH.
NO.
IF WE STOP NOW, IT WAS FOR NOTHING. THAT'S HOW I SEE IT. EVERYTHING I DID... IT WAS FOR THIS. YOU'RE ON THE CUSP OF SOMETHING GREAT--BEING SOMETHING GREAT.
YOU HAVE TO SEE THIS THROUGH.
I'LL FIND A WAY.

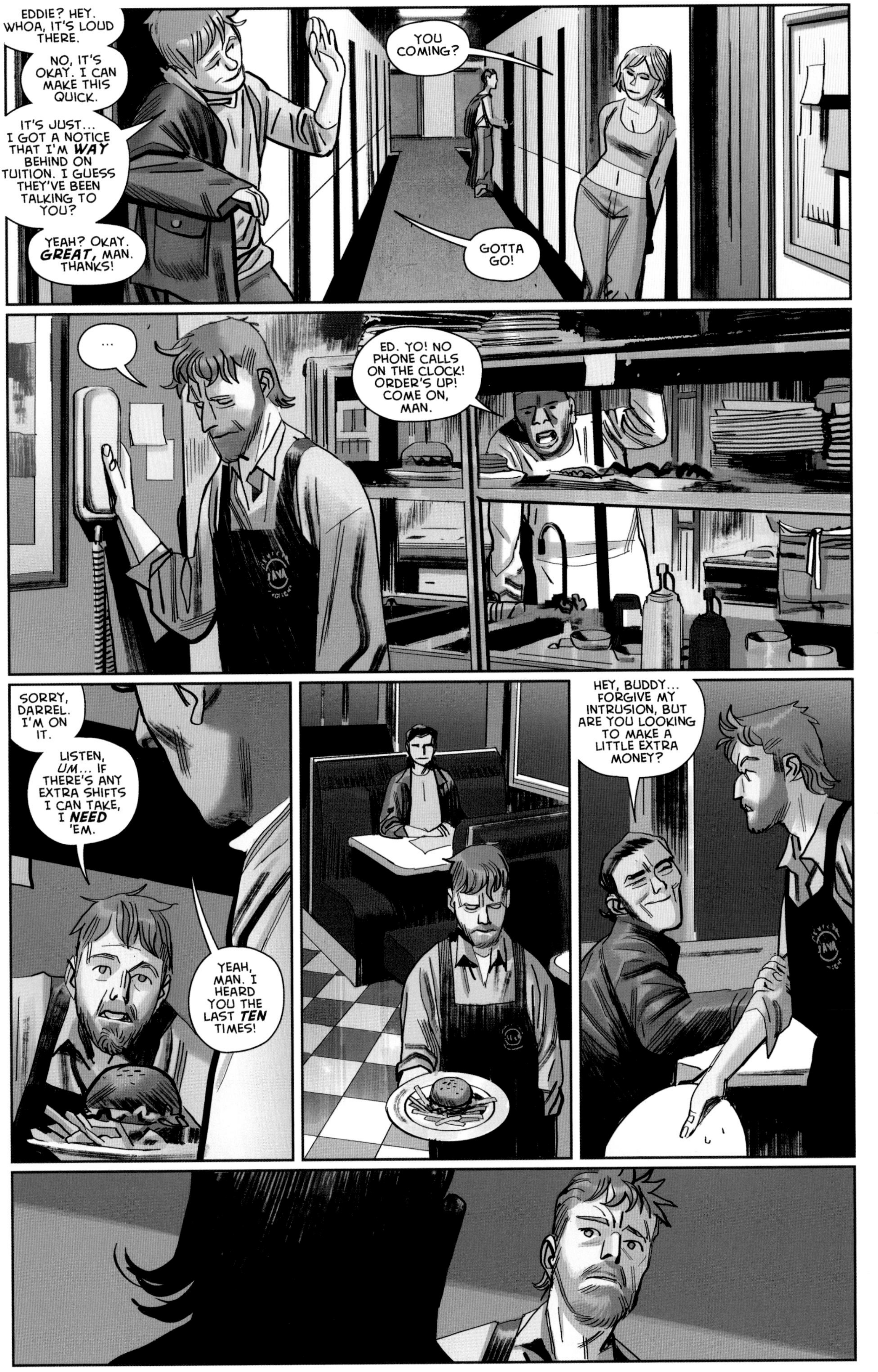
EDDIE? HEY. WHOA, IT'S LOUD THERE.
NO, IT'S OKAY. I CAN MAKE THIS QUICK.
IT'S JUST... I GOT A NOTICE THAT I'M WAY BEHIND ON TUITION. I GUESS THEY'VE BEEN TALKING TO YOU?
YEAH? OKAY. GREAT, MAN. THANKS!
YOU COMING?
GOTTA GO!
...
ED. YO! NO PHONE CALLS ON THE CLOCK! ORDER'S UP! COME ON, MAN.
SORRY, DARREL. I'M ON IT.
LISTEN, UM... IF THERE'S ANY EXTRA SHIFTS I CAN TAKE, I NEED 'EM.
YEAH, MAN. I HEARD YOU THE LAST TEN TIMES!
HEY, BUDDY... FORGIVE MY INTRUSION, BUT ARE YOU LOOKING TO MAKE A LITTLE EXTRA MONEY?

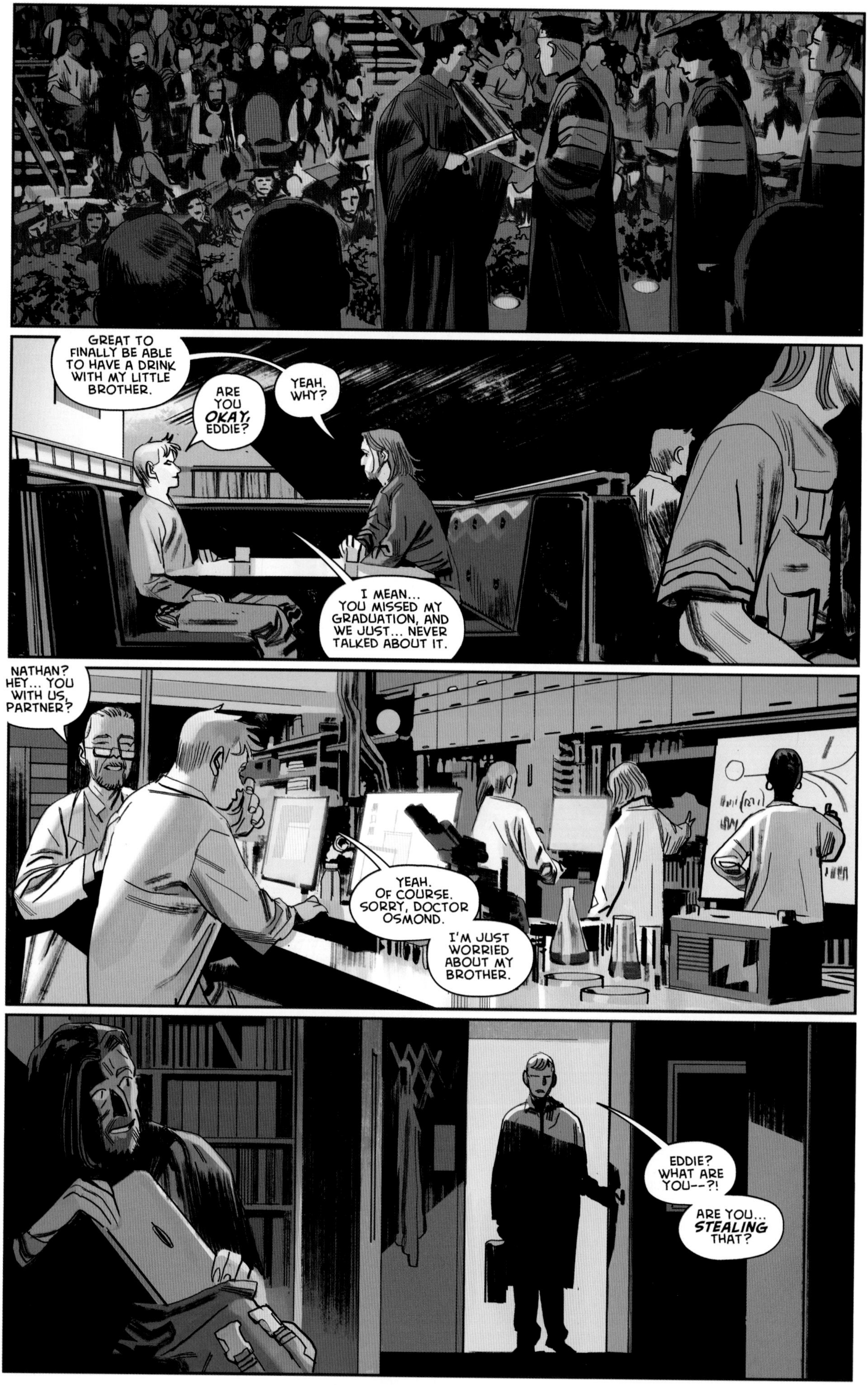
GREAT TO FINALLY BE ABLE TO HAVE A DRINK WITH MY LITTLE BROTHER.
ARE YOU OKAY, EDDIE?
YEAH. WHY?
I MEAN... YOU MISSED MY GRADUATION, AND WE JUST... NEVER TALKED ABOUT IT.
NATHAN? HEY... YOU WITH US, PARTNER?
YEAH. OF COURSE. SORRY, DOCTOR OSMOND.
I'M JUST WORRIED ABOUT MY BROTHER.
EDDIE? WHAT ARE YOU--?!
ARE YOU... STEALING THAT?

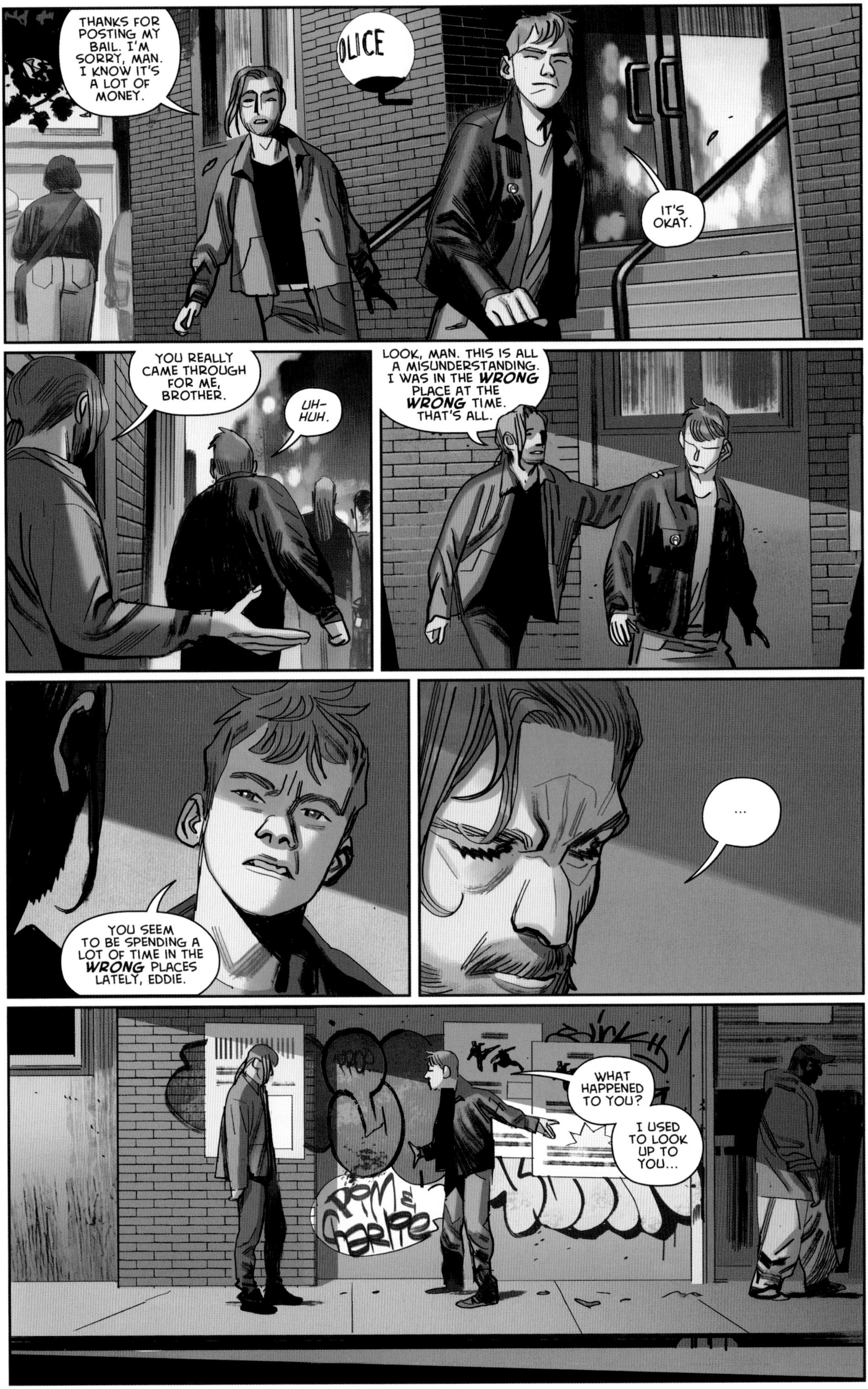

OLICE
THANKS FOR POSTING MY BAIL. I'M SORRY, MAN. I KNOW IT'S A LOT OF MONEY.
IT'S OKAY.
YOU REALLY CAME THROUGH FOR ME, BROTHER.
UH-HUH.
LOOK, MAN. THIS IS ALL A MISUNDERSTANDING. I WAS IN THE **WRONG** PLACE AT THE **WRONG** TIME. THAT'S ALL.
YOU SEEM TO BE SPENDING A LOT OF TIME IN THE **WRONG** PLACES LATELY, EDDIE.
...
WHAT HAPPENED TO YOU?
I USED TO LOOK UP TO YOU...

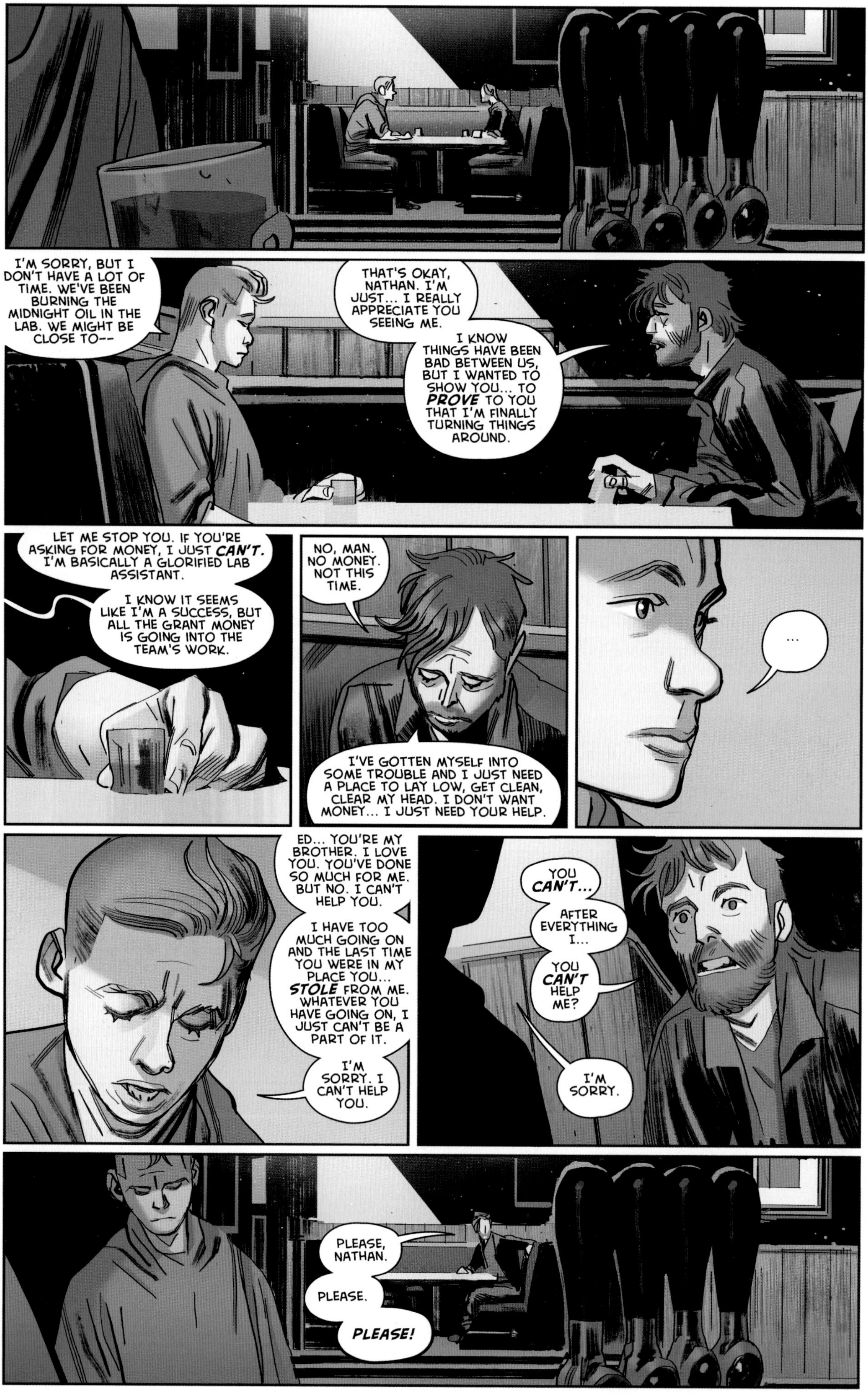
I'M SORRY, BUT I DON'T HAVE A LOT OF TIME. WE'VE BEEN BURNING THE MIDNIGHT OIL IN THE LAB. WE MIGHT BE CLOSE TO--
THAT'S OKAY, NATHAN. I'M JUST... I REALLY APPRECIATE YOU SEEING ME.
I KNOW THINGS HAVE BEEN BAD BETWEEN US, BUT I WANTED TO SHOW YOU... TO PROVE TO YOU THAT I'M FINALLY TURNING THINGS AROUND.
LET ME STOP YOU. IF YOU'RE ASKING FOR MONEY, I JUST CAN'T. I'M BASICALLY A GLORIFIED LAB ASSISTANT.
I KNOW IT SEEMS LIKE I'M A SUCCESS, BUT ALL THE GRANT MONEY IS GOING INTO THE TEAM'S WORK.
NO, MAN. NO MONEY. NOT THIS TIME.
I'VE GOTTEN MYSELF INTO SOME TROUBLE AND I JUST NEED A PLACE TO LAY LOW, GET CLEAN, CLEAR MY HEAD. I DON'T WANT MONEY... I JUST NEED YOUR HELP.
...
ED... YOU'RE MY BROTHER. I LOVE YOU. YOU'VE DONE SO MUCH FOR ME. BUT NO. I CAN'T HELP YOU.
I HAVE TOO MUCH GOING ON AND THE LAST TIME YOU WERE IN MY PLACE YOU... STOLE FROM ME. WHATEVER YOU HAVE GOING ON, I JUST CAN'T BE A PART OF IT.
I'M SORRY. I CAN'T HELP YOU.
YOU CAN'T...
AFTER EVERYTHING I...
YOU CAN'T HELP ME?
I'M SORRY.
PLEASE, NATHAN.
PLEASE.
PLEASE!

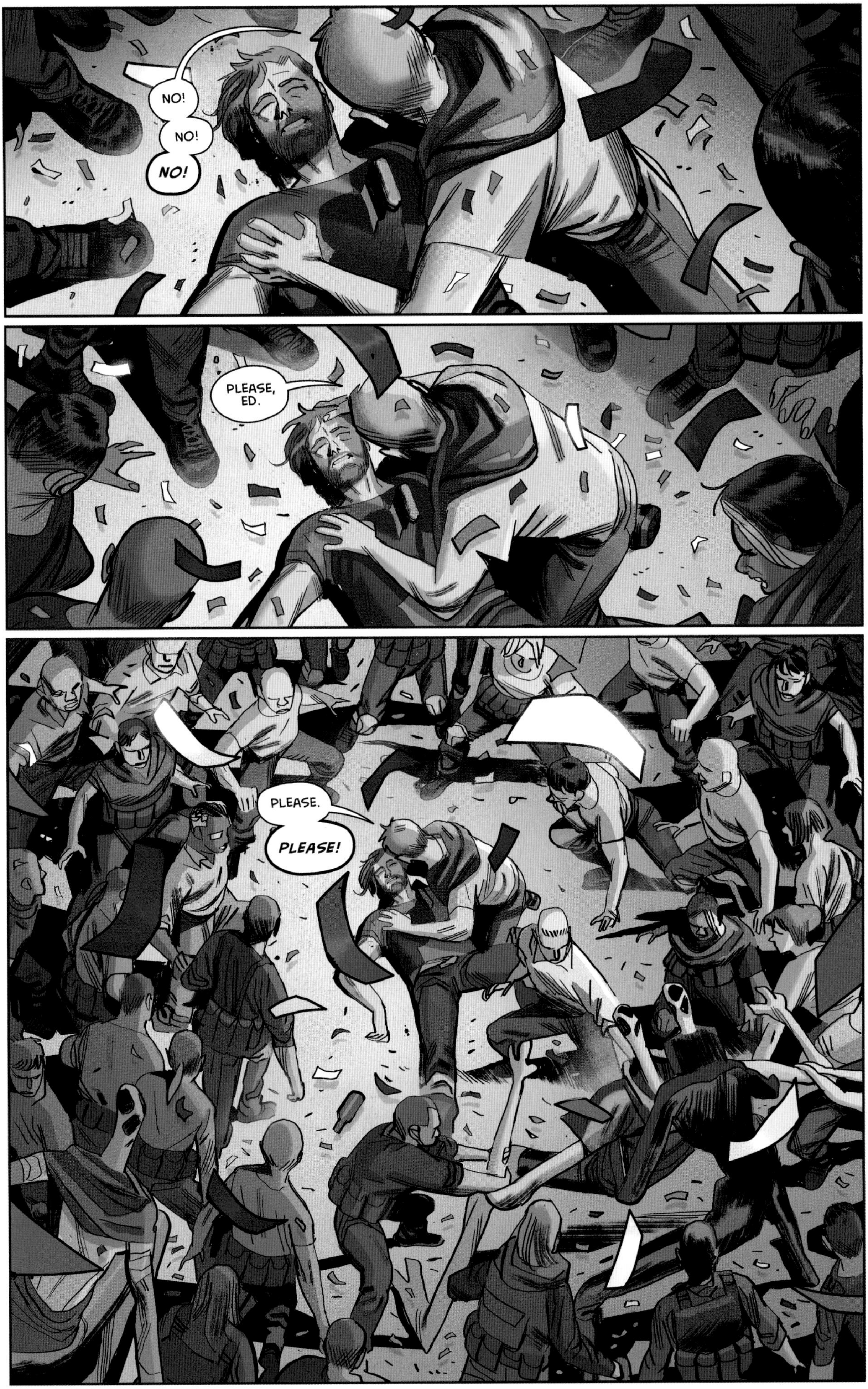
NO!
NO!
NO!
PLEASE, ED.
PLEASE.
PLEASE!

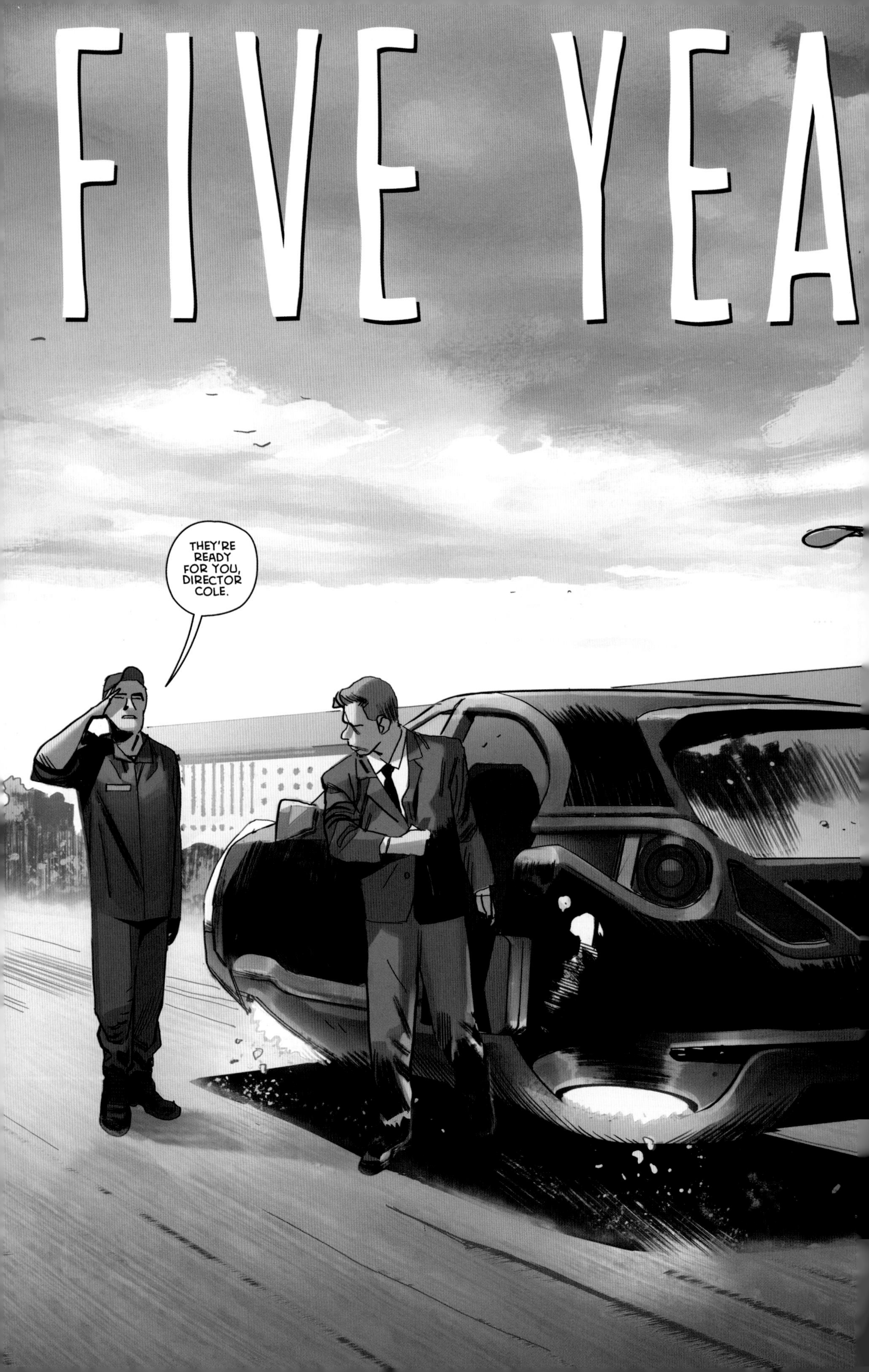
FIVE YEA
THEY'RE READY FOR YOU, DIRECTOR COLE.

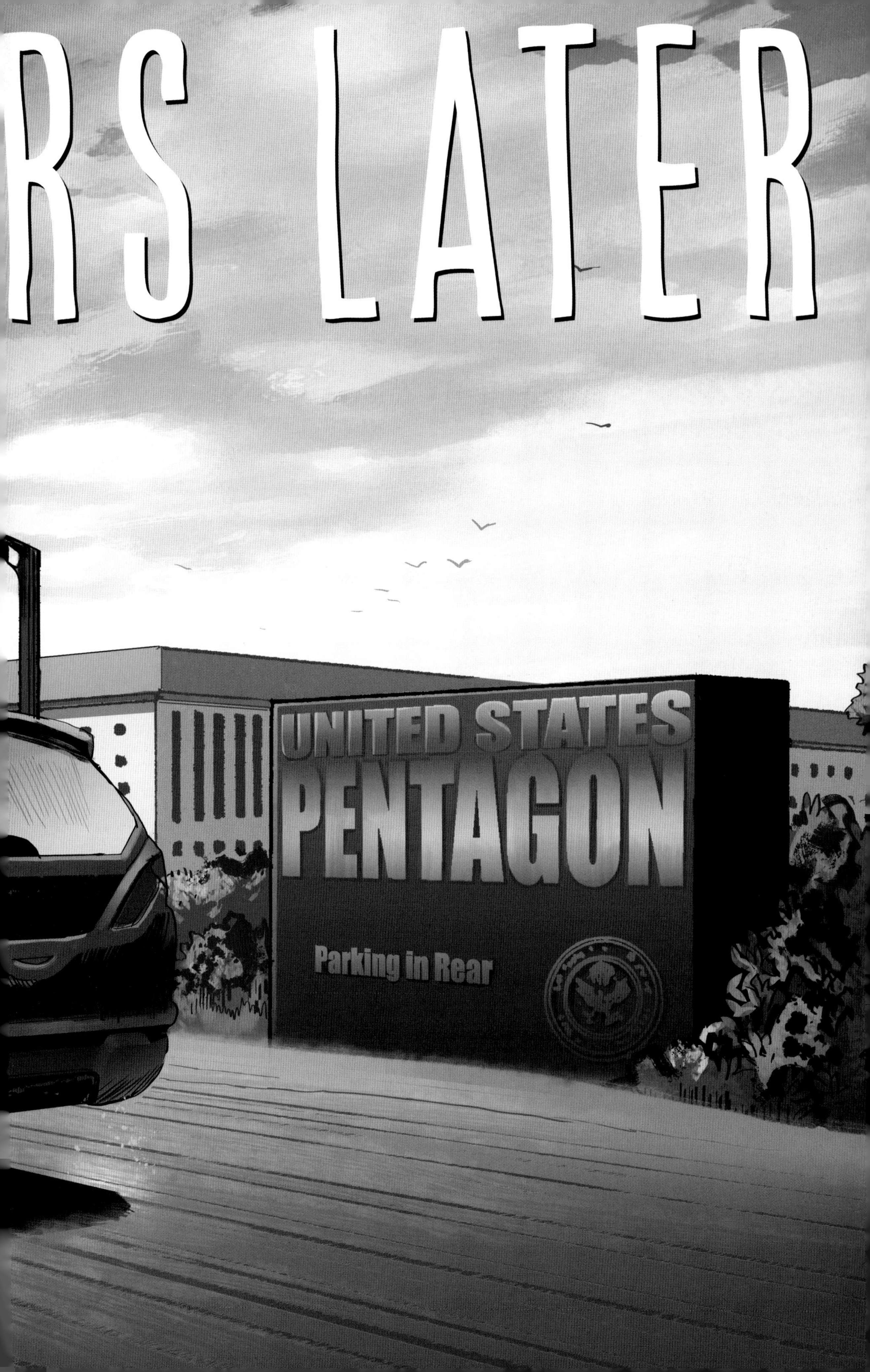
RS LATER
UNITED STATES
PENTAGON
Parking in Rear

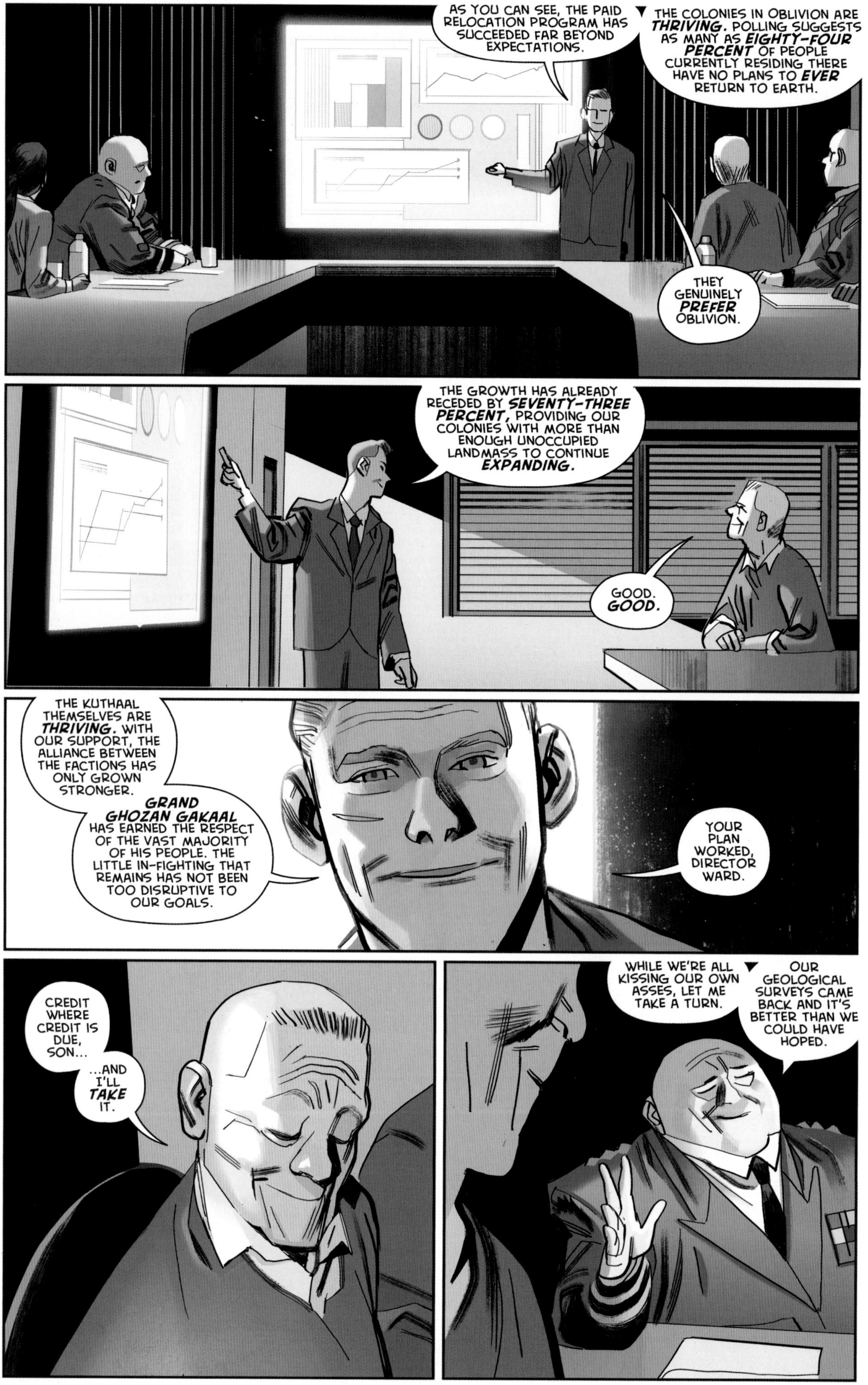
AS YOU CAN SEE, THE PAID RELOCATION PROGRAM HAS SUCCEEDED FAR BEYOND EXPECTATIONS.
THE COLONIES IN OBLIVION ARE THRIVING. POLLING SUGGESTS AS MANY AS EIGHTY-FOUR PERCENT OF PEOPLE CURRENTLY RESIDING THERE HAVE NO PLANS TO EVER RETURN TO EARTH.
THEY GENUINELY PREFER OBLIVION.
THE GROWTH HAS ALREADY RECEDED BY SEVENTY-THREE PERCENT, PROVIDING OUR COLONIES WITH MORE THAN ENOUGH UNOCCUPIED LANDMASS TO CONTINUE EXPANDING.
GOOD. GOOD.
THE KUTHAAL THEMSELVES ARE THRIVING. WITH OUR SUPPORT, THE ALLIANCE BETWEEN THE FACTIONS HAS ONLY GROWN STRONGER.
GRAND GHOZAN GAKAAL HAS EARNED THE RESPECT OF THE VAST MAJORITY OF HIS PEOPLE. THE LITTLE IN-FIGHTING THAT REMAINS HAS NOT BEEN TOO DISRUPTIVE TO OUR GOALS.
YOUR PLAN WORKED, DIRECTOR WARD.
CREDIT WHERE CREDIT IS DUE, SON...
...AND I'LL TAKE IT.
WHILE WE'RE ALL KISSING OUR OWN ASSES, LET ME TAKE A TURN.
OUR GEOLOGICAL SURVEYS CAME BACK AND IT'S BETTER THAN WE COULD HAVE HOPED.

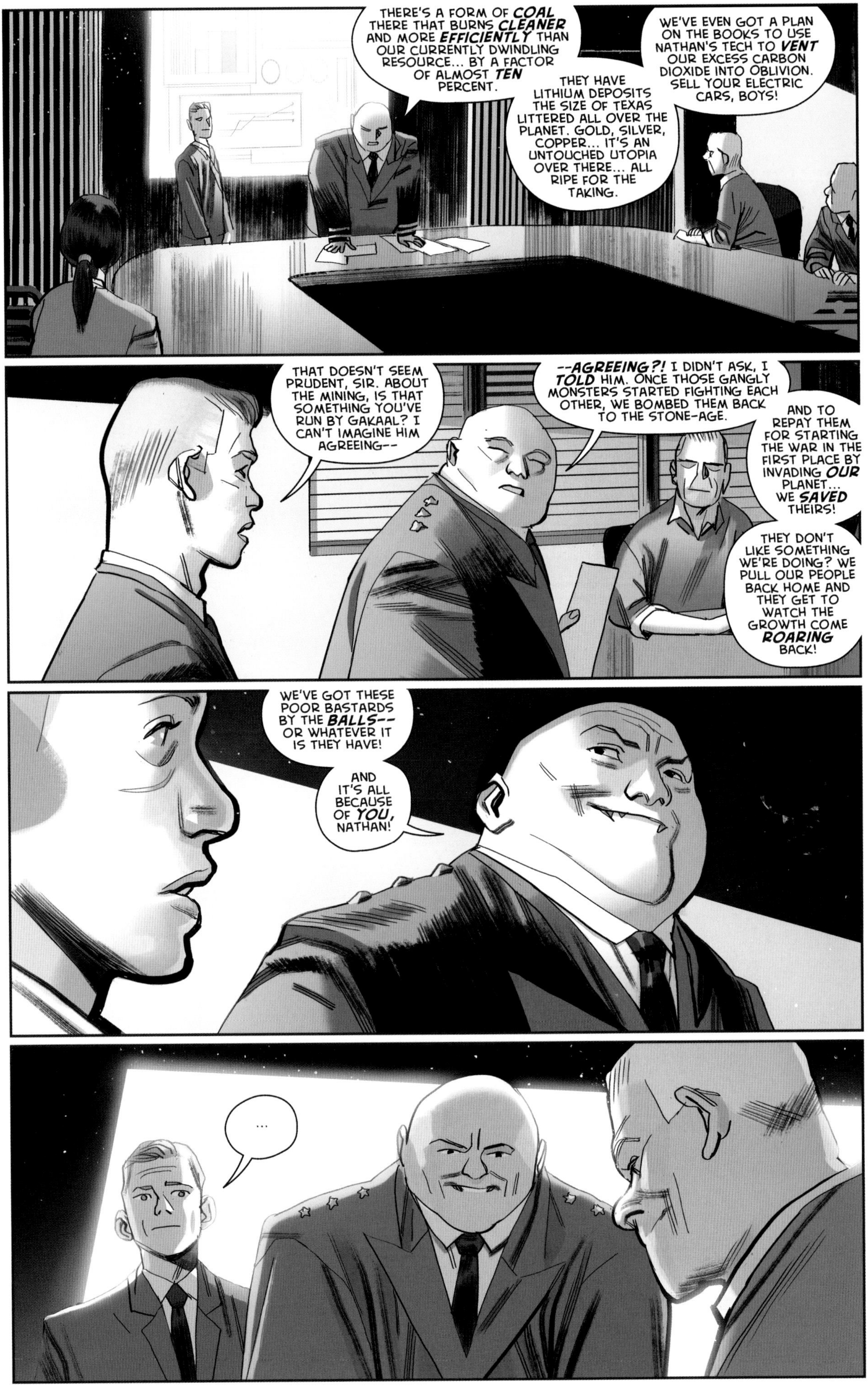
THERE'S A FORM OF COAL THERE THAT BURNS CLEANER AND MORE EFFICIENTLY THAN OUR CURRENTLY DWINDLING RESOURCE... BY A FACTOR OF ALMOST TEN PERCENT.
THEY HAVE LITHIUM DEPOSITS THE SIZE OF TEXAS LITTERED ALL OVER THE PLANET. GOLD, SILVER, COPPER... IT'S AN UNTOUCHED UTOPIA OVER THERE... ALL RIPE FOR THE TAKING.
WE'VE EVEN GOT A PLAN ON THE BOOKS TO USE NATHAN'S TECH TO VENT OUR EXCESS CARBON DIOXIDE INTO OBLIVION. SELL YOUR ELECTRIC CARS, BOYS!
THAT DOESN'T SEEM PRUDENT, SIR. ABOUT THE MINING, IS THAT SOMETHING YOU'VE RUN BY GAKAAL? I CAN'T IMAGINE HIM AGREEING--
--AGREEING?! I DIDN'T ASK, I TOLD HIM. ONCE THOSE GANGLY MONSTERS STARTED FIGHTING EACH OTHER, WE BOMBED THEM BACK TO THE STONE-AGE.
AND TO REPAY THEM FOR STARTING THE WAR IN THE FIRST PLACE BY INVADING OUR PLANET... WE SAVED THEIRS!
THEY DON'T LIKE SOMETHING WE'RE DOING? WE PULL OUR PEOPLE BACK HOME AND THEY GET TO WATCH THE GROWTH COME ROARING BACK!
WE'VE GOT THESE POOR BASTARDS BY THE BALLS-- OR WHATEVER IT IS THEY HAVE!
AND IT'S ALL BECAUSE OF YOU, NATHAN!
...

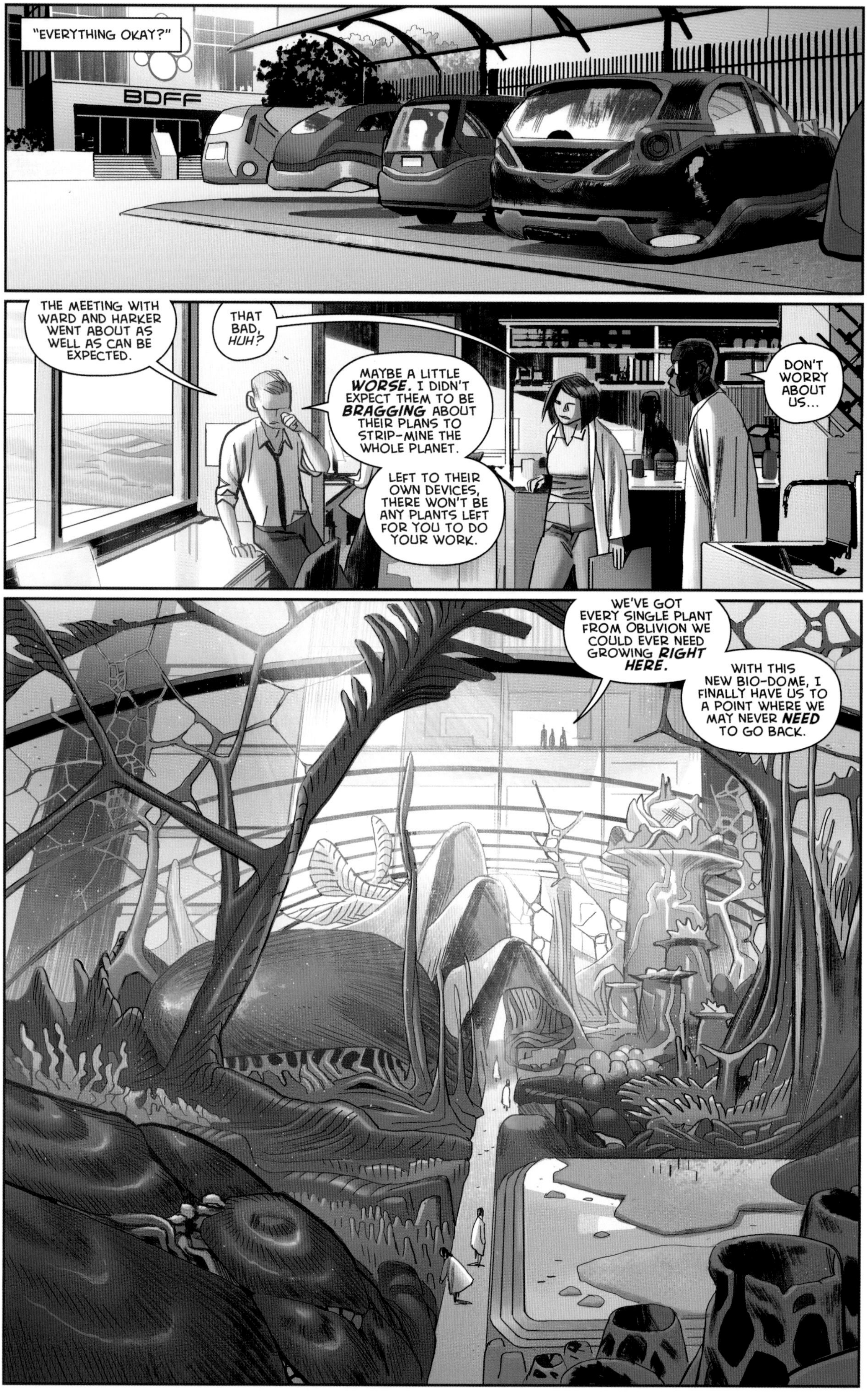
"EVERYTHING OKAY?"
BDFF
THE MEETING WITH WARD AND HARKER WENT ABOUT AS WELL AS CAN BE EXPECTED.
THAT BAD, HUH?
MAYBE A LITTLE WORSE. I DIDN'T EXPECT THEM TO BE BRAGGING ABOUT THEIR PLANS TO STRIP-MINE THE WHOLE PLANET.
LEFT TO THEIR OWN DEVICES, THERE WON'T BE ANY PLANTS LEFT FOR YOU TO DO YOUR WORK.
DON'T WORRY ABOUT US...
WE'VE GOT EVERY SINGLE PLANT FROM OBLIVION WE COULD EVER NEED GROWING RIGHT HERE.
WITH THIS NEW BIO-DOME, I FINALLY HAVE US TO A POINT WHERE WE MAY NEVER NEED TO GO BACK.

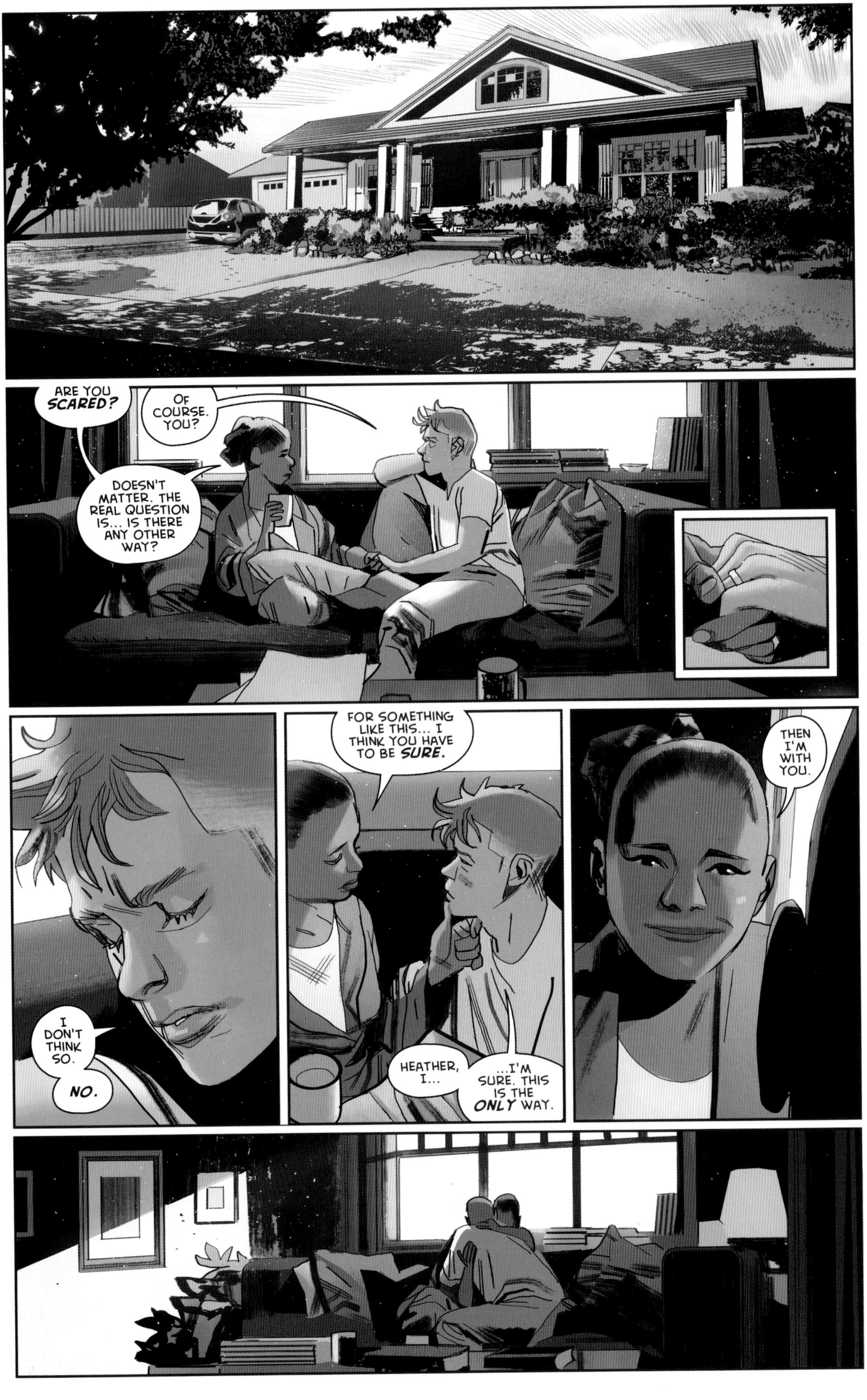
ARE YOU SCARED?
OF COURSE. YOU?
DOESN'T MATTER. THE REAL QUESTION IS... IS THERE ANY OTHER WAY?
I DON'T THINK SO.
NO.
FOR SOMETHING LIKE THIS... I THINK YOU HAVE TO BE SURE.
HEATHER, I...
...I'M SURE. THIS IS THE ONLY WAY.
THEN I'M WITH YOU.

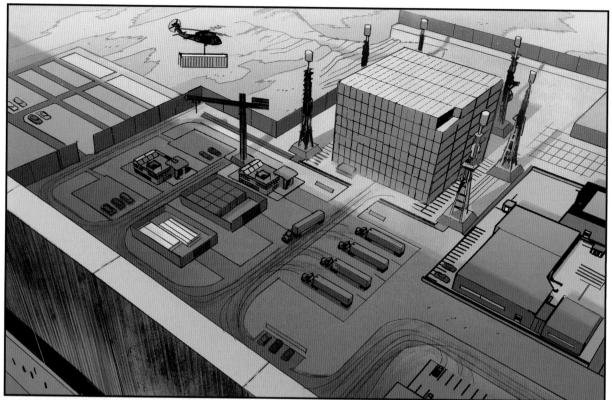

FA-FVVV-VAASH!

HEY, YOU!

WHAT ARE YOU *DOING* UP THERE?!

OH, SORRY.

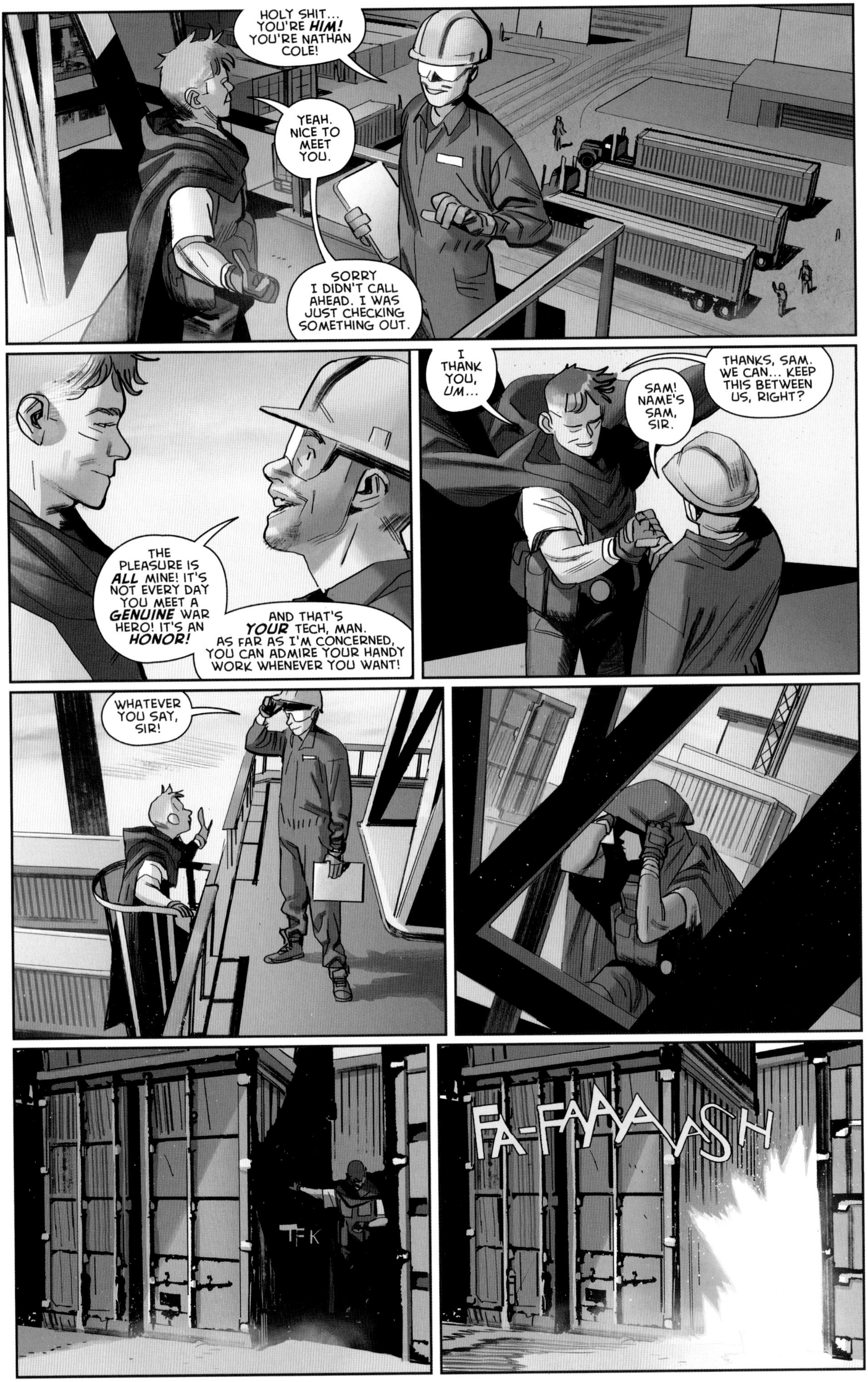
HOLY SHIT... YOU'RE HIM! YOU'RE NATHAN COLE!
YEAH. NICE TO MEET YOU.
SORRY I DIDN'T CALL AHEAD. I WAS JUST CHECKING SOMETHING OUT.
THE PLEASURE IS ALL MINE! IT'S NOT EVERY DAY YOU MEET A GENUINE WAR HERO! IT'S AN HONOR!
AND THAT'S YOUR TECH, MAN. AS FAR AS I'M CONCERNED, YOU CAN ADMIRE YOUR HANDY WORK WHENEVER YOU WANT!
I THANK YOU, UM...
SAM! NAME'S SAM, SIR.
THANKS, SAM. WE CAN... KEEP THIS BETWEEN US, RIGHT?
WHATEVER YOU SAY, SIR!
TFK
FA-FAAAASH

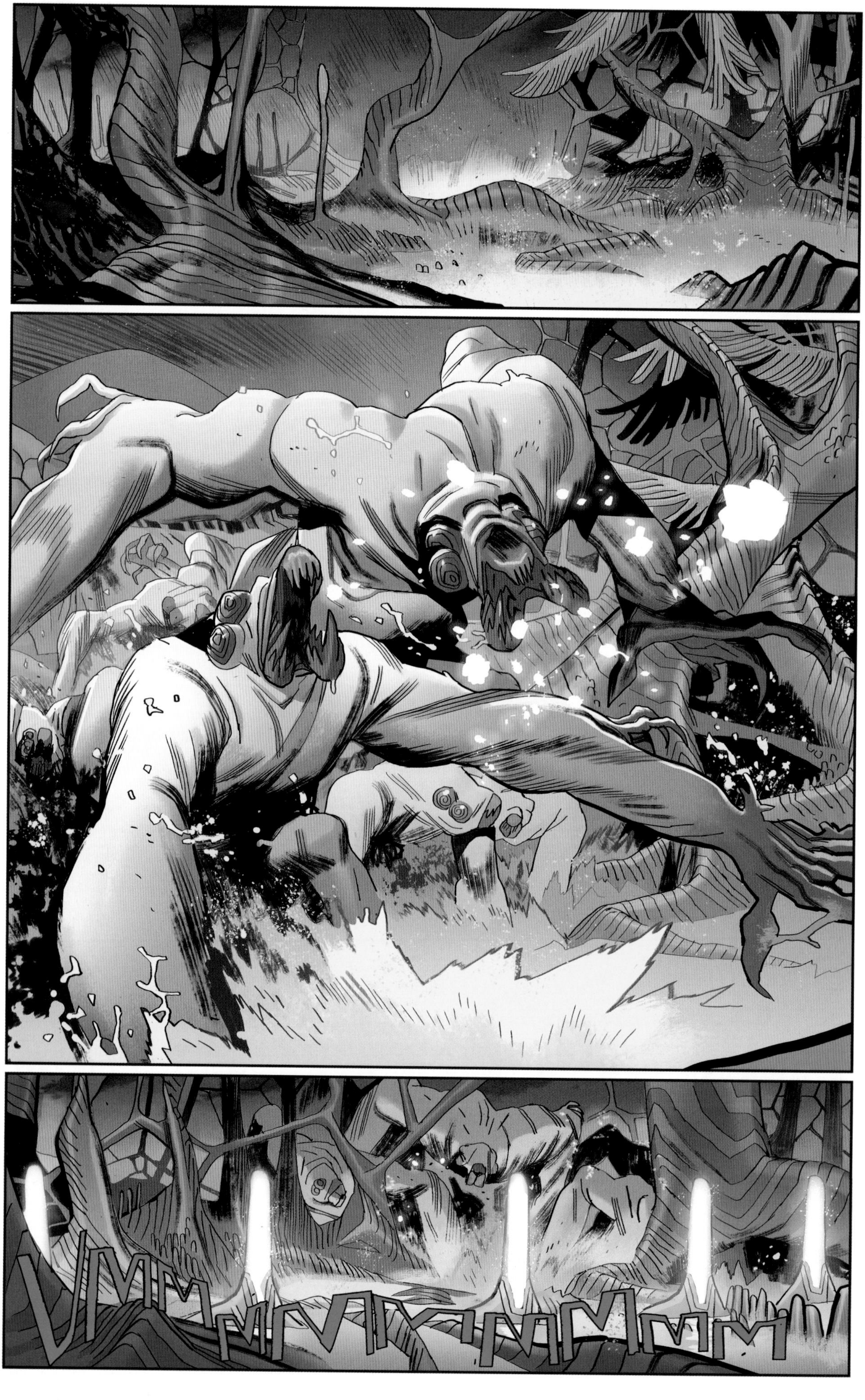
VMMMMMMMMMM

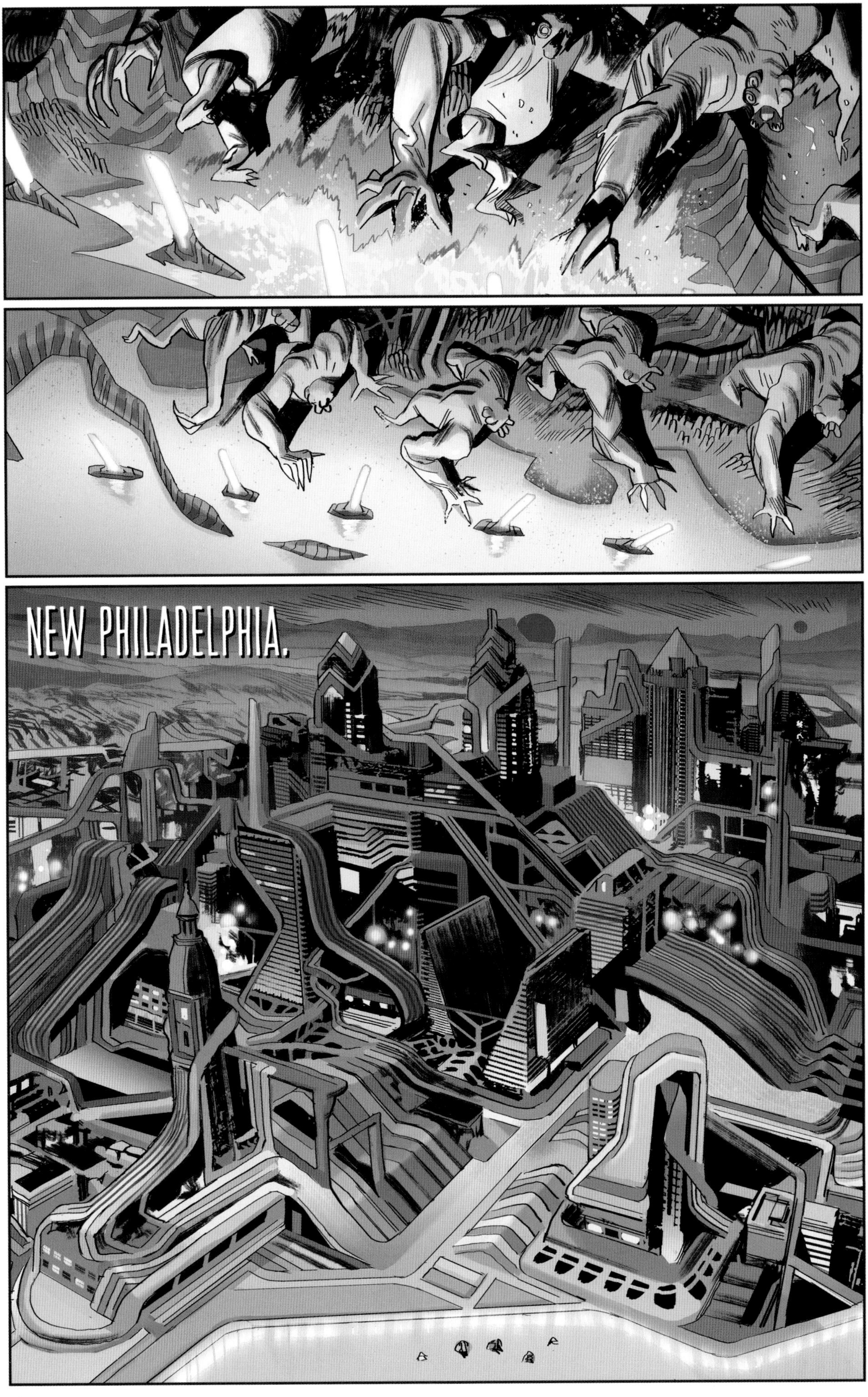
NEW PHILADELPHIA.

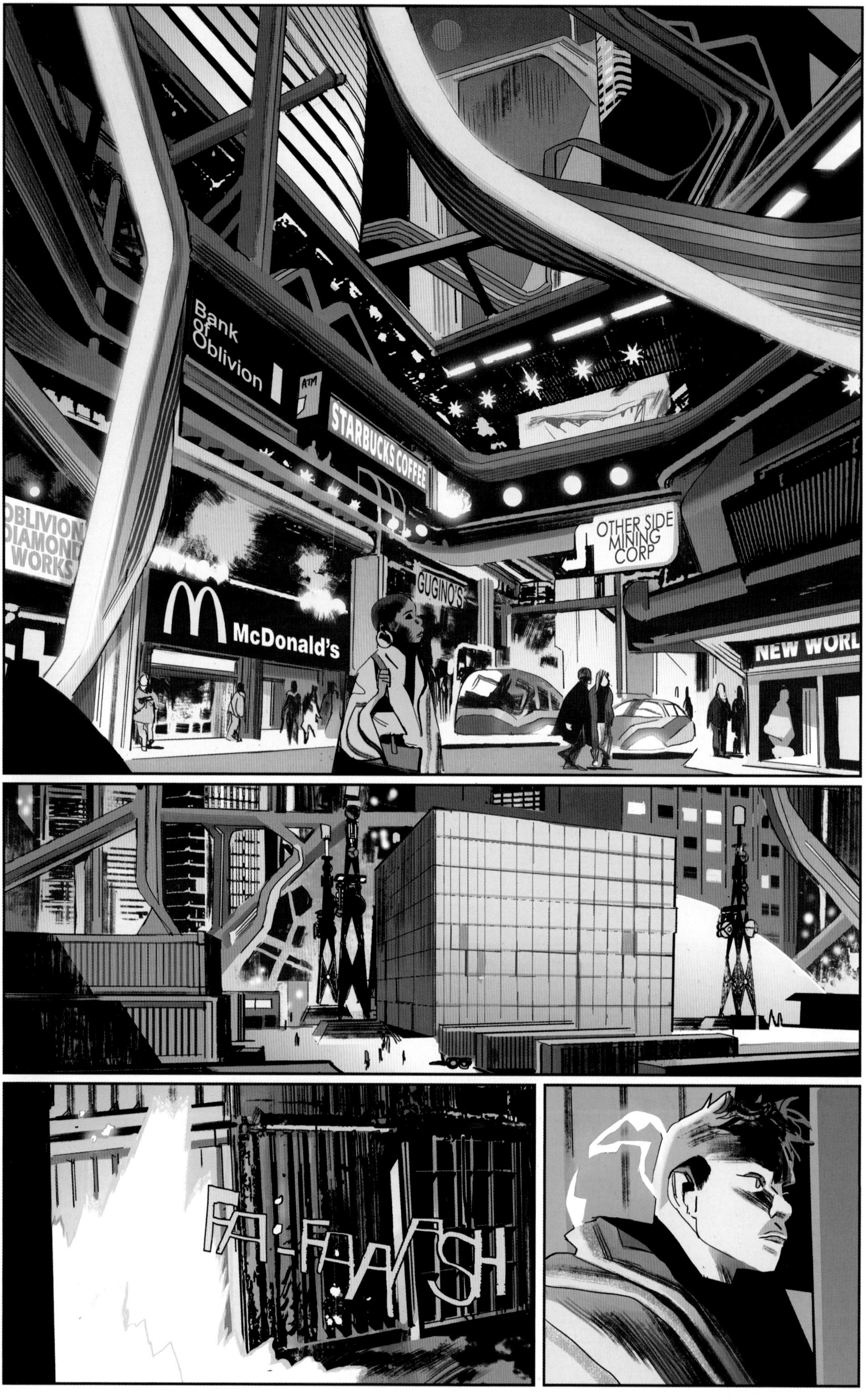
Bank of Oblivion
ATM
STARBUCKS COFFEE
OBLIVION DIAMOND WORKS
McDonald's
GUGINO'S
OTHER SIDE MINING CORP
NEW WORL
FA-FAWSH

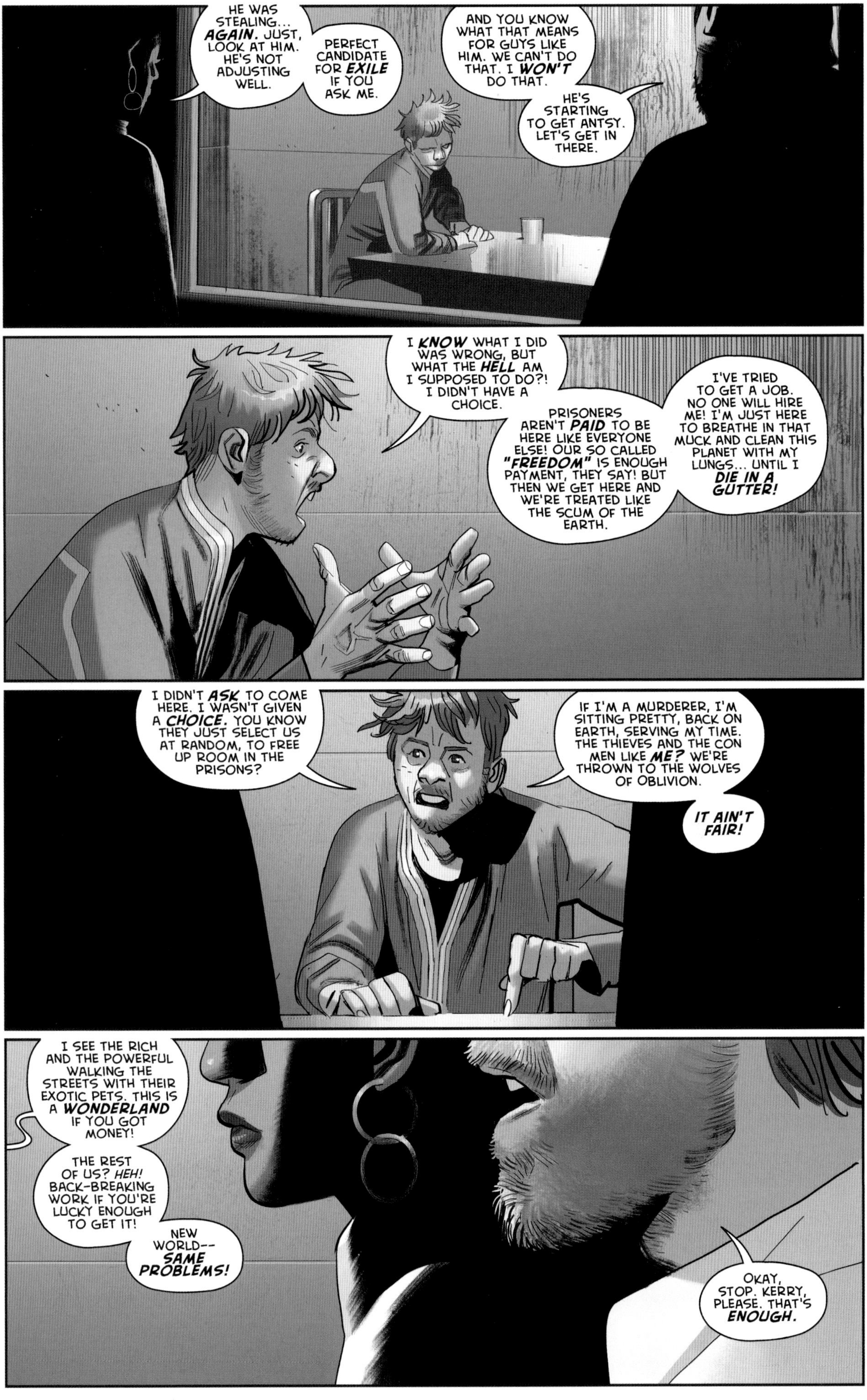
HE WAS STEALING... AGAIN. JUST, LOOK AT HIM. HE'S NOT ADJUSTING WELL.
PERFECT CANDIDATE FOR EXILE IF YOU ASK ME.
AND YOU KNOW WHAT THAT MEANS FOR GUYS LIKE HIM. WE CAN'T DO THAT. I WON'T DO THAT.
HE'S STARTING TO GET ANTSY. LET'S GET IN THERE.
I KNOW WHAT I DID WAS WRONG, BUT WHAT THE HELL AM I SUPPOSED TO DO?! I DIDN'T HAVE A CHOICE.
PRISONERS AREN'T PAID TO BE HERE LIKE EVERYONE ELSE! OUR SO CALLED "FREEDOM" IS ENOUGH PAYMENT, THEY SAY! BUT THEN WE GET HERE AND WE'RE TREATED LIKE THE SCUM OF THE EARTH.
I'VE TRIED TO GET A JOB. NO ONE WILL HIRE ME! I'M JUST HERE TO BREATHE IN THAT MUCK AND CLEAN THIS PLANET WITH MY LUNGS... UNTIL I DIE IN A GUTTER!
I DIDN'T ASK TO COME HERE. I WASN'T GIVEN A CHOICE. YOU KNOW THEY JUST SELECT US AT RANDOM, TO FREE UP ROOM IN THE PRISONS?
IF I'M A MURDERER, I'M SITTING PRETTY, BACK ON EARTH, SERVING MY TIME. THE THIEVES AND THE CON MEN LIKE ME? WE'RE THROWN TO THE WOLVES OF OBLIVION.
IT AIN'T FAIR!
I SEE THE RICH AND THE POWERFUL WALKING THE STREETS WITH THEIR EXOTIC PETS. THIS IS A WONDERLAND IF YOU GOT MONEY!
THE REST OF US? HEH! BACK-BREAKING WORK IF YOU'RE LUCKY ENOUGH TO GET IT!
NEW WORLD-- SAME PROBLEMS!
OKAY, STOP. KERRY, PLEASE. THAT'S ENOUGH.

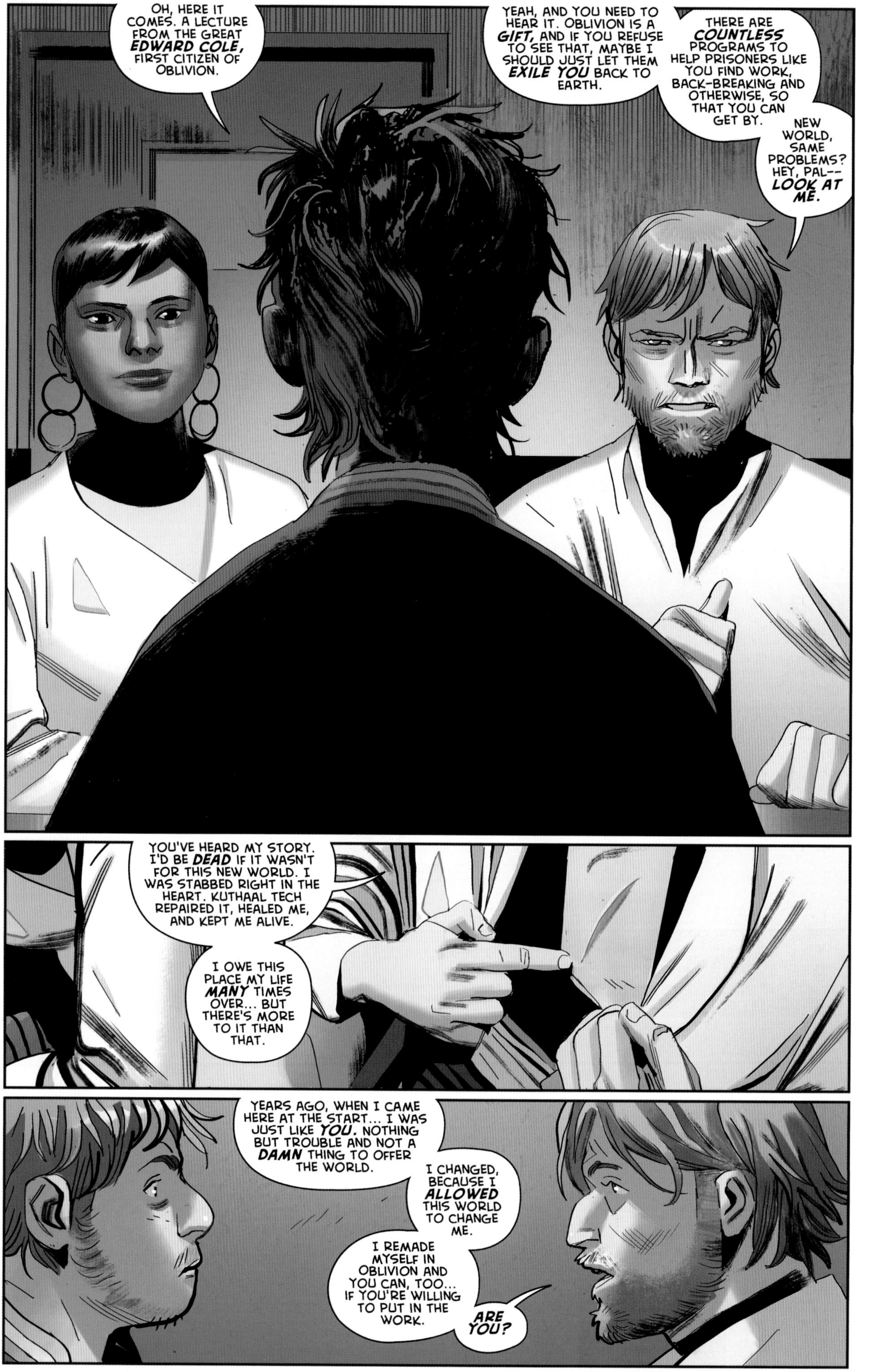
OH, HERE IT COMES. A LECTURE FROM THE GREAT EDWARD COLE, FIRST CITIZEN OF OBLIVION.
YEAH, AND YOU NEED TO HEAR IT. OBLIVION IS A GIFT, AND IF YOU REFUSE TO SEE THAT, MAYBE I SHOULD JUST LET THEM EXILE YOU BACK TO EARTH.
THERE ARE COUNTLESS PROGRAMS TO HELP PRISONERS LIKE YOU FIND WORK, BACK-BREAKING AND OTHERWISE, SO THAT YOU CAN GET BY.
NEW WORLD, SAME PROBLEMS? HEY, PAL-- LOOK AT ME.
YOU'VE HEARD MY STORY. I'D BE DEAD IF IT WASN'T FOR THIS NEW WORLD. I WAS STABBED RIGHT IN THE HEART. KUTHAAL TECH REPAIRED IT, HEALED ME, AND KEPT ME ALIVE.
I OWE THIS PLACE MY LIFE MANY TIMES OVER... BUT THERE'S MORE TO IT THAN THAT.
YEARS AGO, WHEN I CAME HERE AT THE START... I WAS JUST LIKE YOU. NOTHING BUT TROUBLE AND NOT A DAMN THING TO OFFER THE WORLD.
I CHANGED, BECAUSE I ALLOWED THIS WORLD TO CHANGE ME.
I REMADE MYSELF IN OBLIVION AND YOU CAN, TOO... IF YOU'RE WILLING TO PUT IN THE WORK.
ARE YOU?

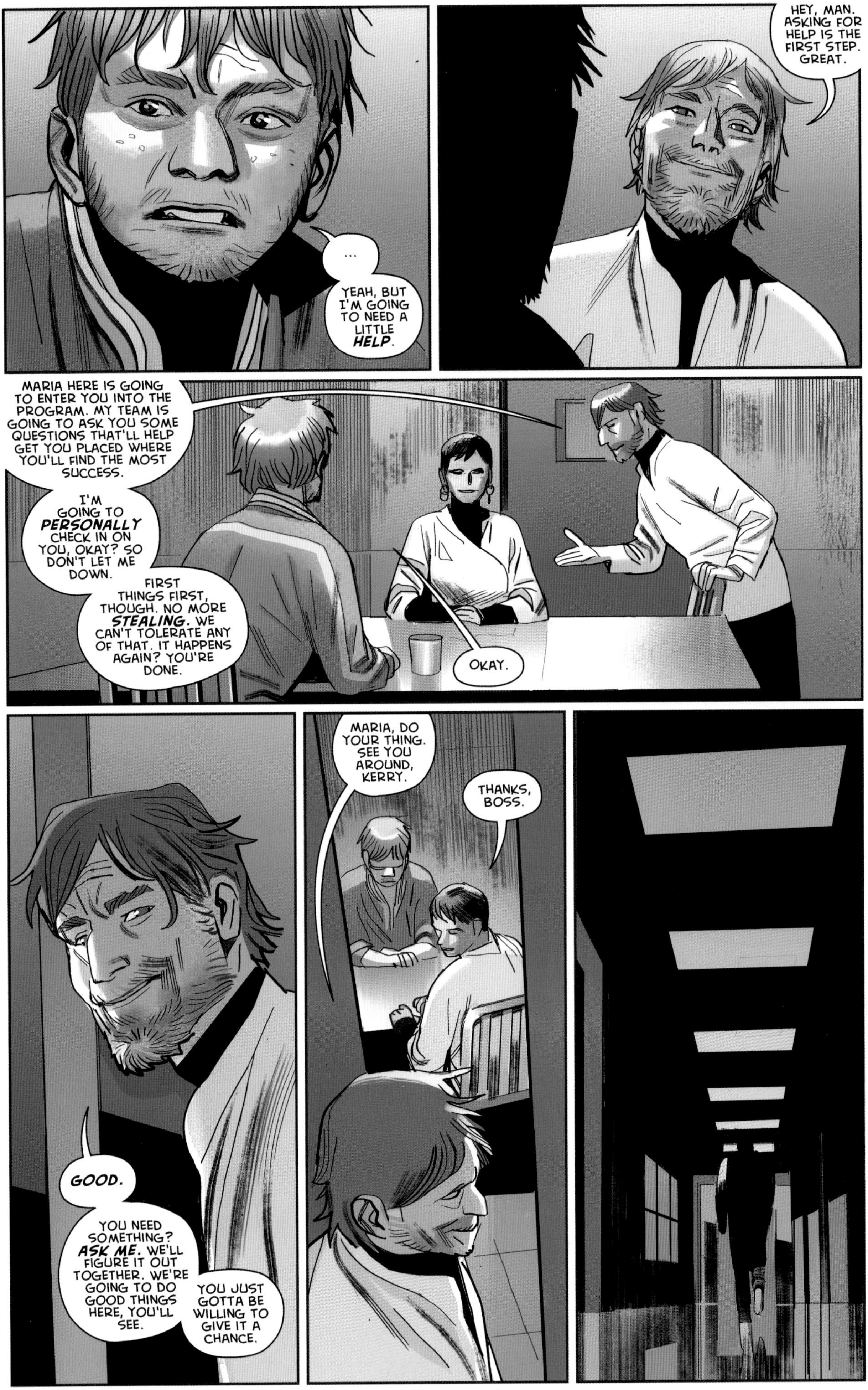
...
YEAH, BUT I'M GOING TO NEED A LITTLE HELP.
HEY, MAN. ASKING FOR HELP IS THE FIRST STEP. GREAT.
MARIA HERE IS GOING TO ENTER YOU INTO THE PROGRAM. MY TEAM IS GOING TO ASK YOU SOME QUESTIONS THAT'LL HELP GET YOU PLACED WHERE YOU'LL FIND THE MOST SUCCESS.
I'M GOING TO PERSONALLY CHECK IN ON YOU, OKAY? SO DON'T LET ME DOWN.
FIRST THINGS FIRST, THOUGH. NO MORE STEALING. WE CAN'T TOLERATE ANY OF THAT. IT HAPPENS AGAIN? YOU'RE DONE.
OKAY.
GOOD.
YOU NEED SOMETHING? ASK ME. WE'LL FIGURE IT OUT TOGETHER. WE'RE GOING TO DO GOOD THINGS HERE, YOU'LL SEE.
YOU JUST GOTTA BE WILLING TO GIVE IT A CHANCE.
MARIA, DO YOUR THING. SEE YOU AROUND, KERRY.
THANKS, BOSS.

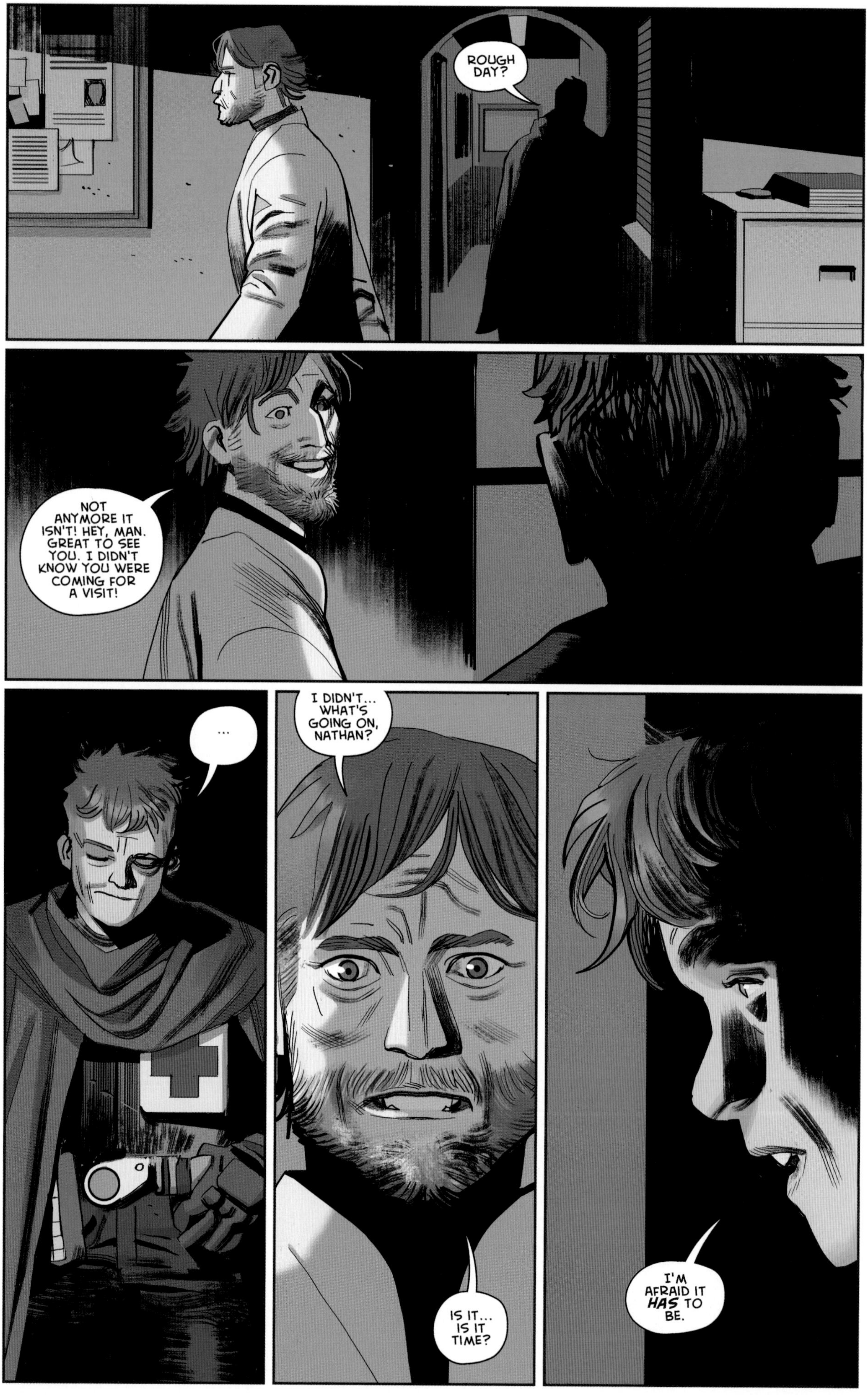
ROUGH DAY?
NOT ANYMORE IT ISN'T! HEY, MAN. GREAT TO SEE YOU. I DIDN'T KNOW YOU WERE COMING FOR A VISIT!
...
I DIDN'T... WHAT'S GOING ON, NATHAN?
IS IT... IS IT TIME?
I'M AFRAID IT *HAS* TO BE.

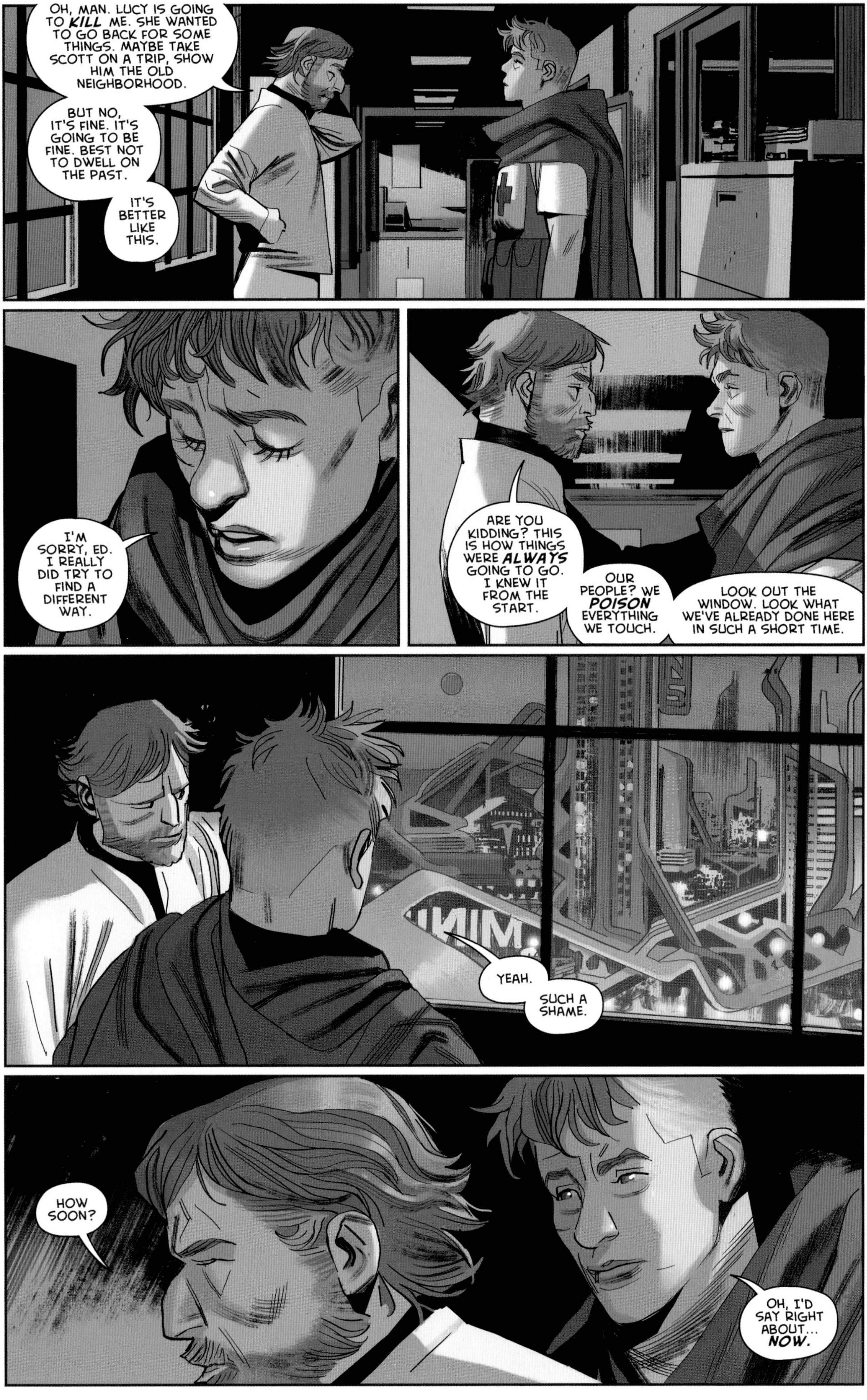
OH, MAN. LUCY IS GOING TO KILL ME. SHE WANTED TO GO BACK FOR SOME THINGS. MAYBE TAKE SCOTT ON A TRIP, SHOW HIM THE OLD NEIGHBORHOOD.
BUT NO, IT'S FINE. IT'S GOING TO BE FINE. BEST NOT TO DWELL ON THE PAST.
IT'S BETTER LIKE THIS.
I'M SORRY, ED. I REALLY DID TRY TO FIND A DIFFERENT WAY.
ARE YOU KIDDING? THIS IS HOW THINGS WERE ALWAYS GOING TO GO. I KNEW IT FROM THE START.
OUR PEOPLE? WE POISON EVERYTHING WE TOUCH.
LOOK OUT THE WINDOW. LOOK WHAT WE'VE ALREADY DONE HERE IN SUCH A SHORT TIME.
YEAH.
SUCH A SHAME.
HOW SOON?
OH, I'D SAY RIGHT ABOUT... NOW.

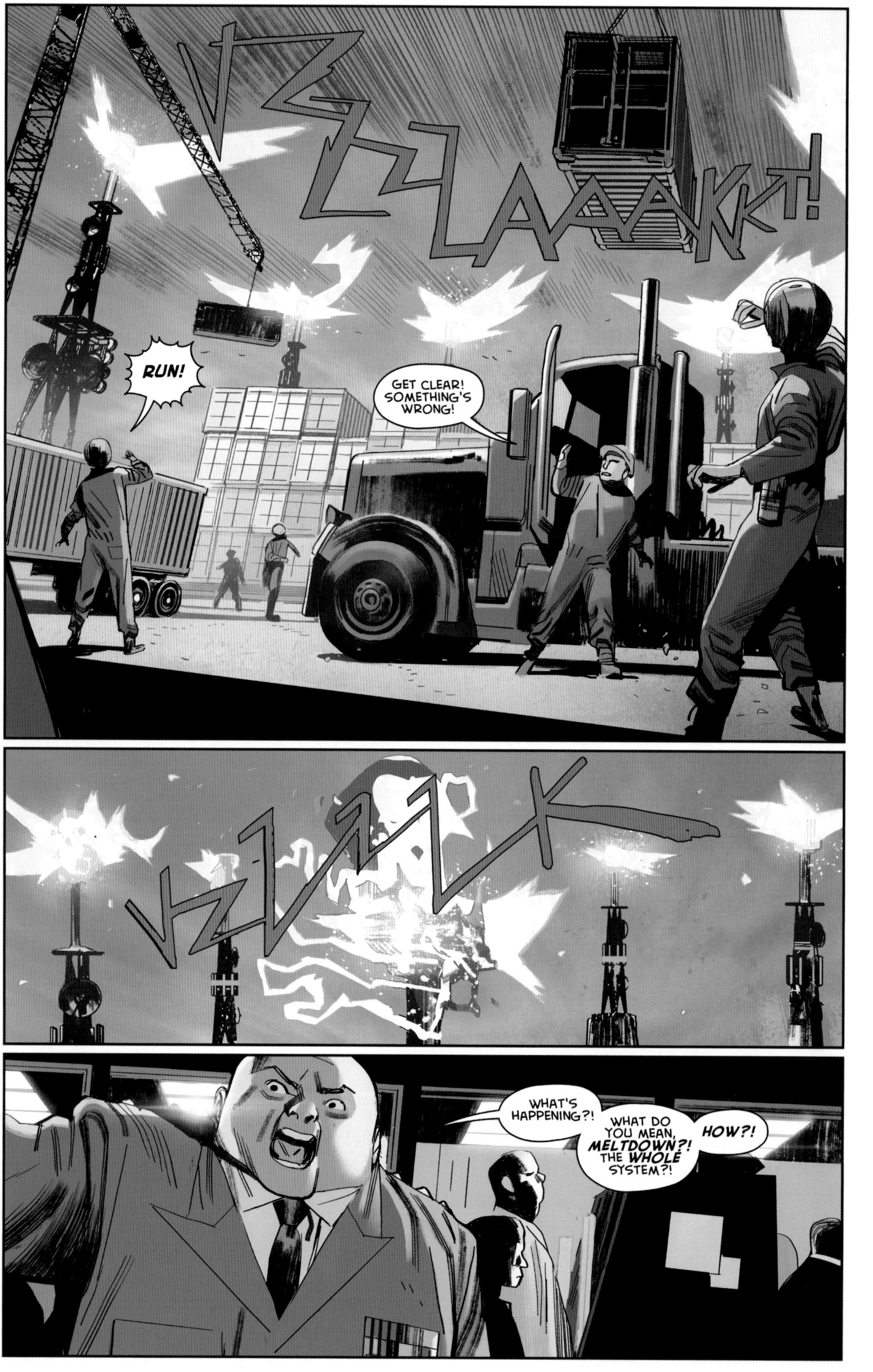

VZZZLAAAKKT!
RUN!
GET CLEAR! SOMETHING'S WRONG!
VZZZZK
WHAT'S HAPPENING?!
WHAT DO YOU MEAN, MELTDOWN?! THE WHOLE SYSTEM?!
HOW?!

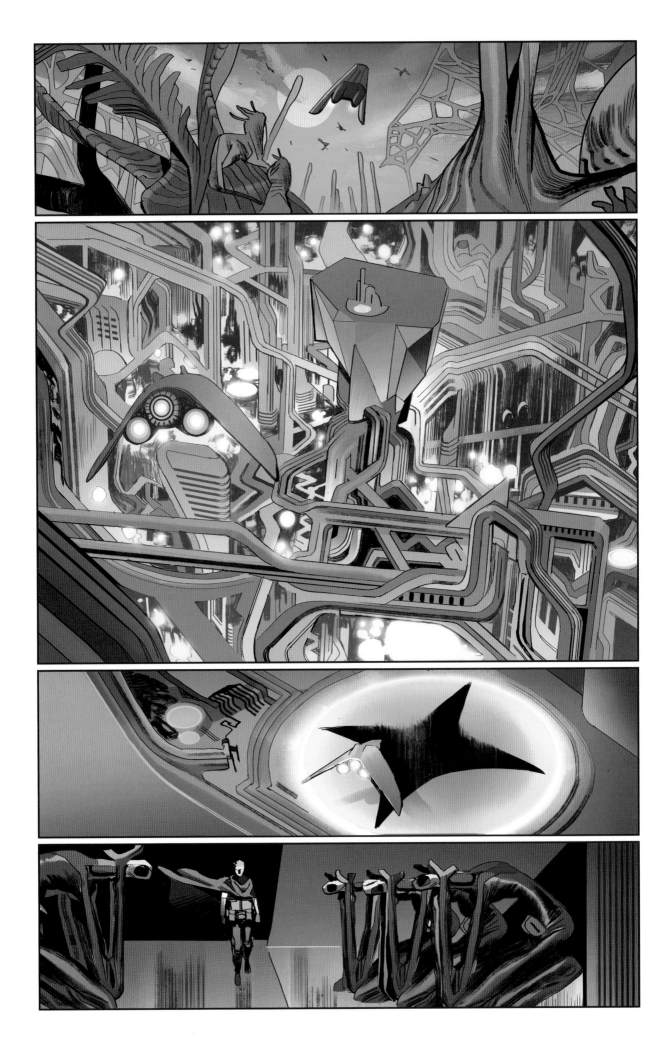

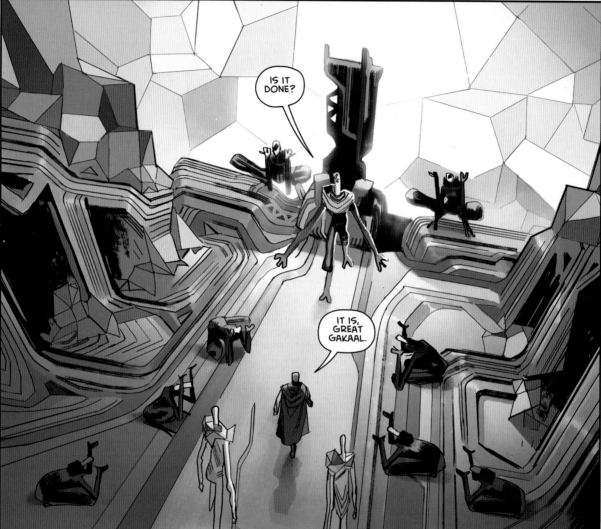

IS IT DONE?

IT IS, GREAT GAKAAL.

YOU HAVE SAVED THIS WORLD ONCE AGAIN, NATHAN COLE. I WILL FOREVER BE IN YOUR DEBT.

YOU UNITED THE TRIBES. YOU BROUGHT THIS WORLD *PEACE.*

I COULDN'T STAND BY WHILE MY PEOPLE TOOK ADVANTAGE OF THAT, STRIPPING THIS WORLD OF VALUE, TO ENRICH THEMSELVES.

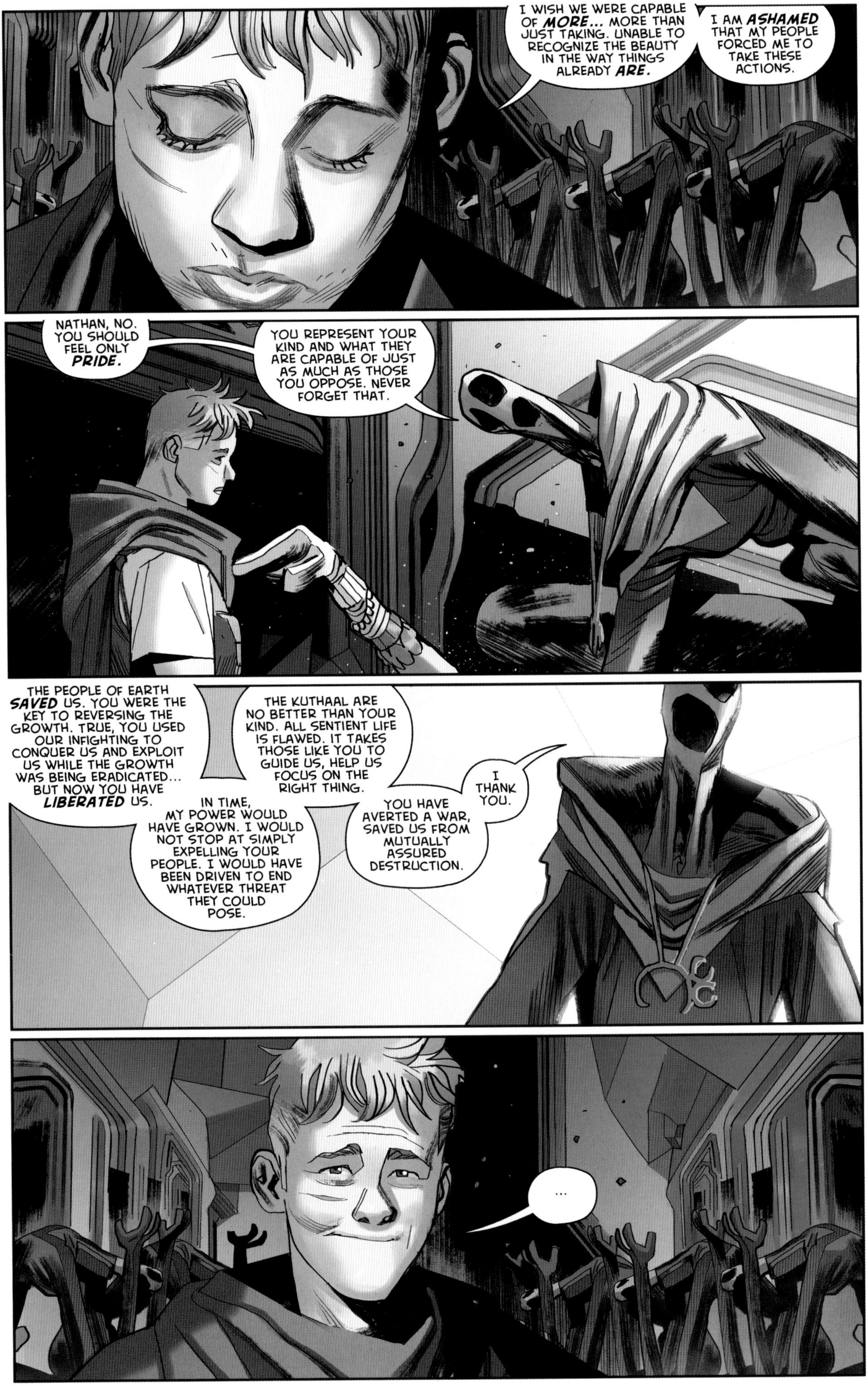
I WISH WE WERE CAPABLE OF MORE... MORE THAN JUST TAKING. UNABLE TO RECOGNIZE THE BEAUTY IN THE WAY THINGS ALREADY ARE.
I AM ASHAMED THAT MY PEOPLE FORCED ME TO TAKE THESE ACTIONS.
NATHAN, NO. YOU SHOULD FEEL ONLY PRIDE.
YOU REPRESENT YOUR KIND AND WHAT THEY ARE CAPABLE OF JUST AS MUCH AS THOSE YOU OPPOSE. NEVER FORGET THAT.
THE PEOPLE OF EARTH SAVED US. YOU WERE THE KEY TO REVERSING THE GROWTH. TRUE, YOU USED OUR INFIGHTING TO CONQUER US AND EXPLOIT US WHILE THE GROWTH WAS BEING ERADICATED... BUT NOW YOU HAVE LIBERATED US.
IN TIME, MY POWER WOULD HAVE GROWN. I WOULD NOT STOP AT SIMPLY EXPELLING YOUR PEOPLE. I WOULD HAVE BEEN DRIVEN TO END WHATEVER THREAT THEY COULD POSE.
THE KUTHAAL ARE NO BETTER THAN YOUR KIND. ALL SENTIENT LIFE IS FLAWED. IT TAKES THOSE LIKE YOU TO GUIDE US, HELP US FOCUS ON THE RIGHT THING.
YOU HAVE AVERTED A WAR, SAVED US FROM MUTUALLY ASSURED DESTRUCTION.
I THANK YOU.
...

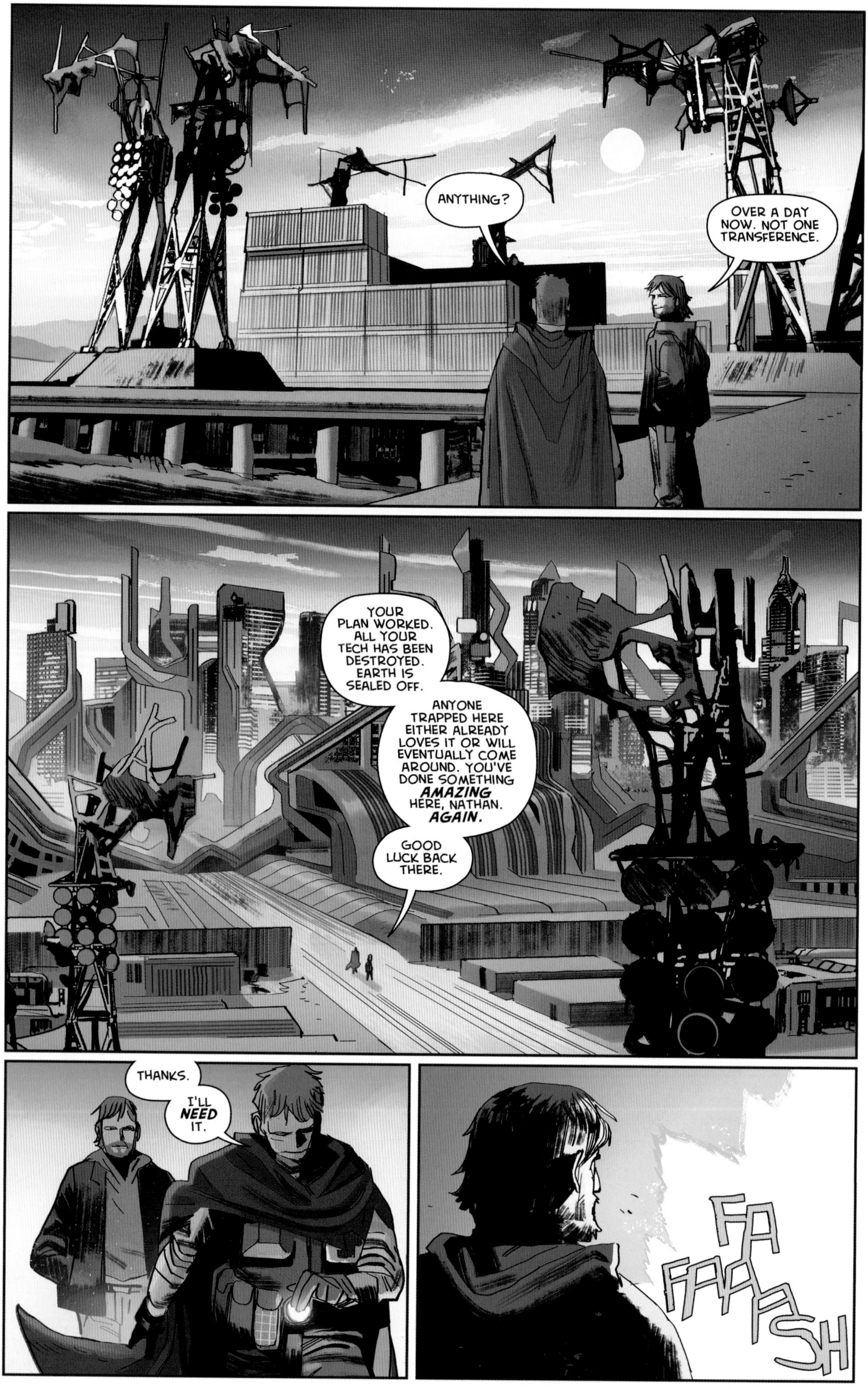
ANYTHING?
OVER A DAY NOW. NOT ONE TRANSFERENCE.
YOUR PLAN WORKED. ALL YOUR TECH HAS BEEN DESTROYED. EARTH IS SEALED OFF.
ANYONE TRAPPED HERE EITHER ALREADY LOVES IT OR WILL EVENTUALLY COME AROUND. YOU'VE DONE SOMETHING **AMAZING** HERE, NATHAN. ***AGAIN.***
GOOD LUCK BACK THERE.
THANKS.
I'LL **NEED** IT.
FA FAAAASH

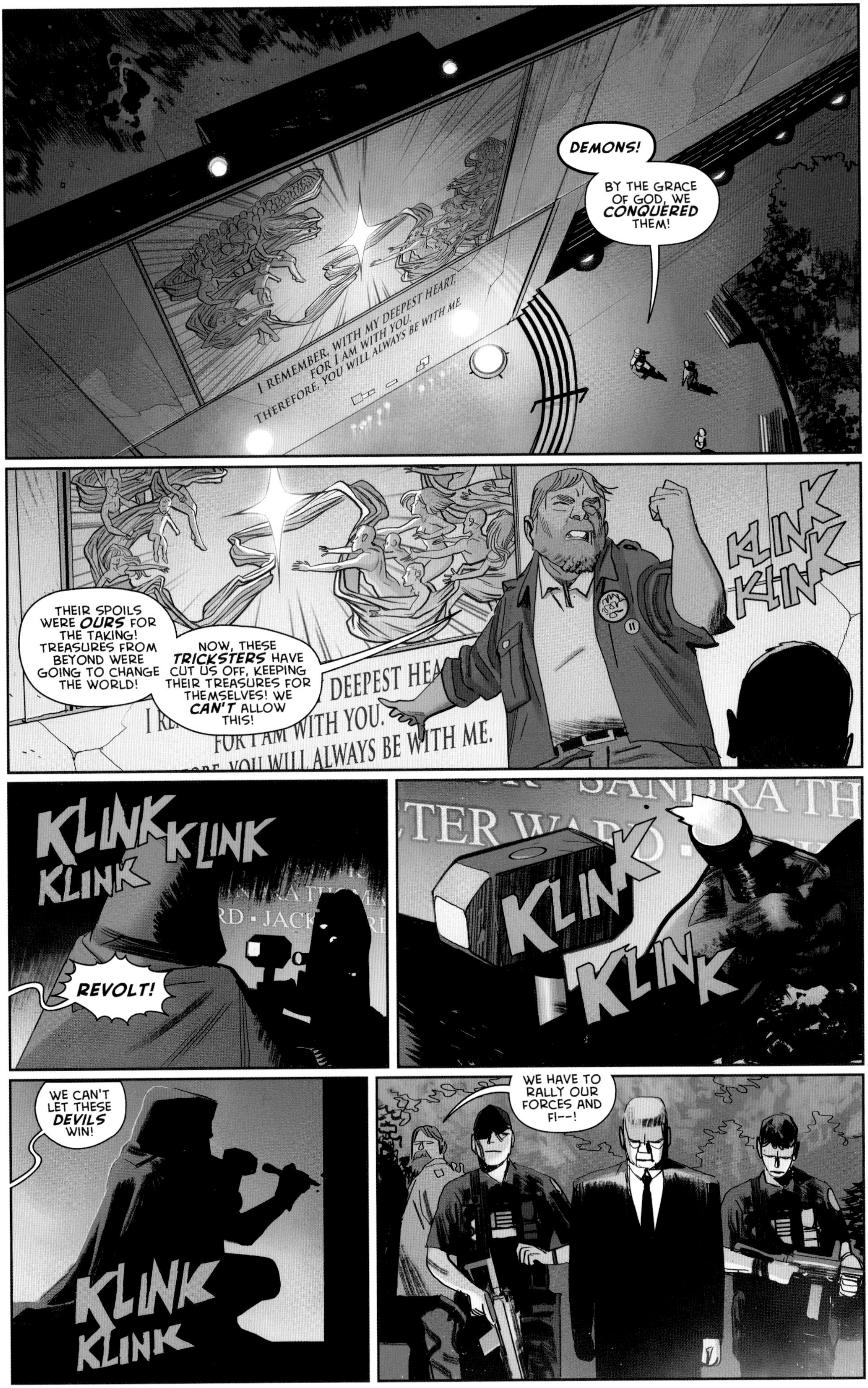

I REMEMBER, WITH MY DEEPEST HEART, FOR I AM WITH YOU. THEREFORE, YOU WILL ALWAYS BE WITH ME.
DEMONS!
BY THE GRACE OF GOD, WE CONQUERED THEM!
THEIR SPOILS WERE OURS FOR THE TAKING! TREASURES FROM BEYOND WERE GOING TO CHANGE THE WORLD!
NOW, THESE TRICKSTERS HAVE CUT US OFF, KEEPING THEIR TREASURES FOR THEMSELVES! WE CAN'T ALLOW THIS!
KLINK KLINK
KLINK KLINK KLINK
REVOLT!
KLINK KLINK
WE CAN'T LET THESE DEVILS WIN!
KLINK KLINK
WE HAVE TO RALLY OUR FORCES AND FI--!

WHAT THE HELL IS *WRONG* WITH YOU?

I MEAN, *SERIOUSLY,* NATHAN. CAN YOU ANSWER THAT QUESTION?

AFTER THE MEETING WITH HARKER THE OTHER DAY... I FEEL LIKE I SHOULD BE ASKING *YOU* THAT SAME QUESTION.

WHY? BECAUSE WE'RE GOING TO USE OBLIVION TO HELP EARTH? LIKE THAT'S SO WRONG? THEY *INVADED* US. GIVE ME A BREAK!

YOU ON THE OTHER HAND... YOU'RE NOW GOING TO BE LOCKED IN A LAB UNTIL YOU'VE REPAIRED ALL THE DAMAGE YOU'VE DONE.

THEN YOU'RE OFF TO *PRISON... AGAIN,* AND NOW THAT YOU'VE *PROVEN* THAT YOU CAN'T BE TRUSTED, THEY'RE GOING TO THROW AWAY THE KEY.

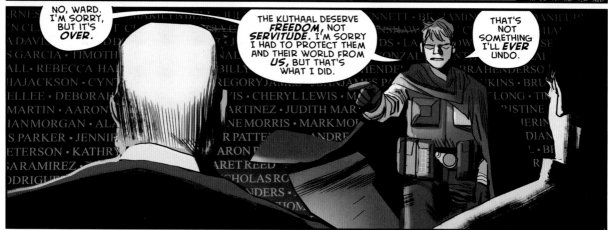

NO, WARD. I'M SORRY, BUT IT'S *OVER.*

THE KUTHAAL DESERVE *FREEDOM,* NOT *SERVITUDE.* I'M SORRY I HAD TO PROTECT THEM AND THEIR WORLD FROM *US,* BUT THAT'S WHAT I DID.

THAT'S NOT SOMETHING I'LL *EVER* UNDO.

HAH.

HAH-- HAH.

OKAY? THAT'S HOW IT'S GOING TO BE, IS IT?

IT IS.

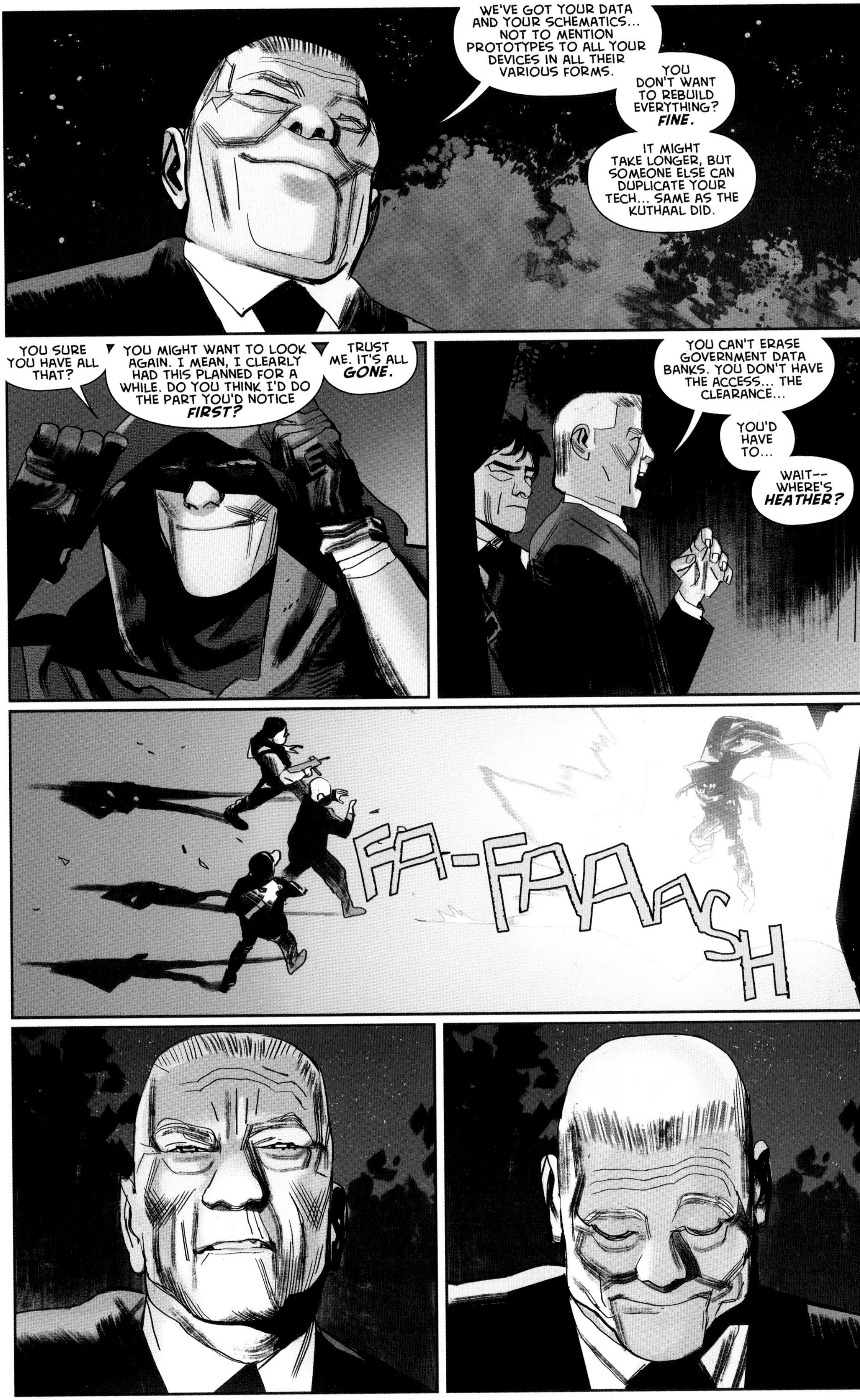
WE'VE GOT YOUR DATA AND YOUR SCHEMATICS... NOT TO MENTION PROTOTYPES TO ALL YOUR DEVICES IN ALL THEIR VARIOUS FORMS.
YOU DON'T WANT TO REBUILD EVERYTHING? FINE.
IT MIGHT TAKE LONGER, BUT SOMEONE ELSE CAN DUPLICATE YOUR TECH... SAME AS THE KUTHAAL DID.
YOU SURE YOU HAVE ALL THAT?
YOU MIGHT WANT TO LOOK AGAIN. I MEAN, I CLEARLY HAD THIS PLANNED FOR A WHILE. DO YOU THINK I'D DO THE PART YOU'D NOTICE FIRST?
TRUST ME. IT'S ALL GONE.
YOU CAN'T ERASE GOVERNMENT DATA BANKS. YOU DON'T HAVE THE ACCESS... THE CLEARANCE...
YOU'D HAVE TO...
WAIT-- WHERE'S HEATHER?
FA-FAAAASH

ERSON · SHAR

REZ · MARGAR

ODRIGUEZ · NIC

CHEZ · FRANK

ER TAYLOR · SA

ER · PETER WAR

NATHAN COLE

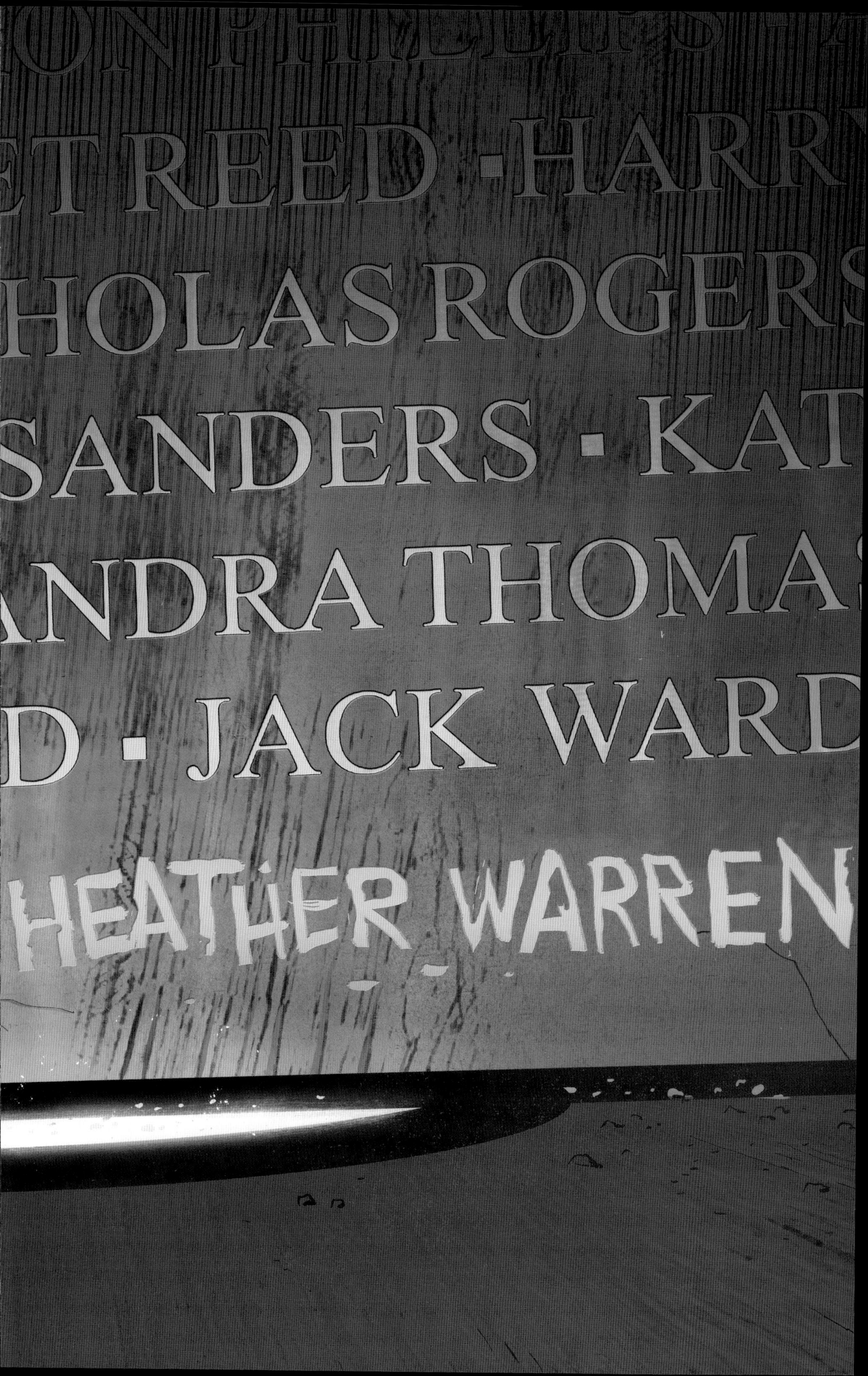
ET REED · HARR
HOLAS ROGERS
SANDERS · KAT
ANDRA THOMAS
D · JACK WARD
HEATHER WARREN

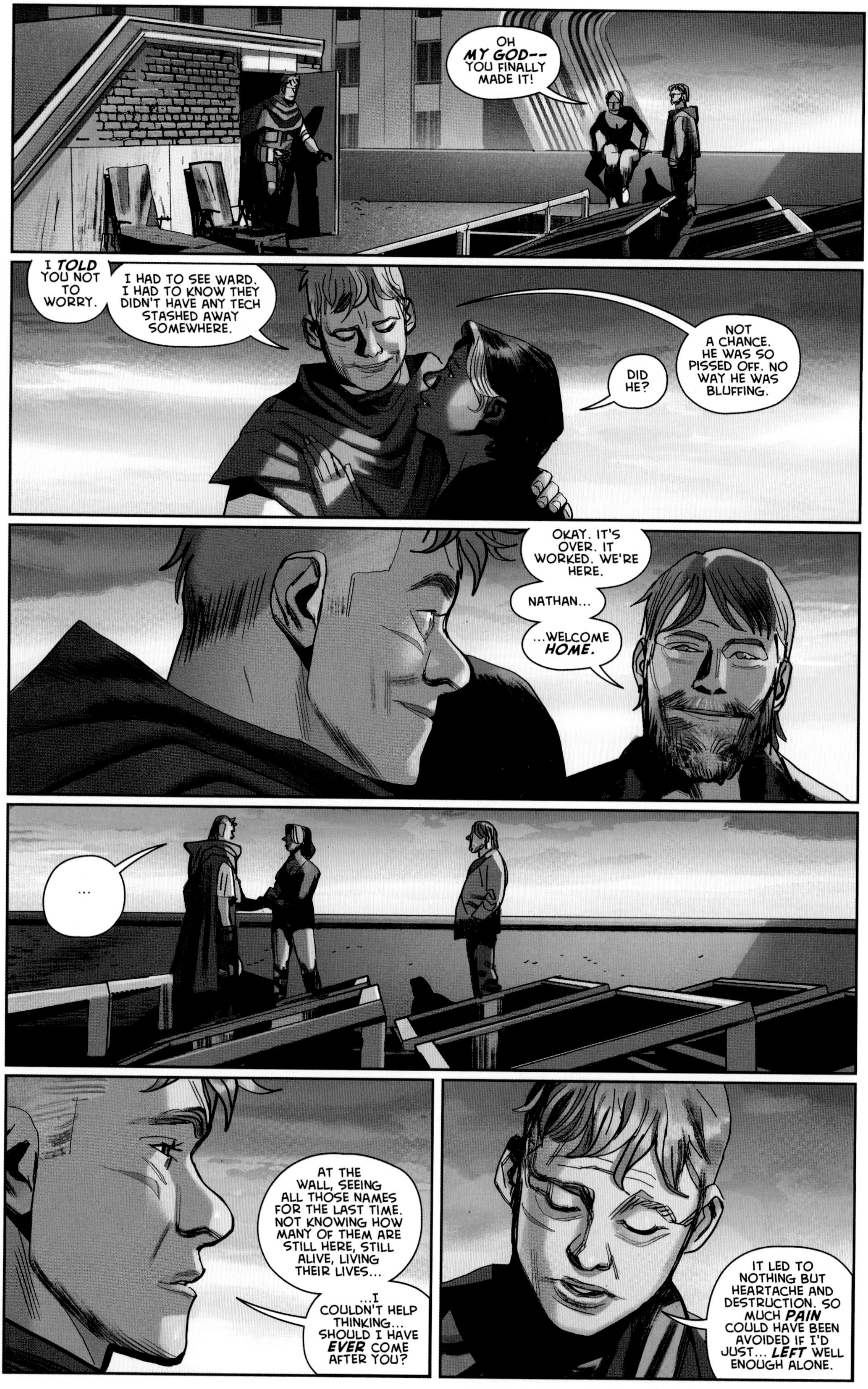
OH MY GOD-- YOU FINALLY MADE IT!
I TOLD YOU NOT TO WORRY.
I HAD TO SEE WARD. I HAD TO KNOW THEY DIDN'T HAVE ANY TECH STASHED AWAY SOMEWHERE.
DID HE?
NOT A CHANCE. HE WAS SO PISSED OFF. NO WAY HE WAS BLUFFING.
OKAY. IT'S OVER. IT WORKED. WE'RE HERE.
NATHAN...
...WELCOME HOME.
...
AT THE WALL, SEEING ALL THOSE NAMES FOR THE LAST TIME. NOT KNOWING HOW MANY OF THEM ARE STILL HERE, STILL ALIVE, LIVING THEIR LIVES...
...I COULDN'T HELP THINKING... SHOULD I HAVE EVER COME AFTER YOU?
IT LED TO NOTHING BUT HEARTACHE AND DESTRUCTION. SO MUCH PAIN COULD HAVE BEEN AVOIDED IF I'D JUST... LEFT WELL ENOUGH ALONE.

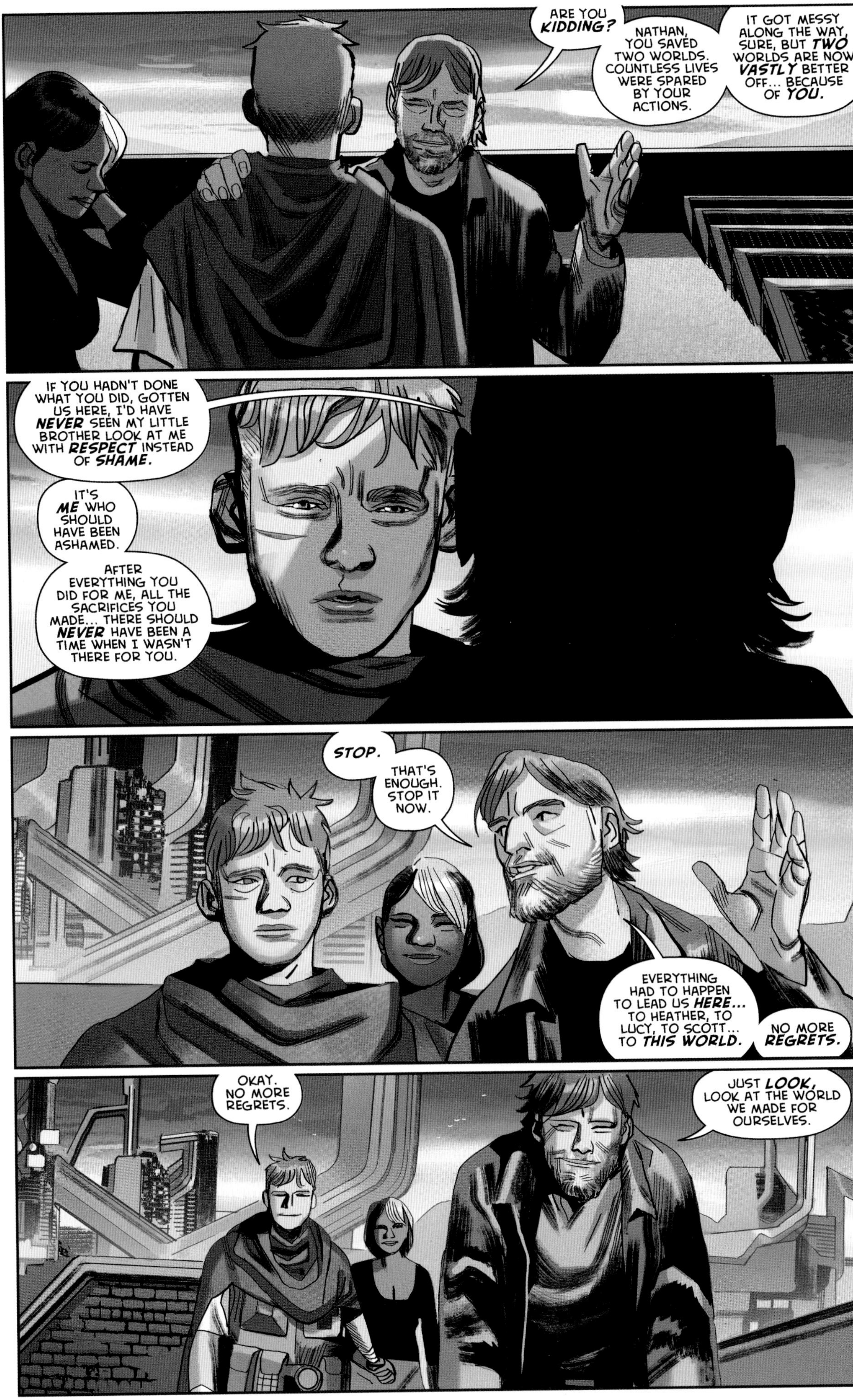
ARE YOU KIDDING?
NATHAN, YOU SAVED TWO WORLDS. COUNTLESS LIVES WERE SPARED BY YOUR ACTIONS.
IT GOT MESSY ALONG THE WAY, SURE, BUT TWO WORLDS ARE NOW VASTLY BETTER OFF... BECAUSE OF YOU.
IF YOU HADN'T DONE WHAT YOU DID, GOTTEN US HERE, I'D HAVE NEVER SEEN MY LITTLE BROTHER LOOK AT ME WITH RESPECT INSTEAD OF SHAME.
IT'S ME WHO SHOULD HAVE BEEN ASHAMED.
AFTER EVERYTHING YOU DID FOR ME, ALL THE SACRIFICES YOU MADE... THERE SHOULD NEVER HAVE BEEN A TIME WHEN I WASN'T THERE FOR YOU.
STOP.
THAT'S ENOUGH. STOP IT NOW.
EVERYTHING HAD TO HAPPEN TO LEAD US HERE... TO HEATHER, TO LUCY, TO SCOTT... TO THIS WORLD.
NO MORE REGRETS.
OKAY. NO MORE REGRETS.
JUST LOOK, LOOK AT THE WORLD WE MADE FOR OURSELVES.

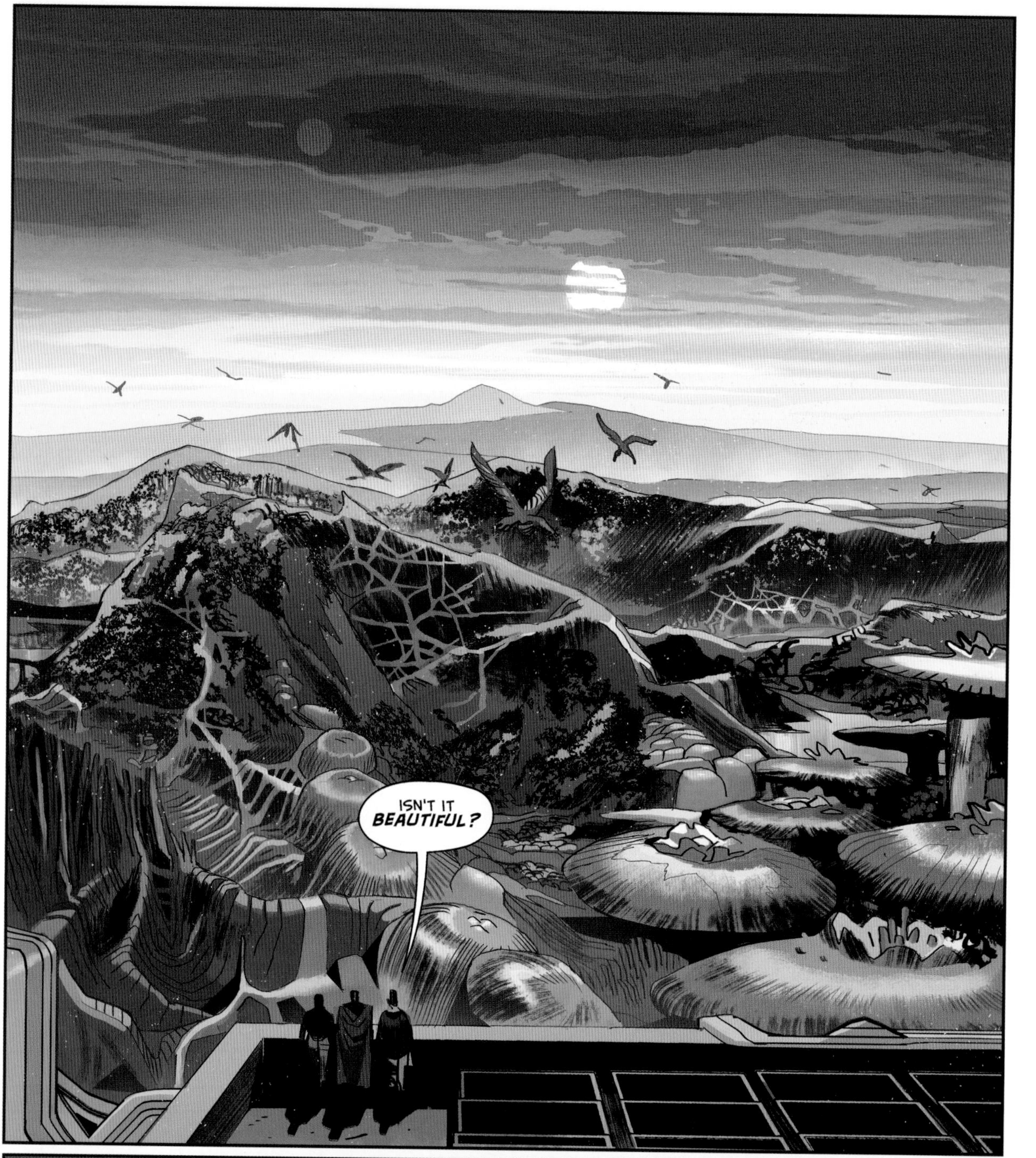
ISN'T IT BEAUTIFUL?

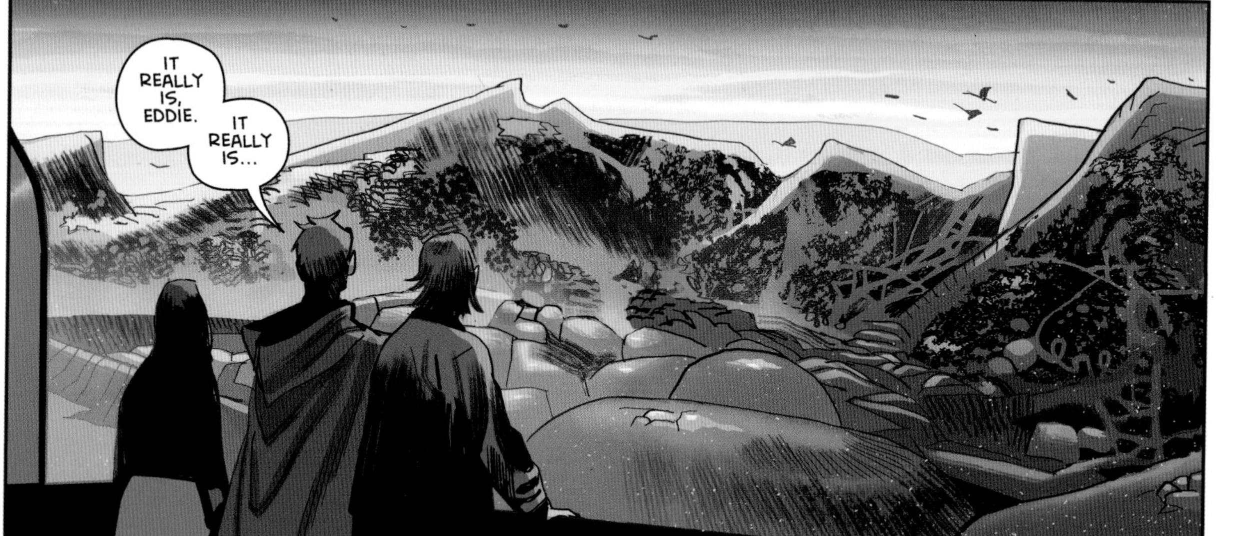
IT REALLY IS, EDDIE.
IT REALLY IS...

THE

END

LORENZO DE FELICI: Here we are, the end of the line! The final book, and there's a lot to talk about. There's another huge time jump between this book and the previous one; a lot of things changed, a bunch of new characters. The first thing to do was to give Nathan a new look. He's been left behind in Oblivion for three years, so he looks like a savage: his beard grew, his hair grew, his cape grew! The cape—which, as mentioned before, is made from the growth itself—makes him look pretty wild and untamed, and it's a lot of fun to draw. But you know, you give Nate a ponytail, and he looks like his usual dapper self.

ROBERT KIRKMAN: It's "wildman of the woods" Nathan! With long running series, or really any series... or really any short story should have as many variations as possible to the look of the main characters. It marks time, shows a progression in the characters, and keeps things interesting. And, man, when you have a collaborator as talented as the world famous Mr. De Felici, those variations are going to look absolutely stunning.

LORENZO: New suits time! The second suit has to be darker than the first one, it's a tradition in comics. Although the red mask makes sure that you can spot the character in every panel, no matter how crowded or complicated it is.

ROBERT: We really should have used this suit more. That was a real mistake. My fault. I suck. Sorry.

LORENZO: In this volume, we keep exploring the Kuthaal and take a look in the heart of their civilization. This time we see a city that has been around for a while, so it's dense and complicated. The huge building where we will meet the Great Kuragg has a massive colorful crystal in the middle, almost like it's been built around it. I liked the look of crystals on the Prism Guard design, so I based the design for the Great Kuragg and his palace around that. It's such a positive look for something ominous.

ROBERT: Is it okay to talk about regrets on this series yet, or too soon? Never got the chance to dive into the crystals of Oblivion. There just never was enough room or the right time to take the time to do it... oh well, maybe someday!

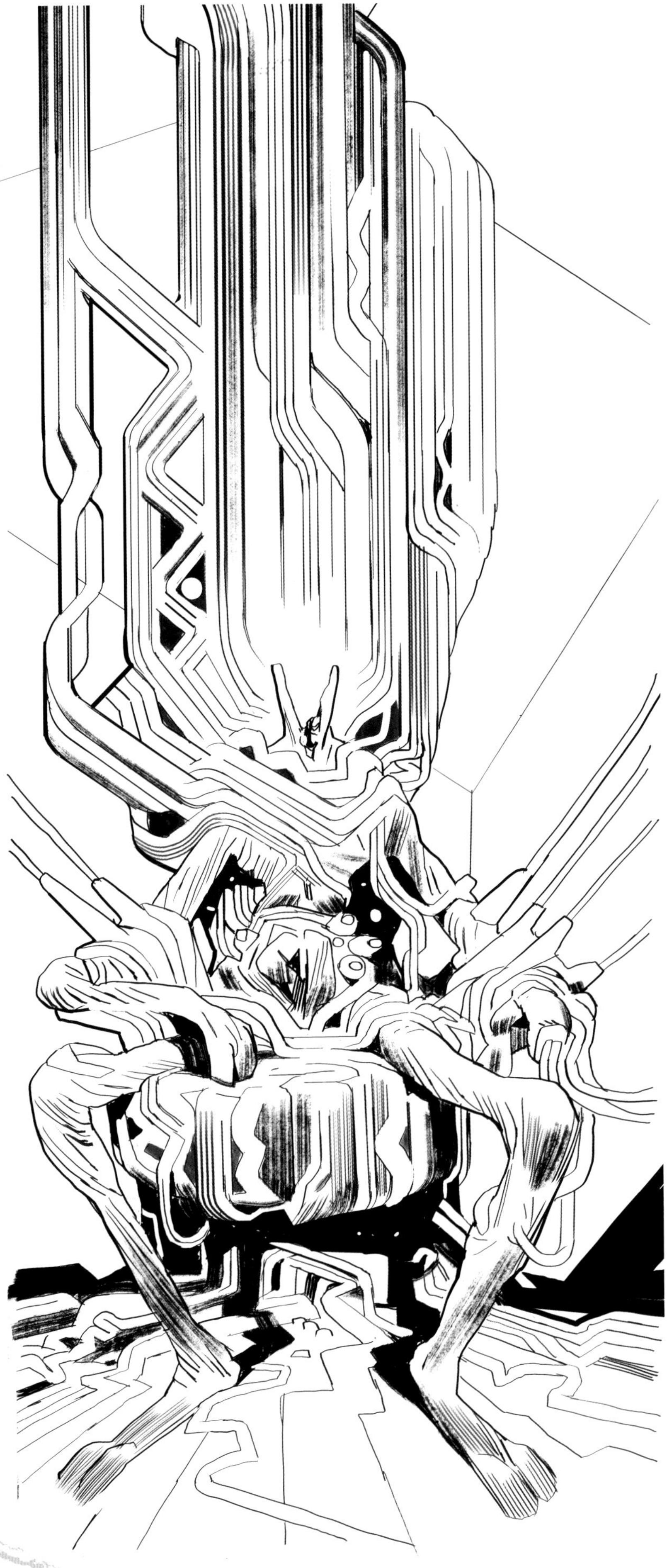

LORENZO: We climb the ranks in the Kuthaal hierarchy to finally get to their leader, the Great Kuragg! Such a powerful name, sounds like a desperate scream. I think that Robert had something completely different in mind, like a bigger guy, a bloated, misshapen Kuthaal. Like 50% Baron Harkonnen, 50% Immortan Joe. However, since I first designed the Kuthaal, I imagined that the more they grow old, the more they look thin and eroded. So, logically, the old king had to be the most fragile and unimposing Kuthaal ever. He's attached to the throne and, as we discover some issues later, without it he just... crumbles away. Sharp political commentary? No, just a weird design idea.

ROBERT: I don't remember what I wrote exactly in the script as a description, but I think all I asked for was an old sickly ruler bound to his chair and kept alive by it. I'll never get over the thrill of just throwing cool ideas out like that, then watching artists spin them into gold. The particular brand of magic Lorenzo worked on this series is awe-inspiring.

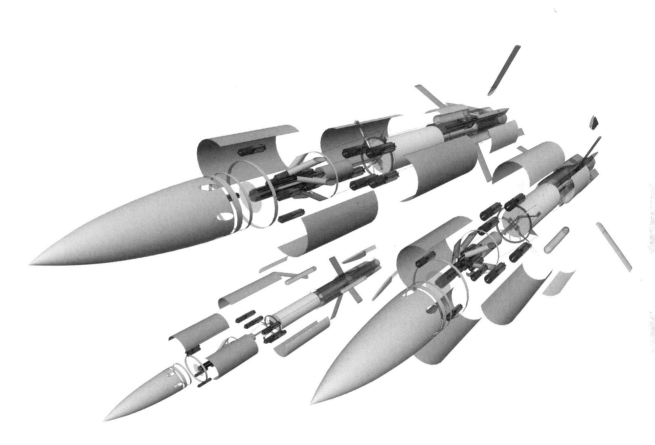

LORENZO: When I read the battle sequence where we see the jet fighters and the missiles opening up and splitting into parts, that's when I realized Robert's silent, sadistic side. Suddenly, I needed to learn what missiles looked like from the inside when I barely knew how they do from the outside... but that's what is truly fun about this job. For the missiles, I had to mish-mash some 3D model so that I could have a realistic, yet interesting depiction of their inside. For the plane, I just winged it.

ROBERT: Sadistic isn't far off... I really was cackling as I wrote those pages. I believe I apologized when I turned that script in... but I didn't mean it.

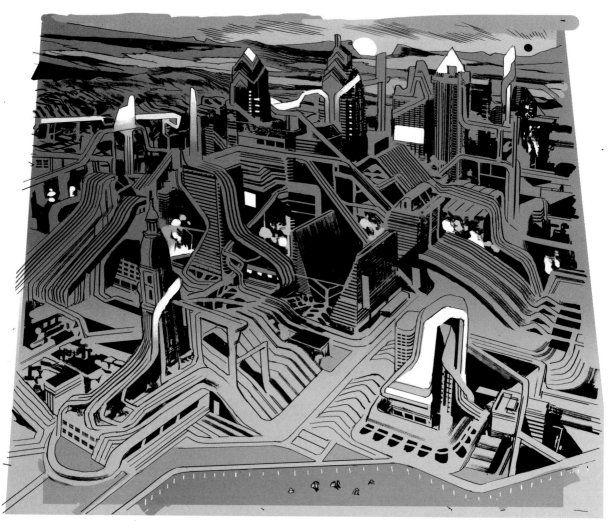

LORENZO: Philadelphia on Oblivion in its final form! This was very fun. There was a delicate balance to aim for. I had to keep the structure and look of Philly visible while showing how it's been contaminated with the Kuthaal architecture.

ROBERT: I really just wanted to show how quickly things advanced in Oblivion with cooperation between humans and Kuthaal. Look how advanced the Oblivion section of Philadelphia is now!

LORENZO: A rejected idea for the cover of issue 28. We were nearly there, the concept was right, but we needed to see them a little better, hence the closer look on the final one. I liked this one though, it's more unsettling and mysterious.

ROBERT: Yeah, I loved this one. The mystery of it is excellent. But I really wanted an "Ed and Mateo are Batman and Robin now" vibe, so we kind of needed to see them.

LORENZO: Rejected cover
for issue 33. I really liked this
one, and I remember putting
it together pretty quickly,
too! The problem was that the
feeling was not the right one.
Heather looked too helpless and
desperate here, when she should
have looked more in control.

ROBERT: I really loved this, but
yeah, wasn't the right vibe.

LORENZO: I felt that the Great Kuragg was the right choice for the third hardcover since I had grown fond of the Kuthaal and their weird look... but yeah, I think all things considered, Ed was a better choice. In my defense, I didn't know what he would have to go through in the last issues!

ROBERT: Sorry about that. I don't like to keep artists in the dark, but sometimes I'm in my little writing hole and I don't come up for air until the script is done. No matter how... late it is...

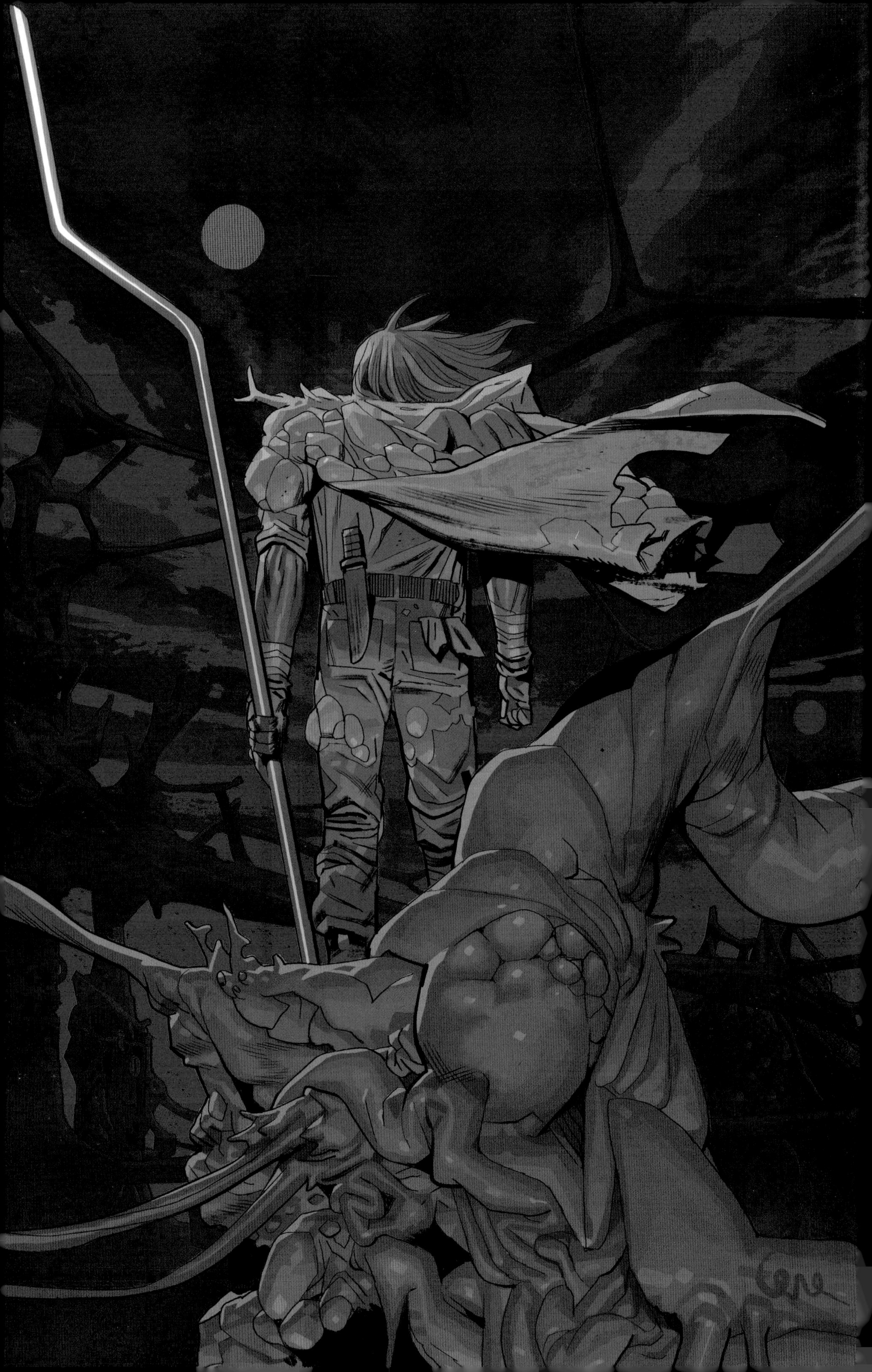

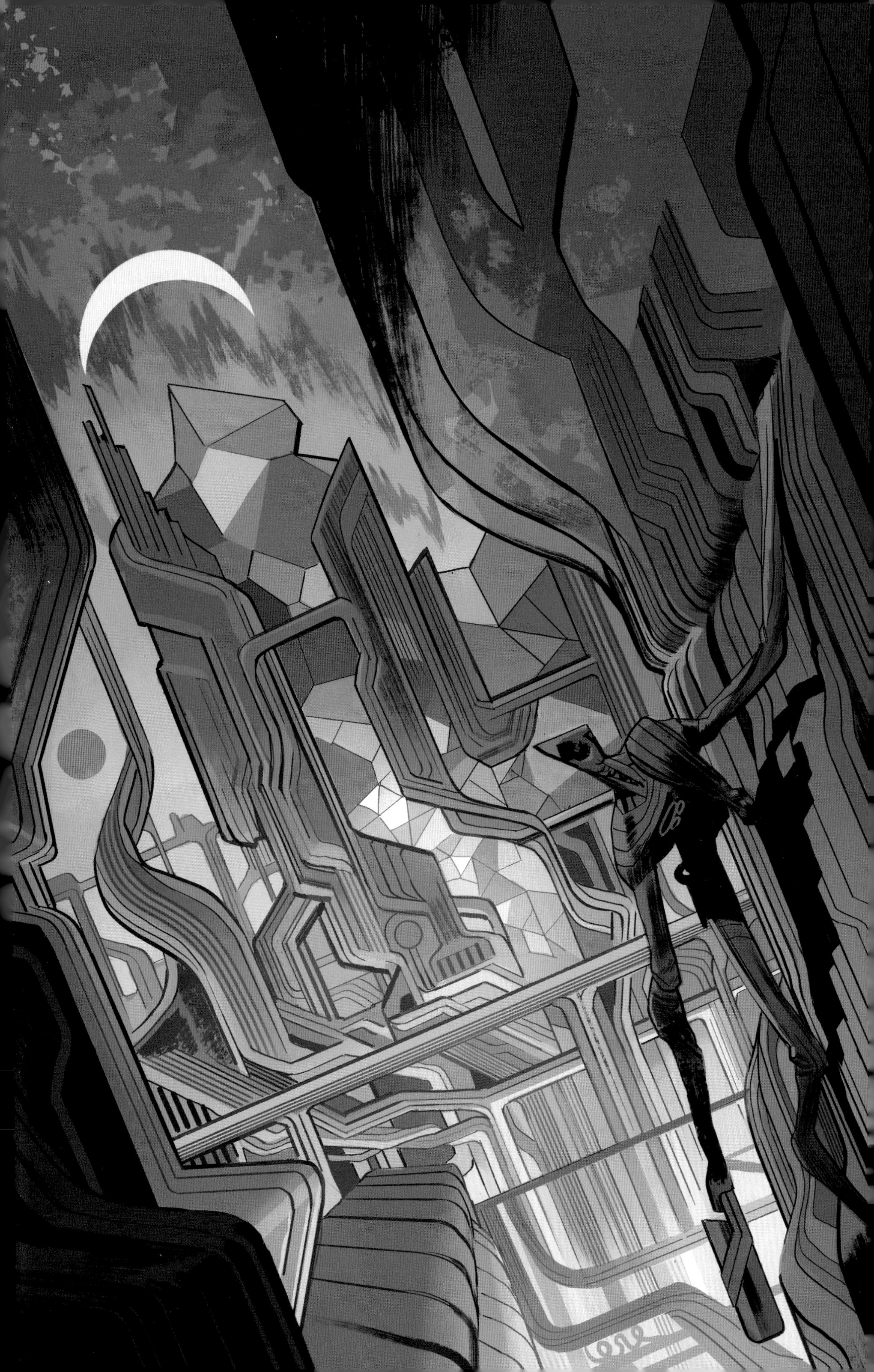

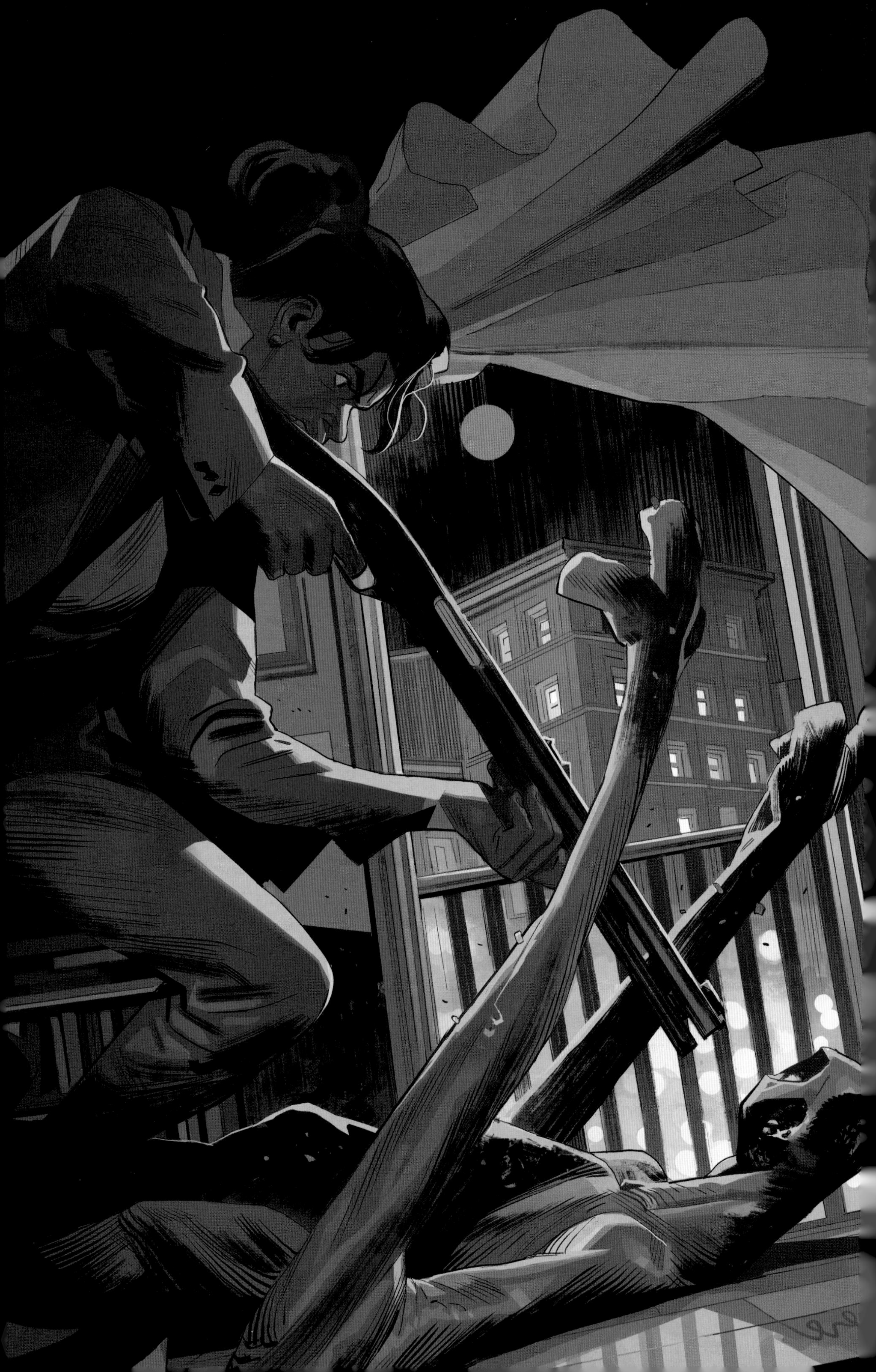

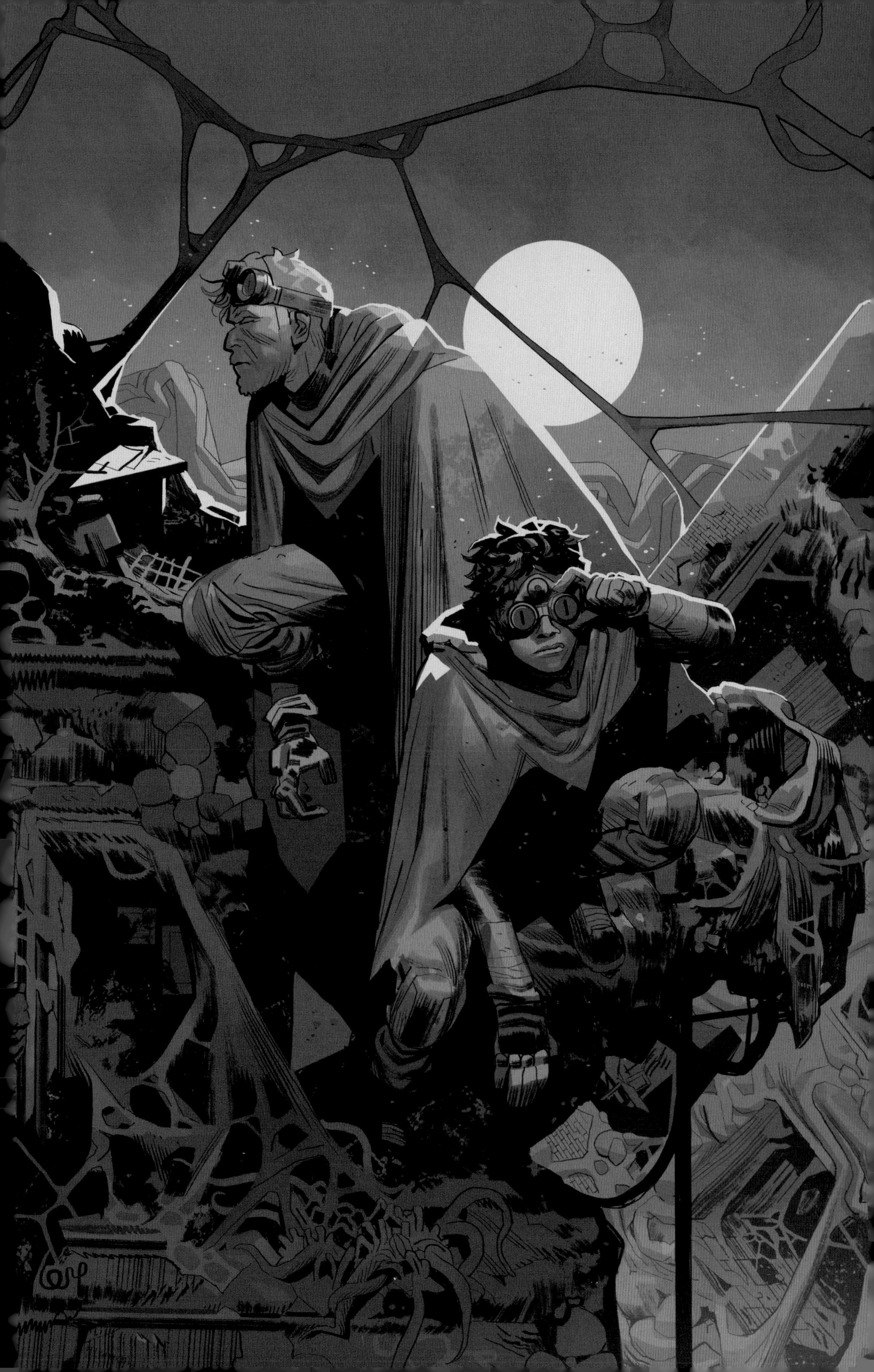

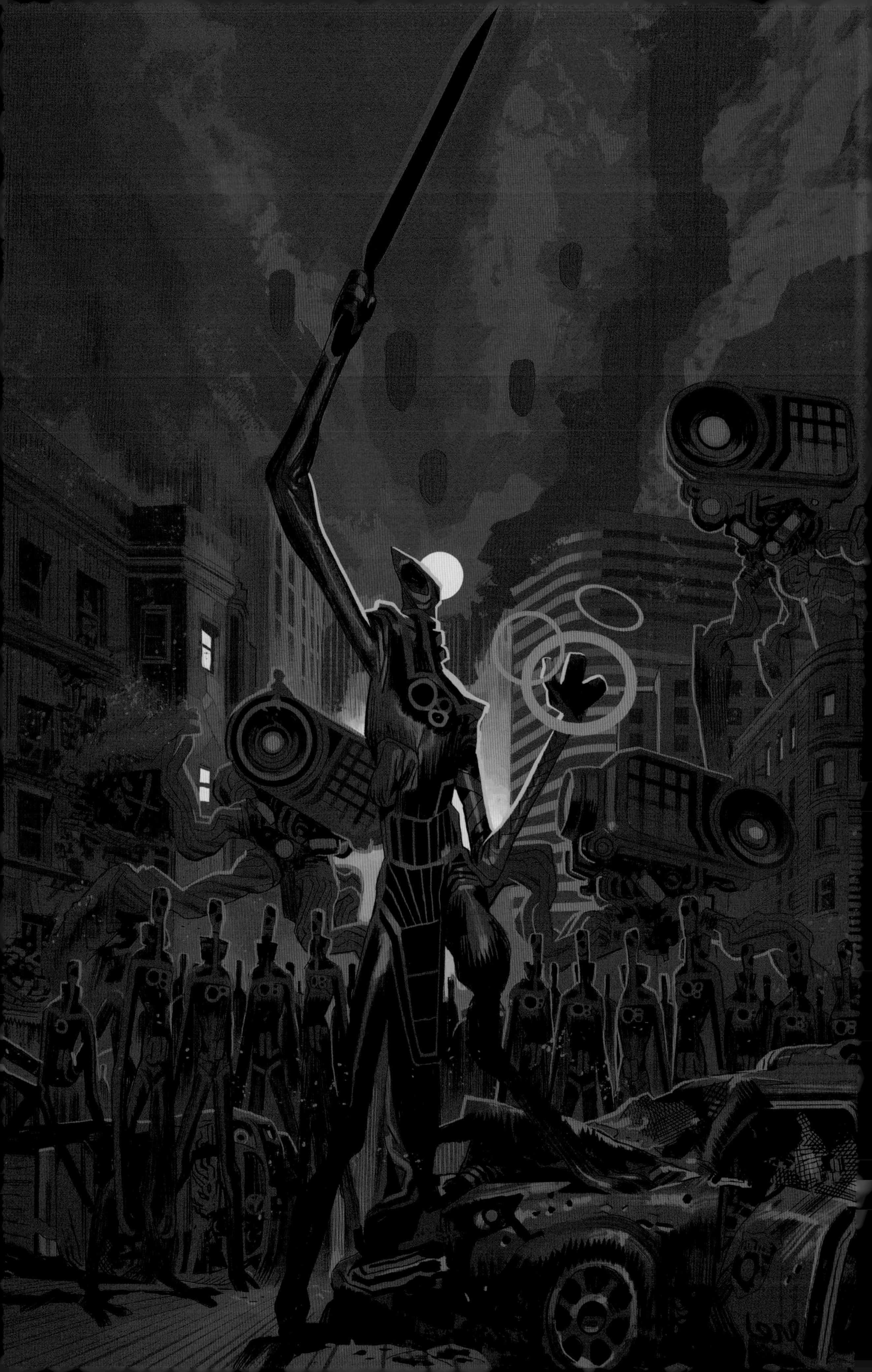

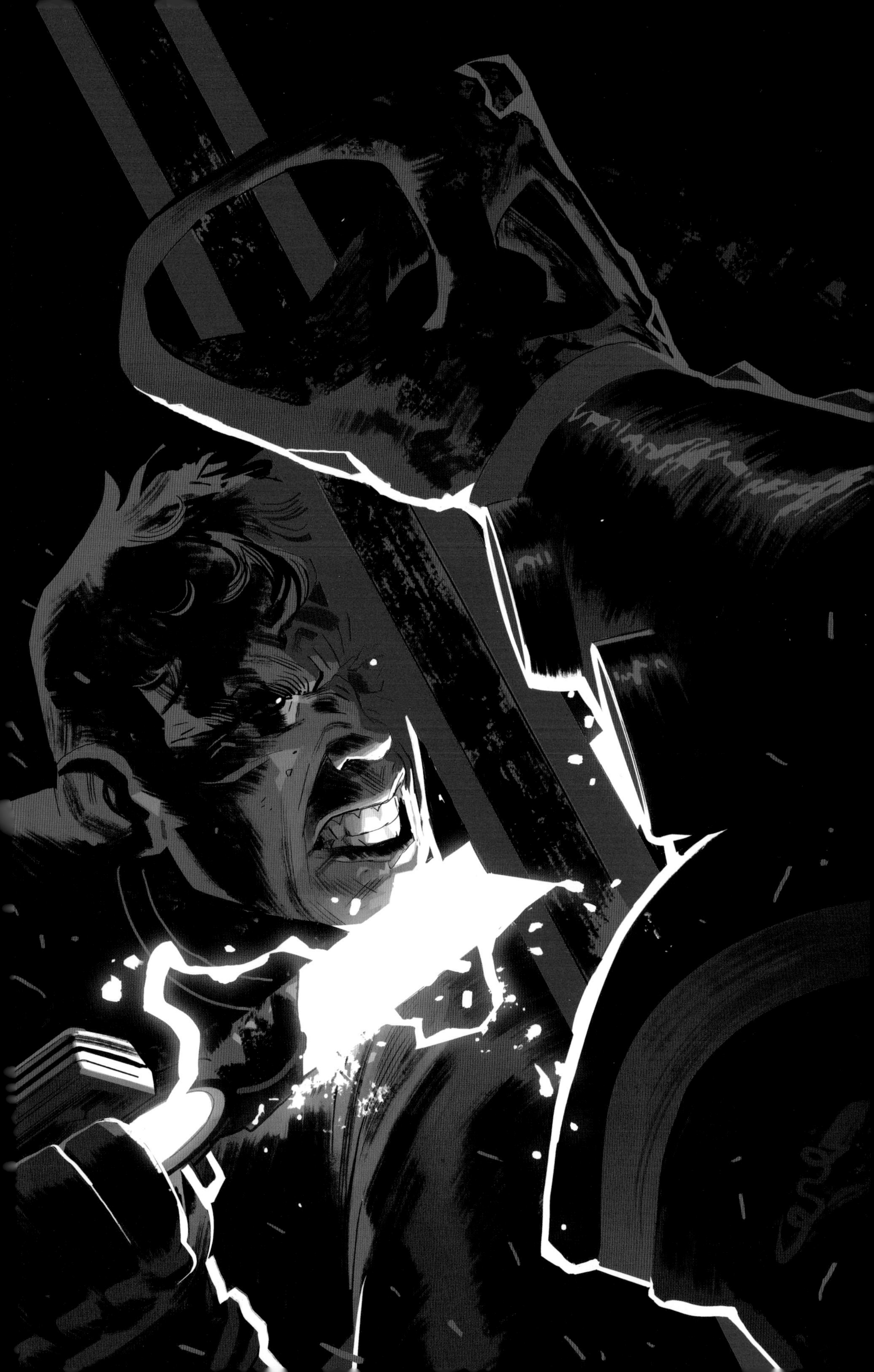

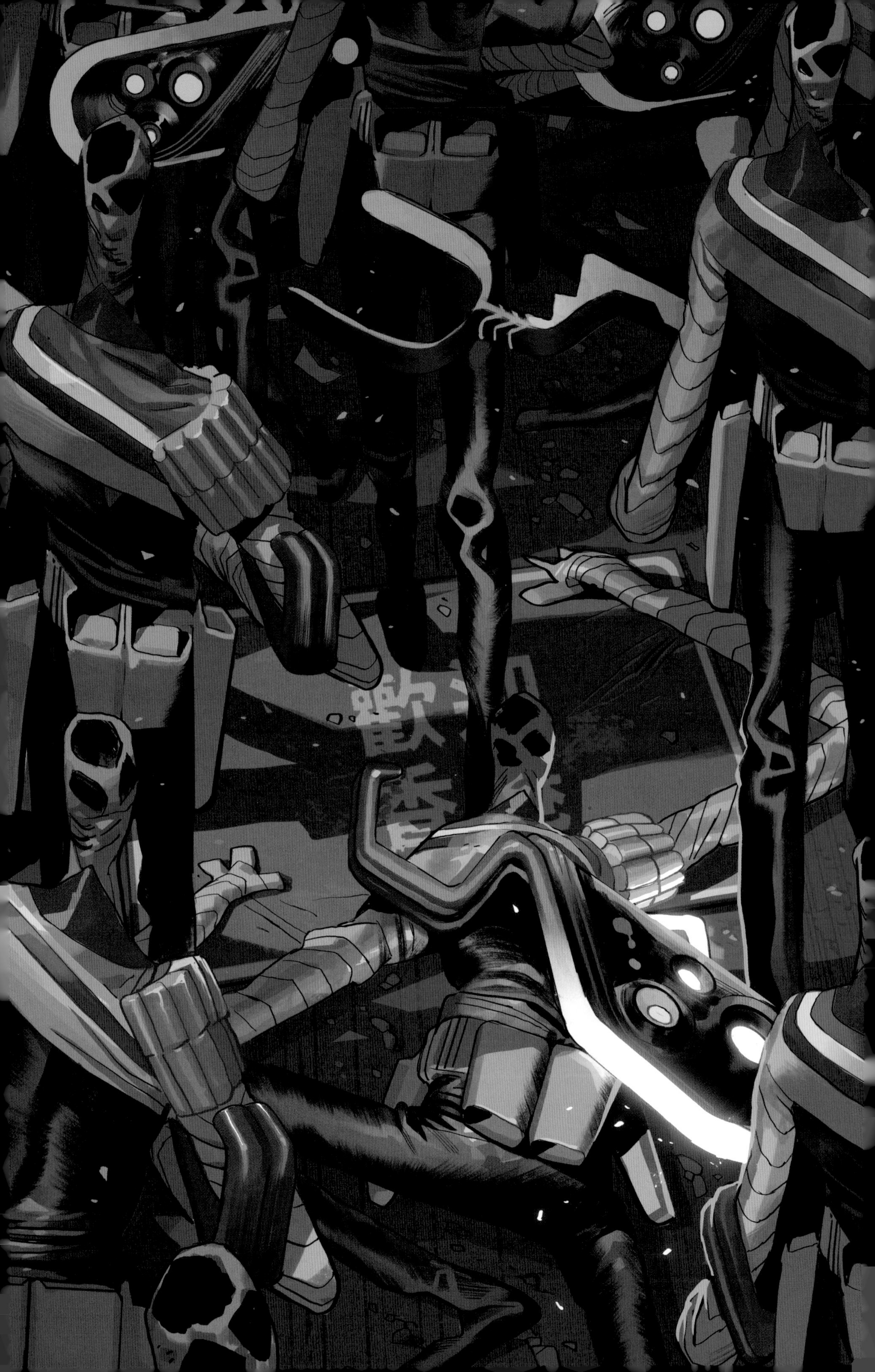
歡

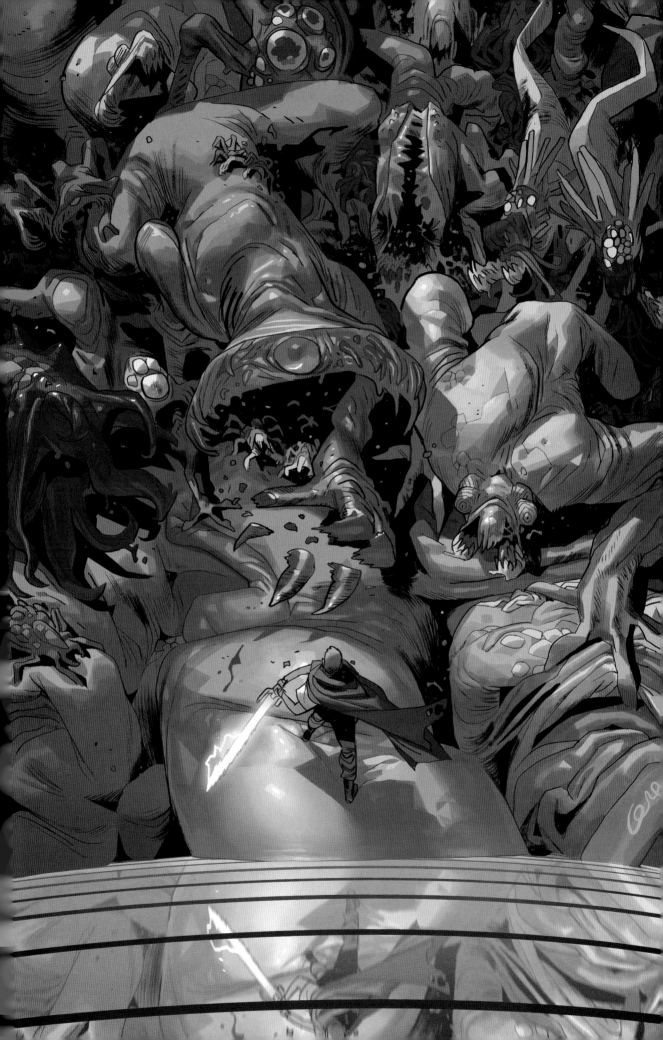

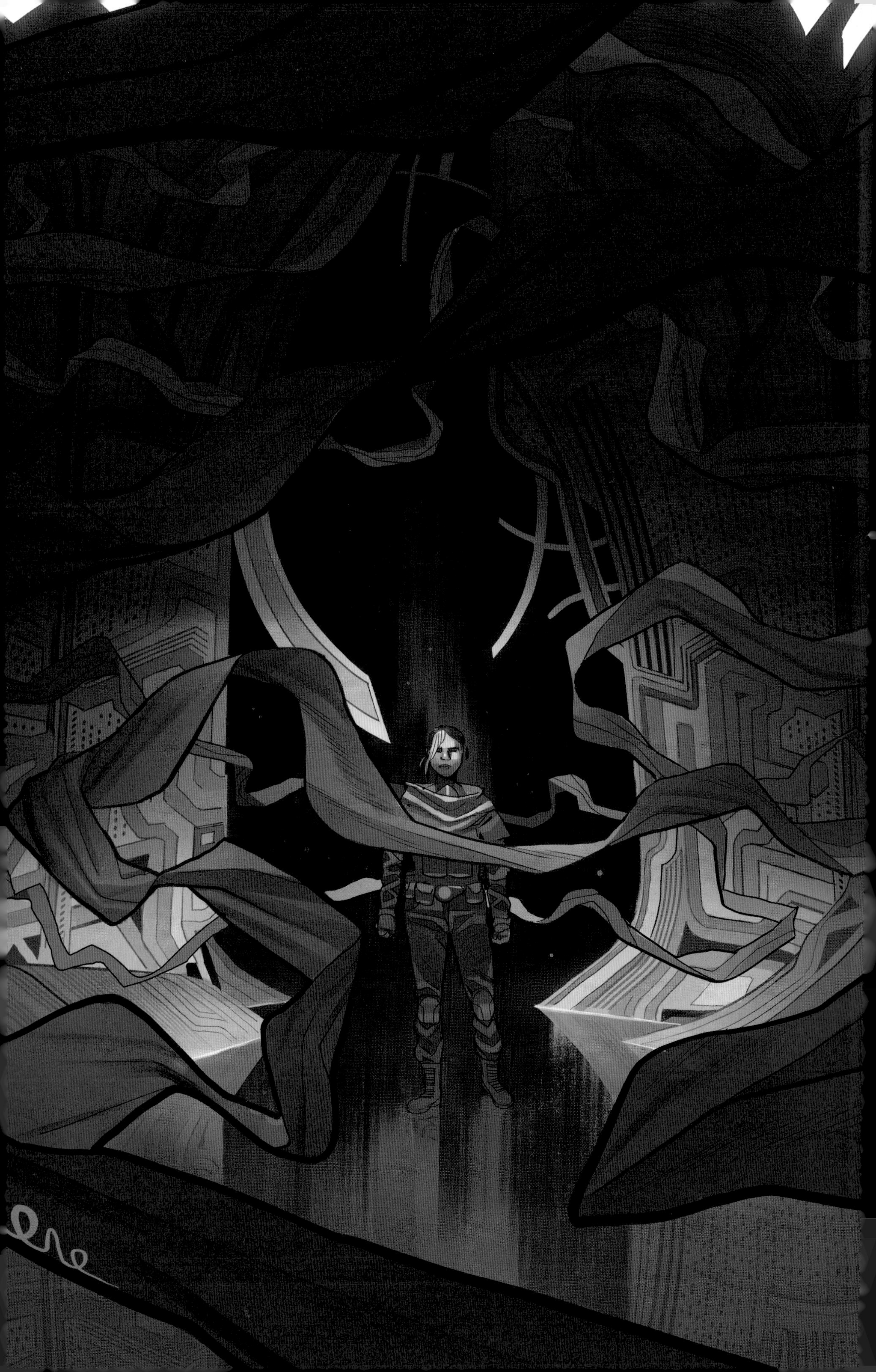

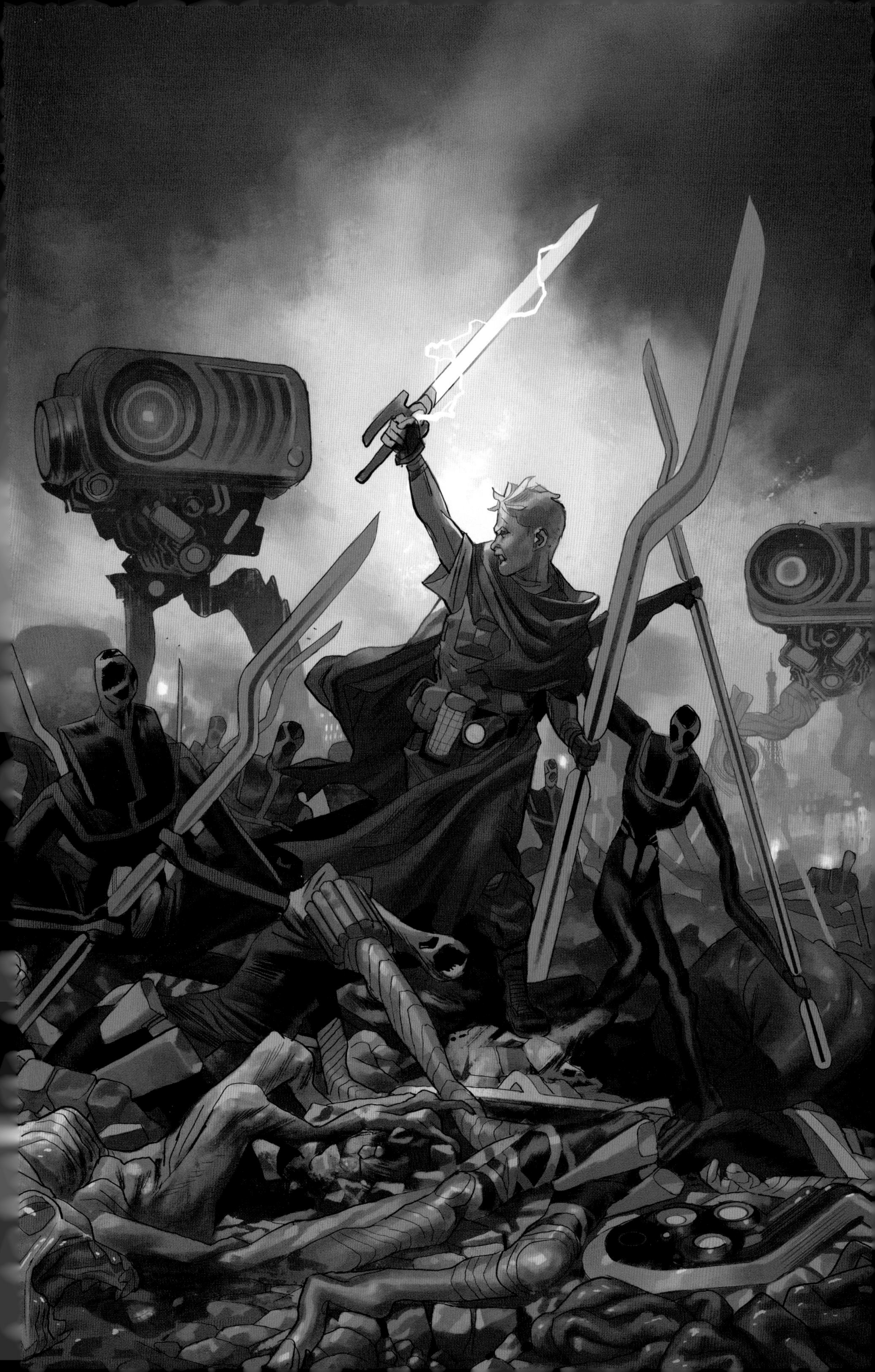

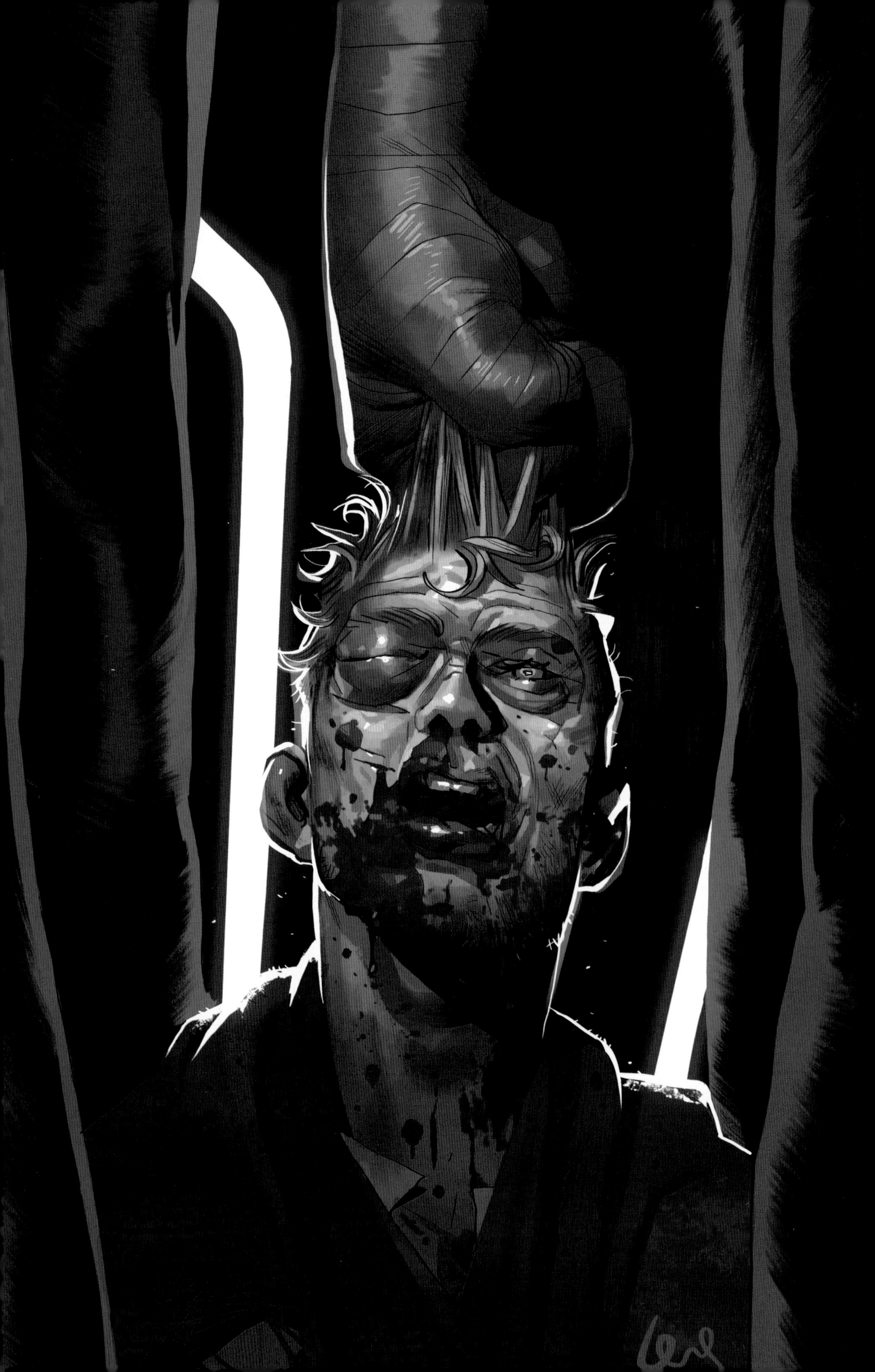

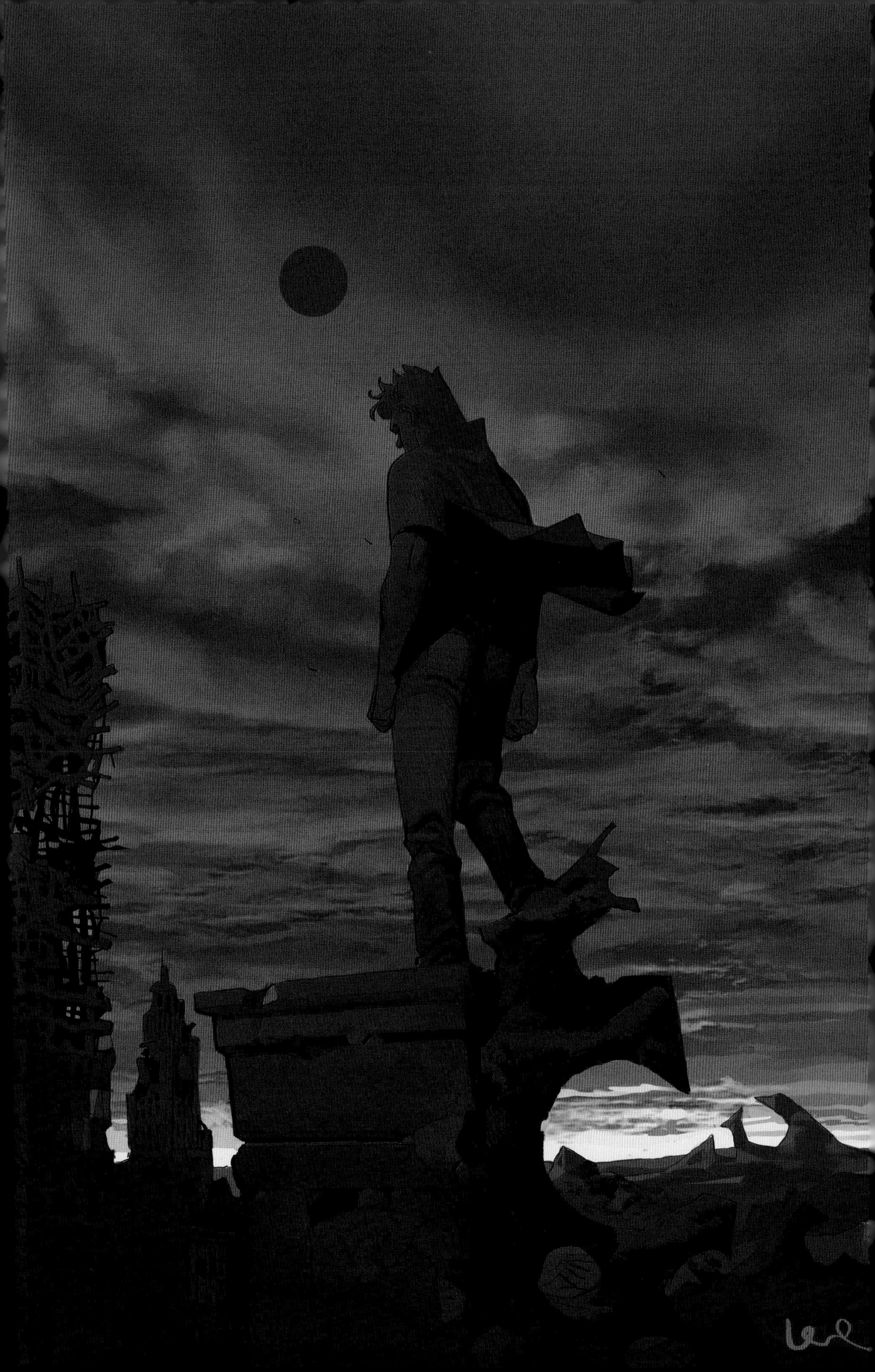

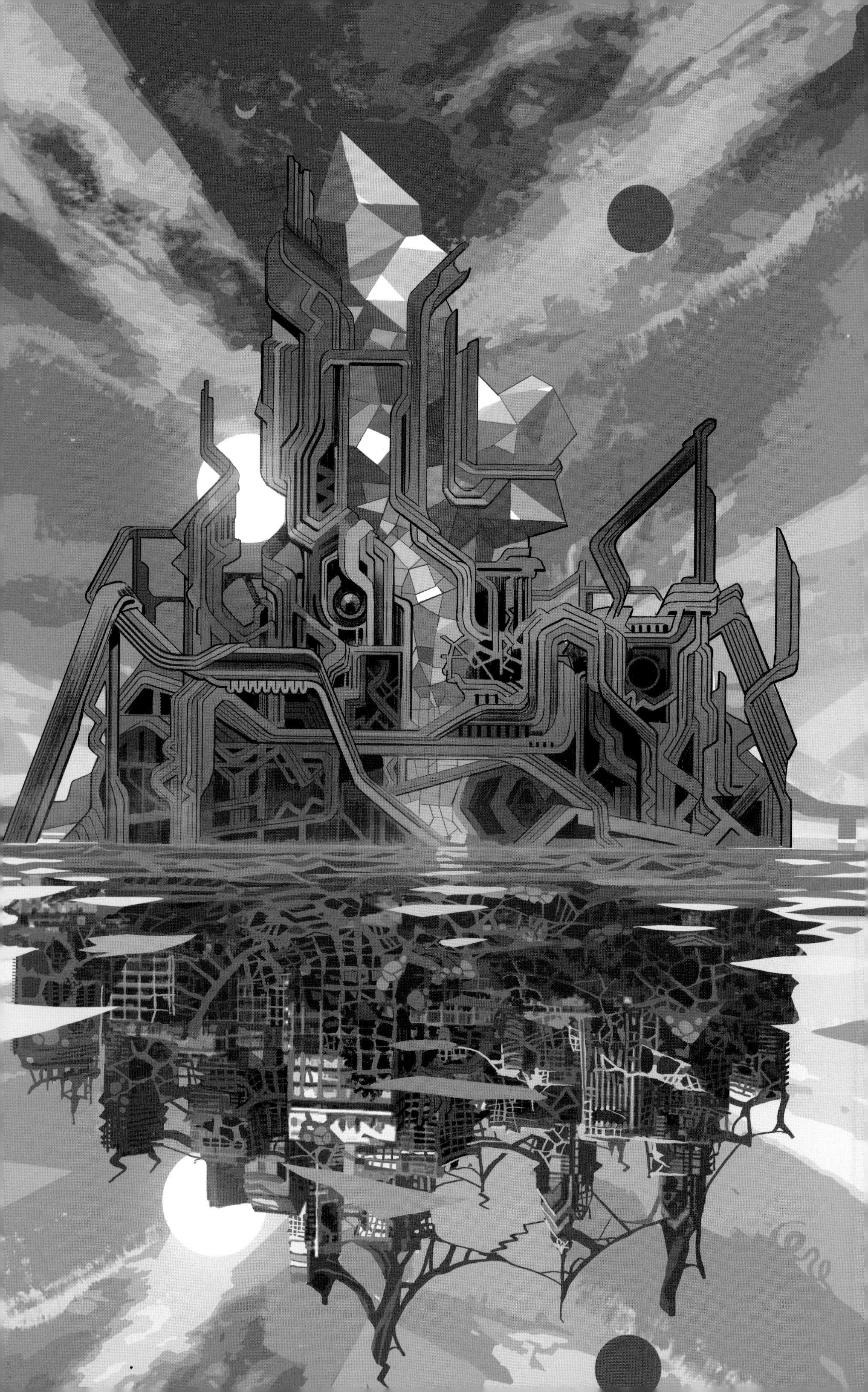

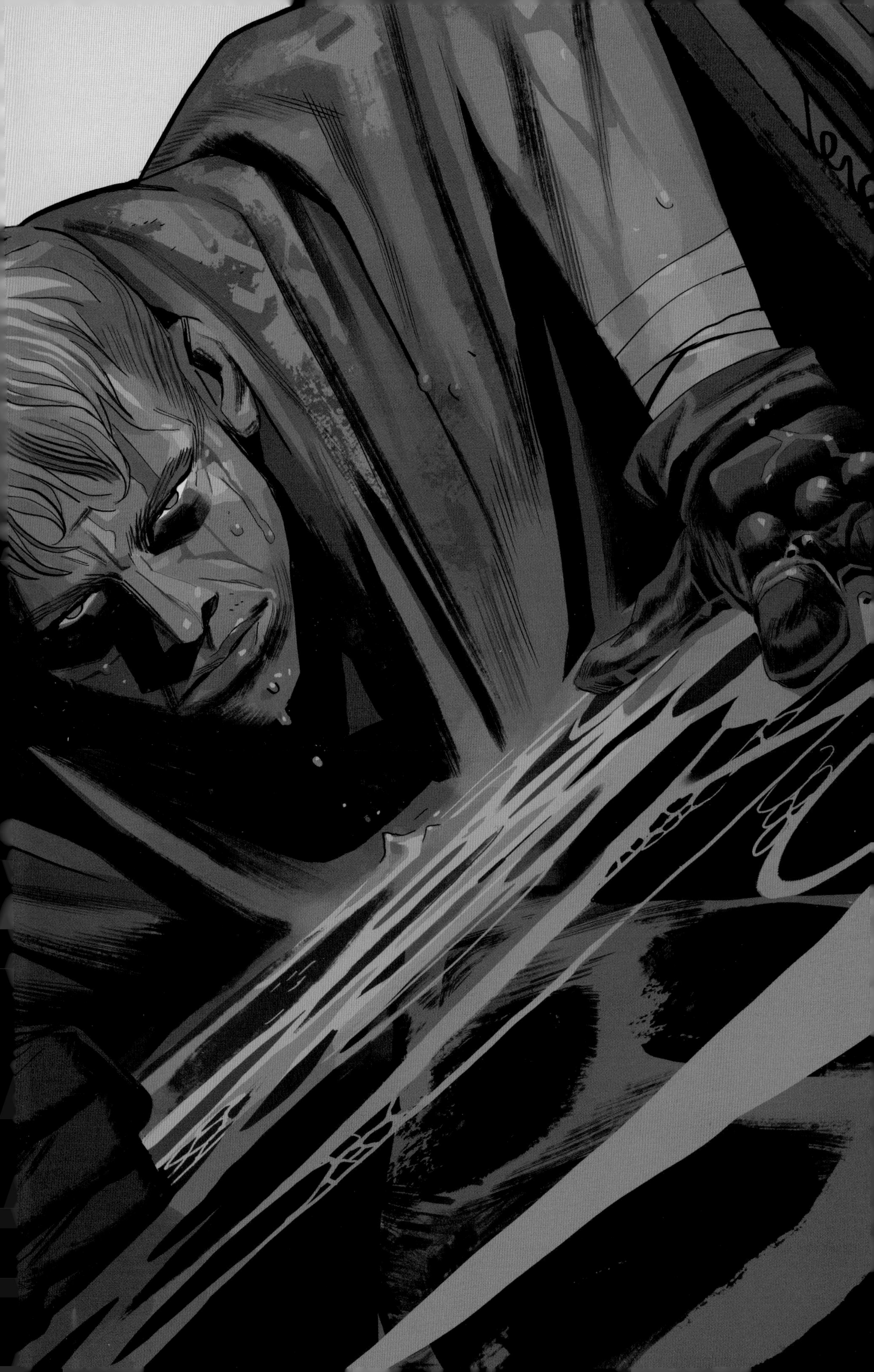

Hi guys!

Between one deadline and another, only now I can stop and realize that one of the jobs I care about most in my life has come to an end.

Seven years of work, in which so many things have happened, but OBLIVION SONG has always been a constant. A few days ago I colored the last page, the last oblivion sky and the last fungus, oh boy...I will miss this strange world with its "lovely" creatures.

I will never be grateful enough for everything this project has given me, especially for allowing me to contribute with this dream team made up of wonderful people.

Thank you, Robert, Sean, Lorenzo, and Rus, it was an honor to contribute with you to create this crazy and exciting universe.

I heartily thank all of you readers who have accompanied us on this journey and supported us enthusiastically, you have been the best encouragement to do better with each issue.

Don't worry, I'm not crying, I just have an Ogre in my eye.

-Annalisa Leoni

o o o o o o o o o o o o o o o

Hey folks!

About time, right? Well... are you happy? You got another Kirkman finale here! I loved it.

It's a bittersweet one, but the bitter and the sweet are definitely in the right places, thanks to Nathan's final, brutal send-off. Man, what a mic drop.

If in reading these pages you felt it's a bummer to say goodbye to OBLIVION SONG, just imagine what I felt while I was working on it, realizing I was drawing the characters I've basically lived with every day for seven years for the last time. It's a bit of a shock!

Your hands, now trembling with emotion I'm sure, are holding the last book of a series that was very different 35 issues ago, and I'm quite positive it's not the only thing that changed in your life - or in the world - in the meantime. It's been quite a ride, these last couple of years.

We really needed an Oblivion to escape to from time to time, and I've been lucky enough to be part of the best expedition team ever. With Robert, Annalisa, Rus, and Sean, we scouted ahead to prepare an interesting trip for you all: I wanna thank them for being such a delight to work with, and you, because you stuck with us this whole time. It's been an honor and a pleasure, y'all!

Now sorry, but I have to transfer back to Oblivion for a while to see these marvelous Annalisa-colored skies once more.

FA-FAAASSH!

-Lorenzo De Felici

o o o o o o o o o o o o o o o

Well, another series of mine has reached an end. I hope you find this ending as meaningful and moving as we all do. It's sad to say goodbye to a project, but it's also nice to reach the end of the road and know the complete story can now live on bookshelves all across the world for as long as we don't all catch on fire. Hopefully that's a long time.

OBLIVION SONG has definitely been one of the most rewarding projects of my career thus far. Getting to work with Lorenzo and Annalisa has been an absolute delight. Seeing this world come to life through their lens has been breathtaking. After years of admiring Lorenzo's work from afar, I didn't know if he was even looking to work in American comics. I could have never guessed what a great collaborator he would turn out to be. One thing that I'm so proud of with this series is how unique it is. The vastly different visual language on display is all Lorenzo, and it is a sight to behold. Annalisa's spectacular color sense really made this world real and helped set this book apart from everything else on the stands these days. She's indisputably one of the best colorists working today. I hope to work with both of these amazing talents again and often as long as they have a slot open in their dance cards for me.

I'm pleased to add this series to the long list of series I've collaborated with Rus Wooton on. He always brings my words to the page with impeccable style. This series is no exception to that.

Andres Juarez provided us with our sweet logo (Did NONE of you notice the "LI" in the logo is the Kuthaal symbol? Shame on you.), and the great graphic design for this series in single issue and collected form. Our hardcovers are some of the best looking books I've ever been a part of. Please do yourself a favor and check those out.

Sean Mackiewicz also worked on this series.

While this is the end of the OBLIVION SONG comic series, I'm confident it's not the end of Oblivion Song as a whole. It will live on in another form maybe soon, or maybe a decade from now. Only time will tell.

Thank you so much, dear reader, for your support over these years, for this series and possibly others. I hope you'll join me on my next journey!

-Robert Kirkman

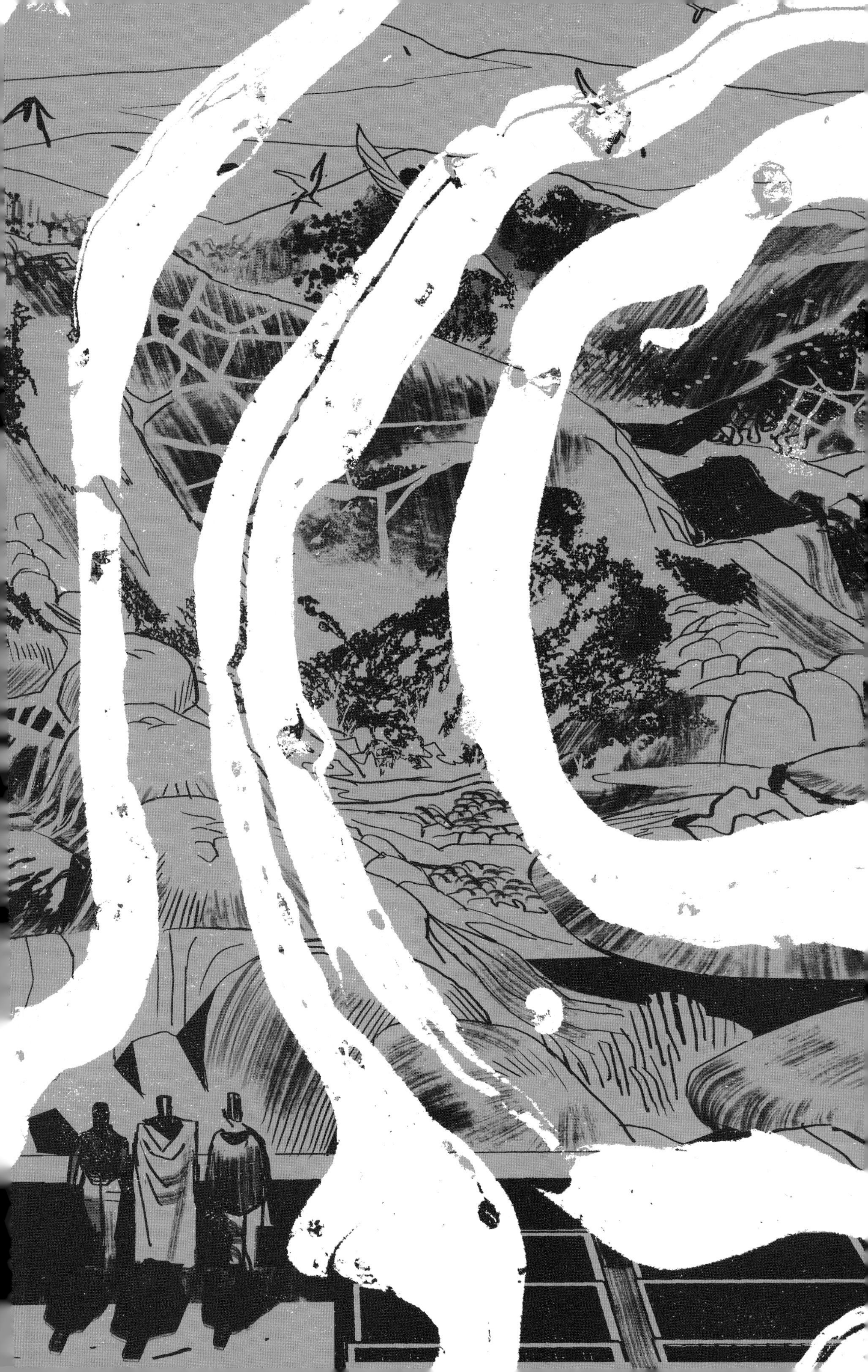

FOR MORE TALES FROM **ROBERT KIRKMAN** AND **SKYBOUND**

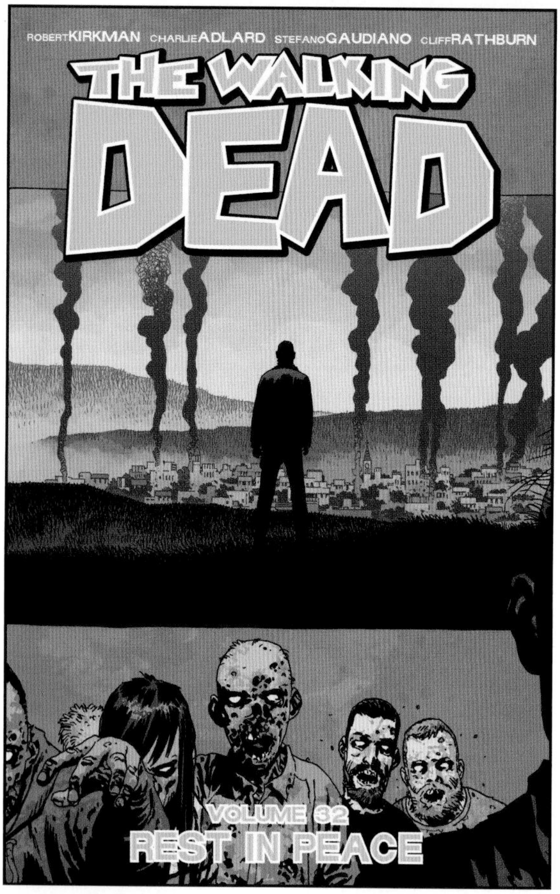
ROBERT KIRKMAN CHARLIE ADLARD STEFANO GAUDIANO CLIFF RATHBURN
THE WALKING DEAD
VOLUME 32
REST IN PEACE

VOL. 1: DAYS GONE BYE TP
ISBN: 978-1-58240-672-5
$14.99

VOL. 2: MILES BEHIND US TP
ISBN: 978-1-58240-775-3
$14.99

VOL. 3: SAFETY BEHIND BARS TP
ISBN: 978-1-58240-805-7
$14.99

VOL. 4: THE HEART'S DESIRE TP
ISBN: 978-1-58240-530-8
$14.99

VOL. 5: THE BEST DEFENSE TP
ISBN: 978-1-58240-612-1
$14.99

VOL. 6: THIS SORROWFUL LIFE TP
ISBN: 978-1-58240-684-8
$14.99

VOL. 7: THE CALM BEFORE TP
ISBN: 978-1-58240-828-6
$14.99

VOL. 8: MADE TO SUFFER TP
ISBN: 978-1-58240-883-5
$14.99

VOL. 9: HERE WE REMAIN TP
ISBN: 978-1-60706-022-2
$14.99

VOL. 10: WHAT WE BECOME TP
ISBN: 978-1-60706-075-8
$14.99

VOL. 11: FEAR THE HUNTERS TP
ISBN: 978-1-60706-181-6
$14.99

VOL. 12: LIFE AMONG THEM TP
ISBN: 978-1-60706-254-7
$14.99

VOL. 13: TOO FAR GONE TP
ISBN: 978-1-60706-329-2
$14.99

VOL. 14: NO WAY OUT TP
ISBN: 978-1-60706-392-6
$14.99

VOL. 15: WE FIND OURSELVES TP
ISBN: 978-1-60706-440-4
$14.99

VOL. 16: A LARGER WORLD TP
ISBN: 978-1-60706-559-3
$14.99

VOL. 17: SOMETHING TO FEAR TP
ISBN: 978-1-60706-615-6
$14.99

VOL. 18: WHAT COMES AFTER TP
ISBN: 978-1-60706-687-3
$14.99

VOL. 19: MARCH TO WAR TP
ISBN: 978-1-60706-818-1
$14.99

VOL. 20: ALL OUT WAR PART ONE TP
ISBN: 978-1-60706-882-2
$14.99

VOL. 21: ALL OUT WAR PART TWO TP
ISBN: 978-1-63215-030-1
$14.99

VOL. 22: A NEW BEGINNING TP
ISBN: 978-1-63215-041-7
$14.99

VOL. 23: WHISPERS INTO SCREAMS TP
ISBN: 978-1-63215-258-9
$14.99

VOL. 24: LIFE AND DEATH TP
ISBN: 978-1-63215-402-6
$14.99

VOL. 25: NO TURNING BACK TP
ISBN: 978-1-63215-659-4
$14.99

VOL. 26: CALL TO ARMS TP
ISBN: 978-1-63215-917-5
$14.99

VOL. 27: THE WHISPERER WAR TP
ISBN: 978-1-5343-0052-1
$14.99

VOL. 28: A CERTAIN DOOM TP
ISBN: 978-1-5343-0244-0
$14.99

VOL. 29: LINES WE CROSS TP
ISBN: 978-1-5343-0497-0
$16.99

VOL. 30: NEW WORLD ORDER TP
ISBN: 978-1-5343-0884-8
$16.99

VOL. 31: THE ROTTEN CORE TP
ISBN: 978-1-5343-1052-0
$16.99

VOL. 32: REST IN PEACE TP
ISBN: 978-1-5343-1241-8
$16.99

BOOK ONE HC
ISBN: 978-1-58240-619-0
$34.99

BOOK TWO HC
ISBN: 978-1-58240-698-5
$34.99

BOOK THREE HC
ISBN: 978-1-58240-825-5
$34.99

BOOK FOUR HC
ISBN: 978-1-60706-000-0
$34.99

BOOK FIVE HC
ISBN: 978-1-60706-171-7
$34.99

BOOK SIX HC
ISBN: 978-1-60706-327-8
$34.99

BOOK SEVEN HC
ISBN: 978-1-60706-439-8
$34.99

BOOK EIGHT HC
ISBN: 978-1-60706-593-7
$34.99

BOOK NINE HC
ISBN: 978-1-60706-798-6
$34.99

BOOK TEN HC
ISBN: 978-1-63215-034-9
$34.99

BOOK ELEVEN HC
ISBN: 978-1-63215-271-8
$34.99

BOOK TWELVE HC
ISBN: 978-1-63215-451-4
$34.99

BOOK THIRTEEN HC
ISBN: 978-1-63215-916-8
$34.99

BOOK FOURTEEN HC
ISBN: 978-1-5343-0329-4
$34.99

BOOK FIFTEEN HC
ISBN: 978-1-5343-0850-3
$34.99

BOOK SIXTEEN HC
ISBN: 978-1-5343-1325-5
$34.99

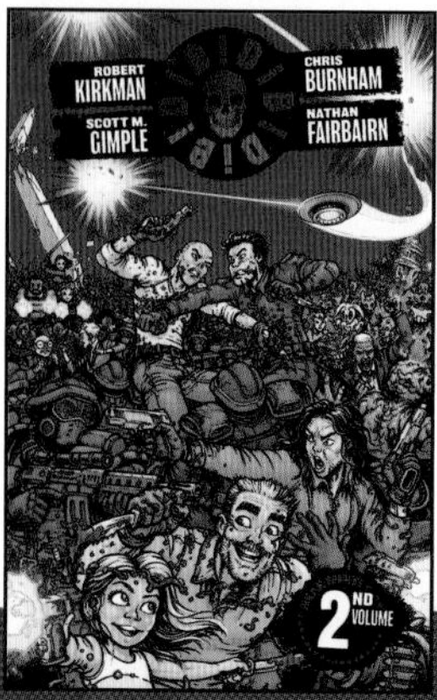
ROBERT KIRKMAN
SCOTT M. GIMPLE
CHRIS BURNHAM
NATHAN FAIRBAIRN
2ND VOLUME

VOLUME 1 TP
ISBN: 978-1-5343-1214-2
$19.99

VOLUME 2 TP
ISBN: 978-1-5343-1707-9
$16.99

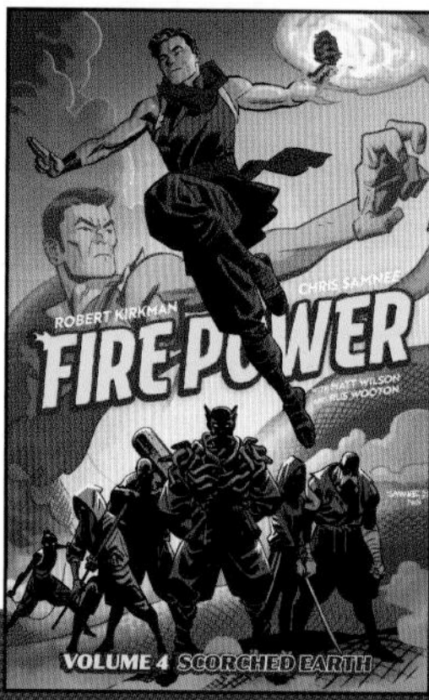
CHRIS SAMNEE
ROBERT KIRKMAN
FIRE POWER
VOLUME 4 SCORCHED EARTH

VOL. 1: PRELUDE
ISBN: 978-1-5343-1655-3
$9.99

VOL. 2: HOME FIRE
ISBN: 978-1-5343-1718-5
$16.99

VOL. 3: FLAME WAR
ISBN: 978-1-5343-1908-0
$16.99

VOL. 4: SCORCHED EARTH
ISBN: 978-1-5343-2103-8
$16.99

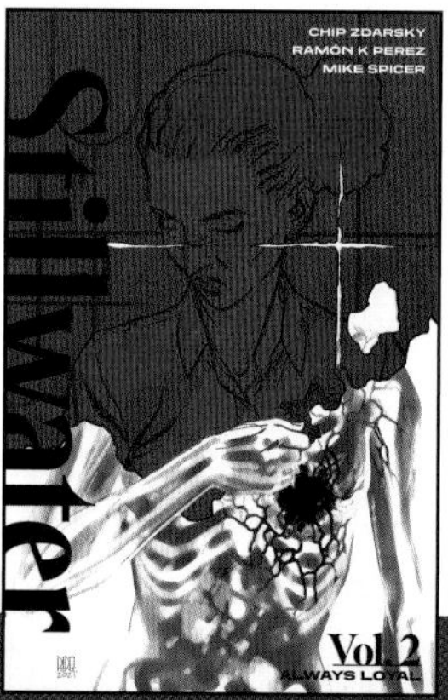
CHIP ZDARSKY
RAMÓN K PÉREZ
MIKE SPICER
Stillwater
Vol. 2
ALWAYS LOYAL

VOL. 1: RAGE, RAGE
ISBN: 978-1-5343-1837-3
$16.99

VOL. 2: ALWAYS LOYAL
ISBN: 978-1-5343-2004-8
$16.99

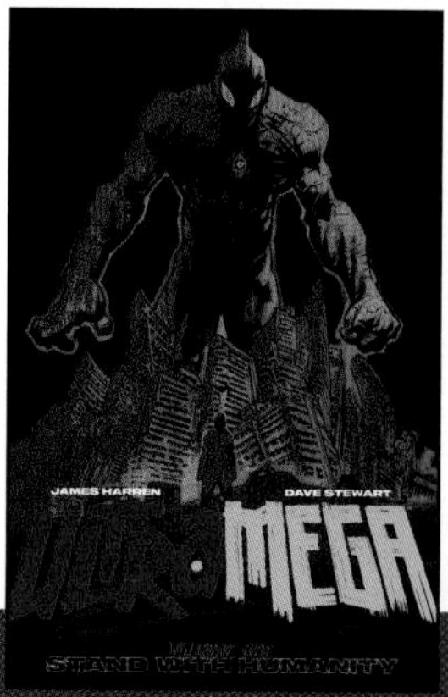
JAMES HARREN
DAVE STEWART

VOL. 1: STAND WITH HUMANITY
ISBN: 978-1-5343-1984-4
$19.99

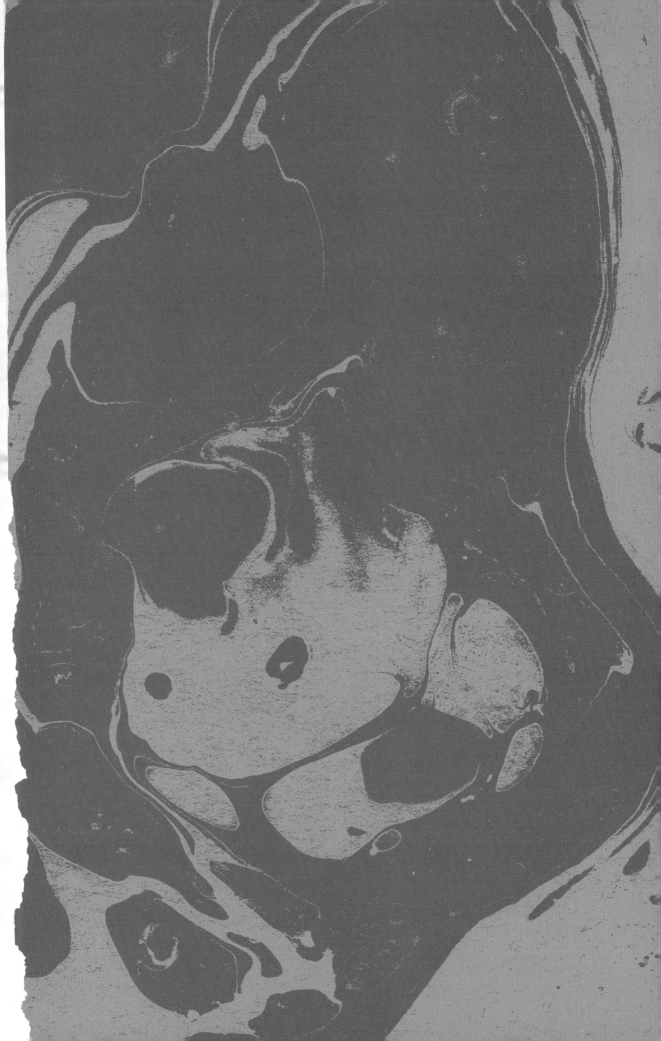

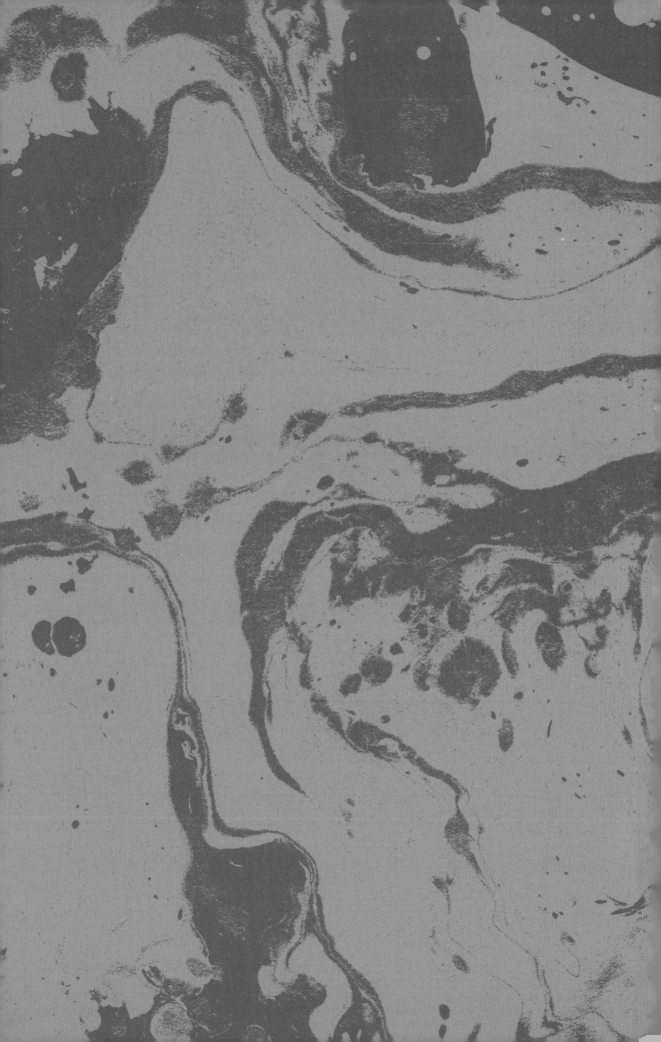